The
French Classical Romances

Complete in Twenty Crown Octavo Volumes

Editor-in-Chief
EDMUND GOSSE, LL.D.

With Critical Introductions and Interpretative Essays by

HENRY JAMES   PROF. RICHARD BURTON   HENRY HARLAND

ANDREW LANG   PROF. F. C. DE SUMICHRAST

THE EARL OF CREWE   HIS EXCELLENCY M. CAMBON

PROF. WM. P. TRENT   ARTHUR SYMONS   MAURICE HEWLETT

DR. JAMES FITZMAURICE-KELLY   RICHARD MANSFIELD

BOOTH TARKINGTON   DR. RICHARD GARNETT

PROF. WILLIAM M. SLOANE   JOHN OLIVER HOBBES

De Beyle (Stendhal)

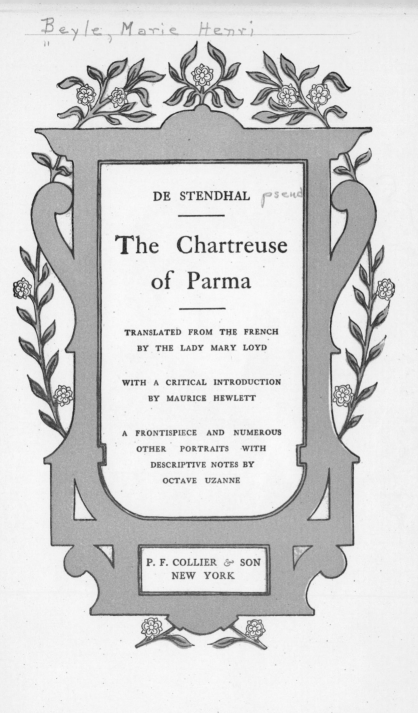

DE STENDHAL *psend*

The Chartreuse of Parma

TRANSLATED FROM THE FRENCH
BY THE LADY MARY LOYD

WITH A CRITICAL INTRODUCTION
BY MAURICE HEWLETT

A FRONTISPIECE AND NUMEROUS
OTHER PORTRAITS WITH
DESCRIPTIVE NOTES BY
OCTAVE UZANNE

P. F. COLLIER & SON
NEW YORK

DE STENDHAL AND *LA CHARTREUSE*

AWARDED the highly honourable task of presenting De Stendhal with his credentials to the English-speaking public, I say that he ought to be greatly received, not only on account of his genius, but on that of the kind his genius is of. A dry point, a whim incarnate, a thinker who drove his passions before him through close walls, he fenced himself about with so many reserves, yet urged so impetuously through them that, had he accomplished no more than this one book (as the fact is, in a technical sense), you would still be sure of the whole of him; it had still been possible to appraise him accurately by the side of his great coeval, Balzac, or his great successor, Mérimée.

He is literally, however, author of two romances and some half-dozen *contes*; of a treatise, *De l'Amour*, which merely articulates theories clothed to better purpose by his fancy; and of various scattered papers of travel (not to be made into books by book-covers), concerning which it is enough here to say that our respect for his acute observation is mainly lost in regrets that he observed such unnecessary detail. On the whole, and this particular work apart, I believe he will be found the most interesting fact in his books. He was of your rare, slow-digesting order of genius, a writer who thought to excess, whose invention was pent up, whose power of production was conditioned by that, whose fastidiousness

I

V

The Chartreuse of Parma

was extreme. It was but seldom that his conception found him high-spirited enough to combat all this; but when it did, as once it did, his audacity catches the breath. Put another way, it was but seldom that his critical faculty was drugged by a great theme; but when it was the immortal part of him, unlimed and unhooded, towered high. You may take it that two ideas moved him profoundly—Italy and Napoleon. In *L'Abbesse de Castro* he had the first, in *Le Rouge et le Noir* the second; but in *La Chartreuse de Parme* he had both, and produced what I soberly believe to be the greatest novel of France.

This is not to say, of course, that Napoleon was his only hero. His heroes are always himself, as he saw himself in his heart's looking-glass, a Napoleon conceived in a library and delivered by a study fire. Seeing Napoleon in himself, the Napoleonic legend captivated him, filled his mind; he could not imagine a great man who should not be a Man of Destiny. Italy worked in with that. Napoleon was the great *condottiere*; no mannish figure could claim De Stendhal which had not Italian simplicity of motive acting upon Italian singleness of design. All his heroes, therefore, are alike at the root. Fabrice del Dongo is Julien in a pallium; give Julien trunk-hose and you have Branciforte, the sublime young brigand of *L'Abbesse*. The differences in them are due to the mind, not to the imagination. Irony was at work in the making of Julien Sorel; irony played with the legend; so Julien came out a little Napoleon of the alcove, whose Austerlitz was Mademoiselle de la Mole, and his Moscow Madame de Rênal. Irony, in fact, and mechanical construction go far to sterilize that magnificent medley called *Le Rouge et le Noir*. I believe that the absence of Italy was fatal to

The Chartreuse of Parma

De Stendhal; he could only breathe freely when the wind
blew from Lombardy, it seems. Yet it must be said—
and not so oddly either—that something of France was
necessary to his completion. If you study the opening
chapters of *La Chartreuse* you will find, I believe, that
Fabrice had French blood in him. Otherwise, for what,
pray, does the Lieutenant Robert, with his old shoes and
his five-franc piece, figure for a year in the company of
the Marchesa del Dongo? And why does Fabrice, on
the plain of Waterloo, encounter the General Comte
d'A——? Why should the general have been so glad to
have known him there? And why does the marchesa
have the habit of writing two or three times a year to
this worthy concerning the education of Fabrice? No;
obviously France had wedded Italy where Fabrice was
concerned. Fortunate conjunction! You have your
Man of Destiny a divine Italian fool salted over with
French wit. The crowning moment of the life of this delightful creature comes when he is fast in prison, in the
Farnese tower and under sentence of death, with poison
imminent, watching through a loophole in his shutter for
Clélia Conti to come and feed her birds. The Fates sit
darkling in the fog with thread and scissors; his beautiful
aunt (who loves him not as aunts use) is scheming in the
court of Ranuce-Ernest V.; he has accomplished none of
his old ambitions and got the stuff for no new ones. Fabrice, at this ill-starred moment, bends himself to en-
trancing problems—Will Clélia come to the window?
Or will she not? Julien Sorel, readers will remember,
was easily absorbed in similar tasks; so was Jules Branciforte, the right-hand man of Prince Colonna. Love, in
the Italian manner, and Destiny (or the conviction of
Destiny) played the mischief with these fine young men.

vii

Looked at thus, broadly and collectively, De Stendhal's heroes have all one texture.

The same monotony does not touch his women. De Stendhal had studied women, as the treatise *De L'Amour* will prove, but not disastrously, as the fate of so many Frenchmen would have it. If he considered them charming fools, pity and love were always his conclusion; nothing of bitter welled up in the mouth. Indeed, if he loved anything made it was the type for which Gina del Dongo and Mademoiselle de la Mole may stand beside Rosalind and Perdita—the girl of character and wit, whose pride it yet is to fold arms over the bosom, be meek toward a man, and turn her radiant armoury to his only service, profit and honour. Mostly he chooses to see the lady kneel in the dust, and from a high seat. Mademoiselle de la Mole comes down very far to meet Julien, the little hypocritical peasant; Hélène de Campireali is many degrees above Jules; Vanina Vanini is a great lady. Clélia Conti is an exception; there is no doubt about Fabrice. Yet when she falls to love him—and this is her reason— he is a condemned prisoner, a reputed assassin, a renegade priest, ostensibly the discredited lover of a little strolling actress. So the exception is not very real. De Stendhal's women are always " kind." The ice about them glitters, crisps, is provocative; but it is there, and very apt to thaw under a beam or two from the bosom's lord. And their wit is equal to their kindness, of the most candid quality. The great example of all is, of course, the Duchess Gina in this book. " Mais savez-vous que ce que vous me proposez là est fort immoral? " she says to Count Mosca; but she does it all the same. The proposal is that she shall marry the old Duke of Sanseverina for the purpose of becoming, with greater convenience, the mistress of Count Mosca. This gentleman, being married himself, is in a position to judge of the convenience, but not of the morality; his reply, ingenious as it is, convinces you of so much. So nice a question as is here involved may be postponed; meantime I beg you to observe the exquisite simplicity of the duchess, neither condemning nor approving, wholly without prepossession, commenting merely, as the conversation flows: " Mais savez-vous. . . ."

Madame de Rênal, wife of the Maire of Verrières, Julien's first victim (and destined to be his undoing), is of another stamp. She is not witty at all, but of your slow, tender, melting, mothering sort of women. She reminds me rather of Madame de Warens, a very naïve lady as Rousseau describes her, though she moves to a more tragic issue. Much of the Madonna (Raphael's: Gina was like Luini's) is in her composition, something, maybe, of the Magdalen, for if she is a sinner it is from excess of benevolence in the first instance; and certainly she must be forgiven for her much loving. Julien Sorel one would gladly kick but for the pain it would cause this generous heart; and to be sure there is Destiny at work, never to be escaped in a book of De Stendhal's. The great scene of this particular book is the last, where you have Mathilde de la Mole and Madame de Rênal together, in accord, about the condemned body of Julien, and this little scamp bored to death with their attentions, absorbed altogether in his own emotion at the approach of his own death. But enough of men and women, since the best of them are here to speak for themselves. No more romantic figures than Fabrice, Clélia and Gina, no finer gentleman than Mosca della Rovere, no duke more Hogarthian than Ranuce-Ernest IV., will stand up in a French novel. Let me, however, grapple with De Stendhal's own person, and find out, if I can, the secret of his force.

Of Stendhal, De Stendhal, Arrigo Beyle *Milanese*, it is proper to record that he was born Beyle, and baptized Henry. For purposes of epitaph he italianated himself; more, he was nice in the business. He would have no more of Enrico than of Henry, but chose a dialect, and not a good dialect, to die in. The churchyard recalls him to your thoughts as Arrigo, which is Milanese for Henry. So he renounced at once orthography and fatherland. This is as if a king of France, preoccupied with English, and local English at that, should be buried in Saint Saviour's at Southwark with the superscription over his head of 'Arry de Bourbon. If it gives a hint of the truth that De Stendhal was apt to let his whims ride him, his books broaden the hint so far that there is danger of seeing, at first blush, little else than whim in them. To be particular, he loved to *documenter* his work. He will have you believe that this *Chartreuse de Parme* is founded upon the memoirs of a canon of Sant' Antonio at Padua. " Je publie cette nouvelle," he says, " sans rien changer au manuscrit de 1830." This is absurd, but immaterial. Otherwise, however, with stories like *Vittoria Accoramboni*, "la traduction fidèle d'un récit fort grave écrit à Padoue en Décembre 1585," or with *L'Abbesse de Castro*, translated (he pretends) "from two voluminous manuscripts, one Roman, the other Florentine." Here two stumbling-blocks disturb the reader: the first, that he attempts to imitate such compositions; the second, that he imitates them so badly. He catches, indeed, nothing but the callosity of the chronicler, gives none of his savour of cheerful pedantry, takes none of the *diverticula amœna* along which he would so easily and so delightfully wander. To his credit, perhaps, De Stendhal could not " fake " (if I may be forgiven); the pity is that he thought he could. I think some or other such attempt is to be found in every published tale of his. Even in *Le Rouge et le Noir*, Julien has to get by heart a long state-paper, which is not in the least degree like a state-paper, which impedes the action, disintegrates the plot, neither convinces nor surprises nor charms. But perhaps something else was at work here.

He was a great reader of these things, it is evident. He knew the Italian analysts well, and admired. From them, as I take it, he got as much strength as weakness. He got his conciseness, his dry light, his blessed reliance upon naked fact, his style of the *procès*, which sets him at such an advantage over the wordy Balzac. I know not how better to expound the man in this particular than to let him speak for himself, as he does in *Vittoria Accoramboni*, "Ainsi, ô lecteur bénévole," he says, " ne cherchez point ici un style piquant, rapide, brillant de fraîches allusions aux façons de sentir à la mode, ne vous attendez point surtout aux émotions entraînantes d'un roman de George Sand; ce grand écrivain eût fait un chef-d'œuvre avec la vie et les malheurs de Vittoria Accoramboni. Le récit sincère que je vous présente ne peut avoir que les avantages plus modestes de l'histoire. Quand par hazard, courant la poste seul à la tombée de la nuit, on s'avise de réfléchir au grand art de connaître le cœur humain, on pourra prendre pour base de ses jugements les circonstances de l'histoire que voici. L'auteur *dit tout, explique tout*, ne laisse rien à faire à l'imagination du lecteur; il écrivit douze jours après la mort de l'héroïne." Then there is a solemn footnote: " Le manuscrit italien est déposé au bureau de la Revue des Deux-Mondes." Pass over the caustic drop on the skin of George Sand, and consider the last sentence. He tells everything, explains everything, leaves nothing to the reader's imagination: this is a way of speaking. What he tells are bare facts, what he explains are credible motives; but in so doing he leaves exactly everything to the reader's imagination, because he records, not describes. The whole secret of good romancing is there. If authors of imagination could only understand for how much facts, well-conceived, count, and for how little descriptions! It is, to my mind, one of De Stendhal's chief claims to honour that he relied upon this romance of fact, and made no attempt to convince by description. Sometimes you may think that he carries his principle to excess, that he condescends to description deliberately jejune. It is true that there are passages whose flowers are the veriest frittering ornaments. A mountain has a majestic summit, a lake has a glassy surface, the forest of La Faggiola has " sombres et magnifiques ombrages." This is when he deigns to touch such affairs at all; the nearest he will ever go is: " Cétait au commencement d'un matin exquis d'Avril." But I think that he gains enormously by this austere handling; he knows so well that the true way of moving the imagination is to give the imagination room in which to move itself. Consider the Waterloo chapters of this book, for instance; there is no pathetic fallacy here, no geography. A clump of willows, a little shot-torn wood, a muddy road, a bridge broken down, a field with mist hanging about its edge. You will find no less in a war bulletin of the day. Yet you know that massed men are moving over broad plains, or cuirassiers in flight; you hear the guns, the rattle of artillery taking up position; the very vagueness of assertion works the spell: this is the landscape of war on a grand scale. Not Livy himself can marshal the facts better, or know more surely when to sound the charge.

The soul is De Stendhal's chosen field; here is the scope for his brushes, here he will give you intimacies in plenty. The very pick of these are in the book which follows; I shall only cite two more—one, the immortal chapter in *Le Rouge et le Noir* where Julien in the twittering dusk takes and retains the hand of Madame de Rênal, a scene so precisely recorded and so closely that you can hear the boy's heart beating, and must swear it autobiography; the second, from *L'Abbesse de Castro*. Here Hélène de Campireali is at the thick of her secret affair with Jules Branciforte, a sad detrimental, being brigand, the son of a brigand. This is discovered, first by her mother, who says nothing, next by her father, who prepares to assassinate Jules. There is a scene of alarm at midnight, in the throes of which Hélène desperately consigns to her mother Jules' letters to keep. The mother hides them in her bed, the father bursts open the girl's chamber, ransacks it, storms, threatens, vulgarizes everything; at last, exhausted, he goes to bed. " Une heure après, quand le seigneur de Campireali fut rentré dans sa chambre à côté de celle de sa femme, et tout étant tranquille dans la maison, la mère dit à sa fille: ' Voilà tes lettres, je ne veux pas les lire, tu vois ce qu'elles ont failli nous coûter! A ta place, je les brûlerais. Adieu, embrasse-moi!' Hélène rentra dans sa chambre, fondant en larmes; *il lui semblait que, depuis ces paroles de sa mère, elle n'aimait plus Jules.*"

You can not go much nearer than that, it seems to me. And yet De Stendhal, in the great scene of this

The Chartreuse of Parma

book between the Duke and the Duchess Gina, not only does go nearer, but holds the cord taut through an entire chapter, a whole night of fence and play of the mind.

Therefore, however arid you find his descriptions, and however tawdry his ornaments, your pains will be rewarded by landscape after landscape, patient, meticulous, extraordinarily accurate, full of interest, of the soul. This, as it was his only concern, should be yours also, if you wish to get the best out of him that he can give you. The study is not always rewarding; some of the souls that he delights to describe seem scarcely worth his trouble. In this *Chartreuse*, for example, one sees in the Marchesa Raversi and her creature Rassi standing dishes of fiction; so in *Le Rouge et le Noir* there are lay figures; and in *L'Abbesse de Castro* the principal character is Prince Colonna, who should be by rights in the second degree. But to take minor parts only, what figures are l'Abbé Blanès, General Fabio Conti, the Princes of Parma, father and son! Real humour went to the making of these; not wit alone, nor perspicacity alone, but genuine, large, benevolent insight; while he laughed the tears were near starting in his eye. You are almost persuaded that De Stendhal loved some of these people: a great concession toward him, for there has been no writer since Dante who has played the deist's God to his invention so consistently as this man of fire cloaked in ice.

Construction may have been often a weakness in De Stendhal. I am not concerned to deny it, since in *La Chartreuse*, at least, there is no lack of design. *Le Rouge et le Noir*, to be sure, is too long; it is diffuse, disjointed, contains episodes enough unrelated to the main stem. Though it have the stuff of great romance, great romance it is not. What is far worse than ill-construction is mechanical construction. Julien Sorel, dreaming of Napoleon, but actually on the threshold of M. de Rênal's service, pauses for a few moments' reflection in the fatal church of Verrières. There on his prie-dieu he sees a scrap of newspaper with the words: " Détails de l'éxécution et des derniers moments de Louis Jenrel, éxécuté à Besançon le. . . ." Louis Jenrel is an anagram for Julien Sorel, and a very bad one. Jenrel is an impossible name, yet there is worse to come. " Le papier était déchiré. Au revers on lisait les deux premiers mots d'une ligne, c'étaient: ' *Le premier pas.*' " This is mere carpentry; yet De Stendhal adds plank to plank. " En sortant, Julien crut voir du sang près du bénitier: c'était de l'eau bénite qu'on avait répandue: le reflet des rideaux rouges qui couvraient les fenêtres la faisait paraître du sang. Enfin, Julien eut honte de sa terreur secrète. ' Serais-je un lâche?' se dit-il: *aux armes!* " All this, packed without significance into the end of Chapter V and designed to balance the tragic events of Chapter LXXV, is unworthy of De Stendhal. If a reader fail to perceive it, it was not worth putting in; if he do perceive it, it was worth at all costs the keeping out. Nothing is worse than machinery in a work of art.

Happily there is little of the sort in *La Chartreuse de Parme*. Fabrice's parentage, perhaps, goes near to danger, and he undoubtedly reads the planets with the Abbé Blanès. Again, on his way to Milan with Gina, he falls in with, and saves from arrest, the General Conti (who is subsequently to prove his jailer) and sees Clélia for the first time. But these are nothings. One of the admirable features of the book is its steady organic growth, its march of circumstance (given certain characters in certain conjunction), and the resultant conviction at the close that what you have been witnessing, unawares, is the whole of the life of a world. Mechanical construction, forced, wilful design, are fatal to such an end.

I have done with the ungrateful task of girding at a great man; the rest must be pure enthusiasm. For irony, of which (in both kinds) he was a master, it is difficult to express one's admiration; luckily, one has only to say, Read. Irony of phrase is, perhaps, the common property of French wits. "Le pouvoir absolu tempéré par des chansons, qu'on appelle la monarchie française," is a pretty instance from *Les Cenci*; but of a higher order is that constructive irony of which De Stendhal affords some great examples. In *L'Abbesse de Castro*, Jules Branciforte and his brigands are going to attack the Convent of the Visitation, and carry away Hélène, if they are lucky. At setting out, the corporal observes: "'Nous allons attaquer un couvent, il y a *excommunication majeure*, et, de plus, ce couvent est sous la protection immédiate de la Madone. . . .'

"'Je vous entends!' s'écria Jules, comme réveillé par ce mot. 'Restez avec moi.'

"Le Caporal ferma la porte, et revint dire le chapelet avec Jules. Cette prière dura une grande heure. A la nuit on se remit en marche."

True, Italian history lends itself to that kind. The ceremony of the exposition of the relics of Saint Clement in *Le Rouge et le Noir* is finer in its way. Julien Sorel, attached for the occasion to the Dean of Chapter, M. Chélan, finds the young Bishop of Agde in the sacristy before a looking-glass. "Julien trouva que le jeune homme avait l'air irrité; de la main droite il donnait gravement des bénédictions du côté du miroir." The poor young man was, in fact, practising. He sends Julien for his mitre, which is under repair, having been damaged in the transit from Paris. Julien, returning with it, grave and proud of his burden, finds the bishop seated before the mirror: "Mais, de temps à autre, sa main droite, quoique fatiguée, donnait encore la bénédiction." Finally, the ceremony begins. The bishop takes his place before the altar of the relics; he kneels in the midst of twenty-four young girls, "chosen from the most distinguished houses of Verrières." Julien was melted to tears. "At this moment he was heart and soul for the Inquisition and the true faith." The king arrives—it was a great occasion for Verrières—throws himself upon his knees; the priests unveil the charming statue of Saint Clement.

"He was recessed under the altar, in the dress of a young Roman soldier. In his neck was a deep wound whence, as it seemed, the blood still flowed. The artist had surpassed himself; the dying eyes, full of grace, were half closed; a dawning moustache enhanced the lovely mouth, half open still, as if in prayer. At the sight of it the young girl by Julien's side shed tears; one of these warm tears fell upon his hand.

"After a moment of prayer in profound silence, broken only by the far sound of bells from all the villages within a circuit of ten miles, the Bishop of Agde begged the king's leave to speak. He ended a touching little sermon with a few simple words, whose effect was all the greater on that account.

"'Never forget, young Christians, that you have seen one of the greatest kings of the earth upon his knees before the servants of the almighty and terrible God. These poor servants, persecuted, murdered on earth, as you see by the still bleeding wound of Saint Clement, are triumphing in heaven. Young Christians, you will remember this day all your lives; you will abhor impiety for ever, will you not? All your lives long you will be true to this God, so great, so terrible, yet so beneficent?'"

"With these words the bishop stood up.

"'You promise?' he asked, holding up his hand, like one inspired.

"'We promise,' said all the young girls, dissolved in tears.

"'I receive your promise in the terrible name of God,' said the bishop in a resonant voice. The ceremony was over.

"Even the king wept. It was a long time before Julien had the hardihood to inquire where had been the bones of the saint sent from Rome to Philip the Good, Duke of Burgundy. He was told that they had been hidden within the charming wax figure.

"His Majesty was graciously pleased to allow the young ladies who had accompanied him in the chapel to wear each a red ribbon embroidered with the words: *War upon Impiety. Perpetual Adoration.*"

I doubt if Voltaire ever used a graver dexterity than that. Indeed, he would have shown his hand. One would have to go to Swift to better it. In Heine's manner, rather, are the last words of *La Chartreuse*, commended by De Stendhal himself "to the Happy Few": "The prisons of Parma were empty, Ernest V. adored by his people. They compared his government to that of the Grand Dukes of Tuscany." But to get the full effect of that culmination the book must be read through. Of a similar quality is the irony of Clélia's vow to the Madonna, that if Fabrice be rescued from prison she will never see him again. This reduces their love-affair, which is never interrupted for a moment, to night, the garden, and the dark. Unfortunately one of the children falls ill, and they meet in the presence of candles; hence the death of the child, and of Clélia, heartbroken over her broken vow.

The greatest irony of all remains: that which is known as tragic irony, and inheres in the very flesh of a tragic book. Each of De Stendhal's three mature romances is permeated with it. So *Le Rouge et le Noir* is a pitiful tragedy, *L'Abbesse de Castro* an heroic tragedy, *La Chartreuse de Parme* a tragi-comedy: futility of earthly endeavour is the end of each. Character is Destiny; the struggles of a strong man with Fate, the rise and fall of conflict, the inevitable end: it seems that we can not better the instruction of the Greeks, save in this, that we can enhance tragedy, sharpen it, make the pain more exquisite by laughter; humane laughter, which may purge the emotions as well as ever terror or tears. Terror was never De Stendhal's weapon; tears he seldom moves. Laughter is his chosen arm, of the noiseless, internal kind. He sides with Cervantes, with whom indeed he has much else in common.

He has (like Cervantes) three of the requisites of romance: love of adventure, quickness of dramatic sense, and feeling for atmosphere. If in addition he had had rapidity of movement (which means high spirits) there need have been no limits to his kingdom. But he never had that. He was of a reflective habit: his bent was analysis, his method patient accumulation of fact, and his chosen style that of the police report. It is impossible to imagine him overflowing with plots; history did not move him; he preferred ideas. At root he was a moralist, never near to Walter Scott. Against this great man he turns his irony more than once or twice.

Judged by method, judged by style, you may set De Stendhal with the classics. His date would put him there. And yet, if you look closely enough, you see him an ultra-romantic born out of due time. He believed himself, I am sure, academic. Actually, there is no more ardent hunter of the strange beauty of romance. His women proclaim it. He goes out armed with the scientist's weapons—the scalpel, the pins and corks; he will impale you any one of his fluttering, lovely, hapless creatures of an hour or so—or so believe it. Really, he sees them in a golden mist; really, he is on his knees. He affects to expound what he treasures under a veil, just as he hides the bones of Saint Clement under a charming wax figure. Madame de Rênal is a goddess to him, a Mater Amabilis; all her pain is but a measure of his preoccupation with her. Does he explain the Duchess Gina? Like Fabrice del Dongo, he loves Clélia most dearly in the dark. Mystery is his business, and if it is not there he will make it. Otherwise why bring in a secret meeting and a state-paper to be committed to memory into the middle of Julien's intrigue with Mademoiselle de la Mole? De Stendhal is as romantic as Balzac; as romantic as any realist alive or dead.

He has the true romantic spirit of adventure. The Waterloo episode is a proof of that; so is Fabrice's flight over the Po after the death of Giletti, his adventures in Bologna, with that wonderful sense of fresh air and open country. He has the " continual slight novelty " which is the only test of romantic invention. Fabrice, going to the wars, disguises himself as a dealer in barometers! Julien has adventures too: the scene in the café at Besançon, with the friendly *dame de comptoir*, the scenes at Strassbourg, the whole account of his leaguer of Madame de Rênal. As for *L'Abbesse de Castro*, it is full of adventurous landscape, with two magnificent battle-pieces—the fight in the wood, and the attack on the Convent of the Visitation. But we come round in the end once more to the truth, which is that De Stendhal will live by one book—*La Chartreuse de Parme*—wherein you have every quality which goes to show him great.

La Chartreuse depicts the Italy of the eighteenth century: the Italy of faded simulacra, of fard and hair powder, of *cicisbei* and curled *abbati*, of *petits-maîtres*, of the Grand Dukes of Tuscany, of Luca Longhi. For the comedian of manners this is the time of times, since manners seemed all, and Italy the place of places, where manners have always been more than all. There was matter for a Molière, matter for a Hogarth (and Longhi took of each); but there was something over. De Stendhal, bringing the wit of one and the irony of the other up to be fed, brought also that something over which neither of these had—dauntless appetite for romance, and the arbitrary dealing—" cet air de maîtrise et ce beau nonchaloir "—of his own genius.

He is moralist since he is thinking man, he is wit since he is Frenchman; more, he is a wizard who quickens the old bones and colours the dead old dust with a wave of mystery. Here is the Italy of Palladian architecture, of Bernini's simpering nymphs, of strutting perukes; here are card-playing *marquises*, and discreet drawing-room Jesuits; here are the Austrians at the gates of Venice, and here the Milanese printing sonnets on rose-coloured silk squares. In the midst of it all the Abbé Blanès consults the stars from his tower-top;

The Chartreuse of Parma

Ranuce-Ernest V. geologizes in his woods, hammer in hand; Clélia Conti feeds her birds, and Fabrice (fetters on his ankles) watches her from the Farnese fortress. The Fiscal-General Rassi schemes for a ribbon, la petite Marietta wheedles for a shawl, Count Mosca della Rovere suffers the gnawing of jealousy in a great marble palace, and the Duchess of Sanseverina, giving herself to Ranuce-Ernest for half an hour by the clock, vows she can not be light-hearted again for a month. Here are colours, here is fragrance for the dead old dust. There is the same variegation of carmine and mildew in Longhi's pictures, the same tragic hint, the same equivocal smile, the same grace, the same dignity. But Longhi can not give you as much as De Stendhal, because he can not get so near. De Stendhal fills you with his own large sense of life, ennobles you with his own large grasp of the great world. He touches the heart through the brain, speaking (as he says) " to the happy few," who possess both these organs.

Not the least interesting point about *La Chartreuse de Parme* is the fact that the Chartreuse itself has nothing to do with the story, and is only mentioned in it twice, on the last page.

MAURICE HEWLETT.

The Charterhouse of Parma

LIFE OF STENDHAL

MARIE HENRI BEYLE, *who called himself* STENDHAL, *was born at Grenoble on the 23d of January, 1783. His father, Joseph Chérubin Beyle, was a lawyer and a member of the parliament of Dauphiné. His childhood and boyhood, excited by echoes of the Revolution, but repressed in the bosom of a royalist and conservative family, were turbulent and distressing; in later years Grenoble was to him " like the recollection of an abominable indigestion." He escaped from it in 1799, and spent a short time in the War Office in Paris. In 1800 he went off to the wars, saw Italy for the first time, was present at the battle of Marengo, and fought his first duel at Milan. From 1801 to 1806 Beyle was in Paris and Grenoble, much occupied with affairs of the heart. In the latter year he entered Napoleon's army, and remained in it until after the retreat from Moscow in 1814. He was made "intendant militaire," and his zeal commended him to the Emperor. On one occasion, called upon to raise five million francs from a German state, Beyle produced seven millions. He seems to have been one of the few officers who kept their heads in the flood of disaster; during the retreat from Russia he was always clean-shaved and perfectly dressed. But the fatigues of 1814 shattered his health, and the ruin of Napoleon his hopes; he was obliged to withdraw to Como to recover his composure. He refused an administrative post in Paris under the new government, and settled definitely at Milan. His career of violent action had exhausted his spirits; he now adopted the mode of life of a dilettante. He gave himself up to music, books, and love. His first work, the "Letters Written from Vienna," appeared*

The Chartreuse of Parma

in 1814; this essay, a musical criticism, was followed in 1817 by the "History of Italian Painting," and "Rome, Naples, and Florence." He became poor, and in 1821, being suspected of Italianism, was expelled from Milan by the Austrian police; he took refuge in Paris. Stendhal's essay on "Love," the earliest of his really remarkable books, was published in 1822, but attracted no attention whatever; in eleven years only seventeen copies of it were sold. His first novel, "Armance," belongs to 1827. In 1830 he was appointed consul at Trieste, and while he was there the great novel, "Le Rouge et le Noir," appeared in Paris without attracting any attention. Stendhal was so miserable at Trieste that he contrived to exchange his consulate for that of Civita Vecchia, which he held until he died. In spite of the complete and astonishing failures of each of his successive books, he continued to add to their number. He had but "one hundred readers" in all Europe, but these he continued to address. In 1838 he published a mystification, the supposed "Memoirs in France" of a commercial traveller. Stendhal did not taste literary success in any degree whatever until, in 1839, and at the age of fifty-six, he produced "La Chartreuse de Parme." This novel gave him fame, but he did not long enjoy it. On the 23d of March, 1842, having reached his sixtieth year, he died in Paris, after a stroke of paralysis. He lies buried at Montmartre, under the epitaph, in Italian, which he had written for the purpose: "Here lies Arrigo Beyle, the Milanese. Lived, Wrote, Died." The life of Stendhal was obscure and isolated throughout; but since his death he has excited boundless curiosity, and his influence has been steadily advancing. He said of himself that he could afford to wait, that he would certainly be appreciated in 1880. He proved himself a true prophet, for it was just forty years after his death that his reputation reached its highest pinnacle, and that, with the discovery of his Correspondence, Stendhal entered into his glory.   E. G.

AUTHOR'S INTRODUCTION

This novel was written in the year 1830, in a place some three hundred leagues from Paris. Many years before that, when our armies were pouring across Europe, I chanced to be billeted in the house of a canon. It was at Padua—a fortunate city, where, as in Venice, men's pleasure is their chief business, and leaves them little time for anger with their neighbours. My stay was of some duration, and a friendship sprang up between the canon and myself.

Passing through Padua again, in 1830, I hurried to the good canon's house. He was dead, I knew, but I had set my heart on looking once more upon the room in which we had spent many a pleasant evening, sadly remembered in later days. I found the canon's nephew, and his wife, who both received me like an old friend. A few acquaintances dropped in, and the party did not break up till a late hour. The nephew had an excellent *sambaglione* fetched from the Café Pedrocchi. But what especially caused us to linger was the story of the Duchess Sanseverina, to which some chance allusion was made, and the whole of which the nephew was good enough to relate, for my benefit.

" In the country whither I am bound," said I to my friends, " I am very unlikely to find a house like this one. To while away the long evenings I will write a novel on the life of your charming Duchess Sanseverina. I will follow in the steps of that old story-teller of yours, Bandello, Bishop of Agen, who would have thought it a crime to overlook the true incidents of his tale, or add others to it."

" In that case," quoth the nephew, " I will lend you my uncle's diaries. Under the head of Parma he mentions some of the court intrigues of that place, at the period when the influence of the duchess was supreme. But beware! it is anything but a moral tale, and now that you French people pique yourselves on your Gospel purity, it may earn you a highly criminal reputation."

I send forth my novel without having made any change in the manuscript written in 1830. This course may present two drawbacks:

The first affects the reader. The characters, being Italian, may not interest him, for the hearts and souls of that nation are very different from the hearts and souls of Frenchmen. The Italians are a sincere and worthy folk, who, except when they are offended, say what they think. Vanity only attacks them in fits. Then it becomes a passion, and is known as *puntiglio*. And, further, among this nation poverty is not considered a cause of ridicule.

The second drawback is connected with the author.

I will avow that I have been bold enough to leave my personages in possession of the natural roughnesses of their various characters. But to atone for this—and I proclaim it loudly—I cast blame of the most highly moral nature upon many of their actions. Where would be the use of my endowing them with the high morality and pleasing charm of the French, who love money above every other thing, and are seldom led into sin either by love or hate? The Italians of my novel are of a very different stamp. And, indeed, it appears to me that every stage of six hundred miles northward from the regions of the South brings us to a different landscape, and to a different kind of novel. The old canon's charming niece had known the duchess, and had even been very much attached to her. She has begged me not to alter anything concerning these adventures of her friend, which are certainly open to censure.

January 23, 1839.

CONTENTS

THE CHARTREUSE OF PARMA

THE CHARTREUSE OF PARMA

CHAPTER I

MILAN IN 1796

ON the 15th of May, 1796, General Bonaparte marched into the city of Milan, at the head of the youthful army which had just crossed the Bridge of Lodi, and taught the world that, after the lapse of centuries, Cæsar and Alexander had found a successor at last.

The prodigies of genius and daring witnessed by Italy in the course of a few months, roused her people from their slumbers. But one week before the arrival of the French, the Milanese still took them for a horde of brigands, whose habit it was to fly before the troops of his Royal and Imperial Majesty. Such, at all events, was the information repeated three times a week in their little newspaper, no bigger than a man's hand, and printed on dirty-looking paper.

In the middle ages, the Milanese had been as brave as the French of the Revolution, and their courage earned the complete destruction of their city by the German emperor. But their chief occupation, since they had become his " *faithful subjects*," was to print sonnets on pink silk handkerchiefs whenever any rich or well-born young lady was given in marriage. Two or three years after that great epoch in her life the said young lady chose herself a *cavaliere servente*; the name of this *cicisbeo*, selected by the husband's family, occasionally held an honoured place in the marriage contract. Between such effeminate habits and the deep emotions stirred by the unexpected arrival of the French army, a great gulf lay. Before long a new and

1

passionate order of things had supervened. On May 15, 1796, a whole people became aware that all it had hitherto respected was supremely ridiculous, and occasionally hateful, to boot. The departure of the last Austrian regiment marked the downfall of the old ideas. To expose one's life became the fashionable thing. People perceived, after these centuries of hypocrisy and insipidities, that the only chance of happiness lay in loving with real passion, and knowing how to risk one's life upon occasion. The continuance of the watchful despotism of Charles V and Philip II had plunged the Lombards into impenetrable darkness. They overthrew these rulers' statues, and forthwith found themselves bathed in light. For fifty years, while Voltaire's Encyclopédie was appearing in France, the monks had been assuring the good folk of Milan that to learn to read, or to learn anything on earth, was idle vexation of the spirit, and that if they would only pay their priest's dues honestly, and tell him all their small sins faithfully, they were almost certain to secure a comfortable place in paradise. To complete the emasculation of this whilom doughty people, the Austrian had sold them, on moderate terms, the privilege of not furnishing recruits to the imperial army.

In 1796, the Milanese army consisted of eighty "*facchini*" in red coats, who kept guard over the town, assisted by four splendid Hungarian regiments. Morals were exceedingly loose, but real passion excessively rare. Apart from the inconvenience of being obliged to tell everything to his priest, the Milanese of the period of 1790 really did not know the meaning of any vehement desire. The worthy citizens were still trammelled by certain monarchical bonds, which had their vexatious side. For instance, the archduke, who resided in the city and governed it in the Emperor's name, had pitched on the very lucrative notion of dealing in corn stuffs. Consequently, no peasant could sell his crops until his Imperial Highness had filled up his granaries.

In May, 1796, three days after the entry of the French, a young miniature painter of the name of Gros, rather a mad fellow—he has since become famous—who had arrived

The Chartreuse of Parma

with the troops, heard somebody at the Café dei Servi, then a fashionable resort, relate the doings of the archduke, who was a very fat man. Seizing the list of ices, printed on a slip of common yellowish paper, he sketched on its blank side the portly archduke, with immoderate quantities of corn, instead of blood, pouring out of the hole in his stomach, made by a French soldier's bayonet. In this land of crafty despotism, that which we call jest or caricature was unknown. The drawing left by Gros on the *café* table acted like a miracle from heaven. During the night the sketch was engraved; on the morrow twenty thousand copies of it were sold.

That same day the walls were posted with the proclamation of a war tax of six millions of francs, levied for the support of the French army, which, though it had just won six battles and conquered twenty provinces, was short of shoes, pantaloons, coats, and hats.

So great was the volume of happiness and pleasure which poured into Lombardy with these Frenchmen, poor as they were, that nobody, save the priests and a few nobles, perceived the weight of the tax, which was soon followed by many others. The French soldiers laughed and sang from morning till night. They were all of them under five-and-twenty, and their general in chief, who numbered twenty-seven years, was said to be the oldest man in his command. All this youth and mirth and gay carelessness made cheery answer to the furious sermons of the monks, who for six months past had been asserting from the pulpit of every sacred edifice that these Frenchmen were all monsters, forced, on pain of death, to burn down everything, and cut off every head, and that for this last purpose a guillotine was borne at the head of every regiment.

In country places the French soldier was to be seen sitting at cottage doors rocking the owner's baby; and almost every evening some drummer would tune up his violin, and dancing would begin. The French square dances were far too difficult and complicated to be taught to the peasant women by the soldiers, who, indeed, knew but little about them. So it was the women who taught

3

The Chartreuse of Parma

the Frenchmen the *monferino*, the *saltarello*, and other Italian dances.

The officers had been billeted, as far as possible, upon rich families. They were in sore need of an opportunity to retrieve past losses. A lieutenant named Robert, for instance, was billeted in the palace of the Marchesa del Dongo. When this officer, a tolerably handy young recruit, entered into occupation of his apartment, his sole worldly wealth consisted of a six-franc piece, which had been paid him at Piacenza. After the passage of the Bridge of Lodi he had stripped a handsome Austrian officer, killed by a round shot, of a splendid new pair of nankeen pantaloons. Never did garment appear at a more appropriate moment! His officer's epaulets were woollen, and the cloth of his coat was sewed to the sleeve linings, to keep the bits together. A yet more melancholy circumstance was that the soles of his shoes were composed of portions of hats, picked up on the battlefield beyond the Bridge of Lodi. These improvised soles were bound to his shoes by strings, which were aggressively visible—so much so, in fact, that when the major-domo of the household made his appearance in Robert's room, to invite him to dine with the marchesa, the lieutenant was cast into a state of mortal confusion. He and his orderly spent the two hours intervening before the dreaded repast in trying to stitch the coat together, and dye the unlucky shoe-strings with ink. At last the awful moment struck. " Never in all my life did I feel so uncomfortable," said Lieutenant Robert to me. " The ladies thought I was going to frighten them—but I trembled much more than they! I kept my eyes on my shoes, and could not contrive to move with ease or grace.

" The Marchesa del Dongo," he added, " was then in the heyday of her beauty. You know what she was, with her lovely eyes, angelic in their gentleness, and the pretty, fair hair, which made so perfect a frame for the oval of her charming face. In my room there was an Herodia, by Leonardo da Vinci, which might have been her portrait. God willed that her supernatural beauty should so overwhelm my senses as to make me quite forget my own

4

appearance. For two years I had been in the Genoese mountains, looking at nothing but ugliness and misery. I ventured to say a few words about my delight.

"But I had too much good sense to dally long with compliments. While I was making mine, I perceived in a palatial marble dining hall some dozen lackeys and men servants, dressed in what then appeared to me the height of magnificence. Think of it! The rascals not only wore good shoes, but silver buckles into the bargain! Out of the corner of my eye I could see their stupid gaze riveted on my coat, and perhaps, too—and this wrung my heart—upon my shoes. With one word I could have terrified the whole set, but how was I to put them in their place without running the risk of alarming the ladies? For to give herself a little courage, the marchesa—she has told me so a hundred times over since—had sent to the convent, where she was then at school, for her husband's sister, Gina del Dongo, who afterward became that charming Contessa Pietranera. No woman was ever more gay and lovable in prosperity, and none ever surpassed her in courage and serenity under Fortune's frowns.

"Gina, who may then have been thirteen, but looked eighteen, frank and lively, as you know, was so afraid of bursting out laughing at my dress that she dared not even eat. The marchesa, on the contrary, overwhelmed me with stiff civilities; she read my impatience and discomfort in my eyes. In a word, I cut a sorry figure. I was chewing the cud of scorn, which no Frenchman is supposed to be capable of doing. At last Heaven sent me a brilliant notion. I began to tell the ladies about my poverty and the misery we had suffered during those two years in the Genoese mountains, where the folly of our old generals had kept us. 'There,' said I, 'they gave us *assignats* which the people would not take in payment, and three ounces of bread a day.' Before I had been talking for two minutes the kind marchesa's eyes were full of tears and Gina had grown quite serious. 'What, lieutenant!' she cried, 'three ounces of bread?'

"'Yes, mademoiselle. But, on the other hand, the

supply failed three times in the week, and as the peasants with whom we lived were even poorer than ourselves, we used to give them a little of our bread.'

"When we rose from table I offered the marchesa my arm, escorted her as far as the drawing-room door, then, hastily retracing my steps, presented the servant who had waited upon me at dinner with the solitary coin on the spending of which I had built such castles in the air.

"A week later," Robert went on, "when it had become quite clear that the French did not guillotine anybody, the Marchese del Dongo returned from Grianta, his country house on Lake Como, where he had valiantly taken refuge when the army drew near, leaving his young and lovely wife and his sister to the chances of war. The marchese's hatred of us was only equalled by his dread. Both were immeasurable. It used to amuse me to see his large, pale, hypocritical face when he was trying to be polite to me. The day after his return to Milan I received three ells of cloth and two hundred francs out of the six millions. I put on fresh plumage and became the ladies cavalier, for ball giving began."

Lieutenant Robert's story was very much that of all the French soldiers. Instead of laughing at the brave fellows' poverty, people pitied them and learned to love them. This period of unforeseen happiness and rapture lasted only two short years. So excessive and so general was the frolic that I can not possibly convey an idea of it, unless it be by means of the following profound historic reflection: This nation had been bored for a century!

The sensuality natural to southern countries had formerly reigned at the courts of those famous Milanese dukes, the Sforza and the Visconti. But since the year 1624, when the Spaniards had seized the province, and held it under the proud, taciturn, distrustful sway of masters who suspected revolt in every corner, merriment had fled away, and the populace, aping its rulers' habits, was much more prone to avenge the slightest insult with a dagger thrust, than to enjoy the moment as it passed.

But between May 15, 1796, when the French entered

6

The Chartreuse of Parma

Milan, and April, 1799, when they were driven out of the city by the battle of Cassano, wild merriment, gaiety, voluptuous pleasure, and oblivion of every sad, or even rational sentiment, reached such a pitch that old millionaire merchants, usurers, and notaries were actually quoted by name as having forgotten their morose and money-getting habits during that period. One might have found a few families of the highest rank that had retired to their country places to sulk at the general cheerfulness and universal joy. And it is a fact, further, that these families had been honoured with a disagreeable amount of attention by the authorities in charge of the war tax, levied for the benefit of the French troops.

The Marchese del Dongo, disgusted at the sight of so much gaiety, had been one of the first to return to his magnificent country seat at Grianta, beyond Como, whither the ladies of his family conducted Lieutenant Robert. This castle, standing in what is probably a unique position, on a plateau some one hundred and fifty feet above the splendid lake, and commanding a great portion of it, had once been a fortress. It had been built, as the numerous marble slabs bearing the family arms attested, during the fifteenth century. The drawbridges were still to be seen, and the deep moats—now dry, to be sure. Still, with its walls eighty feet high and six feet thick, the castle was safe from a *coup de main*, and this fact endeared it to the suspicious marchese. Living there, surrounded by five-and-twenty or thirty servants, whom he believed to be devoted to him— apparently because he never spoke to them without abusing them—he was less harried by fear than at Milan.

This alarm was not entirely unwarranted. The marchese was in active correspondence with an Austrian spy stationed on the Swiss frontier, three leagues from Grianta, to assist the escape of prisoners taken in battle, and the French generals might have taken this exchange of notes very seriously.

The marchese had left his young wife at Milan to manage the family affairs. She it was who had to find means of supplying the contributions levied on the Casa del

The Chartreuse of Parma

Dongo, as it was locally called, and to endeavour to get them reduced, which involved the necessity of her seeing the noblemen who had accepted public positions, and even some very influential persons who were not noble at all. A great event occurred in the family. The marchese had arranged a marriage for his young sister Gina with a gentleman of great wealth and the very highest descent. But he powdered his head. Wherefore Gina received him with shrieks of laughter, and shortly committed the folly of marrying Count Pietranera. He, too, was a high-born gentleman, and very good-looking as well, but he was ruined, as his father had been before him, and—crowning disgrace!— he was an eager partisan of the modern ideas! The marchese's despair was completed by the fact that Pietranera was a lieutenant in the Italian Legion.

After two years of extravagance and bliss, the Paris Directorate, which took on all the airs of a well-established sovereignty, began to manifest a mortal hatred of everything that rose above mediocrity. The incapable generals sent to the Army of Italy lost a series of battles on those very plains of Verona which but two years previously had witnessed the feats of Arcola and Lonato. The Austrians approached Milan; Lieutenant Robert, now a major, was wounded at the battle of Cassano, and came back for the last time to the house of his friend the Marchesa del Dongo. It was a sad farewell. Robert departed with Count Pietranera, who was following the French retreat on Novi. The young countess, whose brother had refused to give up her fortune, followed the retreating army in a cart.

Then began that period of reaction and return to the old ideas which the Milanese call "*i tredici mesi*" (the thirteen months) because their lucky star did not permit this relapse into imbecility to last beyond the battle of Marengo. Everything that was old, bigoted, morose, and gloomy came back to the head of affairs and of society. Before long, those who had remained faithful to the old order were telling the villagers that Napoleon had met the fate he so richly deserved, and had been hanged by the Mamelukes Egypt.

The Chartreuse of Parma

Among the men who had retired to sulk in their country houses, and who now came back, thirsting for vengeance, the Marchese del Dongo distinguished himself by his eagerness. His zeal naturally bore him to the head of the party. The gentlemen composing it, very amiable fellows when they were not in a fright, but who were still in a state of trepidation, contrived to circumvent the Austrian general, who, though rather of a kindly disposition, allowed himself to be persuaded that severity was a mark of statesmanship, and ordered the arrest of a hundred and fifty patriots. They were the best men Italy then possessed.

Soon they were all deported to the Bocche de Cattaro, and cast into subterranean dungeons, where damp and, especially, starvation wreaked prompt and thorough justice on the villains.

The Marchese del Dongo was appointed to an important post; and as the meanest avarice accompanied his numerous other noble qualities, he publicly boasted that he had not sent a single crown to his sister, the Countess Pietranera. This lady, still fathoms deep in love, would not forsake her husband, and was starving with him in France. The kind-hearted marchesa was in despair. At last she contrived to abstract a few small diamonds from her jewel case, which her husband took from her every night and locked up in an iron box under his bed. She had brought him a dowry of eight hundred thousand francs, and he allowed her eighty francs a month for her personal expenses. During the thirteen months of the absence of the French from Milan, this woman, timid as she was, found pretexts of one sort or another which enabled her always to dress in black.

It must be confessed here that, after the example of many serious authors, we have begun the story of our hero a year before his birth. This important personage is no other, in fact, than Fabrizio Valserra, Marchesino del Dongo, as he would be called at Milan.* He had just condescended to come into the world when the French were driven out, the

---

* The habit of the country, borrowed from that of Germany, is that all the sons of a marchese should be called *marchesino*. The son of a count is known as *contino*; each of his daughters is a *contessina*.

The Chartreuse of Parma

chances of his birth making him the second son of that most noble Marchese del Dongo, with whose large, pallid countenance, deceitful smile, and boundless hatred of the new order of ideas, my readers are already acquainted. The whole of the family fortune was entailed on the eldest boy, Ascanio del Dongo, the perfect image of his father. He was eight years old, and Fabrizio two, when, like a flash, that General Bonaparte whom all well-born folk believed to have been hanged long since, descended from Mount St. Bernard. He made his entry into Milan; the event is still unique in history. Conceive a whole population over head and ears in love! A few days later Napoleon won the battle of Marengo. I need not tell the rest. The rapture of the Milanese overflowed the cup. But this time it was mingled with thoughts of vengeance. A good-natured folk had been taught to hate. Soon the remnant of the patriots exiled to Cattaro reappeared, and their return was celebrated by national festivities. Their pale faces, great startled eyes, and emaciated limbs, contrasted strangely with the joy that reigned on every side. Their arrival was the signal for the departure of the families most concerned in their banishment. The Marchese del Dongo was one of the first to flee to his house at Grianta. The heads of the great families were filled with rage and terror, but their wives and daughters, remembering the delights of the first French occupation, sighed regretfully for Milan and the gay balls which, once Marengo was over, were given at the Casa Tanzi. A few days after the victory the French general charged with the duty of maintaining quiet in Lombardy became aware that all the tenants of the noble families, and all the old women in the country, far from dwelling on the wonderful victory which had changed the fate of Italy, and reconquered thirteen fortresses in one day, were thinking of nothing but the prophecy of San Giovità, the chief patron saint of Brescia, according to which sacred pronouncement the prosperity of Napoleon and of the French nation was to end just thirteen weeks after Marengo. Some slight excuse for the Marchese del Dongo and all the sulky country nobility is to be found in the fact that they really and truly did believe in this prophecy. None of these people had read four books in his life. They openly prepared to return to Milan at the end of the thirteenth week, but as time went on, it was marked by fresh successes on the French side. Napoleon, who had returned to Paris, saved the revolution from within by his wise decrees, even as he had saved it from foreign attack at Marengo. Then the Lombard nobles in their country refuges discovered that they had misunderstood the prediction of the patron saint of Brescia. He must have meant thirteen months instead of thirteen weeks! But the thirteen months slipped by, and the prosperity of France seemed to rise higher day by day.

We pass over the ten years of happiness and progress between 1800 and 1810. Fabrizio spent the earliest of them at Grianta, where he dealt out many hard knocks among the little peasant boys, and received them back with interest, but learned nothing—not even to read. Later he was sent to the Jesuit school at Milan. The marchese, his father, insisted that he should learn Latin, not out of those ancient authors who are always holding forth about republics, but out of a splendid tome enriched with more than a hundred and fifty engravings, a masterpiece of seventeenth-century art, the Latin Genealogy of the Valserra, Marchesi del Dongo, published by Fabrizio del Dongo, Archbishop of Parma, in the year 1650. The Valserra were essentially a fighting race, and these engravings represented numerous battles, in which some hero of the name was always depicted as laying about mightily with his sword.

This book was a great delight to young Fabrizio. His mother, who adored him, was allowed now and then to go to Milan to see him, but her husband never offered to pay the cost of these journeys. The money was always lent her by her sister-in-law, the charming Countess Pietranera, who, after the return of the French, had become one of the most brilliant of the ladies at the court of the Viceroy of Italy, Prince Eugene.

After Fabrizio had made his first communion, the countess persuaded the marchese, who still lived in volun-

The Chartreuse of Parma

tary exile, to allow the boy to pay her occasional visits. He struck her as being out of the common, clever, very serious, but handsome, and no discredit to a fashionable lady's drawing-room—though he was utterly ignorant, and hardly knew how to write. The countess, who carried her characteristic enthusiasm into everything she did, promised her protection to the head of the Jesuit house if only her nephew Fabrizio made astonishing progress in his studies, and won several prizes at the close of the year. To put him in the way of earning such rewards, she sent for him every Saturday night, and frequently did not restore him to his teachers till the Wednesday or Thursday following. Though the Jesuits were tenderly cherished by the Viceroy, their presence in Italy was forbidden by the laws of the kingdom, and the Superior of the college, a clever man, realized all the benefits that might accrue from his relations with a lady who was all-powerful at court. He was too wise to complain of Fabrizio's absences, and at the end of the year five first prizes were conferred on the youth, who was more ignorant than ever. In the circumstances, the brilliant Countess Pietranera, attended by her husband, then general in command of one of the divisions of the Guard, and five or six of the most important personages about the Viceroy's court, attended the distribution of prizes in the Jesuit school. The Superior received the congratulations of the heads of his order.

The countess was in the habit of taking her nephew to all the gay fêtes which enlivened the kindly Viceroy's too short reign. She had made him an officer of hussars, on her own authority, and the twelve-year-old boy wore his uniform. One day the countess, delighted with his handsome looks, asked the prince to make him a page, which would have been tantamount, of course, to an acknowledgment of adherence to the new order of things of the Del Dongo family. The next morning she was fain to use all her influence to induce the Viceroy kindly to forget her request, which lacked nothing but the consent of the father of the future page—a consent which would have been loudly refused. As a result of this piece of folly,

which made him shiver, the sulky marchese coined some
pretext for recalling young Fabrizio to Grianta. The
countess nursed a sovereign contempt for her brother,
whom she regarded as a dreary fool, who would be spiteful if he ever had the power. But she doted on Fabrizio,
and after ten years of silence she wrote to the marchese, to
beg that she might have her nephew with her. Her letter
remained unanswered.

When Fabrizio returned to the formidable pile built by
the most warlike of his ancestors he knew nothing about
anything in the world except drill, and riding on horseback.
Count Pietranera, who had been as fond of the child as
his wife, had taught him to ride, and taken him with him
on parade.

When the boy reached Grianta, with eyes still reddened
by the tears he had shed on leaving his aunt's splendid apartments, his only greeting was that of his mother, who covered him with passionate caresses, and of his sisters. The
marchese was shut up in his study with his eldest son, the
Marchesino Ascanio. They were busy writing letters in
cipher, which were to have the honour of being sent to
Vienna, and they were only visible at mealtimes. The
marchese ostentatiously declared that he was teaching his
natural successor to keep the accounts of the revenues of
each of his estates by double entry, but in reality he was
far too jealous by nature to mention such matters to the son
on whom these properties were absolutely entailed. He
really employed him to translate into cipher the despatches
of fifteen or twenty pages which he sent, two or three times a
week, across the Swiss frontier, whence they were conveyed
to Vienna. The marchese claimed that he thus kept his
legitimate sovereign informed as to the internal conditions
of the kingdom of Italy—a subject about which he himself
knew nothing at all. His letters, however, won him great
credit, and for the following reason: He was in the habit
of employing some trusty agent to count up the numbers
of any French or Italian regiment that marched along the
highroad when changing its place of garrison, and in making his report to Vienna he always carefully diminished the

number of men reported present by a full fourth. These letters, then, ridiculous as they otherwise were, had the merit of contradicting others of a more truthful nature, and thus gave pleasure in high quarters. Consequently, not long before Fabrizio's return to Grianta, the marchese had received the star of a famous order—the fifth that adorned his chamberlain's coat. It is true, indeed, that he had to endure the grief of never wearing the said coat outside the walls of his own study, but, on the other hand, he never ventured to dictate any despatch without first enduing his person with the richly embroidered garment, hung with all his orders. Any other course would have seemed to him a failure in respect.

The marchesa was delighted with her boy's charms. But she had kept up the habit of writing, twice or thrice in the year, to General Comte d'A—— (the name then borne by Lieutenant Robert). She had a horror of lying to those she loved; she questioned her son, and was startled by his ignorance.

" If," she argued, " he appears ill-instructed to me, who know nothing, Robert, who knows so much, would think his education an utter failure; and nowadays some merit is indispensable to success!" Another peculiarity, which almost equally astounded her, was that Fabrizio had taken all the religious teaching given him by the Jesuits quite seriously. Though herself a very pious woman, her child's fanaticism made her shiver. " If the marchese has the sense to suspect this means of influencing my son, he will rob me of his love!" She wept many tears, and her passionate love for Fabrizio deepened.

Life in the great country house, with its thirty or forty servants, was very dull; and Fabrizio spent all his days hunting, or skimming over the waters of the lake in a boat. He was soon the sworn ally of all the coachmen and stable assistants—every one of them a vehement partisan of the French—who made open sport of the highly religious valets attached to the persons of the marchese and his elder son. The great joke against these individuals was that, like their masters, they wore powder in their hair.

CHAPTER II

. . . "Alors que Vesper vient embrunir nos yeux
Tout épris de l'avenir, je contemple les cieux,
En qui Dieu nous escrit, par notes non obscures
Les sorts et les destins de toutes créatures.
Car lui, du fond des cieux regardant un humain,
Parfois, mû de pitié, lui montre le chemin ;
Par les astres du ciel, qui sont ses caractères,
Les choses nous prèdit, et bonnes et contraires ;
Mais les hommes, chargés de terre et de trépas,
Méprisent tel écrit, et ne le lisent pas."—*Ronsard*.

THE marchese professed a hearty hatred of knowledge. "Ideas," he said, "have been the ruin of Italy." He was somewhat puzzled to reconcile this holy horror of information with his desire that Fabrizio should perfect the education so brilliantly begun under the auspices of the Jesuits.

To minimize the risk as far as possible, he commissioned the worthy priest of Grianta, Father Blanès, to carry on the boy's Latin studies. To this end the priest should himself have been acquainted with the language. But he thoroughly despised it. His knowledge of it was restricted to the prayers in his missal, which he knew by rote, and the sense of which, or something near it, he was capable of imparting to his flock. None the less was the father respected, and even feared, all over the canton. He had always averred that the famous prophecy of San Giovità, patron saint of Brescia, would not be accomplished either in thirteen weeks or thirteen months. He would confide to his trusted friends that if he dared speak openly he could give the proper interpretation of the number *thirteen*, and that it would cause general astonishment (1813).

The fact is that Father Blanès—a man of primitive virtue and honesty, and a clever one into the bargain—spent

15

most of his nights on the top of his church tower. He had a mania for astrology, and, after calculating the positions and conjunctions of the stars all day, would pass the greater part of his nights in tracing them in the sky. So poor was he that his only instrument was a telescope with a long cardboard tube. My reader will conceive the scorn for linguistic study nursed by a man who spent his life in discovering the precise moment at which empires were to fall, and revolutions, destined to change the face of the whole world, were to begin. "What more do I know about a horse," he would say to Fabrizio, "because somebody tells me its Latin name is *Equus*?"

The peasants dreaded the priest as a mighty magician, and he, through the fear inspired by his tarryings on the top of his tower, prevented them from thieving. His brother priests of the neighbouring parishes envied him his influence, and hated him accordingly. The marchese frankly despised him, because he reasoned too much for a person in so humble a position. Fabrizio worshipped him. To please him he would sometimes spend whole evenings over huge sums in addition or multiplication. And then he would climb up into the tower. This was a great favour—one the priest had never bestowed on any other person. But he loved the boy for the sake of his simplicity. "If you don't become a hypocrite," he would say, "you may turn into a man!"

Twice or thrice in every year, Fabrizio, who was bold and passionate in the pursuit of his pleasures, ran serious risks of drowning in the lake. He was the head and front of all the great expeditions of the peasant boys of Grianta and Cadenabbia. These urchins had provided themselves with a collection of small keys, and when the very dark nights came, they did their best to open the padlocks on the chains by which the fishermen moored their boats to some big stone or tree close to the shore. It must be explained that on the Lake of Como the fisherman puts down his lines at a considerable distance from the edge of the lake. The upper end of each line is fastened to a lath lined with cork, to which is fixed a very flexible hazel rod bearing a little bell, which tinkles as soon as the fish takes the bait and shakes the float.

The great object of the nocturnal raids, in which Fabrizio acted as commander in chief, was to get to these lines before the fishermen heard the tinkling of their little bells. The boys chose stormy seasons, and embarked on their risky enterprises early in the morning, an hour before dawn. They felt convinced, when they got into their boats, that they were rushing into terrible danger—this constituted the splendid aspect of their undertaking—and, like their fathers, they always devoutly recited an *Ave Maria*. Now, it frequently would happen that at the very moment of the start, and the instant after the recital of the *Ave Maria*, Fabrizio would be struck by an omen. This was the fruit, as affecting him, of his friend the priest's astrology, in the actual predictions of which he had no belief at all. To his juvenile imagination these omens were a certain indication of success or failure, and as he was more resolute than any of his comrades, the whole band gradually grew so accustomed to accept such signs that if, just as the boat was shoving off, a priest was seen on the coast line, or a raven flew away on the left, the padlock was hastily put back upon the chain and every boy went home to bed. Thus, though Father Blanès had not imparted his somewhat recondite science to Fabrizio, he had imbued him, all unconsciously, with an unlimited confidence in those signs and portents which may unveil the future.

The marchese was conscious that an accident to his secret correspondence might place him at his sister's mercy. Every year, therefore, when the St. Angela (the Countess Pietranera's feast day) came around, Fabrizio was allowed to spend a week at Milan. All through the year he lived on the hope, or the regretful memory, of those seven days. On so great an occasion, and to defray the expenses of this politic journey, the marchese would give his son four crowns. To his wife, who went with the boy, he gave, as usual, nothing at all. But a cook, six lackeys, and a coachman and pair of horses started for Como the night before the travellers, and while the marchesa was at Milan her carriage was at her disposal, and dinner for twelve persons was served every day.

The sullen retirement in which the Marchese del Dongo elected to live was certainly not an amusing form of existence. But it had one advantage, that of permanently enriching the coffers of the families who chose to adopt it. The marchese owned a revenue of more than two hundred thousand francs; he did not spend a quarter of it. He lived on hope. During the years between 1800 and 1813 he remained in the firm and unceasing expectation that Napoleon would be overthrown before the next six months were out. His joy when he received the news of the catastrophe of the Beresina, in the spring of 1813, may consequently be imagined. The capture of Paris and the fall of Napoleon almost drove him wild with joy, and he ventured on behaviour of the most insulting nature, both to his wife and his sister. At last, after fourteen years of waiting, he tasted the inexpressible delight of seeing the Austrian troops re-enter Milan. The general in command, obeying orders sent from Vienna, received the Marchese del Dongo with a courtesy which almost amounted to respect. One of the highest offices connected with the Government was at once offered him, and he accepted it as the discharge of a just debt. His eldest son was made a lieutenant in one of the finest of the imperial regiments, but Fabrizio would never have anything to do with the cadet's commission which was offered for his acceptance. The marchese's triumph, which he enjoyed with peculiar insolence, lasted but a few months, and was followed by a most humiliating reverse. He had never possessed any business aptitude, and his fourteen years of country life, surrounded by his servants, his notary, and his doctor, coupled with the ill humour which had crept upon him with advancing years, had developed his incapacity to the extremest point. In Austria no important post can be held for long by any person lacking that particular talent demanded by the slow and complicated, but essentially logical, system of administration peculiar to that ancient monarchy. The marchese's blunders scandalized the clerks of his department, and even hampered the progress of business, while his ultra-monarchical vapourings irritated a populace which it was important to lull back into its former state of slumbrous indifference. So, one fine day, he was informed that his Majesty was graciously pleased to accept his resignation of his office, and simultaneously appointed him second grand major-domo of the Lombardo-Venetian Kingdom. The marchese was furious at the abominable injustice of which he was the victim. In spite of his horror of the free press, he printed a Letter to a Friend. Then he wrote to the Emperor, assuring his Majesty that his ministers were playing him false, and were no better than Jacobins. This done, he betook himself sadly back to his home at Grianta. One consolation he possessed. After the downfall of Napoleon certain powerful individuals at Milan had organized a brutal attack on Count Prina, a man of first-class worth, who had acted as minister in the service of the King of Italy. Pietranera risked his own life to save that of the unhappy man, who was thrashed to death with umbrellas, and lingered in agony for five hours. If a certain priest, the Marchese del Dongo's own confessor, had chosen to open the iron gate of the Church of San Giovanni, in front of which Prina had been dragged (and, indeed, he had at one moment been left lying in the gutter running along the middle of the street), the victim might have been saved. But the cleric scornfully refused to unlock the gate, and within six months his patron enjoyed the happiness of securing him a handsome piece of preferment.

The marchese detested his brother-in-law, Count Pietranera, who, though his yearly income did not amount to fifty louis, dared to be fairly merry, ventured to cling faithfully to that which he had loved all his life, and was so insolent as to proclaim that spirit of impersonal justice which Del Dongo was pleased to define as vile Jacobinism. The count had refused to enter the Austrian service. The attention of the authorities was drawn to this refusal on his part, and a few months after the death of Prina the same men who had paid for his assassination procured an order for the imprisonment of General Pietranera. Upon this, his wife sent for a passport and ordered post horses to take her to Vienna, so that she might tell the Emperor the truth. Prina's assassins took fright, and at midnight, just one hour before the countess was to have started for Vienna, one of them, a cousin of her own, brought her the order for her husband's release. The following morning the Austrian general sent for Count Pietranera, received him with every possible respect, and assured him that his retiring pension would shortly be paid on the most satisfactory scale. The worthy General Bubna, who was both a clever and a kind-hearted man, looked thoroughly ashamed of Prina's murder and the count's imprisonment.

After this angry squall had blown over, calmed by Countess Pietranera's firmness, the couple lived in tolerable comfort on the retiring pension, which, thanks to General Bubna's influence, was shortly granted them.

It was a fortunate circumstance that for five or six years previously the countess had lived on terms of great friendship with an exceedingly wealthy young man, who was also her husband's intimate friend, and who placed the finest pair of English horses then to be seen at Milan, his box at the Scala Theatre, and his country house entirely at their service. But the count was conscious of his own valour; he had a generous soul, he was easily moved to anger, and on such occasions indulged in somewhat unusual behaviour. He was out hunting one day with some young men, when one of them, who had served under a different flag, ventured on some joke concerning the courage of the soldiers of the Cisalpine Republic. The count boxed his ears, there was a fracas then and there, and Pietranera, whose opinion found no support among the company present, was killed. This duel, if so it could be called, made a great stir; the persons concerned in it found it more prudent to journey into Switzerland.

That ridiculous kind of courage which men entitle resignation—the courage of the fool, who allows himself to be hanged without opening his lips—was not a quality possessed by the countess. In her rage at her husband's death she would have had Limercati, the wealthy young man who was her faithful adorer, instantly take his way to Switzerland, and there punish Pietranera's murderer either with a rifle bullet or with a hearty cuffing. But Limercati regarded the plan as simply ridiculous, ard forthwith the countess realized that, in her case, love had been killed by scorn.

She grew kinder than ever to Limercati. Her aim was to rekindle his love, and that done, to forsake him and leave him in despair. To explain this plan of vengeance to the French mind, I should say that in Milan, a country far distant from our own, love does still drive men to despair. The countess, whose beauty, heightened by her mourning robes, eclipsed that of all her rivals, set herself to coquette with the best-born young men of the city, and one of them, Count N——, who had always said that Limercati's qualities struck him as being too heavy and stiff to attract so brilliant a woman, fell desperately in love with her. Then she wrote to Limercati:

"Would you like to behave, for once, like a clever man? Imagine that you have never known me. I am, with a touch of scorn, perhaps,
"Your very humble servant,
"GINA PIETRANERA."

When Limercati received this note he departed to one of his country houses; his passion blazed, he lost his head, and talked of shooting himself—an unusual course in countries which acknowledge the existence of a hell.

The very morning after his arrival in the country he wrote to the countess to offer her his hand and his two hundred thousand francs a year. She sent him back his letter, with the seal unbroken, by Count N——'s groom; whereupon Limercati spent three years on his estates, coming back to Milan every two months, but never finding courage to stay there, and boring all his friends with the story of his passionate adoration of the lady and the circumstantial recital of the favour she had formerly shown him. In the earlier months of this period he added that Count N—— would ruin her, and that she dishonoured herself by contracting such an intimacy.

The Chartreuse of Parma

As a matter of fact, the countess had no love of any
kind for N——, and of this fact she apprised him as soon
as she was quite certain of Limercati's despair. The count,
who knew the world, only begged her not to divulge
the sad truth she had confided to him. " If," he added,
" you will have the extreme kindness to continue receiving me with all the external distinctions generally granted
to the reigning lover, I may, perhaps, attain a suitable
position."

After this heroic declaration the countess would make
no further use of Count N——'s horses and opera box. But
for fifteen years she had been accustomed to a life of the
greatest ease. She was now driven to solve the difficult, or
rather impossible, problem of living at Milan on a yearly
pension of fifteen hundred francs. She quitted her palace,
hired two fifth-floor rooms, and dismissed all her servants,
even to her maid, whom she replaced by a poor old char-
woman. The sacrifice was really less heroic and less painful
than it appears. No ridicule attaches to poverty in Milan,
and therefore people do not shrink from it in terror, as the
worst of all possible evils. After some months spent in this
proud penury, bombarded by perpetual letters from Limercati, and even from Count N——, who also desired to marry
her, it came to pass that the Marchese del Dongo, whose
stinginess was usually abominable, was struck by the notion that his own enemies might perhaps be rejoicing over
his sister's sufferings. What! Was a Del Dongo to be reduced to existing on the pension granted by the Viennese
court, against which he had so great a grievance, to its generals' widows?

He wrote that an apartment and an income worthy of
his sister awaited her at Grianta. The versatile-minded
countess welcomed the idea of this new life with enthusiasm.
It was twenty years since she had lived in the venerable pile
which rose so proudly among the old chestnut trees planted
in the days of the Sforzas. " There," she reflected, " I shall
find peace ; and at my age, is that not happiness? (As she
had arrived at the age of one-and-thirty, she believed that
the hour of her retirement had struck.) " I shall find a

happy and peaceful life at last, on the shores of the noble lake beside which I was born."

Whether she was mistaken I know not, but it is certain that this eager-hearted creature, who had just so unhesitatingly refused two huge fortunes, carried happiness with her into the Castle of Grianta. Her two nieces were beside themselves with delight. " You have brought the beautiful days of my youth back to me ! " said the marchesa as she kissed her. " The night before you arrived I felt a hundred years old."

In Fabrizio's company the countess went about revisiting all those enchanting spots near Grianta which travellers have made so famous : the Villa Melzi, on the other side of the lake, opposite the castle, and one of the chief objects in the view therefrom ; the sacred wood of the Sfondrata ; and the bold promontory which divides the branches of the lake, that of Como, so rich in its beauty, and that which runs toward Lecco, of aspect far more severe— a sublime and graceful prospect, equalled, perhaps, but not surpassed, by the most famous view in all the world, that of the Bay of Naples. The countess found the most exquisite delight in calling up memories of her early days, and comparing them with her present sensations. " The Lake of Como," she said to herself, " is not hemmed in, like the Lake of Geneva, by great tracts of land, carefully hedged and cultivated on the best system, reminding one of money and speculation. Here, on every side, I see hills of unequal height, covered with clumps of trees, growing as chance has scattered them, and which have not yet been ruined, and forced to bring in an income, by the hand of man. Amid these hills, with their beautiful shapes and their curious slopes that drop toward the lake, I can carry on all the illusions of the descriptions of Tasso and Ariosto. It is all noble and tender, it all speaks of love ; nothing recalls the hideousness of civilization. The villages set halfway up the hills are sheltered by great trees, and above the tree tops rise the charming outlines of their pretty church spires. Where some little field, fifty paces wide, shows itself here and there among the chestnuts and wild-cherry trees my pleased eye notes plants of more vigorous and willing growth than can .be seen elsewhere. Beyond the hills, on whose deserted crests a happy hermit existence might be spent, the wondering eye rests on the Alpine peaks, covered with eternal snows, and their stern severity reminds one sufficiently of life's misfortunes, to increase one's sense of present delight. The imagination is stirred by the distant sound of the church bells of some little village hidden among the trees. Their tone softens as it floats over the water, with a touch of gentle melancholy and resignation, which seems to say, ' Life slips by. Do not, then, look so coldly on the happiness that comes to you. Make haste to enjoy.' "

The influence of these enchanting spots, unequalled on earth for loveliness, made the countess feel a girl once more. She could not conceive how she had been able to spend so many years without returning to the lake. " Can it be," she wondered, " that true happiness belongs to the beginning of old age? " She purchased a boat, and adorned it with her own hands, assisted by Fabrizio and the marchesa, for no money was to be had, though the household was kept up with the utmost splendour. Since his fall the Marchese del Dongo had doubled his magnificence. For instance, to gain ten paces of ground on the shore of the lake, close to the famous avenue of plane trees leading toward Cadenabbia, he was building an embankment which was to cost eighty thousand francs. At the end of this embankment was rising a chapel, constructed entirely of enormous blocks of granite, after drawings by the celebrated Cagnola, and within the chapel, Marchesi, the fashionable Milanese sculptor, was erecting a tomb on which the noble deeds of the marchese's ancestors were to be represented in numerous bas-reliefs.

Fabrizio's elder brother, the Marchesino Ascanio, tried to join the ladies in their expeditions, but his aunt splashed water over his powdered head, and was forever playing some fresh prank on his solemnity. At last he relieved the merry party of the sight of his heavy sallow countenance. They dared not laugh when he was present, feeling that he was the spy of the marchese, his father, and that it was wise to keep on terms with the stern despot, who had never recovered his temper since his forced resignation.

Ascanio swore to be avenged on Fabrizio.

One day there was a storm, and the boat was in some danger. Though money was scarce enough, the two boatmen were liberally bribed to prevent their saying anything to the marchese, who was very angry already because his daughters had been taken out. Then came a second hurricane. On this beautiful lake storms are both terrible and unexpected. Violent squalls sweep suddenly down the mountain gorges on opposite sides of the shore, and battle over the water. This time, in the midst of the whirlwind and the thunderclaps, the countess insisted on landing; she declared that if she could stand on a lonely rock, as large as a small room, which lay in the middle of the lake, she would enjoy a strange spectacle, and see her stronghold lashed on every side by the furious waves. But, as she sprang from the boat, she fell into the water. Fabrizio plunged in after her, and they were both carried a considerable distance. Drowning is certainly not an attractive death, but boredom, at all events, fled astonished from the feudal castle. The countess had fallen in love with Father Blanès's primitive qualities, and astrological studies. The little money remaining to her after the purchase of her boat had been spent on a small second-hand telescope, and almost every night she mounted, with Fabrizio and her nieces, to the top of one of the Gothic towers of the castle. Fabrizio was the learned member of the party, which would thus spend several very cheerful hours, far from prying eyes.

It must be acknowledged that there were days during which the countess never spoke to anybody, and might be seen walking up and down under the great chestnut trees, plunged in gloomy reverie. She was too clever a woman not to suffer, now and then, from the weariness of never being able to exchange an idea. But the next day she would be laughing again, as she had laughed the day before. It was the lamentations of her sister-in-law which occasionally cast a gloom over her naturally elastic nature. "Are we doomed to spend all the youth left to us in this dreary house?" the marchesa would cry. Before the arrival of the countess she had not even had courage to feel such repinings.

Thus the winter of 1814 to 1815 wore on. Twice, in spite of her poverty, did the countess spend a few days in Milan. She went to see a magnificent ballet by Vigano, produced at the Scala, and the marchese did not forbid his wife to accompany her sister-in-law. The quarterly payments of the little pension were drawn, and it was the poor widow of the Cisalpine general who lent a few sequins to the wealthy Marchesa del Dongo. These expeditions were delightful; the ladies invited their old friends to dinner, and consoled themselves by laughing at everything, like real children. Their light-hearted Italian gaiety helped them to forget the melancholy gloom which the marchese and his elder son shed over everything at Grianta. Fabrizio, then hardly sixteen years old, represented the head of the family in a very satisfactory manner.

On the 17th of March, 1815, the ladies, very lately returned from a delightful little trip to Milan, were walking up and down under the fine avenue of plane trees which had lately been extended down to the very edge of the lake. A boat appeared, coming from the direction of Como, and made some peculiar signals. One of the marchese's agents sprang ashore. Napoleon had just landed in the Gulf of Juan! Europe in general was simple enough to be surprised at this event, which did not astonish the Marchese del Dongo. He wrote his sovereign a letter full of heartfelt expressions of devotion, placed his talents and several millions of money at his service, and reaffirmed that his ministers were all Jacobins, and in league with the Parisian leaders.

On the 8th of March, at six o'clock in the morning, the marchese, adorned with all his insignia, was writing the rough draft of a third political despatch from his son's dictation. Solemnly he transcribed it in his large, careful handwriting, on paper the watermark of which bore his sovereign's effigy. At that very moment Fabrizio was entering the presence of his aunt, the Countess Pietranera.

"I am off!" he cried. "I am going to join the Emperor! He is King of Italy as well! How he loved your husband! I shall go through Switzerland. Last night my friend Vasi, the barometer dealer at Menagio, gave me his passport. Now do you give me a few napoleons, for I have only two of my own. But if it comes to that, I'll walk!"

The countess was weeping with terror and delight. "Good God!" she cried, as she seized Fabrizio's hands, "how did such an idea come into your head?"

She rose from her seat, and from the linen chest, where it had been carefully concealed, took a little bead-embroidered purse, containing all her earthly wealth.

"Take it," she said to her nephew, "but in God's name do not get yourself killed! What would be left to your unhappy mother and to me if you were taken from us? As for Napoleon's success, that, my poor child, is impossible. Did not you hear the story, a week ago, when we were at Milan, of the three-and-twenty well-laid plots for his assassination which he only escaped by a miracle? And in those days he was all powerful! And you have seen it is not the will to destroy him which our enemies lack. France has been nothing since he left her!"

The voice of the countess trembled with the liveliest emotion as she spoke to Fabrizio of Napoleon's future fate. "When I consent to your going to join them," she said, "I sacrifice, for his sake, what I hold dearest in this world!" Fabrizio's eyes grew moist, and his tears fell as he embraced his aunt. But not for an instant did he waver in his determination to depart. He eagerly explained to this beloved friend the reasons which had decided him—reasons which we take the liberty of thinking somewhat comical.

"Yesterday evening, at seven minutes to six o'clock, we were walking, as you know, on the shores of the lake, under the plane trees, below the Casa Sommariva, and our faces were turned southward. Then, for the first time, I noticed, in the far distance, the boat from Como which was bearing the great news to us. As I watched it, without a thought of the Emperor, and simply envying the fate of those who had an opportunity of travelling, I was suddenly overwhelmed by a feeling of deep emotion. The boat had touched the shore, and the agent, after whispering something to my father, who had changed colour, had taken us aside to inform us of the *terrible news*. I turned toward the lake with the simple object of hiding the tears of joy with which my eyes were swimming. Suddenly, on my right, and at an immense height, I perceived an eagle, Napoleon's own bird; it was winging its majestic way toward Switzerland, and consequently toward Paris. ' And I, too,' said I to myself instantly, ' will cross Switzerland, swiftly as an eagle, and will offer that great man a very little thing indeed—but still all that I have to offer—the help of my feeble arm! He would fain have given us a fatherland, and he loved my uncle!' That instant, while I yet watched the eagle, by some strange charm, my tears were dried, and the proof that my idea came from above is that at that very moment, and without hesitation, my resolve was taken, and the method of carrying out the journey became clear to me. In a flash all the melancholy which, as you know, poisons my life, especially on Sundays, was swept away as by some divine breath. I saw the great figure of Italy rising out of the mire into which the Germans have cast her, and strétching out her wounded arms, on which the chains still hung, towards her king and liberator. ' And I too,' I murmured, ' the son, as yet unknown, of that unhappy mother, I will depart, and I will die or win victory beside that Man of Fate, who would have cleansed us from the scorn cast on us by the vilest and most enslaved of the inhabitants of Europe!'

"You know," he added in a lower voice, drawing closer to the countess, and as he spoke he fixed great flashing eyes upon her, " you know the young chestnut tree which my mother planted with her own hands the winter I was born, beside the deep pool in our forest, two leagues off? Before I would do anything I went to see it. ' The spring is not far advanced,' said I to myself; ' well, if there are leaves on my tree, that will be a sign for me, and I too must cast off the torpor in which I languish in this cold and dreary house. Are not these old blackened walls—the symbols now, and once the strongholds, of despotism—a true picture of winter and its dreariness? To me they are what winter is to my tree.'

" Would you believe it, Gina? At half-past seven yesterday evening I had reached my chestnut tree. There were leaves upon it—pretty little leaves of a fair size already! I kissed them, without hurting them, carefully turned the soil round the beloved tree, and then, in a fresh transport, crossed the mountain and reached Menagio. A passport was indispensable, if I was to get into Switzerland. The hours had flown, and it was one o'clock in the morning when I reached Vasi's door. I expected to have to knock for long before I could rouse him; but he was sitting up with three of his friends. At my very first word, ' You are going to Napoleon ! ' he cried, and fell upon my neck; the others, too, embraced me joyfully. ' Why am I married? ' cried one."

The countess had grown pensive; she thought it her duty to put forward some objections. If he had possessed the smallest experience Fabrizio would have perceived that she herself had no faith in the excellent reasons she hastened to lay before him. But though experience was lacking, he had plenty of resolution, and would not even condescend to listen to her expostulations. Before long the countess confined herself to obtaining a promise that at all events his mother should be informed of his plan.

" She will tell my sisters, and those women will betray me unconsciously ! " cried Fabrizio, with a sort of heroic arrogance.

" Speak more respectfully," said the countess, smiling through her tears, " of the sex which will make your fortune. For men will never like you—you are too impulsive to please prosaic beings ! "

When the marchesa was made acquainted with her son's strange project she burst into tears. His heroism did not appeal to her, and she did everything in her power to dissuade him. But she was soon convinced that nothing but prison walls would prevent him from starting, and gave him

what little money she had of her own. Then she recollected
that she had in her possession eight or ten small diamonds,
worth about ten thousand francs, given her the night before by the marchese, so that she might have them reset
the next time she went to Milan. Fabrizio returned the
poor ladies the contents of their slender purses, and his
sisters entered their mother's room while the countess was
sewing the diamonds into our hero's travelling coat. They
were so enthusiastic over his plan, and embraced him with
such noisy delight, that he snatched up a few diamonds,
which had not yet been hidden in his clothes, and insisted
on starting off at once.

"You will betray me without knowing it!" he said to
his sisters, "and as I have all this money I need not take
clothes—I shall find them wherever I go." He kissed his
loved ones, and departed that instant, without even going
back to his room. So rapidly did he walk, in his terror of
being pursued by mounted men, that he reached Lugano
that very evening. He was safe, by God's mercy, in a
Swiss town, and no longer feared that gendarmes in his
father's pay might lay violent hands on him in the lonely
road. From Lugano he wrote a fine letter to the marchese,
a childish performance which increased that gentleman's
fury. Then he took horse, crossed the St. Gothard, travelled rapidly, and entered France by Pontarlier. The Emperor was in Paris, and in Paris Fabrizio's misfortunes
began. He had started with the firm intention of getting
speech with the Emperor, the idea that this might be difficult
never entering his head. At Milan he had seen Prince Eugène a dozen times a day, and could have spoken to him each
time if he would. In Paris he went every day of his life
to watch the Emperor review his troops in the court of the
Tuileries, but never could get near him. Our hero believed every Frenchman must be as deeply moved as he
was himself by the extreme danger in which the country
stood. At the table of the hotel in which he lived, he made
no secret of his plans or his devotion. He found himself
surrounded by young men of agreeable manners, and still
more enthusiastic than himself, who succeeded, before many

days were passed, in relieving him of every penny he possessed. Fortunately, and out of sheer modesty, he had not mentioned the diamonds given him by his mother. One morning, when, after a night's orgie, it became quite clear to him that he had been robbed, he bought himself two fine horses, engaged an old soldier, one of the horse dealer's grooms, as his servant, and, overflowing with scorn for the young Parisians who talked so fine, started to join the army. He had no information save that it was concentrating near Maubeuge. Hardly had he reached the frontier, when it struck him as absurd that he should stay indoors and warm himself at a good fire while soldiers were bivouacking in the open air. In spite of the remonstrances of his servant, who was a sensible fellow, he insisted, in the most imprudent manner, on joining the military bivouac on the farthest edge of the frontier toward Belgium. He had hardly reached the first battalion, lying beside the road, when the soldiers began to stare at the young civilian, whose dress had not a touch of uniform about it. Night was falling, and the wind was very cold. Fabrizio drew near to a fire, and offered to pay for leave to sit by it. The soldiers looked at each other in astonishment, especially at this offer of pay, but made room for him good-naturedly, and his servant extemporized a shelter for him. But an hour later, when the adjutant of the regiment passed within hail of the bivouac, the soldiers reported the arrival of the stranger who talked bad French. The adjutant questioned Fabrizio, who told him of his worship for the Emperor in an accent of the most doubtful description, whereupon the officer requested that he would accompany him to the colonel, who was quartered in a neighbouring farm. Fabrizio's servant at once brought up the two horses. The sight of them seemed to produce such an effect upon the noncommissioned officer that he immediately changed his mind, and began to question the servant as well. The man, an old soldier, suspected his interlocutor's plan of campaign, and spoke of his master's influence in high quarters, adding that his fine horses could not easily be taken from him. Instantly, at a sign from the adjutant, one soldier seized him by the collar, another took charge of the horses, and Fabrizio was sternly ordered to follow his captor and hold his tongue.

After making him march a good league through darkness that seemed all the blacker by contrast with the bivouac fires, which lighted up the horizon on every side, the adjutant handed Fabrizio over to an officer of gendarmerie, who gravely demanded his papers. Fabrizio produced his passport, which described him as a " dealer in barometers, travelling with his merchandise."

" What fools they are ! " cried the officer ; " this really is too much ! "

He questioned our hero, who talked about the Emperor and liberty in terms of the most ardent and enthusiastic description ; whereupon the officer fell into fits of laughter. " Upon my soul ! " he cried, " they are anything but clever ; to send us greenhorns such as you is a little too much, really ! " And in spite of everything Fabrizio could say, and his desperate assurances that he really was not a dealer in barometers, he was ordered to the prison of B——, a small town in the neighbourhood, where he arrived at three o'clock in the morning, bursting with anger, and half dead with fatigue.

Here he remained, astonished, first of all, and then furious, and utterly unable to understand what had happened, for thirty-three long days. He wrote letter after letter to the commandant of the fortress, the jailer's wife, a handsome Flemish woman of six-and-thirty, undertaking to deliver them ; but as she had no desire whatever to see so good-looking a young fellow shot, and as, moreover, he paid her well, she invariably put his letters in the fire. Very late at night she would condescend to come to listen to his complaints—she had informed her husband that the simpleton had money, whereupon that prudent functionary had given her *carte blanche*. She availed herself of his permission, and gleaned several gold pieces ; for the adjutant had only taken the horses, and the police officer had confiscated nothing at all. One fine afternoon Fabrizio caught the sound of a heavy though distant cannonade. Fighting had begun at last ! His heart thumped with impatience. He heard a great deal of noise, too, in the streets. An important military movement was, in fact, in course of execution. Three divisions were marching through the town. When the jailer's wife came to share his sorrows, at about eleven o'clock that night, Fabrizio made himself even more agreeable than usual. Then, taking her hands in his, he said: "Help me to get out! I swear on my honour I'll come back to prison as soon as the fighting is over."

"That's all gammon!" she replied. "Have you any *quibus* (cash)?" He looked anxious, not understanding what the word *quibus* meant. The woman, seeing his expression, concluded his funds were running low, and, instead of talking about gold napoleons, as she had intended, only mentioned francs.

"Listen!" she said. "If you can raise a hundred francs, I will blind both eyes of the corporal who will relieve the guard to-night, with a double napoleon. Then he will not see you get out of prison, and if his regiment is to be off during the day, he will make no difficulties." The bargain was soon struck; the woman even agreed to hide Fabrizio in her own room, out of which it would be easier for him to slip in the early morning.

The next day, before dawn, she said to our hero, and there was real feeling in her tone: "My dear boy, you are very young to ply this horrible trade of yours. Believe me, don't begin it again!"

"What!" repeated Fabrizio. "Is it wicked, then, to want to fight for one's own country?"

"Enough! But always remember I have saved your life. Your case was a clear one. You would certainly have been shot. But never tell anybody, for we should lose our place, my husband and I. And, above all, never repeat your silly tale about being a Milanese gentleman disguised as a dealer in barometers; it is too foolish! Now, listen carefully. I am going to give you the clothes of a hussar who died in the prison the day before yesterday. Never open your lips unless you are obliged to. If a sergeant or an officer questions you so that you have to reply, say you have been lying ill in the house of a peasant, who found you shaking with fever in a ditch, and sheltered you out of charity. If this answer does not satisfy them, say you are working your way back to your regiment. You may be arrested because of your accent. Then say you were born in Piedmont, that you are a conscript, and were left behind in France last year, etc."

For the first time, after his three-and-thirty days of rage and fury, Fabrizio understood the meaning of what had befallen him. He had been taken for a spy! He reasoned with the jailer's wife, who felt very tenderly toward him that morning, and at last, while she, armed with a needle, was taking in the hussar's garments for him, frankly told her his story. For a moment she believed it—he looked so simple and was so handsome in his hussar uniform!

"As you had set your heart on fighting," she said, half convinced at last, "you should have enlisted in some regiment as soon as you got to Paris. That job would have been done at once if you had taken any sergeant to a tavern and paid his score there." She added a great deal of good advice for his future, and at last, just as day was breaking, let him out of the house, after making him swear again and again, a hundred times over, that, whatever happened to him, her name should never pass his lips. As soon as Fabrizio had got clear of the little town and began stepping out boldly along the highroad, with his sabre tucked under his arm, a shadow fell upon his soul. "Here I am," he reflected, "with the clothes and the route papers of a hussar who died in prison, where he was put, I understand, for stealing a cow and some silver spoons and forks! I have inherited, so to speak, his existence, and that without any wish or intention of my own. Look out for prisons! The omen is clear—I shall suffer many things from prisons!"

Hardly an hour after he had bidden farewell to his benefactress the rain began to fall with such violence that the newly fledged hussar, hampered by the heavy boots which had never been made for his feet, could hardly contrive to walk. He came across a peasant riding a sorry nag, and bought the horse, bargaining by signs, for the jailer's wife had advised him to speak as little as possible, on account of his foreign accent.

That day the army, which had just won the battle of Ligny, was in full march on Brussels. It was the eve of the battle of Waterloo. Toward noon, while the rain still poured down, Fabrizio heard artillery firing. In his happiness he forgot all the terrible moments of despair he had endured in his undeserved prison. He travelled on, far into the night, and, as he was beginning to learn a little sense, he sought shelter in a peasant's hut, quite off the main road. The peasant was crying, and saying that he had been stripped of everything he had. Fabrizio gave him a crown, and discovered some oats. "My horse is no beauty," the young man reflected, "but still some adjutant fellow might take a fancy to him," and he lay down in the stable beside his mount. An hour before daylight next morning he was on the road again. By dint of much coaxing he wheedled his horse into a trot. Toward five o'clock he heard heavy firing. It was the beginning of Waterloo.

CHAPTER III

FABRIZIO soon came upon some *cantinières*, and the deep gratitude he felt toward the jailer's wife incited him to address them. He inquired of one of them as to where the Fourth Regiment of Hussars, to which he belonged, might be.

"You would do much better not to be in such a hurry, my young fellow," replied the woman, touched by Fabrizio's pallor and the beauty of his eyes. "Your hand is not steady enough yet for the sword play that this day must see! Now, if you had only a gun, I don't say but that you might fire it off as well as any other man."

The advice was not pleasing to Fabrizio, but, however much he pressed his horse, he could not get it to travel any faster than the sutler's cart. Every now and then the artillery fire seemed to grow closer, and prevented each from hearing what the other said, for so wild was the boy with enthusiasm and delight that he had begun to talk again. Every word the woman dropped increased his joy, by making him realize it more fully. He ended by telling the woman, who seemed thoroughly kind-hearted, the whole of his adventures, with the exception of his real name and his flight from prison. She was much astonished, and could make neither head nor tail of the handsome young soldier's story.

"I have it!" she cried at last, with a look of triumph. "You are a young civilian, in love with the wife of some captain in the Fourth Hussars! Your ladylove has given you the uniform you wear, and you are tearing about after her. As sure as God reigns above us, you are no soldier; you have never been a soldier! But, like the brave fellow

The Chartreuse of Parma

you are, you are determined to be with your regiment while it is under fire rather than be taken for a coward."

Fabrizio agreed to everything. That was the only method by which he could secure good advice. "I know nothing of these French people's ways," said he to himself, "and if somebody doesn't guide me I shall get myself into prison again, or some fellow will steal my horse from me!"

"In the first place, my boy," said the *cantinière*, who was growing more and more friendly, "you must admit you are under twenty—I don't believe you are an hour over seventeen!"

That was true, and Fabrizio willingly admitted it.

"Then you're not even a conscript—it's simply and solely for the lady's sake that you are risking your bones. Bless me, she's not oversqueamish! If you still have any of the yellow boys she has given you in your pocket, the first thing you must do is to buy yourself another horse. Look how that brute of yours pricks up her ears whenever the guns growl a little close to her! That's a peasant's horse; it'll kill you the moment you get to the front. See that white smoke yonder, over the hedge? That means musket volleys! Therefore, my fine fellow, make ready to be in a horrible fright when you hear the bullets whistling over your head. You had far better eat a bit now, while you have the time."

Fabrizio acted on her advice, and, pulling a napoleon out of his pocket, requested the *cantinière* to pay herself out of it.

"It's a downright pity!" cried the good woman; "the poor child doesn't even know how to spend his money! 'Twould serve you right if I pocketed your napoleon and made my Cocotte start off at full trot. Devil take me if your beast could follow her! What could you do, you simpleton, if you saw me make off? Let me tell you that when the big guns begin to grumble nobody shows his gold pieces. Here," she went on, "I give you back eighteen francs and fifty centimes; your breakfast costs you thirty sous. Soon we shall have horses to sell. Then you'll give

37

ten francs for a small one, and *never* more than twenty, not even for the best!"

The meal was over, and the *cantinière*, who was still holding forth, was interrupted by a woman who had been coming across the fields, and now passed along the road.

"Halloo! Hi!" she shouted. "Halloo, Margot! Your Sixth Light Regiment is on the right!"

"I must be off, my boy," said the *cantinière*; "but really and truly I am sorry for you! Upon my soul, I feel friendly to you. You know nothing about anything; you'll be wiped out, as sure as God is God; come along with me to the Sixth!"

"I understand very well that I know nothing at all," said Fabrizio; "but I mean to fight, and I am going over there to that white smoke."

"Just look how your mare's ears are wagging! The moment you get her down there she'll take the bit in her teeth, weak as she is, and gallop off, and God knows where she'll take you to! Take my advice, as soon as you get down to the soldiers, pick up a musket and an ammunition pouch, lie down beside them, and do exactly as they do. But, Lord! I'll wager you don't even know how to bite open a cartridge!"

Fabrizio, though sorely galled, truthfully answered that his new friend had guessed aright.

"Poor little chap, he'll be killed at once! God's truth, it won't take long! You must and shall come with me," she added with an air of authority.

"But I want to fight."

"So you shall fight! The Sixth is a first-rate regiment, and there'll be fighting for every one to-day."

"But shall we soon get to your regiment?"

"In a quarter of an hour, at the outside."

"If this good woman vouches for me," reasoned Fabrizio, "I shall not be taken for a spy on account of my universal ignorance, and I shall get a chance of fighting." At that moment the firing grew heavier, the reports following closely one upon the other, "like the beads in a rosary," said Fabrizio to himself.

The Chartreuse of Parma

"I begin to hear the volleys," said the *cantinière*, whipping up her pony, which seemed quite excited by the noise. She turned to the right, along a cross-road leading through the meadow; the mud was a foot deep, and the little cart almost stuck in it. Fabrizio pushed at the wheels. Twice over his horse fell down. Soon the road grew dryer, and dwindled into a mere foot-path across the sward. Fabrizio had not ridden on five hundred paces when his horse stopped short—a corpse lying across the path had startled both beast and rider.

Fabrizio, whose face was naturally pale, turned visibly green; the *cantinière*, looking at the dead man, said, as though talking to herself, "Nobody of our division," and then, raising her eyes to our hero's face, burst out laughing.

"Ha, ha, my child!" she cried, "here's a lollypop for you!"

Fabrizio sat on, horror-struck. What most impressed him was the mud on the feet of the corpse, which had been stripped of its shoes, and of everything else, indeed, except a wretched pair of blood-stained trousers.

"Come," said the *cantinière*, "tumble off your horse; you must get used to it. Ha," she went on, "he got it through the head!" The corpse was hideously disfigured. A bullet had entered near the nose and passed out at the opposite temple. One eye was open and staring.

"Now, then, get off your horse, boy," cried the *cantinière*, "shake him by the hand, and see if he'll shake yours back."

At once, though sick almost to death with horror, Fabrizio threw himself from his horse, seized the dead hand and shook it well. Then he stood in a sort of dream; he felt he had not strength to get back upon his horse; the dead man's open eye, especially, filled him with horror.

"This woman will take me for a coward," thought he to himself bitterly. Yet he felt that he could not stir; he would certainly have fallen. It was a terrible moment. Fabrizio was just going to faint dead away. The *cantinière* saw it, jumped smartly out of her little cart, and without a word proffered him a glass of brandy, which he swallowed at a gulp. After that he was able to remount, and rode along without opening his lips. Every now and then the woman looked at him out of the corner of her eye.

"You shall fight to-morrow, my boy," she said at last. "To-day you shall stay with me. You see now that you must learn your soldier's trade."

"Not at all. I want to fight now, at once," cried our hero, and his look was so fierce that the. *cantinière* augured well from it. The artillery fire grew heavier, and seemed to draw nearer. The reports began to form a sort of continuous bass, there was no interval between them, and above this deep note, which was like the noise of a distant torrent, the musketry volleys rang out distinctly.

Just at this moment the road turned into a grove of trees. The *cantinière* noticed two or three French soldiers running toward her as hard as their legs would carry them. She sprang nimbly from her cart, and ran to hide herself some fifteen or twenty paces from the road. There she concealed herself in the hole left by the uprooting of a great tree. "Now," said Fabrizio to himself, "I shall find out whether I am a coward." He halted beside the forsaken cart and drew his sword. The soldiers paid no attention to him, but ran along the wood on the left side of the road.

"Those are some of our men," said the *cantinière* coolly, as she came back panting to her little cart. "If your mare had a canter in her I would tell you to ride to the end of the wood, and see if there is any one on the plain beyond." Fabrizio needed no second bidding. He tore a branch from a poplar tree, stripped off the leaves, and belaboured his mount soundly. For a moment the brute broke into a canter, but it soon went back to its usual jog-trot. The *cantinière* had forced her pony into a gallop. "Stop! stop! I say!" she shouted to Fabrizio. Soon they both emerged from the wood. When they reached the edge of the plain they heard a most tremendous noise. Heavy guns and musketry volleys thundered on every hand—right, left, and behind them—and as the grove from which they had just emerged crowned a hillock some eight or ten feet higher than the plain, they had a fair view of a corner of the battle-field. But the meadow just beyond the wood was empty. It was bounded, about a thousand paces from where they stood, by a long row of very bushy willow trees. Beyond these hung a cloud of white smoke, which now and then eddied up toward the sky.

"If I only knew where the regiment was!" said the woman, looking puzzled. "We can't go straight across that big meadow. By the way, young fellow," she said to Fabrizio, "if you see one of the enemy, stick him with the point of your sword; don't amuse yourself by trying to cut him down."

Just at that moment she caught sight of the four soldiers of whom we have already spoken. They were coming out of the wood on to the plain to the left of the road. One of them was on horseback.

"Here's what you want," said she to Fabrizio. Then, shouting to the mounted man, "Halloo, you! Why don't you come and drink a glass of brandy?" The soldiers drew nearer.

"Where's the Sixth Light Regiment?" she called out.

"Over there, five minutes off, in front of the canal that runs along those willows. And Colonel Macon has just been killed."

"Will you take five francs for that horse of yours?"

"Five francs! That's a pretty fair joke, my good woman! Five francs for an officer's charger that I shall sell for five napoleons before the hour's out!"

"Give me one of your napoleons," whispered the *cantinière* to Fabrizio; then, going close up to the man on horseback, "Get off, and look sharp about it!" she said; "here's your napoleon."

The soldier slipped off, and Fabrizio sprang gaily into his saddle, while the *cantinière* unfastened the little valise he had carried on the other.

"Here! why don't you help me, you fellows?" said she to the soldier. "What do you mean by letting a lady work!" But the captured charger no sooner felt the valise than he began to plunge, and Fabrizio, who was a first-rate horseman, had to use all his skill to retain his seat. "That's a good sign," said the *cantinière*; "the gentleman's not accustomed to the tickling of valises!"

"It's a general's horse," cried the soldier who had sold it. "That horse is worth ten napoleons if it's worth a farthing."

"Here are twenty francs for you," said Fabrizio, who was beside himself with joy at feeling a spirited animal between his legs.

Just at this moment a round shot came whizzing slantwise through the row of willows, and Fabrizio enjoyed the curious sight of all the little branches flying left and right as if they had been mowed off with a scythe. "Humph!" said the soldier, as he pocketed his twenty francs, "the worry's beginning." It was about two o'clock in the day.

Fabrizio was still lost in admiration of this curious spectacle, when a group of generals, escorted by a score of hussars, galloped across one of the corners of the wide meadow on the edge of which he was standing. His horse neighed, plunged two or three times, and pulled violently at the curb. "So be it, then," said Fabrizio to himself. He gave the animal the rein, and it dashed, full gallop, up to the escort which rode behind the generals.

Fabrizio counted four plumed hats.

A quarter of an hour later he gathered from some words spoken by the hussar next him that one of these generals was the famous Marshal Ney. That crowned his happiness; yet he could not guess which of the four was the marshal. He would have given all the world to know, but he remembered he must not open his lips. The escort halted to cross a large ditch, which the rain of the preceding night had filled with water. It was skirted by large trees, and ran along the left side of the meadow at the entrance of which Fabrizio had bought his horse. Almost all the hussars had dismounted. The sides of the ditch were steep and exceedingly slippery, and the water lay quite three or four feet below the level of the meadow. Fabrizio, wrapped up in his delight, was thinking more about Marshal Ney and glory than about his horse, which, being very spirited, jumped into the watercourse, splashing the water up to a considerable height.

The Chartreuse of Parma

One of the generals was well wetted, and shouted with an oath, " Devil take the damned brute! " This insult wounded Fabrizio deeply. " Can I demand an explanation? " he wondered. Meanwhile, to prove that he was not so stupid as he looked, he tried to force his horse up the opposite side of the ditch, but it was five or six feet high, and most precipitous. He was obliged to give it up. Then he followed up the current, the water rising to his horse's head, and came at last to a sort of watering-place, up the gentle slope of which he easily passed into the field on the other side of the cutting. He was the first man of the escort to get across, and trotted proudly along the bank. At the bottom of the ditch the hussars were floundering about, very much puzzled what to do with themselves, for in many places the water was five feet deep. Two or three of the horses took fright and tried to swim, which created a terrible splashing. Then a sergeant noticed the tactics followed by the greenhorn, who looked so very unlike a soldier. " Turn up the stream," he shouted; " there's a watering-place on the left! " and by degrees they all got over.

When Fabrizio reached the farther bank, he found the generals there all alone. The roar of the artillery seemed to him louder than ever. He could hardly hear the general he had so thoroughly drenched, who shouted into his ear: " Where did you get that horse? "

Fabrizio was so taken aback that he answered in Italian: " *L'ho comprato poco fa!* " (" I have just bought it.")

" What do you say? " shouted the general again.

But the noise suddenly grew so tremendous that Fabrizio could not reply. At this moment, it must be acknowledged, our hero felt anything but heroic. Still, fear was only a secondary sensation on his part. It was the noise that hurt his ears and disconcerted him so dreadfully. The escort broke into a gallop. They were crossing a wide stretch of ploughed land, which lay beyond the canal. The field was dotted with corpses.

" The red-coats! the red-coats! " shouted the hussars joyfully. Fabrizio did not understand them at first. Then he perceived that almost all the corpses were dressed in red, and also, which gave him a thrill of horror, that a great many of these unhappy " red-coats " were still alive. They were crying out, evidently asking for help, but nobody stopped to give it to them. Our hero, in his humanity, did all he could to prevent his horse from treading on any red uniform. The escort halted. Fabrizio, instead of attending to his duty as a soldier, galloped on, with his eye on a poor wounded fellow.

" Will you pull up, you idiot ? " shouted the troop sergeant-major. Then Fabrizio became aware that he was twenty paces in advance of the generals' right, and just in the line of their field-glasses. As he rode back to the rear of the escort, he saw the most portly of the officers speaking to his next neighbour, also a general, with an air of authority, and almost of reprimand. He swore. Fabrizio could not restrain his curiosity, and, in spite of the advice of his friend the jailer's wife, never to speak if he could help it, made up a neat and correct little French sentence. " Who's that general blowing up the one next him ? " he asked.

" Why, that's the marshal, to be sure ! "

" What marshal ? "

" Marshal Ney, you fool ! Where in thunder have you been serving up to now ? "

Touchy though he was by nature, Fabrizio never dreamed of resenting the insult. Lost in boyish admiration, he feasted his eyes on the " bravest of the brave," the famous Prince of the Moskowa.

Suddenly every one broke into a gallop. In a few minutes Fabrizio saw another ploughed field, about twenty paces in front of him, the surface of which was heaving in a very curious manner. The furrows were full of water, and the damp earth of the ridges was flying about, three or four feet high, in little black lumps. Fabrizio just noticed this odd appearance as he galloped along; then his thoughts flew back to the marshal and his glory. A sharp cry rang out close to him; two hussars fell, struck by bullets, and when he looked at them, they were already twenty paces behind the escort. A sight which seemed horrible to him was that of a horse, bathed in blood, struggling on the ploughed earth, with its feet caught in its own entrails. It was trying to follow the others. The blood was pouring over the mud.

"Well, I am under fire at last," he thought. "I have seen it!" he reiterated, with a glow of satisfaction. "Now I am a real soldier!" The escort was now galloping at full speed, and our hero realized that it was shot which was tossing up the soil. In vain he gazed in the direction whence the fusillade came. The white smoke of the battery seemed to him an immense way off, and amid the steady and continuous grumble of the artillery fire he thought he could distinguish other reports, much nearer. He could make nothing of it at all.

At that moment the generals and their escort entered a narrow lane, sunk about five feet below the level of the ground. It was full of water.

The marshal halted, and put up his glass again. This time Fabrizio had a good view of him. He saw a very fair man with a large red head. "We have no faces like that in Italy," he mused. "With my pale face and chestnut hair I shall never be like him," he added sadly. To him those words meant, "I shall never be a hero!" He looked at the hussars. All of them except one had fair mustaches. If Fabrizio stared at them, they stared at him as well. He coloured under their scrutiny, and, to ease his shyness, turned his head toward the enemy. He saw very long lines of red figures, but what astonished him was that they all looked so small. Those long files, which were really regiments and divisions, seemed to him no higher than hedges. A line of red-coated horsemen was trotting toward the sunken road, along which the marshal and his escort had begun to move slowly, splashing through the mud. The smoke made it impossible to see anything ahead. Only, from time to time, hurrying horsemen emerged from the white smoke.

Suddenly Fabrizio saw four men come galloping as hard as they could tear from the direction in which the enemy lay. "Ah!" said he to himself, "we are going to be attacked!" Then he saw two of these men address the marshal, and one of the generals in attendance upon him galloped off toward the enemy, followed by two hussars of the escort, and the two men who had just ridden up. On the other side of a small water-course, which everybody now crossed, Fabrizio found himself riding alongside a good-natured-looking sergeant. " I really must speak to this man," he said to himself. " Perhaps if I do that, they'll stop staring at me." After considerable meditation he said to the sergeant: " This is the first time I have ever seen a battle. But is it really a battle?"

" I should think so! But who on earth are you?"

" I am brother to a captain's wife."

" And what's the captain's name?"

Our hero was in a hideous difficulty; he had never expected that question. Luckily for him, the sergeant and the escort began to gallop again.

" What French name shall I say?" he wondered. At last he bethought him of the name of the man who had owned the hotel in which he had lodged in Paris. He brought his horse up close beside the sergeant's charger, and shouted at the top of his voice:

" Captain Meunier."

The other, half deafened by the noise of the artillery, answered, " What! Captain Teulier? Well, he's been killed!"

" Bravo!" said Fabrizio to himself. " Captain Teulier! I must look distressed."

" Oh, my God!" he cried, and put on a pitiful face. They had left the sunken road, and were crossing a small meadow. Every one tore at full gallop, for the bullets were pelting down again. The marshal rode toward a cavalry division; the escort was surrounded, now, by dead and wounded men, but our hero was already less affected by the sight; he had something else to think about.

While the escort was halting he noticed a *cantinière* with her little cart; his affection for that excellent class of women overrode every other feeling, and he galloped off toward the vehicle. " Stop here, you——" shouted the sergeant.

" What harm can he do me?" thought Fabrizio, and he galloped on toward the cart. He had felt some hope, as he spurred his horse onward, that its owner might be the good woman he had met in the morning—the horse and cart looked very much like hers. But the owner of these was quite a different person, and very forbidding-looking into the bargain. As he drew close to her he heard her say, "Well, he was a very handsome chap."

A hideous sight awaited the newly made soldier. A cuirassier, a splendid fellow, nearly six feet high, was having his leg cut off. Fabrizio shut his eyes and drank off four glasses of brandy one after the other. "You don't stint yourself, my little fellow!" quoth the *cantinière*. The brandy gave him an idea. "I must buy my comrades' good-will. Give me the rest of the bottle," he said to the woman.

"But d'ye know that on such a day as this the rest of the bottle will cost you six francs?"

As he galloped back to the escort, "Aha! you were fetching us a dram. 'Twas for that you deserted!" exclaimed the sergeant. "Hand over!"

The bottle went round, the last man throwing it into the air after he had drained it. "Thankye, comrade," he shouted to Fabrizio. Every eye looked kindly on him, and these glances lifted a hundred-weight off his heart, one of those overdelicate organs which pines for the friendship of those about it. At last, then, his comrades thought no ill of him; there was a bond between them. He drew a deep breath, and then, turning to the sergeant, calmly inquired:

"And if Captain Teulier has been killed, where am I to find my sister?" He thought himself a young Macchiavelli when he said Teulier instead of Meunier.

"You'll find that out to-night," replied the sergeant.

Once more the escort moved forward, in the direction of some infantry divisions. Fabrizio felt quite drunk; he had swallowed too much brandy, and swayed a little in his saddle. Then he recollected, very much in season, a remark he had frequently heard made by his mother's coachman: "When you've lifted your little finger you must always look between your horse's ears, and do what your next

47

neighbour does." The marshal halted for some time close to several bodies of cavalry, which he ordered to charge. But for the next hour or two our hero was hardly conscious of what was going on about him; he was overcome with weariness, and when his horse galloped he bumped in his saddle like a lump of lead.

Suddenly the sergeant shouted to his men:

"Don't you see the Emperor, you——" and instantly the escort shouted "Vive l'Empereur" at the top of their voices. My readers may well imagine that our hero stared with all his eyes, but all he saw was a bevy of generals galloping by, followed by another escort. The long, hanging plumes on the helmets of the dragoons in attendance prevented him from making out any faces. "So, thanks to that cursed brandy, I've missed seeing the Emperor on the battle-field." The thought woke him up completely. They rode into another lane swimming with water, and the horses paused to drink.

"So that was the Emperor who passed by?" he said to the next man.

"Why, certainly; the one in the plain coat. How did you miss seeing him?" answered his comrade good-naturedly.

Fabrizio was sorely tempted to gallop after the Emperor's escort and join it. What a joy it would have been to serve in a real war in attendance on that hero! Was it not for that very purpose that he had come to France? "I am perfectly free to do it," he reflected, "for indeed the only reason for my doing my present duty is that my horse chose to gallop after these generals."

But what decided him on remaining was that his comrades the hussars treated him in a friendly fashion; he began to believe himself the close friend of every one of the soldiers with whom he had been galloping the last few hours; he conceived himself bound to them by the noble ties that united the heroes of Tasso and Ariosto. If he joined the Emperor's escort he would have to make fresh acquaintances, and perhaps he might get the cold shoulder, for the horsemen of the other escort were dragoons, and he, like all those in attendance on the marshal, wore hussar uniform. The manner in which the troopers now looked at him filled our hero with happiness. He would have done anything on earth for his comrades; his whole soul and spirit were in the clouds. Everything seemed different to him now that he was among friends, and he was dying to ask questions.

"But I am not quite sober yet," he thought. "I must remember the jailer's wife." As they emerged from the sunken road he noticed that they were no longer escorting Marshal Ney; the general they were now attending was tall and thin, with a severe face and a merciless eye.

He was no other than the Count d'A——, the Lieutenant Robert of May 15, 1796. What would have been his delight at seeing Fabrizio del Dongo!

For some time Fabrizio had ceased to notice the soil flying hither and thither under the action of the bullets. The party rode up behind a regiment of cuirassiers; he distinctly heard the missiles pattering on the cuirasses, and saw several men fall.

The sun was already low, and it was just about to set, when the escort, leaving the lane, climbed a little slope which led into a ploughed field. Fabrizio heard a curious little noise close to him, and turned his head. Four men had fallen with their horses; the general himself had been thrown, but was just getting up, all covered with blood. Fabrizio looked at the hussars on the ground; three of them were still moving convulsively, the fourth was shouting "Pull me out!" The sergeant and two or three troopers had dismounted to help the general, who, leaning on his aide-de-camp, was trying to walk a few steps away from his horse, which was struggling on the ground and kicking furiously.

The sergeant came up to Fabrizio. Just at that moment, behind him and close to his ear, he heard somebody say, "It's the only one that can still gallop." He felt his feet seized and himself lifted up by them, while somebody supported his body under the arms. Thus he was drawn over his horse's hind quarters, and allowed to slip on to the ground, where he fell in a sitting posture. The aide-de-camp caught hold of the horse's bridle, and the general, assisted by the sergeant, mounted and galloped off, swiftly followed by the six remaining men. In a fury, Fabrizio jumped up and ran after them, shouting, *" Ladri! ladri!"* (" Thieves! thieves!") There was something comical about this running after thieves over a battle-field. The escort and General Count d'A—— soon vanished behind a row of willow trees. Before very long Fabrizio, still beside himself with rage, reached a similar row, and just beyond it he came on a very deep watercourse, which he crossed. When he reached the other side he began to swear again at the sight—but a very distant sight—of the general and his escort disappearing among the trees. " Thieves! thieves!" he shouted again, this time in French. Broken-hearted—much less by the loss of his horse than by the treachery with which he had been treated—weary, and starving, he cast himself down beside the ditch. If it had been the enemy which had carried off his fine charger he would not have given it a thought, but to see himself robbed and betrayed by the sergeant he had liked so much, and the hussars, whom he had looked on as his brothers, filled his soul with bitterness. The thought of the infamy of it was more than he could bear, and, leaning his back against a willow, he wept hot, angry tears. One by one his bright dreams of noble and chivalrous friendship—like the friendships of the heroes of Jerusalem Delivered—had faded before his eyes! The approach of death would have been as nothing in his sight if he had felt himself surrounded by heroic and tender hearts, by noble-souled friends, whose hands should have pressed his while he breathed out his last sigh. But how was he to keep up his enthusiasm when he was surrounded by such vile rascals? Fabrizio, like every angry man, had fallen into exaggeration. After a quarter of an hour spent in such melancholy thoughts, he became aware that the bullets were beginning to fall among the row of trees which sheltered his meditation. He rose to his feet, and made an effort to discover his whereabouts. He looked at the meadow, bounded by a broad canal and a line of bushy willows, and thought he recognised the spot. Then he noticed a body of infantry which was crossing the ditch and debouching into the meadows some quarter of a league ahead of him. "I was nearly caught napping," thought he. "I must take care not to be taken prisoner." And he began to walk forward very rapidly. As he advanced, his mind was relieved; he recognised the uniform. The regiments which he feared might have cut off his retreat belonged to the French army; he bore to the right, so as to reach them.

Besides the moral suffering of having been so vilely deceived and robbed, Fabrizio felt another, the pangs of which were momentarily increasing—he was literally starving. It was with the keenest joy, therefore, that after walking, or rather running, for ten minutes, he perceived that the body of infantry, which had also been moving very rapidly, had halted, as though to take up a position. A few minutes more and he was among the nearest soldiers.

"Comrades, could you sell me a piece of bread?"

"Halloo, here's a fellow who takes us for bakers!"

The rude speech and the general titter that greeted it overwhelmed Fabrizio. Could it be that war was not, after all, that noble and general impulse of souls thirsting for glory which Napoleon's proclamations had led him to conceive it? He sat down, or rather let himself drop upon the sward; he turned deadly pale. The soldier who had spoken, and who had stopped ten paces off to clean the lock of his gun with his handkerchief, moved a little nearer, and threw him a bit of bread; then, seeing he did not pick it up, the man put a bit of the bread into his mouth. Fabrizio opened his eyes, and ate the bread without having strength to say a word; when at last he looked about for the soldier, intending to pay him, he saw he was alone. The nearest soldiers to him were some hundred paces off, marching away. Mechanically he rose and followed them; he entered a wood. He was ready to drop with weariness, and was already looking about for a place where he might lay him down, when to his joy he recognized first the horse, then the cart, and finally the *cantinière* he had met in the morning. She ran to him, quite startled by his looks.

"March on, my boy," she said. "Are you wounded? and where's your fine horse?" As she spoke she led him toward her cart, into which she pushed him, lifting him under the arms. So weary was our hero that before he had well got into the cart he had fallen fast asleep.

CHAPTER IV

NOTHING woke him, neither the shots that rang out close to the little cart, nor the jolting of the horse, which the good woman whipped up with all her might. The regiment, after having believed all day long that victory was on its side, had been unexpectedly attacked by clouds of Prussian cavalry, and was retreating, or rather flying, toward the French border.

The colonel, a handsome, well-set-up young man, who had succeeded to Macon's command, was cut down. The major who took his place, an old fellow with white hair, halted the regiment. " Come," he shouted to his men, " in the days of the Republic none of us ran away till the enemy forced us to it. You must dispute every inch of the ground, and let yourselves be killed! " he added with an oath. " It's our own country that these Prussians are trying to invade now."

The little cart stopped short, and Fabrizio woke with a jump. The sun had disappeared long ago, and he noticed to his surprise that it was almost dark. The soldiers were running hither and thither in a state of confusion, which greatly astonished our hero. It struck him that they all looked very crestfallen.

" What's the matter? " said he to the *cantinière*.

" Nothing at all. The matter is that we're done for, my boy ; that the Prussian cavalry is cutting us down—that's all. The fool of a general took it for our own at first. Now then, look sharp! Help me to mend the trace ; Cocotte has broken it ! "

Several musket shots rang out ten paces off. Our hero, now thoroughly rested, said to himself : " But really, all this whole day through I have never fought at all! All I have done was to ride escort to a general. I must go and fight," said he to the woman.

"Make your mind easy; you'll fight more than you want. We're all done for!"

"Aubry, my boy," she shouted to a corporal who was passing by, "give an eye to the little cart now and then."

"Are you going to fight?" said Fabrizio to Aubry.

"No; I'm going to put on my pumps and go to the ball."

"I'm after you."

"Look after the little hussar," shouted the *cantinière*; "he's a plucky young chap."

Corporal Aubry marched on without saying a word; eight or ten soldiers ran up and joined him. He led them up behind a big oak with brambles growing all round it. Once there, he stationed them, still without opening his lips, in a very open line, along the edge of the wood, each man at least ten paces from his neighbour.

"Now, then, you fellows," he said, and it was the first time his voice had been heard, "don't you fire until you hear the word of command. Remember, you've only three cartridges apiece."

"But what is happening?" wondered Fabrizio to himself. At last, when he was alone with the corporal, he said, "I have no musket."

"Hold your tongue, to begin with. Go forward fifty paces beyond the wood; you'll find some of our poor fellows who've just been cut down. Take a musket and ammunition-pouch off one of them. But mind you don't take them from a wounded man; take the gun and pouch from some man who is quite dead. And look sharp, for fear you should get shot at by our own people!"

Fabrizio started off at a run, and soon came back with a musket and ammunition-pouch.

"Load your musket, and get behind this tree; and above all, don't fire till I give the word."

"Great God!" said the corporal, breaking off, "he doesn't even know how to load his weapon!" He came to Fabrizio's rescue, and went on talking as he did it. "If

any of the enemy's cavalry ride at you to cut you down,
slip round your tree, and don't fire your shot till your man's
quite close—not more than three paces off; your bayonet
must almost touch his uniform. But will you chuck that
great sword of yours away?" exclaimed the corporal. "Do
you want it to throw you down? 'Sdeath, what soldiers
they send us nowadays!" And as he spoke he snatched
at the sword himself and threw it angrily away. "Here,
wipe the flint of your gun with your handkerchief. But
have you ever fired a gun off?"

"I am a sportsman."

"God be praised!" said the corporal, with a sigh of
relief. "Well, mind you don't fire till I give the word,"
and he departed.

Fabrizio was filled with joy. "At last," said he to himself, "I am really going to fight and kill an enemy! This
morning they were shooting at us, and all I did was to expose myself—a fool's errand!" He looked about in every
direction with the most eager curiosity. After a moment
seven or eight musket shots rang out close to him, but as
he received no order himself he stood quietly behind his
tree. It had grown almost quite dark; he could have fancied he was hunting bears in the Tramezzina, above Grianta. He bethought him of a hunter's trick: took a cartridge from his pouch and extracted the ball. "If I get a
sight of him," said he, "I mustn't miss him," and he
slipped the extra ball down the barrel of his gun. He heard
two shots fired close to his tree, and at the same moment
he beheld a trooper dressed in blue galloping in front of
him from right to left. "He's more than three paces off,"
said he, "but at this distance I can't well miss him." He
covered the horseman with his musket, and pulled the trigger. The horse fell, and his rider with him. Our hero
fancied he was hunting, and ran joyfully up to the quarry
he had just bagged. He had got quite close to the man,
who seemed to him to be dying, when two Prussian troopers
rode down upon him at the most astounding rate, with their
swords lifted to cut him down. Fabrizio took to his heels,
and ran for the wood, throwing away his gun so that he

might run the quicker. The Prussian troopers were not more than three paces behind him when he reached a plantation of young oaks, very straight growing, and about as thick as a man's arm, which skirted the wood. The little oaks checked the horsemen for a moment, but they soon got through them and pursued Fabrizio across a clearing. They were quite close on him again when he managed to slip between seven or eight big trees. Just at that moment his face was almost scorched by the fire from five or six muskets just in front of him. He lowered his head, and when he raised it again he found himself face to face with the corporal.

"Have you killed yours?" said the corporal.

"Yes, but I've lost my musket."

"Muskets are not the thing we are short of. You're a good chap, though you do look like a muff. You've done well to-day, and these fellows have just missed the two who were after you, and were riding straight upon them. I didn't see them.

"Now we must make off. The regiment must be half a mile away; and, besides, there's a little bit of meadow to cross, where we may be taken in flank." As he talked the corporal marched swiftly along at the head of his ten men, some two hundred paces farther on. As he entered the little meadow of which he had spoken they came upon a wounded general supported by his aide-de-camp and a servant. "You must give me four men," said he to the corporal, and his voice was faint. "I must be carried to the ambulance; my leg is shattered."

"You may go to the devil," replied the corporal; "you and all the rest of the generals. You've all of you betrayed the Emperor this day."

"What!" cried the general in a fury; "you won't obey my orders? Do you know that I am General Count B——, commanding your division?" and so forth, with a string of invectives.

The aide-de-camp rushed at the soldier. The corporal thrust at him with his bayonet, and then made off at the double, followed by his men.

The Chartreuse of Parma

" May they all be like you ! " he repeated with an oath.
" With their legs shattered and their arms too ! A pack of
rascals, sold to the Bourbons and traitors to the Emperor,
every one of them ! "

Fabrizio heard the hideous accusation with astonishment.

Toward ten o'clock in the evening the little party came
upon the regiment, at the entrance to a big village consist-
ing of several narrow streets. But Fabrizio noticed that
Corporal Aubry avoided speaking to any of the officers.
" It's impossible to get on ! " cried the corporal. Every
street was crowded with infantry, cavalry, and especially
with artillery caissons and baggage wagons. The corporal
tried to get up three of these streets, but after about twenty
paces he was forced to stop. Everybody was swearing,
and everybody was in a rage.

" Some other traitor must be in command ! " cried the
corporal. " If the enemy has the sense to move round the
village we shall all be taken like dogs. Follow me, men ! "
Fabrizio looked; there were only six soldiers left of the
corporal's party. Through a big, open doorway they passed
into a great poultry-yard, and thence into a stable, from
which a little door admitted them into a garden. Here
they lost their way for a moment, and wandered hither and
thither. But at last, climbing over a hedge, they found
themselves in a huge field of buckwheat, and within less
than half an hour, following the noise of shouting and other
confused sounds, they had got back into the high-road on
the other side of the village.

The ditches on either side of the road were full of
muskets which had been thrown away, and Fabrizio
took one for himself. But the road, broad as it was,
was so crowded with carts and fugitives that in half
an hour the corporal and Fabrizio had hardly got five
hundred paces forward. They were told that the road
would lead them to Charleroi. As the village clock struck
eleven—

" Let us strike across country again," cried the corporal. The little band now only consisted of three privates,

the corporal, and Fabrizio. When they had got about a quarter of a league from the high-road—

" I'm done up ! " said one of the soldiers.

" And so am I," said another.

" That's fine news ! We're all in the same boat," said the corporal. " But do as I tell you, and you'll be the better for it." He caught sight of five or six trees growing beside a little ditch in the middle of an immense field of corn.

" Make for the trees," said he to his men. " Lie down here," he added when they had reached them, " and, above all, make no noise. But before we go to sleep, which of you has any bread ? "

" I have," said one of the soldiers.

" Hand it over," commanded the corporal, with a masterful air. He divided the bread into five pieces, and took the smallest for himself.

" A quarter of an hour before daybreak," he said as he munched, " you'll have the enemy's cavalry upon you. The great point is not to get yourselves run through. On these great plains one man alone with cavalry at his heels is done for, but five men together may save themselves. All of you stick faithfully to me, don't fire except at close quarters, and I'll undertake to get you into Charleroi to-morrow night." An hour before daybreak the corporal roused them ; he made them reload their weapons. The noise on the highway still continued ; it had been going on all night, like the noise of a distant torrent.

" It's like the noise sheep make when they are running away," said Fabrizio to the corporal, with an artless air.

" Will you hold your tongue, you greenhorn ? " said the corporal angrily, and the three privates, who, with Fabrizio, composed the whole of his army, looked at our hero with an expression of indignation, as if he had said something blasphemous. He had insulted the nation !

" This is rather strong," thought our hero to himself. " I noticed the same sort of thing at Milan under the viceroy. They are not running away—oh, dear, no ! With these Frenchmen you must never tell the truth if it hurts their vanity. But as for their angry looks, I don't care a farthing for them, and I must make them understand it." They were still marching along some five hundred paces from the stream of fugitives which blocked the high-road. A league farther on the corporal and his party crossed a lane running into the high-road, in which many soldiers were lying. Here Fabrizio bought a tolerable horse for forty francs, and from among the numerous swords that were lying about he carefully chose a long, straight weapon. " As I am told I must thrust," he thought, " this will be the best." Thus equipped, he put his horse into a canter, and soon came up with the corporal, who had gone forward; he settled himself in his stirrups, seized the sheath of his sword with his left hand, and addressed the four Frenchmen. " These fellows who are fleeing along the highway look like a flock of sheep; they move like frightened sheep ! "

In vain did he dwell upon the word sheep; his comrades had quite forgotten that only an hour previously it had kindled their ire. Here we perceive one of the contrasts between the French and the Italian character; the Frenchman is doubtless the happier of the two—events glide over him; he bears no spite.

I will not conceal the fact that Fabrizio was very much pleased with himself after he had talked about those sheep. They marched along, keeping up a casual conversation. Two leagues farther on the corporal, who was very much astonished at seeing nothing of the enemy's cavalry, said to Fabrizio:

" You are our cavalry, so gallop toward that farm on the hillock yonder, and ask the peasant if he'll sell us some breakfast. Be sure you tell him there are only five of us. If he demurs, give him five francs of your money, on account; but make your mind easy, we'll take the silver piece back after we've had our breakfast."

Fabrizio looked at the corporal; his gravity was imperturbable, and he really wore an appearance of moral superiority. He obeyed, and everything fell out just as the commander-in-chief had foretold, only Fabrizio insisted the peasant should not be forced to return the five-franc piece he had paid him.

"The money is my own," said he to his comrades. "I'm not paying for you; I'm paying for the corn he has given my horse."

Fabrizio's French was so bad that his comrades thought they detected a tone of superiority about his remark; they were very much offended, and from that instant they began to hatch a quarrel with him. They saw he was very different from themselves, and that fact displeased them. Fabrizio, on the contrary, began to feel exceedingly friendly toward them. They had been marching along silently for about two hours when the corporal, looking toward the high-road, shouted in a transport of delight, "There's the regiment!" They were soon on the high-road themselves, but alas, there were not two hundred men round the eagle! Fabrizio soon caught sight of the *cantinière*; she was walking along with red eyes, and every now and then her tears overflowed. In vain did Fabrizio peer about, looking for Cocotte and the little cart.

"Pillaged! lost! stolen!" cried the poor woman, in answer to our hero's inquiring glance. Without a word he threw himself from his horse, took him by the bridle, and said to her, "Get on his back!" She didn't wait for a second invitation. "Shorten the stirrups for me," she said. Once she was comfortably settled on horseback, she began to tell Fabrizio all the disasters of the preceding night.

After an endless story, eagerly listened to, however, by our hero, who could make nothing of it, we must admit, but who had a deep feeling of regard for the good-natured *cantinière*, she added, "And to think that it should be Frenchmen who have robbed, and beaten, and ruined me!"

"What! it wasn't the enemy?" cried Fabrizio, with an artlessness which made his handsome face, so grave and pale, look more charming than ever.

"What a silly you are, my poor child!" returned the woman, smiling through her tears; "and silly as you are, you are a very good fellow."

"And however silly he may be, he pulled his Prussian

down well yesterday," added Corporal Aubry, who had happened to find his way through the crowd to the other side of the horse on which the good woman was riding. " But he's proud," said the corporal. Fabrizio started a little. " And what's your name? " continued he. " For, after all, if any report is sent in, I should like to give it."

" My name is Vasi," answered Fabrizio, with rather an odd look. " I mean," correcting himself hastily, " Boulot."

Boulot had been the name of the owner of the route papers the jailer's wife had given him. Two nights before, as he marched along, he had studied them carefully, for he was beginning to reflect a little, and was not so astonished by everything that happened to him as he had been at first. In addition to poor Boulot's papers he had also carefully kept the Italian passport according to which he claimed the noble name of Vasi, dealer in barometers. When the corporal had taxed him with being proud it had been on the tip of his tongue to reply, " Proud! I, Fabrizio Valserra, Marchesino del Dongo, who is willing to bear the name of a dealer in barometers called Vasi? "

While he was considering all this and saying to himself, " I must really remember that my name is Boulot, or I shall find myself in the prison with which Fate threatens me," the corporal and the *cantinière* had been exchanging ideas about him.

" Don't take what I say for mere curiosity," said the *cantinière*, and she dropped the second person singular, which, in her homely fashion, she had hitherto been using. " I'm going to ask you these questions for your own good. Who are you, really and truly? "

Fabrizio was silent for a moment; he was considering that he might never come across better friends from whom to ask advice, and advice he sorely needed. " We are going into a fortified town; the governor will want to know who I am, and if my answers show that I know nothing about the hussar regiment, the uniform of which I wear, I shall be thrown into prison at once." Being an Austrian subject, Fabrizio realized all the importance of his passport. The members of his own family, highly born and religious as they were, had suffered frequent annoyance in this particular. The good woman's questions were not, therefore, the least displeasing to him, but when he paused before replying to choose out his clearest French expressions, the *cantinière*, pricked with eager curiosity, added by way of encouragement, " We'll give you good advice about your behaviour, Corporal Aubry and I."

" I'm sure of that," answered Fabrizio. " My name is Vasi, and I belong to Genoa; my sister, who was a famous beauty, married a captain. As I am only seventeen, she sent for me that I might see France and improve myself. I did not find her in Paris, and knowing she was with this army I followed it, and have hunted in every direction without being able to find her. The soldiers, struck by my foreign accent, had me arrested. I had money at that time; I gave some to the gendarme in charge of me. He gave me papers and a uniform, and said, ' Be off with you, and swear you'll never mention my name to a living soul.' "

" What was his name? " said the *cantinière*.

" I gave my word," said Fabrizio.

" He's right," said the corporal. " The gendarme was a blackguard, but our comrade mustn't tell his name. And what was the name of the captain who married your sister? If we knew his name we might find him."

" Teulier, of the Fourth Hussars," answered our hero.

" Then," said the corporal rather sharply, " your foreign accent made the soldiers take you for a spy? "

" That's the vile word! " cried Fabrizio, and his eyes flamed. " I, who worship the Emperor and the French— that insult hurts me more than anything! "

" There's no insult; there's where you're mistaken," replied the corporal gravely. " The soldiers' mistake was very natural."

Then he explained, with more than a little pedantry, that in the army every man must belong to a regiment and wear a uniform, and, failing that, would certainly be taken for a spy.

" The enemy," he said, " has sent us heaps of them. In this war traitors abound."

The Chartreuse of Parma

The scales fell from Fabrizio's eyes, and for the first time he understood that in everything that had happened to him during the past two months he himself had been at fault.

"But the boy must tell us the whole story," said the *cantinière*, whose curiosity was momentarily growing keener.

Fabrizio obeyed, and when he had finished—

"The fact is," said she seriously, and addressing the corporal, "the child knows nothing about soldiering. This war will be a wretched war, now that we are beaten and betrayed. Why should he get his bones broken, *gratis pro Deo!*"

"And with that," said the corporal, "he doesn't even know how to load his gun, either in slow time or in quick! It was I who put in the bullet that killed his Prussian for him."

"And, besides," added the *cantinière*, "he lets everybody see his money, and he'll be stripped of everything as soon as he leaves us."

"And the first cavalry sergeant he comes across," the corporal went on, "will take possession of him and make him pay for his drinks, and he may even be recruited for the enemy, for there's treachery everywhere. The first man he meets will tell him to follow him, and follow him he will! He would do much better to enlist in our regiment."

"Not so, I thank you, corporal," cried Fabrizio eagerly. "I'm much more comfortable on horseback; and, besides, I don't know how to load a musket, and you've seen that I can manage a horse."

Fabrizio was very proud of this little speech of his. I will not reproduce the long discussion as to his future which ensued between the corporal and the *cantinière*.

Fabrizio remarked that in the course of it they repeated all the incidents of his story three or four times over—the soldiers' suspicions; the gendarme who sold him the uniform and the papers; the manner in which he had fallen in with the marshal's escort on the previous day; the story of the horse, etc. The *cantinière*, with feminine curiosity, con-

The Chartreuse of Parma

stantly harked back to the manner in which he had been
robbed of the good horse she had made him buy.

"You felt somebody seize your feet, you were drawn
gently over your horse's tail, and were left sitting on the
ground."

"Why is it," wondered Fabrizio, "that they keep going
over things which we all know perfectly well!" He had not
yet learned that this is the method whereby the humbler
folk in France think a matter out.

"How much money have you?" inquired the *cantinière*
of him. Fabrizio answered unhesitatingly; he was sure of
this woman's noble-heartedness—that is the finest side of the
French character.

"I may have about thirty napoleons in gold, and eight
or ten five-franc pieces, altogether."

"In that case your course is clear," cried the *cantinière*.
"Get yourself out of this routed army, turn off to one side,
take the first tolerable road you can find on the right, ride
steadily forward, away from the army always. Buy yourself
civilian clothes at the first opportunity. When you are eight
or ten leagues off, and you see no more soldiers about you,
take post-horses, get to some good town, and rest there for
a week, and eat good beefsteaks. Never tell any one that
you have been with the army; the gendarmes would take
you up at once as a deserter, and, nice fellow as you are,
my boy, you are not sharp enough yet to take in the
gendarmes. Once you have civilian clothes upon your
back, tear your route papers into little bits, and take back
your real name. Say you're Vasi—and where should he say
he comes from?" she added, appealing to the corporal.

"From Cambray, on the Scheldt—it's a good old town,
very small, do you hear? with a cathedral—and Fénelon."

"That's it," said the *cantinière*, "and never let out that
you've been in the battle, never breathe a word about
B—— nor the gendarme who sold you the papers. When
you want to get back to Paris, go first of all to Versailles,
and get into the city from that side, just dawdling along on
your feet as if you were out for a walk. Sew your money
into your trousers, and when you have to pay for anything,

mind you only show just the money you need for that. What worries me is that you'll be made a fool of, and you'll be stripped of everything you have. And what is to become of you without money, seeing you don't even know how to behave?"

The good woman talked on and on, the corporal backing her opinions by nodding his head, for she gave him no chance of getting in a word. Suddenly the crowd upon the high-road quickened its pace, and then, like a flash, it crossed the little ditch on the left-hand side and fled at full speed.

"The Cossacks, the Cossacks!" rang out on every side.

"Take back your horse," cried the *cantinière*.

"God forbid!" said Fabrizio. "Gallop! be off! I give him to you. Do you want money to buy another little cart? Half of what I have is yours."

"Take back your horse, I say," said the good woman in a rage, and she tried to get off. Fabrizio drew his sword. "Hold on tight!" he cried, and he struck the horse two or three times with the flat of the blade. It broke into a gallop and followed the fugitives.

Our hero looked at the high-road. Only a few minutes before it had been crowded with some two or three thousand people, packed like peasants in a religious procession.

Since that cry of "Cossacks" there was not a soul upon it. The fugitives had thrown away their shakos, their muskets, and their swords.

Fabrizio, thoroughly astonished, climbed about twenty or thirty feet into a field on the right of the road; thence he looked up and down the high-road and across the plain. There was not a sign of any Cossack. "Queer people, these Frenchmen," said he to himself. Then he went on: "As I am to go to the right, I may as well start at once. These people may have had some reason for bolting which I don't know." He picked up a musket, made sure it was loaded, shook the powder in the priming, cleaned the flint, then chose himself a well-filled cartridge pouch and looked all round him again. He stood literally alone in the middle of the plain, which had lately been so packed with people. In the far distance he saw the fugitives still running along and beginning to disappear behind the trees. " This really is very odd," he said. And remembering the corporal's manœuvre on the preceding night, he went and sat down in the middle of a cornfield. He would not go far away, because he hoped to rejoin his friends the corporal and the *cantinière*.

Sitting in the corn, he discovered he had only eighteen napoleons left, instead of thirty, but he had a few little diamonds which he had hidden in the lining of his hussar boots on the morning of his parting with the jailer's wife. He concealed his gold pieces as best he could, and pondered deeply the while over this sudden disappearance of his fellow-travellers.

" Is it a bad omen for me? " he wondered. His chief vexation was that he had not asked Corporal Aubry the following question: " Have I really been in a battle? " He thought he had, and he would have been perfectly happy if he could have been quite certain of it.

" In any case," he said, " I was present at it under a prisoner's name, and I had the prisoner's route papers in my pocket, and even his coat upon my back. All that is fatal for my future. What would Father Blanès have said of it? And that unlucky Boulot died in prison, too. It all looks very ominous. My destiny will lead me to a prison! " Fabrizio would have given anything in the world to know whether Boulot had really been guilty. He had a recollection that the jailer's wife had told him the hussar had been locked up, not only for stealing spoons and forks, but for having robbed a peasant of his cow, and further beaten the said peasant unmercifully. He had no doubt that he himself would some day find himself in prison for misdoings of the same nature as those of the hussar. He thought of his friend the priest. What would he not have given to be able to consult him! Then he recollected that he had not written to his aunt since he left Paris. " Poor Gina! " he said, and the tears rose to his eyes. All at once he heard a slight noise close to him. It was a soldier feeding three horses, whose bridles he had removed and who seemed half dead with hunger; on the growing corn.

He was holding them by the snaffle. Fabrizio flew up like a partridge, and the soldier was startled. Our hero, perceiving it, could not resist the pleasure of playing the hussar for a moment. "Fellow," he shouted, "one of those horses is mine, but I will give you five francs for the trouble you've taken to bring it to me!" "I wish you may get it," said the soldier. Fabrizio, who was within six paces, levelled his musket at him. "Give up the horse, or I'll blow your brains out!" The soldier had his musket slung behind him; he twisted his shoulder back to get at it. "If you stir a step you're a dead man!" shouted Fabrizio, rushing at him. "Well, well! hand over the five francs, and take one of the horses," said the soldier, rather crestfallen, after glancing regretfully up and down the road, on which not a soul was to be seen. Fabrizio, with his gun still raised in his left hand, threw him three five-franc pieces with the right. "Get down, or you're a dead man! Put the bit on the black horse, and move off with the others. I'll blow your brains out if you shuffle!" With an evil glance the man obeyed. Fabrizio came close to the horse and slipped the bridle over his left arm without taking his eyes off the soldier, who was slinking slowly away. When he saw he was about fifty paces off our hero sprang upon the horse's back. He had hardly got into the saddle, and his foot was still searching for the right stirrup, when a bullet whistled close beside his head; it was the soldier who had fired his musket at him. Fabrizio, in a fury, galloped toward him. He took to his heels, and was soon galloping away on one of his horses. "Well, he's out of range now," said Fabrizio to himself. The horse he had just bought was a splendid animal, but it seemed to be almost starving. Fabrizio went back to the high-road, which was still quite deserted; he crossed it, and trotted on toward a little undulation in the ground on the left, where he hoped he might find the *cantinière*, but when he reached the top of the tiny eminence he could only see a few scattered soldiers more than a league away. He sighed. "It is written," he said, "that I am never to see that good kind woman again!" He went to a farm which he had noticed in the distance, on the right of the road. Without dismounting he fed his poor horse with oats, which he paid for beforehand. It was so starving that it actually bit at the manger. An hour later he was trotting along the high-road, still in the vague hope that he might find the *cantinière*, or at all events come across Corporal Aubry. As he pushed steadily forward, looking about on every side, he came to a marshy stream, spanned by a narrow wooden bridge. Near the entrance to the bridge and on the right-hand side of the road stood a lonely house, which displayed the sign of the White Horse. "I'll have my dinner there," said Fabrizio to himself. Beside the bridge was a cavalry officer with his arm in a sling. He was sitting on his horse and looked very sad. Ten paces from him three dismounted troopers were busy with their pipes.

"Those fellows," said Fabrizio to himself, "look very much as if they might be inclined to buy my horse even cheaper than the price I've paid for him." The wounded officer and the three men on foot were watching him, and seemed to be waiting for him. "I really ought to avoid that bridge and follow the river bank on the right; that's what the *cantinière* would advise me to do, to get out of the difficulty. Yes," said our hero to himself, "but if I take to flight I shall be ashamed of it to-morrow. Besides, my horse has good legs, and the officer's horse is probably tired out. If he tries to dismount me I'll take to my heels." Reasoning thus, Fabrizio shook his horse together and rode on as slowly as possible.

"Come on, hussar!" shouted the officer, with a voice of authority. Fabrizio came on a few steps, and then halted. "Do you want to take my horse from me?" he called out.

"Not a bit of it! Come on!"

Fabrizio looked at the officer. His mustache was white, he had the most honest face imaginable, the handkerchief which supported his left arm was covered with blood, and his right hand was also wrapped in a bloody bandage. "It's those men on foot who will snatch at the horse's bridle," thought Fabrizio; but when he looked closer he saw that the men on foot were wounded as well.

"In the name of all that's honourable," said the officer, who wore a colonel's epaulettes, "keep watch here, and tell every dragoon, light-cavalry man, and hussar you may see that Colonel Le Baron is in the inn there, and that he orders them to report themselves to him." The old colonel looked broken-hearted. His very first words had won our hero's heart, and he replied very sensibly, "I'm very young, sir; perhaps nobody would listen to me. I ought to have a written order from you."

"He's right," said the colonel, looking hard at him. "Write the order, La Rose; you can use your right hand." Without a word, La Rose drew a little parchment-covered book from his pocket, wrote a few words, tore out the leaf, and gave it to Fabrizio. The colonel repeated his orders, adding that Fabrizio would be relieved after two hours, as was only fair, by one of the wounded soldiers who were with him. This done, he went into the tavern with his men. Fabrizio, so greatly had he been struck by the silent and dreary sorrow of the three men, sat motionless at the end of the bridge, watching them disappear. "They were like enchanted genii," said he to himself. At last he opened the folded paper, and read the following order:

"Colonel Le Baron, Sixth Dragoons, commanding the Second Brigade of the First Cavalry Division of the Fourteenth Corps, orders all cavalry, dragoons, light-cavalry men, and hussars not to cross the bridge, and to report themselves to him at his headquarters, the White Horse Tavern, close to the bridge.

"*Dated.* Headquarters, close to the bridge over the Sainte. June 19, 1815.

"*Signed* for Colonel Le Baron, wounded in the right arm, and by his orders.

"SERGEANT LA ROSE."

Fabrizio had hardly kept guard on the bridge for half an hour when six light-cavalry men mounted, and three on foot, approached him. He gave them the colonel's order. "We are coming back," said four of the mounted men, and they crossed the bridge at full trot. By that time Fabrizio was engaged with the two others. While the altercation grew warmer the three men on foot slipped over the bridge. One of the two remaining mounted men ended by asking to see the order, and carried it off, saying, "I'll take it to my comrades, who are sure to come back; you wait patiently for them," and he galloped off with his companion after him. The whole thing was done in an instant.

Fabrizio, in a fury, beckoned to one of the wounded soldiers who had appeared at one of the tavern windows. The man, whom Fabrizio observed to be wearing a sergeant's stripes, came downstairs, and shouted, as he drew near him, "Draw your sword, sir! Don't you know you're on duty?" Fabrizio obeyed, and then said, "They've carried off the order!"

"They're still savage over yesterday's business," answered the other drearily. "I'll give you one of my pistols. If they break through again fire it in the air, and I'll come down, or the colonel will make his appearance."

Fabrizio had noticed the gesture of surprise with which the sergeant had received the intelligence that the order had been carried off. He had realized that the incident was a personal insult to himself, and was resolved that nothing of the sort should happen in future. He had gone back proudly to his post, armed with the sergeant's pistol, when he saw seven hussars come riding up. He had placed himself across the entrance to the bridge. He gave them the colonel's order, which vexed them very much. The boldest tried to get across. Fabrizio, obeying the wise advice of his friend the *cantinière*, who had told him the previous morning that he must cut and not thrust, lowered the point of his big straight sword, and made as though he would have run through anybody who disobeyed the order.

"Ha! the greenhorn wants to kill us, as if we had not been killed enough yesterday!" They all drew their swords, and fell upon Fabrizio. He gave himself up for dead, but he remembered the look of surprise on the sergeant's face, and resolved he would not be despised a second time. He backed slowly over his bridge, trying to thrust with his point as he went. He looked so queer, with his great straight cavalry sword, much too heavy for him, and which he did not know how to handle, that the hussars soon saw who they had to do with. Then they tried not to wound him, but to cut his coat off his back. He thus received three or four small sword cuts on the arm. Meanwhile, faithful to the *cantinière's* advice, he kept on thrusting with all his might. Unluckily one of his lunges wounded a hussar in the hand. The man, furious at being touched by such a soldier, replied with a violent thrust which wounded Fabrizio in the thigh. The wound was all the deeper because our hero's charger, instead of escaping from the *mêlée*, seemed to delight in it, and to throw himself deliberately on the assailants. The hussars, seeing Fabrizio's blood running down his right arm, were afraid they had gone too far, and, forcing him over to the left parapet of the bridge, they galloped off. The instant Fabrizio was free for a moment he fired his pistol in the air to warn the colonel.

Four mounted hussars and two on foot belonging to the same regiment as the last had been coming toward the bridge, and were still two hundred paces off when the pistol shot rang out. They were carefully watching what happened on the bridge, and thinking Fabrizio had fired upon their comrades, the four mounted men galloped down upon him, brandishing their swords; it was a regular charge. Colonel Le Baron, summoned by the pistol shot, opened the tavern door, rushed on to the bridge just as the hussars galloped up to it, and himself ordered them to halt.

" There's no colonel here," cried one of the men, and he spurred his horse. The colonel in his anger broke off his remonstrance, and seized the rein of the horse on the off side with his wounded hand. " Halt, sir! " he cried to the hussar. " I know you. You belong to Captain Henriet's company."

" Well, then, let the captain give me his orders! Captain Henriet was killed yesterday," he added with a sneer, " and

you may go and be damned!" As he spoke he tried to
force his way through, and knocked over the old colonel,
who fell in a sitting posture on the floor of the bridge.
Fabrizio, who was two paces farther on the bridge, but
facing the tavern, urged his horse furiously forward, and
while the hussar's horse overthrew the colonel, who still
clung to the off rein, he thrust vehemently and angrily at
its rider. Luckily the man's horse, which was dragged
downward by the bridle, on to which the colonel was still
hanging, started to one side, so that the long blade of Fabrizio's heavy cavalry sword slipped along the hussar's
waistcoat and came right out under his nose. The hussar,
in his fury, turned round and hacked at Fabrizio with all
his strength, cutting through his sleeve and making a deep
wound in his arm. Our hero tumbled off his horse. One
of the dismounted hussars, seeing the two defenders of the
bridge lying on the ground, seized his opportunity, sprang
on to Fabrizio's horse, and would have galloped it off the
bridge and away, but the sergeant, who had hurried up from
the tavern, had seen his colonel fall, and believed him to
be seriously wounded. He ran after Fabrizio's horse, and
plunged the point of his sword into the thief's back, so that
he, too, fell. Then the hussars, seeing nobody but the sergeant standing on the bridge, galloped across it and rode
rapidly away.

The sergeant went to look after the wounded. Fabrizio
had already picked himself up; he was not in much pain, but
he was losing a great deal of blood. The colonel rose to his
feet more slowly; he was quite giddy from his fall, but he
was not wounded at all.

"The only thing that hurts me," he said to his sergeant,
"is the old wound in my hand." The hussar whom the sergeant had wounded was dying.

"The devil may take him!" cried the colonel. "But,"
said he to the sergeant and the two other troopers who now
hurried up, "look after this boy, whose life I did wrong
to endanger. I will stay at the bridge myself, and try to stop
these madmen. Take the young fellow to the inn and dress
his arm. Use one of my shirts for bandages."

CHAPTER V

THE whole affair had not lasted more than a minute. Fabrizio's wounds were of the most trifling description; his arm was bound up in strips torn off one of the colonel's shirts. He was offered a bed in the upper story of the inn.

"But while I am lying comfortably here," said Fabrizio to the sergeant, "my horse will feel lonely in the stable, and may take himself off with another master."

"Not bad, for a recruit," said the sergeant, and he settled Fabrizio on some clean straw in the very manger to which his horse was tied.

Then, as Fabrizio felt very faint, he brought him a bowl of hot wine and talked to him for a while. Certain compliments included in this conversation made our hero feel as happy as a king.

It was near daybreak on the following morning when Fabrizio awoke. The horses were neighing long and loud, and making a terrible racket. The stable was full of smoke. At first Fabrizio could make nothing of the noise, and did not even realize where he was. At last, when the smoke had half stifled him, it struck him that the house was on fire; in the twinkling of an eye he was out of the stable and on his horse's back. He looked up and saw the smoke pouring out of the two windows above the stable, and the roof of the house hidden in a black, whirling cloud. A good hundred fugitives had reached the tavern during the night, and all of them were shouting and swearing at once. The five or six who were close to Fabrizio seemed to him to be completely drunk. One of them tried to stop him, shouting, "Where are you taking my horse?"

When Fabrizio had gone about a quarter of a league he looked back. Nobody was following him; the house was blazing. He recognised the bridge, thought of his wound, and touched his arm, which felt hot and tight in the bandages. And what had become of the old colonel? "He gave his shirt to bind up my arm." That morning our hero was the coolest and most collected man in the world; the quantities of blood he had lost had washed all the romantic qualities out of his character.

"To the right," said he, "and let us be off." He quietly followed the course of the river, which, after passing under the bridge, flowed toward the right side of the road. He remembered the good *cantinière's* advice. "What true friendship!" said he to himself; "what an honest soul!"

After an hour he began to feel very weak. "Now then," he thought, "am I going to faint? If I faint somebody will steal my horse, and perhaps my clothes, and with my clothes my valuables." He had not strength to guide his horse, and was doing his best to keep steady in the saddle, when a peasant digging in a field hard by the highroad noticed his pallor, and offered him a glass of beer and a bit of bread.

"Seeing you so pale," said the man, "I thought you might have been wounded in the great battle." Never did help come more in the nick of time. When Fabrizio began to chew that morsel of black bread his eyes had begun to sting when he looked in front of him. When he had pulled himself together a little he thanked his benefactor. "And where am I?" he inquired. The peasant informed him that three quarters of a league farther on he would find the little town of Zonders, where he would be well cared for. Fabrizio reached the town without well knowing what he was doing, his only care being how not to fall off at every step his horse took. He saw a big gate standing open and rode through it; it led to a tavern, The Currycomb. The good-natured mistress of the house, an exceedingly fat woman, ran forward, calling for help in a voice that shook with pity. Two young girls assisted Fabrizio to dismount. Before he was well out of his saddle he fainted dead away. A surgeon was summoned and he was bled. On that day and those following it he hardly knew what was being done to him. He slept almost incessantly.

The Chartreuse of Parma

The puncture in his leg threatened to turn into a serious abscess. Whenever he was in his senses he begged that care might be taken of his horse, and frequently reiterated that he would pay well, which mightily offended the good hostess and her daughters. He had been admirably tended for a fortnight, and was beginning to collect his thoughts a little, when he noticed, one evening, that his nurses seemed very much disturbed. Presently a German officer entered his room. The language in which his questions were answered was one which Fabrizio did not understand, but he clearly perceived that he himself was the subject of the conversation; he pretended to be asleep. Some time afterward, when he thought the officer must have departed, he called his hostess.

" Did not that officer come to write my name down on a list and take me prisoner? "

With tears in her eyes his hostess admitted the fact.

"Well, then," he cried, raising himself up in his bed, "there's money in my pocket. Buy me civilian clothes, and this very night I'll ride away. You've saved my life once already by taking me in when I should have fallen and died in the street. Save it again by helping me to get back to my mother."

At this point the landlady's daughters both burst into tears. They trembled for Fabrizio's safety, and as they could hardly understand any French, they came close to his bed to question him. They held a discussion with their mother in Flemish, but every moment their wet eyes turned pityingly upon our hero. He thought he gathered that his flight might compromise them seriously, but that they were ready to take the risk. He clasped his hands together and thanked them earnestly.

A local Jew undertook to provide him with a suit of clothes, but when he brought it, about ten o'clock that night, the young ladies discovered, by comparing the coat with Fabrizio's hussar jacket, that it was a great deal too large for him. They set to work on it at once; there was no time to be lost. Fabrizio showed them several napoleons hidden in his garments, and begged them to sew them into those which had just been bought. With the suit the Jew had brought a fine pair of new boots. Fabrizio did not hesitate to ask the kind-hearted girls to cut open his hussar boots at the place he showed them, and his little diamonds were soon hidden in the lining of his new foot-gear.

A singular result of his loss of blood, and his consequent weakness, was that Fabrizio had almost entirely forgotten his French. He talked to his hostesses in Italian, and as they spoke nothing but their Flemish *patois*, intercourse was really carried on solely by signs. When the young girls, perfectly disinterested as they were, beheld the diamonds, their admiration for our hero knew no bounds. They were convinced he was a prince in disguise. Aniken, the younger and more artless of the two, kissed him without further ceremony. Fabrizio, for his part, thought them charming, and toward midnight, when, in consideration of the journey he was about to take, the surgeon had allowed him to drink a little wine, he was half inclined not to depart at all.

"Where could I be better off than I am here?" he said. Nevertheless, about two o'clock in the morning he got up and dressed. Just as he was leaving his room the kindly hostess informed him that his horse had been carried off by the officer who had searched the house a few hours previously.

"Ah, the blackguard!" cried Fabrizio, "to play such a trick on a wounded man!" and he began to swear. Our young Italian was not enough of a philosopher to recollect the price he himself had paid for the horse.

Aniken told him, through her tears, that a horse had been hired for him. If she could have had her will he would not have started at all. The parting was a tender one. Two tall young fellows, the good landlady's kinsmen, lifted Fabrizio into his saddle and walked along, holding him up, while a third preceded the little party by a few hundred paces, on the lookout for any suspicious patrol upon the road. After two hours' journey a halt was made at the house of a cousin of the hostess of The Currycomb. In spite of all Fabrizio could say he could not induce the

The Chartreuse of Parma

young men to leave him. Nobody, they declared, knew the paths through the forest as well as they!

"But to-morrow morning, when my escape becomes known, and you are not seen in the neighbourhood, your absence will get you into trouble," urged Fabrizio.

A fresh start was made, and by good luck, when daylight came, a heavy fog shrouded the plain. Toward eight o'clock in the morning they were near a small town. One of the young men went on to see whether the post-horses had all been stolen. The postmaster had been able to hide them, and to fill up his stables with vile screws instead. Two horses were fetched out of the swamps where they had been concealed, and three hours later Fabrizio clambered into a little cabriolet, shabby enough, but drawn by two excellent posters. He felt stronger already; his parting with the hostesses' young kinsmen was pathetic in the extreme. Never—not under one of the friendly pretexts Fabrizio could invent—could he induce them to accept a halfpenny.

"In your condition, sir, you need it much more than we do," was the honest young fellows' invariable reply. They departed at last, bearing letters in which Fabrizio, somewhat steadied by the excitement of his journey, had endeavoured to express all he felt for his benefactresses. The tears were in his eyes as he wrote, and in his letter to little Aniken some love passages certainly occurred.

Nothing extraordinary happened during the rest of his journey. When he reached Amiens the sword thrust in his thigh was causing him great suffering. The country surgeon had not thought of keeping the wound open, and in spite of the bleeding, an abscess had formed. During the fortnight Fabrizio spent in the inn at Amiens, kept by an obsequious and covetous family, the allies were overrunning France, and so deeply did our hero reflect upon his late experiences that he became another man. There was only one point on which he still remained a child. Had the fighting he had seen really been a battle? and, secondly, Was it the battle of Waterloo?

For the first time in his life he found pleasure in reading; he was always hoping to discover in the newspapers or the descriptions of the battle something which would enable him to recognise the ground he had ridden over with Marshal Ney's and the other general's escort. During his stay at Amiens he wrote almost every day to his good friends of the Currycomb Inn. As soon as he was cured he went to Paris. At his former hotel he found twenty letters from his mother and his aunt, all beseeching him to return as quickly as possible. The last one from the Countess Pietranera was couched in a sort of enigmatic tone which alarmed him very much. This letter dispelled all his tender dreams. To a man of his nature a word sufficed to stir up apprehensions of the gravest kind, and his imagination immediately depicted misfortunes aggravated by the most gruesome details.

"Be careful not to sign your letters when you write us news of yourself," said the countess. "When you return you must not come straight to the Lake of Como. Stop in Swiss territory, at Lugano." He was to arrive at that little town under the name of Cavi; there, at the principal inn, he was to find his aunt's man-servant, who would tell him what he was to do next. The countess closed her letter with the following words: "Use every means to conceal the folly you have committed, and, above all, keep no paper, whether written or printed, about you! In Switzerland you will be surrounded by the friends of Ste.-Marguerite.* If I have money enough I will send somebody to the Hôtel des Balances, at Geneva, to give you details which I can not write, and which, nevertheless, you must have before you arrive. But for God's sake, not another day in Paris; our spies there will recognise you!"

Fabrizio's imagination began to picture the most extraordinary things, and the only pleasure of which he was capable was that of trying to guess what the amazing fact might be, with which his aunt desired to acquaint him. Twice, during his journey across France, he was arrested,

---

* This name, thanks to Signor Pellico, is known all over Europe. It is that of the street in Milan in which the Ministry of Police and the prisons are situated.

but each time he contrived to obtain his release. These annoyances he owed to his Italian passport, and that strange title of " dealer in barometers," which tallied so ill with his youthful countenance, and his arm in a sling.

At Geneva, at last, he met one of his aunt's serving-men, who told him, from her, that he, Fabrizio, had been denounced to the Milanese police, as having gone over to Napoleon with proposals formulated by a huge conspiracy organized in his late Kingdom of Italy. " If this was not the object of his journey," said his accuser, " why should he have taken a false name?" His mother would endeavour to prove the truth; firstly, that he had never gone beyond Switzerland, and, secondly, that he had left the castle hastily in consequence of a quarrel with his elder brother.

When Fabrizio heard the story, his first feeling was one of pride. " I've been taken for a sort of ambassador to Napoleon; I am supposed to have had the honour of speaking to that great man. Would to God it had been so!" He recollected that his ancestor seven generations back, grandson of that Valserra who had come to Milan with Sforza, underwent the honour of having his head cut off by the duke's enemies, who laid hands upon him as he was going into Switzerland, to carry proposals to the cantons and to collect recruits. He could see, in his mind's eye, the engraving recording this fact in the family genealogy. When Fabrizio cross-questioned the man-servant, he found him in a fury about a matter which he let slip at last, in spite of the fact that the countess had told him several times over to hold his tongue about it. It was Fabrizio's elder brother, Ascanio, who had denounced him to the Milanese police. This cruel fact threw our hero into a state bordering on madness. To get into Italy from Geneva, it was necessary to pass through Lausanne. He insisted on starting instantly on foot, and walking ten or twelve leagues, although the diligence from Geneva to Lausanne was to depart within two hours. Before he left Geneva, he had a quarrel in one of the dreary *cafés* of the place, with a young man who, so he declared, had looked at him strangely. It was perfectly true. The phlegmatic, sensible young citizen, who never thought of anything but making money, believed him to be mad. When Fabrizio entered the *café*, he had cast wild glances about him on every side, and then spilled the cup of coffee he had ordered over his trousers. In this quarrel, Fabrizio's first instinctive movement was quite in the style of the sixteenth century. Instead of suggesting a duel to the young Genevan, he drew his dagger and threw himself upon him to strike him. In that moment of fury Fabrizio forgot everything he had learned concerning the code of honour, and fell back on the instinct—or I should rather say on the memories—of his early boyhood.

The confidential servant whom he met at Lugano increased his rage by relating fresh details. Fabrizio was very much loved at Grianta, and nobody would ever have mentioned his name. But for his brother's spiteful proceeding every one would have pretended to believe he was at Milan, and the attention of the police would never have been drawn to his absence. "You may be quite certain that the customs officers hold a description of your appearance," said his aunt's messenger, "and if we travel by the high-road you will be stopped on the frontier."

Fabrizio and his attendants knew every mountain-path between Lugano and the Lake of Como. They disguised themselves as hunters—in other words, as smugglers—and as they were three together, and resolute-looking fellows into the bargain, the customs officers they met did no more than greet them civilly. Fabrizio arranged matters so as to arrive at the castle about midnight. At that hour his father and all the servants with powdered heads were sure to be safe in their beds. Without any difficulty he dropped into the deep ditch and entered the castle by a small window opening out of a cellar. Here his mother and his aunt were awaiting him. Very soon his sisters joined them. For a long time they were all in such a transport of tenderness and tears, that they had hardly begun to talk sensibly before the first rays of dawn warned these beings, who believed themselves unhappy, that time was slipping by.

"I hope your brother will not have suspected your return!" said the Countess Pietranera. "I have hardly spoken to him since this fine prank of his, and his vanity did me the honour of being very much hurt. To-night, at supper, I condescended to address him—I had to find some pretext for hiding my wild delight, which might have roused his suspicions. Then, when I perceived how proud he was of this sham reconciliation, I took advantage of his satisfaction to make him drink a great deal more than was good for him, and he will certainly not have thought of lying in ambush to carry on his spying operations."

" It's in your room that we must hide our hussar," said the marchesa. " He can not start at once. We have not collected our thoughts sufficiently as yet, and we must choose the best way of throwing that terrible Milanese police off the scent."

This idea was promptly put into practice. But on the following day the marchese and his eldest son remarked that the marchesa spent all her time in her sister-in-law's apartment. We will not depict the passion of joy and tenderness that filled these happy beings' hearts during the whole of that day. The Italian nature is much more easily wrung than ours by the suspicions and wild fancies born of a feverish imagination. But its joys, on the other hand, are far deeper than ours, and last much longer. During the whole of that day the countess and the marchesa were absolutely beside themselves; they made Fabrizio begin all his stories over and over again. At last, so difficult did any further concealment of their feelings from the sharp eyes of the marchese and his son Ascanio appear, that they decided to betake themselves to Milan, and there conceal their mutual ecstasy.

The ladies took the usual boat belonging to the castle as far as Como; any other course would have aroused innumerable suspicions. But when they reached the port of Como, the marchesa recollected that she had left papers of the most important description at Grianta. She sent the boatmen back at once, and they were thus deprived of all opportunity of noticing the manner in which the two ladies employed their time at Como. The moment the latter arrived, they hired one of the carriages that always stand near the high tower, built in the middle ages, which rises above the Milan gate, and started off at once, without giving the coachman time to speak to a soul. About a quarter of a league beyond the town, they fell in with a young sportsman of their acquaintance, who, as they had no gentleman with them, was good-natured enough to attend them to the gates of Milan, whither he himself was bound, shooting on the way. Everything promised well, and the ladies were talking most merrily to the young traveller when, just where the road bends round the base of the pretty hill and wood of San Giovanni, three gendarmes in disguise sprang to the horses' heads. "Ah!" cried the marchesa, "my husband has betrayed us!" and she fainted away.

A sergeant of gendarmes, who had been standing somewhat in the background, approached the carriage. He stumbled as he walked, and spoke in a voice that was redolent of the tavern: "I am sorry to have to perform this duty, but I arrest you, General Fabio Conti!" Fabrizio thought the sergeant was poking fun at him by calling him general. "I'll pay you out for this," thought he to himself. He had his eye on the gendarmes, and was watching his opportunity to leap from the carriage and take to his heels across the fields.

The countess smiled—at a venture, as I think—and then said to the sergeant, "But, my good sergeant, do you take this child of sixteen years old to be General Conti!"

"Are you not the general's daughter?" said the sergeant.

"Behold my father!" said the countess, pointing to Fabrizio. The gendarmes burst into a roar of laughter.

"Show your passports, and don't bandy words!" said the sergeant, nettled by the general mirth.

"These ladies never take any passport to go to Milan," said the coachman, with a cool and philosophic air; "they are coming from their house at Grianta. This one is the Countess Pietranera, and that one is the Marchesa del Dongo."

The sergeant, quite put out of countenance, went to the horses' heads, and there held council with his men. The conference had lasted quite five minutes, when the countess begged the carriage might be moved a few paces farther into the shade; the heat was overwhelming, though it was only eleven o'clock in the day. Fabrizio, who had been looking about carefully in all directions, with a view to making his escape, noticed, emerging from a field path which led on to the dusty road, a young girl of fourteen or fifteen, with her handkerchief to her face, shedding frightened tears. She walked between two gendarmes in uniform, and three paces behind her, also flanked by gendarmes, came a tall, bony man, who gave himself dignified airs, like a prefect walking in a procession.

" But where did you find them? " said the sergeant, who now appeared quite drunk.

" Running away across the fields, and not a passport between them ! " The sergeant seemed to have quite lost his bearings. He had five prisoners now, instead of the two he had been sent out to take. He retired a little distance, leaving only one man to look after the prisoner with the majestic demeanour, and another to keep the horses from moving on.

" Stay here," whispered the countess to Fabrizio, who had already jumped out of the carriage. " It will all come right."

They heard a gendarme exclaim : " What does it matter? If they have no passports we have a right to take them up."

The sergeant did not seem quite so sure. The name of Pietranera had alarmed him. He had known the general, and he was not aware of his death. " The general," he reflected, " is not the man to forego his vengeance if I arrest his wife without authority."

During this deliberation, which was somewhat lengthy, the countess had entered into conversation with the young girl, who was still standing in the dust, on the road beside the carriage. She had been struck by her beauty.

" The sun will do you harm, signorina. That honest soldier," she added, addressing the gendarme standing at the horses' heads, " will let you get into the carriage, I am sure ! " Fabrizio, who was prowling round the carriage, came forward to help the young lady into it. She had her foot on the step, and Fabrizio's hand was under her arm, when the imposing individual, who was standing six paces behind the carriage, called out, in a voice that his desire to look dignified made yet more rasping: " Stop on the road! Do not get into a carriage which does not belong to you! " Fabrizio had not heard this order. The young girl, instead of trying to get up, tried to get down, and as Fabrizio still held her, she fell into his arms. He smiled, and she blushed deeply; for a moment after the girl had freed herself from his clasp they stood looking into each other's eyes.

" What a charming prison companion! " said Fabrizio to himself. " What deep thoughts lie behind that brow! That woman would know how to love! "

The sergeant approached with an air of importance.

" Which of these ladies is called Clelia Conti? "

" I," said the young girl.

" And I," exclaimed the elderly man, " I am General Fabio Conti, Chamberlain to his Serene Highness the Prince of Parma, and I think it most improper that a man of my position should be hunted like a thief! "

" The day before yesterday, when you embarked at the port of Como, did you not send the police inspector, who asked you for your passport, about his business? Well, to-day the inspector prevents you from going about your business."

" My boat had already pushed off from the shore. I was in a hurry, a storm was coming on, a man without a uniform shouted to me from the pier to come back into the port. I told him my name, and I went on my way."

" And this morning you sneaked out of Como! "

" A man in my position does not take out a passport to go from Milan to see the lake. This morning, at Como, I was told I should be arrested at the gate. I left the town on foot with my daughter. I hoped I might meet with some carriage on the road, which would take me to Milan, where my first visit will certainly be to the general commanding the province, to lay my complaint before him."

The Chartreuse of Parma

The sergeant seemed relieved of a great weight.

"Very good, general, you are under arrest, and I shall take you to Milan.—And who are you?" he said, turning to Fabrizio.

"My son," put in the countess, "Ascanio, son of General Pietranera."

"Without a passport, madam?" said the sergeant, very much more politely.

"He is so young! He has never had one; he never travels alone; he is always with me!"

While this colloquy was proceeding, General Conti had been growing more and more dignified, and more and more angry with the gendarmes.

"Not so many words!" said one of them at last; "you're arrested, and there's an end of it."

"You'll be very lucky," said the sergeant, "if we give you leave to hire a horse from some peasant! Otherwise, in spite of the dust and the heat, and your chamberlain-ship, you'll just march along among our horses."

The general began to swear.

"Will you hold your tongue?" said the gendarme. "Where's your uniform? Any man who chooses can say he is a general."

The general grew more and more furious. In the carriage, meanwhile, matters were going far better.

The countess was making all the gendarmes run about as if they had been her servants. She had just given one of them a crown to go and fetch her some wine, and above all some cool water, from a villa which stood about two hundred paces off. She had found time to pacify Fabrizio, who was most anxious to bolt into the wood that clothed the hill. "I have two good pistols," he kept saying. She persuaded the angry general to let his daughter get into her carriage. On this occasion the general, who was fond of talking of himself and his family, informed the ladies that his daughter was only twelve years old, having been born on October 27, 1803, but that she was so sensible that every one took her for fourteen or fifteen.

"Quite a common person," was the verdict which the

countess's eyes telegraphed to the marchesa's. In an hour's time, thanks to the former lady, everything was settled. One of the gendarmes, who had business in the adjoining village, hired his horse to General Conti, after the countess had told him he would have ten francs for it.

The sergeant departed alone with the general, and his comrades remained under a tree, with four huge bottles of wine which the gendarme, with the assistance of a peasant, had brought back from the villa. The worthy chamberlain authorized Clelia Conti to accept a seat in the ladies' carriage back to Milan, and the idea of arresting the gallant General Pietranera's son never entered anybody's head. After the first moments devoted to general civilities, and remarks on the little incident just brought to a close, Clelia Conti noticed the touch of enthusiasm evident in the beautiful countess's manner when she spoke to Fabrizio. Clelia was sure she was not his mother. More especially was her attention attracted by the constant allusions to something bold, heroic, dangerous in the highest degree, which he had lately done. But what that might be the young girl, clever as she was, could not divine. She gazed in wonder on the young hero, whose eyes still seemed to sparkle with the fire of action. He, on his side, was somewhat taken aback by the singular beauty of the twelve-year-old girl, and his glances brought the colour to her cheeks.

About a league from Milan, Fabrizio took leave of the ladies, saying he must go and see his uncle. "If ever I get out of my difficulties," said he, addressing Clelia, "I shall go and see the great pictures at Parma. Will you deign, then, to remember this name—Fabrizio del Dongo?"

"Very good!" said the countess. "So that's how you keep your incognito! Signorina, be good enough to remember that this scamp is my son, and that his name is Pietranera, and not Del Dongo!"

That evening, very late, Fabrizio entered Milan by the Renza gate, which leads to a fashionable promenade. The very modest hoards amassed by the marchesa and her sister had been exhausted by the expense of sending servants into

The Chartreuse of Parma

Switzerland. Luckily Fabrizio still had a few napoleons, and one of the diamonds, which they decided to sell.

The two ladies were much beloved, and knew everybody in the city. The leading members of the Austrian and religious party spoke to Baron Binder, the chief of the police, in Fabrizio's favour. These gentlemen could not understand, they declared, how the prank of a boy of sixteen, who had quarrelled with his elder brother and left his father's house, could be taken seriously.

"My business is to take everything seriously," gently replied the baron, a wise and melancholy man. He was then engaged in organizing the far-famed Milan police, and had undertaken to prevent a revolution like that of 1746, which drove the Austrians out of Genoa. This Milanese police, which afterward became celebrated by its connection with the adventures of Pellico and Andryana, was not exactly cruel, but it carried laws of great severity into logical and pitiless execution. The Emperor Francis II was determined to strike terror into these bold Italian imaginations.

"Give me," said Baron Binder to Fabrizio's friends, "the proved facts as to what the young Marchesino del Dongo has been doing every day, from the moment he left Grianta, on the 8th of March, until his arrival last night in this city, where he is hidden in a room in his mother's apartment, and I am ready to look upon him as the most charming and frolicsome young fellow in the town. But if you can not give me information as to the young man's goings and comings for every day since his departure from Grianta, is it not my duty to have him arrested, however high may be his birth, and however deep my respect for the friends of his family? And am I not bound to keep him in prison until he has proved to me that he did not convey a message to Napoleon from the few malcontents who may exist among his Majesty, the Emperor-King's, Lombard subjects? And further, gentlemen, note well, that even if young Del Dongo contrives to justify himself on this point, he will still remain guilty of having gone abroad without a regular passport, and also of passing under a false name, and knowingly using a passport issued to a mere artisan—

that is to say, to an individual of a class infinitely inferior to his own."

This declaration, merciless in its logic, was accompanied by all that show of deference and respect due from the head of the police to the exalted position of the Marchesa del Dongo and of the important personages who had come forward on her behalf.

When the marchesa heard the baron's reply she was in despair.

"Fabrizio will be arrested!" she exclaimed, bursting into tears; "and once he is in prison, God only knows when he will come out! His father will cast him off!"

The two ladies took counsel with two or three of their closest friends, and in spite of everything they said, the marchesa wished to insist on sending her son away the following night.

"But," said the countess, "you must surely see that Baron Binder knows quite well that your son is here. He is not a spiteful man."

"No, but he desires to please the Emperor Francis."

"But if he thought he could serve his own ends by putting Fabrizio into prison, he would have done it already, and if you insist on the boy's taking to flight, you insult him by your want of confidence."

"But the very fact that he admits he knows Fabrizio's whereabouts is as good as telling us to send him away. No, I shall never breathe freely as long as I can say to myself, 'In a quarter of an hour my boy may be shut up between four walls!' Whatever Baron Binder's ambition may be," added the marchesa, "he thinks his personal position in this country will be strengthened by an affected consideration for a man of my husband's rank, and the strange frankness with which he avows that he knows where to lay his hand on my son proves this to me. And besides, the baron calmly sets forth the two offences of which Fabrizio stands accused according to his brother's vile denunciation, and explains that either of these entails imprisonment. Is not that as good as telling us that if we prefer exile to prison we have only to choose it?"

The Chartreuse of Parma

"If you choose exile," repeated the countess, "we shall never see the boy again." Fabrizio, who had been present at the whole discussion with one of the marchesa's oldest friends, now one of the councillors of the Austrian Tribunal, was strongly in favour of making himself scarce, and that very evening, in fact, he left the palace, concealed in the carriage which was to convey his mother and aunt to the Scala.

The coachman, whom they did not trust, betook himself, as usual, to a neighbouring tavern, and while the footman, a faithful servant, held the horses, Fabrizio, disguised as a peasant, slipped out of the carriage and out of the town. By the next morning he had crossed the frontier with equal success, and a few hours later he was safe in a country house belonging to his mother in Piedmont, near Novara, at a place called Romagnano, where Bayard met his death.

The amount of attention bestowed by the two ladies on the theatrical performance after they reached their box may be easily conceived. They had only gone to the theatre to secure an opportunity of consulting several of their friends of the Liberal party, whose appearance at the Palazzo del Dongo would have stirred suspicion on the part of the police. The council in the box decided on making a fresh appeal to Baron Binder. There could be no question of offering money to the magistrate, who was a perfectly upright man. And besides, the ladies were very poor; they had obliged Fabrizio to take all the money remaining over from the sale of the diamond with him. Nevertheless, it was very important to know the baron's final word. The countess's friends reminded her of a certain Canon Borda, a very agreeable young man, who had formerly tried to pay her court, and had behaved in a somewhat shabby fashion to her. When he found his advances were rejected, he had gone to General Pietranera, had told him of his wife's friendship with Limercati, and was forthwith turned out of the house for his pains. Now, the canon played cards every evening with Baroness Binder, and was, naturally, her husband's close friend. The countess made up her mind to the horribly disagreeable step of paying a visit to the canon, and the next morning early, before he had gone out, she appeared in his rooms.

When the canon's only servant pronounced the name of the Countess Pietranera, his master was so agitated that his voice almost failed him, and he made no attempt to rearrange a morning costume of the most extreme simplicity.

"Show the lady in, and then go," he said huskily. The countess entered the room, and Borda cast himself on his knees before her.

"It is in this position only that an unhappy madman like myself can dare to receive your orders," said he to the countess, who looked irresistibly charming in her morning dress, which was half a disguise.

Her deep grief at the idea of Fabrizio's exile and the violence she did her own feelings in appearing under the roof of a man who had once behaved like a traitor to her, combined to make her eyes shine with an extraordinary light.

"It is in this position," cried the canon again, "that I must receive your orders—for some service you must desire of me, otherwise the poor dwelling of this unhappy madman would never have been honoured by your presence. Once upon a time, wild with love and jealousy, and seeing he had no chance of finding favour in your eyes, he played a coward's part toward you."

The words were sincerely spoken, and were all the nobler because at that moment the canon was in a position of great power. The countess was touched to tears; her heart had been frozen with humiliation and dread, but these feelings were replaced, in an instant, by a tender emotion and a ray of hope. From a condition of great misery she passed, in the twinkling of an eye, to one that was almost happiness.

"Kiss my hand," she said, and she held it to the canon's lips, "and stand up. I have come to ask you to obtain mercy for my nephew Fabrizio. Here is the truth, without the smallest disguise, just as it should be told to an old friend. The boy, who is only sixteen years and a half old, has committed an unspeakable folly. We were living at the Castle of Grianta, on the Lake of Como. One night, at seven o'clock, a boat from Como brought us the news that the Emperor had landed in the Gulf of Juan. The next morning Fabrizio started for France, after having induced one of his humble friends, a dealer in barometers of the name of Vasi, to give him his passport. As he by no means looks like a dealer in barometers, he had hardly travelled ten leagues through France when he was arrested. His outbursts of enthusiasm, expressed in very bad French, were thought suspicious. After some time he escaped, and contrived to get to Geneva. We sent to meet him at Lugano."

"At Geneva, you mean," said the canon, smiling.

The countess finished her story.

"Everything that is humanly possible I will do for you," replied the canon earnestly. "I place myself entirely at your orders. I will even risk imprudences," he added. "Tell me, what am I to do at this moment, when my poor room is to be bereft of the celestial vision which marks an epoch in the history of my life?"

"You must go to Baron Binder; you must tell him you have loved Fabrizio from his babyhood, that you saw the child at the time of his birth, when you used to come to our house, and that you beseech Binder, in the name of his friendship for you, to set all his spies to discover whether before Fabrizio departed into Switzerland he ever had the shortest interview with any of the suspected Liberals. If the baron is at all decently served he will be convinced that this whole business has been nothing but a childish freak. You know that when I lived in the Palazzo Dugnani I had quantities of engravings of Napoleon's battles. My nephew learned to read from the inscriptions on those pictures. When he was only five years old my poor husband would describe the battles to him; we used to put the general's helmet on the child's head, and he would drag his great sword about the room. Well, one fine day the boy hears that the man my husband worshipped, the Emperor, is back in France. Like the young madcap he is, he started off to join him, but he did not succeed. Ask your baron what punishment he can possibly inflict for that one moment of folly."

"I was forgetting something," cried the canon. "You shall see that I am not quite unworthy of your gracious pardon. Here," he said, hunting about among the papers on his table, "here is the denunciation of that vile *col-torto* [hypocrite]—look! It is signed 'Ascanio Valserra del Dongo'—which is at the bottom of the whole business. I got it yesterday in the police office, and I went to the Scala, hoping to meet somebody who was in the habit of going to your box, by whom I might send it to you. The copy of this paper reached Vienna long ago. This is the enemy we have to fight!" The canon and the countess read the document together, and agreed that in the course of the day he was to send her a copy by a safe hand. Then the countess went back rejoicing to the Palazzo del Dongo.

"No one could have behaved more perfectly than this man, who once behaved so ill," said she to the marchesa. "To-night, at the Scala, when the theatre clock strikes a quarter to eleven, we will turn everybody out of our box, we will shut our door, and at eleven o'clock the canon will come himself, and tell us what he has been able to do. This plan seemed to us the one least likely to compromise him."

The canon was no fool; he took good care not to break his appointment, and having kept it, he gave proofs of a thorough kind-heartedness and absolute straightforwardness rarely seen save in countries where vanity does not override every other feeling. His accusation of the Countess Pietranera to her own husband had caused him constant remorse, and he hailed the opportunity for atonement.

That morning, when the countess left him, he had said to himself bitterly, "Now there she is, in love with her nephew!" and his old wound was not healed. "Otherwise, proud as she is, she would have never come to me. When poor Pietranera died she refused all my offers of service with horror, though they were couched in the most polite terms and transmitted to her by Colonel Scotti, who had been her lover. To think of the beautiful Pietranera living on fifteen hundred francs!" he added, as he walked rapidly

The Chartreuse of Parma

up and down his room, " and then settling herself at Grianta with an odious *secatore* like the Marchese del Dongo! But that is all explained now. That young Fabrizio is certainly very attractive—tall, well-built, with a face that is always gay, and, what's better, with a sort of tender voluptuous look about him—a Correggio face!" added the canon bitterly.

"The difference of age—not too great, after all! Fabrizio was born after the French came here—about '98, I think. The countess may be seven or eight and twenty. No woman could be prettier, more delightful. Even in this country, where there are so many lovely women, she beats them all—the Marini, the Gherardi, the Ruga, the Aresi, the Pietragrua—she is better-looking than any of them! They were living happily together on the banks of that lovely Lake of Como when the young man insisted on following Napoleon. Ah, there are hearts in Italy still, in spite of what every one may do! Beloved country! No," he mused, and his breast swelled with jealousy, "there is no other possible means of explaining her willingness to vegetate in the country and endure the disgusting sight, every day and at every meal, of the Marchese del Dongo's hideous countenance, and the vile sallow face of the Marchesino Ascanio, who will be much worse than his father, on the top of it! Ah, well! I will serve her faithfully. At all events, I shall have the satisfaction of seeing her nearer than through my opera-glasses."

Canon Borda explained the matter very clearly to the ladies. In his heart Binder was disposed to do all he could for them. He was heartily glad that Fabrizio had taken himself off before definite orders had arrived from Vienna, for Baron Binder could decide nothing himself; on this matter, as on every other, he was obliged to wait for orders. Every day he sent an exact copy of all his information to Vienna, and awaited the imperial reply.

During his exile at Romagnano, Fabrizio was to be sure, in the first place, to go to mass every day, to choose some intelligent man, devoted to the cause of the monarchy, as his confessor, and in confession to be careful to confide

6

none but the most irreproachable sentiments to his ear; secondly, he was not to consort with any man who had the reputation of being clever, and, when occasion offered, he was to speak of rebellion with horror, as a thing that should never be permitted; thirdly, he was never to be seen in a *café*, he was never to read any newspaper except the Turin and Milan Official Gazettes, he was to express dislike of reading in general, and he was never to peruse any work printed later that 1720, the only possible exception being Sir Walter Scott's novels; " and lastly," said the canon, with just a touch of spite, " he must not fail to pay open court to some pretty woman in the district—one of noble birth, of course. That will prove he has none of the gloomy and discontented spirit of the juvenile conspirator."

Before going to bed that night, the countess and the marchesa wrote Fabrizio two voluminous letters, which explained, with an anxiety that was most endearing, all the advice imparted by the canon.

Fabrizio had not the slightest wish to conspire. He loved Napoleon, believed himself destined, as a nobleman, to be more fortunate than most men, and despised the whole middle class.

Since he had left college he had never opened a book, and while there, had only read books arranged by the Jesuits. He took up his residence at some distance from Romagnano, in a magnificent palace which had been one of the masterpieces of the famous architect San Michele. But it had been left untenanted for thirty years, so that the rain came through all the ceilings, and there was not a window that would shut. He took possession of the agent's horses, and rode them all day long, just as it suited him. He never opened his lips, and thought a great deal. The suggestion that he should take a mistress in some *ultra* family tickled his fancy, and he obeyed it to the letter. He chose for his confessor a young and intriguing priest, who aimed at becoming a bishop (like the confessor of the Spielberg).*

---

* In Andryana's curious memoirs. which are as amusing as a fairy-tale and should be as immortal as the works of Tacitus.

The Chartreuse of Parma

But he travelled three leagues on foot, and wrapped himself in what he believed to be impenetrable mystery, so as to read the Constitutionnel, which he thought sublime—"as fine as Alfieri and Dante," he would often exclaim. Fabrizio resembled young Frenchmen in this particular, that he thought much more about his horse and his newspaper than about his high-born mistress. But there was no room, as yet, for any imitation of others in that simple and steadfast soul, and he made no friends in the society to be found in the town of Romagnano. His simplicity was taken for pride; nobody could understand his nature; "a younger son, who is discontented because he is not the eldest," said the parish priest.

CHAPTER VI

WE will honestly admit that the canon's jealousy was not utterly unfounded. When Fabrizio returned from France he appeared in Countess Pietranera's eyes as a handsome stranger with whom she had once been intimately acquainted. If he had made love to her she would have fallen in love with him, and the admiration she already nursed for both his person and his acts was passionate, and I might almost say unbounded. But Fabrizio kissed her with so much innocent gratitude and simple affection that she herself would have been horrified at the idea of seeking any other feeling in a regard that was almost filial. "After all," said the countess to herself, "some few old friends who knew me six years ago at the viceroy's court may still consider me pretty, and even young; but to this boy I am a respectable woman, and frankly, without any regard for my vanity, a middle-aged woman, too!" The countess laboured under a certain illusion with regard to her time of life, but it was not the illusion of the ordinary woman. "Besides," she added, "at Fabrizio's age a man is inclined to exaggerate the effect produced by the ravages of time. Now, an older man than he——"

The countess, who had been walking up and down her drawing-room, paused before a mirror, and smiled. My readers must be informed that for several months past serious siege had been laid to Gina Pietranera's heart, and that by a man quite out of the ordinary category. A short time after Fabrizio's departure for France the countess, who, though she did not quite acknowledge it to herself, was already very much interested in him, had fallen into a condition of the deepest melancholy. All her former occupations seemed to have lost their attraction, and if I may so describe it, their flavour. She told herself that Napoleon, in his desire to win the affections of the Italian people, would certainly take Fabrizio for his aide-de-camp! "He's lost to me!" she exclaimed, weeping. "I shall never see him again! He will write to me, but what can I be to him ten years hence?"

While she was in this frame of mind she made a trip to Milan, in the hope of obtaining more direct news of Napoleon, and possibly further news of Fabrizio. Though she did not admit it, her eager soul was growing very weary of the monotony of her country life. "I do not live there," said she to herself. "I only keep myself from dying." She shuddered at the thought of the powdered heads she must behold every day—her brother, her nephew Ascanio, and their serving-men; what would her trips on the lake be without Fabrizio? The affection that bound her to the marchesa was her only consolation. But for some time past her intimacy with Fabrizio's mother, who was older than herself, and had no future outlook, had brought her less satisfaction.

Such was the Countess Pietranera's peculiar position. Now that Fabrizio was gone, she expected but little future happiness, and she hungered for consolation and for novelty. When she reached Milan she developed a passionate fondness for the opera then in fashion. She shut herself up alone for long hours at a stretch in her old friend's, General Scotti's, box at the Scala. The men whose acquaintance she sought, in the hope of obtaining news of Napoleon and his army, struck her as coarse and vulgar. When she came home at night she would extemporize on her piano till three o'clock in the morning. One evening she went to the Scala, and was sitting in a box belonging to one of her lady friends, whither she had gone to try and gather news from France. The Minister of Parma, Count Mosca, was presented to her. He was an agreeable man, who spoke of France and of Napoleon in a manner which made her heart thrill afresh with hope and fear. The following day she returned to the same box. The clever statesman returned also, and during the whole of the performance she talked to him, and found pleasure in the conversation. Never, since Fabrizio's departure, had she thought an evening so enjoyable. The man who thus diverted her thoughts, Count Mosca della Rovere Sorezana, was then Minister of War, of Police, and of Finance to Ernest IV, that famous Prince of Parma, so celebrated for his severity, which Milanese Liberals termed cruelty. Mosca might have been forty or forty-five years of age. He was a large-featured man, without a vestige of self-importance and a simple cheery manner, which prepossessed people in his favour. He would have been very good-looking, if his master's whim had not obliged him to powder his hair, as an earnest of the propriety of his political views. In Italy, where the fear of wounding the vanity of others is little felt, people soon fall into intimacy, and proceed to make personal remarks. The corrective for this habit consists in not meeting again, if feelings happen to be hurt.

"Tell me, count," said Countess Pietranera on the third occasion of their meeting, "why you wear powder? Powder on a man like you—delightful, still young, and who fought with us in Spain!"

"Because I brought no booty away with me from Spain. After all, a man must live. I was mad for glory; one word of praise from Gouvion-St. Cyr, the French general who commanded us, was all I cared for in those days. When Napoleon fell, I discovered that while I had been spending all my fortune in his service, my father, who had a lively imagination, and dreamed of seeing me a general, had been building me a palace at Parma; and in 1813 I discovered that the whole of my worldly wealth consisted of a big unfinished palace and a pension."

"A pension! Three thousand five hundred francs, I suppose, like my poor husband's."

"Count Pietranera was a full general. My poor major's pension was never more than eight hundred francs, and until I became Minister of Finance I was never paid even that!"

As the only other occupant of the box was its owner, a lady of exceedingly liberal opinions, the conversation was continued in the same strain of intimacy. In answer to the countess's questions, Count Mosca spoke of his life at

The Chartreuse of Parma

Parma: "In Spain, under General St. Cyr, I braved volleys
of musketry fire for the sake of the Cross of Honour, and
afterward to win a little glory. Now I dress myself up like
a character in a comedy to secure a great establishment and
a certain number of thousand francs. When I played my
first moves in this game of chess the insolence of my superiors nettled me, and I resolved to reach one of the highest places. I have gained my object, but my happiest days
are always those I am able to spend, now and then, at
Milan. Here, as it seems to me, the heart of the old army of
Italy still throbs."

The frankness and *disinvoltura* with which the minister
referred to so greatly-dreaded a prince piqued the countess's
curiosity. She had expected to meet a self-important
pedant; instead of that she found a man who seemed rather
ashamed of his solemn position. Mosca had promised to
keep her informed of all the news from France he could
collect. This was a great indiscretion for any one living at
Milan the month before Waterloo. At that moment the
fate of Italy hung in the balance, and every one in Milan
was in a fever of hope or fear. In the midst of the universal
agitation, the countess made inquiries concerning the man
who spoke thus lightly of a position so universally envied,
and one which was his own sole subsistence. She learned
things that were curious, whimsical, and interesting. Count
Mosca della Rovere Sorezana, she was told, is on the point
of becoming the Prime Minister and acknowledged favourite of Ernest IV, absolute ruler of the state of Parma, and
one of the richest princes in Europe into the bargain. The
count could already have attained this supreme position
if he would only have assumed a more serious demeanour.
The prince, it is said, has frequently remonstrated with him
on this point. "How can my ways matter to your Highness," he answers boldly, "so long as I transact your
business?"

"The favourite's good fortune," continued her infor-
mant, "is not without its thorns. He has to please a sovereign who, though certainly a man of sense and cleverness,
appears to have lost his head since the day he ascended an

absolute throne, and who, for instance, nurses suspicions really unworthy even of a woman."

"Ernest IV's bravery is limited to that he has displayed in war. Twenty times over, and in the most gallant fashion, he has led a column to the attack. But since his father, Ernest III, has died, and he himself has taken up his residence within his dominions—where, unluckily for himself, he enjoys unlimited power—he has begun to hold forth in the wildest way against Liberals and liberty. He soon took it into his head that his subjects hated him, and at last, in a fit of temper, and egged on by a wretch by the name of Rassi, a sort of Minister of Justice, he caused two Liberals, whose guilt was probably of the slightest, to be hanged.

"Since that fatal moment, the sovereign's whole life seems changed, and he is harried by the most extraordinary suspicions. He is not yet fifty, but terror has so degraded him, if one may so describe it, that when he begins to talk about the Jacobins and the plans of their Central Committee in Paris his face grows like that of a man of ninety, and he falls back into all the fanciful terrors of babyhood. His favourite, Rassi, the head of his judicial department (or chief justice) has no influence except through his master's terrors. As soon as he begins to tremble for his own credit, he instantly discovers some fresh conspiracy of the blackest and most fanciful description. If thirty imprudent souls meet to read a number of the Constitutionnel, Rassi declares they are conspiring, and sends them as prisoners to that famous Citadel of Parma, which is the terror of the whole of Lombardy. As this citadel is very high—one hundred and eighty feet, they say—it is seen from an immense distance all over the huge plain, and the outline of the prison, about which horrible stories are told, frowns like a merciless sovereign over the whole tract of country from Milan to Bologna."

"Would you believe it," said another traveller to the countess, "at night Ernest IV sits shivering with terror in his room on the third story of his palace, where he is guarded by eighty sentries, who shout a whole sentence instead of a password every quarter of an hour. With ten

The Chartreuse of Parma

bolts shot on each of his doors, and the rooms above and below his apartments filled with soldiers, he is still terrified of the Jacobins! If a board in the floor creaks he snatches at his pistols and is convinced a Liberal must be hidden underneath his bed. Instantly every bell in the castle begins to ring, and an aide-de-camp hurries off to wake Count Mosca. When the Minister of Police reaches the castle he knows better than to deny the existence of the conspiracy. Armed to the teeth, he and the prince go alone round every corner of the apartments, look under all the beds, and, in a word, perform a number of ridiculous antics worthy of an old woman. In those happy days when the prince was a soldier, and had never killed a man except in war, all these precautions would have struck him as exceedingly degrading. Being an exceedingly intelligent and clever man, he really is ashamed of them. Even at the moment of taking them they appear ridiculous to him. And the secret of Count Mosca's immense credit is that he applies all his skill to prevent the prince from ever feeling ashamed in his presence. It is he, Mosca, who, as Minister of Police, insists on search being made under every bit of furniture, and, as people at Parma declare, even in musical instrument cases. It is the prince who objects, and jokes his minister on his extreme punctiliousness. ' This is a matter of honour to me,' Mosca replies. ' Think of the satirical sonnets the Jacobins would rain down upon us if we let them kill you! We have to defend not only your life, but our own reputation.' Still the prince appears to be only half taken in by it all, for if any one in the town ventures to say there has been a sleepless night in the castle, Rassi forthwith sends the unseasonable joker to the citadel, and once the prisoner is shut up in that high and airy dwelling, it is only by a miracle that any one recollects his existence. It is because Mosca is a soldier, who, during the Spanish campaigns, saved his own life twenty times over, pistol in hand, and surrounded by pitfalls, that the prince prefers him to Rassi, who is far more pliable and cringing. The unhappy prisoners in the citadel are kept in the most strict and solitary confinement. All sorts of stories are current about them. The Liberals declare that Rassi has invented a plan whereby the jailers and confessors are ordered to convince them that almost every month one of them is led out to execution. On that day they are allowed to mount on to the terrace of the huge tower, one hundred and eighty feet high, and thence they see a departing procession, in which a spy represents the poor wretch supposed to be going out to meet his fate."

These tales and a score more of the same nature, and not less authentic, interested the countess deeply. The day after hearing them she questioned the count, and jested at his answers. She thought him most entertaining, and kept assuring him that he certainly was a monster, though he might be unconscious of the fact. One day, as the count was going home to his inn, he said to himself: "Not only is the Countess Pietranera a charming woman, but when I spend the evening in her box I contrive to forget certain things at Parma, the memory of which stabs me to the heart!" This minister, in spite of his lively air and brilliant manners, had not the soul of a Frenchman. He did not know how to forget his sorrows. "When there was a thorn in his pillow he was forced to break it and wear it down by thrusting it into his own throbbing limbs." I must apologize for introducing this sentence, translated from the Italian. The morning following on his discovery, the count became aware that in spite of the business which had called him to Milan, the day was extraordinarily long; he could not stay quiet anywhere, and tired his carriage horses out. Toward six o'clock he rode out to the Corso. He had hoped he might have met the Countess Pietranera there. He could not see her, and recollected that the Scala opened at eight o'clock. Thither he betook himself, and did not find more than ten persons in the whole of the great building. He felt quite shy at being there. "Can it be?" he mused, "that at five-and-forty I am committing follies for which a subaltern officer would blush? Luckily nobody suspects it." He fled, and tried to pass away the time by walking about the pretty streets in the neighbourhood of the Scala Theatre. They are full of *cafés*, which at that hour are

The Chartreuse of Parma

teeming with customers. In front of each, a crowd of idlers sits on chairs, spreading right out into the street, eating ices and criticising the passers-by. The count was a passer-by of considerable notoriety, and he had the pleasure of being recognised and accosted. Three or four importunate individuals, of that class which it is not easy to shake off, seized this opportunity of obtaining an audience from the powerful minister. Two of them thrust petitions into his hands, a third contented himself with giving him long-winded advice as to his political conduct.

"So clever a man as I am must not go to sleep, and a person so powerful as I should not walk in the streets," he reflected. He went back to the theatre, and it occurred to him to take a box on the third tier. Thence he could gaze unnoticed right into the box on the second tier, in which he hoped to see the countess appear. Two full hours of waiting did not seem too long to this man who was in love. Safely screened from observation, he gave himself up to the enjoyment of his passionate dream. "What is old age!" he said to himself. "Surely, above all other things, it means that the capacity for this exquisite foolery is lost!"

At last the countess made her appearance. Through his opera-glasses he watched her adoringly. "Young, brilliant, blithe as a bird," he said, "she does not look five-and-twenty. Her beauty is the least of her charms. Where else could I discover a creature of such perfect sincerity, one whose actions are never governed *by prudence*, who gives herself up bodily to the feelings of the moment, and asks nothing better than to be whirled off by some fresh object? I can understand all Count Nani's wild behaviour!"

The count gave himself excellent reasons for his extravagant feelings so long as he only thought of attaining the happiness he saw before his eyes. But his arguments were not so cogent when he began to consider his own age, and the anxieties, some of them gloomy enough, which clouded his existence. "A clever man, whose terrors override his intelligence, gives me a great position and large sums of money for acting as his minister. But supposing he were to dismiss me to-morrow? I should be nothing but an elderly and needy man; in other words, just the sort of man that every one is inclined to despise. A nice sort of individual to offer to the countess!" These thoughts were too dreary, and he turned his eyes once more upon the object of his affections. He was never tired of gazing at her, and he refrained from going to her box so that he might contemplate her more undisturbedly. "I have just been told," he mused, "that she only encouraged Nani to play a trick on Limercati, who would not take the trouble to run her husband's murderer through, or have him stabbed by somebody else. I would fight twenty duels for her!" he murmured in a passion of adoration. He kept continually glancing at the Scala clock, with its luminous figures standing out on a black ground, which, as each five minutes passed, warned the spectators that the hour of their admission into some fair friend's box had duly arrived.

The count ruminated again: "I have only known her such a short time that I dare not spend more than half an hour in her box. If I stay longer than that I shall attract attention, and then, thanks to my age, and still more to the cursed powder in my hair, I shall look as foolish as a pantaloon!" But a sudden thought forced him to a decision. "Supposing she were to leave her box to pay a visit to another; I should be well punished for the stinginess with which I had meted out my pleasure to myself!" He rose to his feet, meaning to go down to the box in which the countess was sitting. Suddenly he felt that his desire to enter it had almost entirely disappeared. "Now this really is delightful," he exclaimed, and he stopped on the staircase to laugh at himself. "I am positively frightened! Such a thing hasn't happened to me for five-and-twenty years!" He had almost to make a conscious effort to go into the box, and like a clever man he took advantage of the circumstance.

He made no attempt whatever to appear at his ease, or to show off his wit by plunging headlong into some joking conversation. He had the courage to be shy, and applied his mind to letting his agitation betray itself without rendering him ridiculous. "If she takes it amiss," said he to himself, "I am done for forever! What! Shyness in a man with powdered hair—hair which would be gray if the powder did not cover it! But it is the truth, therefore it can not be ridiculous unless I exaggerate it, or wave it like a trophy before her eyes." The countess had so often been bored at the Castle of Grianta, among the powdered heads of her brother, her nephew, and some tiresome neighbours of the right way of thinking, that she never gave a thought to the fashion in which her new adorer dressed his hair.

Her good sense, then, saved her from bursting out laughing when he entered, and her whole attention was absorbed by the French news which Mosca always confided to her particular ear when he entered her box. Some of this news, no doubt, he invented. As she talked it over with him that evening she noticed his glance, which was open and kindly.

"I fancy," she said, "that when you are at Parma, surrounded by your slaves, you do not look at them in so kindly a manner. That would spoil everything, and give them some hope of not being hanged."

The total absence of pretension on the part of a man who bore the reputation of being the foremost diplomatist in Italy struck the countess as peculiar, and even endowed him with a certain charm in her eyes. On the whole, and considering how well and brilliantly he talked, she was not at all displeased that he should have taken it into his head to play the part of her attentive swain for this one evening, and with no serious ulterior intentions.

A great point had been gained, and a very risky one. Fortunately for the minister, who at Parma never saw his advances rejected, the countess had only just returned from Grianta, and her mind was still numb with the dulness of her rural life. She had forgotten, so to speak, how to be merry, and everything connected with the elegancies and frivolities of life wore an appearance of novelty which almost made them sacred in her eyes. She had no inclination to laugh at anything, not even at a shy man of five-and-forty who had fallen in love with her. A week later the count's boldness might have met with quite a different reception.

As a rule no visit paid to a box in the Scala lasts more

than twenty minutes. The count spent the whole evening in that in which he had been so happy as to find the Countess Pietranera. "This woman," said he to himself, "brings me back to all the follies of my youth," yet he felt the danger of his position. "Will she forgive my folly for the sake of my reputation as an all-powerful pasha at a place forty leagues off? How tiresome that life of mine at Parma is!" Nevertheless, as each quarter struck, he vowed to himself he would depart.

"You must consider, signora," he said laughingly to the countess, "that I am bored to death at Parma, and that therefore I must be allowed to drink deep draughts of pleasure whenever pleasure lies in my path. Thus, for this one evening, and without making any ulterior claim on your kindness, give me leave to pay my court to you. In a few days, alas! I shall be far from this box, where I forget all my sorrows, and you will say, perhaps, all the proprieties."

A week after that lengthy visit to the box at the Scala, which had been followed by various little incidents too numerous to relate here, Count Mosca was madly in love, and the countess was beginning to think that his age need be no objection if he pleased her in other respects. Matters had reached this point, when Mosca was recalled by a courier from Parma. It was as though his prince had grown frightened at being left alone. The countess went back to Grianta. That beautiful spot, no longer idealized, now, by her imagination, seemed to her a desert. "Have I really grown fond of this man?" said she to herself. Mosca wrote, and found himself at a loss; separation had dried up the springs of his ideas. His letters were amusing, and there was a quaintness connected with them which did not fail to please. So as to avoid the remarks of the Marchese del Dongo, who was not fond of paying for the delivery of letters, these were sent by messengers, who posted them at Como, Lecco, Varese, and the other pretty little towns in the near neighbourhood of the lake. One object of this manœuvre was that the couriers might bring back answers. It was successfully attained.

Before long the countess began to watch for the days

when the post arrived. The couriers brought her flowers, fruit, little presents of no value, but which entertained her and her sister-in-law as well. Her memory of the count began to be mingled with thoughts of his great power, and the countess grew curious about everything that was said concerning him. Even the Liberals paid homage to his talents.

The chief ground of the count's evil reputation rested on the fact that he was considered the head of the *ultra* party at the court of Parma, where the Liberal party was led by an intriguing woman, capable of anything, even of success, and very rich into the bargain—the Marchesa Raversi. The prince was very careful not to discourage whichever of the two parties was not in power. He knew well enough that he would always be master, even with a ministry chosen out of the Marchesa Raversi's circle. Numerous details of these intrigues were related at Grianta. Mosca, whom all the world described as a minister of first-rate talent and a man of action, was not present, and therefore the countess was free to forget the hair powder, which in her eyes symbolized everything that is most slow and dreary. That, after all, was an infinitesimal detail, one of the obligations imposed by the court at which he otherwise played so noble a part. "A court is an absurd thing," said the countess to the marchesa, "but it's amusing. It's an interesting game, but it must be played according to the rules. Did anybody ever think of rebelling against the rules of piquet? Yet once one has grown accustomed to them, there is great enjoyment in beating one's adversary."

The countess gave many a thought to the writer of all those pleasant letters. The days on which she received them were bright days to her. She would call for her boat, and go and read them at the most beautiful spots on the lake—at Pliniana, at Belano, or in the wood of the Sfondrata. These letters seemed to bring her some consolation for Fabrizio's absence. At any rate, she could not deny the count the right to be desperately in love with her, and before the month was out she was thinking of him with a very tender affection. Count Mosca, on his part, was very nearly in earnest when he offered to send in his resignation, leave the ministry, and spend his life with her at Milan or elsewhere. "I have four hundred thousand francs," he said; "that would always give us fifteen thousand francs a year."

"An opera-box and horses again," reflected the countess. The dream was a tempting one.

The charms of the sublime scenery round Como appealed to her afresh. On the shores of the lake she dreamed again over the strange and brilliant existence which, contrary to all appearances, was opening once more before her. She saw herself in Milan, on the Corso, happy and gay as she had been in the days of the viceroy. "My youth would come back to me. My life would be full, at all events."

Her ardent imagination sometimes deceived her, but she had never laboured under those voluntary illusions which are the result of cowardice. Above all things, she was perfectly straightforward with herself. "If I am a little beyond the age for committing follies, envy—which can deceive as well as love—may poison the happiness of my life at Milan. After my husband's death, my proud poverty and my refusal of two great fortunes were admired. This poor little count of mine has not a twentieth part of the wealth those two simpletons, Limercati and Nani, laid at my feet. The tiny widow's pension, obtained with so much difficulty, the sending away of my servants, the little room on the fifth story, which brought twenty coaches to the door of the house—all that was curious and interesting at the time. But I shall have some disagreeable moments, however cleverly I may manage, if with no more private fortune than my widow's pension, I go back to Milan, and live there in the modest middle-class comfort which the fifteen thousand francs a year that will remain to Mosca after his resignation will insure us. One curious objection, which will become a terrible weapon in the hands of the envious, is, that though the count has been separated from his wife for years, he is married. At Parma everybody is aware of this, but at Milan it will be news, and it will be ascribed to me. Therefore, farewell, my beautiful Scala! my heavenly Lake of Como, fare thee well!"

The Chartreuse of Parma

In spite of all her forebodings, if the countess had had the smallest fortune of her own, she would have accepted Mosca's offer to resign. She believed herself to be growing old, and the idea of a court alarmed her. But the fact which, on this side of the Alps, will appear incredible to the last degree, is that the count would have given in his resignation most joyfully. At least he contrived to convince his friend that so it was. Every letter of his besought her, with ever-growing eagerness, to grant him another interview at Milan. She did so. " If I were to swear that I loved you madly," she said to him, " I should lie to you. I should be only too happy if, now that I am past thirty, I could love as I loved at two-and-twenty. But too many things which I believed eternal have faded from my sight. I have the most tender affection for you, I feel the most unbounded confidence in you, and I prefer you to every other man I know." She believed herself perfectly sincere, but the close of this declaration was not absolutely truthful. It may be that if Fabrizio had chosen he might have swept everything else out of her heart, but Fabrizio, in Count Mosca's eyes, was no more than a child. The minister arrived in Milan three days after the young madcap had departed for Novara, and lost no time in speaking to Baron Binder in his favour. The count's opinion was, that there was no chance of saving the youth from banishment.

He had not come to Milan alone. In his carriage had travelled the Duke Sanseverina-Taxis—a nice-looking little old man of sixty-eight, gray-haired, polished, well-groomed, immensely rich, but of inadequate birth. His grandfather had amassed millions of money by farming the revenues of the state of Parma. His father had induced the then reigning prince to appoint him his ambassador at a certain court, by means of the following argument: " Your Highness allows your envoy at the court of —— thirty thousand francs a year, and he cuts a very poor figure on the money. If your Highness will appoint me I will be content with a salary of six thousand francs; I will never spend less than a hundred thousand francs a year on my embassy, and my man of business shall pay twenty thousand francs a year to the Department of Foreign Affairs at Parma. This sum will be the salary of any secretary of my embassy selected by the government. I shall show no jealousy about being informed as to diplomatic secrets, if any such exist. My object is to shed honour on my family, which is still a new one, and to increase its dignity by holding a great official position." The present duke, son of the ambassador, had been clumsy enough to betray some Liberal tendencies, and for the last two years he had been in a state of despair. He had lost two or three millions in Napoleon's time, by his obstinate insistence on remaining abroad, and notwithstanding this he had failed, since the sovereigns had been reestablished in Europe, to obtain a certain great order which figured in his father's portrait. The absence of this order was wasting him away with sorrow.

So complete is the intimacy which in Italy results on love, that personal vanity could be no stumbling-block between the two friends. It was, therefore, with the most perfect simplicity that Mosca said to the woman he worshipped: " I have two or three plans to suggest to you, all of them fairly well laid. I have dreamed of nothing else for the last three months. First, I can resign, and we will live quietly at Milan, Florence, Naples, or where you will. We have fifteen thousand francs a year, independently of the prince's bounty to us, which will last for a time, at all events. Second, if you will condescend to come to the country where I have some power, you will buy a country place— let us say Sacca, for instance, a charming house in the forest overlooking the Po; you can have the contract of sale duly signed within a week. The prince will give you a position at his court. But here a great difficulty comes in. You would be well received at court, nobody would venture to hesitate as to that in my presence, and besides, the princess thinks she is unfortunate, and I have just rendered her several services with an eye to your benefit. But there is one capital objection of which I must remind you. The prince is exceedingly religious, and, as you know, I am, unluckily, a married man. This would give rise to innumerable small difficulties. You are a widow, and that charming title must be exchanged for another. Here my third proposal comes in.

"It would be easy enough to find a husband who would give us no trouble, but, above all things, we must have a man of considerable age—for why should you refuse me the hope of taking his place some day? Well, I have arranged this curious business with the Duke Sanseverina-Taxis, who is quite ignorant, of course, of the name of his future duchess. All he knows about her is that she will make him an ambassador and will procure him the order his father held, and without which he himself is the most unhappy of men. Apart from that mania the duke is by no means a fool. He gets his coats and wigs from Paris; he is not at all the kind of man who deliberately plots wickedness. He honestly believes that his honour is involved in wearing that particular order, and he is ashamed of his money. A year ago he came and proposed to me to build a hospital, so as to get his order. I laughed at him, but he did not laugh at me when I proposed this marriage. My first condition, of course, was that he was never to set his foot in Parma again."

"But do you know that the suggestion you make to me is exceedingly immoral?" said the countess.

"Not more immoral than everything else at our court, and at twenty others. There's one convenience about absolute power, that it sanctifies everything in the eyes of the people. Now where is the importance of an absurdity that nobody notices? Our policy for the next twenty years will consist in being afraid of the Jacobins, and what a terror it will be! Every year we shall believe ourselves on the brink of another '93. Some day, I hope, you will hear the remarks I make on that subject at my receptions; they are really fine! Everything which may tend to diminish this terror, however little, will be *superlatively moral* in the eyes of the nobles and the bigots. Now, at Parma every one who is not either noble or a bigot is in prison, or on the road thither. You may be quite sure that till the day I am disgraced no one will think this marriage the least extraordinary. The arrangement involves no dishonesty to any one, and that, I imagine, is the great point. The prince, whose favour is our stock in trade, has only imposed one condition to insure his consent—that the future duchess should be of noble birth. Last year, as far as I can reckon, my post brought me in a hundred and seven thousand francs, and my whole income must have been a hundred and twenty-two thousand. I have invested a sum of twenty thousand francs at Lyons. Now, you must choose between a life of splendour, with a hundred and twenty-two thousand francs a year to spend—which in Parma would be as much as four hundred thousand in Milan (but in this case you must accept the marriage which will give you the name of a very decent man, whom you will never see except at the altar)—or a modest existence on fifteen thousand francs a year at Florence or Naples—for I agree with you, you have been too much admired at Milan. We should be tormented by envy there, and it might end by making us unhappy. The life at Parma would, I hope, have some charm of novelty, even for you who have seen the court of Prince Eugène. It would be worth your while to make acquaintance with it before we close that door. Do not think I desire to influence your decision. As far as I am concerned, my choice is made. I would rather live with you on a fourth floor than continue alone in my great position."

The possibility of this strange marriage was discussed daily between the lovers. The countess saw the duke at a ball at the Scala, and thought him very presentable. In one of their last conversations, Mosca thus summed up the matter: "We must take some decisive step if we want to spend our lives happily, and not to grow old before our time. The prince has given his approbation. Sanseverina is really rather attractive than otherwise. He owns the finest palace in Parma and a huge fortune; he is sixty-eight years old, and is madly in love with the Collar of an Order; but there is one great blot upon his life—he bought a bust of Napoleon by Canova, for ten thousand francs. His second misdoing, which will be the death of him if you do not come to his rescue, is that he once lent twenty-five napoleons to Ferrante Palla, a madman, from our country, but

a man of genius all the same, whom we have since condemned to death—by default, I am happy to say. This
Ferrante once wrote two hundred lines of poetry, which are
quite unrivalled. I will recite them to you; they are as fine
as Dante. The prince will send Sanseverina to the court of
———. He will marry you the day he starts, and in the
second year of his journey—which he calls an embassy—
he will receive the collar of the order for which he sighs.
In him you will find a brother, whom you will not dislike.
He is ready to sign every document I give him beforehand,
and, besides, you will see him hardly ever, or never, just
as you choose. He will be glad not to show himself in
Parma, where the memory of his grandfather, the farmer
general, and his own imputed liberalism make him feel uncomfortable. Rassi, our persecutor, declares that the duke
subscribed secretly to the Constitutionnel, through Ferrante, the poet; and for a long time this calumny was a
serious obstacle in the way of the prince's consent."

Why should the historian be blamed for faithfully re-
producing the smallest details of the story he has heard?
Is it his fault if certain persons, led away by a passion
which he, unfortunately for himself, does not share, stoop to
actions of the deepest immorality? It is true, indeed, that
this sort of thing is no longer done in a country where the
only passion—that which has survived all others—is the
love of money, which is the food of vanity?

Three months after the events above related, the Duchess
Sanseverina-Taxis was astonishing the court of Parma by
her easy charm and the noble serenity of her intellect. Her
house was beyond all comparison the most agreeable in the
city. This fulfilled the promise made by Count Mosca to his
master. The reigning prince, Ranuzio-Ernest IV, and the
princess, his wife, to whom the duchess was presented by
two of the greatest ladies in the country, received her with
the utmost respect. She had been curious to see the prince,
the arbiter of the fate of the man she loved. She desired to
please him, and succeeded only too well. She beheld a
man of tall and somewhat heavy build; his hair, mustaches,
and huge whiskers were of what his courtiers called a beau-

tiful golden colour; elsewhere their dull tinge would have earned the unflattering title of tow. From the middle of a large face there projected, very slightly, a tiny, almost feminine nose. But the duchess remarked that to realize all these various uglinesses a close examination of the royal features was necessary. Taking him altogether, the prince had the appearance of a clever and resolute man. His air and manner were not devoid of majesty, but very often he took it into his head to try and impress the person to whom he was speaking; then he grew confused himself, and rocked almost perpetually from one leg to the other. Apart from this, Ernest IV's glance was penetrating and authoritative. There was something noble about the gesture of his arm, and his speech was both measured and concise.

Mosca had warned the duchess that the prince's audience chamber contained a full-length portrait of Louis XIV and a very fine Florentine scagliola table. The imitation struck her very much. It was evident that the prince sought to reproduce the noble look and utterance of Louis XIV, and that he leaned against the scagliola table so as to make himself look like Joseph II. Immediately after his first words to the duchess he seated himself, so as to give her an opportunity of making use of the tabouret which her rank conferred on her. At this court the only ladies who have a right to sit are duchesses, princesses, and wives of Spanish grandees. The rest all wait until the prince or princess invites them to be seated, and these august persons are always careful to mark the degree of rank by allowing a short interval to elapse before giving this permission to a lady of less rank than a duchess. The duchess thought the prince's imitation of Louis XIV was occasionally somewhat too marked, as, for instance, when he threw back his head and smiled good-naturedly.

Ernest IV wore a dress-coat of the fashion then reigning in Paris. Every month he received from that city, which he abhorred, a dress-coat, a walking-coat, and a hat. But on the day of the duchess's visit he had attired himself, with a whimsical mixture of styles, in red pantaloons, silk stockings, and very high shoes, such as may be observed in the pictures of Joseph II.

He received the lady graciously, and said several sharp and witty things to her. But she saw very clearly that civil as her reception was, there was no excessive warmth about it. "And do you know why?" said Count Mosca, when she returned from her audience. "It is because Milan is a larger and finer city than Parma. He was afraid that if he received you as I expected, and as he had given me reason to hope, you would take him for a provincial person, in ecstasies over the charms of a fine lady just arrived from the capital. Doubtless, too, he is vexed by a peculiarity which I hardly dare express to you. The prince sees no lady at his court who can compete with you in beauty; last night, when he was going to bed, that was the sole subject of his conversation with Pernice, his chief valet, who is a friend of mine. I foresee a small revolution in matters of etiquette. My greatest enemy at this court is a blockhead who goes by the name of General Fabio Conti. You must imagine an extraordinary creature who has spent one full day of his whole life, perhaps, on active service, and who therefore gives himself the airs of a Frederick the Great; and, further, because he is the head of the Liberal party here (God alone knows how liberal they are!), endeavours to reproduce the noble affability of General Lafayette."

"I know Fabio Conti," said the duchess. "I had a glimpse of him at Como; he was quarrelling with the gendarmes." She related the little incident, which my readers may possibly recollect.

"Some of these days, madam—if your intellect ever contrives to probe the depths of our etiquette—you will become aware that no young lady is presented at this court till after her marriage. Well, so fervent is our prince's patriotic conviction of the superiority of his own city of Parma over every other, that I am ready to wager anything he will find means to have young Clelia Conti, our Lafayette's daughter, presented to him. She is a charming creature, on my honour, and only a week ago was

supposed to be the loveliest person in the prince's dominions.

" I do not know," the count went on, " whether the horrible stories put about by our sovereign's enemies have
travelled as far as Grianta. He is described as a monster
and an ogre. As a matter of fact, Ernest IV is full of good
commonplace virtues, and it might be added that if he had
been as invulnerable as Achilles he would have continued
to be a model potentate. But in a fit of boredom and bad
temper, and a little, too, for the sake of imitating Louis
XIV, who found some hero of the Fronde living quietly
and insolently in a country house close to Versailles fifty
years after the close of that rebellion, and forthwith cut off
his head, Ernest IV had two Liberals hanged. These impudent fellows were in the habit, it appears, of meeting on
certain days to speak evil of the prince and earnestly implore Heaven to send a plague on Parma, and so deliver
them from the tyrant. The use of the word " tyrant " was
absolutely proved. Rassi declared this was a conspiracy;
he had them sentenced to death, and the execution of one
of them, Count L——, was a horrible business. All this
happened before my time. Ever since that fatal moment,"
continued the count, dropping his voice, " the prince has
been subject to fits of terror which are unworthy of any
man, but which are the sole and only source of the favour
I enjoy. If it were not for the sovereign's alarms, my
particular style of excellence would be too rough and
rugged to suit this court, where stupidity reigns supreme.
Will you believe that the prince looks under every bed in
his apartments before he gets into his own, and spends a
million yearly—which at Parma is what four millions would
be at Milan—to insure himself a good police force. The
head of that terrible police force, madam, now stands before
you. Through the police—that is to say, through the
prince's terrors—I have become Minister of War and of
Finance; and as the Minister of the Interior is my nominal
chief—insomuch as the police falls within his department—
I have caused that portfolio to be bestowed on Count Zurla-
Contarini, an idiot who delights in work, and is never so

happy as when he can write eighty letters in a day. This very morning I have received one on which the count has had the pleasure of writing No. 20,715 with his own hand."

The Duchess Sanseverina was presented to the melancholy-looking Princess of Parma, Clara Paolina, who, because her husband had a mistress (the Marchesa Balbi, a rather pretty woman), thought herself the unhappiest, and had thus become the most tiresome woman, perhaps, in the universe.

The duchess found herself in the presence of a very tall and thin woman, who had not reached the age of six-and-thirty, and who looked fifty. Her face, with its noble and regular features, might have been thought beautiful, in spite of a pair of large round eyes, out of which she could hardly see, if the princess had not grown so utterly careless of her personal appearance. She received the duchess with such evident shyness that certain of the courtiers, who hated Count Mosca, ventured to remark that the sovereign looked like the woman who was being presented, and the duchess like the sovereign who received her. The duchess, surprised and almost put out of countenance, did not know what terms she should employ to indicate the inferiority of her own position to that which the princess chose to take up. The only thing she could devise to restore some composure to the poor princess, who was really not lacking in intelligence, was to begin and carry on a long dissertation on the subject of botany. The princess really knew a great deal about the subject; she had very fine hot-houses filled with tropical plants. The duchess, while simply attempting to get out of her own difficulty, made a lasting conquest of the Princess Clara Paolina, who, timid and nervous as she had been at the opening of the audience, was so perfectly at her ease before its close that, contrary to every rule of etiquette, this first reception lasted no less than an hour and a quarter. The very next day the duchess purchased quantities of exotic plants, and gave herself out as a great lover of botany.

The princess spent all her time with the venerable Father Landriani, Archbishop of Parma, a learned and even a witty

The Chartreuse of Parma

man, and a perfectly well-mannered man into the bargain.
But it was a curious sight to see him, enthroned in the
crimson velvet chair which he occupied by virtue of his
office, opposite the arm-chair in which the princess sat,
surrounded by her ladies of honour and her two ladies in
waiting. The aged prelate, with his long white hair, was
even more shy, if that were possible, than the princess.
They met every day of their lives, and every audience
began with a full quarter of an hour of silence—to such a
point indeed, that one of the ladies in waiting, the Countess Alvizi, had become a sort of favourite because she
possessed the knack of encouraging them to open their
lips, and making them break the stillness.

To wind up her presentations, the duchess was received
by the hereditary prince, who was taller than his father, and
even shyer than his mother. He was sixteen years old, and
an authority on mineralogy. When the duchess appeared
he blushed scarlet, and was so put out that he was quite
unable to invent anything to say to the fair lady. He was
very good-looking, and spent his whole life in the woods
with a hammer in his hand. When the duchess rose to her
feet to bring the silent audience to a close,

"Heavens, madam," he cried, "how beautiful you
are!" and the lady who had been presented to him did not
think the remark altogether ill-chosen.

The Marchesa Balbi, a young woman of five-and-twenty,
might, some two or three years before the arrival of the
duchess in Parma, have been quoted as a most perfect type
of Italian beauty. She still had the loveliest eyes in the
world, and the most graceful little gestures. But close observation showed her skin to be covered with innumerable
tiny wrinkles, which made her into a young-looking old
woman. Seen from a distance, in her box at the theatre,
for instance, she was still beautiful, and the good people
in the pit thought the prince showed very good taste. He
spent all the evenings in the Marchesa Balbi's house, but
frequently without opening his lips, and her consciousness
that the prince was bored had worried the poor woman into
a condition of extraordinary thinness. She gave herself

The Chartreuse of Parma

airs of excessive cleverness, and was always smiling archly. She had the most beautiful teeth in the world, and in season and out she endeavoured to smile people into the belief that she meant something different from what she was saying. Count Mosca declared it was this perpetual smile—while she was yawning in her heart—which had given her so many wrinkles. The Balbi had her finger in every business, and the state could not conclude a bargain of a thousand francs without a " remembrance," so it was politely termed at Parma, for the marchesa. According to public report she had invested six millions of francs in England, but her fortune, which was certainly a thing of recent growth, did not really exceed one million five hundred thousand francs. It was to protect himself from her cunning and to keep her dependent on him that Mosca had made himself Minister of Finance. The marchesa's sole passion was fear, disguised in the shape of sordid avarice. " I shall die destitute," she would sometimes say to the prince, who was furious at the very idea. The duchess remarked that the splendid gilded antechamber of the Balbi's palace was lighted by a solitary candle, which was guttering down on to a precious marble table, and her drawing-room doors were blackened by the servants' fingers. " She received me," said the duchess to her friend, " as if she expected me to give her a gratuity of fifty francs ! "

The tide of these successes was somewhat checked by the reception the duchess received at the hands of the cleverest woman at the court of Parma, the celebrated Marchesa Raversi, a consummate *intrigante*, who led the party opposed to Count Mosca. She was bent on his overthrow, and had been so more especially during the last few months, for she was the Duke Sanseverina's niece, and was afraid the charms of the new duchess might diminish her own share of his inheritance.

" The Raversi is by no means a woman to be overlooked," said the count to his friend. " So great is my opinion of her capacity that I separated from my wife simply and solely because she insisted on taking one of the marchesa's friends, the Cavaliere Bentivoglio, as her lover."

The Chartreuse of Parma

The Marchesa Raversi, a tall, masterful woman, with very black hair, remarkable for the diamonds which she wore even in the daytime, and for the rouge with which she covered her face, had declared her enmity to the duchess beforehand, and was careful to begin hostile operations as soon as she beheld her. Sanseverina's letters betrayed so much satisfaction with his embassy, and especially such delight in his hope of obtaining his much-coveted order, that his family feared he might leave part of his fortune to his wife, on whom he showered a succession of trifling presents. The Raversi, though a thoroughly ugly woman, had a lover, Count Baldi, the best-looking man about the court. As a general rule she succeeded in everything she undertook.

The duchess kept up a magnificent establishment. The Palazzo Sanseverina had always been one of the most splendid in Parma, and the duke, in honour of his embassy and his expected decoration, was spending large sums on improvements. The duchess superintended all these changes.

The count had guessed aright. A few days after the duchess's presentation the young Clelia Conti appeared at court; she had been created a canoness. To parry the blow the conferring of this favour might appear to have given the count's credit, the duchess, under pretext of opening the gardens of her palace, gave a fête, and in her graceful way made Clelia, whom she called her "little friend from the Lake of Como," the queen of the revels. Her initials appeared, as though by chance, on all the chief transparencies which adorned the grounds. The youthful Clelia, though a trifle pensive, spoke in the most charming fashion of her little adventure on the shore of the lake, and of her own sincere gratitude. She was said to be very devout and fond of solitude. "I'll wager," said the count, "she's clever enough to be ashamed of her father!" The duchess made a friend of the young girl; she really felt drawn toward her. She did not wish to appear jealous, and included her in all her entertainments. She made it her rule to endeavour to soften all the various hatreds of which the count was the object.

The Chartreuse of Parma

Everything smiled on the duchess. The court existence, over which the storm-cloud always hangs threateningly, entertained her. Life seemed to have begun afresh for her; she was tenderly attached to the count, and he was literally beside himself with delight. His private happiness had endued him with the most absolute composure regarding matters which only affected his ambition, and hardly two months after the duchess's arrival he received his patent as Prime Minister, and all the honours appertaining to that position, which fell but little short of those rendered to the sovereign himself. The count's influence over his master's mind was all powerful. A striking proof of the fact was soon to become evident in Parma.

Ten minutes' walk from the town, toward the southeast, rises the far-famed citadel, renowned all over Italy, the great tower of which, some hundred and eighty feet high, may be descried from an immense distance. This tower, built toward the beginning of the sixteenth century by the Farnese, grandsons of Paul III, in imitation of the Mausoleum of Adrian at Rome, is so thick that room has been found on the terrace at one end of it, to build a palace for the governor of the citadel, and a more modern prison, known as the Farnese Tower. This citadel, built in honour of Ranuzio-Ernest II, who had been his own stepmother's favourite lover, has a great reputation in the country, both for its beauty and as a curiosity. The duchess took a fancy to see it. On the day of her visit, the heat in Parma had been most oppressive. At the altitude on which the prison stood she found a breeze, and was so delighted that she remained there several hours. Rooms in the Farnese Tower were immediately opened for her convenience.

On the terrace of the great tower she met a poor imprisoned Liberal, who had come up to enjoy the half-hour's walk allowed him every third day. She returned to Parma, and not having yet attained the discretion indispensable at an autocratic court, she talked about the man, who had told her his whole story. The Marchesa Raversi's party laid hold of the duchess's remarks, and made a great deal of them, in the eager hope that they would give umbrage to the prince. As a matter of fact, Ernest IV was fond of reiterating that the great point was to strike people's imaginations. "*Forever*," he would say, "is a great word, and sheds more terror in Italy than anywhere else." Consequently he had never granted a pardon in his life. A week after her visit to the fortress, the duchess received a written commutation of a prisoner's sentence, signed by the prince and minister, and with the name left blank. Any prisoner whose name she might insert was to recover his confiscated property, and to be allowed to depart to America and there spend the remainder of his days. The duchess wrote the name of the man to whom she had spoken. By ill-luck he happened to be a sort of half-rascal, a weak-hearted fellow. It was on his confessions that the celebrated Ferrante Palla had been condemned to death.

The peculiar circumstances connected with this pardon crowned the Duchess Sanseverina's success. Count Mosca was deliriously happy. It was one of the brightest moments in his life, and had a decisive influence on Fabrizio's future. The young man was still at Romagnano, near Novara, confessing his sins, hunting, reading nothing at all, and making love to a high-born lady—according to the instructions given him. The duchess was still somewhat disgusted by this last stipulation. Another sign, which was not a good one for the count, was that though on every other subject she was absolutely frank with him, and, in fact, thought aloud in his presence, she never mentioned Fabrizio without having carefully prepared her sentence beforehand.

"If you wish it," said the count to her one day, " I will write to that delightful brother of yours on the Lake of Como, and with a little trouble on my own part and that of my friends, I can certainly force the Marchese del Dongo to sue for mercy for your dear Fabrizio. If it be true— and I should be sorry to think it was not—that the boy is somewhat superior to the majority of the young men who ride their horses up and down the streets of Milan, what a life lies before him! that of a man who at eighteen years old has nothing to do, and never expects to have any occupation. If Heaven had granted him a real passion for anything on the face of the earth—even for rod-fishing—I would respect it. But what is to become of him at Milan, even if he is pardoned? At one particular hour of the day he will ride out upon the horse he will have brought over from England; at another fixed hour sheer idleness will drive him into the arms of his mistress, whom he will care for less than he does for his horse. Still, if you order me to do it, I will endeavour to procure your nephew the opportunity of leading that kind of life."

"I should like him to be an officer," said the duchess.

"Could you advise any sovereign to confer such a position, which may at any moment become one of some importance, on a young man who, in the first place, is capable of enthusiasm, and, in the second, has proved his enthusiasm for Napoleon to the extent of going to join him at Waterloo? Consider what we should all be now if Napoleon had won that battle! True, there would be no Liberals for us to dread, but the only way in which the sovereigns of the ancient families could retain their thrones would be by marrying his marshals' daughters. For Fabrizio the military career would be like the life of a squirrel in a cage—constant movement and no advancement; he would have the vexation of seeing his services outweighed by those of any and every plebeian. The indispensable quality for every young man in the present day—that is to say, for the next fifty years, during which time our terrors will last, and religion will not yet be firmly re-established—must be lack of intelligence and incapacity for all enthusiasm. I have thought of one thing—but you will begin by crying out at the very idea—and it is a matter which would give me infinite trouble, that would last for many a day. Still, it is a folly that I am ready to commit for you—and tell me, if you can, what folly I would not commit for the sake of a smile from you?"

"Well?" said the duchess.

"Well! Three Archbishops of Parma have been members of your family—Ascanio del Dongo, who wrote a book in 16—; Fabrizio, who was here in 1699; and another Ascanio, in 1740. If Fabrizio will enter the Church, and give proofs of first-rate merit, I will first of all make him bishop of some other place, and then archbishop here, provided my influence lasts long enough. The real objection is this: Shall I continue in power sufficiently long to realize this fine plan? It will take several years. The prince may die, or he may have the bad taste to dismiss me. Still, after all, this is the only means I can perceive of doing anything for Fabrizio which will be worthy of you."

There was a long discussion; the idea was very repugnant to the duchess.

"Prove to me once again," said she to the count, "that no other career is possible for Fabrizio."

The count repeated his arguments, and he added: "What you regret is the gay uniform. But in that matter I am powerless."

The duchess asked for a month to think it over, and then, with a sigh, she accepted the minister's wise counsels. "He must either ride about some big town on an English horse, with a stuck-up air, or take up a way of life which is not unsuitable to his birth. I see no middle course," repeated the count. "A nobleman, unfortunately, can not be either a doctor or a lawyer, and this is the century of lawyers. But remember, madam," he continued, "that it is in your power to give your nephew the same advantages of life in Milan as are enjoyed by the young men of his age who are considered to be Fortune's favourites. Once his pardon is granted, you can allow him fifteen, twenty, or thirty thousand francs a year; the sum will matter little; neither you nor I expect to put away money."

But the duchess pined for glory; she did not want her nephew to be a mere spendthrift. She gave in her adhesion to her lover's project.

"Observe," the count said to her, "that I do not the least claim that Fabrizio should become an exemplary priest, like so many that you see about you. No. First and foremost, he remains an aristocrat; he can continue perfectly ignorant if he so prefers it, and that will not prevent him from becoming a bishop and an archbishop if the prince only continues to consider me a useful servant. If your will condescends to change my proposal into an immutable decree," he continued, our *protégé* must not appear at Parma in any modest position. His ultimate honours would give umbrage if he had been seen here as an ordinary priest. He must not appear at Parma without the violet stockings * and all the appropriate surroundings. Then everybody will guess that your nephew is going to be a bishop, and nobody will find fault. If you will be ruled by me, you will send Fabrizio to Naples for three years to study theology. During the vacations he can, if he chooses, go and see Paris and London, but he must never show himself at Parma."

This last sentence made the duchess shiver. She sent a courier to her nephew, desiring him to meet her at Piacenza. I need hardly say that the messenger carried all the necessary funds and passports.

Fabrizio, who was the first to arrive at Piacenza, ran to meet the duchess, and kissed her in a transport of affection, which made her burst into tears. She was glad the count was not present. It was the first time since the beginning of their *liaison* that she had been conscious of such a sensation.

Fabrizio was greatly touched, and deeply distressed, also, by the plans the duchess had made for him. His hope had always been that, once his Waterloo escapade had been excused, he might yet become a soldier.

One thing struck the duchess and increased her romantic admiration for her nephew; he absolutely refused to lead the ordinary life of young men in large Italian cities.

"Don't you see yourself at the Corso, in Florence, or Naples," said the duchess, "riding your thorough-bred English horses, and then in the evening your carriage, and beautiful rooms, and so forth?" She dwelt with delight on her description of the commonplace enjoyments from which she saw Fabrizio turn in disdain. "He is a hero," thought she to herself.

"And after ten years of that delightful life," said Fa

---

* In Italy, young men who are learned or protected in high quarters are created *monsignori* and *prelates*, which does not mean that they are bishops. They then wear violet stockings. A *monsignore* takes no vows, and can relinquish his violet stockings if he desires to marry.

brizio, "what shall I have done? What shall I be? Nothing but a middle-aged young man who will have to make way for the first good-looking youth who rides into society on another English horse."

At first he would not hear of going into the Church. He talked of going to New York, obtaining citizenship, and serving as a soldier in the republic of America.

"What a mistake you will make! You will have no fighting, and you will just fall back into the old *café* life, only without elegance, without music, and without love-making," replied the duchess. "Believe me, your life in America would be a sad business, both for you and me." And she explained what dollar worship was, and the respect necessarily paid to the artisan class, on whose votes everything depended. They went back again to the Church plan.

"Before you lose your temper over it," said the duchess, "try to understand what the count asks you to do. It is not at all a question of your living a poor and more or less exemplary life, like Father Blanès. Remember the history of your ancestors, who were Archbishops of Parma. Read the notices of their lives in the Appendix to the Genealogy. The man who bears a great name must be first and foremost a true nobleman, high-hearted, generous, a protector of justice, destined from the outset to stand at the head of his order, guilty of but one piece of knavery in his life, and that a very useful one."

"Alas!" cried Fabrizio, "so all my illusions have vanished into thin air!" and he sighed deeply. "It is a cruel sacrifice. I confess I never reckoned with the horror of enthusiasm and intelligence, even when used in their own service, which will reign for the future among all absolute sovereigns."

"Consider that a proclamation, or a mere freak of the affections, may drive an enthusiastic man into the opposite party to that in the service of which he has spent his whole life."

"Enthusiastic! I!" repeated Fabrizio. "What an extraordinary accusation! I can not even contrive to fall in love!"

The Chartreuse of Parma

" What! " exclaimed the duchess.

" When I have the honour of paying my court to a beautiful woman, even though she be religious and of the highest birth, I never can think of her except when I am looking at her."

This confession had a very peculiar effect upon the duchess.

" Give me a month," said Fabrizio, " to take leave of Signora C—— at Novara, and, what is far more difficult, to bid farewell to the dreams of all my life. I will write to my mother, who will be good enough to come and see me at Belgirate, on the Piedmontese shore of the Lago Maggiore, and on the one-and-thirtieth day from this one I will be at Parma *incognito*."

" Do not dream of such a thing," exclaimed the duchess; she had no wish that Count Mosca should see her with Fabrizio.

They met once more at Piacenza. This time the duchess was sorely agitated. A storm had broken at court. The Marchesa Raversi's party was on the brink of triumph; it was quite on the cards that Count Mosca might be replaced by General Fabio Conti, the head of what was known at Parma as the Liberal party. With the exception of the name of the rival whose favour was thus growing with the prince, the duchess told Fabrizio everything. She discussed all his future chances over again, even to the possibility that the count's all-powerful protection might fail him.

" I am to spend three years at the Ecclesiastical Academy at Naples," exclaimed Fabrizio. " But as I am to be first and foremost a young man of family, and as you do not expect me to lead the severe life of a virtuous seminarist, the idea of my stay at Naples does not alarm me. The life there will, at all events, be no worse than that at Romagnano. The best company in that place was beginning to look on me as a Jacobin. During my exile I have discovered that I know nothing—not even Latin—nay, not even how to spell! I had determined to begin my education afresh at Novara. I shall be glad to study theology at Naples; it is a complicated science."

The Chartreuse of Parma

The duchess was overjoyed. "If we are dismissed," she said, "we will go and see you at Naples. But as, for the moment, you accept the idea of the violet stockings, the count, who knows the present condition of Italy thoroughly, has given me a hint for you. Believe whatever is taught you or not, as you choose, *but never express any objection.* Tell yourself you are being taught the rules of whist; would you make any demur about the rules of whist? I told the count you were a believer, and he was very glad of it; it is useful both in this world and in the next. But do not, because you believe, fall into the vulgarity of speaking with horror of Voltaire, Diderot, Raynal, and all the other wild Frenchmen who were the precursors of the two Chambers. Those names should hardly ever be pronounced by you. But if the necessity should arise, you must refer to them with the calmest irony, as people whose theories have long since been rejected, and whose attacks are no longer of the slightest consequence. Accept everything you are told at the academy with the blindest faith. Recollect that there are individuals within its walls who will take faithful note of your most trifling objections. A little love affair, if judiciously managed, will be forgiven you, but a doubt, never! Advancing years suppress the tendency to love-making and increase that toward doubt. When you go to confession act on this principle. You will have a letter of recommendation to the bishop who acts as factotum to the Cardinal Archbishop of Naples. To him alone you will confess your escapade in France, and your presence near Waterloo on the 18th of June. And even so, shorten the matter, make little of the adventure; only confess it so that nobody may be able to reproach you with having concealed it—you were so young when it happened. The second hint which the count sends you is this: If a brilliant argument occurs to you, or a crushing reply which would change the course of a conversation, do not yield to the temptation to shine; keep silence. Clever people will read your intelligence in your eyes. It will be time enough for you to be witty when you are a bishop."

Fabrizio began life at Naples with a quiet-looking carriage and four faithful Milanese servants, sent him by his aunt. After a year's study, no one called him a clever man; he rather bore the reputation of being an aristocrat, studious, very generous, and something of a libertine.

The year, which had been a fairly pleasant one to Fabrizio, had been terrible for the duchess. Two or three times over the count had been within an inch of ruin. The prince, who, being ill, was more timorous than ever, fancied that by dismissing him he would get rid of the odium of the executions which had taken place before the count became minister. Rassi was the favourite with whom the sovereign was determined not to part. The count's peril made the duchess cling to him with passionate affection; she never gave a thought to Fabrizio. To give some colour to their possible retirement, she discovered that the air of Parma, which is, indeed, somewhat damp, like that of the whole of Lombardy, was quite unsuited to her health. At last, after intervals of disgrace, during which the Prime Minister sometimes spent three weeks without seeing his master privately, Mosca won the day. He had General Fabio Conti, the so-called Liberal, appointed governor of the citadel in which the Liberals sentenced by Rassi were imprisoned. " If Conti shows any indulgence to his prisoners," said Mosca to his mistress, " he will be disgraced as a Jacobin, whose political views have made him forget his duty as a soldier. If he proves severe and merciless, which, as I fancy, is the direction in which he will most likely lean, he ceases to be the leader of his own party, and alienates all the families whose relations are imprisoned in the citadel. The poor wretch knows how to put on an air of the deepest respect whenever he appears before the prince; he can change his clothes four times a day, he can discuss a question of etiquette, but his head is not strong enough to guide him along the difficult path which is the only one that can lead him to safety. And anyhow, I am on the spot."

The day after General Fabio Conti's appointment, which closed the ministerial crisis, it was noised abroad that an ultra-monarchical newspaper was to be published in Parma.

The Chartreuse of Parma

"What quarrels this newspaper will cause!" said the duchess.

"The idea of publishing this newspaper is perhaps the best I ever had," replied the count with a laugh. "Little by little, and in spite of myself, I shall let the ultra-furies take the management out of my hands. I have had good salaries attached to all the positions connected with the editorial staff—people will apply to be appointed from all quarters—the matter will keep us busy for a month or two, and so my late dangers will be forgotten. Those serious personages P—— and D—— have already joined the staff."

"But the whole thing will be too revoltingly absurd!"

"I hope so, indeed," replied the count. "The prince shall read it every morning, and admire the doctrine of the newspaper I have founded. As regards the details, he will approve of some and find fault with others; that will take up two of his working hours. The newspaper will get into difficulties, but by the time the serious troubles begin, eight or ten months hence, it will be entirely in the hands of the ultras. Then that party, which is a trouble to me, will have to answer for it, and I shall make complaints against the newspaper. On the whole, I would rather have a hundred vile absurdities than see a single man hanged. Who will remember an absurdity two years after its publication in the official newspaper? Whereas, if I have to hang a man, his son and his whole family vow a hatred against me which will last my whole life, and may shorten it."

The duchess, who was always passionately interested in one thing or another, constantly active and never idle, was cleverer than the whole court of Parma together. But she had not the patience and calmness indispensable to success in intrigue; nevertheless, she contrived to follow the working of the various coteries with eager interest, and was even beginning to enjoy some personal credit with the prince. The reigning princess, Clara Paolina, who was loaded with honours, but, girt about with the most superannuated etiquette, looked on herself as the unhappiest of women. The Duchess Sanseverina paid court to her, and undertook to convince her she was not so very wretched after all. It must be explained that the prince never saw his wife except at dinner. This repast lasted about twenty minutes, and sometimes for weeks and weeks the prince never opened his lips to Clara Paolina. The duchess endeavoured to change all this. She herself amused the prince, all the more so because she had managed to preserve her independence. Even if she had desired it she could not have contrived never to displease any of the fools who swarmed at court. It was this utter incapacity on her part that caused her to be detested by the common herd of courtiers, all of them men of title, most of them enjoying incomes of about five thousand francs a year. She realized this misfortune during her first days at Parma, and turned her exclusive attention to pleasing the prince and his consort, who completely swayed the hereditary prince. The duchess knew how to amuse the sovereign, and took advantage of the great attention he paid to her lightest word, to cast hearty ridicule on the courtiers who hated her. Since the follies into which Rassi had led him—and bloodstained follies cannot be repaired—the prince was occasionally frightened, and very often bored. This had brought him to a condition of melancholy envy. He realized that he was hardly ever amused, and looked glum if he thought other people were amusing themselves. The sight of happiness drove him wild. "We must hide our love," said the duchess to her lover, and she allowed the prince to surmise that her affection for the count, charming fellow though he was, was by no means so strong as it had been.

This discovery insured his Highness a whole day of happiness. From time to time the duchess would let fall a word or two concerning a plan she had for taking a few months' holiday every year, and spending the time in seeing Italy, for she did not know the country at all. She would pay visits to Naples, Florence, and Rome. Now, nothing in the world could possibly be more displeasing to the prince than any idea of such desertion. This was one of his ruling weaknesses—any action which might be imputed to scorn of his native city stabbed him to the heart. He felt he had no means of detaining the Duchess Sanseverina, and the

The Chartreuse of Parma

Duchess Sanseverina was by far the most brilliant woman at Parma. People even came back from their country houses in the neighbourhood to be present at her Thursday parties, a wonderful effort for these idle Italians. These Thursday gatherings were real *fêtes*, at which the duchess almost always produced some fresh and attractive novelty. The prince was dying to see one of these parties, but how was he to set about it? To go to a private house was a thing which neither he nor his father had ever done.

On a certain Thursday it was raining and bitterly cold. All through the evening the duke had been listening to the carriages rattling across the pavement of the square in front of his palace, on their way to the Palazzo Sanseverina. A fit of impatient anger seized him. Other people were amusing themselves, and he, their sovereign prince and absolute lord, who ought to amuse himself more than anybody in the world, was feeling bored.

He rang for his aide-de-camp. It took a little time to station a dozen trusty servants in the street leading from the palace of his Highness to the Palazzo Sanseverina. At last, after an hour, which to the prince seemed like a century, and during which he had been tempted, twenty times over, to set forth boldly without any precaution whatsoever, and take his chance of dagger thrusts, he made his appearance in the Duchess Sanseverina's outer drawing-room. If a thunderbolt had fallen in that drawing-room, it could not have caused such great surprise. In the twinkling of an eye, as the prince passed forward, a stupor of silence fell upon the rooms which had just been so noisy and so gay. Every eye was fixed on the prince, and stared wider and wider. The courtiers seemed put out of countenance; the duchess alone did not appear astonished. When the power of speech returned, the great anxiety of all the company present was to decide the important question whether the duchess had been warned of the impending visit, or whether it had taken her, like everybody else, by surprise.

The prince amused himself, and my readers will now be able to realize the impulsive nature of the duchess, and the infinite power which the vague ideas of possible departure she had so skilfully dropped had enabled her to attain.

As she accompanied the departing prince to the door, he addressed her in the most flattering strain. A strange notion entered her head, and she ventured to say, quite simply, and as though it were the most ordinary matter in the world:

"If your Most Serene Highness would address two or three of the gracious expressions you have showered on me to the princess, you would ensure my happiness far more thoroughly than by telling me, here, that I am pretty. For I would not, for all the world, that the princess should look askance at the signal mark of favour with which your Highness has just honoured me." The prince looked hard at her, and responded dryly:

"I suppose I am free to go where I choose."

The duchess coloured.

"My only desire," she instantly replied, "was to avoid giving your Highness the trouble of driving out for nothing, for this Thursday will be my last. I am going to spend a few days at Bologna or Florence."

When she passed back into the drawing-rooms, every one thought she had reached the very height of court favour, and she had just dared what no one in the memory of man had ever dared at Parma. She made a sign to the count, who left his whist table and followed her into a small room, which, though lighted up, was empty.

"What you have done is very bold," he said. "I should not have advised you to do it. But when a man's heart is really engaged," he added with a laugh, "happiness increases love, and if you start to-morrow morning, I follow you to-morrow night! The only thing which will delay me is this troublesome Finance Ministry, which I have been foolish enough to undertake. But in four hours of steady work I shall be able to give over a great many cash boxes. Let us go back, dear friend, and show off our ministerial conceit freely and unreservedly; it may be the last performance we shall give in this city. If the man thinks he is being set at defiance he is capable of anything; he will call that *making an example!* When all these people have departed we will see about barricading you in for the night. Perhaps your best plan would be to start at once for your house at Sacca, near the Po, which has the advantage of being only half an hour's journey from the Austrian states."

It was an exquisite moment, both for the duchess's love, and for her vanity. She looked at the count, and her eyes were moist with tears. That so powerful a minister, surrounded by a mob of courtiers who overwhelmed him with homage equal to that they paid to the prince himself, should be ready to leave everything for her, and that so cheerfully!

When she went back to her rooms she was giddy with delight; every one bowed down before her.

"How happiness does change the duchess!" said the courtiers on every side; "one would hardly know her again. At last that Roman soul, which as a rule scorns everything, actually condescends to appreciate the exceeding favour which the sovereign has just shown her."

Toward the end of the evening the count came to her. "I must tell you some news." Immediately the persons close to the duchess retired to a distance.

"When the prince returned to the palace," the count went on, "he sent to the princess to announce his arrival. Imagine her astonishment! 'I have come,' he said, 'to give you an account of a really very pleasant evening which I have just spent with the Sanseverina. It is she who begged me to give you details of the manner in which she has rearranged that smoky old palace.' And then the prince, seating himself, began to describe each of your rooms. He spent more than five-and-twenty minutes with his wife, who was shedding tears of joy. In spite of her cleverness, she could not find a word to carry on the conversation in the light tone which it was his Highness's pleasure to give it."

The prince was not a bad man, whatever the Italian Liberals might say of him. He had, it is true, cast a certain number of them into prison, but this was out of fright, and he would sometimes reiterate, as though to console himself for certain memories, "It is better to kill the devil than to let the devil kill us." On the morrow after the party to which we have just referred he was quite joyous; he had done two good actions—had been to the party, and had talked to his wife. At dinner he spoke to her again. In a word, that Thursday party at the Sanseverina palace brought about a domestic revolution which resounded all over Parma. The Raversi was dismayed, and the duchess tasted a twofold joy. She had been able to serve her lover, and she had found him more devoted than ever.

" And all that because a very imprudent notion came into my head," said she to the count. " I should have more freedom, no doubt, at Rome or at Naples, but could I find any existence so fascinating as this? No, my dear count, and, in good truth, I owe my happiness to you."

CHAPTER VII

Any history of the four years that now elapsed would have to be filled up with small court details, as insignificant as those we have just related. Every spring the marchesa and her daughters came to spend two months either at the Palazzo Sanseverina or at the duchess's country house at Sacca, on the banks of the Po. These were very delightful visits, during which there was much talk of Fabrizio. But the count would never allow him to appear at Parma. The duchess and the Prime Minister found it necessary to repair an occasional blunder, but on the whole Fabrizio followed the line of conduct mapped out for him with tolerable propriety. He was the great nobleman studying theology, who did not reckon absolutely upon his virtue to insure his advancement. At Naples he had taken a strong fancy to antiquarian studies. He made excavations, and this passion almost took the place of his fondness for horses. He sold his English horses so as to continue his researches at Miseno, where he found a bust of the youthful Tiberius, which soon ranked as one of the finest known relics of antiquity. The discovery of this bust was almost the keenest pleasure Fabrizio knew while he was at Naples. He was too proud-spirited to imitate other young men, and, for instance, to play the lover's part with a certain amount of gravity. He had mistresses, certainly, but they were of no real consequence to him, and in spite of his youth he might have been said not to know what love was. This only made the women love him more. There was nothing to prevent him from behaving with the most perfect coolness, for in his case one young and pretty woman was always as good as any other young and pretty woman; only the one whose acquaintance he had last made seemed to him the most attractive. During the last year of his sojourn, one of the most admired beauties in Naples had committed imprudences for his sake. This had begun by amusing him, and ended by boring him to death; and that to such a point that one of the joys connected with his departure was that it delivered him from the pursuit of the charming Duchess of ——. It was in 1821 that, his examination having been passed with tolerable success, the director of his studies received a decoration and a pecuniary acknowledgment, and he himself started, at last, to see that city of Parma of which he had often dreamed. He was a monsignore, and had four horses to his carriage. At the last posting station before Parma he took two horses instead, and when he reached the town he stopped before the Church of St. John. It contained the splendid tomb of the Archbishop Ascanio del Dongo, his great-great-uncle, author of the Latin Genealogy. He prayed beside the tomb, and then went on foot to the palace of the duchess, who did not expect him till several days later. Her drawing-room was very full. Soon she was left alone.

"Well, are you pleased with me?" he said, and threw himself into her arms. "Thanks to you, I have been spending four fairly happy years at Naples, instead of boring myself at Novara with the mistress the police authorized me to take."

The duchess could not get over her astonishment; she would not have known him if she had met him in the street. She thought him, what he really was, one of the best-looking men in Italy. It was his expression, especially, that was so charming.

When she had sent him to Naples he had looked a reckless daredevil; the riding-whip which never left his hand seemed an inherent portion of his being. Now, when strangers were present, his manner was the most dignified and guarded imaginable, and when they were alone she recognised all the fiery ardour of his early youth. Here was a diamond which had lost nothing in the cutting. Hardly an hour after Fabrizio's arrival Count Mosca made his appearance; he had come a little too soon. The young man spoke so correctly about the Parmesan order conferred on his tutor, and expressed his lively gratitude for other benefits to which he dared not refer in so open a manner with such perfect propriety, that at the first glance the minister judged him correctly. "This nephew of yours," he murmured to the duchess, "is born to adorn all the dignities to which you may ultimately desire to raise him." Up to this point all had gone marvellously well. But when the minister, who had been very much pleased with Fabrizio, and until then had given his whole attention to his behaviour and gestures, looked at the duchess, the expression in her eyes struck him as strange.

"This young man makes an unusual impression here," said he to himself. The thought was a bitter one. The count had passed his fiftieth year—a cruel word, the full meaning of which can only be realized, perhaps, by a man who is desperately in love. He was exceedingly kind-hearted, very worthy to be loved, except for his official severity. But in his eyes that cruel phrase, *my fiftieth year*, cast a black cloud over all his life, and might even have driven him to be cruel on his own account. During the five years which had elapsed since he had persuaded the duchess to settle in Parma, she had often roused his jealousy, more especially in the earlier days. But she had never given him any cause for real complaint. He even believed, and he was right, that it was with the object of tightening her hold upon his heart that the duchess had bestowed apparent favour on certain of the young beaux about the court. He was sure, for instance, that she had refused the advances of the prince, who, indeed, had dropped an instructive remark on the occasion.

"But," the duchess had objected laughingly, "if I accepted your Highness's attentions, how should I ever dare to face the count again?"

"I should be almost as much put out of countenance as you. The poor dear count—my friend! But that is a difficulty very easily surmounted, and which I have already considered. The count should be shut up in the citadel for the rest of his life!"

The Chartreuse of Parma

At the moment of Fabrizio's arrival, the duchess was so transported with delight that she gave no thought at all to the ideas her looks might stir in the count's brain. Their effect was deep, and his consequent suspicion ineradicable.

Two hours after his arrival Fabrizio was received by the prince. The duchess, foreseeing the good effect of this impromptu audience on the public mind, had been soliciting it for two months beforehand. This favour placed Fabrizio, from the very outset, above the heads of all his equals. The pretext had been that he was only passing through Parma on his way to see his mother in Piedmont. Just at the very moment when a charming little note from the duchess brought the prince the information that Fabrizio was waiting on his pleasure, his Highness was feeling bored. "Now," said he to himself, "I shall behold a very silly little saint; he will be either empty-headed or sly." The commandant of the fortress had already reported the preliminary visit to the archbishop uncle's tomb. The prince saw a tall young man enter his presence; but for his violet stockings he would have taken him for a young officer.

This little surprise drove away his boredom. "Here," thought he to himself, "is a fine-looking fellow, for whom I shall be asked God knows what favours—all and any that are at my disposal. He has just arrived; he must feel some emotion. I'll try a little Jacobinism, and we shall see what kind of answers he'll give."

After the first few gracious words spoken by the prince, "Well, monsignore," said he to Fabrizio, "are the inhabitants of Naples happy? Is the King beloved?"

"Most Serene Highness," replied Fabrizio, without a moment's hesitation, "as I passed along the streets I used to admire the excellent demeanour of the soldiers of his Majesty's various regiments. All good society is respectful, as it should be, to its masters; but I confess I have never in my life permitted people of the lower class to speak to me of anything but the labour for which I pay them."

"The deuce!" thought the prince; "what a priestling! Here's a well-trained bird! The Sanseverina's own wit!" Thoroughly piqued, the prince used all his skill to draw

The Chartreuse of Parma

Fabrizio into talk upon this risky subject. The young man, stimulated by the danger of his position, was lucky enough to find admirable answers. " To put forward one's love for one's king," said he, " is almost an insolence. What we owe him is blind obedience." The sight of so much prudence almost made the prince angry. " This young man from Naples seems to be a clever fellow, and I don't like the breed. It's all very well for a clever man to behave according to the best principles, and even to believe in them honestly—somehow or other he is always sure to be first cousin to Voltaire and Rousseau ! "

The prince felt there was a sort of defiance of himself in the correct manners and unassailable answers of this youth just leaving college ; things were by no means turning out as he had foreseen. In the twinkling of an eye he changed his tone to one of simple good-nature, and going back, in a few words, to the great principles of society and government, he reeled off, applying them to the occasion, certain sentences from Fénelon which had been taught him in his childhood for use at public audiences.

" These principles surprise you, young man," said he to Fabrizio (he had addressed him as monsignore at the beginning of the audience, and proposed to repeat the title when he dismissed him, but during the course of the conversation he considered it more skilful and more favourable to the development of the feelings to use a more intimate and friendly term), " these principles, young man, surprise you. I confess they have no close resemblance with the *slices of absolutism* (he used the very words) which are served up every day in my official newspaper. But, good God ! why do I quote that to you ? You know nothing of the writers in that paper ! "

" I beg your Most Serene Highness's pardon. Not only do I read the Parma newspaper, which seems to me fairly well written, but I share its opinion, that everything which has been done since the death of Louis XIV in 1715, is at once a folly and a crime. Man's foremost interest is his own salvation—there can not be two opinions on that score —and that bliss is to last for all eternity. The words *liberty*,

The Chartreuse of Parma

justice, happiness of the greatest number, are infamous and criminal; they give men's minds a habit of discussion and disbelief. A Chamber of Deputies *mistrusts* what those people call the *ministry.* Once that fatal habit of *distrust* is contracted, human weakness applies it to everything. Man ends by distrusting the Bible, the commands of the Church, tradition, etc., and thenceforward he is lost. Even supposing—and it is horribly false and criminal to say it— this distrust of the authority of the princes set up by God could insure happiness during the twenty or thirty years of life on which each of us may reckon, what is half a century, or even a whole century, compared with an eternity of torment?"

The manner in which Fabrizio spoke showed that he was endeavouring to arrange his ideas so that his auditor might grasp them as easily as possible. He was evidently not repeating a lesson by rote.

Soon the prince ceased to care about coping with the young man, whose grave and simple manner made him feel uncomfortable.

"Farewell, monsignore," he said abruptly. "I see that the education given in the Ecclesiastical Academy at Naples is an admirable one, and it is quite natural that when these excellent teachings are sown in so distinguished an intelligence, brilliant results should be obtained. Farewell!" And he turned his back on him.

"That fool is not pleased with me," said Fabrizio to himself.

"Now," thought the prince, as soon as he was alone, "it remains to be seen whether that handsome young fellow is susceptible of any passion for anything; in that case he will be perfect. Could he possibly have repeated his aunt's lessons more cleverly? I could have fancied I heard her speaking! If there was a revolution here it would be she who would edit the Moniteur, just as the San Felice did it in old days at Naples. But, in spite of her five-and-twenty years and her beauty, the San Felice was hanged for good and all—a warning to ladies who are too clever!"

When the prince took Fabrizio for his aunt's pupil he

made a mistake. Clever folk born on the throne, or close behind it, soon lose all their delicacy of touch. They proscribe all freedom of conversation around them, taking it for coarseness; they will not look at anything but masks, and yet claim to be judges of complexion; and the comical thing is that they believe themselves to be full of tact. In this particular case, for instance, Fabrizio did believe very nearly everything we have heard him say. It is quite true that he did not bestow a thought on those great principles more than twice in a month. He had lively tastes, he had intelligence, but he also had faith.

The taste for liberty, the fashion for and worship of the happiness of the greatest number, which is one of the manias of the nineteenth century, was in his eyes no more than a heresy, which would pass away like others, after slaying many souls, just as the plague, while it rages in any particular region, kills many bodies. And in spite of all this, Fabrizio delighted in reading the French newspapers, and even committed imprudences for the sake of procuring them.

When Fabrizio returned, rather in a flutter, from his audience at the palace, and began to relate the prince's various attacks upon him to his aunt, "You must call at once," she said, "on Father Landriani, our excellent archbishop. Go to his house on foot, slip quietly up the stairs, don't make much stir in the antechamber, and if you have to wait, all the better—a thousand times better. Be *apostolic*, in a word."

"I understand," said Fabrizio; "the man is a Tartuffe."

"Not the least in the world; he is the very embodiment of virtue."

"Even after what he did at the time of Count Palanza's execution?" returned Fabrizio in astonishment.

"Yes, my friend, even after what he did then. Our archbishop's father was a clerk in the Ministry of Finance, quite a humble, middle-class person; that explains everything. Monsignore Landriani is a man of intelligence, lively, far-reaching, and profound. He is sincere, he loves

The Chartreuse of Parma

virtue. I am convinced that if the Emperor Decius were
to come back to earth he would cheerfully endure martyrdom, like Polyeuctus, in the opera that was performed here
last week. There you have the fair side of the medal; here is
the reverse: The moment he enters the sovereign's presence,
or even the presence of his Prime Minister, he is dazzled by
so much grandeur, he flushes, grows confused, and it becomes physically impossible to him to say 'No.' This accounts for the things he has done and which have earned him
his cruel reputation all over Italy. But what is not generally
known is that when public opinion opened his eyes as to
Count Palanza's trial, he voluntarily imposed on himself the
penance of living on bread and water for thirteen weeks—as
many weeks as there are letters in the name Davide Palanza.
There is at this court an exceedingly clever rascal of the
name of Rassi, the prince's chief justice, or head of the
Law Department, who, at the period of Count Palanza's
death, completely bewitched Father Landriani. While he
was doing his thirteen weeks' penance, Count Mosca, out
of pity, and a little out of spite, used to invite him to dinner
once or twice a week. To please his host the good archbishop ate his dinner like anybody else—he would have
thought it rebellion and Jacobinism to parade his repentance
of an action approved by his sovereign. But it was quite
well known that for every dinner which his duty as a faithful
subject had forced him to eat like everybody else, he endured a self-imposed penance of two days on bread and
water. Monsignore Landriana, though his mind is superior
and his knowledge first-class, has one weakness—*he likes
to be loved*. You must look at him tenderly, therefore, and
at your third visit you must be frankly fond of him. This,
together with your birth, will make him adore you at once.
Show no surprise if he accompanies you back to the head
of the stairs; look as if you were accustomed to his ways—
he is a man who was born on his knees before the nobility.
For the rest, be simple, apostolic—no wit, no brilliancy, no
swift repartee. If you do not startle him he will delight
in your company. Remember, it is on his own initiative
that he must appoint you his grand vicar; the count and

143

The Chartreuse of Parma

I will appear surprised, and even vexed, at your too rapid promotion. That is essential on account of the sovereign."

Fabrizio hurried to the archiepiscopal palace.

By remarkable good luck the good prelate's servant, who was a trifle deaf, did not catch the name of Del Dongo. He announced a young priest called Fabrizio. The archbishop was engaged with a priest of not very exemplary morals, whom he had summoned in order to reprimand him. He was in the act of administering a reproof—a very painful effort to him, and did not care to carry the trouble about with him any longer. He therefore kept the great-nephew of the famous Archbishop Ascanio del Dongo waiting for three quarters of an hour.

How shall I reproduce his excuses and his despair when, having conducted the parish priest as far as the outermost antechamber, he inquired, as he passed back toward his apartment, *what he could do for* the young man who stood waiting, caught sight of his violet stockings, and heard the name Fabrizio del Dongo?

The matter struck our hero in so comic a light that even on this first visit he ventured, in a passion of tenderness, to kiss the saintly prelate's hand. It was worth something to hear the archbishop reiterating in his despair " That a Del Dongo should have waited in my antechamber ! " He felt obliged, in his own excuse, to relate the whole story of the parish priest, his offences, his replies, and so forth.

" Can that really be the man," said Fabrizio to himself, as he returned to the Palazzo Sanseverina, " who hurried on the execution of that poor Count Palanza ? "

" What does your Excellency think ? " said Count Mosca laughingly, as he entered the duchess's room. (The count would not allow Fabrizio to call him " your Excellency.")

" I am utterly amazed ! I know nothing about human nature. I would have wagered, if I had not known his name, that this man could not bear to see a chicken bleed."

" And you would have won," replied the count. " But when he is in the prince's presence, or even in mine, he can not say ' No.' As a matter of fact, I must have my yellow ribbon across my coat if I am to produce my full effect upon him; in morning dress he would contradict me, and I always put on my uniform before I receive him. It is no business of ours to destroy the prestige of power—the French newspapers are demolishing it quite fast enough. The *respectful mania* will hardly last out our time, and you, nephew, you'll outlive respect—you'll be a good-natured man."

Fabrizio delighted in the count's society. He was the first superior man who had condescended to converse with him seriously, and, further, they had a taste in common—that for antiques and excavations. The count, on his side, was flattered by the extreme deference with which the young man listened to him, but there was one capital objection—Fabrizio occupied rooms in the Palazzo Sanseverina; he spent his life with the duchess, and let it appear, in all innocence, that this intimacy constituted his great happiness, and Fabrizio's eyes and skin were distressingly brilliant.

For a long time Ranuzio-Ernest IV, who seldom came across an unaccommodating fair, had been nettled by the fact that the duchess, whose virtue was well known at court, had made no exception in his favour. As we have seen, Fabrizio's intelligence and presence of mind had displeased him from the very outset; he looked askance at the extreme affection, somewhat imprudently displayed, between aunt and nephew. He listened with excessive attention to the comments of his courtiers, which were endless. The young man's arrival, and the extraordinary audience granted him, were the talk and astonishment of the court for a good month. Whereupon the prince had an idea.

In his guard there was a private soldier who could carry his wine in the most admirable manner. This man spent his life in taverns, and reported the general spirit of the military direct to the sovereign. Carlone lacked education, otherwise he would long ago have been promoted. His orders were to be in the palace every day when the great clock struck noon.

The Chartreuse of Parma

The prince himself went a little before noon to arrange something about the sun-blind in a room on the mezzanine connected with the apartment in which his Highness dressed. He returned to this room a little after noon had struck, and found the soldier there. The prince had a sheet of paper and an ink-bottle in his pocket. He dictated the following note to the soldier:

"Your Excellency is a very clever man, no doubt, and it is thanks to your deep wisdom that we see this state so well governed. But, my dear count, such great successes can not be obtained without rousing a little envy, and I greatly fear there may be some laughter at your expense, if your sagacity does not guess that a certain handsome young man has had the good fortune to inspire, in spite of himself, it may be, a most extraordinary passion. This fortunate mortal is, we are told, only twenty-three years of age, and, dear count, what complicates the question is that you and I are much more than double that. In the evening, and at a certain distance, the count is delightful, sprightly, a man of wit, as charming as he can be; but in the morning, and in close intimacy, the newcomer may, if we look at matters closely, prove more attractive. Now, we women think a great deal of that freshness of youth, especially when we ourselves are past thirty. Is there not talk already of settling the charming young man at our court in some great position? and who may the person be who most constantly mentions the subject to your Excellency?"

The prince took the letter and gave the soldier two crowns.

"These over and above your pay," he said, with a gloomy look. "You will keep absolute silence to everybody, or you will go to the dampest of the lower dungeons in the citadel."

In his writing-table the prince kept a collection of envelopes addressed to the majority of the people about his court by the hand of this same soldier, who was supposed not to know how to write, and never did write even his police reports. The prince chose out the envelope he wanted.

A few hours later Count Mosca received a letter through the post. The probable hour of its arrival had been carefully calculated, and at the moment when the postman, who had been seen to go in with a letter in his hand, emerged from the minister's palace, Mosca was summoned to the presence of his Highness. Never had the favourite appeared wrapped in so black a melancholy. To enjoy it more thoroughly the prince called out as he entered: " I want to divert myself by gossiping with my friend, not to work with my minister. I am enjoying the most frightful headache tonight, and I feel depressed into the bargain."

Must I describe the abominable temper that raged in the breast of Count Mosca della Rovere, Prime Minister of Parma, when he was at last permitted to take leave of his august master? Ranuzio-Ernest IV possessed a finished skill in the art of torturing the human heart, and I should not do him much injustice if I were to compare him here with a tiger who delights in playing with his victim.

The count had himself driven home at a gallop, called out that not a soul was to be admitted, sent word to the auditor in waiting that he was dismissed (the very thought of a human being within hearing distance of his voice was odious to him), and shut himself up in his great picture gallery. There, at last, he could give rein to all his fury, and there he spent his evening, walking to and fro in the dark, like a man beside himself. He tried to silence his heart, so as to concentrate all the strength of his attention on the course he should pursue. Plunged in an anguish which would have stirred the pity of his bitterest enemy, he mused: " The man I hate lives with the duchess, spends every moment of his time with her. Must I try to make one of her women speak? Nothing could be more dangerous— she is so kind, she pays them well, they adore her (and who, great God! does not adore her?). Here lies the question," he began again passionately. " Must I let her guess the jealousy which devours me, or must I hide it?

" If I hold my peace, no attempt at concealment will

be made. I know Gina; she is a woman who always follows her first impulse; her behaviour is unforeseen even by herself; if she tries to trace out a plan beforehand, she grows confused; at the moment of action some new idea always occurs to her, which she follows delightedly as being the best in the world, and which ruins everything.

"If I say nothing of my martyrdom, then nothing is hidden from me, and I see everything which may happen.

"Yes, but if I speak, I call other circumstances into existence; I make them reflect, I prevent many of the horrible things which may happen. . . . Perhaps he will be sent away " (the count drew a breath). " Then I shall almost have won my cause. Even if there were a little temper at first, I could calm that down. . . . And if there were temper, what could be more natural? . . . She has loved him like a son for the last fifteen years. There lies all my hope— *like a son!* . . . But she has not seen him since he ran away to Waterloo; but when he came back from Naples, to her, especially, he was a different man! *A different man!*" he reiterated furiously, "and a charming man, too! Above all, he has that tender look and smiling eye which give so much promise of happiness. And the duchess can not be accustomed to seeing such eyes at our court. Their place is taken here by glances that are either dreary or sardonic. I myself, worried by business, ruling by sheer influence only, over a man who would fain turn me into ridicule— what eyes must I often have! Ah, whatever care I take, it is my eyes, after all, that must have grown old. Is not my very laughter always close on irony? . . . I will go further —for here I must be sincere—does not my merriment betray its close association with absolute power and . . . wickedness? Do not I say to myself, sometimes—especially when I am exasperated—' I can do what I choose '? And I even add a piece of foolishness—' I must be happier than others, because in three matters out of four I possess what others have not, sovereign power. . . . Well, then, let me be just. This habit of thought must spoil my smile—must give me a look of satisfied selfishness. . . . And how charming is that smile of his! It breathes the easy happiness of early youth, and sheds that happiness around him."

Unfortunately for the count, the weather that evening was hot, oppressive, close on a thunder-storm—the sort of weather, in a word, which in those countries inclines men to extreme resolves. How can I reproduce all the arguments, all the views of what had happened to him, which for three mortal hours tortured the passionate-hearted man? At last prudent counsels prevailed, solely as a result of this reflection: "In all probability I am out of my mind. When I think I am arguing I am not arguing at all. I am only turning about in search of a less cruel position, and I may pass by some decisive reason without perceiving it. As the excess of my suffering blinds me, let me follow that rule approved by all wise men, which is called *prudence*.

"Besides, once I have spoken the fatal word *jealousy*, my line is marked out for good and all. If, on the contrary, I say nothing to-day, I can always speak to-morrow, and everything remains in my hands." The excitement had been too violent; the count would have lost his reason if it had lasted. He had a moment's relief—his attention had just fixed itself on the anonymous letter. Whence could it come? Hereupon supervened a search for names, and a verdict on each as it occurred, which created a diversion. At last the count recollected the spiteful flash in the sovereign's eye when he had said, toward the close of the audience: "Yes, dear friend, there can be no doubt that the pleasures and cares of the most fortunate ambition, and even of unlimited power, are nothing compared with the inner happiness to be found in the relations of a tender and loving intercourse. Myself, I am a man before I am a prince, and when I am so happy as to love, it is the man, and not the prince, that my mistress knows."

The count compared that twinkle of spiteful pleasure with the words in the letter, "*It is thanks to your deep wisdom that we see this state so well governed.*"

"The prince wrote that sentence!" he exclaimed. "It is too gratuitously imprudent for any courtier. The letter comes from his Highness."

The Chartreuse of Parma

That problem once solved, the flush of satisfaction caused by the pleasure of guessing it soon faded before the cruel picture of Fabrizio's charms, which once more rose up before him. It was as though a huge weight had fallen back upon the heart of the unhappy man. "What matters it who wrote the anonymous letter?" he cried in his fury. "Does it make the fact it reveals to me any less true? This whim may change my whole life," he added, as though to excuse his own excitement. "At any moment, if she cares for him in a certain way, she may start off with him to Belgirate, to Switzerland, or to any other corner of the world. She is rich, and, besides, if she had only a few louis a year to live on, what would that matter to her? Did she not tell me, only a week ago, that she was tired of her palace, well arranged and magnificent as it is? That youthful nature must have novelty! And how simply this new happiness offers itself to her! She will be swept away before she has thought of the danger—before she has thought of pitying me! and yet I am so wretched!" he exclaimed, bursting into tears.

He had sworn he would not go to see the duchess that evening, but he could not resist the temptation. Never had his eyes so thirsted for the sight of her. About midnight he entered her rooms. He found her alone with her nephew. At ten o'clock she had dismissed all her company and closed her doors.

At the sight of the tender intimacy between the two, and the unaffected delight of the duchess, a frightful difficulty, and an unexpected one, rose up before the count's eyes; he had not thought of it during his lengthy ponderings in the picture gallery. *How* was he to conceal his jealousy?

Not knowing what pretext to adopt, he pretended he had found the prince exceedingly prejudiced against him that evening, contradicting everything he said, and so forth. He had the pain of perceiving that the duchess hardly listened to him, and paid no attention to circumstances which only two nights before would have led her into a whole train of argument. The count looked at Fabrizio. Never had that handsome Lombard countenance seemed to him so simple and so noble. Fabrizio was paying much more attention than the duchess to the difficulties he was relating.

"Really," said he to himself, "that face combines extreme kind-heartedness with a certain expression of tender and artless delight which is quite irresistible. It seems to say, 'The only serious matters in this world are love and the happiness it brings.' And yet if any detail which demands intelligence occurs, his eye kindles, and one is quite astonished and amazed.

"In his eyes everything is simple, because everything is sent from above. My God, how am I to struggle against such an enemy? And after all, what will my life be without Gina's love? With what delight she seems to listen to the charming sallies of that young intellect, which, to a woman's mind, must seem unique!"

A frightful thought clutched the count like a cramp. "Shall I stab him there, in her sight, and kill myself afterward?" He walked up and down the room; his legs were shaking under him, but his hand closed convulsively upon the handle of his dagger. Neither of the others were paying any attention to him. He said he was going to give an order to his servant. They did not even hear him; the duchess was laughing fondly at something Fabrizio had just said to her. The count went under a lamp in the outer drawing-room, and looked to see whether the point of his dagger was sharp. "My manner to the young man must be gracious and perfectly polite," he thought, as he returned and drew close to them.

His brain was boiling. They seemed to him to be bending forward and exchanging kisses there in his very sight. "That is not possible under my eyes," he thought. "My reason is going. I must compose myself. If I am rough the duchess is capable, out of sheer pique to her vanity, of following him to Belgirate, and there, or during the journey, a chance word may give a name to what they feel for each other; and then, in a moment, all the consequences must come.

"Solitude will make that one word decisive, and besides, what is to become of me once the duchess is far away from me? And if, after a great many difficulties with the prince, I should go and show my aged and careworn face at Belgirate, what part should I play between those two in their delirious happiness?

" Even here, what am I but the *terzo incommodo* (our beautiful Italian language was made for the purposes of love)! *Terzo incommodo* (the third party, in the way)! What anguish for a man of parts to feel himself in this vile position, and not to have strength of mind to get up and go away!"

The count was on the point of breaking out, or at all events of betraying his suffering by the disorder of his countenance. As he walked round the drawing-room, finding himself close to the door, he took to flight, calling out, in good-natured and friendly fashion, " Good-bye, you two!—I must not shed blood," he murmured to himself.

On the morrow of that horrible evening, after a night spent partly in revolving Fabrizio's advantages, and partly in the agonizing paroxysms of the most cruel jealousy, it occurred to the count to send for a young man-servant of his own. This man was making love to a girl named Cecchina, one of the duchess's waiting-maids, and her favourite. By good luck, this young servant was exceedingly steady in his conduct, even stingy, and was anxious to be appointed doorkeeper in one of the public buildings at Parma. The count ordered this man to send instantly for Cecchina. The man obeyed, and an hour later the count appeared unexpectedly in the room occupied by the girl and her lover. The count alarmed them both by the quantity of gold coins he gave them; then, looking into the trembling Cecchina's eyes, he addressed her in the following words: " Are there love passages between the duchess and monsignore?"

" No," said the girl, making up her mind after a moment's silence. " No, *not yet*; but he often kisses the signora's hands. He laughs, I know, but he kisses them passionately."

This testimony was borne out by a hundred answers to as many questions put by the distracted count. His passionate anxiety ensured the poor folks honest earning of the money he had given them. He ended by believing what they told him, and felt less wretched. " If ever the duchess suspects this conversation of ours," he said to Cecchina, " I will send your lover to spend twenty years in the fortress, and you will never see him again till his hair is white."

A few days went by, during which it became Fabrizio's turn to lose all his cheerfulness.

" I assure you," he kept saying to the duchess, " Count Mosca has an antipathy to me."

" So much the worse for his Excellency! " she replied with a touch of peevishness.

This was not the real cause of the anxiety which had driven away Fabrizio's gaiety. " The position," he mused, " in which chance has placed me is untenable. I am quite sure she will never speak—a too significant word would be as horrifying to her as an act of incest. But supposing that one evening, after a day of imprudence and folly, she should examine her own conscience! What will my position be if she believes I have guessed at the inclination she seems to feel toward me? I shall simply be the casto Giuseppe " (an Italian proverb alluding to Joseph's ridiculous position with regard to the wife of the eunuch Potiphar).

" Shall I make her understand by confiding to her frankly that I am quite incapable of any serious passion? My ideas are not sufficiently well ordered to enable me to express the fact so as to prevent its appearing a piece of deliberate impertinence. My only other resource is to simulate a great devotion for a lady left behind me in Naples, and in that case I must go back there for four-and-twenty hours. This plan is a wise one, but what a trouble it will be! I might try some obscure little love affair here at Parma. This might cause displeasure, but anything is preferable to the horrible position of the man who will not understand. This last expedient may, indeed, compromise my future. I must try to diminish that danger by my prudence, and by buying discretion." The cruel thought, amid all these considerations, was that Fabrizio really cared for the duchess far more than he did for anybody else in the world. " I must be awkward indeed," said he to himself angrily, " if I am so afraid of not being able to convince her of what is really true."

He had not wit to extricate himself from the difficulty, and he soon grew gloomy and morose. " What would become of me, great heavens, if I were to quarrel with the only being on earth to whom I am passionately attached ? "

On the other hand, Fabrizio could not make up his mind to disturb so delightful a condition of felicity by an imprudent word. His position was so full of enjoyment, his intimate relations with so charming and so pretty a woman were so delightful! As regarded the more trivial aspects of life, her protection insured him such an agreeable position at the court, the deep intrigues of which, thanks to the explanations she gave him, amused him like a stage play. " But at any moment," he reflected, " I may be wakened as by a thunderclap. If one of these evenings, so cheerful and affectionate, spent alone with this fascinating woman, should lead to anything more fervent, she will expect to find a lover in me. She will look for raptures and wild transports, and all I can ever give her is the liveliest affection, without any love. Nature has bereft me of the capacity for that sort of sublime madness. What reproaches I have had to endure on that score already! I fancy I still hear the Duchess of A——, and I could laugh at the duchess! But she will think that I fail in love for her, whereas it is love which fails in me; and she never will understand me. Often, when she has told me some story about the court, with all the grace and frolicsomeness that she alone possesses—and a story, besides, which it is indispensable for me to know—I kiss her hands and sometimes her cheek as well. What should I do if her hand pressed mine in one particular way ? "

Fabrizio showed himself daily in the most esteemed and dullest houses in Parma. Guided by his aunt's wise counsels, he paid skilful court to the two princes, father and son, to the Princess Clara Paolina, and to the archbishop. Success came to him, but this did not console him for his mortal terror of a misunderstanding with the duchess.

CHAPTER VIII

Thus, only a month after his arrival at court, Fabrizio was acquainted with all the worries of a courtier, and the intimate friendship which had been the happiness of his life was poisoned. One evening, harassed by these thoughts, he left the duchess's apartments, where he looked far too much like the reigning lover, and, wandering aimlessly through the town, happened to pass by the theatre, which was lighted up. He went in. This, for a man of his cloth, was a piece of gratuitous imprudence, and one he had fully intended to avoid while at Parma, which, after all, is only a small town of forty thousand inhabitants. It is true, indeed, that from the first days of his residence there he had put aside his official dress, and in the evenings, unless he was going to very large parties, he wore plain black, like any man in mourning.

At the theatre he took a box on the third tier, so as not to be seen. The piece was Goldoni's "Locandiera." He was looking at the architecture of the house, and had hardly turned his eyes upon the stage. But the numerous audience was in a state of constant laughter. Fabrizio glanced at the young actress who was playing the part of the Locandiera, and thought her droll; he looked at her more attentively, and she struck him as being altogether pretty, and, above all, exceedingly natural. She was a simple young creature, the first to laugh at the pretty things Goldoni had put into her mouth, which seemed to astonish her as she spoke them. He inquired her name, and was told it was Marietta Valserra.

"Ah," thought he to himself, " she has taken my name! How odd!" Contrary to his intention, he did not leave the theatre until the play was over. The next day he came back.

Three days after that he had found out where Marietta Valserra lived.

On the very evening of the day on which, with a good deal of difficulty, he had procured this address, he noticed that the count looked at him in the most pleasant manner. The poor jealous lover, who had hard work to restrain himself within the bounds of prudence, had set spies upon the young man's conduct, and was delighted at his freak for the actress. How shall I describe the count's delight when, the day after that on which he had been able to force himself to be gracious to Fabrizio, he learned that the young man—partly disguised, indeed, in a long blue overcoat—had climbed to the wretched apartment on the fourth floor of an old house behind the theatre, in which Marietta Valserra lived. His delight increased twofold when he knew that Fabrizio had presented himself under a false name, and was honoured by the jealousy of a good-for-nothing fellow of the name of Giletti, who played third-rate servants' parts in the city, and danced on the tight rope in the neighbouring villages. This noble lover of Marietta's was heaping volleys of abuse on Fabrizio, and vowed he would kill him.

Opera companies are formed by an impresario, who engages the artists he can afford to pay, or finds disengaged, from all quarters, and the company thus collected by chance remains together for a season or two, at the outside. This is not the case with comedy companies. These, though they move about from town to town, and change their place of residence every two or three months, continue, nevertheless, as one family, the members of which either love or hate each other. These companies frequently comprise couples, living in constant and close relations, which the beaux of the towns in which they occasionally perform find it very difficult to break up. This is exactly what happened to our hero. Little Marietta liked him well enough, but she was horribly afraid of Giletti, who claimed to be her lord and master, and kept a close eye upon her. He openly declared that he would kill the monsignore, for he had dogged Fabrizio's steps, and had succeeded in finding out his name.

The Chartreuse of Parma

This Giletti was certainly the most hideous of beings, and the least attractive imaginable as a lover. He was enormously tall, hideously thin, deeply pitted with small-pox, and had something of a squint into the bargain. Notwithstanding this, he was full of the graces peculiar to his trade, and would make his entry on the wings, where his comrades were assembled, turning wheels on his hands and feet, or performing some other pleasing trick. His great parts were those in which the actor appears with his face whitened with flour, and receives or inflicts innumerable blows with a stick. This worthy rival of Fabrizio's received a salary of thirty-two francs a month, and thought himself very well off indeed.

To Count Mosca it was as though he had been brought back from the gates of the tomb, when his watchers brought him the proofs of all these details. His good-nature reasserted itself; he was gayer and better company than ever in the duchess's rooms, and took good care not to tell her anything of the little adventure which had restored him to life. He even took precautions to prevent her hearing anything of what was happening until the latest possible moment; and finally, he gathered courage to listen to his reason, which for a month had been vainly assuring him that whenever a lover's merits fade, that lover should take a journey.

Important business summoned him to Bologna, and twice a day the cabinet couriers brought him, not so much the necessary papers from his offices, as news of little Marietta's amours, of the redoubtable Giletti's fury, and of Fabrizio's undertakings.

Several times over one of the count's agents bespoke performances of " Arlecchino scelettro e pasta," one of Giletti's triumphs (he emerges from the pie just as his rival Brighella is going to eat it, and thrashes him soundly). This made a pretext for sending him a hundred francs. Giletti, who was over head and ears in debt, took good care to say nothing about this windfall, but his pride reached an astonishing pitch.

What had been a whim in Fabrizio's case, now became a

matter of piqued vanity. (Young as he was, his anxieties had already driven him to indulge in *whims*.) His vanity led him to the theatre; the little girl acted very well and amused him. When the play was over he was in love for quite an hour. The count, receiving news that Fabrizio was in real danger, returned to Parma. Giletti, who had served as a dragoon in the fine "Napoleon" regiment, was seriously talking of murdering Fabrizio, and was making arrangements for his subsequent flight into the Romagna. If my reader be very young, he will be scandalized by my admiration for this fine trait of virtue. Yet it involved no small effort of heroism on the count's part to leave Bologna. For too often, indeed, in the mornings, his complexion looked sorely jaded, and Fabrizio's was so fresh and pleasant to look at! Who could have reproached him with Fabrizio's death if it had occurred in his absence, and on account of so foolish a business? But to his rare nature, the thought of a generous action, which he might have done, and which he had not performed, would have been an eternal remorse; and, further, he could not endure the idea of seeing the duchess sad, and by his fault.

When he arrived, he found her taciturn and gloomy. This is what had happened. Her little maid Cecchina, tormented by remorse and gauging the importance of her own fault by the large sum she had been paid for committing it, had fallen sick. One night the duchess, who had a real regard for her, went up to her room. The young girl could not resist this mark of kindness. She burst into tears, begged her mistress to take back the money still remaining to her out of what she had received, and at last gathered courage to tell her the story of the count's questions and her own replies. The duchess ran across to the lamp and put it out. Then she told Cecchina that she would forgive her, but only on condition that she never said a word about the strange scene to anybody on earth. "The poor count," she added carelessly, "is afraid of looking ridiculous—all men are alike."

The duchess hurried down to her own apartments. She had hardly shut herself into her own room before she burst into tears. The idea of love passages with Fabrizio, at whose birth she had been present, was horrible to her, and yet what other meaning could her conduct bear?

Such had been the first cause of the black depression in which the count found her plunged. When he arrived, she had fits of impatience with him, and almost with Fabrizio; she would have liked never to have seen either of them again. She was vexed by Fabrizio's behaviour with little Marietta, which seemed to her ridiculous. For the count—who, like a true lover, could keep nothing from his mistress—had told her the whole story. She could not grow accustomed to this disaster; there was a flaw in her idol. At last, in a moment of confidence, she asked the count's advice. It was an exquisite instant for him, and a worthy reward for the upright impulse which had brought him back to Parma.

"What can be more simple?" said the count, with a smile. "These young fellows fall in love with every woman they see, and the next morning they have forgotten all about her. Ought he not to go to Belgirate to see the Marchesa del Dongo? Very well, then. Let him start. While he is away I shall request the comedy company to remove itself and its talents elsewhere, and will pay its travelling expenses. But we shall soon see him in love again with the first pretty woman chance may throw across his path. That is the natural order of things, and I would not have it otherwise. If it is necessary, let the marchesa write to him."

This suggestion, emitted with an air of the most complete indifference, was a ray of light to the duchess; she was afraid of Giletti.

That evening the count mentioned, as though by chance, that one of his couriers was about to pass through Milan on his way to Vienna.

Three days later Fabrizio received a letter from his mother.

He departed, very much annoyed because Giletti's jealousy had hitherto prevented him from taking advantage of the friendly feelings of which Marietta had assured him through her *mamaccia*, an old woman who performed the functions of her mother.

Fabrizio met his mother and one of his sisters at Belgirate, a large Piedmontese village on the right bank of the Lago Maggiore. The left bank is in Milanese territory, and consequently belongs to Austria.

This lake, which is parallel to the Lake of Como, and, like it, runs from north to south, lies about thirty miles farther westward. The mountain air, the calm and majestic aspect of the splendid lake, which recalled that near which he had spent his childhood, all contributed to change Fabrizio's annoyance, which had verged upon anger, into a gentle melancholy. The memory of the duchess rose up before him, clothed with infinite tenderness. It seemed to him, now he was far from her, that he was beginning to love her with that love which he had never yet felt for any woman. Nothing could have been more painful to him than the thought of being parted from her forever, and if, while he was in this frame of mind, the duchess had condescended to the smallest coquetry—such, for example, as giving him a rival—she would have conquered his heart.

But far from taking so decisive a step, she could not help reproaching herself bitterly because her thoughts hovered so constantly about the young traveller's path. She upbraided herself for what she still called a fancy, as if it had been an abomination. Her kindness and attention to the count increased twofold, and he, bewitched by all these charms, could not listen to the healthy reason which prescribed a second trip to Bologna.

The Marchesa del Dongo, greatly hurried by the arrangements for the wedding of her eldest daughter with a Milanese duke, could only spend three days with her beloved son. Never had she found him so full of tender affection. Amid the melancholy which was taking stronger and yet stronger hold of Fabrizio's soul, a strange and even absurd idea had presented itself to him, and was forthwith carried into effect. Dare we say he was bent on consulting Father Blanès? The good old man was perfectly incapable of understanding the sorrows of a heart torn by various boyish passions of almost equal strength; and besides, it would have taken a week to give him even a faint idea of the various interests at Parma which Fabrizio was forced to consider. Yet when Fabrizio thought of consulting him, all the fresh feelings of his sixteenth year came back to him. Shall I be believed when I affirm that it was not simply to the wise man and the absolutely faithful friend that Fabrizio longed to speak? The object of this excursion and the feelings which agitated our hero all through the fifty hours of its duration are so absurd, that for the sake of my story I should doubtless do better to suppress them. I fear Fabrizio's credulity may deprive him of the reader's sympathy. But thus he was. Why should I flatter him more than another? I have not flattered Count Mosca nor the prince.

Fabrizio, then, if the truth must be told, accompanied his mother to the port of Laveno, on the left bank of the Lago Maggiore, the Austrian side, where she landed about eight o'clock at night. (The lake itself is considered neutral, and no passports are asked of any one who does not land.) But darkness had hardly fallen before he, too, had himself put ashore on that same Austrian bank, in a little wood which juts out into the water. He had hired a *sediola*—a sort of country gig which travels very fast—in which he was able to follow about five hundred paces behind his mother's carriage. He was disguised as a servant belonging to the Casa del Dongo, and none of the numerous police or customs officers thought of asking him for his passport. A quarter of a league from Como, where the Marchesa del Dongo and her daughter were to spend the night, he took a path to the left, which, after running round the village of Vico, joined a narrow newly made road along the very edge of the lake. It was midnight, and Fabrizio had reason to hope he would not meet any gendarmes. The black outline of the foliage on the clumps of trees through which the road constantly passed stood out against a starry sky, just veiled by a light mist. A profound stillness hung over the waters and the sky. Fabrizio's soul could not resist this sublime beauty; he stopped and seated himself on a rock which jutted out into the lake and formed a little promontory. Nothing broke the universal silence, save the little waves that died out at regular intervals upon the beach. Fabrizio had the heart of an Italian. I beg the fact may be forgiven him. This drawback, which will make him less attractive, consisted, above all, in the following fact: he was only vain by fits and starts, and the very sight of sublime beauty filled his heart with emotion, and blunted the keen and cruel edge of his sorrows. Sitting on his lonely rock, no longer forced to keep watch against police agents, sheltered by the darkness of the night and the vast silence, soft tears rose in his eyes, and he enjoyed, at very little cost, the happiest moments he had known for many a day.

He resolved he would never tell a lie to the duchess; and it was because he loved her to adoration at that moment that he swore an oath never to tell her that he *loved her*; never would he drop into her ear that word *love*, because the passion to which the name is given had never visited his heart. In the frenzy of generosity and virtue which made him feel so happy at that moment, he resolved, on the earliest opportunity, to tell her the whole truth—that his heart had never known what love might be. Once this bold decision had been adopted, he felt as though a huge weight had been lifted off him. " Perhaps she will say something to me about Marietta. Very good; then I will never see little Marietta again," he answered his own thought, joyously.

The morning breeze was beginning to temper the overwhelming heat which had prevailed the whole day long. The dawn was already outlining the Alpine peaks which rise over the northern and eastern shores of the Lake of Como with a pale faint light. Their masses, white with snow, even in the month of June, stand out sharply against the clear blue of a sky which, at those great heights, no cloud ever dims. A spur of the Alps running southward toward the favoured land of Italy separates the slopes of Como from those of Garda. Fabrizio's eye followed all the branchings of the noble range; the dawn, as it drove away the light mists rising from the gorges, revealed the valleys lying between.

He had resumed his way some minutes previously; he climbed the hill which forms the Durini promontory, and at last his eyes beheld the church tower of Grianta, from which he had so often watched the stars with Father Blanès. " How crassly ignorant I was in those days!" he thought. " I couldn't even understand the absurd Latin of the astrological treatises my master thumbed; and I believe the chief reason of my respect for them was that, as I only comprehended a word here and there, my imagination undertook to supply their meaning after the most romantic fashion."

Gradually his reverie wandered into another direction. Was there anything real about this science? Why should it be different from others? A certain number of fools and of clever people, for instance, agree between themselves that they understand the Mexican language. By this means they impose on society, which respects them, and on governments, who pay them. They are loaded with favours, just because they are stupid, and because the people in power need not fear their disturbing the populace, and stirring interest and pity by their generous sentiments. " Look at Father Bari, on whom Ernest IV has just bestowed a pension of four thousand francs and the cross of his order, for having reconstituted nineteen lines of a Greek dithyramb!

" But, after all, what right have I to think such things absurd? " he exclaimed of a sudden, stopping short. " Has not that very same cross been given to my own tutor? " Fabrizio felt profoundly uncomfortable. The noble passion for virtue which had lately thrilled his heart was being transformed into the mean satisfaction of enjoying a good share in the proceeds of a robbery. " Well," said he at last, and his eyes grew dim as the eyes of a man who is discontented with himself, " since my birth gives me a right to profit by these abuses, I should be an arrant fool if I did not take my share; but I must not venture to speak evil of them in public places." This argument was not devoid of sense, but Fabrizio had fallen a long way below the heights of sublime delight on which he had hovered only an hour before. The thought of his privileges had scorched that always delicate plant which men call happiness.

" If I must not believe in astrology," he went on, making an effort to divert his thoughts, " if, like three-fourths of the non-mathematical sciences, this one is no more than an association of enthusiastic simpletons with clever humbugs, paid by those they serve, how comes it that I dwell so often, and with so much emotion, upon that fatal episode? I did escape, long since, from the jail at B——, but I was wearing the clothes and using the papers of a soldier who had been justly cast into prison."

Fabrizio's reasoning would never carry him any farther than this. He revolved the difficulty in a hundred ways, but he never could surmount it. He was too young as yet. During his leisure moments, his soul was steeped in the delight of tasting the sensations arising out of the romantic circumstances with which his imagination was always ready to supply him. He by no means employed his time in patiently considering the real peculiarities of things, and then discovering their causes. Reality still seemed to him dull and dirty. I can conceive its not being pleasant to look at. But then one should not argue about it. Above all things, one should not put forward one's own various forms of ignorance as objections.

Thus it was that, though Fabrizio was no fool, he was not able to realize that his half belief in omens really was a religion, a profound impression received at his entrance into life. The thought of this belief was a sensation and a happiness, and he obstinately endeavoured to discover how it might be *proved* a science which really did exist, like that of geometry, for instance. He eagerly ransacked his memory for the occasions on which the omens he had observed had not been followed by the happy or unfortunate event they had appeared to prognosticate. But though he believed himself to be following out a course of argument, and so drawing nearer to the truth, his memory dwelt with delight on those cases in which the omen had, on the whole, been followed by the accident, good or evil, which he had believed it to foretell, and his soul was filled with emotion and respect. And he would have felt an invincible repugnance toward any one who denied the existence of such signs, more especially if he had spoken of them jestingly.

The Chartreuse of Parma

Fabrizio had been walking along without any regard for distance, and he had reached this point in his powerless arguments when, raising his head, he found himself confronted by the wall of his own father's garden. This wall, which supported a fine terrace, rose more than forty feet above the road, on the right-hand side. A course of dressed stone, running along the top, close to the balustrade, gave it a monumental appearance. "It's not bad," said Fabrizio coldly to himself. "The architecture is good; very nearly Roman in style." He was applying his new antiquarian knowledge. Then he turned away in disgust—his father's severity and, above all, his brother Ascanio's denunciation after his return from France, came back to his mind.

"That unnatural denunciation has been the origin of my present way of life. I may hate it, I may scorn it, but, after all, it has changed my fate. What would have become of me once I had been sent to Novara, where my father's man of business could hardly endure the sight of me, if my aunt had not fallen in love with a powerful minister? and then, if that same aunt had possessed a hard and unfeeling nature, instead of that tender passionate heart which loves me with a sort of frenzy that astounds me? Where should I be now if the duchess had been like her brother, the Marchese del Dongo?"

Lost in these bitter memories, Fabrizio had been walking aimlessly forward. He reached the edge of the moat, just opposite the splendid façade of the castle. He scarcely cast a glance at the huge time-stained building. The noble language of its architecture fell on deaf ears; the memory of his father and his brother shut every sensation of beauty out of his heart. His only thought was that he must be on his guard in the presence of a dangerous and hypocritical enemy. For an instant, but in evident disgust, he glanced at the little window of the third-floor room he had occupied before 1815. His father's treatment had wiped all the charm out of his memories of early days. "I have never been back in it," he thought, "since eight o'clock at night on that seventh of March. I left it to get the passport from Vasi, and the next morning, in my terror of spies, I hurried on my departure. When I came back, after my journey to France, I had not time even to run up and look once at my prints; and all that thanks to my brother's accusation."

Fabrizio turned away his head in horror. " Father Blanès is more than eighty-three now," he mused sadly; " he hardly ever comes to the castle, so my sister tells me. The infirmities of years have laid their hand upon him; that noble steady heart is frozen by old age. God knows how long it may be since he has been in his tower! I'll hide myself in his cellar, under the vats or the wine-press, until he wakes; I will not disturb the good old man's slumbers! Probably he will even have forgotten my face—six years makes so much difference at my age. I shall find nothing but the shell of my old friend. And it really is a piece of childishness," he added, " to have come here to face the odious sight of my father's house."

Fabrizio had just entered the little square in front of the church. It was with an astonishment that almost reached delirium that he saw the long, narrow window on the second story of the ancient tower lighted up by Father Blanès's little lantern. It was the father's custom to place it there when he went up to the wooden cage which formed his observatory, so that the light might not prevent him from reading his planisphere. This map of the sky was spread out on a huge earthenware vase, which had once stood in the castle orangery. In the orifice at the bottom of the vase was the tiniest of lamps, the smoke of which was carried out of the vase by a slender tin tube, and the shadow cast by this tube on the map marked the north. All these memories of simple little things flooded Fabrizio's soul with emotion and filled it with happiness.

Almost unthinkingly he raised his two hands and gave the little low, short whistle which had once been the signal for his admission. At once he heard several pulls at the cord running from the observatory, which controlled the latch of the tower door. In a transport of emotion he bounded up the stairs and found the father sitting in his accustomed place in his wooden arm-chair. His eye was fixed on the little telescope. With his left hand the father signed to him not to interrupt his observation. A moment afterward he noted down a figure on a playing card; then, turning in his chair, he held out his arms to our hero, who cast himself into them, bursting into tears. The Abbé Blanès was his real father.

" I was expecting you," said Blanès when the first outburst of tenderness had subsided. Was the abbé posing as a wise man, or was it that thinking of Fabrizio so often as he did, some astrological sign had warned him, by a mere chance, of his return?

" The hour of my death draws near," said Father Blanès.

" What! " exclaimed Fabrizio, much affected.

" Yes," returned the father, and his tone was serious, but not sad. " Five months and a half, or six months and a half, after I have seen you again, my life, which will have attained its full measure of happiness, will fade out, ' *come face al mancar dell'alimento* ' " (even as the little lamp when the oil fails in it).

" Before the closing moment comes I shall probably be speechless for one month or two. After that I shall be received into our Father's bosom, provided, indeed, that he is satisfied that I have fulfilled my duty at the post where he set me as sentinel.

" You are worn out with weariness, your agitation makes you inclined for sleep. Since I have expected you I have hidden a loaf and a bottle of brandy in the large case which contains my instruments. Support your life with these, and try to gather enough strength to listen to me for a few moments more. I have it in my power to tell you several things before this night has altogether passed into the day. I see them far more distinctly now, than I may, perhaps, see them to-morrow, for, my child, we are always weak, and we must always reckon with this weakness. To-morrow, it may be, the old man, the earthly man, in me, will be making ready for my death, and to-morrow night, at nine o'clock, you must leave me."

When Fabrizio had obeyed him in silence, as was his

wont, " It is true, then," the old man resumed, " that when you tried to see Waterloo, all you found at first was a prison? "

" Yes, father," replied Fabrizio, much astonished.

" Well, that was a rare good fortune, for your soul, warned by my voice, may make itself ready to endure another prison, far more severe, infinitely more terrible. You will probably only leave it through a crime, but, thanks be to Heaven! the crime will not be committed by your hand. Never fall into crime, however desperately you may be tempted. I think I see that there will be some question of your killing an innocent man, who, without knowing it, has usurped your rights. If you resist this violent temptation, which will seem justified by the laws of honour, your life will be very happy in the eyes of men . . . and reasonably happy in the eyes of the wise," he added, after a moment's reflection. " You will die, my son, like me, sitting on a wooden seat, far from all luxury, and undeceived by it. And, like me, without having any serious reproach upon your soul.

" Now future matters are ended between us; I am not able to add anything of much importance. In vain I have sought to know how long your imprisonment will last—whether it will be six months, a year, ten years. I can not discover anything. I must, I suppose, have committed some sin, and it is the will of Heaven to punish me by the sorrow of this uncertainty. I have only seen that after the prison—yet I do not know whether it is at the very moment of your leaving it—there will be what I call a crime; but, happily, I think I may be sure that it will not be committed by you. If you are weak enough to dabble in that crime, all the rest of my calculations are but one long mistake. Then you will not die with peace in your soul, sitting on a wooden chair and dressed in white! " As he spoke these words the father tried to rise, and then it was that Fabrizio became aware of the ravages time had worked on his frame. He took almost a minute to get up and turn toward Fabrizio. The young man stood by, motionless and silent. The father threw himself into his arms, and strained him close to him several times over with the utmost tenderness. Then, with all the old cheerfulness, he said: " Try to sleep in tolerable comfort among my instruments. Take my fur-lined wrappers; you will find several which the Duchess Sanseverina sent me four years ago. She begged me to foretell your future to her, but I took care to do nothing of the kind, though I kept her wrappers and her fine quadrant. Any announcement of future events is an infringement of the rule, and involves this danger—that it may change the event, in which case the whole science falls to the ground, and becomes nothing more than a childish game. And, besides, I should have had to say some hard things to the ever-lovely duchess. By the way, do not let yourself be startled in your sleep by the frightful noise the bells will make in your ear, when they ring for the seven o'clock mass; later on they will begin to sound the big bell on the lower floor, which makes all my instruments rattle. To-day is the feast of San Giovità, soldier and martyr. You know our little village of Grianta has the same patron saint as the great city of Brescia, which, by the way, led my illustrious master, Jacopo Marini, of Ravenna, into a very comical error. Several times over he assured me I should attain a very fair ecclesiastical position; he thought I was to be priest of the splendid Church of San Giovità at Brescia, and I have been priest of a little village numbering seven hundred and fifty souls. But it has all been for the best. I saw, not ten years since, that if I had been priest of Brescia, my fate would have led me to a prison, on a hill in Moravia, the Spielberg. To-morrow I will bring you all sorts of dainty viands, stolen from the great dinner which I am giving to all the neighbouring priests, who are coming to sing in my high mass. I will bring them into the bottom of the tower, but do not try to see me, do not come down to take possession of the good things until you have heard me go out again; you must not see me *by daylight*, and as the sun sets at twenty-seven minutes past seven to-morrow, I shall not come to embrace you till toward eight o'clock. And you must depart while the hours are still counted by nine—that is to say, before the clock has struck ten. Take care you are not seen at the tower windows; the gendarmes hold a description of your person, and they are, in a manner, under the orders of your brother, who is a thorough tyrant. The Marchese del Dongo is breaking," added Blanès sadly, " and if he were to see you, perhaps he would give you something from his hand directly into yours. But such benefits, with the stain of fraud upon them, are not worthy of a man such as you, whose strength one day will be in his conscience. The marchese hates his son Ascanio, and to that son the five or six millions of his property will descend. That is just. When he dies you will have four thousand francs a year, and fifty yards of black cloth for your servants' mourning."

CHAPTER IX

THE old man's discourse, Fabrizio's deep attention to it, and his own excessive weariness, had thrown him into a state of feverish excitement. He found it very difficult to sleep, and his slumber was broken by dreams which may have been omens of the future. At ten o'clock next morning, he was disturbed by the rocking of the tower, and a frightful noise which seemed to be coming from without. Terrified, he leaped to his feet, and thought the end of the world must have come. Then he fancied himself in prison, and it was some time before he recognised the sound of the great bell which forty peasants had set swinging in honour of the great San Giovità. Ten would have done it just as well.

Fabrizio looked about for a place whence he might look on without being seen. He observed that from that great height he could look all over his father's gardens, and even into the inner courtyard of his house. He had forgotten it. The thought of his father, now nearing the close of his life, changed all his feelings toward him. He could even distinguish the sparrows hopping about in search of a few crumbs on the balcony of the great dining-room. "They are the descendants of those I once tamed," he thought. This balcony, like all the others, was adorned with numerous orange trees, set in earthenware vases, large and small. The sight of them touched him. There was an air of great dignity about this inner courtyard, thus adorned, with its sharply cut shadows standing out against the brilliant sunshine.

The thought of his father's failing health came back to him. "It really is very odd!" he said to himself. "My father is only thirty-five years older than I am—thirty-five

171

and twenty-three only make fifty-eight." The eyes which were gazing at the windows of the room occupied by the harsh parent, whom he had never loved, brimmed over with tears. He shuddered, and a sudden chill ran through his veins when he fancied he recognised his father crossing an orange-covered terrace on the level of his chamber. But it was only a man-servant. Just beneath the tower a number of young girls in white dresses, and divided into several groups, were busily outlining patterns in red, blue, and yellow flowers on the soil of the streets along which the procession was to pass. But there was another sight which appealed yet more strongly to Fabrizio's soul. From his tower he could look over the two arms of the lake for a distance of several leagues, and this magnificent prospect soon made him forget every other sight. It stirred the most lofty feelings in his breast. All his childish memories crowded on his brain; and that day spent prisoned in a church tower was perhaps one of the happiest in his life.

His felicity carried him to a frame of thought considerably higher than was as a rule natural to him. Young as he was, he pondered over the events of his past life as though he had already reached its close. "I must acknowledge that never, since I came to Parma," he mused at last, after several hours of the most delightful reverie, "have I known calm and perfect delight such as I used to feel at Naples, when I galloped along the roads of Vomero, or wandered on the coasts of Misena.

" All the complicated interests of that spiteful little court have made me spiteful, too. . . . I find no pleasure in hating anybody; I even think it would be but a poor delight to me to see my enemies humiliated, if I had any. But, hold!" he cried; "I have an enemy—Giletti! Now, it is curious," he went on, " that my pleasure at the idea of seeing that ugly fellow going to the devil should have outlived the very slight fancy I had for little Marietta. . . . She is not to be compared to the Duchess d'A——, to whom I was obliged to make love, at Naples, because I had told her I had fallen in love with her. Heavens, how bored I used to be during those long hours of intimacy with which the fair duchess used to honour me! I never felt anything of that sort in the shabby room—bedroom and kitchen, too—in which little Marietta received me twice, and for two minutes each time!

"And heavens, again! What do those people eat? It was pitiful! I ought to have given her *mamaccia* a pension of three beefsteaks a day. . . . That little Marietta," he added, "distracted me from the wicked thoughts with which the neighbourhood of the court had inspired me.

"Perhaps I should have done better to take up with the *'café* life,' as the duchess calls it. She seemed rather to incline to it, and she is much cleverer than I am. Thanks to her bounty—or even with this income of four thousand francs a year, and the interest of the forty thousand francs invested at Lyons, which my mother intends for me—I should always have been able to keep a horse and to spend a few crowns on making excavations and forming a collection. As I am apparently never destined to know what love is, my greatest pleasures will always lie in that direction. I should like, before I die, to go back once to the battle-field of Waterloo, and try to recognise the meadow where I was lifted from my horse in such comical fashion, and left sitting on the grass. Once that pilgrimage had been performed, I would often come back to this noble lake. There can be nothing so beautiful in the whole world—to my heart, at all events! Why should I wander so far away in search of happiness? It lies here, under my very eyes.

"Ah," said Fabrizio again, "but there is a difficulty—the police forbid my presence near the Lake of Como. But I am younger than the people who direct the police. Here," he added with a laugh, "I shall find no Duchess d'A——, but I should have one of the little girls who are scattering flowers down yonder, and I am sure I should love her just as much. Even in love matters, hypocrisy freezes me, and our fine ladies aim at too much sublimity in their effects. Napoleon has given them notions of propriety and constancy.

"The devil!" he exclaimed a moment later, pulling his

head in suddenly, as if afraid he might be recognised, in spite of the shadow cast by the huge wooden shutters which kept the rain off the bells. " Here come the gendarmes in all their splendour ! " Ten gendarmes, in fact, four of whom were non-commissioned officers, had appeared at the head of the principal street of the village. The sergeant posted them a hundred paces apart, along the line the procession was to follow. " Everybody here knows me. If I am seen, I shall be carried at one bound from the shores of Como to the Spielberg, where I shall have a hundred-and-ten-pound weight of fetters fastened to each of my legs. And what a grief for the duchess ! "

It was two or three minutes before Fabrizio was able to realize that, in the first place, he was eighty feet above other people's heads, that the spot where he stood was compara-tively dark, that anybody who might glance upward would be blinded by the blazing sun, and, last of all, that every eye was staring wide about the village streets, the houses of which had been freshly whitewashed in honour of the feast of San Giovità. In spite of the cogency of these argu-ments, Fabrizio's Italian soul would have been incapable of any further enjoyment if he had not interposed a rag of old sacking, which he nailed up in the window, between himself and the gendarmes, making two holes in it so that he might be able to look out.

The bells had been crashing out for ten minutes, the procession was passing out of the church, the *mortaretti* were exploding loudly. Fabrizio turned his head and looked at the little esplanade, surrounded by a parapet, on which his childish life had so often been endangered by the *mortaretti*, fired off close to his legs, because of which his mother always insisted on keeping him beside her, on feast days.

These *mortaretti* (or little mortars), it should be ex-plained, are nothing but gun barrels sawn off in lengths of about four inches. It is for this purpose that the peas-ants so greedily collect the musket barrels which Euro-pean policy, since the year 1796, has sown broadcast over the plains of Lombardy. When these little tubes are cut into four-inch lengths, they are loaded up to the very muzzle, set on the ground in a vertical position, and a train of powder is laid from one to the other; they are ranged in three lines, like a battalion, to the number of some two or three hundred, in some clear space near the line of procession. When the Holy Sacrament approaches, the train of powder is lighted, and then begins a sharp, dropping fire of the most irregular and ridiculous description, which sends all the women wild with delight. Nothing more cheery can be imagined than the noise of these *mortaretti*, as heard from a distance across the lake, and softened by the rocking of the waters. The curious rattle which had so often been the delight of his childhood put the overserious notions which had assailed our hero to flight. He fetched the Father's big astronomical telescope, and was able to recognise most of the men and women taking part in the procession. Many charming little girls, whom Fabrizio had left behind him as slips of eleven and twelve years old, had now grown into magnificent-looking women, in all the flower of the most healthy youth. The sight of them brought back our hero's courage, and for the sake of exchanging a word with them, he would have braved the gendarmes willingly.

When the procession had passed, and re-entered the church by a side door, which was out of Fabrizio's range of vision, the heat at the top of the tower soon became intense. The villagers returned to their homes, and deep silence fell over the place. Several boats filled with peasants departed to Bellagio, Menaggio, and other villages on the shores of the lake. Fabrizio could distinguish the sound of every stroke of the oars. This detail, simple as it was, threw him into a perfect ecstasy; his delight at that moment was built up on all the unhappiness and discomfort which the complicated life of courts had inflicted upon him. What a pleasure would it have been, at that moment, to row a league's distance over that beautiful calm lake, in which the depths of the heavens were so faithfully reflected! He heard somebody open the door at the bottom of the tower— Father Blanès's old servant, laden with a big basket; it was as much as he could do to refrain from going to speak to her. "She has almost as much affection for me as her master has," he thought. "And I am going away at nine o'clock to-night. Would she not keep silence, as she would swear to me to do, even for those few hours? But," said Fabrizio to himself, "I should displease my friend; I might get him into trouble with the gendarmes." And he let Ghita depart without saying a word to her. He made an excellent dinner, and then lay down to sleep for a few minutes. He did not wake till half-past eight at night. Father Blanès was shaking his arm, and it had grown quite dark.

Blanès was exceedingly weary; he looked fifty years older than on the preceding night; he made no further reference to serious matters. Seating himself in his wooden chair, "Kiss me," he said to Fabrizio. Several times over he clasped him in his arms. At last he spoke: "Death, which will soon end this long life of mine, will not be so painful as this separation. I have a purse which I shall leave in Ghita's care, with orders to use its contents for her own need, but to make over whatever it may contain to you, if you should ever ask her for it. I know her; once I have given her this command she is capable, in her desire to save for you, of not eating meat four times in the year, unless you give her explicit orders on the subject. You may be reduced to penury yourself, and then your old friend's mite may be of service to you. Expect nothing but vile treatment from your brother, and try to earn money by some labour that will make you useful to society. I foresee strange tempests; fifty years hence, perhaps, no idle man will be allowed to live. Your mother and your aunt may fail you; your sisters must obey their husbands' will——" Then suddenly, he cried: "Go! Go! Fly!" He had just heard a little noise in the clock, a warning that it was about to strike ten. He would not even give Fabrizio time for a farewell embrace.

"Make haste! make haste!" he cried. "It will take you at least a minute to get down the stairs. Take care you do not fall; that would be a terrible omen." Fabrizio rushed down the stairs, and once out on the square, he began to run.

He had hardly reached his father's castle before the clock struck ten.

Every stroke echoed in his breast, and filled him with a strange sense of agitation. He paused to reflect, or rather to give rein to the passionate feelings inspired by the contemplation of the majestic edifice at which he had looked so coolly only the night before. His reverie was disturbed by human footsteps; he looked up, and saw himself surrounded by four gendarmes. He had two excellent pistols, the priming of which he had renewed during his dinner; the click he made as he cocked them attracted one of the gendarme's notice, and very nearly brought about his arrest. He recognised his danger, and thought of firing at once. He would have been within his rights, for it was his only chance of resisting four armed men. Fortunately for him, the gendarmes, who were going round to clear the wine-shops, had not treated the civilities offered them in several of these hospitable meeting-places with absolute indifference. They were not sufficiently quick in making up their minds to do their duty. Fabrizio fled at the top of his speed. The gendarmes ran a few steps after him, shouting, "Stop! stop!" Then silence fell on everything once more. Some three hundred paces off Fabrizio stopped to get his breath. "The noise of my pistols very nearly caused my arrest. It would have served me right if the duchess had told me—if ever I had been allowed to look into her beautiful eyes again—that my soul delights in contemplating things that may happen ten years hence, and forgets to look at those which are actually under my nose."

Fabrizio shuddered at the thought of the danger he had just escaped. He hastened his steps, but soon he could not restrain himself from running, which was not over-prudent, for he attracted the attention of several peasants on their homeward way. Yet he could not prevail upon himself to stop till he was on the mountain, over a league from Grianta, and even then he broke into a cold sweat, whenever he thought of the Spielberg.

"I've been in a pretty fright!" said he to himself, and at the sound of the word he felt almost inclined to be ashamed.

" But does not my aunt tell me that the thing I need most is to learn how to forgive myself? I am always comparing myself with a perfect model, which can have no real existence. So be it, then. I will forgive myself my fright, for, on the other hand, I was very ready to defend my liberty, and certainly those four men would not all have been left to take me to prison. What I am doing at this moment," he added, " is not soldierly. Instead of rapidly retiring after having fulfilled my object, and possibly roused my enemy's suspicions, I am indulging a whim which is perhaps more absurd than all the good father's predictions."

And, in fact, instead of returning by the shortest road, and gaining the banks of the Lago Maggiore, where the boat awaited him, he was making a huge detour for the purpose of seeing his tree—my readers will perhaps recollect Fabrizio's affection for a chestnut tree planted by his mother some three-and-twenty years previously. " It would be worthy of my brother," he thought, " if he had had that tree cut down; but such creatures as he have no feeling for delicate matters. He will not have thought of it, and besides," he added resolutely, " it would not be an evil omen." Two hours later there was consternation in his glance; mischievous hands, or a stormy wind, had broken off one of the chief branches of the young tree, and it was hanging withered. With the help of his dagger Fabrizio cut it off carefully, and closely pared the wound, so that the rain might not enter the trunk. Then, though time was very precious to him, for it was nearly dawn, he spent a good hour in digging up the ground round the *beloved tree*. When all these follies were accomplished, he rapidly proceeded on his way toward the Lago Maggiore. He did not feel depressed on the whole; the tree was doing well, it was stronger than ever, and in five years it had almost doubled in size. The broken branch was a mere accident, of no consequence.

Now that it had been lopped off, the tree would not suffer, and would even grow the taller, as its limbs divided at a greater height.

Before Fabrizio had travelled a league, a brilliant strip

of white light in the east outlined the peaks of the Resegon di Lek, a well-known mountain in that country. The road he was now following was full of peasants, but instead of thinking of military matters, Fabrizio was filled with emotion by the sublime or touching aspects of the forest round the Lake of Como. They are perhaps the most lovely in the world. I do not mean those which bring in the greatest number of "*new crowns*," as they say in Switzerland, but those which appeal most strongly to the human soul. For a man in Fabrizio's position, exposed to all the attentions of the gendarmes of Lombardy and Venetia, it was mere childishness to listen to their language. At last he said to himself: "I am half a league from the frontier. I shall meet the customs officers and the gendarmes making their round. This fine cloth coat of mine will rouse their suspicions; they will ask me for my passport. The said passport bears a name doomed to a prison, written in fair characters, and so I find myself under the agreeable necessity of committing murder. If the gendarmes walk two together, as they generally do, I dare not wait till one of them seizes me by the collar before I fire; if he should hold me for one instant before he falls, I shall find myself at the Spielberg."

Fabrizio—filled with a special horror at the idea of firing first, and possibly on an old soldier who had served under his uncle, Count Pietranera—ran to hide himself in the hollow trunk of a huge chestnut tree. He was putting fresh caps into his pistols when he heard a man coming through the wood, singing, as he came, in a charming voice, a delightful air by Mercadante, then fashionable in Italy.

"That's a good omen!" said Fabrizio to himself; he listened attentively to the melody, and the sound of it wiped out the little touch of anger which had begun to season his arguments. He looked carefully up and down the highroad and saw nobody. "The singer will come up some side road," thought he to himself. Almost at that very moment he saw a servant, very neatly dressed in the English style, ride slowly up the road on a hack, leading a very fine blood-horse, perhaps a trifle too thin.

The Chartreuse of Parma

"Ah," said Fabrizio to himself, "if I had reasoned like Mosca, who is perpetually telling me that the risk a man runs always marks the ratio of his rights over his neighbour, I should crack this serving-man's skull with a pistol-shot, and once I was on that horse, I should snap my fingers at all the gendarmes in the world. Then, as soon as I got back to Parma, I would send money to the man or his widow. But that would be an abominable action."

CHAPTER X

EVEN as he moralized, Fabrizio sprang upon the high-road from Lombardy to Switzerland, which, at this spot, is quite four or five feet below the level of the forest. " If my man takes fright," said our hero to himself, " he will start off at a gallop, and I shall be left here, looking a sorry fool." By this time he was not more than ten paces from the servant, who had stopped singing. Fabrizio read in his eyes that he was frightened; perhaps he was going to turn his horses round. Without any conscious intention, Fabrizio made a bound, and seized the near horse by the bridle.

" My friend," said he to the serving-man, " I am not a common thief, for I am going to begin by giving you twenty francs; but I am obliged to borrow your horse. I shall be killed if I do not clear out at once. The four brothers Riva, those great hunters whom you doubtless know, are on my heels. They have just caught me in their sister's bedroom. I jumped out of the window, and here I am. They have turned out into the forest, with their hounds and their guns. I had hidden myself in that big hollow chestnut tree because I saw one of them cross the road; their hounds will soon be on my track. I am going to get on your horse and gallop a league beyond Como; thence I shall go to Milan, to cast myself at the viceroy's feet. If you consent with a good grace, I'll leave your horse at the posting-house, with two napoleons for yourself. If you make the slightest difficulty I shall kill you with these pistols. If, when I am once off, you set the gendarmes after me, my cousin, the brave Count Alari, the Emperor's equerry, will see to your bones being broken for you."

Fabrizio invented his speech as he delivered it, which

he did in the most gentle manner. "For the rest," he said, laughing, "my name is no secret. I am the Marchesino Ascanio del Dongo. My home is close by, at Grianta. Now, then," he cried, raising his voice, "let the horse go!" The stupefied servant said never a word. Fabrizio put up the pistol he had held in his left hand, laid hold of the bridle, which the man had dropped, sprang on the horse, and cantered off. When he had ridden three hundred paces he perceived he had forgotten to give him the twenty francs he had promised. He pulled up; the road was still empty, except for the servant, who was galloping after him. He waved him forward with his handkerchief, and when he was within fifty paces threw a handful of silver coins upon the road, and started off again. Looking back from a distance, he saw the servant picking up the silver. "Now, that really is a sensible man," said Fabrizio, laughing; "not a useless word did he say." He rode rapidly southward, halted at a lonely house, and started forth again a few hours later. By two o'clock in the morning he had reached the Lago Maggiore. He soon saw his boat, standing on and off. He made the signal agreed on, and she approached the shore. He could find no peasant with whom he might leave the horse, so he turned the noble creature loose, and three hours later, he was at Belgirate. Once in a friendly country, he took some repose. He was full of joy, for he had been thoroughly successful. Dare we mention the true cause of his delight? His tree was growing splendidly, and his soul had been refreshed by the deep emotion he had felt in Father Blanès's arms. "Does he really believe," said he to himself, "in all the predictions he has made to me? Or is it that as my brother has given me the reputation of a Jacobin, a man who knows neither truth nor law, and capable of any crime, he simply desired to induce me to resist the temptation of taking the life of some villain who may do me an evil turn?" The day after the next, Fabrizio was at Parma, where he vastly entertained the duchess and the count by relating with the greatest exactness, as was his wont, the whole story of his journey.

When Fabrizio arrived, he found the porter and all the

servants at the Palazzo Sanseverina garbed in the deepest mourning.

"Whose loss do we mourn?" he inquired of the duchess.

"That excellent man who was known as my husband has just died at Baden. He has left me the palace—that was a settled thing; but, as a proof of his regard, he has added a legacy of three hundred thousand francs, and this places me in a serious difficulty. I will not give it up for the benefit of his niece, the Marchesa Raversi, who plays me the vilest of tricks every day of her life. You, who understand art, must really find me some good sculptor, and I will put up a monument to the duke which shall cost three hundred thousand francs." The count began to tell stories about the Raversi.

"In vain have I striven to soften her by kindness," said the duchess. "As for the duke's nephews, I have had them all made colonels or generals, and in return, never a month passes without their sending me some abominable anonymous letter. I have been obliged to hire a secretary to read all my letters of that description."

"And their anonymous letters are the least of all their sins," continued Count Mosca. "They carry on a regular manufacture of vile accusations. Twenty times over I ought to have had the whole set brought before the courts, and your Excellency" (turning to Fabrizio) "will guess whether my worthy judges would have condemned them or not."

"Well, that's what spoils all the rest, to me," replied Fabrizio, with that artlessness that sounded so comical at court. "I would much rather see them sentenced by magistrates who would judge them according to their own consciences."

"If you, who travel to improve your mind, would give me the addresses of a few such magistrates, you would do me a real kindness. I would write to them before I went to bed to-night."

"If I were a minister this lack of upright judges would wound my vanity."

"But it strikes me," rejoined the count, "that your Excellency, who is so fond of the French, and once upon a time even lent them the help of your invincible arm, is forgetting one of their great maxims, 'It is better to kill the devil than that the devil should kill you?' I should very much like to see how anybody could govern these eager beings who read the history of the French Revolution all day long, with judges who would acquit the persons I accused. They would end by acquitting rascals whose guilt was perfectly evident, and every man of them would think himself a Brutus. But I have a bone to pick with you. Does not your sensitive soul feel some remorse concerning that fine horse, rather too lean, which you have just turned loose on the shores of the Maggiore?"

"I certainly intend," said Fabrizio very gravely, "to send the owner of the horse whatever sum may be necessary to pay him the expenses of advertising, and any others he may have incurred in recovering the beast from the peasants who must have found it. I propose to read the Milanese newspaper carefully, so as to find any advertisement touching a strayed horse. I am quite familiar with the appearance of this one."

"He really is *primitive*," said the count to the duchess. "And what would have become of your Excellency," he continued, laughing, "if, while you were galloping along on that horse's back, he had happened to stumble? You would have found yourself at the Spielberg, my dear young nephew, and with all my credit, I should barely have contrived to get some thirty pounds struck off the weight of the shackles on each of your legs. In that delightful retreat you would have spent quite ten years; your legs would possibly have swelled and mortified. Then they would have been neatly cut off for you."

"Ah, for pity's sake, don't carry the wretched story any further," broke in the duchess with tears in her eyes. "He is back, and safe——"

"And I am even more glad of it than you, you may be sure of that," responded the minister very gravely. "But pray, since this boy was set on going into Lombardy, why did he not ask me to get him a passport in a fitting name?

The Chartreuse of Parma

The moment I heard of his arrest I should have hurried off to Milan, and my friends there would have been willing enough to close their eyes and pretend their police had taken up one of the Prince of Parma's subjects. The story of your trip is entertaining and amusing enough, I am quite ready to admit that," the count continued, and his tone grew less gloomy. "Your leap on to the high-road decidedly enchants me. But between ourselves, since that serving-man held your life in his hands, you had a right to deprive him of his. We propose to raise your Excellency to a brilliant position—at least, such are the orders this lady gives me, and I do not think my bitterest enemies can accuse me of ever having neglected her commands. What a heartbreak it would have been to her if that lean horse of yours had happened to make a false step while you were riding a steeple-chase upon his back! It would almost have been better if he had broken your neck outright."

"You are very tragic to-night, dear friend," said the duchess, quite overcome.

"Because tragic events are happening all around us," replied the count, and he, too, was moved. "This is not France, where everything ends with a song or a sentence of imprisonment, and I really am wrong to laugh when I talk to you of such matters. Well, nephew mine, granting that I find a chance some day of making you a bishop—for, frankly, I can not begin with making you Archbishop of Parma, as the duchess here would very reasonably have me do. Supposing you were settled in your bishopric, and far from the sound of our wise counsels; tell us what your policy would be."

"I would kill the devil sooner than let him kill me, as my friends the French so sensibly say," answered Fabrizio, with shining eyes. "I would hold the position you gave me by every means, even with my pistols. I have read the story of our ancestor, who built Grianta, in the Del Dongo Genealogy. Toward the end of his life his good friend Galeazzo, Duke of Milan, sent him to inspect a fortified castle on our lake. There was some fear of a fresh invasion by the Swiss. 'I really must send a civil word to the commandant of the fortress,' said the duke, just as he was dismissing him. He wrote two lines, and gave him the letter; then he took it back. 'It will be more courteous if I seal it,' said the prince. Vespasiano del Dongo departed. But as he was sailing over the lake he remembered an old Greek story, for he was a learned man. He opened his good master's letter, and found it was an order to the commandant of the fortress to put him to death the moment he arrived. So absorbed had Sforza been in his effort to make the deception he had been playing on our ancestor life-like, that he had left a considerable space between the last line of his note and his signature. Vespasiano del Dongo inserted an order to recognise him as governor-general of all the lake castles, in the blank space, and tore the upper part of the letter off. When he had reached the fortress, and his authority had been duly acknowledged, he threw the commandant down a well, declared war on Sforza, and, after a few years, exchanged his strong castle for the huge estates which have enriched every branch of our family, and which will one day benefit me to the extent of four thousand francs a year."

"You talk like an academician!" cried the count laughingly. "You have told the story of a splendid prank. But it is not once in ten years that the delightful opportunity for doing such startling things presents itself. A man who may be stupid at times, but is watchful and prudent always, may often enjoy the pleasure of outwitting men of imagination. It was a freak of the imagination that led Napoleon to put himself into the hands of the prudent John Bull, instead of trying to escape to America. John Bull sat in his counting-house, and laughed at the Emperor's letter and his reference to Themistocles. The mean Sancho Panzas of this world will always triumph over the noble-hearted Don Quixotes. If you will consent not to do anything extraordinary, I don't doubt you may be a highly respected, if not a highly respectable, bishop. Nevertheless, I hold to my previous observation. In this matter of the horse your Excellency behaved very foolishly. You have been within an ace of imprisonment for life."

The Chartreuse of Parma

Fabrizio shuddered at the words. He sat on, plunged in a deep astonishment. "Was that the imprisonment which threatens me?" he mused. "Is that the crime I was not to commit?" Father Blanès's predictions, the prophetic value of which he had despised, began to assume all the importance of real omens in his eyes.

"Well," cried the duchess, quite surprised, "what is the matter with you? The count has cast you into a very gloomy reverie."

"The light of a new truth has fallen upon my mind, and instead of rebelling against it, I am adopting it. It is quite true. I have been very near a prison that never would have opened its doors again. But the servant lad looked so handsome in his English livery it would have been a sin to kill him."

The count was delighted with his air of youthful wisdom.

"He is satisfactory in every way," he said, looking at the duchess. "I must tell you, my boy, that you have made a conquest, and perhaps the most desirable one you could possibly have made."

"Ha!" thought Fabrizio, "now I shall hear some jest about little Marietta." He was mistaken. The count went on: "Your evangelic simplicity has won the heart of our venerable archbishop, Father Landriani. One of these days you will be made a grand vicar, and the beauty of the joke is that the three present grand vicars, all of them men of parts and hard-working, and two of them, I believe, grand vicars before you were born, are about to send a fine letter to their archbishop, begging you may take rank above them all. These gentlemen base this request on your virtuous qualities, in the first place, and in the second, on the fact that you are great-nephew to the famous Archbishop Ascanio del Dongo. When I heard of the respect your virtues had inspired, I instantly promoted the senior grand vicar's nephew to a captaincy. He had remained a lieutenant ever since he had served at the siege of Tarragona, under Marshal Suchet."

"Go at once, just as you are, in your travelling dress, and pay an affectionate call on your archbishop," exclaimed the duchess. "Tell him all about your sister's marriage. When he knows she is going to be a duchess he will think you more *apostolic* than ever. Of course, you will forget everything the count has just confided to you about your approaching appointment."

Fabrizio hurried off to the archiepiscopal palace. His behaviour there was both modest and simple. This was a tone he could assume only too easily. For him the effort was when he had to play the nobleman. While he was listening to Monsignore Landriani's somewhat lengthy dissertations he kept saying to himself, "Ought I to have fired my pistol at the man-servant who was leading the lean horse?" His reason replied in the affirmative. But he could not reconcile his heart to the thought of that handsome young fellow dropping disfigured from his saddle.

"That prison which would have swallowed me up if the horse had stumbled—was it the prison with which so many omens threaten me?"

The question was of sovereign importance to him. And the archbishop was enchanted with his air of deep attention.

CHAPTER XI

WHEN Fabrizio left the archiepiscopal palace he hurried off to Marietta's dwelling. In the distance he heard Giletti's rough voice. He had sent out for wine, and was carousing with his friends the prompter and the candle snuffer. The *mamaccia*, who performed the functions of a mother to Marietta, was the only person who answered his signal.

"Things have happened while you have been away," she cried. "Two or three of our actors have been accused of having held an orgy in honour of the great Napoleon's birthday, and our unlucky company has been given the name of Jacobin. So we have been ordered to clear out of the dominion of Parma, and, *Evriva Napoleone!* But the Prime Minister is supposed to have paid our reckoning. Giletti certainly has money in his pocket. I don't know how much, but I have seen him with a handful of crown pieces. The manager has given Marietta five crowns for her travelling expenses to Mantua and Venice, and one for mine. She is still very much in love with you, but she is afraid of Giletti. Three days ago, at her last performance, he really would have killed her. He boxed her ears soundly twice over, and, what is abominable, he tore her blue shawl. If you would give her a blue shawl it would be very good-natured of you, and we would say we had won it in the lottery. The drum master of the carabineers is holding a competition to-morrow—you will see the hour advertised at every street corner. Come and see us then. If Giletti goes to the match, and we can hope he will stay away for any time, I will be at the window, and will beckon you to come up. Try to bring us something very pretty. And Marietta dotes upon you."

As he descended the winding stairs that led from the vile

garret, Fabrizio's soul was filled with compunction. "I am not a bit altered," he thought. "All those fine resolutions I made on the shores of the lake, when I looked at life with so much philosophy, have flown away. I was not in my normal condition then. It was all a dream, which disappears when I have to face stern realities. This would be the moment for action," he went on, as he re-entered the Sanseverina Palace about eleven o'clock at night. But in vain did he search his heart for that noble sincerity which had seemed so easy of attainment during the night he had spent on the shores of Como. "I shall displease the person I love best in the world. If I speak, I shall look like an inferior play-actor. I really never am worth anything, except in certain moments of excitement."

"The count is wonderfully good to me," said he to the duchess, after he had given her an account of his visit to the archbishop. "I value his kindness all the more highly because I fancy I notice that he does not particularly care about me. Therefore I must be all the more correct in my behaviour to him. I know he has excavations at Sanguigna in which he still delights—judging, at least, by his expedition the day before yesterday, galloping twelve leagues to spend two hours with his workmen. He is afraid that if they find fragments of statuary in the antique temple, the foundations of which he has just laid bare, they may steal them. I should like to offer to go and spend thirty-six hours at Sanguigna. I am to see the archbishop to-morrow, about five o'clock. I could start in the evening, and take advantage of the cool hours of the night for my ride."

The duchess made no answer at first. Presently she said to him in a very tender voice : " It looks as if you were seeking pretexts for getting away from me ; you are hardly back from Belgirate, and you find out a reason for starting off again."

"Here's a fine opportunity for me," thought Fabrizio. "But I was a little mad when I was sitting by the lake. In my passion for truthfulness I overlooked the fact that my compliment winds up with an impertinence. I should have to say, ' I regard you with the most devoted friendship, etc.,

but my heart is not capable of real love.' Is not that tantamount to saying: 'I see you are in love with me. But pray
take care! I can not return it to you in kind.' If the
duchess has any passion for me, she will be vexed at my
having guessed it. If her feeling for me is one of mere
friendship she will be disgusted by my impudence, and such
offences are never forgiven."

While he was weighing these important considerations
Fabrizio was walking, quite unconsciously, up and down the
room, looking grave and proud, like a man who sees misfortune hovering within ten paces of him.

The duchess gazed at him with admiration. This was
not the child she had known from his birth, the nephew
ever ready to obey her commands. This was a serious man
—a man whose love would be an exquisite possession. She
rose from the ottoman on which she had been sitting, and
threw herself passionately into his arms.

"Are you bent on leaving me?" she cried.

"No," said he, looking like a Roman emperor, "but I
want to behave well."

The phrase was susceptible of several interpretations.
Fabrizio had not courage to go farther, and run the risk
of wounding the adorable woman before him. He was too
young, too easily moved. His mind did not suggest any
well-turned expression which might convey his meaning.
In a fit of passion, which was natural enough, and in spite
of his reason, he clasped the charming creature in his arms
and rained kisses upon her. Just at that moment the count's
carriage was heard in the courtyard, and almost instantly
he entered the room. He looked quite affected.

"You inspire very strange devotions," said he to Fabrizio, who was almost stunned by the phrase. "This
evening the archbishop was received in audience by the
prince, as he is regularly every Thursday. The prince
has just informed me that the archbishop, who seemed
greatly agitated, began by making a very prosy speech,
evidently learned by heart, of which the prince could make
nothing at all. Landriani ended by saying that it was important for the sake of the Church in Parma that Monsi-

gnore Fabrizio del Dongo should be appointed his chief
grand vicar, and afterward, as soon as he had reached his
five-and-twentieth year, his coadjutor, *and his ultimate successor.*

"This idea alarmed me, I confess," said the count. "It
is somewhat precipitate, and I was afraid it might throw the
prince into a fit of ill-humour. But he looked at me and
laughed, and said to me in French, '*Ce sont là vos coups,
monsieur!*'

"'I will take my oath before God and your Highness,'
I cried with the utmost possible fervour, 'that I was utterly
ignorant of the idea of the "future succession."' Then I
went on to tell the real truth, as we talked it over here a
few hours since, and I added impulsively that I should have
considered his Highness had conferred an overwhelming
favour on me if he had ultimately granted you a modest
bishopric to begin with. The prince must have believed
me, for it pleased him to be gracious. He said to me in
the simplest possible way : 'This is an official affair between
me and the archbishop. You have nothing whatever to do
with it. The old gentleman has sent me in a very long and
tolerably tiresome report, which he winds up with a formal
proposal. I replied that the individual was still very young,
and more especially a very new arrival at my court; that
I should almost look as if I were honouring a letter of
credit drawn on me by the Emperor if I bestowed the re-
version of so high a dignity on the son of one of the great
officials of his Lombardo-Venetian kingdom. The archbishop protested there had been no pressure of any such
kind. It was a pretty piece of folly to say that to me. It
surprised me in a man who is generally so intelligent. But
he always loses his head completely when he talks to me,
and to-night he was more nervous than ever, which led me
to think he passionately desired what he asked for. I told
him that nobody knew better than myself that there had
been no attempt in high quarters to put forward Del Dongo,
that nobody about my court denied his powers, that his
reputation for virtue was a fair one, but that I feared he
was capable of *enthusiasm,* and that I had made a vow I

would never place madmen of that kind, on whom rulers
never can rely, in any exalted position. Then,' his Highness
continued, 'I had to endure a pathetic appeal nearly as
long as the first. The archbishop sang the praises of enthusiasm for God's house. "Bungler," said I to myself,
"you are risking the appointment you were very near getting! You should have cut it short, and thanked me fervently." Not a bit, he went on pouring out his homily with
a bravery that was ridiculous. I cast about for an answer
that would not be too unfavourable to young Del Dongo's
cause. I found it, and a fairly apposite one, as you will
perceive.

" '"Monsignore," I said, "Pius VII was a great Pope,
and a great saint. He was the only one of all the sovereigns
who dared to say *No* to the tyrant at whose feet Europe
grovelled. Well, he was capable of enthusiasm, and this
led him, when he was Bishop of Imola, into writing that
famous pastoral of the Citizen-Cardinal Chiaramonti, in support of the Cisalpine Republic."

" 'My poor archbishop was struck dumb, and to complete his stupefaction I said to him, very gravely: "Farewell, monsignore; I will take four-and-twenty hours to think
over your proposal." The poor man added a few more
entreaties, which were both ill-expressed and, considering I
had bidden him "Farewell," somewhat inopportune. Now,
Count Mosca della Rovere, I desire you will inform the
duchess that I will not delay for four-and-twenty hours a
matter which may give her pleasure. Sit you down here,
and write the archbishop the note of approval which will
close the whole business.' I wrote the note, he signed it,
and he said, 'Take it to the duchess instantly.' Here,
madam, is the note, and to it I owe the happiness of seeing
you again to-night."

The duchess perused the paper with delight. While the
count had been telling his long story Fabrizio had had time
to collect himself. He did not appear astonished by the incident. He took it like a true aristocrat, who had always
believed in his own right to that extraordinary advancement,
those lucky chances which might very well throw a com-

mon man off his balance. He expressed his gratitude, but in measured language, and ended by saying to the count:

"A good courtier should flatter the ruling passion. Yesterday you expressed your fear that your workmen at Sanguigna might steal the fragments of antique statuary they may unearth. I delight in excavations. If you will give me leave, I will go and look after those workmen. To-morrow evening, after I have paid the necessary visits, to return thanks, at the palace, and to the archbishop, I will start for Sanguigna."

"But can you imagine," said the duchess, "any reason for the good archbishop's sudden devotion to Fabrizio?"

"There is no need of any imagination. The grand vicar whose brother is a captain said to me, yesterday, 'Father Landriani argues on this unvarying principle, that the holder of the title is superior to the coadjutor, and he is beside himself with delight at having a Del Dongo at his orders, and under an obligation conferred by himself. Everything that draws attention to Fabrizio's high birth increases his private satisfaction—that is the man he has under him. In the second place, he likes Monsignore Fabrizio. He does not feel shy in his presence. And, finally, for the last ten years he has been nursing a hearty hatred of the Bishop of Piacenza, who openly avows his expectation of succeeding him at Parma, and who is, besides, the son of a miller. It is with an eye to this future succession that the Bishop of Piacenza has entered into close relations with the Marchesa Raversi, and this intimacy makes our archbishop tremble for his pet plan—that of seeing a Del Dongo on his staff, and of issuing his orders to him.'"

Very early on the next morning but one, Fabrizio was overlooking the workers on the excavations at Sanguigna, opposite Colorno (the Versailles of the Parmese princes). These excavations stretched across the plain close to the high-road leading from Parma to the bridge of Casal-Maggiore, the nearest Austrian town. The workmen were cutting a long ditch along the plain. It was eight feet deep, and as narrow as might be. The object was to find, alongside the old Roman road, the ruins of a second temple, which, according to local tradition, had been still standing in the middle ages. Notwithstanding the prince's authority, many peasants looked with a jealous eye on the long trenches cut across their land. In spite of everything they were told, they fancied search was being made for some treasure, and Fabrizio's presence was particularly valuable as a check on any little outbreak on their part. He was not at all bored. He watched the work with passionate interest. Now and then some medal was turned up, and he was resolved he would not give the labourers time to agree among themselves to pilfer it.

It was about six o'clock in the morning of a lovely day. He had borrowed an old single-barrelled gun. He shot at a few larks. One of them fell wounded on the high-road. Fabrizio, when he followed it, saw a carriage in the distance, coming from Parma, and travelling toward Casal-Maggiore. He had just reloaded his gun when the vehicle, a very shabby one, came slowly up to him, and in it he recognised little Marietta. With her were the ungainly Giletti and the old woman she passed off as her mother.

Giletti took it into his head that Fabrizio had set himself thus in the middle of the road, gun in hand, with the idea of insulting him, and perhaps of carrying off little Marietta. Like a bold fellow, he jumped out of the carriage instantly. In his left hand he grasped a large and very rusty pistol, and in his right a sword, still in its scabbard, which he was in the habit of wearing when necessity obliged the manager of his company to allot him some nobleman's part in a play.

" Ha, villain," he cried, " I'm heartily glad to catch you here, only a league from the frontier! I'll soon settle your business for you; your violet stockings won't protect you here."

Fabrizio had been making signs to little Marietta, and scarcely paying any attention to Giletti's jealous shrieks. Suddenly he saw the muzzle of the rusty pistol within three feet of his own chest. He had only time to strike at the pistol with his gun, using it as if it had been a stick; the pistol went off, but nobody was wounded.

"Stop, you fool!" shrieked Giletti to the *vetturino*, skilfully contriving at the same time to spring at the barrel of his adversary's gun and hold it away from his own body. He and Fabrizio each tugged at the gun with all his strength. Giletti, who was much the stronger of the two, kept slipping one hand over the other toward the lock, and had very nearly got possession of the weapon when Fabrizio, to prevent his using it, touched the trigger. He had previously noticed that the muzzle was over three inches above Giletti's shoulder. The shot went off close to the man's ear; he was a little startled, but pulled himself together in a moment.

"Oho! you'd like to blow my brains out, you scoundrel! I'll soon settle you!"

Giletti threw away the scabbard of his sword, and fell upon Fabrizio with the most astonishing swiftness. Fabrizio, who was unarmed, gave himself up for lost.

He bolted toward the carriage, which had stopped some paces behind Giletti, and, turning to the left, he caught hold of the springs, ran quickly round it, and past the right-hand door, which was open. Giletti, tearing along on his long legs, and not having thought of catching at the carriage springs, ran several steps in his original direction before he could stop himself. Just as Fabrizio ran past the open door he heard Marietta say in an undertone: "Look out for yourself; he'll kill you! Here!" and at the same moment he saw a great hunting-knife fall out of the carriage. He bent down to pick it up, but just at that moment a sword thrust from Giletti touched him on the shoulder. When Fabrizio stood up he found himself within six inches of Giletti, who gave him a furious blow in the face with the pommel of his sword. So violent was this blow that Fabrizio was quite dazed, and at that moment he was very near being killed. Fortunately for him, Giletti was still too close to be able to thrust at him. When Fabrizio recovered his wits he took to flight at the top of his speed. As he ran he threw away the sheath of the hunting-knife, and then, turning sharp round, he found himself within three paces of Giletti, who was tearing after him. Giletti was running as fast as he could go; Fabrizio made a thrust at him, and though Giletti had time to strike up the hunting-knife a little, he received the thrust full in his cheek. He passed close to Fabrizio, who felt himself wounded in the thigh; this was by Giletti's knife, which he had found time to open. Fabrizio made a spring to the right, turned round, and at last the adversaries found themselves within reasonable fighting distance.

Giletti was swearing furiously. " Ah, I'll cut your throat for you, you scoundrel of a priest! " he cried over and over again. Fabrizio was quite out of breath, and could not speak; the blow on his face with the pommel of the sword hurt him dreadfully, and his nose was pouring blood. He parried various blows with his hunting-knife, and delivered several thrusts without well knowing what he was about. He had a sort of vague idea that he was performing in a public assault-at-arms. This idea had been suggested to him by the presence of his workmen, who, to the number of five-and-twenty or thirty, had formed a ring round them, but at a very respectful distance, for both of the combatants kept running hither and thither, and then rushing upon each other.

The fight seemed to be growing less fierce, the thrusts rather less rapidly exchanged, when Fabrizio said to himself, " Judging by the way my face hurts me he must have disfigured me." Stung to fury by the thought, he rushed at his enemy, holding the hunting-knife in front of him. The point entered Giletti's chest on the right, and passed out near his left shoulder. At the same moment the whole length of Giletti's sword ran through the upper part of Fabrizio's arm, but as the sword slipped beneath the skin the wound was quite a trifling one.

Giletti had fallen. Just as Fabrizio went toward him, with his eye on his left hand, which held the knife, that hand unclosed mechanically, and the weapon dropped from its grasp.

" The rascal is dead," said Fabrizio to himself. He looked at the face; the blood was pouring from Giletti's mouth.

The Chartreuse of Parma

Fabrizio ran to the carriage. "Have you a looking-glass?" he cried to Marietta. Marietta, very pale, was staring at him, and did not answer. The old woman, with the greatest coolness, opened a green workbag and handed Fabrizio a small mirror about the size of a man's hand, with a handle to it. Fabrizio felt his face all over as he peered into the glass. "My eyes are all right," said he. "That's a great thing." Then he looked at his teeth; they were not broken. "Then why does it hurt me so?" he murmured.

The old woman replied: "Because the top of your cheek has been crushed between Giletti's sword and the bone we all have there. It's all blue and horribly swelled. Put on leeches at once, and it will be nothing at all."

"Ah, leeches at once," said Fabrizio, laughing, and he recovered all his self-possession. He saw the workmen gathering round Giletti, looking at him without daring to touch him.

"Why don't you help the man?" he shouted. "Take his coat off him!" He would have proceeded, but raising his eyes he saw, some three hundred paces off, five or six men advancing along the high-road, with slow and measured step, toward the spot on which he stood.

"Those are gendarmes," thought he to himself, "and as there's a man dead they will arrest me, and I shall have the pleasure of making my solemn entry into the city of Parma with them! What a nice story for the courtiers who are the Raversi's friends and hate my aunt!" Instantly, and as quick as lightning, he threw all the money he had in his pockets to the astonished workmen, and jumped into the carriage.

"Prevent those gendarmes from following me," he shouted to the men, "and I will make your fortunes. Tell them I am innocent, that the man attacked me and would have killed me. And you," he added to the *vetturino*, "make your horses gallop! You shall have four gold napoleons if you get across the Po before those fellows can reach me."

"All right," said the *vetturino*; "don't be in a fright! Those men yonder are on foot, and if my little horses only trot they will be left far behind." As he spoke he shook them up into a gallop.

Our hero was much offended by the coachman's use of the word fright. He really had been in a horrible fright after receiving the blow from the sword pommel in his face.

"We may meet people on horseback coming this way," said the *vetturino*, thinking of his four napoleons, "and the men who are following us may shout to them to stop us." This meant "Reload your weapons."

"Ah, how brave you are, my little abbé!" cried Marietta, and she kissed Fabrizio. The old woman had thrust her head out of the window; presently she drew it in again.

"Nobody is following you, sir," she said to Fabrizio very coolly, "and there is nobody on the road in front of you. You know how precise the Austrian police officials are; if they see you come galloping up to the embankment beside the Po you may be perfectly certain they will stop you."

Fabrizio put his head out of the window. "You can trot now," said he to the coachman. Then, turning to the old woman, "What passport have you?"

"Three instead of one," replied she, "and each of them cost us four francs. Isn't that cruel for poor play-actors, travelling all the year round? Here is a passport for Signor Giletti, a dramatic artist—that shall be you—and here are Mariettina's and mine. But Giletti had all our money in his pocket. What is to become of us?"

"How much had he?" said Fabrizio.

"Forty good crowns of five francs each," said the old woman.

"That is to say, six crowns and some small change," laughed Marietta. "I won't have my little abbé imposed upon."

"Is it not quite natural, sir," returned the old woman with the greatest calmness, "that I should try to do you out of four-and-thirty crowns? What are thirty-four crowns to you? And as for us, we've lost our protector. Who is to look after our lodgings now, and bargain with the *vetturino* when we travel, and keep everything in order? Giletti was not a beauty, but he was useful, and if this child

here had not been a fool and fallen in love with you at
first sight, Giletti would never have noticed anything, and
you would have given us good silver crowns. I can assure
you we are very poor."

Fabrizio was touched. He took out his purse and gave
the old woman several gold pieces.

"You see," he said, "that I have only fifteen left, so it
will be useless to try and get any more out of me."

Little Marietta threw her arms round his neck and the
old woman kissed his hands. The carriage was still trotting slowly forward, when the yellow barriers, striped with
black, which marked the Austrian frontier, appeared in
sight. The old woman addressed Fabrizio.

"You would do well to pass on foot with Giletti's passport in your pocket. We will stop a few minutes, on the
pretext of making ourselves look tidy. And besides, the
customs officers will open our baggage. If you will take
my advice, you had better walk lazily through Casal-Maggiore; even turn into the *café* and drink a glass of brandy.
Once you are out of the village make off. The police on
Austrian territory are devilishly sharp; they will soon find
out that a man has been killed. You are travelling with a
passport which does not belong to you; for less than that
you might get two years in prison. When you leave the
town turn to the right, and get to the banks of the Po. Hire
a boat, and take refuge at Ravenna or Ferrara. Get out of
the Austrian states as quickly as ever you can. Two louis
will buy you another passport from some custom-house
officer; this one would be the ruin of you. Remember
you've killed the man!"

Fabrizio carefully reread Giletti's passport as he walked
toward the bridge of boats at Casal-Maggiore. Our hero
was seriously alarmed; he had a vivid recollection of all
Count Mosca had told him concerning the risk he would
run if he re-entered Austrian territory, and only two paces
in front of him he saw the fateful bridge which was to
admit him to those dominions, the capital of which, in his
eyes, was the Spielberg. But what else was he to do? By
an express convention between the two states the duchy

of Modena, which bounds the dominion of Parma on the south, returned all fugitives who passed over its borders. The Parmese frontier running up into the mountain country near Genoa was too distant; his misadventure would be known at Parma before he could reach those mountains. Nothing remained to him, therefore, except the Austrian states on the left bank of the Po. Thirty-six hours or two days would probably elapse before there could be time to write to the Austrian authorities and request his arrest. On the whole, Fabrizio thought it wiser to burn his own passport, which he lighted at the end of his cigar. He would be safer on Austrian ground as a vagabond than as Fabrizio del Dongo, and there was the possibility of his being searched.

Apart from his very natural repugnance to the idea of staking his life on the unhappy Giletti's passport, the document itself presented some material difficulties. Fabrizio's stature did not, at the most, exceed five foot five, instead of the five foot ten described in the passport. He was nearly twenty-four, and looked younger. Giletti was thirty-nine. We will confess that our hero spent a full half-hour walking up and down an embankment on the river, close by the bridge of boats, before he could make up his mind to go down upon it. "What advice should I give to another man in my place?" said he to himself at last. "Clearly, to go across. It is dangerous to stay in Parma. A gendarme may be sent in pursuit of the man who has killed another, even against his own will." Fabrizio turned out his pockets, tore up all his papers, and kept literally nothing except his handkerchief and his cigar case. It was important to shorten, by every possible means, the examination he would have to undergo. He thought of a terrible difficulty which might be made, and to which he could find no good answer. He was going to call himself Giletti, and all his linen was marked F. D.

Fabrizio, as will be observed, was one of those unhappy beings who are tortured by their own imaginations, a somewhat common weakness among intelligent people in Italy. A French soldier of equal or even inferior courage would have set about crossing the bridge at once, without thinking of any difficulty beforehand, and he would have done it with perfect composure, whereas Fabrizio was very far from being composed when, at the far end of the bridge, a little man dressed in gray said to him, " Go into the police office and show your passport."

The office had dirty walls, studded with nails on which the officials' pipes and greasy hats were hung. The big deal writing-table at which they sat was covered with ink stains and wine stains. Two or three big green leather registers also showed stains of every shade of colour, and the edges of the pages were blackened by dirty hands. On these registers, which were piled one upon the other, lay three splendid laurel wreaths, which had been used the night before, in honour of one of the Emperor's fête days.

Fabrizio was struck by all these details; they sent a pang through his heart. This was the price he paid for the splendid luxury and freshness of his beautiful rooms in the Palazzo Sanseverina. He was obliged to enter the dirty office and stand there like an inferior. He was soon to be cross-questioned.

The official who stretched out a yellow hand to receive his passport was a short, dark man, with a brass jewel in his neckcloth. " Here's a common man, in a bad temper," said Fabrizio to himself. He seemed very much surprised when he read the passport, and the perusal lasted quite five minutes.

" You've had an accident," said he to the stranger, looking at his cheek.

" The *vetturino* upset us over the river embankment." Then silence fell again, and the official cast strange glances at the traveller.

" I have it," said Fabrizio to himself; " he's going to tell me that he's sorry to have to give me an unpleasant piece of news, and that I am arrested."

All sorts of wild notions crowded on to our hero's brain. His logic at that moment was of the weakest description. He thought, for instance, of bolting through the office door, which was standing open. " I would get rid of my coat, I would jump into the Po, and I have no doubt I could swim across. Anything is better than the Spielberg."

While he weighed his chances of succeeding in this prank, the police officer was looking hard at him; their two faces were a study. The presence of danger inspires a sensible man with genius, raising him, so to speak, above himself. In the case of the man of imagination, it inspires him with romances, which may indeed be bold, but which are frequently absurd.

Our hero's look of indignation under the scrutinizing glance of this police officer with the brass jewellery was something worth seeing. "If I were to kill him," said Fabrizio to himself, " I should be sentenced to twenty years at the galleys or to death. That would be far less awful than the Spielberg, with a chain weighing a hundred and twenty pounds on each foot, and eight ounces of bread for my daily food. And it would last twenty years, so that I should be forty-four before I came out." Fabrizio's logical mind overlooked the fact that as he had burned his own passport, there was nothing to acquaint the police officer with the detail of his being the rebel Fabrizio del Dongo.

Our hero was tolerably frightened, as my readers perceive. His alarm would have been far greater if he had been aware of the thoughts passing in the official's mind. The man was a friend of Giletti's; his surprise at seeing his passport in the hands of another person may therefore be imagined. His first impulse had been to arrest the stranger. Then he reflected that very likely Giletti had sold the passport to the good-looking young fellow, who had probably just got into some scrape at Parma. " If I arrest him," said he to himself, " Giletti will get into trouble. It will easily be discovered that he has sold his passport. But, on the other hand, what will my superiors say if they find out that I, who am a friend of Giletti's, have countersigned his passport when presented by another person?" The officer stood up with a yawn, and said to Fabrizio, " Wait here, sir!" Then, as was natural to a policeman, he added, "There is a difficulty." Fabrizio said within himself, "What there is going to be, is my flight."

The Chartreuse of Parma

The official, indeed, had left the office, leaving the door open, and the passport was still lying on the deal table. "There's no doubt about my danger," thought Fabrizio to himself. "I will take up my passport, and walk quietly back across the bridge. If the gendarme questions me I will tell him I have forgotten to get it countersigned by the police officer at the last village in the dominion of Parma." The passport was actually in Fabrizio's hand when, to his inexpressible astonishment, he heard the clerk with the brass jewellery say:

"Upon my soul! I am done up; I'm choking with heat; I am going to get a cup of coffee at the *café*. When you've finished your pipe just go into the office; there's a passport to be signed. The traveller is waiting."

Fabrizio, who was just stepping out on tiptoe, found himself face to face with a good-looking young fellow, who was humming a tune, and heard him say, "Very good. We'll see to their passport. I'll oblige them with my flourish."

"Where do you wish to go, sir?"

"To Mantua, Venice, and Ferrara."

"Ferrara let it be," answered the official, whistling; he took up a stamp, printed the *visa* upon the passport in blue ink, and rapidly inserted the words "Mantua, Venice, and Ferrara" in the blank space left by the stamp. Then he waved his hand in the air several times, signed his name, and dipped his pen in the ink again to make his flourish, a feat he performed slowly and with infinite care. Fabrizio watched every motion of his pen. The clerk looked complacently at his flourish, added five or six dots, and then returned the passport to Fabrizio, saying indifferently, "A pleasant journey to you, sir."

Fabrizio was departing with a rapidity which he was attempting to conceal when he felt himself stopped by a touch on his left arm. Instinctively his hand sought the handle of his dagger, and if he had not seen houses all round him he might have been guilty of a blunder. The man who had touched his left arm, seeing his startled look, said apologetically:

The Chartreuse of Parma

"But I spoke to you three times, sir, and you did not answer. Have you anything to declare at the custom-house?"

"I've nothing on me but my handkerchief; I am going to shoot with one of my relations, quite close by."

He would have been sorely puzzled if he had been asked to mention that relation's name.

Thanks to the great heat and his own emotions, Fabrizio was dripping as if he had fallen into the Po. "I am brave enough when I have to do with play-actors, but custom-house clerks with brass jewellery drive me beside myself. I'll write the duchess a comic sonnet on that subject."

Fabrizio entered the town of Casal-Maggiore and immediately turned to the right, down a shabby street leading to the Po. "I am in sore need," said he to himself, "of the assistance of Bacchus and Ceres," and he entered a shop, over the door of which a gray cloth hung from a pole. On this cloth was inscribed the word *Trattoria*. A ragged bed sheet, supported by two thin wooden hoops and hanging within three feet of the ground, sheltered the door of the *trattoria* from the direct blaze of the sun. Within it a half-naked and very pretty woman received our hero respectfully, a fact which gave him the keenest satisfaction. He lost no time in telling her that he was starving with hunger. While the woman was preparing his breakfast a man of about thirty years of age came into the room. On his first entrance he made no sign of greeting, but suddenly he rose from the bench on which he had cast himself with an easy gesture, and said to Fabrizio:

"*Eccellenza! la riverisco!*" (I salute your Excellency!) Fabrizio felt exceedingly cheerful at that moment, and instead of at once expecting something gloomy he answered with a laugh:

"And how the devil do you know my Excellency?"

"What! doesn't your Excellency recollect Ludovico, one of the Duchess Sanseverina's coachmen? At Sacca, the country house where we went every year, I always got fever, so I asked my mistress to give me a pension, and I retired. I am rich now, for instead of the pension of twelve crowns a year, which was the very most I could have expected, my mistress told me that to give me leisure to write sonnets (for I am a poet in the vulgar tongue) she would allow me four-and-twenty crowns; and the signor count told me that if ever I was in need I had only to come and tell him. I had the honour of driving monsignore for a stage when he went to make his retreat, like a good churchman, at the Carthusian monastery at Velleia."

Fabrizio looked at the man, and began to recall him a little. He had been one of the smartest coachmen at the Casa Sanseverina; now that he was rich, as he affirmed, his only garments were a coarse, tattered shirt and a pair of canvas nether garments, which hardly reached his knees, and had once been dyed black. A pair of shoes and a very bad hat completed his costume; and further, he had not been shaved for a fortnight. Fabrizio, as he ate his omelet, chatted with him on absolutely equal terms. He thought he perceived that Ludovico was his hostess's lover. He soon despatched his meal, and then said to Ludovico in an undertone, "I have a word for you."

"Your Excellency can speak freely before her; she is a really good woman," said Ludovico, with a tender glance.

"Well, then, my friends," said Fabrizio at once, "I am in trouble, and I want your help. To begin with, there is nothing political about my business. I have simply killed a man who tried to murder me because I was speaking to his mistress."

"Poor young fellow!" quoth the hostess.

"Your Excellency may reckon on me," cried the coachman, with eyes that shone with the most fervent devotion. "Where does your Excellency desire to go?"

"To Ferrara. I have a passport, but I would rather not face the gendarmes, who may know something of what has happened."

"When did you put the fellow out of the way?"

"At six o'clock this morning."

"Is there no blood on your Excellency's clothes?" said the hostess.

" I was thinking of that," replied the coachman; " and besides, the cloth is too fine. Such stuff as that is not often seen in our country. It would attract attention. I will go and buy clothes from the Jew. Your Excellency is about my height, only thinner."

" For mercy's sake, don't call me your Excellency! That will attract attention."

" Yes, your Excellency," replied the coachman, as he went out of the shop.

" Halloo! halloo! " shouted Fabrizio. " What about the money? Come back! "

" Don't talk of money," said the hostess. " He has sixty-seven crowns, which are very much at your service, and I," she added, dropping her voice, " have forty, which I offer you with all my heart. One does not always happen to have money about one when such accidents as these occur."

When Fabrizio had entered the *trattoria* he had taken off his coat on account of the heat.

" If any one should come in, that waistcoat of yours might get us into difficulties; that fine English cloth would be remarked."

She gave the fugitive one of her husband's waistcoats, made of canvas dyed black. A tall young man entered the shop through an inner door; there was a touch of elegance about his dress.

" This is my husband," said the hostess.—" Pietro Antonio," said she to her husband, " this gentleman is a friend of Ludovico's. He had an accident this morning on the other side of the river; he wants to escape to Ferrara."

" Oh, we'll get him through," said the husband very civilly. " We have Carlo Giuseppe's boat."

Another weakness of our hero's character, which we will confess as frankly as we have related his fright in the police office at the end of the bridge, now caused his eyes to brim with tears.

The absolute devotion he had met with among these peasants moved him deeply. He thought, too, of his aunt's characteristic kind-heartedness. He would have liked to have been able to make all these people's fortunes. Ludovico now came back, carrying a bundle.

" Good-bye to this other fellow," said the husband in the most friendly fashion.

" That's not it at all," replied Ludovico, in a very anxious voice. " People are beginning to talk about you. It was noticed when you left the main street and turned down our *vicolo* that you hesitated, like a man who wanted to hide himself."

" Get up quickly to the room above," said the husband. This room was a very large and handsome one. The two windows were filled with gray linen instead of glass. It contained four beds, each about six feet wide and five feet high.

" And quick! and quick!" said Ludovico. " There's a conceited fool of a gendarme lately arrived here who wanted to make love to the pretty woman below stairs, and I warned him that when next he went out patrolling on the roads he would very likely meet a bullet. If that dog hears your Excellency mentioned, he'll want to play us a trick; he'll try to get you arrested here, so as to bring disrepute on Theodolinda's *trattoria*. What!" Ludovico went on, when he saw Fabrizio's shirt all stained with blood and his wounds tied up with handkerchiefs; " so the *porco* defended himself! This is enough to get us arrested a hundred times over. I didn't buy a shirt." Unceremoniously he opened the husband's cupboard, and handed over one of his shirts to Fabrizio, who was soon dressed as a rich middle-class countryman. Ludovico unhooked a net which was hanging on the wall, put Fabrizio's clothes into the basket for holding the fish, ran down the stairs, and went swiftly out by a back door, Fabrizio following him.

" Theodolinda," he called out, as he hurried past the shop, " hide what we've left upstairs. We'll go and wait in the willows, and you, Pietro Antonio, make haste and send us a boat. It will be well paid for."

Ludovico led Fabrizio over more than twenty ditches; the widest of these were bridged by very long and very elastic wooden boards. Ludovico pulled these planks over

as fast as they crossed them. When they reached the last
cutting he pulled the plank away eagerly. " Now we can
breathe," he said. " That dog of a policeman will have to
go more than two leagues round before he can reach your
Excellency. But you've turned white! " said he to Fabrizio. " I've not forgotten to bring a little bottle of
brandy."

" I shall be very glad of it; the wound in my thigh
is beginning to hurt, and besides, I was in a horrible
fright while I was in the police office at the end of the
bridge."

" I should think so indeed," said Ludovico. " With a
bloody shirt like yours, I don't understand how you ever
dared to go into such a place. As for the wounds, I know
all about that sort of thing. I'll take you to a nice cool place
where you can sleep for an hour; the boat will come to
fetch us there, if there's a boat to be had. If not, when
you're a little rested we'll go on two short leagues farther,
and I'll take you to a mill where I can get a boat myself.
Your Excellency knows a great deal more than I do; my
mistress will be in despair when she hears of the accident.
She will be told you are mortally wounded, or perhaps that
you have killed the other treacherously. The Marchesa
Raversi will not fail to put about every kind of spiteful report to distress my mistress. Your Excellency might
write."

" And how shall I send my letter? "

" The men at the mill to which we are going earn twelve
sous a day; they can get to Parma in a day and a half—that
means four francs for the journey, and two francs for the
wear and tear of their shoes. If the message was carried for
a poor man like myself it would cost six francs; as it will
be done for a nobleman, I will give twelve."

When they reached the resting-place, in a thicket of
alder and willow trees, very cool and shady, Ludovico went
on an hour's distance to fetch paper and ink. " Heavens!
how comfortable I am here! " exclaimed Fabrizio; " fortune, farewell! I shall never be an archbishop."

When Ludovico returned he found him sound asleep,

and would not wake him. The boat did not come till near sunset. As soon as Ludovico saw it appearing in the distance, he roused Fabrizio, who wrote two letters.

"Your Excellency is very much wiser than I am," said Ludovico, with a look of distress, "and I am afraid you will be displeased with me at the bottom of your heart, whatever you may say, if I add a certain thing."

"I am not such an idiot as you think," said Fabrizio. "And whatever you may say to me, I shall always look upon you as a faithful servant of my aunt's, and a man who has done everything in the world to help me out of a very terrible difficulty."

A good many further protestations were necessary before Ludovico could be induced to speak, and when he finally made up his mind he began with a preface which lasted quite five minutes. Fabrizio grew impatient, and then he thought : " Whose fault is this? The fault of our vanity, which this man has seen very clearly from his coach-box?" At last Ludovico's devotion induced him to run the risk of speaking frankly.

"What would not the Marchesa Raversi give the runner you are going to send to Parma for those two letters? They are written by your own hand, and therefore can be used as evidence against you. Your Excellency will take me for an indiscreet and curious person, and besides, you will be ashamed, perhaps, to let the duchess see a poor coachman's handwriting. But for the sake of your safety, I am forced to speak, even if you do think it an impertinence. Could not your Excellency dictate those two letters to me? Then I should be the only person compromised, and very little compromised at that, for I could always say that you made your appearance in front of me in a field, with an inkhorn in one hand and a pistol in the other, and ordered me to write."

"Give me your hand, my dear Ludovico," cried Fabrizio; "and to convince you I have no desire to keep anything secret from such a friend, you shall copy these two letters just as they are." Ludovico realized the full extent of this mark of confidence, and was very much touched by

it, but at the end of a few lines, seeing the boat coming
rapidly toward them—

"These letters will be finished more quickly," said he
to Fabrizio, "if your Excellency would take the trouble of
dictating them to me." As soon as the letters were finished,
Fabrizio wrote an A and a B on the bottom line, and on a
little scrap of paper which he afterward crumpled up, he
wrote in French, "*Croyez A et B.*" The messenger was to
hide this scrap of paper in his clothes.

When the boat was within hailing distance, Ludovico
shouted to the boatmen, using names which were not their
own. They did not reply, but approached the bank about
a thousand yards lower down, looking about on every side,
lest any custom-house officer should have caught sight of
them.

"I am at your orders," said Ludovico to Fabrizio.
"Would you wish me to take the letters to Parma myself?
Would you like me to go with you to Ferrara?"

"To come with me to Ferrara is a service which I did
not venture to ask of you. I shall have to land and try to
get into the town without showing my passport. I don't
mind telling you that I have the greatest repugnance to the
idea of travelling under Giletti's name, and nobody that I
can think of, except yourself, can procure me another passport."

"Why did you not speak of that at Casal-Maggiore? I
know a spy there who would have sold us an excellent passport, and not dear either, for forty or fifty francs."

One of the two boatmen, who had been born on the right
bank of the Po, and consequently needed no passport to get
him to Parma, undertook to deliver the letters. Ludovico,
who knew how to handle an oar, pledged himself to manage
the boat with the other man's assistance.

"Lower down the river," he said, "we shall meet several
armed police-boats, and I know how to keep out of their
way." A dozen times they had to hide themselves in the
midst of low islets covered with willows; three times they
landed, to let the empty boat pass in front of the police
boats. Ludovico took advantage of these long spells of

idleness to recite several of his sonnets to Fabrizio. They were good enough as regarded feeling, but this was weakened by the form of expression, and none of them were worth writing down. The curious thing was that the ex-coachman's passions and conception were lively and picturesque, but the moment he began to write he grew cold and commonplace. " The very opposite," said Fabrizio to himself, " of what we see in the world. There everything is gracefully expressed, but the heart has nothing to do with it." He discovered that the greatest pleasure he could do to his faithful servant was to correct the spelling of his sonnets.

" When I lend my manuscript to anybody I get laughed at," said Ludovico. " But if your Excellency would condescend to dictate the spelling of the words to me, letter by letter, envious people would have to hold their tongues. Spelling is not genius."

It was not till the evening of the second day that Fabrizio was able to land, in perfect safety, in an alder copse a league from Ponte-Lago-Oscuro. All the day long he lay hid in a hemp field, and Ludovico went on to Ferrara, where he hired a little lodging in the house of a needy Jew, who at once realized that there was money to be earned if he would hold his tongue. In the evening, as the darkness was falling, Fabrizio rode into Ferrara on a pony. He was in urgent need of care. The heat on the river had made him ill; the knife thrust in his thigh and the sword thrust Giletti had given him in the shoulder, at the beginning of their fight, had both become inflamed, and made him feverish.

CHAPTER XII

THE Jew landlord of their lodgings brought them a discreet surgeon, who, soon coming to the conclusion that there was money to be made, informed Ludovico that his conscience obliged him to report the wounds of the young man, whom Ludovico called his brother, to the police.

"The law is clear," he added. "It is quite evident that your brother has not hurt himself, as he declares, by falling off a ladder with an open knife in his hand."

Ludovico coldly answered the worthy surgeon to the effect that if he ventured to listen to the promptings of his conscience, he, Ludovico, would have the honour, before he left Ferrara, of falling upon him with an open knife in his hand. When he related the incident to Fabrizio he blamed him severely. But there was not an instant to be lost about decamping. Ludovico told the Jew he was going to try what an airing would do for his brother. He fetched a carriage, and our friends left the house, never to return to it again. My readers doubtless find these descriptions of all the steps necessitated by the lack of a passport very lengthy. But in Italy, and especially in the neighbourhood of the Po, everybody's talk is about passports. As soon as they had slipped safely out of Ferrara, as if they were merely taking a drive, Ludovico dismissed the carriage, re-entered the town by a different gate, and then came back to fetch Fabrizio in a *sediola*, which he had hired to take them twelve leagues. When they were near Bologna, our friends had themselves driven across country, to the road leading into the city from Florence. They spent the night in the most wretched tavern they could discover, and the next morning, as Fabrizio felt strong enough to walk a little, they entered Bologna on foot. Giletti's passport had been burned. The actor's death must now be known, and it was less dangerous to be arrested for having no passport, than for presenting one belonging to a man who had been killed.

Ludovico knew several servants in great houses at Bologna. It was agreed that he should go and collect intelligence from them. He told them he had come from Florence with his young brother, who, being overcome with sleep, had let him start alone an hour before sunrise. They were to have met in the village where Ludovico was to halt during the sultry midday hours, but when his brother did not arrive, Ludovico had resolved to retrace his steps. He had found him wounded by a blow from a stone and several knife thrusts, and robbed into the bargain, by people who had picked a quarrel with him. The brother was a good-looking young fellow; he could groom and manage horses, and would be glad to take service in some great house. Ludovico intended to add, if necessity should arise, that when Fabrizio had fallen down, the thieves had taken to flight, and had carried off a little bag containing their linen and their passports.

When Fabrizio reached Bologna he felt very weary, and not daring to go into an inn without a passport, he turned into the large Church of San Petronio. It was deliciously cool within the building, and he soon felt quite recovered. " Ungrateful wretch that I am," said he to himself suddenly; " I walk into a church, and just sit myself down as if I were in a *café*." He threw himself on his knees, and thanked God fervently for the protection He had so evidently extended to him since he had had the misfortune of killing Giletti. The danger which still made him shudder was that of being recognised in the police office at Casal-Maggiore. " How was it," he thought, " that the clerk, whose eyes were so full of suspicion, and who read my passport three times over, did not perceive that I am not five foot ten tall, that I am not eight-and-thirty years old, and that I am not deeply pitted with the small-pox? What mercies do I owe thee, oh, my God! and I have waited until now to lay my nothingness at Thy feet. My pride would fain have believed it was to vain human prudence that I owed the happiness of escaping the Spielberg, which was already yawning to engulf me."

More than an hour did Fabrizio spend in the deepest emotion at the thought of the immense goodness of the Most High. He did not hear Ludovico approach him and stand in front of him. Fabrizio, who had hidden his face in his hands, raised his head, and his faithful servant saw the tears coursing down his cheeks.

"Come back in an hour," said Fabrizio to him with some asperity.

Ludovico forgave his tone in consideration of his piety. Fabrizio recited the seven penitential psalms, which he knew by heart, several times over, making long pauses over the verses applicable to his present position.

Fabrizio asked pardon of God for many things, but it is a remarkable fact that it never occurred to him to reckon among his faults his plan of becoming an archbishop simply and solely because Count Mosca was a prime minister, and considered this dignity, and the great position it conferred, suitable for the duchess's nephew. He had not indeed desired the thing at all passionately, but still he had considered it exactly as he would have considered his appointment to a ministry or a military command. The thought that his conscience might be involved in the duchess's plan had never struck him. This is a remarkable feature of the teaching he owed to the Jesuits at Milan. This form of religion deprives men of courage to think of unaccustomed matters, and more especially forbids self-examination, as the greatest of all sins—a step toward Protestantism. To discover in what one is guilty, we must ask questions of one's priest, or read the list of sins as printed in the book entitled Preparation for the Sacrament of Penitence. Fabrizio knew the Latin list of sins, which he had learned at the Ecclesiastical Academy at Naples, by heart, and when, as he repeated this list, he came to the word "Murder," he had honestly accused himself before God of having killed a man, though in defence of his own life. He had run rapidly, and without the smallest attention, through the various clauses relating to the sin of simony (the purchase of ecclesiastical dignities with money). If he had been invited to give a hundred louis to become grand vicar to the Archbishop of Parma, he would have shrunk from the idea with horror. But although he neither lacked intelligence nor, more especially, logic, it never once came into his head that the employment of Count Mosca's credit in his favour constituted a simony. Herein lies the triumph of the Jesuits' teaching; it instils the habit of paying no attention to things which are as clear as day. A Frenchman brought up amid Parisian self-interest and scepticism might honestly have accused Fabrizio of hypocrisy at the very moment when our hero was laying open his heart before his God with the utmost sincerity, and the deepest possible emotion.

Fabrizio did not leave the church until he had prepared the confession which he had resolved to make the very next morning. He found Ludovico sitting on the steps of the huge stone peristyle which rises on the great square before the façade of San Petronio. Just as the air is purified by a great thunder-storm, so Fabrizio's heart felt calmer, happier, and, so to speak, cooler. "I am much better. I hardly feel my wounds at all," he said, as he joined Ludovico. "But, first of all, I must ask your forgiveness; I answered you crossly when you came to speak to me in the church. I was examining my conscience. Well, how does our business go?"

"It's going right well. I've engaged a lodging—not at all worthy of your Excellency, indeed—kept by the wife of one of my friends, who is a very pretty woman, and in close intimacy, besides, with one of the principal police agents. To-morrow I shall go and report that our passports have been stolen. This declaration will be well received, but I shall pay the postage of a letter which the police will send to Casal-Maggiore to inquire whether there is a man there of the name of San Micheli, who has a brother named Fabrizio in the service of the Duchess Sanseverina of Parma. It's all done, *siamo à cavallo*" (an Italian proverb, meaning "we are saved").

Fabrizio had suddenly become very grave. He asked

The Chartreuse of Parma

Ludovico to wait for him a moment, returned to the church almost at a run, and had hardly got inside when he cast himself once more upon his knees and humbly kissed the stone pavement. "This is a miracle," he cried, with tears in his eyes. "Thou sawest my soul ready to return to the path of duty, and Thou hast saved me. O God, I may be killed some day in a scuffle. Remember, O Lord, when my dying moment comes, the condition of my heart at this moment." In a passion of the liveliest joy, Fabrizio once more recited the seven penitential psalms. Before he left the church, he approached an old woman who sat in front of a great Madonna and beside an iron triangle set vertically on a support of the same metal. The edges of this triangle bristled with little spikes, destined to support the small tapers which the faithful burn before Cimabue's famous Madonna.

Only seven tapers were burning when Fabrizio approached. He noted the fact in his memory, so as to reflect on it when he should have time.

"How much do the tapers cost?" said he to the woman.

"Two *baiocchi* each."

And, indeed, they were no thicker than a penholder, and not a foot high.

"How many tapers will your triangle hold?"

"Sixty-three, since there are seven already."

"Ha!" said Fabrizio. "Sixty-three and seven make seventy; I must remember that, too." He paid for the tapers, set up and lighted the first seven himself, and then knelt down to make his offering. As he rose from his knees he said to the old woman, "It is for a mercy bestowed."

"I am dying of hunger," said Fabrizio to Ludovico as he rejoined him.

"Don't let us go into a tavern; let us go to the lodgings," said his servant. "The mistress of the house will go out and buy you what you want for breakfast; she'll cheat us out of a score of sous, and that will make her feel all the more kindly to the new arrival."

The Chartreuse of Parma

"That means that I shall have to go on starving for another hour," said Fabrizio, laughing as merrily as a child, and he entered a tavern close to San Petronio. To his extreme astonishment he beheld, sitting at a table close to his own his aunt's principal man-servant, Pepe, the very man who had once been sent to meet him at Geneva. Fabrizio signed to him to keep silence; then, after a hasty repast, with a happy smile trembling on his lips, he rose to his feet. Pepe followed him, and for the third time our hero passed into San Petronio. Ludovico discreetly held back, and walked up and down the square.

"Oh, monsignore, how are your wounds? The duchess is in dreadful anxiety. For one whole day she believed you were dead, and cast away on some island in the river. I must send a messenger to her instantly. I have been hunting for you for six days; I spent three of them at Ferrara, going to all the inns."

"Have you a passport for me?"

"I have three. One with all your Excellency's names and titles, one with nothing but your name, and the third with a false name, Giuseppe Bossi. Each of the passports will serve your Excellency's purpose, whether you choose to arrive from Florence or from Modena. All you have to do is to walk out beyond the town. The count would be glad if you would lodge at the Albergo del Pellegrino, which is kept by a friend of his."

Fabrizio walked, as though by chance, up the right aisle of the church to the spot where his tapers were burning. He fixed his eyes on the Cimabue Madonna, then, kneeling down, he said to Pepe, "I must thank God for a moment." Pepe followed his example. As they left the church Pepe noticed that Fabrizio gave a twenty-franc piece to the first beggar who asked charity of him. The beggar set up a shout of gratitude, which attracted the crowds of indigent people of every sort who generally collect on the square of San Petronio all round the charitable donor. Everybody wanted his or her share of the napoleon. The women, despairing of getting through the press round the lucky mendicant, fell upon Fabrizio, shrieking to him to say it was true he had given his gold piece to be divided among all the poor beggars. Pepe brandished his gold-headed cane, and ordered them to leave " his Excellency " alone.

"Oh, your Excellency," screamed all the women at once, even louder than before, " give the poor women another gold piece." Fabrizio quickened his pace; the women ran after him, calling aloud, and many male beggars ran up from side streets, so that quite a little disturbance ensued. The whole of the filthy and noisy crowd kept shouting "Your Excellency!" Fabrizio found it by no means easy to get out of the press. The scene recalled his imagination to earth. "I am only getting what I deserve," thought he. "I have been rubbing shoulders with the common folk."

Two of the women followed him as far as the Saragossa Gate, through which he passed out of the town. There Pepe stopped them by threatening them seriously with his cane and throwing them some small coins. Fabrizio climbed the pretty hill of San Michele in Bosco, walked partly round the town, outside the walls, turned into a footpath, which, five hundred paces farther on, ran into the road from Florence, returned to Bologna, and gravely presented a passport containing a very accurate description of his person to the police commissary. This passport described him as Giuseppe Bossi, student of theology. Fabrizio noticed a little splash of red ink that seemed to have been dropped by accident on the lower right-hand corner of the paper. Two hours later he had a spy upon his heels, on account of the title " your Excellency " applied to him by his companion in the presence of the beggars at San Petronio, although his passport detailed none of those honours which entitle a man to be addressed as " Excellency " by his servants.

Fabrizio perceived the spy, and snapped his fingers at him. He gave not a thought, now, either to passports or police officers, and was as amused as a child with everything about him. When Pepe, who had been ordered to stay with him, saw how well pleased he was with Ludovico, he thought his own best course was to carry the good news to the duchess himself. Fabrizio wrote two long letters to his dear ones. Then he bethought him of writing a third to the venerable Archbishop Landriani. This letter produced a most extraordinary effect. It contained the exact history of his fight with Giletti. The good archbishop, quite overcome by his emotion, did not fail to go and read the letter to the prince, whose curiosity to know how the young monsignore would set about excusing so terrible a murder made him willing to listen. Thanks to the Marchesa Raversi's many friends, the prince, like the whole city of Parma, believed Fabrizio had obtained the assistance of some twenty or thirty peasants to kill an inferior actor who had ventured to dispute his possession of little Marietta. At despotic courts truth lies at the mercy of the first clever schemer, just as in Paris it is ruled by fashion.

"But, devil take it," said the prince to the archbishop, "one has those things done by a third person. It is not customary to do them oneself. And then actors like Giletti are not killed; they are bought."

Fabrizio had not the smallest suspicion of what was going on at Parma. As a matter of fact, the death of a player who only earned thirty-two francs a month in his lifetime was going near to overthrow the *ultra* ministry, with Count Mosca at its head.

When the news of Giletti's death reached him, the prince, nettled by the airs of independence which the duchess gave herself, had ordered Rassi, his Minister of Justice, to deal with the whole trial as if the accused person had been a Liberal. Fabrizio, for his part, believed that a man of his rank was above all law. The fact that in countries where the bearers of great names are never punished, there is nothing that can not be achieved, even against such persons, by intrigue, had not entered into his calculations. He would often talk to Ludovico of his perfect innocence, which was soon to be proclaimed. His great argument was that he was not guilty. At last, one day, Ludovico said to him: "I can not conceive why your Excellency, who is so clever and knows so much, takes the trouble of saying such things to me, who am his devoted servant. Your Excellency is too cautious. Such things are only good for use in public or before the judges."

" This man believes I am a murderer, and he does not love me the less," mused Fabrizio, thunder-struck.

Three days after Pepe's departure, Fabrizio was astonished to receive a huge letter bound with a silken cord, like those used in Louis XIV's time, and addressed to " His Most Reverend Excellency, Monsignore Fabrizio del Dongo, Chief Grand Vicar of the Diocese of Parma, Canon, etc."

" But am I all that already? " he said to himself with a laugh. Archbishop Landriani's epistle was a masterpiece of perspicacity and logic. It covered no less than nineteen large sheets, and gave a very good account of everything that had happened at Parma with regard to Giletti's death.

" The march of a French army on the town, under the command of Marshal Ney, would not have made more stir," wrote the good archbishop. " Every soul, my very dear son, except the duchess and myself, believes you killed the actor Giletti because you wanted to do it. If that misfortune had befallen you, it would have been one of those matters that can be hushed up by means of a couple of hundred louis and an absence of six months. But the Raversi is bent on using the incident to overthrow Count Mosca. It is not the terrible sin of murder for which the public blames you, it is simply for your awkwardness, or rather insolence, in not having condescended to employ a *bulo* [a kind of inferior bully]. I give you the clear substance of the talk I hear all round me. For since this most deplorable event I go every day to three of the most important houses in this city, so as to find opportunity for justifying you, and never have I felt I was making a holier use of what little eloquence Heaven has bestowed on me."

The scales began to fall from Fabrizio's eyes. The numerous letters he received from the duchess, all throbbing with affection, never condescended to report anything of what was happening around her. The duchess assured him she would leave Parma forever, unless he soon returned there in triumph. " The count," she wrote, in a letter which reached him together with the archbishop's, " will do all that is humanly possible for you. As for me, this last prank of yours has changed my nature; I have grown as stingy as Tombone, the banker. I have discharged all my workmen. I have done more—I have dictated the inventory of my belongings to the count, and I find I have very much less than I thought. After the death of that excellent Pietranera (whose murder, by the way, you would have done far better to avenge, than to risk your life against such a creature as Giletti), I was left with twelve hundred francs a year, and debts amounting to five thousand. Among other things, I remember, I had thirty pairs of white satin slippers which had come from Paris, and only one single pair of walking shoes. I have almost made up my mind to take the three hundred thousand francs the duke left me, and which I had intended to lay out entirely on a magnificent monument to his memory. For the rest, it is the Marchesa Raversi who is your bitterest enemy, and therefore mine. If you are bored at Bologna, you have only to say one word, and I will go to you there. Here are four more bills of exchange."

The duchess never told Fabrizio a word about the opinion concerning his business which prevailed at Parma. Her first object was to console him, and in any case the death of such an absurd person as Giletti did not strike her as matter of any serious reproach to a Del Dongo.

"How many Gilettis have our ancestors sent into the next world!" she would say to the count; "and nobody ever dreamed of finding fault with them for it."

Fabrizio, filled with astonishment, and perceiving for the first time the real condition of things, set himself to study the archbishop's letter. Unfortunately the archbishop himself believed him better informed than he really was. As Fabrizio understood the matter, the Marchesa Raversi's triumph rested on the impossibility of discovering any eye-witnesses of the fatal scuffle. His own servant, who had been the first to bring the news to Parma, had been inside the village tavern at Sanguigna when the incident occurred. Little Marietta, and the old woman who acted as her mother, had disappeared, and the marchesa had bought over the man who had driven the carriage, and who was now making a deposition of the most abominable kind. " Although the proceedings are wrapped in the deepest mystery," wrote the good archbishop in his Ciceronian style, " and directed by Rassi, of whom Christian charity forbids me to speak evil, but who has made his fortune by pursuing unfortunate beings accused of crime, even as the hound pursues the hare; though Rassi, I say, whose baseness and venality you can not overrate, has been charged with the management of the trial by an angry prince, I have obtained a sight of the *vetturino's* three depositions. By a signal piece of good fortune the wretch has flatly contradicted himself, and I will add, seeing I speak to my vicar-general, who will rule this diocese when I am gone, that I sent for the priest of the parish in which this wandering sinner dwells. I will confide to you, my very dear son, though under the secret of the confessional, that the priest already knows, through the *vetturino's* wife, the actual number of crowns her husband has received from the Marchesa Raversi. I will not dare to say that the marchesa has insisted on his slandering you, but that is very likely. The crowns were paid over by a miserable priest who performs very dubious functions in the marchesa's service, and whom I have been obliged, for the second time, to prohibit from saying mass. I will not weary you with the recital of several other steps which you might fairly have expected from me, and which, indeed, it was only my duty to take. A canon, a colleague of yours at the cathedral, who is occasionally too apt to remember the influence conferred on him by the possession of the family fortune, of which, by God's will, he has become the sole inheritor, ventured to say, in the house of Count Zurla, Minister of the Interior, that he considered this trifle clearly proved against you (he was speaking of the unhappy Giletti's murder). I summoned him to my palace, and there, in presence of my three other vicars-general, of my chaplain, and of two priests who happened to be in my waiting-room, I requested him to enlighten us, his brothers, as to the grounds on which he based the complete conviction he declared himself to have acquired, of the guilt of one of his colleagues at the cathedral. The only reasons the poor wretch could articulate were very inconclusive. Every one present rose up against him, and although I did not think it necessary to add more than a very few words, he burst into tears, and before us all made a full confession of his complete error. Whereupon I promised him secrecy, in my own name and that of all those who had been present at the conference, on condition, however, that he should use all his zeal to rectify the false impression produced by the remarks he had been making during the past fortnight.

"I will not repeat, my dear son, what you must have known for long—that out of the four-and-thirty peasants working on Count Mosca's excavation, and who, according to the Raversi, were paid to assist you in your crime, thirty-two men were hard at work at the bottom of their ditch at the moment when you seized the hunting-knife and used it to defend your life against the man who had so unexpectedly attacked you. Two of them who were not in the ditch shouted to them, 'He is murdering monsignore!' This one exclamation is a brilliant testimony to your innocence. Well, Rassi declares that these two men have disappeared, and further, eight of the men who were in the trench have been found. When they were first examined six of these declared they had heard the shout, 'He is murdering monsignore!' I know indirectly that when they were examined for the fifth time, yesterday evening, five of them asserted that they could not remember whether they had actually heard the exclamation, or whether they had been told of it afterward, by one of their comrades. Orders have been given which will make me acquainted with the localities in which these workmen live, and their priest will make them understand that if they allow themselves to be tempted to wrest the truth, for the sake of earning a few crowns, they will be damned everlastingly."

The good archbishop proceeded with infinite detail, as may be judged by what we have already reported. Then he added these lines in Latin:

"This business is nothing less than an attempt to turn out the ministry. If you are sentenced it can only be to the galleys or to execution. In that case I should intervene, and declare, with all the weight of my archiepiscopal authority, that I know you to be innocent; that you have simply defended your life against a rascal; and further, that I have forbidden you to return to Parma as long as your enemies triumph there. I even propose to brand the Minister of Justice as he deserves; the hatred felt for that man is as common as esteem for his character is rare. But on the eve of the day whereon the minister pronounces so unjust a sentence, the Duchess of Sanseverina will leave the city, and perhaps even the dominion of Parma. In that case, no one doubts that the count will immediately hand in his resignation. Then, most probably, General Fabio Conti will be made minister, and the Marchesa Raversi will triumph. The great difficulty about your business is that no capable man has been placed in charge of the steps indispensable for the demonstration of your innocence, and for the frustration of the attempts being made to suborn witnesses. The count thinks he is doing this himself, but he is too great a gentleman to condescend to certain details, and besides, his position as Minister of Police obliged him, at the very outset, to issue the severest orders against you. And finally—dare I say it?—our sovereign master believes you guilty, or simulates the belief, at all events, and imports a certain bitterness into the affair." (The words corresponding to *our sovereign master* and *simulates the belief* were in Greek characters, and Fabrizio was infinitely grateful to the archbishop for having dared to write them at all. He cut the line out of the letter with his penknife, and instantly destroyed it.)

Twenty times over Fabrizio broke off in the perusal of this letter. He was filled with the deepest and most lively gratitude, and instantly wrote a letter of eight pages in reply. Often he had to lift his head, so as to prevent the tears from dropping on his paper. The next morning, just as he was about to seal his missive, he bethought him that it was too worldly in tone. "I will write it in Latin," said he to himself; "it will seem more correct to the worthy archbishop." But while he was striving to turn fine long Latin phrases, careful imitations of Cicero, he remembered that one day, when the archbishop had been speaking to him of Napoleon, he had made it a point to call him " *Buonaparte.*" That instant every trace of the emotion which, only the night before, had affected him even to tears, fled utterly. " Oh, King of Italy! " he cried, " the faith so many swore to you in your lifetime shall be kept by me, now that you are no more. He cares for me, no doubt, but that is because I am a Del Dongo and he the son of a common man." So that his fine Italian letter might not be wasted, Fabrizio made some necessary changes in it, and despatched it to Count Mosca.

That very some day, Fabrizio met little Marietta in the street. She reddened with delight, and signed to him to follow without speaking to her. She took her way swiftly toward a lonely portico; once there, she drew forward the black lace which covered her head, in the fashion of that country, so that no one could recognise her, and then, turning round sharply—

" How is it," said she to Fabrizio, " that you are walking about freely in the streets? " Fabrizio told her his story.

" Great heavens, you've been to Ferrara! And I have been hunting for you everywhere. You must know that I quarrelled with the old woman because she wanted to take me to Venice, where I knew quite well you would never go, because you are on the Austrian black list. I sold my gold necklace to get to Bologna. Something told me I should have the happiness of meeting you here, and the old woman arrived two days after me. I would not advise you to visit us, because she would make more of those shabby attempts to get money out of you, of which I am so ashamed. We have lived very comfortably since that fatal day you know of, and we have not spent a quarter of what you gave her. I should not like to go to see you at the Albergo del Pellegrino; that would be a *publicity.* Try to hire some little room in a lonely street, and at the *Ave Maria* (nightfall) I will be here under this same portico."

Having said these words, she took to flight.

CHAPTER XIII

THE unexpected appearance of this charming young person drove every serious thought away. Fabrizio lived on at Bologna with a sense of the deepest delight and security. His artless propensity to find happiness in anything which filled his life, betrayed itself in his letters to the duchess, and to such a point as to annoy her.

Fabrizio hardly noticed it; only he noted in abbreviated signs on the dial plate of his watch, "When I write to the duchess I must never say 'when I was a prelate, when I was a churchman'—it vexes her." He had bought a pair of ponies, with which he was very much pleased, and harnessed them to a hired chaise whenever little Marietta had a fancy to go and see one of the delightful spots in the neighbourhood of Bologna. Almost every evening he drove her to the Reno Cascade. On the way back he would stop at the house of the good-natured Crescentini, who rather believed himself to be Marietta's father.

"Faith," said Fabrizio to himself, "if this be the *café* life which struck me as being so absurd for any serious man to lead, I did wrong to turn up my nose at it." He forgot that he never went near a *café* except to read the Constitutionnel, and that as he was utterly unknown to any one in Bologna, the pleasures of vanity had nothing to do with his present state of felicity. When he was not with little Marietta, he was to be seen at the observatory, where he was attending a course of astronomy. The professor had taken a great fancy to him, and Fabrizio would lend him his horses on a Sunday, so that he and his wife might go and ruffle it in the Corso of the Montagnola.

He had a horror of making any one unhappy, however unworthy the person might be. Marietta would not hear

227

of his seeing the *mamaccia*, but one day, when she was in church, he went up to the old woman's room. She flushed with anger when she saw him enter. " I must play the Del Dongo here," said Fabrizio to himself. " How much does Marietta earn a month when she has an engagement? " he called out, with very much the same air as that with which a self-respecting young Parisian takes his seat in the *balcon* at the Opéra Bouffe.

" Fifty crowns."

" You lie, as usual. Tell me the truth, or, by God, you'll not get a centime."

" Well, she was earning twenty-two crowns in our company at Parma, when we were so unlucky as to meet you. I earned twelve crowns, and we each gave Giletti, our protector, a third of our earnings; on that Giletti made Marietta a present almost every month — something like two crowns——"

" You lie again; you only earned four crowns. But if you are good to Marietta, I will engage you as if I were an *impresario*. You shall have twelve crowns for yourself every month, and twenty-two for her, but if I see her eyes red once I shall go bankrupt."

" You're mighty proud of yourself! Well, let me tell you, your fine generosity is ruining us," rejoined the old woman furiously. " We are losing *l'avviamento* [our custom]. When we have the crushing misfortune of losing your Excellency's protection, no comedy company will know anything about us. They will all be full, we shall find no engagement, and, thanks to you, we shall die of hunger."

" Go to the devil! " said Fabrizio, departing.

" I will not go to the devil, you ungodly wretch! But I will go straight to the police, and they shall know from me that you are a monsignore who has cast away his cassock, and that Giuseppe Bossi is no more your name than it's mine."

Fabrizio had already descended several steps; he turned and came back. " In the first place, the police probably know my real name better than you do. But, if you venture to denounce me, if you dare to do anything so infamous," he said very seriously, " Ludovico will talk to you, and it will not be six knife thrusts that you will have in your old carcass, but four times six, and you will spend six months in hospital, and without tobacco."

The hag turned pale, rushed at Fabrizio's hand, and tried to kiss it

" I accept what you are ready to do for me and Marietta thankfully; you looked so good-natured that I took you for a simpleton. And consider this well; other people might make the same mistake. I would advise you to look more like a great gentleman, as a rule." Then she added, with the most admirable impudence, " You will think over this piece of good advice, and, as winter is not far off, you will make Marietta and me each a present of a good coat of that ·fine English stuff in the big shop on the Piazza San Petronio."

The pretty Marietta's love offered Fabrizio all the charms of the most tender friendship, and this made him think of the happiness of the same description he might have found in the company of the duchess.

" But is it not a very comical thing," said he to himself, " that I am not capable of that exclusive and passionate preoccupation which men call love? Amid all my chance *liaisons*, at Novara or at Naples, did I ever meet a woman whose presence I preferred, even in the earliest days, to a ride on a good-looking horse that I had never mounted before? Can it be," he added, " that what is called 'love' is yet another lie? I love, of course, just as I am hungry at six o'clock in the evening. Can it be that this somewhat vulgar propensity is what these liars have lifted into the love of Othello and the love of Tancred? Or must I believe that my organization is different from that of other men. What if no passion should ever touch my heart? That would be a strange fate! "

At Naples, especially toward the close of his residence there, Fabrizio had met women who, proud of their rank, their beauty, and the worldly position of the adorers they had sacrificed to him, had tried to govern him. At the very first inkling of their plans Fabrizio had broken with them in the promptest and most scandalous manner. "Now," said he, "if I ever allow myself to be carried away by the pleasure, no doubt a very keen one, of being on good terms with that pretty woman known as the Duchess Sanseverina, I am exactly like the blundering Frenchman who killed the hen that laid the golden eggs. To the duchess I owe the only happiness with which a tender feeling has ever inspired me. My affection for her is my life; and besides, apart from her what am I? A miserable exile condemned to a hand-to-mouth existence, in a ruinous castle near Novara. I remember that when the great autumn rains came I used to be obliged to fasten an umbrella over the head of my bed, for fear of accidents. I used to ride the agent's horses, and he just allowed it out of respect for my blue blood (and my muscular strength). But he was beginning to think I had stayed there too long. My father allowed me twelve hundred francs a year, and thought himself damned because he was supporting a Jacobin. My poor mother and my sisters went without gowns so as to enable me to make some trifling presents to my mistresses. This kind of generosity used to wring my heart, and besides, my state of penury was beginning to be suspected, and the young noblemen in the neighbourhood would soon have been pitying me. Sooner or later some coxcomb would have betrayed his scorn for a poor and unsuccessful Jacobin, for in their eyes I was nothing else. I should have bestowed or received some hearty sword thrust, which would have brought me to the fortress of Fenestrella or forced me to take refuge in Switzerland once more—still with my twelve hundred francs a year. To the duchess I owe the happiness of having escaped all these ills, and further, she it is who feels for me those transports of affection which I ought to feel for her.

"Instead of the ridiculous and shabby existence which would have turned me into that sorry animal, a fool, I have spent four years in a great city, and with an excellent carriage, which has prevented me from feeling envy, and other low provincial sentiments. This aunt, in her extreme kindness, is always scolding me because I do not draw enough money from her banker. Shall I spoil this admirable position forever? Shall I lose the only friend I have in the world? All I have to do is to tell her a lie, and say to a charming woman, who probably has not her equal in the world, and for whom I have the most passionate regard, 'I love you.' This from me, who do not know what real love means! She would spend whole days reproaching me with the absence of those transports which I have never known. Now, Marietta, who can not see into my heart, and who takes a caress for an outburst of passion, thinks me madly in love with her, and believes herself the happiest of living women."

" As a matter of fact, the only slight acquaintance that I have ever had with that tender absorption which is, I believe, denominated *love*, was for that young girl Aniken, at the inn at Zonders, near the Belgian frontier."

It is with much regret that we must here relate one of Fabrizio's worst actions. In the midst of his tranquil life, a foolish sting to his vanity took possession of the heart which love could not vanquish, and carried him quite off his feet. Living in Bologna at the same time as himself, was the celebrated Fausta F——, undoubtedly one of the first singers of our time, and perhaps the most capricious woman ever seen. The gifted Venetian poet Burati had written a famous satirical sonnet concerning her, which, at that time, was in the mouth of every one, from princes to the lowest urchins in the street :—

" To will and not to will, to adore and detest in one and the same day, to find no happiness save in inconstancy, to scorn that which the world adores, so long as the world adores it—Fausta has all these faults and many more. Wherefore, never cast your eyes upon the serpent; if once thou seest her, oh, imprudent man, all her caprices are forgotten. If thou hast the happiness of hearing her, thou forgettest even thyself, and love, at that moment, makes of thee what Circe once made the comrades of Ulysses."

Just at that moment this miracle of beauty was so fascinated by the huge whiskers and overweening insolence of the young Count M—— that even his abominable jealousy

did not revolt her. Fabrizio saw the count in the streets
of Bologna, and was nettled by the air of superiority with
which he swaggered along the pavements, and graciously
condescended to show off his charms before the public. The
young man was very rich, believed he might venture anything, and as his *prepotenzi* had earned him several threats,
he hardly ever appeared unaccompanied by eight or ten
buli (a sort of ruffian) who wore his liveries, and came
from his property near Brescia.

Once or twice, when he had chanced to hear the Fausta
sing, Fabrizio had crossed glances with the doughty count.
He was astonished by the angelic sweetness of her voice;
he had never dreamed of anything like it. It gave him sensations of supreme delight, a fine contrast to the placidity of
his existence. "Can this, at last, be love?" said he to himself. Full of curiosity to feel the passion, and amused, too,
by the idea of braving the count, who looked far more
threatening than any drum-major, our hero committed the
childish folly of appearing much too frequently in front of
the Palazzo Tanari, in which the count had installed the
Fausta.

One day, toward nightfall, Fabrizio, who was trying to
make Fausta look at him, was greeted by shrieks of laughter, evidently intentional, from the count's *buli*, who were
standing round the door of the palace. He hurried home,
armed himself well, and returned.

Fausta, hidden behind her sun-blinds, was expecting this
return, and noted it down to his credit. The count, who was
jealous of everybody on earth, became especially jealous of
Signor Giuseppe Bossi, and indulged in all sorts of absurd
threats, whereupon our hero sent him a letter every morning containing nothing but these words: "Signor Giuseppe
Bossi destroys vermin, and lives at the Pellegrino, in the Via
Larga, No. 79."

Count M——, inured to the respect ensured him everywhere by his great fortune, his blue blood, and the bravery
of his thirty serving-men, refused to understand the language of the little note.

Fabrizio wrote more notes to the Fausta. M—— set

spies upon his rival, who was not, perhaps, unpleasing to the lady. He first of all learned his real name, and that, for the moment, at all events, he did not dare to show his face in Parma. A few days later Count M——, with his *buli*, his splendid horses, and Fausta, all departed to Parma.

Fabrizio, warming to the game, followed them next morning. In vain did the faithful Ludovico remonstrate pathetically with him. Fabrizio would not listen, and Ludovico, who was a brave man himself, admired him for it. Besides, this journey would bring him nearer his own pretty mistress at Casal-Maggiore. By Ludovico's care, eight or ten old soldiers who had served in Napoleon's regiments, entered Signor Giuseppe Bossi's service, nominally as servants.

" If," said Fabrizio to himself, " when I commit this folly of going after the Fausta, I only hold no communication with the Minister of Police, Count Mosca, nor with the duchess, I risk no one but myself. Later on I will tell my aunt that I did it all in search of love, that beautiful thing that I have never been able to discover. The fact is that I do think about Fausta, even when I don't see her; but is it the memory of her voice that I love, or is it her person? "

As he had given up all thoughts of the Church as a career, Fabrizio had grown moustaches and whiskers almost as tremendous as those of Count M——, and these somewhat disguised him. He established his headquarters, not at Parma—that would have been too imprudent—but in a village hard by, on the road to Sacca, where his aunt's country house was situated. Advised by Ludovico, he gave himself out in the village as the valet of a very eccentric English nobleman who spent a hundred thousand francs a year on sport, and who was shortly to arrive from the Lake of Como, where he was detained by the trout-fishing.

Fortunately the pretty little palace which Count M—— had hired for the fair Fausta stood at the southernmost end of the town of Parma, and just on the Sacca road, and Fausta's windows looked on to the fine avenues of tall trees which stretch away below the high tower of the citadel.

Fabrizio was not known in that lonely quarter of the

town. He did not fail to have Count M—— followed, and one day, when he had just left the exquisite singer's house, Fabrizio was bold enough to appear in the street in broad daylight. He was well armed, indeed, and mounted on an excellent horse. Musicians, such as are constantly found in the Italian streets, and who occasionally are very good indeed, ranged themselves with their instruments under the Fausta's windows, and, after some introductory chords, sang, very fairly, a cantata in her honour. Fausta appeared at the window, and her attention was easily caught by a very courteous young gentleman, who first of all saluted her, and then began to bombard her with most significant glances. In spite of the exaggeratedly English dress Fabrizio had donned, she soon recognised the sender of the passionate letters which had brought about her departure from Bologna. " This is a strange being," said she to herself. " I fancy I am going to fall in love with him. I have a hundred louis in my pocket. I can very well afford to break with the terrible count. He really has no intelligence, and there is nothing novel about him; the only thing that rather entertains me is the frightful appearance of his followers."

The next morning Fabrizio, having heard that the Fausta went to mass every day about eleven o'clock, in that very church of San Giovanni which contained the tomb of his great-uncle, the Archbishop Ascanio del Dongo, ventured to follow her there. It must be said that Ludovico had provided him with a fine English wig of the brightest red hair. *À propos* to the colour of these locks—that of the flame which devoured his heart—he wrote a sonnet which delighted the Fausta. An unknown hand had laid it carefully on her piano. This manœuvring went on for quite a week, but Fabrizio felt that in spite of all his various efforts, he was making no real progress.

Fausta refused to receive him. He had overdone his eccentricity, and she has since acknowledged that she was afraid of him. Fabrizio still retained a faint hope of arriving at the sensation which is known as love, but in the meanwhile, he was very often sorely bored.

"Sir, let us take ourselves off," said Ludovico to him over and over again. "You are not the least in love; your coolness and reasonableness are quite hopeless, and besides, you make no progress whatsoever. Let us decamp, for very shame."

In the first flush of disgust, Fabrizio was on the very point of departing. Then he heard that the Fausta was to sing at the Duchess Sanseverina's house. "Perhaps that sublime voice will really set my heart on fire at last," thought he, and he actually dared to introduce himself, in disguise, into his aunt's palace, where every one knew him.

The emotion of the duchess may be imagined, when, quite toward the end of the concert, she noticed a man in a chasseur's livery standing near the door of the great drawing-room; something in his appearance stirred her memory. She sought Count Mosca, and it was not until then that he informed her of Fabrizio's extraordinary and really incomprehensible folly. He took the matter very well—this love for somebody who was not the duchess was very agreeable to him—and the count, who, politics apart, was a man of perfect honour, acted on the maxim that his own happiness depended entirely on that of the duchess. "I will save him from himself," said he to his friend. "Imagine our enemies' delight if he were arrested in this very palace! So I have posted a hundred men of my own in the house, and it was on this account that I asked you to give me the keys of the great water-tank. He gives himself out as being desperately in love with the Fausta, and hitherto he has not been able to carry her off from Count M——, who gives the giddy creature all the luxuries of a queen."

The liveliest sorrow was painted on the features of the duchess.

Fabrizio was nothing more than a libertine, then—incapable of any tender or serious feeling! "And not to see us! That is what I shall never be able to forgive him," she said at last. "And I, who am writting to him every day, to Bologna——"

"I give him great credit for his self-restraint," said the count. "He does not desire to compromise us by his freak, and it will be very amusing to hear his account of it later."

The Fausta was too giddy-pated to be able to hold her tongue about anything which occupied her thoughts. The morning after the concert, during which she had sung all her airs at the tall young man dressed as a chasseur, she referred, in conversation with the count, to an unknown and attentive individual. "Where do you see him?" inquired the count in a fury. "In the streets, in church," replied the Fausta, in confusion. She immediately tried to repair her imprudence, or at all events to remove any idea which could recall Fabrizio's person. She launched into an endless description of a tall red-haired young man with blue eyes, some very rich and clumsy Englishman, doubtless, or else some prince. At this word the count, the definiteness of whose impressions was their only virtue, jumped to the conclusion—a delightful one for his vanity—that his rival was none other than the hereditary Prince of Parma. This poor melancholy youth, watched over by five or six governors, sub-governors, tutors, etc., who never allowed him to go out without holding a preliminary council, was in the habit of casting strange looks at every decent-looking woman whom he was allowed to approach. At the duchess's concert he had been seated, as his rank demanded, in front of all the other auditors, in a separate arm-chair, and three paces from the fair Fausta, and had gazed at her in a manner which had caused excessive vexation to the count. This delightful piece of wild vanity, the idea of having a prince for his rival, entertained Fausta vastly, and she amused herself by strengthening it with a hundred details, imparted in the most apparently artless fashion.

"Is your family," said she to the count, "as old as that of the Farnese, to which this young man belongs?"

"As old! What do you mean? There are no bastards in my family." *

---

* Pietro Luigi, the first sovereign of the Farnese family, so famous for his virtues, was, as is well known, the natural son of Pope Paul III.

The Chartreuse of Parma

It so fell out that Count M—— never could get a clear view of his pretended rival, and this confirmed his flattering conviction that he had a prince for his antagonist. As a matter of fact, Fabrizio, when the necessities of his enterprise did not summon him to Parma, spent his time in the woods near Sacca, and on the banks of the Po. Count M—— had grown more haughty than ever, but far more prudent, too, since he had believed himself to be disputing Fausta's affections with a prince. He besought her very earnestly to behave with the utmost reserve in everything she did.

After casting himself at her feet, like a jealous and passionate lover, he told her very plainly that his honour demanded that she should not be duped by the young prince.

"Excuse me," she replied. "I should not be his dupe if I loved him. I have never yet seen a prince at my feet."

"If you yield," he responded, with a haughty look, "I may not, perhaps, be able to avenge myself on the prince, but vengeance I will have, you may be certain," and he went out, banging the doors behind him. Had Fabrizio made his appearance at that moment, he would have won his cause.

"If you value your life," said Count M—— to her that evening, as he took leave of her after the play, "see to it that I never find out that the young prince has entered your house. I can do nothing to him, but s'death, madam, do not force me to remember that I can do anything I please to you!"

"Ah, my little Fabrizio," exclaimed the Fausta, "if I only knew where to lay my hand on you!"

Wounded vanity may drive a wealthy young man, who has been surrounded by flatterers since his birth, into many things. The very real passion with which the Fausta had inspired Count M—— burned up again furiously. The dangerous prospect of a struggle with the only son of the sovereign in whose country he was sojourning did not daunt him, and at the same time he was not clever enough to make any attempt to get a sight of the prince, or at least have him followed. As he could discover no other method of attack, M—— ventured on the idea of making him look ridiculous.

" I shall be banished forever from the dominion of Parma,"
said he. " Well, what matter? "

If he had made any attempt to reconnoitre the enemy's
position, Count M—— would have discovered that the poor
young prince never went out of doors except in the company of three or four old men, the tiresome guardians of
official etiquette, and that the only pleasure of his own
choice in which he was allowed to indulge, was his taste for
mineralogy. Both in the daytime, and at night, the little
Palazzo occupied by Fausta, and to which the best company
in Parma crowded, was surrounded by watchers. M——
was kept informed, hour by hour, of what she was doing,
and especially of what was done by those about her. One
point, at least, was praiseworthy, in the precautions taken
by the jealous man—the lady, whimsical as she was, had
no suspicion, at first, of the increasing watchfulness about
her. All Count M——'s agents reported that a very young
man, wearing a wig of red hair, constantly appeared under
the Fausta's windows, but every time in some fresh disguise. " Clearly that is the young prince," said M—— to
himself; " otherwise why should he disguise himself?
Egad, I am not the man to make way for him! But for the
usurpations of the Venetian republic I should now be a
reigning prince like him."

On San Stefano's Day the spies' reports grew more
gloomy; they seemed to indicate that the Fausta was beginning to respond to her unknown admirer's attentions. " I
might depart instantly, and take the woman with me," said
M—— to himself, " but I fled from Bologna before Del
Dongo. Here I should flee before a prince, and what would
the young man say? He might think he had contrived to
frighten me, and on my soul, my family is as good as his! "

M—— was beside himself with rage, and to crown his
misery, his great object was to prevent his jealousy from
making him look ridiculous in the eyes of Fausta, with
whose jeering disposition he was well acquainted. Therefore, on San Stefano's Day, after having spent an hour with
her, and received a welcome which seemed to him the very
acme of falsehood, he left her, toward eleven o'clock, when

she was dressing to go and hear mass at the Church of San Giovanni. Count M—— returned to his rooms, put on the shabby black dress of a young theological student, and hurried off to San Giovanni. He chose out a place behind one of the tombs which adorned the third chapel on the right. Under the arm of a cardinal, who was represented kneeling on this tomb, he could see everything that went on in the church. The statue blocked the light within the chapel, and concealed him very sufficiently. Soon he saw Fausta enter, looking more beautiful than ever. She was in full dress, and twenty admirers of the highest rank attended her. Smiles and delight shone on her lips and in her eyes. " Clearly," thought the unhappy man, " she is expecting to meet the man she loves, and whom, thanks to me, she has perhaps not been able to see for a long time."

Suddenly the liveliest expression of happiness shone in Fausta's eyes. " My rival is here," said M—— to himself, and the fury of his wounded vanity knew no bounds. "What am I doing here, acting as counter-weight to a young prince who puts on disguises? " But, hard as he tried, he could not discover the rival whom his hungry glance sought on every side. Every instant the Fausta, after looking all round the church, would fix her eyes, heavy with love and happiness, on the dark corner in which M—— stood concealed. In a passionate heart, love is apt to exaggerate the very slightest things, and deduce consequences of the most ridiculous nature. Thus, poor M—— ended by persuading himself that the Fausta had caught sight of him, and that, having perceived his mortal jealousy, in spite of his desperate efforts to conceal it, she was seeking, by her tender glances, at once to reproach and to console him.

The cardinal's tomb, behind which he had taken up his post of observation, was raised some four or five feet above the marble pavement of San Giovanni. When, toward one o'clock, the fashionable mass was brought to a close, most of the congregation departed, and the Fausta dismissed the city beaux on the pretext that she desired to perform her devotions. She remained kneeling on her chair, and her eyes, which had grown softer and more brilliant than ever, rested on M——. Now that only a few persons remained in the church, she did not take the trouble of looking all round it before allowing them to dwell with delight on the cardinal's statue. "What delicacy!" said Count M——, who thought she was gazing at him. At last the Fausta rose and went quickly out of church, after having made some curious motions with her hands.

M——, drunk with love, and almost wholly cured of his foolish jealousy, was leaving his place to fly to his mistress's palace and overwhelm her with his gratitude, when, as he passed in front of the cardinal's tomb, he noticed a young man all in black. This fatal being had remained kneeling close against the epitaph on the tomb in such a position that the lover's jealous eyes had passed over his head, and so failed to catch sight of him.

The young man rose, moved quickly away, and was instantly surrounded by seven or eight rather awkward and odd-looking fellows, who seemed to belong to him. M—— rushed after him, but, without any too evident effort, the clumsy men, who seemed to be protecting his rival, checked his progress in the little procession necessitated by the wooden screen round the entrance door. When, at last, he got out into the street behind them, he had only time to see the door of a sorry-looking carriage, which, by an odd contrast, was drawn by two excellent horses, swiftly closed, and in a moment it was out of sight.

He went home, choking with fury. He was soon joined by his spies, who coolly informed him that on that day the mysterious lover, disguised as a priest, had knelt very devoutly close up against a tomb standing at the entrance of a dark chapel in the Church of San Giovanni; that the Fausta had remained in the church until it was almost empty, and that she had then swiftly exchanged certain signs with the unknown person, making something like crosses with her hands. M—— rushed to the faithless woman's house. For the first time she could not conceal her confusion. With all the lying simplicity of a passionate woman, she related that she had gone to San Giovanni as usual, but had not seen her persecutor there. On these words M——, beside himself, told her she was the vilest of creatures, related all he had seen himself, and, as the more bitterly he accused her, the more boldly she lied to him, he drew his dagger and would have fallen upon her. With the most perfect calmness the Fausta said:

"Well, everything you complain of is perfectly true, but I have tried to hide it from you, so as to prevent your boldness from carrying you into mad plans of vengeance which may be the ruin of us both. Let me tell you, once for all, I take this man who persecutes me with his attentions to be one who will find no obstacle to his will, in this country, at all events." Then, having skilfully reminded M—— that, after all, he had no rights over her, the Fausta ended by saying that she should probably not go again to the Church of San Giovanni. M—— was desperately in love; it was possible that a touch of coquetry might have mingled with prudence in the young woman's heart. He felt himself disarmed. He thought of leaving Parma; the young prince, powerful as he was, would not be able to follow him, or, if he followed him, he would be no more than his equal. Then his pride reminded him once more that such a departure would always look like flight, and Count M—— forbade himself to think of it again.

"He has not an idea of my little Fabrizio's existence," thought the delighted singer. "And now we shall be able to laugh at him most thoroughly."

Fabrizio had no suspicion of his own good fortune. The next morning, when he saw the fair lady's windows all carefully closed, and could not catch sight of her anywhere, the joke began to strike him as lasting rather too long. His conscience began to prick him. "Into what a position am I putting poor Count Mosca, the Minister of Police? He will be taken for my accomplice, and my coming to this country will be the ruin of his fortunes. But if I give up a plan I have followed for so long, what will the duchess say when I tell her of my attempts at love-making?"

One night when, feeling sorely inclined to give up the game, he thus reasoned with himself, as he prowled up and down under the great trees which divide the palace in which

Fausta was living from the citadel, he became aware that he was being followed by a spy of exceedingly small stature. In vain did he walk through several streets in his endeavour to get away from him. He could not shake off the tiny form which seemed to dog his steps. Losing patience at last, he moved quickly into a lonely street, running along the river, in which his servants were lying in wait. At a signal from him they sprang upon the poor little spy, who threw himself at their feet. It turned out to be Bettina, the Fausta's waiting-woman. After three days of boredom and retirement she had disguised herself in man's attire, to escape Count M——'s dagger—which both she and her mistress greatly dreaded—and had undertaken to come and tell Fabrizio that he was passionately loved and intensely longed for, but that any reappearance at the Church of San Giovanni was quite impossible. "It was high time," thought Fabrizio to himself. "Well done, my obstinacy!"

The little waiting-woman was exceedingly pretty, a fact which soon weaned Fabrizio from his communings with morality. She informed him that the public promenade and all the streets through which he had passed that evening, were carefully, though secretly, guarded by spies in the count's pay. They had hired rooms on the ground floor and on the first floor, and, hidden behind the window shutters, they watched everything that went on in the streets, even those which seemed the loneliest, and heard everything that was said.

"If the spies had recognised my voice," said little Bettina, "I should have been stabbed without mercy as soon as I got home, and my poor mistress with me, perhaps." Fabrizio thought her terror increased her charms.

"Count M——," she added, "is furious, and my mistress knows he is capable of anything. . . . She bade me tell you that she wishes she were with you, and a hundred leagues from here."

Then she told the story of all that had happened on San Stefano's Day and of the fury of the count, who had not missed one of the loving glances and signs which the Fausta, who had been quite beside herself with passion that day, had bestowed on Fabrizio. The count had unsheathed his dagger, had caught hold of Fausta by the hair, and but for her presence of mind would certainly have killed her.

Fabrizio conducted the pretty waiting-maid to a lodging he had hard by. He told her that he was the son of a great Turinese nobleman who chanced to be at Parma at that moment, and that therefore he was obliged to act with the greatest caution. Bettina answered laughingly that he was a much greater man than he chose to appear. It was some time before our hero contrived to understand that the charming girl took him for no less a person than the hereditary prince himself. The Fausta was beginning to take alarm, and also to care for Fabrizio. She had resolved not to tell her waiting-maid his real name, and had spoken of him to her as "the prince." Fabrizio ended by confessing to the pretty girl that she had guessed aright. "But if my name is noised abroad," he added, "in spite of my great passion for your mistress, of which I have given her so many proofs, I shall not be able to see her any more; and my father's ministers, those spiteful wretches whom I shall one day send about their business, will not fail to give her instant orders to clear out of the country which she has hitherto embellished by her presence."

Toward morning, Fabrizio and the fair waiting-maid laid several plans for meeting, so as to enable him to get to Fausta. He sent for Ludovico and another of his men, a very cunning fellow, who arrived at an understanding with Bettina, while he was writing the most exaggerated letter to Fausta. Tragic exaggeration quite fitted in with the situation, and Fabrizio used it without stint. It was not till daybreak that he parted with the pretty waiting-maid, who was highly delighted with the treatment she had received at the hands of the young prince.

A hundred times over they had agreed that now the Fausta had entered into communication with her lover, he was not to appear under the windows of the little palace until she was able to admit him, when he would be duly warned. But Fabrizio, who was now in love with Bettina and believed himself near success with Fausta, could not stay quietly in his village two leagues from Parma. Toward midnight on the morrow, he came on horseback, with a sufficient train of servants, and sang, under the Fausta's windows, an air then fashionable, to which he had put words of his own. " Is not this a common practice among lovers? " said he to himself.

Now that the Fausta had given him to understand that she desired a meeting, this long pursuit seemed very wearisome to Fabrizio. " No, this is not love," said he to himself as he sang, not particularly well, under the windows of the little palace. " Bettina seems to me a hundred times more attractive than Fausta, and it is she whom I should best like to see at this moment." He was returning to his village, feeling rather bored, when, about five hundred paces from Fausta's palace, he was sprung upon by some fifteen or twenty men. Four of them seized his horse's bridle, two others took hold of his arms. Ludovico and Fabrizio's *bravi* were attacked, but contrived to escape, and several pistols were fired. The whole affair was over in an instant. Then, as though by magic, and in the twinkling of an eye, fifty men, bearing lighted torches, appeared in the street, every man well armed. Fabrizio, in spite of the people who were holding him, had jumped off his horse, and struggled fiercely to get free. He even wounded one of the men, who was holding his arms in a vice-like grasp, but he was very much astonished to hear the fellow say, in the most respectful tone :

" Your Highness will give me a good pension for this wound, and that will be far better for me than to fall into the crime of high treason by drawing my sword against my prince."

" Now here comes the chastisement of my folly," thought Fabrizio. " I shall have damned myself for a sin which did not even strike me as attractive."

Hardly had the attempted scuffle come to an end, when several lackeys, dressed in magnificent liveries, brought forward a sedan-chair, gilt and painted in a most extraordinary manner. It was one of those grotesque conveyances used by masks during carnival time. Six men, dagger in

hand, requested " his Highness " to get in, saying the cold
night air might hurt his voice. The most respectful forms
of address were used, and the title " prince " was constantly
repeated, and almost shouted aloud. The procession began
to move on. Fabrizio counted more than fifty men carrying lighted torches down the street. It was about one o'clock
in the morning, all the world was looking out of window,
there was a certain solemnity about the whole affair. " I
was afraid Count M—— might treat me to dagger thrusts,"
said Fabrizio to himself, " but he contents himself with
making game of me. I should not have accused him of so
much taste. But does he really believe he has to do with
the prince? If he knows I am only Fabrizio, I must beware
of the stiletto."

The fifty torch-bearers and the twenty armed men, having made a long halt under the Fausta's windows, paraded
up and down in front of the finest palaces in the city. From
time to time the major-domos who walked by the side of
the sedan-chair inquired whether " his Highness " had any
orders to give them. Fabrizio did not lose his head. He
could see by the torch-light that Ludovico and his men were
following the procession as closely as they could. Fabrizio
argued to himself: " Ludovico has only eight or ten men;
he does not dare to attack." From within his sedan-chair
Fabrizio saw plainly enough that the people charged with
the execution of this doubtful joke were armed to the teeth.
He affected to laugh with the major-domos in attendance
on him. After more than two hours of this triumphal
march he perceived that they were about to cross the street
in which the Palazzo Sanseverina stood. Just as they
passed by the street leading to the palace he suddenly
opened the door in the front of the chair, jumped over one
of the staves, overthrew one of the footmen, who thrust his
torch into his face, with a dagger thrust, received one himself in the shoulder, a second footman singed his beard with
his lighted torch, and finally, Fabrizio reached Ludovico,
to whom he shouted, " Kill! kill every one who carries a
torch!" Ludovico hacked with his sword, and saved him
from two men who were trying to pursue him. Fabrizio

rushed up to the entrance of the Palazzo Sanseverina. The porter, in his curiosity, had opened the little door three feet high, set in the large one, and was staring in astonishment at the great train of torches. Fabrizio bounded through the tiny door, slammed it behind him, ran to the garden, and escaped by another door opening on to a deserted street. An hour later he was beyond the city walls; when day broke he was over the frontier into the state of Modena, and in perfect safety; by the evening he was back in Bologna. "Here's a pretty expedition!" said he to himself. "I have not even succeeded in getting speech with my flame." He lost no time about writing letters of excuse to the count and to the duchess, prudent missives which, though they described his emotions, furnished no clew that any enemy could lay hold of. "I was in love with love," he wrote to the duchess. "I have done everything in the world to make its acquaintance. But nature, it appears, has refused me a heart capable of love and melancholy; I can not rise above vulgar enjoyment, etc." The stir this adventure made in Parma can not be described. The mystery of it whetted the general curiosity. Numbers of people had seen the torches and the sedan-chair, but who was the man who had been carried off and treated with such formal ceremony? No well-known personage was missing from the city on the following day.

The humble folk living in the street in which the prisoner made his escape declared they had seen a corpse. But when broad daylight came, and the inhabitants ventured to emerge from their houses, the only trace of the struggle they could discover was the quantity of blood which stained the paving stones. More than twenty thousand sightseers visited the street during the day. The dwellers in Italian towns are accustomed to see strange sights, but the *how* and *why* is always clearly known to them. What annoyed the Parmese about this incident, was that even a whole month after, when the torch-light procession had ceased to be the only subject of general conversation, no one, thanks to Count Mosca's prudence, had been able to discover the name of the rival who would fain have carried the Fausta off from Count

The Chartreuse of Parma

M——. This jealous and vindictive lover had taken to flight as soon as the procession had set forth on its way. By the count's orders, the Fausta was shut up in the citadel. The duchess was vastly entertained by a little piece of injustice in which the count was forced to indulge, to check the curiosity of the prince, who might otherwise have tried to discover Fabrizio's name.

A learned man had just arrived at Parma from the north, with the intention of writing a history of the middle ages. He was searching for manuscripts in various libraries, and the count had given him all possible facilities. But this learned man, who was still very young, was of an irascible temper. He fancied, for instance, that every soul in Parma desired to turn him into ridicule. It is true that the street boys did occasionally run after him, attracted by the waving locks of pale red hair which he proudly displayed. This learned gentleman believed that his innkeeper charged him abnormal prices for everything, and he would never pay for the most trifling article without looking up its price in Mrs. Starke's Travels, a book which has reached its twentieth edition, because it gives the prudent Englishman the price of a turkey, an apple, a glass of milk, and so forth.

On the very evening of the day on which Fabrizio had taken his involuntary part in the torch-light procession, the red-haired *savant* fell into a rage at his inn, and pulled a pair of pocket pistols out of his pocket to take vengeance on a *camérier* who had asked him two sous for an inferior peach. He was immediately arrested, for it is a great crime, in Parma, to carry pocket pistols.

As this irascible gentleman was tall and thin, it occurred to the count, next morning, to pass him off on the prince as the foolhardy being who had endeavoured to carry off the Fausta, and on whom a trick had been played by her lover. In Parma the punishment for carrying pocket pistols is three years at the galleys, but the penalty is never exacted. After a fortnight in prison, during which he saw nobody but a lawyer, who filled him with the deepest terror of the abominable laws directed by the cowardice of the people in power against the bearers of concealed weapons, he was visited by a second lawyer, who told him the story of the mock procession in which Count M—— had forced a rival, whose identity had not been discovered, to bear a part. "The police do not want to confess to the prince that they can not find out who this rival is. Say that you desired to find favour in the Fausta's eyes, that fifty rascals laid hands on you while you were singing beneath her windows, and that you were carried about in a sedan-chair for an hour by people who only spoke to you in a most respectful manner. There is nothing humiliating about this avowal, and one word is all that is asked of you. The instant you say it, and get the police out of this difficulty, you will be put into a post-chaise, taken to the frontier, and allowed to depart in peace."

For a whole month the learned man held out. Two or three times over, the prince was on the point of having him brought before the Minister of the Interior, and himself presiding at the examination. But he had forgotten all about it before the historian, wearied out, made up his mind to confess everything, and was conducted to the frontier. The prince remained convinced that Count M——'s rival possessed a mass of red hair.

Three days after the procession, while Fabrizio, with his faithful Ludovico, in his hiding-place at Bologna, was plotting means of discovering Count M——, he learned that the count was in hiding, too, in a mountain village on the road to Florence, and that only three of his *buli* were with him. Next day, as he was returning from a ride, the count was seized by eight masked men, who informed him they were police agents from Parma. He was conducted, after his eyes had been bandaged, to an inn some two leagues farther up in the mountains, where he was received with every attention, and found a liberal supper ready. The best Italian and Spanish wines were served.

"Pray, am I a state prisoner?" inquired the count.

"Not the least in the world," was the polite response of Ludovico, who wore a mask. "You have insulted a private individual by venturing to have him carried about in a sedan-chair. To-morrow morning he means to fight a duel with you. If you kill him, you will be provided with money and good horses, and there will be relays ready for you all the way to Genoa."

"What may this ruffian's name be?" quoth the count in a rage.

"His name is Bombace. You will have the choice of weapons, and good seconds, thoroughly loyal men; but one or the other of you must die."

"It's a murder, then!" cried Count M—— in alarm.

"God forbid! It is simply a duel to the death, with a young man whom you carried about the streets of Parma in the middle of the night, and who would be dishonoured if you lived on. The earth is not large enough for both of you. Therefore do your best to kill him. You will have swords, pistols, rapiers—all the weapons it has been possible to collect within a few hours, for time is precious; the Bolognese police are very diligent, as you know, and there must be no interference with this duel, for the sake of the honour of this young man, whom you have turned into ridicule."

"But if the young man is a prince?"

"He is a private individual, like yourself, and indeed a much less rich man than you. But he is resolved to fight to the death, and he will force you to fight, I warn you."

"I am not afraid of anything on earth," exclaimed Count M——.

"That is what your adversary most earnestly desires," replied Ludovico. "Make yourself ready to defend your life to-morrow, very early in the morning; to be attacked by a man who has good reason to be furious with you, and who will not spare you. I tell you again, you will have the choice of weapons, and now, make your will!"

About six o'clock the next morning, Count M——'s breakfast was served. Then one of the doors of the room in which he had been kept was opened, and he was requested to enter the courtyard of a country inn. This court was surrounded with tolerably high hedges and walls, and all the entrances had been carefully closed.

On a table in one corner, which the count was requested

to approach, stood several bottles of wine and brandy, two pistols, two rapiers, two swords, paper, and ink. About a score of peasants were at the windows of the tavern, which looked on to the yard. The count besought their pity. "These people want to murder me," he cried; "save my life!"

"You are deceived, or else you desire to deceive," shouted Fabrizio, who was standing in the opposite corner of the courtyard, beside a table covered with weapons. He had taken off his coat, and his face was hidden under one of those wire masks used in fencing-rooms.

"I advise you," added Fabrizio, "to put on the wire mask you will find beside you, and then advance either with a rapier or with pistols. As you were told yesterday morning, you have the choice of weapons." The count made endless difficulties, and seemed very unwilling to fight. Fabrizio, on his side, was afraid the police would arrive, although they were up in the mountains, and five full leagues from Bologna. He ended by hurling such frightful insults at his rival, that he had the satisfaction of goading Count M—— into fury. He snatched up a rapier, and advanced upon Fabrizio. The beginning of the fight was somewhat slack.

After a few minutes it was interrupted by a great noise. Our hero had been quite conscious that he was undertaking an enterprise which might be made a subject of reproach, or at all events of slanderous imputations upon him, all through his life. He had sent Ludovico into the fields to beat up witnesses. Ludovico gave money to some strangers who were working in a neighbouring wood, and they hurried up, shouting, under the impression that they were expected to kill an enemy of the man who had paid them. When they reached the inn, Ludovico begged them to watch with all their eyes, and see whether either of the young men did anything treacherous, or took any unfair advantage of the other.

The fight, which had been checked for a moment by the peasants' shouts, again hung fire. Once more Fabrizio rained insults on the count's self-conceit. "Signor Conte," he cried, " when you are insolent, you must be brave as well. I know that is a hard matter for you; you would far rather pay other people to be brave." The count, stung to fresh fury, yelled out that he had been a constant frequenter of the fencing school at Naples, kept by the famous Battistino, and that he would soon chastise his opponent's impudence. Now that Count M——'s fury had revived, he fought with tolerable resolution, but this did not prevent Fabrizio from giving him a fine sword thrust in the chest, which kept him several months in bed. As Ludovico bent over the count to put a temporary bandage on his wound, he whispered in his ear, " If you dare to let the police know of this duel, I will have you stabbed in your bed."

Fabrizio fled to Florence. As he had remained in hiding at Bologna, it was not till he reached Florence that he received all the duchess's reproachful letters. She could not forgive him for coming to her concert, and not attempting to obtain speech of her. Fabrizio was delighted with Count Mosca's letters; they breathed frank friendship and the noblest feelings. He guessed that the count had written to Bologna to dispel the suspicions of him which the duel might have caused. The police behaved with perfect justice. It reported that two strangers, only one of whom, the wounded man, was recognised (Count M——), had fought with rapiers in the presence of more than thirty peasants, joined, toward the end of the fight, by the village priest, who had unsuccessfully endeavoured to separate the combatants. As the name of Giuseppe Bossi had never been mentioned, Fabrizio ventured, before two months were out, to return to Bologna, more convinced than ever that he was fated never to make acquaintance with the noble and intellectual side of love. This he did himself the pleasure of explaining to the duchess, in very lengthy terms. He was very tired of his lonely life, and passionately longed to go back to the delightful evenings he had spent with his aunt and the count. He had not tasted the delights of good company since he had parted from them.

" I have brought so much worry upon myself on account of the love I had hoped to enjoy, and of the Fausta," wrote he to the duchess, "that now, if her fancy still turned my way, I would not ride twenty leagues to claim the fulfilment of her bond. Therefore, have no fear, as you say you have, that I may go to Paris, where I see she is appearing with the most brilliant success. I would ride any possible number of leagues to spend an evening with you and with the count, who is always so good to his friends."

CHAPTER XIV

WHILE Fabrizio was prosecuting his search for love in a village near Parma, Rassi, all unconscious of his vicinity, continued dealing with the young man's case as if it had been that of a Liberal. He pretended it was impossible to find any witnesses for the defence, or rather, he browbeat those he did find. Finally, after protracted and skilful labour, lasting nearly a year, the Marchesa Raversi, one Friday evening some two months after Fabrizio's last visit to Bologna, publicly announced in her drawing-room—that on the very next day young Del Dongo's sentence, which had been pronounced just an hour before, would be presented for the prince's signature, and would receive his approval.

Within a very few minutes the duchess was apprised of her enemy's announcement. "The count's agents must serve him very ill," said she to herself. "Even this morning he thought the sentence could not be pronounced for another week. It would not break his heart, perhaps, to see my young grand vicar banished from Parma. But," she added, and she began to sing, "we shall see him come back, and he will be our archbishop some day!" The duchess rang the bell. "Call all the servants together into the anteroom," said she to her footman, "even the cooks. Go to the commandant of the fortress and get a permit from him for four post-horses, and see that those same horses are harnessed to my carriage before half an hour is out." All the waiting-women in the house were busy packing trunks, the duchess hurriedly slipped on a travelling dress— all this without sending any warning to the count. The idea of making sport of him a little filled her with delight.

"My friends," she said to the servants, who were now assembled, "I have just heard that my poor nephew is about to be sentenced, by default, for having had the impudence to defend his life against a madman. It was Giletti who would have killed him. You have all of you had opportunities of seeing how gentle and inoffensive Fabrizio is by nature. Infuriated, as I have a right to be, by this vile insult, I start instantly for Florence. I leave each of you ten years' wages. If you fall into difficulties, write to me, and as long as I have a sequin, there will be something for you."

The duchess thought exactly what she said, and at her last words, her servants burst into tears. Her own eyes were wet, and she added, in a voice that trembled with emotion, " Pray to God for me, and for Monsignore del Dongo, chief grand vicar of the diocese, who will be sentenced to-morrow morning to the galleys, or, which would be less ridiculous, to the penalty of death."

The servants' tears fell faster, and their sobs changed by degrees into shouts that were almost seditious. The duchess entered her coach, and had herself driven to the prince's palace. In spite of the unwonted hour, she requested General Fontana, the aide-de-camp in waiting, to beg the prince to grant her an audience. The aide-de-camp observed, with great astonishment, that she was not in full court dress. As for the prince, he was not the least surprised, and even less displeased, by the request for an audience. " Now we shall see tears shed by lovely eyes," said he to himself, rubbing his hands. " She comes to sue for mercy; this proud beauty is going to humble herself at last. And, indeed, she was quite unbearable, with her little airs of independence. Whenever the smallest thing displeased her, those speaking eyes seemed always to tell me ' it would be far pleasanter to live at Naples, or at Milan, than in your little town of Parma.' It is true I do not reign over Naples, nor over Milan, but at any rate this fine lady is coming to beg me for something which depends on me alone, and which she pines to obtain. I have always thought that the nephew's arrival would help me to get something out of her."

While the prince was smiling at his own thoughts, and indulging in these pleasing forecasts, he kept walking up and down his study, at the door of which General Fontana still stood, upright and stiff, like a soldier shouldering arms. When he saw the prince's shining eyes and recollected the duchess's travelling garments, he felt convinced the monarchy was about to drop to pieces, and his astonishment exceeded all limits when he heard the prince address him thus: "You will ask the duchess to be good enough to wait for a quarter of an hour or so." The aide-de-camp turned to the right about, like a soldier on parade, and the prince smiled again. "Fontana is not accustomed," said he to himself, "to see the haughty duchess kept waiting. His face of astonishment when he tells her to wait for a quarter of an hour will pave the way for the affecting tears that will shortly be shed in this study." That quarter of an hour was an exquisite one to the prince. He walked up and down, with steady and even step; he reigned in very deed. "It is important that nothing should be said which is not perfectly correct. Whatever may be my feelings toward the duchess, I must not forget that she is one of the greatest ladies of my court. How did Louis XIV address the princesses, his daughters, when he had reason to be displeased with them?" and his glance lingered on the great king's portrait.

The comical thing was that the prince never thought of asking himself whether he should show mercy to Fabrizio, and what kind of mercy he should extend. At last, after the lapse of twenty minutes, the faithful Fontana appeared once more at the door, this time without saying a word. "The Duchess Sanseverina is permitted to enter," exclaimed the prince, with a theatrical air. "Now the tears will begin," said he, and as though to prepare himself for the sight, he pulled out his own handkerchief.

Never had the duchess looked so active or so pretty; she did not seem more than five-and-twenty. When the poor aide-de-camp saw her float across the carpet which her light foot hardly appeared to touch, he very nearly lost his head altogether. "I have all sorts of apologies to make your Most Serene Highness," said the duchess in her clear blithe voice. "I've taken the liberty of presenting myself in a dress which is not exactly correct, but your Highness has so accustomed me to your kindnesses, that I have dared to hope you would grant me this favour."

The duchess spoke rather slowly, so as to give herself time to enjoy the expression of the prince's countenance, which was exquisite, by reason of his overwhelming astonishment and the remains of pomposity still indicated by the pose of his head and the position of his arms. The prince was thunder-struck. Every now and then he exclaimed almost inarticulately, in his little shrill, unsteady voice, " What! what! "

When the duchess had come to the end of her speech, she paused respectfully, as though to give him an opportunity of replying. Then she continued, " I venture to hope your Most Serene Highness will pardon the incongruity of my costume," but even as she spoke the words, her mocking eyes shot out such brilliant shafts that the prince could not endure their glance. He stared at the ceiling, which, in his case, was always a sign of the most extreme embarrassment.

" What! what! " said he again. Then he was lucky enough to think of a remark.

" Duchess, pray be seated," and he himself offered her a chair, and with considerable grace. The duchess was not unmoved by this politeness, and her indignant glance softened.

" What! what! " repeated the prince once more, fidgeting in his chair as though he could not settle himself firmly into it.

" I am going to take advantage of the coolness of the night hours to travel by post," continued the duchess, " and as my absence may be of considerable duration, I would not leave your Most Serene Highness's dominions without thanking you for all the kindness you have condescended to show me during the last five years." At these words the prince understood at last, and turned pale. No man in the world suffered more than he, at the idea of having been mistaken in his forecast, but he took on an air of majesty quite worthy of the picture of Louis XIV which hung in front of him. "Ah, very good," thought the duchess; "this is a man."

"And what may be the reason of this sudden departure?" said the prince in a fairly steady voice.

"The plan is an old one," replied the duchess, "and a petty insult which is being put on Monsignore del Dongo, who is to be sentenced either to death or to the galleys to-morrow, has hastened my departure."

"And to what town do you proceed?"

"To Naples, I think." Then, rising, she added: "All that now remains for me to do is to take leave of your Most Serene Highness, and to thank you, most humbly, for your *former* kindnesses." Her tone was now so resolute that the prince clearly perceived that in two seconds everything would be over. Once the rupture of her departure had taken place, he knew any arrangement would be hopeless. She was not a woman to undo what she had once done. He hurried after her.

"But you know very well, duchess," he said, taking her hand, "that I have always liked you, and that if you had chosen, that affection would have borne another name. A murder has been committed; that can not be denied. I employed my best judges to carry on the trial——"

At these words the duchess drew herself up to her full height. Like a flash every semblance of respect and even of urbanity disappeared. The offended woman stood unveiled before him, and an offended woman speaking to a being whom she knew to be false. With an expression of the liveliest anger and even scorn, she addressed the prince, laying stress on every word:

"I am leaving your Most Serene Highness's dominions forever, so that I may never again hear the names of Rassi and of the other vile assassins who have passed sentence of death on my nephew, and on so many others. If your Most Serene Highness does not desire to mingle a feeling of bitterness with the memory of the last moments I have to spend in the presence of a prince who is both courteous and witty, when he is not deceived, I very humbly beseech your Highness not to remind me of those shameless judges who sell themselves for a decoration, or for a thousand crowns." The ring of nobility, and above all of truth, in her words, made the prince shiver. For a moment he feared his dignity might be compromised by a yet more direct accusation. But on the whole, his sensation soon became one of pleasure. He admired the duchess; her whole person, at that moment, breathed a beauty that was sublime. "Good God, how beautiful she is!" said the prince to himself; "something must be forgiven to such a woman —there is probably not another like her in Italy. . . . Well, with a little careful policy, I may not find it impossible to make her my mistress some day. Such a creature would be very different from that doll-faced Balbi, who steals at least three hundred thousand francs a year from my poor subjects into the bargain. . . . But did I hear aright?" thought he suddenly. "She said, 'sentenced my nephew and so many others'!" Then rage got the upper hand, and it was with a haughtiness worthy of his supreme position that the prince said, after a silence, "And what must be done to prevent the duchess from departing?"

"Something of which you are not capable," replied the duchess, and the most bitter irony and the most open scorn rang in her voice.

The prince was beside himself, but the habit of reigning with absolute authority had brought him strength to resist his first impulses. "I must possess this woman," thought he; "I owe it to myself. And then I must kill her with my scorn. If she leaves this study I shall never see her again." But wild as he was, at that moment, with rage and hatred, how was he to pitch on a phrase which would at once fulfil what was due to himself, and induce the duchess not to forsake his court that instant? "A gesture," thought he, "can neither be repeated nor turned into ridicule," and he put himself between the duchess and the door of the room. Soon after he heard somebody tapping at the door. "Who is the damned fellow," he exclaimed, swearing with all the strength of his lungs, "who is the damned fellow who wants to intrude his idiotic person here?" Poor General Fontana put in a pale and completely puzzled countenance.

The Chartreuse of Parma

With a face like the face of a dying man he murmured inarticulately, "His Excellency Count Mosca craves the honour of an audience."

"Let him come in," shouted the prince, and as Mosca bowed before him, "Well," said he, "here is the Duchess Sanseverina, who says she is instantly leaving Parma to go and settle in Naples, and who has been making impertinent remarks to me into the bargain."

"What!" said Mosca.

"What! You knew nothing about the plan of departure?"

"Not a single word. When I left the duchess at six o'clock she was cheerful and gay." The words produced an incredible effect upon the prince. First of all he looked at Mosca, whose increasing pallor proved that he had spoken the truth, and had nothing to do with the duchess's sudden freak. "In that case," said he to himself, "she is lost to me forever. My pleasure and my vengeance both fly away together. At Naples she and her nephew Fabrizio will write epigrams on the mighty rages of the little Prince of Parma." Then he looked at the duchess; the most violent scorn and anger were struggling in her breast, her eyes were riveted on Count Mosca, and the delicate lines of her beautiful mouth expressed the bitterest disdain. Her whole expression seemed to say "Cringing courtier!"

"Thus," thought the prince after having scrutinized her, "I have lost the means of recalling her to my country. Once more, if she leaves the study at this moment, she is lost to me. God only knows what she will say about my judges at Naples. And with the wit and divine powers of persuasion Heaven has given her, she will make everybody believe her. Thanks to her, I shall bear the reputation of an undignified tyrant, who gets up in the night to look under his bed." Then, by a skilful manœuvre, as if he were walking about to calm his agitation, the prince once more placed himself in front of the study door. The count was at his right, some three paces off, pale, discomposed, and trembling to such an extent that he was obliged to support himself by leaning on the back of the arm-chair which

the duchess had occupied during the beginning of the audience, and which the prince had pushed away with an angry
gesture.

The count was in love. " If the duchess goes," he was
saying to himself, " I shall follow her. But will she allow
me to follow her? That is the question." On the prince's
left the duchess stood erect, her arms folded tightly across
her bosom, superbly angry, watching him. The brilliant
colour which had lately flushed her beautiful face had faded
into the deepest pallor. The prince's face, unlike those of
the other two actors in the scene, was red, and he looked
worried. His left hand convulsively jerked the cross fastened to the ribbon of his order, which he wore under his
coat; his right hand caressed his chin.

" What is to be done? " said he to the count, hardly
knowing what he said, and carried away by his habit of
consulting Mosca about everything.

" Truly I know not, your Most Serene Highness," said
the count, like a man who was breathing out his last sigh;
he could hardly speak the words. The tone of his voice was
the first consolation to his wounded pride which the prince
had enjoyed during the audience, and this small piece of
good fortune inspired him with a remark that was very
grateful to his vanity.

" Well," said he, " I am the most sensible of us three.
I am willing to completely overlook my own position in the
world. I shall speak *as a friend*," and he added, with a
noble smile of condescension—a fine imitation of the good
old times of Louis XIV—" as a *friend speaking to his
friends*. Duchess," he added, " what must I do to induce
you to forget this untimely decision? "

" Truly, I know not," said the duchess with a great sigh;
" truly I know not, so hateful is Parma to me." There was
not the smallest epigrammatic intention in her words; her
sincerity was quite evident. The count turned sharply
toward her; his courtier's soul was horrified. Then he cast
a beseeching glance toward the prince. The prince paused
for a moment; then, turning with great dignity and calmness
to the count, " I see," said he, " that your charming friend

is quite beside herself; that is quite natural—she *adores* her nephew." Then to the duchess—speaking in the most gallant manner, and at the same time with the sort of air with which a man quotes the key word of a comedy—he added, "*What must I do to find favour in those fair eyes?*"

The duchess had had time to reflect. In a slow and steady voice, as if she had been dictating her ultimatum, she replied: "Your Highness would write me a gracious letter, such as you so well know how to write, in which you would say that, not being convinced of the guilt of Fabrizio del Dongo, chief grand vicar to the archbishop, you will not sign the sentence when it is presented to you, and that these unjust proceedings shall have no further effect."

"What! unjust?" said the prince, reddening up to the whites of his eyes and falling into a rage again.

"That is not all," replied the duchess with all the dignity of a Roman matron. "*This very evening*, and," she added, looking at the clock, "it is already a quarter past eleven— this very evening your Most Serene Highness would send word to the Marchesa Raversi that you advise her to go to the country to recover from the fatigue which a certain trial, of which she was talking in her drawing-room early this evening, must doubtless have caused her."

The prince was raging up and down his study like a fury.

"Did any one ever see such a woman?" he cried. "She actually fails in respect to my person!"

The duchess replied with the most perfect grace: "Never in my life did it enter my head to fail in respect to your Most Serene Highness. Your Highness was so extremely condescending as to say that you would speak *as a friend to his friends*. And, indeed, I have no desire to remain in Parma," she added, shooting a glance of the most ineffable scorn at the count. That glance decided the prince, who had been hitherto very uncertain in his mind, although his words might have been taken to indicate an undertaking, —but words meant little to him.

A few more remarks were exchanged, but at last Count Mosca received orders to write the gracious note for which the duchess had asked. He omitted the sentence: "*These unjust proceedings shall have no further effect.*" "It will be quite enough," said the count to himself, "if the prince promises not to sign the sentence when it is presented to him." As the prince signed the paper he thanked him with a glance.

The count made a great blunder. The prince was tired out, and he would have signed everything. He flattered himself he had got through the scene very well, and the whole matter was overshadowed in his mind by the thought, "If the duchess goes away the court will grow tiresome to me in less than a week." The count noticed that his master had corrected the date, and inserted that of the next day. He glanced at the clock; it was almost midnight. The correction only struck the minister as a proof of the prince's pedantic desire to show his exactness and careful government. As to the exile of the Marchesa Raversi, he made no difficulty at all. The prince took a particular delight in banishing people.

"General Fontana!" he called out, half opening the door. The general appeared, wearing a face of such astonishment and curiosity that a swift glance of amusement passed between the count and the duchess, and in that glance, peace was made between them.

"General Fontana," said the prince, "you will get into my carriage, which is waiting under the colonnade, you will go to the Marchesa Raversi's house, you will send up your name. If she is in bed you will add that you come from me, and when you reach her room, you will say these exact words, and no others: 'Signora Marchesa Raversi, his Most Serene Highness invites you to depart to-morrow, before eight o'clock in the morning, to your castle at Velleia. His Highness will inform you when you may return to Parma.'" The prince's eyes sought those of the duchess, who, without thanking him, as he had expected, made him an exceedingly respectful courtesy and went swiftly out of the room.

"What a woman!" said the prince, turning toward Count Mosca.

The count, who was delighted at the Marchesa Raversi's

exile, which immensely facilitated all his ministerial actions, talked for a full half-hour, like the consummate courtier he was; his great object was to heal the sovereign's vanity, and he did not take leave until he had thoroughly convinced him that there was no finer page in the anecdotic history of Louis XIV than that which he had just furnished for his own future historians.

When the duchess got home she closed her doors, and gave orders that nobody was to be admitted—not even the count. She wanted to be alone, and to make up her mind as to what she ought to think of the scene that had just taken place. She had acted at random, just as her fancy led her at the moment. But whatever step she might have been carried away into undertaking, she would have adhered to it steadily. She never would have blamed herself, and much less repented, when her coolness had returned. It was to these characteristics that she owed the fact that she was still, at six-and-thirty years of age, the prettiest woman at the court.

At that moment she was dreaming over all the charms Parma might possess, as she might have done on her way back there, after a long absence, so sure had she been, from nine to eleven o'clock, that she was about to leave the city forever.

"That poor dear count did cut a comical figure when he heard of my departure in the prince's presence! He really is a charming fellow, and one does not come across such a heart as his every day. He would have resigned all his portfolios to follow me. But, then, for five whole years he has never once had to complain of any want of attention on my part. How many regularly married women could say the same to their lord and master? I must admit there is no self-importance nor pedantry about him; he never makes me feel I should like to deceive him. He always seems ashamed of his power when he is with me. How droll he looked before his lord and master! If he were here I would kiss him. But nothing on earth would induce me to undertake the task of amusing a minister who has lost his portfolio. That is an illness which nothing but death can cure, and which kills other folks. What a misfortune it must be to be a minister when you are young! I must write to him. He must know this thing officially before he quarrels with his prince. But I was forgetting my poor servants."

The duchess rang the bell. Her women were still busy filling trunks, the carriage was standing underneath the portico, and the men were packing it. All the servants who had no work to do were standing round the carriage with tearful eyes. Cecchina, the only person allowed to enter the duchess's room on solemn occasions, informed her mistress of all these details.

"Send them upstairs," said the duchess. A moment later she herself went into the anteroom. "I have received a promise," said she, addressing them, "that the sentence against my nephew will not be signed by the sovereign" (the Italian mode of expression). "I have put off my departure. We shall see whether my enemies have enough credit to get this decision altered."

There was silence for a moment. Then the servants began to shout "Long live our lady the duchess!" and clapped their hands furiously. The duchess, who had retired into the next room, reappeared, like a popular actress, dropped a little graceful courtesy to her people, and said, "My friends, I thank you." At that moment, on the slightest hint from her, they would all have marched in a body to attack the palace. She beckoned to one of her postillions, a former smuggler, and most trusty servant, who followed her out.

"You must dress yourself as a well-to-do peasant, you must get out of Parma as best you can; then hire a *sediola*, and get to Bologna as quickly as possible. You will enter Bologna, as if you were taking an ordinary walk, by the Florence gate, and you will deliver a packet, which Cecchina will give you, to Fabrizio, who is living at the Pellegrino. Fabrizio is in hiding there, and calls himself Signor Giuseppe Bossi. Do not betray him by any imprudence; do not appear to know him. My enemies may set spies upon your heels. Fabrizio will send you back here in a few hours, or a few days. It is on your way back, especially, that you must be careful not to betray him."

"Ah, the Marchesa Raversi's servants, you mean," exclaimed the postillion. "We're ready for them, and if it were the signora's will they should soon be exterminated."

"Some day, perhaps. But for your life beware of doing anything without my orders." It was the copy of the prince's note that the duchess wanted to send to Fabrizio. She could not deny herself the pleasure of amusing him, and she added a few words concerning the scene of which the note had been the outcome. These few words swelled into a letter of ten pages. She sent for the postillion again. "You can not start," she said, "until four o'clock, when the gates open."

"I thought I would get out by the main sewer; the water would be up to my chin, but I could get through."

"No," said the duchess. "I will not let one of my most faithful servants run the risk of a fever. Do you know any one in the archbishop's household?"

"The second coachman is a friend of mine."

"Here is a letter for the holy prelate; slip quietly into his palace, and have yourself taken to his valet—I would not have his Grace disturbed. If he is already shut up in his own room, spend the night at the palace, and as he always gets up at daybreak, send in to-morrow at four o'clock, say you have been sent by me, ask the holy archbishop's blessing, give him this packet, and take the letters he may possibly give you to Bologna." The duchess was sending the archbishop the original of the prince's letter, requesting him, as the note concerned his chief grand vicar, to place it among the archiepiscopal archives, where she hoped her nephew's colleagues, the other grand vicars and canons, would take note of its existence—all this under seal of the most profound secrecy.

The duchess wrote to Monsignore Landriani in a style of familiarity which was certain to delight that worthy man; her signature took up three lines. The letter, couched in the most friendly terms, ended with the words:

The Chartreuse of Parma

"Angelina Cornelia Isola Valserra del Dongo, Duchess Sanseverina."

"I don't believe I have written my name in full," said the duchess, laughing, "since I signed my marriage contract with the poor duke. But it is trifles such as these that impress people, and common folk take caricature for beauty."

She could not resist winding up her evening by yielding to the temptation of writing a tormenting letter to the poor count. She announced to him, *officially*, and *for his guidance*, so she expressed it, *in his intercourse with crowned heads*, that she did not feel herself equal to the task of entertaining a disgraced minister. "You are afraid of the prince," she wrote. "When you can no longer see him, shall you expect me to frighten you?" She despatched the letter instantly.

The prince, on his side, sent, at seven o'clock the next morning, for Count Zurla, Minister of the Interior, and said: "Give fresh and most stringent orders to every *podestà* to arrest Fabrizio del Dongo. I hear there is some chance that he may venture to reappear in my dominions. The fugitive is at Bologna, where he seems to brave the action of our law courts. You will therefore place police officers who are personally acquainted with his appearance: 1. In the villages on the road from Bologna to Parma. 2. In the neighbourhood of the Duchess Sanseverina's house at Sacca and her villa at Castelnovo. 3. All round Count Mosca's country-house. I venture, Count, to rely on your great wisdom to conceal all knowledge of your sovereign's orders from discovery by Count Mosca. Understand clearly that I will have Fabrizio del Dongo arrested."

As soon as this minister had departed, Rassi, the chief justice, entered the prince's study by a secret door, and came forward, bent well-nigh double, and bowing at every step. The rascal's face was a study for a painter, worthy of all the vileness of the part he played, and while the swift and disturbed glance of his eye betrayed his consciousness of his own value, the grinning expression of arrogant self-confidence upon his lips showed that he knew how to struggle against scorn.

The Chartreuse of Parma

As this individual is destined to exert great influence over Fabrizio's fate, I may say a word of him here. He was tall, with fine and very intelligent eyes, but his face was seamed by small-pox. As for intelligence, he had plenty of it, and of the sharpest. His thorough knowledge of legal matters was uncontested, but his strongest point was his resourcefulness. Whatever might be the aspect of a matter, he always, with the greatest ease and in the shortest space of time, discovered the most logical and well-founded means of obtaining a sentence or an acquittal. He was, above all things, a past master in attorney's tricks.

This man, whose services mighty monarchs would have envied the Prince of Parma, had only one great passion—to talk familiarly with exalted personages, and entertain them with buffooneries. Little did he care whether the great man laughed at what he said, or at his own person, or even made disgusting jokes about his wife. So long as he saw him laugh, and was himself treated with familiarity, he was content. Sometimes, when the prince had exhausted all possible means of belittling his chief justice's dignity, he would kick him heartily. If the kicks hurt him, the chief justice would cry. But the instinct of buffoonery was so strong in him that he continued to prefer the drawing-room of a minister who scoffed at him, to his own, where he held despotic sway over the whole legal profession. Rassi had made himself quite a peculiar position, owing to the fact that not the most insolent noble in the country could humiliate him. His vengeance for the insults showered on him all the day long consisted in retailing them to the prince, to whom he had acquired the privilege of saying everything. It is true that the prince's answer frequently consisted in a hearty box on the ear, which hurt him horribly, but to that he never took exception. The presence of the chief justice distracted the prince's thoughts in his hours of bad temper, and he would then amuse himself by ill treating him. My readers will perceive that Rassi was almost the perfect man for a court. He had no honour and no humour.

"Secrecy, above all things!" exclaimed the prince, with-

out any recognition of his salutation. The most courteous
of men, as a rule, he treated Rassi like the merest varlet.
" What is the date of your sentence? "

" Yesterday morning, your Most Serene Highness."

" How many of the judges signed it? "

" All five."

" And the penalty? "

" Twenty years in the fortress, as your Most Serene
Highness told me."

" A death sentence would have horrified people," said
the prince, as though talking to himself. " A pity! What
a shock it would have been to that woman! But he is a
Del Dongo, and the name is honoured in Parma because of
the three archbishops who came almost one after the other.
. . . Twenty years in the fortress, you say? "

" Yes, your Most Serene Highness," replied Rassi, who
was still standing doubled up in an attitude of obeisance.
" To be preceded by a public apology before a portrait of
your Most Serene Highness; and besides, a fast of bread
and water every Friday and on the eves of all the chief
feast days, because of *the prisoner's notorious impiety*. This
with a view to the future, and to break the neck of his
career."

" Write," said the prince, " ' His Most Serene Highness,
having deigned to grant a favourable hearing to the very
humble petitions of the Marchesa del Dongo, mother of
the culprit, and the Duchess Sanseverina, his aunt, who have
represented that at the period of the crime their son and
nephew was very young, and carried away by his mad passion for the wife of the unfortunate Giletti, has condescended, notwithstanding his horror of the murder, to
commute the penalty to which Fabrizio del Dongo has
been condemned to that of twelve years' detention in the
fortress.'

" Give the paper to me to sign." The prince added his
signature and the date of the preceding day. Then, handing the sheet back to Rassi, he said : " Write just below my
signature : ' The Duchess Sanseverina having once more
cast herself at his Highness's feet, the prince has granted the

culprit permission to walk for an hour, every Thursday, on the platform of the square tower, vulgarly called the Farnese Tower.'

"Sign that," said the prince, "and keep your lips sealed, whatever you may hear in the town. You will tell Councillor de' Capitani, who voted for two years' imprisonment, and even held forth in support of his ridiculous opinion, that I advise him to read over the laws and regulations. Now, silence again, and good-night to you."

Chief-Justice Rassi made three deep bows, very slowly indeed, and the prince never even looked at them.

All this happened at seven o'clock in the morning. A few hours later, the news of the Marchesa Raversi's exile had spread all over the town and the *cafés*. Everybody was talking at once about the great event. For some time, thanks to the marchesa's banishment, that implacable enemy of small cities and small courts, known as boredom, fled from the town of Parma. General Fabio Conti, who had believed himself sure of the ministry, pretended he had the gout, and never showed his nose outside his fortress for several days. The middle class, and consequently the populace, concluded from current events that the prince had resolved to confer the archbishopric of Parma on Monsignore del Dongo. The more cunning *café* politicians went so far as to declare that Archbishop Landriani had been invited to feign serious illness, and send in his resignation. He was to be compensated with a large pension, charged on the tobacco duties. They were quite certain of this. The rumour reached the archbishop, who was very much disturbed, and for some days his zeal in our hero's cause was largely paralyzed in consequence. Some two months later, this fine piece of news appeared in the Paris press, with the trifling alteration that it was Count Mosca, the Duchess Sanseverina's nephew, who was supposed to be likely to be appointed archbishop.

Meanwhile the Marchesa Raversi was raging at her country house at Velleia. There was nothing womanish about her. She was not one of those weak creatures who fancy they slake their vengeance when they pour out violent diatribes against their enemies. The very day after her disgrace, Cavaliere Riscara and three other friends of hers waited on the prince, and sued permission to go and see her in her country place. His Highness received these gentlemen with the utmost graciousness, and their arrival at Velleia was a great consolation to the marchesa.

Before the second week was out she had gathered quite thirty persons about her—all those who would have obtained office in the Liberal government. Every evening the marchesa sat in council with the best-informed of her adherents. One day, when she had received numerous letters from Parma and Bologna, she retired at a very early hour. Her favourite waiting-woman introduced to her presence first of all her acknowledged lover, Count Baldi, a young man of great beauty and utter futility, and later on Cavaliere Riscara, who had been Baldi's predecessor. This last was a short man, dusky, both physically and morally speaking, who had begun life by teaching geometry in the Nobles' College at Parma, and was now a councillor of state, and knight of several orders.

" I have the good habit," said the marchesa to the two men, " of never destroying any paper, and it serves me well now. Here are nine letters which the Sanseverina has written to me on various occasions. You will both of you start for Genoa; there, among the convicts at the galleys, you will seek out an ex-notary whose name is Burati, like the great Venetian poet, or, it may be, Durati. You, Count Baldi, will be pleased to sit down at my table, and write at my dictation :

" ' An idea has just struck me, and I send you a word. I am going to my hut near Castelnovo. If you like to come and spend twelve hours there with me, it will make me very happy. I do not think there is any great danger in this, after what has happened. The clouds are growing lighter. Nevertheless, stop before you go into Castelnovo. You will meet one of my servants on the road. They are all passionately devoted to you. Of course you will keep the name of Giuseppe Bossi for this little expedition. I am told you have a beard worthy of the most splendid Capuchin, and at Parma you have only been seen with the decent countenance of a grand vicar.'

" Do you understand, Riscara? "

" Perfectly. But the journey to Genoa is a quite unnecessary luxury. I know a man in Parma who has not been to the galleys yet, indeed, but who can not fail to get there. He will forge the Sanseverina's handwriting in the most successful manner."

At these words Count Baldi opened his fine eyes desperately wide. He was only beginning to understand.

" If you know this worthy gentleman at Parma, whose interests you hope to advance," said the marchesa to Riscara, " he probably knows you too. His mistress, his confessor, his best friend, may be bought by the Sanseverina. I prefer to delay my little joke for a few days, and run no risk whatsoever. Start within two hours, like two good little lambs, don't see a soul at Genoa, and come back as quickly as you can." Cavaliere Riscara sped away, laughing, and talking through his nose like Pulcinello. " I must pack up," he cried, cantering off with the most ludicrous gestures.

He wanted to leave Baldi alone with the fair lady. Five days later, Riscara brought the marchesa back her lover, very stiff and sore. To save six leagues, he had made him cross a mountain on mule-back. He swore nobody should ever catch him making a long journey again. Baldi brought the marchesa three copies of the letter she had dictated, and six others, in the same hand, of Riscara's composition, and which might come in usefully later. One of these letters contained some very pleasing jokes about the prince's terrors at night, and the deplorable thinness of his mistress, the Marchesa Balbi, who, so it declared, left a mark like that of a pair of tongs on the cushion of every arm-chair in which she sat. Anybody would have sworn these missives were all in the Duchess Sanseverina's handwriting.

" Now," said the marchesa, " I know, without any possibility of doubt, that the duchess's best beloved, her Fabrizio, is at Bologna, or in the neighbourhood."

" I am too ill," interrupted Count Baldi. " I beseech

you to excuse me from making another journey, or, at all events, let me rest for a few days, and recover my health."

" I will plead your cause," said Riscara. He rose, and said something to the marchesa in an undertone.

" Very good; I consent to that," she answered with a smile.

" Make your mind easy. You will not have to go away," said the marchesa to Baldi, with a somewhat scornful look.

" Thanks," he cried, and his tone was heart-felt. Riscara did, in fact, set off alone, in a post-chaise. He had hardly been two days at Bologna before he caught sight of Fabrizio and Marietta in a carriage. " The devil! " he cried. " Our future archbishop does not appear to deny himself any pleasure. This must be revealed to the duchess, who will be delighted." All Riscara had to do, to discover Fabrizio's residence, was to follow him there. The very next morning, the post brought the young man the letter of Genoese manufacture. He thought it a little short, but no idea of suspicion occurred to him. The idea of seeing the duchess and the count again sent him frantic with delight, and in spite of all Ludovico's remonstrances, he hired a post-horse and started off at a hand gallop. All unknown to himself, he was followed by Riscara, who, when he reached the posting-station before Castelnovo, about six leagues from Parma, had the pleasure of seeing a crowd collected in the square in front of the local prison. Its doors had just closed upon our hero, who had been recognised, as he was changing horses, by two myrmidons of the law, chosen and sent out by Count Zurla.

Riscara's small eyes twinkled with delight. With the most exemplary patience, he verified every incident connected with the affair that had just taken place in the little village, and then sent off a messenger to the marchesa Raversi. After which, by dint of walking about the streets as though to visit the church—a very interesting building—and to hunt up a picture by Parmegiano which, he had heard, existed in that neighbourhood, he contrived to come across the *podestà*, who hastened to pay his respects to a councillor of state. Riscara appeared surprised that the

The Chartreuse of Parma

podestà had not despatched the conspirator, on whom he had so luckily laid his hand, straight to the citadel.

"There is some risk," Riscara added unconcernedly, "that his many friends, who were out looking for him yesterday, to help him to get across the dominions of his Most Serene Highness, might meet the gendarmes. There were quite twelve or fifteen of the rebels, all mounted."

"*Intelligenti pauca!*" exclaimed the *podestà*, with a knowing look.

CHAPTER XV

Two hours later, poor unlucky Fabrizio, securely hand-cuffed, and fastened by a long chain to his own *sediola*, into which he had been thrust, started for the citadel at Parma, under the guard of eight gendarmes. These men had been ordered to collect all the gendarmes stationed in the villages through which the procession might pass as they went along, and the *podestà* himself attended the important prisoner. Toward seven o'clock in the evening the *sediola*, escorted by all the little boys in Parma, and guarded by thirty gendarmes, was driven across the beautiful promenade, past the little palace in which the Fausta had lived a few months previously, and stopped before the outer gate of the citadel just as General Fabio Conti and his daughter were about to issue from it. The governor's carriage stopped before reaching the drawbridge, to allow the *sediola* to which Fabrizio was bound to pass across it. The general at once shouted orders to close the citadel gate, and hastened down to the doorkeeper's office to make inquiries. He was more than a little surprised when he recognised the prisoner, whose limbs had grown quite stiff from being bound to the *sediola* during the long journey. Four gendarmes had picked him up, and were carrying him to the jailer's office. "It appears, then," said the self-sufficient governor to himself, "that the celebrated Fabrizio del Dongo, the man to whom the best society in Parma has seemingly sworn to devote its whole thoughts for the past year, is in my power."

The general had met him a score of times—at court, in the duchess's house, and elsewhere—but he took good care to make no sign of recognition; he would have been afraid of compromising himself.

274

The Chartreuse of Parma

"Draw up a most circumstantial report of the prisoner's delivery into my hands by the worthy *podestà* of Castelnovo," he called out to the prison clerk.

Barbone, the clerk in question, a most alarming-looking person, with his huge beard and generally martial air, began to look even more self-important than usual; he might have been taken for a German jailer. Believing that it was the Duchess Sanseverina's influence which had prevented his master, the governor, from becoming Minister of War, he was even more insolent than usual to this particular prisoner, addressing him in the second person plural, which, in Italy, is the tense used in speaking to servants. "I am a prelate of the Holy Roman Church," said Fabrizio steadily, "and grand vicar of this diocese; my birth alone entitles me to respect."

"I know nothing about that," replied the clerk impudently. "Prove your assertions by producing the patents which give you a right to those highly respectable titles." Fabrizio had no patents to show, and held his peace. General Fabio Conti, standing beside the clerk, watched him write without raising his own eyes to the prisoner's face, so that he might not be obliged to say he really was Fabrizio del Dongo.

Suddenly Clelia Conti, who was waiting in the carriage, heard a terrible noise in the guard-room. Barbone, after writing an insolent and very lengthy description of the prisoner's person, had ordered him to open his clothes, so that he might verify and note down the number and condition of the scratches he had received in his affair with Giletti.

"I can not," said Fabrizio with a bitter smile. "I am not in a position to obey this gentleman's orders; my handcuffs prevent it."

"What!" cried the general; "the prisoner is handcuffed inside the fortress! That's against the rules; there must be a distinct order. Take off the handcuffs!"

Fabrizio looked at him. "Here's a pretty Jesuit," thought he to himself; "for the last hour he has been looking at me in these handcuffs, which make me hor-

ribly uncomfortable, and now he pretends to be astonished."

The gendarmes at once removed the handcuffs. They
had just found out that Fabrizio was the Duchess Sanseverina's nephew, and lost no time in treating him with a
honeyed politeness which contrasted strongly with the
clerk's rudeness. This seemed to annoy the clerk, and he
said to Fabrizio, who had not moved:

" Now then, make haste. Show us those scratches poor
Giletti gave you at the time of his murder."

With a bound Fabrizio sprang upon the clerk, and gave
him such a cuff that Barbone fell off his chair across the
general's legs. The gendarmes seized Fabrizio's arms, but
he did not move. The general himself, and the gendarmes
who were close to him, hastily picked up the clerk, whose
face was streaming with blood. Two others, who were
standing a little farther off, ran to shut the office door,
thinking the prisoner was trying to escape. The non-commissioned officer in command was convinced young Del
Dongo could not make any very successful attempt at flight,
seeing he was now actually within the citadel, but at any
rate, with the instincts of his profession, and to prevent any
scuffle, he moved over to the window. Opposite this open
window, and about two paces from it, the general's carriage was drawn up. Clelia had shrunk far back within it,
so as to avoid witnessing the sad scene that was being en-
acted in the office. When she heard all the noise she
looked out.

" What is happening? " said she to the officer.

" Signorina, it is young Fabrizio del Dongo, who has
just cuffed that impudent rascal Barbone."

" What! is it Signor del Dongo who is being taken to
prison? "

" Why, there's no doubt about that," said the officer.
" It's on account of the poor fellow's high birth that there
is so much ceremony. I thought the signorina knew all
about it." Clelia continued to look out of the carriage
window. Whenever the gendarmes round the table scattered a little she could see the prisoner.

"Who would have dreamed," thought she, "when I met him on the road near the Lake of Como, that the very next time I saw him he would be in this sad position? He gave me his hand then, to help me into his mother's coach. Even then he was with the duchess. Can their love story have begun at that time?"

My readers must be informed that the Liberal party, led by the Marchesa Raversi and General Conti, affected an absolute belief in the tender relations supposed to exist between Fabrizio and the duchess; and the gullibility of Count Mosca, whom it loathed, was a subject of never-ending pleasantry on its part.

"Well," thought Clelia, "here he is a prisoner, and the captive of his enemies. For, after all, Count Mosca, even if one takes him to be an angel, must be delighted at seeing him caught."

A peal of loud laughter burst forth in the guard-room.

"Jacopo," said she to the officer, in a trembling voice, "what can be happening?"

"The general asked the prisoner angrily why he struck Barbone, and Monsignore Fabrizio answered very coldly: 'He called me a murderer; let him show the patents which authorize him to give me that title,' and then everybody laughed."

Barbone's place was taken by a jailer who knew how to write.

Clelia saw the clerk come out of the guard-room, mopping up the blood that streamed from his hideous face with his handkerchief; he was swearing like a trooper. "That d—d Fabrizio," he shouted at the top of his voice, "shall die by no hand but mine! I'll cheat the executioner of his job," and so forth. He had stopped short between the guard-room window and the carriage to look at Fabrizio, and his oaths grew louder and deeper.

"Be off with you!" said the officer; "you've no business to swear in that way before the signorina." Barbone raised his head to glance into the carriage; his eyes and Clelia's met, and she could not restrain an exclamation of horror. She had never had so close a view of so vile a countenance.

" He will kill Fabrizio," said she to herself. " I must warn
Don Cesare."

This was her uncle, one of the most respected priests
in the town. His brother, General Conti, had obtained
him the appointment of steward and chief chaplain of the
prison.

The general got back into the carriage. " Would you
rather go home? " said he to his daughter, " or sit and wait
for me, perhaps for a long time, in the courtyard of the
palace? I must go and report all this to the sovereign."

Fabrizio, escorted by the gendarmes, was just leaving
the guard-room to go to the room allotted to him. Clelia
was looking out of the carriage; the prisoner was quite
near her. Just at that moment she answered her father's
question in these words: " I will go with you." Fabrizio,
hearing them spoken so close to him, raised his eyes, and
met the young girl's glance. The thing that struck him
most was the expression of melancholy on her face. " How
beautiful she has grown since we met at Como! " he thought.
" What deep thoughtfulness in her expression! Those who
compare her with the duchess are quite right. What an angelic face! "

Barbone, the gory clerk, who had his own reasons for
keeping near the carriage, stopped the three gendarmes
in charge of Fabrizio with a gesture, and then, slipping
round the back of the carriage so as to get to the window
on the general's side, he said: " As the prisoner has used
violence within the citadel, would it not be well to put the
handcuffs on him for three days, by virtue of Article 157
of the regulations? "

" Go to the devil! " shouted the general, who saw difficulties ahead of him in connection with this arrest. He
could not afford to drive either the duchess or Count Mosca
to extreme measures, and besides, how was the count likely
to take this business? After all, the murder of a man like
Giletti was a mere trifle, and would have been nothing at all
but for the intrigue that had been built upon it.

During this short dialogue, Fabrizio stood, a superb
figure, amid the gendarmes. Nothing could exceed the

pride and nobility of his mien. His delicate, well-cut features, and the scornful smile which hovered on his lips, contrasted delightfully with the common appearance of the gendarmes who stood round him. But all that, so to speak, was only the external part of his expression. Clelia's celestial beauty transported him with delight, and his eyes spoke all his surprise. She, lost in thought, had not withdrawn her head from the window. He greeted her with the most deferential of half smiles, and then, after an instant—

" It strikes me, signorina, that some time ago, and near a lake, I had the honour of meeting you, attended by gendarmes."

Clelia coloured, and was so confused that she could not find a word in reply. " How noble he looked among those rough men ! " she had been saying to herself, just when he spoke to her. The deep pity, and we might almost say emotion, that overwhelmed her, deprived her of the presence of mind which should have helped her to discover an answer. She became aware of her own silence, and blushed still more deeply. Just at this moment the bolts of the great gate of the citadel were shot back with much noise. Had not his Excellency's carriage been kept waiting for a minute at least? So great was the echo under the vaulted roof that even if Clelia had thought of any reply, Fabrizio would not have been able to hear her words.

Whirled away by the horses, which had broken into a gallop as soon as they had crossed the drawbridge, Clelia said to herself, " He must have thought me very absurd "; and then suddenly she added: " Not absurd only. He must have thought me a mean-souled creature. He must have fancied I did not return his salutation because he is a prisoner, and I am the governor's daughter."

This idea threw the high-minded young girl into despair. " What makes my behaviour altogether degrading," she added, " is that when we first met, long ago, and also attended by gendarmes, as he said, it was I who was a prisoner, and he rendered me a service—and helped me out of a great difficulty. Yes, I must acknowledge it; my behaviour lacks nothing; it is full of vulgarity and ingratitude.

The Chartreuse of Parma

Alas, for this poor young fellow! Now that misfortune has overtaken him, every one will be ungrateful to him. I remember he said to me then, 'Will you remember my name at Parma?' How he must despise me now! I might so easily have said a civil word. Yes, I must acknowledge it, my conduct to him has been abominable. But for his mother's kindly offer to take me in her carriage, I should have had to walk after the gendarmes through the dust, or, which would have been far worse, to ride on horseback behind one of the men. Then it was my father who was arrested, and I who was defenceless. Yes, indeed, there is nothing lacking to my behaviour, and how bitterly such a being as he must have felt it! What a contrast between his noble face and my actions! what dignity! what composure! How like a hero he looked, surrounded by his vile enemies! I can understand the duchess's passion for him now. If this is the effect he produces in the midst of a distressing event, which must lead to terrible results, what must he be when his heart is full of happiness?"

The governor's carriage waited for more than an hour in the courtyard of the palace, and yet, when the general came down from the prince's study, Clelia did not think he had stayed too long.

"What is his Highness's will?" inquired Clelia.

"His lips said 'imprisonment,' but his eyes said 'death.'"

"Death! Great God!" exclaimed Clelia.

"Come, come! hold your tongue," said the general angrily. "What a fool I am to answer a child's questions!"

Meanwhile Fabrizio had climbed the three hundred and eighty steps which led to the Farnese Tower, a new prison built at an immense height on the platform of the great tower. He never gave one thought—one distinct thought, at all events—to the great change which had just taken place in his life. "What eyes!" he kept saying to himself. "How much they express! what depths of pity! She seemed to be saying: 'Life is such a vale of misery; don't grieve too much over what happens to you. Are we not sent here on earth to be unhappy?' How those lovely eyes of hers gazed at me, even when the horses moved forward so noisily under the arch!"

Fabrizio was quite forgetting to be miserable.

That night Clelia accompanied her father to several great houses. In the earlier part of the evening nobody knew anything about the arrest of the *great culprit*—this was the name the courtiers bestowed on the rash and unlucky young man only two hours later. That evening it was noticed that Clelia's face showed more animation than usual. Now animation, the air of taking an interest in what was going on about her, was the one thing generally wanting to this beautiful creature. When comparisons were drawn between her beauty and that of the duchess, it was this unmoved appearance, this look of being above everything, which turned the scale in her rival's favour. In England or France, the homes of vanity, this opinion would probably have been completely reversed. Clelia Conti was a young girl, too slight as yet to permit of her being compared to Guido's exquisite figures; we will not conceal the fact that, according to the rules of antique beauty, her features were somewhat too strongly marked. Her lips, for instance, exquisitely graceful as their outline was, were somewhat too full.

The delightful peculiarity of her face, that shone with the artless charm and celestial impress of the noblest nature, was that, in spite of its rare and most extraordinary beauty, it bore no resemblance whatever to the heads of the old Greek statues. The beauty of the duchess, on the contrary, was almost too much on the lines of the recognised ideal, and her essentially Lombard type recalled the voluptuous smile and tender melancholy of Lionardo da Vinci's pictures of the fair Herodias. While the duchess was sprightly, bubbling over with wit and merriment, interesting herself personally, if I may so say, in every subject which the current of conversation brought before her mental eye, Clelia, to an equal extent, was calm and slow to betray emotion—either because she scorned her surroundings, or because she regretted some absent dream. For a long time it had been believed she would end by embracing the religious life. She was now twenty. She disliked going to balls, and when she did accompany her father to such gatherings, she did it in obedience to his command, and in order to serve the interests of his ambition.

"Will it really never be possible for me," the vulgar-minded general would often think, "to turn this daughter of mine, the most beautiful and the most virtuous creature in our sovereign's dominions, to some account for my own advancement? My life is too isolated; I have nobody but her in the whole world, and a family which would give me social support is a necessity to me, in order that in a certain number of houses my worth, and, above all, my fitness for ministerial functions, may be accepted as the indispensable basis of every political argument. Well, my daughter—beautiful, good, and pious as she is—loses her temper whenever any young man in a good position about court attempts to induce her to accept his advances. As soon as the suitor is dismissed, she takes a less gloomy view of his character, and she is almost gay until another marrying man puts in an appearance. The handsomest man at court, Count Baldi, paid his addresses, and failed to please her. The wealthiest man in his Highness's dominions, the Marchese Crescenzi, has succeeded him. She vows he would make her wretched."

At other times the general would muse thus: "There is no doubt about it, my daughter's eyes are much finer than the duchess's, especially because their expression now and then is infinitely deeper. But when is that splendid expression of hers to be seen? Never in a drawing-room, where it might make her fortune, but when we are out of doors, and she is moved to pity, for instance, by the sufferings of some wretched rustic. 'Pray keep some memory of that splendid glance for the drawing-rooms in which we shall appear to-night,' I sometimes say to her. Not a bit of it. If she does condescend to go out with me, her pure and noble countenance bears a somewhat haughty, and anything but encouraging, expression of passive obedience." The general had spared no pains, as my readers will perceive, to

provide himself with a suitable son-in-law. But he spoke
the truth.

Courtiers, having nothing to look at within their own
souls, are very observant of external matters. The Parmese courtiers had remarked that it was especially when
Clelia could not persuade herself to cast off her beloved
reveries, and feign interest in outside things, that the duchess
was fond of hovering near her, and tried to make her talk.
Clelia had fair hair, which contrasted, very softly, with her
delicate colouring, somewhat too pale, as a general rule.
A careful observer would have judged, from the very shape
of her forehead, that her look of dignity, and her general
demeanour, so far above any vulgar seeking after graceful
effect, were the outcome of her profound indifference to all
vulgar things. They arose from an absence of any interest in anything—not from any incapacity for such interest. Since her father had held the governorship of the
citadel, Clelia had lived happy, or, at all events, free from
sorrow, in her rooms in that lofty building. The huge number of steps leading to the governor's palace, which stood on
the terrace of the great tower, kept away tiresome visitors,
and for this reason Clelia enjoyed a quite conventual freedom. This almost constituted the ideal of happiness which
she had once thought of seeking in the religious life. A
sort of horror seized her at the very idea of placing her
beloved solitude, and her inmost thoughts, at the mercy of
a young man whose title of "husband" would give him
the right to disturb her whole inner life. If her solitude
had not brought her happiness, it had at all events enabled
her to avoid sensations which would have been too painful.

The day Fabrizio had been taken to the fortress, the
duchess met Clelia at a party given by the Minister of the
Interior, Count Zurla. There was a ring of admirers round
them. That evening, Clelia looked even more beautiful
than the duchess. There was a look in the young girl's
eyes, so strange, so deep, as to be well-nigh indiscreet.
There was pity in that look. There was indignation, too,
and anger. The gay talk and brilliant fancies of the duchess
seemed at moments to throw Clelia into a state of distress

which almost amounted to horror. " What sobs and moans that poor woman will pour out when she hears that her lover—that noble-hearted and noble-looking young man— has been cast into prison! And the sovereign's eyes, that condemned him to death. Oh, absolute power, when wilt thou cease to crush our Italy? Oh, vile, base beings! And I—I am a jailer's daughter; and I did not fail to act up to that noble part when I would not condescend to answer Fabrizio. And once he was my benefactor! What can he think of me now, as he sits alone in his room, beside his little lamp? "

Sickened by the thought, Clelia gazed, with horror in her eyes, round the minister's splendidly lighted rooms.

" Never," whispered the circle of courtiers who gathered round the two reigning beauties, and strove to join in their conversation, " never have they talked together so eagerly, and at the same time with such an air of intimacy. Can it be that the duchess, who is always trying to soothe the hatreds roused by the Prime Minister, has pitched on some great marriage for Clelia? " This conjecture was strengthened by a circumstance which had never, hitherto, been noticed at court. There was more light, so to speak, more passion, in the young girl's eyes than in those of the lovely duchess. She, on her side, was astonished, and to her credit we may say it, delighted, by the new charms she was discovering in the youthful recluse. For over an hour she had been gazing at her with a pleasure such as is not often felt at the sight of a rival.

" But what can be happening? " wondered the duchess. " Never has Clelia looked so lovely, and I may say, so touching. Can it be that her heart has spoken? . . . But if it be so, her love is an unhappy one; there is a gloomy pain at the bottom of this new-found animation. . . . But an unhappy love keeps silence. Is she trying to tempt back some faithless swain by her social successes? " And the duchess scrutinized all the young men standing round. She noted no very striking expression in any one of them. They all wore the same appearance of more or less self-satisfied conceit. " There is some miracle here," thought the

duchess, nettled at not being able to guess what it all meant.
Where is Count Mosca, that cleverest of beings? No,
I am not mistaken. Clelia certainly does look at me as if
I had roused quite a new sense of interest in her. Is it the
result of the bestowal of some order on that crawling courtier, her father? I fancied her young and high-souled nature
incapable of descending to matters of pecuniary gain.
Can General Fabio Conti have any important request to
make to the count?"

Toward ten o'clock one of the duchess's friends came
up to her and murmured something in a low voice. She
turned very white. Clelia took her hand, and ventured to
squeeze it.

"I thank you, and now I understand you. . . . You
have a noble heart," said the duchess with a great effort.
She was hardly able to say the few words. She smiled pro-
fusely at the lady of the house, who left her seat to conduct her to the door of the outer drawing-room. Such an
honour was due to princesses of the blood only, and the
duchess felt its cruel irony in connection with her present
position. So she smiled and smiled to the Countess Zurla;
but though she tried desperately hard, she could not articulate a single word.

Clelia's eyes filled with tears as she watched the duchess
pass out of the rooms, crowded with all the most brilliant
society of the city. "What will become of that poor
woman," she thought, "when she finds herself alone in her
carriage? It would be indiscreet of me to offer to go with
her. I dare not. . . . How it would console the poor prisoner, sitting in some miserable room, if he could know how
deeply he is loved! Into what horrible solitude they have
cast him! And we are here, in these brightly lighted rooms.
It is monstrous! Could I find means of sending him a line?
Good heavens! That would be to betray my father. His
position between the two parties is so delicate. What will
become of him if he exposes himself to the hatred of the
duchess, who rules the Prime Minister, the master of three
parts of the business of the state? And then, the prince
keeps a close eye on everything that happens in the fortress,

and he will have no joking on that subject. Terror makes people cruel. . . . In any case, Fabrizio " (Clelia had ceased saying Monsignore del Dongo) " is far more to be pitied. . . . He has much more at stake than the mere danger of losing a lucrative appointment. And the duchess! . . . What a frightful passion love is! And yet all these liars in society talk of it as a source of happiness. One hears old women pitied because they can no longer feel love nor inspire it. Never shall I forget what I have just seen—that sudden change. How the duchess's eyes, so lovely, so shining, grew sad and dim after the Marchese N—— whispered those fatal words in her ear! Fabrizio must be very worthy to be so much loved."

Amid these very serious reflections, which quite filled Clelia's mind, the complimentary remarks around her were more offensive to her than ever. To escape them she moved toward an open window, half shaded by a silken curtain. She had a hope that no one would dare to follow her into this retreat. The window opened on a little grove of orange trees, planted in the ground; as a matter of fact, it was necessary to roof them over every winter. Clelia breathed the perfume of the flowers with the greatest delight, and with this enjoyment, a certain amount of peace came back into her heart. " I thought him a very noble-looking fellow," she mused. " But imagine his inspiring so remarkable a woman with such a passion! She has had the glory of refusing the prince's own advances; and if she had condescended to desire it she might have been the queen of these dominions. My father says that the sovereign's passion was so great that he would have married her if ever he had been free. And this love of hers for Fabrizio has lasted so long. For it is quite five years since we met them near the Lake of Como. Yes, quite five years," she reiterated after a moment's thought. " It struck me even then, when so many things were unperceived by my childish eyes. How both those ladies seemed to admire Fabrizio!"

Clelia noticed with delight that none of the young men who were so eager to talk to her had ventured to come near her balcony. One of them, the Marchese Crescenzi, had made a few steps in her direction, and then had stopped beside a card-table. "If only," she said, "I could see some pretty orange trees like these out of my window in the palace in the fortress—the only one which has any shade at all—my thoughts might be less sad. But there is nothing to be seen but those great hewn stones of the Farnese Tower. Ah!" she said, starting, "perhaps that is where they have put him! How I long for a talk with Don Cesare; he will be less strict than the general. My father will certainly tell me nothing as we drive back to the fortress, but I shall get everything out of Don Cesare. I have some money. I might buy a few orange trees, and set them under the window of my aviary, so that they would prevent me from seeing the great walls of the Farnese Tower. How much more I shall hate them now that I know one of the persons shut up within them! . . . Yes, this is the third time I have seen him: once at court, at the princess's birth-day ball; to-day, standing with three gendarmes round him, while that horrible Barbone was asking that the handcuffs might be put upon him; and then that time at the Lake of Como—that is quite five years ago. What a young rascal he looked then! How he looked at the gendarmes, and how strangely his mother and his aunt looked at him! There was some secret that day, certainly—something they were hiding among themselves. I had an idea at the time that he, too, was afraid of the gendarmes." Clelia shuddered. "But how ignorant I was! No doubt, even then, the duchess was interested in him. . . . How he made us laugh after a few minutes when, in spite of their evident anxiety, the two ladies had grown somewhat accustomed to a stranger's presence! . . . And this evening I could not answer anything he said to me. . . . Oh, ignorance and timidity, how often you resemble the vilest things on earth! And that is my case even now, when I am past twenty. . . . I was quite right to think of taking the veil—I am really fit for nothing but the cloistered life. 'Worthy daughter of a jailer,' he must have said to himself. He despises me, and as soon as he is able to write to the duchess he will tell her of my unkindness, and the duchess will think me a very deceitful girl, for this evening she may have believed I was full of sympathy for her misfortune."

Clelia perceived that somebody was drawing near, with the apparent intention of standing beside her on the iron balcony in front of the window. This vexed her, though she reproached herself for the feeling. The dreams thus disturbed were not devoid of a certain quality of sweetness. "Here comes some intruder. I'll give him a cold reception," she thought. She turned her head with a scornful glance, and perceived the archbishop's timorous figure edging toward her balcony by almost invisible degrees. "This holy man has no knowledge of the world," thought Clelia to herself. "Why does he come and disturb a poor girl like me? My peace is the only thing I have!" She was greeting him with a respect not untinged with haughtiness when the prelate spoke:

"Signorina, have you heard the dreadful news?"

The expression of the young girl's eyes had completely changed already, but, obedient to her father's instructions, reiterated a hundred times over, she replied, with an air of ignorance which her eyes utterly belied:

"I have heard nothing, monsignore."

"My chief grand vicar, poor Fabrizio del Dongo, who is no more guilty of the death of that ruffian Giletti than I am, has been carried off from Bologna, where he was living under the name of Giuseppe Bossi, and shut up in your citadel. He arrived there *chained* to the carriage which brought him. A kind of jailer of the name of Barbone, who was pardoned years ago, after having murdered one of his own brothers, tried to use personal violence to Fabrizio, but my young friend is not a man to endure an insult. He threw the vile fellow on the ground, and was immediately carried down to a dungeon, twenty feet below the earth, with handcuffs on his wrists."

"Not handcuffs. No."

"Ah, you know something," exclaimed the archbishop, and the old man's features lost their expression of deep despondency; "but before all things, since somebody might come near this balcony, and interrupt us, would you do me the charity of giving Don Cesare this pastoral ring of mine with your own hands?" The young girl had taken the ring and did not know where to bestow it so as to avoid the risk of losing it. "Put it on your thumb," said the archbishop, and he slipped it on himself. "May I rely on your giving him this ring?"

"Yes, monsignore."

"Will you promise me secrecy as to what I am going to add, even if you should not think it proper to grant my request?"

"Yes, indeed, monsignore," replied the young girl, alarmed by the grave and gloomy aspect assumed by the old man. "Our honoured archbishop," she added, "can give me no orders that are not worthy of himself and of me."

"Tell Don Cesare that I recommend my adopted son to his care. I know that the police officers who carried him off did not even give him time to take his breviary; I beg Don Cesare to give him his own, and if your uncle will send to-morrow to the palace, I undertake to replace the book given by him to Fabrizio. I also beg Don Cesare to pass on the ring, now on your pretty hand, to Monsignore del Dongo." The archbishop was here interrupted by General Fabio Conti, who came to fetch his daughter and take her to her carriage. A short conversation ensued, during which the prelate showed himself to be not devoid of cunning. Without referring in the smallest degree to the newly made prisoner, he contrived that the current of talk should lead up to his own enunciation of certain political and moral sentiments, as, for instance: "There are certain critical moments in court life which decide the existence of important personages for considerable periods. It would be eminently imprudent to transform a condition of political coolness, which is a frequent and very simple result of party opposition, into a personal hatred." Then the archbishop, somewhat carried away by the great grief which this unexpected arrest had occasioned him, went so far as to say that while a man must certainly preserve the position he enjoyed, it would be wanton imprudence to bring down desperate hatreds on his own head by allowing himself to be drawn into certain things which **never** could be forgotten.

When the general was in his **coach with** his daughter—" These may be called threats," he cried. " Threats, to a man like me!" Not another word was exchanged between father and daughter during their twenty minutes' drive.

When Clelia had received the pastoral ring from the archbishop, she had fully determined that when she was in the carriage with her father she would speak to him of the trifling service the prelate had asked of her. But when she heard the word " threats," and the furious tone in which it was uttered, she became convinced that her father would intercept the message. She hid the ring with her left hand and clasped it passionately. All the way from the minister's house to the citadel she kept asking herself whether it would be a sin not to speak to her father. She was very pious, very timid, and her heart, usually so quiet, was throbbing with unaccustomed violence. But the challenge of the sentinel on the rampart above the gate rang out over the approaching carriage before Clelia could pitch on words appropriate to persuade her father not to refuse, so great was her fear that he might do so. Neither could she think of any as she climbed the three hundred and eighty steps which led up to the governor's palace.

She lost no time in speaking to her uncle; he scolded her, and refused to have anything to do with the business.

CHAPTER XVI

"WELL," cried the general, as soon as he caught sight of his brother Don Cesare, "here is the duchess ready to spend a hundred thousand crowns to make a fool of me and save the prisoner."

But for the present we must leave Fabrizio in his prison, high up in the citadel of Parma. He is well guarded there, and when we come back we shall find him safe enough, though perhaps a trifle changed. We must now turn all our attention to the court, where his fate is to be decided by the most complicated intrigues, and, above all, by the passions of a most unhappy woman. As Fabrizio, watched by the governor, climbed the three hundred and eighty steps which led to his dungeon in the Farnese Tower he felt, greatly as he had dreaded that moment, that he had no time to think of his misfortune.

When the duchess reached home after leaving Count Zurla's party she waved her women from her, and then, throwing herself, fully dressed, upon her bed, she moaned aloud: "Fabrizio is in the hands of his enemies, and, because of me, perhaps they will poison him." How can I describe the moment of despair which followed this summing up of the situation in the heart of a woman so unreasonable, so enslaved by the sensation of the moment, and, though she did not acknowledge it to herself, so desperately in love with the young prisoner?

There were inarticulate exclamations, transports of rage, convulsive movements, but not one tear. She had sent away her women that they might not see her weep. She had thought she must burst into sobs the moment she was left alone, but tears, the first relief of a great sorrow, were denied her utterly. Her haughty soul was too full of rage, indignation, and the sense of her own inferiority to the prince.

"Is not this humiliation enough?" she cried. "I am insulted, and, what is far worse, Fabrizio's life is risked! And shall I not avenge myself? Beware, my prince! you may destroy me—so be it; that is in your power—but after you have done it, I will have your life. Alas, my poor Fabrizio, and what good will that do you? What a change from the day on which I was about to leave Parma! And yet I thought myself unhappy then. . . . What blindness! I was on the point of breaking up all the habits of a pleasant life. Alas, all unknowingly, I stood on the brink of an event which was to settle my fate forever. If the count's vile habits of slavish toadyism had not made him suppress the words '*unjust proceedings*' in that fatal note which I had wrung from the prince's vanity, we should have been safe. More by good luck than by good guidance, I must acknowledge, I had nettled his vanity about his beloved city of Parma. Then it was I who threatened to depart. Then I was free. . . . My God! now I am nothing but a slave. Here I lie, nailed to this vile sewer; and Fabrizio lies chained in the citadel—that citadel which has been death's antechamber to so many men. And I—I can no longer hold that wild beast by his fear of seeing me forsake his lair!

"He is too clever not to feel that I shall never go far from the hateful tower to which my heart is fettered. The man's wounded vanity may inspire him with the most extraordinary notions; their whimsical cruelty would only tickle his astounding vanity. If he puts forward his nauseous attempts at love-making again, if he says, 'Accept the homage of your slave or else Fabrizio dies,' well, then it will be the old story of Judith. . . . Yes, but though that would be suicide for me, it would be murdering Fabrizio. That booby who would come after him, our prince royal, and Rassi, his infamous torturer, would hang Fabrizio as my accomplice."

The duchess cried out in her distress. This alternative, from which she could see no escape, put her agonized heart

to torture. Her bewildered mind could see no other probability in the future. For some ten minutes she tossed about
like a mad woman; this horrible restlessness was followed
at last, for a few moments, by the slumber of exhaustion;
she was worn out. But in a few minutes she woke again,
with a start, and found herself sitting on her bed. She had
fancied the prince was cutting off Fabrizio's head before her
very eyes. The duchess cast distracted glances all about
her. When she had convinced herself, at last, that neither
the prince nor Fabrizio were in her presence, she fell back
upon her bed, and very nearly fainted. So great was her
physical weakness that she had not strength to alter her
position. " O God, if only I could die!" she said. " But
what cowardice! Could I forsake Fabrizio in his misfortunes? My brain must be failing. Come, let me look at the
truth; let me coolly consider the horrible position into
which I have sprung, as though to please myself. What
mad folly to come and live at the court of an absolute
prince, a tyrant who knows every one of his victims! To
him every glance they give seems a threat against his own
power. Alas! neither the count nor I thought of that when
I left Milan. All I considered were the attractions—a pleasant court, something inferior, indeed, still somewhat resembling the happy days under Prince Eugène.

" One has no idea, at a distance, of what the authority of
a despot, who knows all his subjects by sight, really means.
The external forms of despotism are the same as those of
other governments. There are judges, for instance, but
they are men like Rassi. The monster! He would not
think it the least odd to hang his own father at the prince's
order. . . . He would call it his duty. . . . I might buy
over Rassi, but—unhappy that I am—I have no means of
doing it. What have I to offer him? A hundred thousand
francs, perhaps. And the story goes that when Heaven's
wrath against this unhappy country last saved him from a
dagger thrust, the prince sent him ten thousand gold sequins
in a casket. And besides, what sum of money could possibly tempt him? That grovelling soul, which has never
read anything but scorn in other men's eyes, has the pleas-

ure, now, of being looked at with fear, and even with respect. He may become Minister of Police—and why not? Then three quarters of the inhabitants of the country will pay him abject court, and tremble before him as slavishly as he himself trembles before the sovereign.

"As I can not fly this odious place, I must be useful to Fabrizio. If I live on alone, solitary, despairing, what, then, am I to do for Fabrizio? No! forward, miserable woman! Do your duty. Go out into the world. Pretend you have forgotten Fabrizio. Pretend to forget you, dear angel?"

At the words the duchess burst into tears—she could weep at last. After an hour claimed by the natural weakness of humanity, she became aware, with some sense of consolation, that her ideas were beginning to grow clearer. "If I had a magic carpet," said she, "if I could carry off Fabrizio from the citadel, and take refuge with him in some happy country where they could not pursue us—in Paris, for instance—we should have the twelve hundred francs his father's agent sends me with such comical regularity, to live on, at first; and I am sure I could get together another three hundred thousand, out of the remnants of my fortune." The imagination of the duchess dwelt with inexpressible delight upon all the details of the life she would lead three hundred leagues from Parma. "There," thought she to herself, "he might enter the army under an assumed name. In one of those brave French regiments, young Valserra would soon make himself a reputation, and he would be happy at last."

These dreams of delight brought back her tears again, but this time, they were softer. There was still such a thing as happiness, then, somewhere. This frame of mind continued for a long time. The poor woman shrank with horror from the contemplation of the terrible reality. At last, just as the dawn began to show a white light above the tree tops in her garden, she made a great effort. "Within a few hours," said she to herself, "I shall be on the battle-field. I shall have to act, and if anything irritating should happen to me, if the prince took it into his head to say anything about Fabrizio, I am not sure that I shall be able to keep my self-control. Therefore, here and without delay, I must take my resolution.

" If I am declared a state criminal, Rassi will seize everything there is in the palace. On the first of the month, the count and I, according to our custom, burned all the papers of which the police might take advantage—and he is Minister of Police; there lies the beauty of the joke. I have three rather valuable diamonds. To-morrow Fulgenzio, my old boatman from Grianta, shall go to Geneva and place them in safe-keeping. If ever Fabrizio escapes (O God! be favourable to me!" and she crossed herself), " the Marchese del Dongo will perceive, in his unspeakable meanness, that it is a sin to provide support for a man who has been prosecuted by a legitimate prince. Then Fabrizio will get my diamonds, and so he will have bread at all events.

" I must dismiss the count. . . . After what has happened I never could bear to be alone with him again. Poor fellow! he is not wicked—far from it—he is only weak. His commonplace soul can not rise to the height of ours. My poor Fabrizio, would you could be with me for an instant, so that we might take counsel together about our danger!

" The count's scrupulous prudence would interfere with all my plans, and besides, I must not drag him down into my own ruin. . . . For why should not that tyrant's vanity make him cast me into prison? I shall have conspired . . . what is more easy to prove? If he would only send me to his citadel, and I could contrive to buy even one instant's conversation with Fabrizio, how bravely we would go to death together! But a truce to such folly—his Rassi would advise him to get rid of me by poison. My appearance in the streets, dragged along in a cart, might touch the hearts of his dear subjects . . . but what! more fancies? Alas! such foolery must be forgiven to a poor woman whose real fate is so sad. The truth in all this is that the prince will not send me to death, but nothing would be easier for him than to cast me into prison and keep me there. He can have all sorts of compromising papers hidden in a corner of my palace, as was done in the case of poor L——. Then three judges—who need not be too great rogues, for there will be authentic evidence—and a dozen false witnesses, will do the rest. Thus I may be sentenced to death for conspiracy, and the prince, in his boundless mercy, and considering that I had formerly had the honour of being received by him, will commute the penalty to ten years in the fortress. But I, not to belie the violent character which has drawn so many foolish remarks from the Marchesa Raversi and my other enemies, shall coolly poison myself—so, at least, the public will kindly believe. But I will undertake that Rassi will make his appearance in my dungeon, and politely offer me a phial of strychnine or laudanum, in the prince's name.

" Yes, I must have a very open rupture with the count, for I will not drag him down with my own fall. That would be infamy. The poor man has loved me so sincerely. It was my own folly which led me to believe any true courtier's soul had room in it for love. The prince will very probably find some pretext for throwing me into prison. He will be afraid of my perverting public opinion with regard to Fabrizio. The count has a deep sense of honour; that instant he will do what the court hangers-on, in their overwhelming astonishment, will style an act of madness— he will leave the court. I braved the prince's authority the night he wrote that note; I must be prepared for anything from his wounded self-love. Can a man who was born a prince ever forget the sensation I gave him that evening? And besides, if the count is at variance with me, he will be in a better position to serve Fabrizio. But supposing the count, whom my decision will throw into despair, were to avenge himself. . . . But that is an idea that would not occur to him. He is not an intrinsically mean man, like the prince. The count may countersign an infamous decree, and groan as he does it, but he is honourable. And then, what should he avenge? The fact that after having loved him for five years, and never given his love a single cause for complaint, I say to him: ' Dear count, I was happy enough to love you. Well, the flame has burned out; I do not love you any more. But I know the very bottom of your heart; I have the deepest regard for you, and you will always be the dearest of all my friends.'

" What reply can an honourable gentleman make to such a declaration?

" I will take a new lover, or, at all events, the world will think so. I will say to that lover: ' After all, the prince is quite right to punish Fabrizio's blunder. But on his fête day our gracious sovereign will, no doubt, set him at liberty!' Thus I shall gain six months. This new lover, whom prudence recommends, should be that venal judge, that vile torturer, Rassi. He would be ennobled, and as a matter of fact, I should give him the *entrée* into the best society. Forgive me, Fabrizio, dearest, that effort is beyond my powers. What! that monster! still stained with the blood of Count P—— and of D——? I should swoon with horror if he came near me, or, rather, I should seize a knife and plunge it into his vile heart. Ask me not things which are impossible!

" Yes, above all things, I must forget Fabrizio. I must not betray a shadow of anger against the prince. I must be as cheerful as ever. And my cheerfulness will seem yet more attractive to these sordid souls. First, because I shall appear to submit to their sovereign with a good grace; and secondly, because, far from making game of them, I shall take pains to show off their pretty little points—for instance, I will compliment Count Zurla on the beauty of the white feather in the hat he has just sent a courier to fetch from Lyons, and which is his great delight.

" I might choose a lover in the Raversi's party. If the count retires, that will be the ministerial party, and there the power will lie. The man who rules the citadel will be a friend of the Raversi, for Fabio Conti will be one of the ministers. How will the prince, a well-bred man, a clever man, accustomed to the count's delightful methods, endure doing business with that ox, that arch-fool, whose whole life has been taken up with the all-important problem of whether his Highness's soldiers ought to wear seven buttons on the breasts of their tunics, or nine? It is such idiotic brutes as these—all very jealous of me, and there lies your danger, my dear Fabrizio—it is such idiotic brutes as these who will decide my fate and yours. Therefore the count will not resign. He always fancies resignation is the greatest sacrifice that can be made by a Prime Minister, and every time his looking-glass tells him he is growing old, he offers to make that sacrifice for me. Therefore my rupture with him must be complete. Yes, and there must be no reconciliation unless that should appear my only means of preventing his retirement. I will dismiss him, indeed, with all the kindness possible. But after his courtier-like suppression of the words '*unjust proceedings*' in the prince's note, I feel that if I am not to hate him I must spend some months without seeing him at all. On that decisive evening I had no need of his intelligence; all he had to do was to write under my dictation. He had only to write that one sentence, which I had won by my own resolution. His cringing courtier's instinct was too much for him. He told me next morning that he could not ask his prince to sign anything so ridiculous—that he would have had to issue letters of pardon. But, good heavens, when one has to deal with such people—those monsters of vanity and spite known as the Farnese—one takes what one can get."

At the thought, the anger of the duchess blazed up afresh. "The prince deceived me," she said, "and how basely! . . . There is no excuse for that man. He has intellect, he has cleverness, he has logic; the only mean things in him are his passions. We have remarked it a score of times, the count and I. He is never vulgar-minded, except when he thinks there has been an intention to insult him. Well, Fabrizio's crime has nothing to do with politics; it is a mere trifle of an assassination, such as occur by the hundred every year within his happy dominions, and the count has sworn to me that he has made the most careful inquiries, and that Fabrizio is innocent. Giletti was not devoid of courage. When he saw himself close to the frontier, he was suddenly tempted to get rid of a rival who found favour in the eyes of his mistress."

The duchess pondered long over the question of Fabrizio's possible culpability. Not that she considered it a very heavy sin on the part of a nobleman of her nephew's rank to rid himself of an impertinent actor, but, in her despair, she was beginning to have a vague feeling that she would have to struggle desperately to prove Fabrizio's innocence. "No," said she at last, "here is a decisive proof. He is like poor Pietranera; he always carries arms in his pockets, and that day all he had was a broken-down single-barrelled gun, which he had borrowed from one of the workmen.

"I hate the prince, because he has deceived me, and deceived me after the most cowardly fashion. After he had signed his pardon, he had the poor boy carried off from Bologna. But this account shall be settled between us."

Toward five o'clock in the morning the duchess, worn out by her long fit of despair, rang for her women. When they entered her room they screamed aloud. Seeing her stretched on her bed, fully dressed, with all her diamonds, her face white as her sheets, and her eyes closed, they almost fancied she was lying in state after her death. They would have thought her in a dead faint, if they had not recollected that she had just rung. Every now and then a slow tear coursed down her cheeks; her women understood, on a sign from her, that she desired to be put to bed.

Twice that morning, after Count Zurla's party, the count had called upon the duchess. Finding no admittance, he wrote that he desired her advice for himself. Ought he to continue minister after the affront which had been put upon him? "The young man is innocent; but even if he had been guilty, ought he to have been arrested without any warning to me, his declared protector?"

The count had no virtue; we may even add that what Liberals understand by *virtue* (to seek the happiness of the greatest number) seemed to him folly. He believed his first duty to be to seek the happiness of Count Mosca della Rovere; but when he spoke of resigning, he was thoroughly honourable and perfectly sincere. Never in all his life had he spoken an untruth to the duchess. She, however, paid not the slightest attention to his letter. Her course, and a very painful one, was settled: she was to pretend to forget Fabrizio. After that effort, everything else was quite indifferent to her.

Toward noon next morning the count, who had called quite ten times at the Palazzo Sanseverina, was at last admitted. He was thunder-struck when he saw the duchess. "She looks forty," said he to himself, "and yesterday she was so brilliant, so young; every one tells me that during her long conversation with Clelia Conti she looked quite as young as she, and far more bewitching."

The duchess's voice and manner of speaking were just as strange as her appearance. Her tone—passionless, devoid of all human interest, of any touch of anger—drove the colour from the count's face. It reminded him of one of his friends who, a few months previously, when on the point of death, and after having received the sacrament, had desired to speak with him. After a few minutes, the duchess was able to speak to him. She looked at him, but her eyes were still dim.

"Let us part, my dear count," she said, in a voice that was weak, but quite articulate, and which she did her best to render kind. "Let us part! It must be done. Heaven is my witness that for the last five years my conduct toward you has been above reproach. You have given me a brilliant life in place of the boredom which would have been my dreary lot at Grianta. But for you, old age and I would have met together some years earlier. . . . On my part, my one care has been to endeavour to make you happy. It is because I care for you that I propose this separation, '*à l'amiable*,' as they say in France."

The count did not understand her. She was obliged to repeat herself several times over. Then he grew deadly pale, and, casting himself on his knees beside her bed, he poured out all that the deepest astonishment, followed by the liveliest despair, could inspire in the heart of a clever man who was desperately in love. Over and over again he offered to send in his resignation, and follow his friend to some safe retreat a thousand leagues from Parma.

"You dare to speak to me of departure," she cried at

last, "and Fabrizio is here!" But seeing that the name of Fabrizio pained the count, she added, after a moment's rest, and with a slight pressure of his hand: "No, dear friend, I will not tell you that I have loved you with those passionate transports which nobody, it appears to me, can feel after thirty, and I am long past that age. You will have been told that I love Fabrizio, for I know that story has been rife at this *wicked* court." For the first time during this conversation, her eyes flashed as she spoke the word *wicked*. "I swear to you, before God, and on Fabrizio's life, that not the smallest thing has ever happened between him and me, which a third person might not have seen. Neither will I tell you that I love him exactly as a sister would love him. I love him, so to speak, by instinct. I love his courage, so simple and so perfect that he may be said to be unaware of it himself. I remember that this admiration began when he returned from Waterloo. He was still a child, in spite of his seventeen years. His great anxiety was to know whether he really had been present at the battle; and if that were so, whether he could say he had fought, seeing he had not shared in the attack on any battery or any column of the enemy's forces. It was during our serious discussion of this important subject that I began to notice his perfect charm. His great soul was revealed to me. What skilful lies a well-brought-up young man would have put forward in his place! Well, if he is not happy, I can not be happy. There; that sentence exactly describes the condition of my heart. If it is not the truth, it is, at all events, as much of the truth as I can see." Encouraged by her tone of frankness and friendliness, the count tried to kiss her hand. She drew it away with a sort of horror. "Those days are over," she said. "I am a woman of seven-and-thirty; I am on the threshold of old age. I feel all its despondency already; perhaps, indeed, I am very near my grave. That moment is a terrible one, so I have heard, and yet I think I long for it. I have the worst symptom of old age. This horrible misfortune has killed my heart; there is no love left in me. When I look at you, dear count, I only seem to see the shadow of some one who was once dear to me! I will say more. It is only my gratitude which makes me speak to you thus."

"What is to become of me?" reiterated the count; "of me, who feel I love you more passionately than when I first saw you at the Scala?"

"Shall I tell you something, dear friend? Your talk of love wearies me, and strikes me as indecent. Come," she said, and she tried to smile, but failed, "take courage; act like a clever man, a judicious man, full of resource to meet events. Be with me that which you really are in the eyes of the outside world—the cleverest man and the greatest politician whom Italy has produced for centuries."

The count rose to his feet and walked up and down for some moments in silence.

"Impossible, dear friend," said he at last. "I am torn in pieces by the most violent passion, and you ask me to appeal to my own reason. There is no reason for me at present."

"Let us not speak of passion, I beg of you," she replied in a hard tone, and for the first time in their two hours' conversation there was some expression in her voice. In spite of his own despair, the count endeavoured to console her.

"He has deceived me," she exclaimed, without making any answer to the reasons for hope which the count was putting before her; "he has deceived me in the basest manner," and for an instant her deadly pallor disappeared. But the count remarked that even at that moment she had not strength to raise her arms.

"Good God!" thought he, "can it be possible that she is only ill? In that case this must be the beginning of some very serious illness." And, overcome with anxiety, he proposed sending for the famous Razori, the chief physician of that country, and the best in Italy.

"Would you, then, give a stranger the pleasure of knowing all the depths of my despair? . . . Is that the counsel of a traitor or of a friend?" and she looked at him with wild eyes.

"It is all over," said he to himself in despair. "She

has no more love for me, and, what is worse, she does not even reckon me among men of ordinary honour."

"I must tell you," added the count, speaking rapidly, "that I was determined, in the first instance, to know all the details of the arrest which has thrown us into despair, and, curiously enough, I know nothing positive as yet. I have had the gendarmes at the next post questioned. They saw the prisoner come in by the road from Castelnovo, and were ordered to follow his *sediola*. I immediately sent off Bruno, with whose zeal and devotion you are acquainted. He has orders to go back from one post to another, and to find out where and how Fabrizio was arrested."

At the sound of Fabrizio's name the duchess was seized with a slight convulsion.

"Excuse me, my friend," she said to the count, as soon as she could speak. "These details interest me. Tell them all to me; help me to understand the smallest incidents."

"Well, signora," continued the count, striving to speak lightly, in the hope of distracting her thoughts a little. "I am rather tempted to send a confidential message to Bruno, and tell him to push on as far as Bologna. It is there, perhaps, that they may have laid hands upon our young friend. What is the date of his last letter?"

"Tuesday; that is five days ago."

"Had it been opened in transmission?"

"There was not a sign of that. I must tell you that it was written on the most horrible paper; the address is in a woman's handwriting, and bears the name of an old washerwoman who is related to my waiting-maid. The washerwoman believes the letters have to do with a love affair, and Cecchina repays her the charges for delivery, and gives her nothing more." The count, who had now quite taken up the tone of a business man, endeavoured, in talking the matter over with the duchess, to discover on what day Fabrizio might have been carried off from Bologna. It was only then that he, generally so full of tact, discovered that this was the tone he had better take. These details interested the unhappy woman, and seemed to distract her thoughts a little. If the count had not been so desperately in love, this simple idea would have occurred to him as soon as he entered her room.

The duchess dismissed him, so that he might send orders to the faithful Bruno without delay. When they touched, for a moment, on the question of finding out whether the sentence had actually been pronounced, when the prince had signed the note addressed to the duchess, she, with a sort of eagerness, seized the opportunity of saying to the count: "I will not reproach you with having omitted the words *'unjust proceedings'* from the note which you wrote, and he signed. That was your courtier's instinct, which was too strong for you. Unconsciously, you were preferring the interests of your master to the interests of your friend. Your acts, my dear count, have been subservient to my orders, and that for a very long time. But it is not within your power to change your nature. As a minister you have great talents, but you have the instincts of your trade as well. The suppression of the word 'unjust' has worked my ruin. But far be it from me to reproach you with it in any way. The fault lay with your instincts, and not with your will.

"Remember," she added in an altered voice, and in the most imperious fashion, "that I am not too much overwhelmed by Fabrizio's imprisonment, that it has never occurred to me to leave this country, and that my feeling for the prince is one of the most profound respect. That is what you have to say. And this is what I have to say to you: As I propose, in future, to direct my course alone, I wish to part from you *'à l'amiable'*—that is to say, as good old friends. You must consider that I am sixty years old, that youth is dead within me, that I can never feel anything very strongly again, that love is no longer possible to me. But I should be still more miserable than I am if I should happen to compromise your future. It may become part of my plans to give myself the appearance of having taken a young lover, and I should not like to see you pained on that account. I can swear to you, on Fabrizio's happiness"—and she paused a minute on the words—"that I have never been unfaithful to you once in all these five years

—that is a very long time," she said. She tried to smile; there was a movement on her pallid cheeks, but there was no curve upon her lips. "I will even swear to you that I have never planned such a thing, nor even thought of it. Now I have made that clear, so pray leave me."

The count left the Palazzo Sanseverina in a state of despair. He saw the duchess was thoroughly resolved to separate from him, and he had never been so desperately in love with her. This is one of the matters to which I am constantly obliged to return, because, outside Italy, their improbability is so great. As soon as he reached his own house he sent off six different people along the road from Castelnovo and Bologna, all of them carrying letters. " But this is not all," said the unhappy count to himself. " The prince may take it into his head to have the unhappy boy executed, just to avenge himself for the tone the duchess took with him on the day of that fatal note. I felt then that the duchess had overstepped a boundary beyond which one should never go, and it was to patch things up that I fell into the incredible folly of suppressing the words ' *unjust proceedings*,' the only ones which bound the sovereign. But pooh! is there anything that binds a man in his position? It was certainly the greatest mistake of my whole life, and has risked everything which made it worth living to me. I must use all my activity and skill to repair the blunder now. But if I utterly fail to gain anything, even by sacrificing a certain amount of my dignity, I will leave this man in the lurch, and we'll see whom he will find to replace me, and realize his mighty political dreams, and his idea of making himself constitutional King of Lombardy! Fabio Conti is a mere fool, and Rassi's talent amounts to finding legal reasons for hanging a man whom the ruler dislikes."

Once the count had thoroughly made up his mind to resign his post if the severity with which Fabrizio was treated exceeded that of an ordinary imprisonment, he said to himself: " If an imprudent defiance of that man's vain whim costs me my life, I will preserve my honour at all events. . . . By the way, now that I snap my fingers at my ministerial portfolio, I can venture to do a hundred things which would have seemed impossible to me, even this morning. For instance, I will attempt anything within the bounds of human possibility to help Fabrizio to escape. . . . Good God!" exclaimed the count, breaking off suddenly, and his eyes dilated immensely, as if he had caught sight of some unexpected joy. "The duchess said nothing about escape to me! Can she have failed in sincerity for once in her life, and is her quarrel with me merely founded on her desire that I should deceive the prince? My faith, the thing is done!"

The count's eyes had regained their old expression of satirical shrewdness. "That charming creature Rassi is paid by his master for all those sentences of his which dishonour us in the eyes of Europe. But he is not the man to refuse payment from me for betraying his master's secrets. The brute has a mistress and a confessor. But the mistress is too vile a creature for me to converse with; all the fruit hucksters in the neighbourhood would know the details of our interview by the next morning." The count, revived by this gleam of hope, was already on his way to the cathedral. Astounded at the hastiness of his own action, he laughed, in spite of his sorrow. "See what it is," he said, "to be no longer minister."

This cathedral, like many Italian churches, was used as a passage from one street to another. In the distance the count noticed one of the archbishop's grand vicars crossing the aisle.

"As I have met you," said he, "I am sure you will be good enough to save my gouty feet from the deadly fatigue of climbing up the archbishop's staircase. I should be profoundly grateful to him if he would be so kind as to come down to the sacristy." The archbishop was delighted at the message. He had a thousand things to say to the minister about Fabrizio; but the minister guessed these things were nothing but empty phrases, and would not listen to any of them.

"What sort of a man is Dugnani, the curate of San Paolo?"

The Chartreuse of Parma

"A small mind and a huge ambition," replied the archbishop; "very few scruples, and excessive poverty, because of his vices."

"Zounds! Monsignore," exclaimed the minister, "your descriptions are worthy of Tacitus," and he took leave of him with a smile. As soon as he was back in his palace he sent for Father Dugnani.

"You direct the conscience of my excellent friend Chief-Justice Rassi. Is there not anything he would like to say to me?" and without more words, or further ceremony, he dismissed the priest.

CHAPTER XVII

THE count considered himself as already out of office. "Let me see," thought he to himself, "how many horses shall we be able to keep after my disgrace, for that is what my retirement will be called?" The count reckoned up his fortune. When he had entered the ministry he had possessed eighty thousand francs. He now discovered, to his great astonishment, that his whole possessions did not amount to five hundred thousand francs. "That makes twenty thousand francs a year at the most," he mused. "I really am a terrible blunderer. There is not a vulgar fellow at Parma who does not believe I have saved a hundred and fifty thousand francs a year. And on that particular point the prince is more vulgar-minded than anybody else. When they see me in poverty they will only say I am very clever about concealing my wealth. By Jove!" he exclaimed, "if I am in office for three months longer that fortune shall be doubled!" This idea suggested an excuse for writing to the duchess, and he seized it eagerly. But to gain forgiveness for writing at all, in their present terms, he filled his letter up with figures and calculations. "We shall only have twenty thousand francs a year," he said, "to keep us all three at Naples—Fabrizio, you, and I. Fabrizio and I will keep one saddle horse between us." The minister had only just sent his letter off, when Chief-Justice Rassi was announced. He received him with a haughtiness that bordered closely on impertinence.

"How is this, sir?" he cried; "you have a conspirator in whom I am interested carried off from Bologna, and you would fain cut off his head, and all this without a word to me. May I inquire if you know my successor's name? Is he to be General Conti or yourself?"

Rassi was struck dumb. He had too little social experience to be able to judge whether the count was speaking seriously or not. He turned very red, and mumbled some unintelligible words. The count watched him, and enjoyed his confusion.

All at once Rassi gave himself a shake, and exclaimed with perfect glibness, just like Figaro when he is caught red-handed by Almaviva:

"Upon my word, count, I'll not mince matters with you. What will you give me if I answer all your questions just as I would answer those of my confessor?"

"The Cross of St. Paul" (the Parmese order), "or, if you can furnish me with a pretext for granting it to you, I will give you money."

"I would rather have the Cross of St. Paul, because that gives me noble rank."

"What, my dear sir! You still have some regard for our poor advantages?"

"If I had been nobly born," replied Rassi, with all the impudence of his trade, "the relations of the people whom I have hanged would hate me, but they would not despise me."

"Well," returned the count, "I will save you from their scorn. Do you enlighten my ignorance. What do you intend to do with Fabrizio?"

"Indeed, the prince is sorely puzzled. He is very much afraid that, tempted by Armida's lovely eyes—excuse this glowing language, I use the sovereign's own words—he is afraid that, fascinated by those exquisite eyes, of which he himself has felt the charm, you may leave him in the lurch, and you are the only man capable of managing this Lombard business. I will even tell you," added Rassi, lowering his voice, "that you have a fine opportunity here, quite worth the Cross of St. Paul that you are giving me. The prince would confer on you, as a reward from the nation, a fine property worth six hundred thousand francs, which he would cut off his own domains, or else a grant of three hundred thousand crowns, on condition of your undertaking not to interfere about Fabrizio del Dongo, or at all events only to mention the matter to him in public."

"I expected something better than that," said the count. "If I don't interfere about Fabrizio I must quarrel with the duchess."

"Well, that again is just what the prince says. Between ourselves, the fact is that he is furiously angry with the duchess, and he is afraid that to console yourself for your quarrel with that charming lady you may ask him, now that your wife is dead, to grant you the hand of his cousin, Princess Isota—she is not more than fifty years old."

"He has guessed aright," replied the count. "Our master is the cleverest man in his own dominions."

Never had the whimsical notion of marrying this elderly princess entered the count's head. Nothing could have been more uncongenial to a man with his mortal hatred of court ceremonial. He began rapping his snuff-box on the top of a little marble table, close to his arm-chair.

Rassi took his perplexed gesture to be the possible harbinger of a stroke of good fortune; his eyes shone.

"I beg of you, count," he cried, "if your Excellency proposes to accept either the property worth six hundred thousand francs, or the money grant, not to choose anybody but myself to negotiate the matter for you. I would undertake," he added, dropping his voice, "to get the money grant increased, or even to add a considerable tract of forest to the landed property. If your Excellency would only condescend to impart a little gentleness and caution into your manner of speaking of the brat shut up yonder, the landed property bestowed on you by the nation's gratitude might be turned into a duchy. I tell your Excellency again, the prince, at the present moment, loathes the duchess. But he is in a very great difficulty—to such a point, indeed, that I have sometimes imagined there must be some secret matter which he does not dare to acknowledge to me. At any rate, there is a perfect gold mine for us both in the business, for I can sell you his most private secrets, and very easily, too, seeing I am looked on as your sworn enemy. After all, furious though he is with the duchess, he believes, as we all do, that you are the only person in the world who can successfully carry through the secret arrangements

The Chartreuse of Parma

about the Milanese territory. Will your Excellency give
me leave to repeat the sovereign's expression, word for
word?" said Rassi, growing more eager. "Often there
are features in the mere positions of words which no para-
phrase can render, and you may see more in them than
I do."

"I give you full leave," said the count, who was still
rapping the marble table absently with his gold snuff-box;
"I give you full leave, and I shall be grateful."

"If you will give me an hereditary patent of nobility,
independently of the Cross, I shall be more than satisfied.
When I mention the idea of nobility to the prince, he answers: 'Turn a rascal like you into a noble! I should
have to shut up shop the very next day; not a soul in Parma
would ever seek for rank again.' To come back to the
Milanese business, the prince said to me, only three days
ago: 'That knave is the only man who can carry on the
thread of our intrigues. If I turn him away, or if he follows
the duchess, I may as well give up all hope of one day
seeing myself the Liberal and adored ruler of all Italy.'"

At these words the count breathed more freely. "Fabrizio will not die," said he to himself.

Never before, in the whole of his life, had Rassi been
admitted to familiar conversation with the Prime Minister.
He was beside himself with delight. He felt himself on the
eve of bidding farewell to that cognomen of Rassi, which
had become synonymous with everything that was mean
and vile throughout the whole country. The common
people called all mad dogs *Rassi*; only quite lately soldiers
had fought duels because the name had been applied to them
by some of their comrades. Never a week passed that the
unlucky name did not appear in some piece of low dog-
gerel. His son, an innocent schoolboy of sixteen years of
age, dared not show himself in the *cafés* because of his name.

The scalding memory of all these delightful features of
his position drove him to commit an imprudence.

"I have a property," said he to the count, edging his
seat close to the Prime Minister's arm-chair; "it is called
Riva. I should like to be Baron Riva."

"Why not?" said the Prime Minister. Rassi quite lost his head.

"Well, then, count, I will dare to be indiscreet; I will venture to guess the object of your desire. You aspire to the hand of Princess Isota, and that is a noble ambition. Once you are related to the prince, you are safe from all disgrace; you have a tight hold upon our friend. I will not conceal from you that the idea of this marriage with Princess Isota is odious to him. But if your business were in the hands of a skilful man, well paid, we need not despair of success."

"I, my dear Baron, should certainly despair. I repudiate beforehand everything you may say in my name. But, on the day when that illustrious alliance at last crowns my earnest hopes, and raises me to that mighty position in the state, I will either give you three hundred thousand francs of my own, or else I will advise the prince to show you some mark of favour, which you yourself may prefer to that sum of money."

This conversation may seem a lengthy one to the reader, yet we have suppressed more than half of it. It lasted for another two hours. Rassi left the count's house, half delirious with delight. The count remained, with great hopes of saving Fabrizio, and more determined than ever to resign.

He felt convinced it would be a good thing to renew his credit by the presence of such men as Rassi and Conti in power. He dwelt with the keenest delight on a method of revenging himself on the prince which had just occurred to him. "He may drive the duchess out," he exclaimed, "but, by my soul! he shall give up his hope of being constitutional King of Lombardy." The whole idea was a ridiculous fancy; the prince, though a clever man, had dreamed over it till he had fallen desperately in love with it.

The count flew on wings of delight to retail this conversation with the chief justice to the duchess. He found her door closed; the porter hardly dared to tell him that he had received the order from his mistress's own lips. Sadly the count retraced his steps to the ministry; the mis-

fortune which had befallen him had quite wiped out the joy
caused by his conversation with the prince's confidant. Too
disheartened to do anything else, he was wandering drearily
up and down his picture gallery, when, a quarter of an
hour later, the following note was delivered to him:

"Since it is true, dear and kind friend, that we are now
no more than friends, you must only come to see me three
times a week. After a fortnight we will reduce these visits,
to which my heart still clings, to two in the month. If you
desire to please me, you will give publicity to this rupture of
ours. If you would bring back almost all the love I once
felt for you, you would choose another woman to be your
friend. As for me, I intend to be very gay; I propose to
go out a great deal; perhaps I shall even find some clever
man who may help me to forget my sorrows. As a friend,
indeed, you will always hold the first place in my heart, but
I do not wish it to be said that my action has been dictated by your wisdom. And above all things, I wish it to
be well known that I have lost all influence over your decisions. In a word, dear count, believe that you will always
be my dearest friend, and never anything else. I beg you
will not nurse any thought of change; this is the very end.
You may reckon on my unchanging regard."

The last words were too much for the count's courage;
he wrote an eloquent letter to the prince, resigning all his
posts, and sent it to the duchess, with the request that she
would send it over to the palace. In a few moments his
resignation came back to him, torn into four pieces, and on
one of the blank spaces on the paper the duchess had condescended to write, "No! a thousand times No!"

It would be difficult to describe the poor minister's despair. "She is right. I admit it," he reiterated over and
over again. "My omission of the words '*unjust proceedings*' is a terrible misfortune. It will end, perhaps, in Fabrizio's death, and that will involve my own."

It was with a sick weight at his heart that the count, who
would not appear at the palace without being sent for, wrote
out, with his own hand, the *motu proprio* which appointed
Rassi a Knight of the Order of St. Paul, and conferred on

him a title of hereditary nobility. To this document the count added a report, covering half a page, which laid the state reasons rendering this step desirable, before the prince. It was a sort of melancholy pleasure to him to make fair copies of these two papers, and send them to the duchess.

His brain was full of conjectures. He strove to guess at the future line of conduct of the woman he loved. "She knows nothing about it herself," he thought. "Only one thing is certain—that nothing in the world would induce her to relinquish the decisions she has once expressed." His misery was increased by the fact that he could not contrive to see that the duchess was in the wrong. "She conferred a favour on me when she loved me. She loves me no longer because of a fault, involuntary, indeed, but which may have horrible consequences. I have no right to complain." The next morning the count heard the duchess had begun to go into society again. She had appeared the night before in all the houses that had been open to guests. What would have become of him if he had met her in the same drawing-room? How was he to speak to her? The following day was terribly gloomy. The general report was that Fabrizio was to be put to death; the whole town was stirred. It was added that the prince, out of regard to his high birth, had condescended to give orders that his head should be cut off.

"It is I who will have killed him," thought the count. "I can never expect to see the duchess again." In spite of this somewhat simple reasoning, he could not refrain from calling at her house three times over. It must be said that he went on foot so as to avoid comment. In his despair he even dared to write to her. He had sent twice for Rassi, but the chief justice had not appeared. "The rascal is playing me false," said the count to himself.

The next morning three great pieces of news stirred the upper ranks, and even the middle classes, of Parma. Fabrizio's execution was more than ever certain, and a very curious thing in connection with this information was that the duchess did not seem overmuch distressed about her

young lover. At all events she took admirable advantage
of the pallor resulting from a somewhat serious indisposi-
tion, from which she had suffered just at the moment of
Fabrizio's arrest. In these details the middle classes were
sure they recognised the dried-up heart of a great court
lady. Yet, out of decency, or as a sacrifice to the memory
of young Fabrizio, she had broken with Count Mosca.
"What immorality!" exclaimed the Jansenists of Parma.
But already the duchess (and this was incredible) seemed inclined to listen to the addresses of the handsomest young men
about the court. Among other symptoms it was remarked
that she had held a very merry conversation with Count Baldi, the Raversi's lover, and had rallied him greatly on his constant expeditions to Velleia. The lower middle class and the
populace were furious about Fabrizio's death, which the
worthy folk ascribed to Count Mosca's jealousy. Court
society also devoted a great deal of attention to the count,
but only to mock at him. The third of the great pieces of
intelligence to which we have referred was no other, indeed,
than the count's resignation. Everybody laughed at this
absurd lover of fifty-six, who was sacrificing a magnificent
position to the grief of seeing himself forsaken by a heart-
less woman, who, for a considerable time, had preferred a
younger man to himself. The archbishop was the only
man whose intelligence—or shall we say his heart?—enabled him to guess that the count's honour forbade him to
continue Prime Minister in a country the ruler of which
was about to behead a young man who had been his *protégé*,
without even consulting him. The news of the count's
resignation cured General Fabio Conti's gout, as we shall
duly relate, when we speak of the manner in which Fabrizio
was spending his time in the citadel, while all the town was
expecting to hear the hour fixed for his execution.

The following day the count saw Bruno, the trusty
agent whom he had sent to Bologna. The count was greatly
moved when the man entered his study. The sight of him
brought back the memory of his own happiness, the day
he had despatched him to Bologna at the request of the
duchess. Bruno had just arrived from Bologna, where he

had found out nothing at all. He had not been able to dis-cover Ludovico, whom the *podestà* of Castelnovo had de-tained in the prison of his village.

" I shall send you back to Bologna," said the count to Bruno. " The duchess will value the sad pleasure of know-ing every detail of Fabrizio's misfortune. Apply to the officer commanding the gendarmes at Castelnovo——"

" But, no ! " cried .the count, breaking off suddenly. " You shall start instantly for Lombardy, and there you shall distribute money, and plenty of it, to all our correspondents. My object is to have reports of the most encouraging na-ture sent in by all those people."

Bruno, having thoroughly realized the object of his mission, set to work to write out his letters of credit. The count, just as he was giving him his last instructions, re-ceived a thoroughly deceitful letter, but admirably expressed. It might have been taken for a missive from one friend, ask-ing another to do him a service. The friend who wrote this letter was none other than the prince. He had heard some talk of resignation, and besought his friend Count Mosca to continue at his post. He begged him to do this in the name of friendship, and the dangers threatening the country, and as his master, he commanded him. He added that the King of * * * had just placed two ribbons of his Order at his disposal; he was keeping one for himself, and sent the other to his dear friend Count Mosca.

" This creature is my curse ! " exclaimed the count in his fury, and to Bruno's amazement. " He thinks he can take me in with the very same hypocritical phrases we have so often strung together to catch some fool." He declined the proffered Order, and in his reply, wrote that the state of his health left him very little hope of being able to per-form the arduous duties of his ministry much longer. The count was frantic. A moment afterward, Chief-Justice Rassi was announced; he treated him like a negro slave.

" How now ! Because I have made you a noble, you grow insolent. Why did you not come yesterday to thank me, as was your merest duty, Sir Rascal ? "

Rassi was far above such abuse. The prince's behaviour

to him, every day, was the same as that. But he wanted to be a baron, and he justified himself skilfully—nothing was easier.

"The prince kept me nailed to a writing-table the whole of yesterday; I never could get out of the palace. His Highness set me to copy a whole heap of diplomatic documents in my crabbed lawyer's writing. So silly were they, and so prolix, that I really believe his sole object was to keep me prisoner. When I was dismissed at last, half-starved, at five o'clock, he ordered me to go straight home, and not to go out again the whole evening. And as a matter of fact I saw one of his private spies, whom I know well, walking up and down my street till midnight. This morning, the moment I could, I sent for a carriage, in which I drove to the door of the cathedral. I got out of the carriage very slowly, and then I walked quickly across the church, and here I am. At this moment your Excellency is the one man in the world I most passionately desire to please."

"And I, you rogue, am not in the least taken in by any of your more or less well-concocted stories. Yesterday you refused to talk to me about Fabrizio; I respected your scruples and your oaths of secrecy—though to such as you, oaths are no more, at the outside, than useful pretexts. To-day I will have the truth. What are these absurd stories according to which this youth has been condemned to death for the murder of the man Giletti?"

"No one can inform your Excellency concerning these reports better than I, seeing it is I myself who have put them about, according to the sovereign's orders. And now I come to think of it, it was perhaps to prevent me from telling you of this incident that the prince kept me a prisoner yesterday. The prince, who does not think me a madman, could not but be sure I would bring you my cross, and beg you to fasten it to my buttonhole."

"Come down to facts," exclaimed the minister, "and make me no speeches."

"No doubt the prince would be very glad to have young Del Dongo sentenced to death. But, as you doubtless know, all he has to go upon is a sentence to twenty years in chains, which he himself commuted, the very day after it was pronounced, to twelve years in the fortress, with fasting on bread and water every Friday, and certain other religious observances."

"It is just because I knew the sentence was only one of imprisonment that the reports of his approaching execution current all over the town alarmed me. I remembered Count Palanza's death, which you juggled so cleverly."

"That's when I ought to have had the cross," exclaimed Rassi, not the least disconcerted. "I ought to have put on the screw while I held it in my hand, and the man was anxious for the count's death. I behaved like a simpleton then, and that experience emboldens me to advise you not to do likewise now." This comparison appeared most offensive to the count, who had much ado to restrain himself from kicking Rassi.

"First of all," the latter proceeded, with all the logic of a juris-consult, and all the perfect assurance of a man whom no insult can offend, "first of all, there can be no execution of the said Del Dongo; the prince would not venture on it; times are very much changed. And then I, who am now a nobleman, and hope through you to become a baron, I would not put my hand to it. Now it is only from me, as your Excellency knows, that the chief executioner can get his orders, and I swear to you that the Cavaliere Rassi will never give an order to hurt Signor del Dongo."

"And you will do well," said the count, looking him over sternly.

"Let there be no confusion," replied Rassi with a smile. "My concern is only with an official demise, and if Monsignore del Dongo should die of a colic you must not ascribe that to me. The prince is mad—why, I know not—against the Sanseverina " (only three days previously Rassi would have said "the duchess;" but, like everybody else in the city, he was aware of her rupture with the Prime Minister). The count was struck by the suppression of the title in such a mouth, and my readers may conceive the pleasure he felt! He flashed a look of the bitterest hatred

at Rassi. "My dearest angel," said he in his heart, "the
only way I can prove my love, is by blindly obeying your
command!"

"I will confess to you," said he to the lawyer, "that
I take no very passionate interest in the duchess's various
whims. Nevertheless, as it was she who introduced that
good-for-nothing young Fabrizio to me—he would have
done far better to have stayed at Naples, and never to
have come here to throw all our affairs into confusion.
—I am anxious he should not be put to death in my time,
and I am ready to give you my word that you shall be
a baron within a week of the time when he gets out of
prison."

"In that case, count, I shall not be a baron till twelve
years are out, for the prince is furious, and his hatred for
the duchess is so intense that he endeavours to hide it."

"His Highness is more than good. What need has he
to conceal his hatred, since his Prime Minister no longer
extends his protection to the duchess? Only I will not give
any one the chance of accusing me of meanness, or, above
all, of jealousy. It was I who brought the duchess to this
country, and if Fabrizio dies in prison, you will certainly not
be a baron, but you may possibly be stabbed. But enough
of this trifling. I have reckoned up my fortune; I find I
have barely twenty thousand francs a year, and I now propose humbly to send in my resignation to the sovereign. I
have some hope of being employed by the King of Naples.
That great city will offer me recreations which I need just
now, and which are not to be found in a hole like Parma.
The only thing that would induce me to remain would be
if I were given the hand of Princess Isota," etc., and the
conversation ran endlessly on this subject. When Rassi
rose to go, the count said to him, with a very careless air:
"You know it has been said that Fabrizio deceived me, in
the sense that he had been one of the duchess's lovers. I do
not admit the truth of this report. As a contradiction of it,
I wish you to hand this purse to Fabrizio."

"But, count," said Rassi in alarm, looking into the
purse, "there is a huge sum here, and the regulations——"

The Chartreuse of Parma

"To you, my good fellow, it may seem huge," replied the count, with an air of royal scorn. "When a man of your class sends ten sequins to a friend in prison he thinks he has ruined himself. Now, I choose that Fabrizio shall have these six thousand francs, and especially I choose that nobody at the palace shall know anything about it."

When the startled Rassi would have replied, the count slammed the door impatiently behind him. "Such men as he," said he to himself, "never recognise power unless they see insolence." This over, the mighty minister indulged in a performance so absurd that we hardly know how to relate it. Hurrying over to his writing-table, he took out a miniature of the duchess, and covered it with passionate kisses. "Forgive me, dearest angel," he exclaimed, "for not having thrown the rascal who ventured to speak of you with a tinge of familiarity out of the window with my own hands. But if I show this excessive patience it is only out of obedience to your will, and he will lose nothing by my delay."

After a long conversation with the portrait, the count, who felt his heart dead within his breast, was struck with an absurd idea, and proceeded, with childish eagerness, to put it into action. He sent for a dress-coat and decorations, and betook himself to wait upon the elderly Princess Isota. Never in his life had he done such a thing, except on New Year's Day. He found her surrounded by a number of pet dogs, dressed up in her fine clothes, and even adorned with her diamonds, as if she had been going to court. When the count expressed some fear that he was disturbing her Highness's plans, as she was probably thinking of going out, her Highness responded that a Princess of Parma owed it to herself to be always in full dress. For the first time since his misfortune had occurred, the count felt a touch of amusement. "I did well to come here," thought he to himself, "and I will avow my passion this very day." The princess had been delighted at the visit of a man who was so famous for his wit, and Prime Minister to boot. The poor old lady was not accustomed to attentions of that kind. The count opened with a skilful speech about the immense distance which must always part a mere noble-man from the members of a reigning family.

"Some distinction should be made," said the princess. "The daughter of a King of France, for instance, never has any hope of succeeding to the throne. But this is not the case with the Parma family. That is the reason why we of the Farnese race must always keep up a certain external dignity. Even I, poor princess as I am, can not say it is absolutely impossible that you may one day be my Prime Minister."

The whimsical unexpectedness of this remark made the poor count feel quite cheerful again, for an instant. As the minister emerged from Princess Isota's apartment (she had blushed furiously when he had confessed his passion for her), he met one of the quartermasters from the palace. The prince had sent for him in a great hurry.

"I am ill," replied the minister, delighted to have the chance of being rude to the prince. "Ha, ha!" he cried, in a rage. "You drive me distracted, and then you expect me to serve you! But you shall learn, my prince, that in this century, the mere fact of having received your author-ity from Providence does not suffice you. You must have great powers of mind, and a noble character, if you want to be a successful despot."

Having dismissed the quartermaster, who was highly scandalized by the sick man's appearance of perfect health, the count was pleased to call on the two men about the court who had most influence with Fabio Conti. What made the minister shudder, and shook all his confidence, was that the governor of the citadel was supposed to have got rid of a certain captain, who had been his personal enemy, by means of the "Acquetta di Perugia."

For a week, the count was aware, the duchess had been spending immense sums of money to get into communica-tion with the citadel. But he did not think her likely to attain success. Everybody was too much on the alert as yet. We will not weary our readers with all the distracted woman's attempts at bribery. She was in despair, and her efforts were seconded by agents of every kind, and the most absolute devotion. But there is just one kind of business that is thoroughly well done in a small despotic court, and that is the watch kept over political prisoners. The only result produced by the money the duchess laid out was that eight or ten men of every rank were dismissed from the citadel service.

CHAPTER XVIII

THUS, in spite of their absolute devotion to the prisoner's interests, neither the duchess nor the Prime Minister had been able to do more than a very little for him. The prince was furious with Fabrizio; and both the court and the public had a grudge against him, and were delighted to see him in trouble—his luck had been too remarkable. The duchess, though she had scattered money broadcast, had not been able to advance one step in her siege of the citadel. Never a day passed but that the Marchesa Raversi or Cavaliere Riscara found some fresh word to drop into General Conti's ear. Thus they strengthened his weakness.

As we have already said, Fabrizio, on the day of his imprisonment, was conducted, in the first place, to the governor's palace. This is a pretty little building erected during the last century, after a design by Vanvitelli, who placed it at an elevation of a hundred and eighty feet, on the platform of the huge Round Tower. From the windows of this little palace, set like a camel's hump on the back of the great tower, Fabrizio looked far out over the country, and to the Alps in the distance. At the foot of the citadel he could mark the course of the Parma, a sort of torrent which bends to the right, about four leagues from the city, and casts itself into the Po. Beyond the left bank of that river, which formed a succession of immense white stains upon the verdant green of the surrounding country, his delighted eye could distinctly recognise the peaks of the mighty wall of the Alps, running right across the north of Italy. These peaks, which, even in the month of August, as it then was, are always covered with snow, cast a sort of memory of coolness across the blazing country. Every detail of their outline can be followed, and yet they are more than thirty leagues from the citadel of Parma.

The wide view from the governor's charming palace is broken, at one of its southern corners, by the Farnese Tower, in which a room was being hastily prepared for Fabrizio. This second tower was built, as my readers will perhaps remember, on the platform of the great .tower, in honour of a certain hereditary prince, who, far from following the example of Hippolytus, the son of Theseus, had turned a by no means deaf ear to the blandishments of a youthful stepmother. The princess died within a few hours; the son of the prince only regained his liberty some seventeen years later, when he ascended the throne after his father's death. This Farnese Tower, to which Fabrizio was conducted after waiting some three-quarters of an hour, is externally a very ugly building, rising some fifty feet above the platform of the great tower, and adorned with a number of lightning conductors.

The prince, who had reason to be displeased with his wife, and who had caused the prison, which was visible from every quarter, to be constructed, conceived the strange notion of persuading his subjects that it had already been in existence for many years, and for this reason he dubbed it the Farnese Tower. Any reference to the progress of the building was forbidden; yet, from every corner of the city of Parma, and of the plains around it, the masons might be seen laying every stone that went to the composition of the pentagonal edifice. To prove its ancient origin a magnificent bas-relief, representing Alessandro Farnese, the famous general, forcing Henry IV to retire from Paris, was placed above the doorway, two feet wide and four high, which formed the entrance to the building. The Farnese Tower, standing in this prominent position, consists of a ground floor apartment, at least forty paces long, broad in proportion, and full of very squat pillars, for the room, disproportionately large as it is, is not more than fifteen feet high. This is used as the guard-room, and in the middle of it the staircase runs up round one of the pillars—quite a small, open-work iron staircase, very light, and hardly two feet wide. Up this staircase, which shook under the weight of the jailers who guarded him, Fabrizio was led into some huge rooms more than twenty feet high, which formed a magnificent first floor. They had once been furnished with the utmost splendour for the young prince who had spent the seventeen best years of his life in them. At one end of these rooms the new prisoner was shown a chapel of the greatest magnificence—the walls and vaulted ceiling were entirely cased with black marble; the pillars, which were also black, and of the most noble proportions, were set in rows along the black walls, though not touching them; these walls were adorned with a number of skulls of colossal proportions, beautifully chiselled in white marble, and each supported by two crossed bones. "That was certainly invented by the hatred of a man who did not dare to kill," said Fabrizio to himself. "What a devilish notion to show it to me!"

Another very light open-work iron staircase, also wound round a pillar, led to the second story of this prison, and it was in these second-story rooms, about fifteen feet high, that General Fabio Conti's genius had been displaying itself for the past year. Under his directions, to begin with, the windows of the rooms, which had originally been occupied by the prince's servants, and are over thirty feet above the stone flags forming the roof of the great Round Tower, were all securely covered with gratings. These rooms, each of which has two windows, are reached by a dark passage, running through the centre of the building, and across this very narrow passage Fabrizio noticed three successive gates, made of huge iron bars, and carried right up into the vaulted ceiling. The plans, sections, and elevations of all these fine inventions had secured the general a weekly audience with his master for the two previous years. A conspirator immured in one of these dungeons could not well appeal to public opinion on the score of inhuman treatment, and yet he was precluded from holding communication with any one on earth, or from making the smallest movement without being overheard. In each of these rooms the general had placed thick oaken planking, which formed something like benches, three feet high; and here came in his great invention, that which established his claim to be appointed Minister of Police. On these planks he had built a kind of wooden shed, ten feet high, and very resounding, which only touched the wall on the window side of the room. On the three other sides a narrow passage, some four feet wide, ran between the original walls of the prison, built of enormous hewn stones, and the wooden sides of the shed. These sides, made of four thicknesses of walnut wood, oak, and deal, were strongly bound together by iron bolts, and innumerable nails.

It was into one of these rooms, which had been prepared a year previously, was considered General Fabio Conti's masterpiece, and had received the resounding title of "Passive Obedience," that Fabrizio was conducted. The view out of the barred windows was sublime. Only one small corner of the horizon, that toward the northwest, was concealed by the balustraded roof of the governor's pretty palace, which was only two stories high. The ground floor was occupied by the officers of his staff, and Fabrizio's eye was at once caught by one of the upper-floor windows, round which hung a great number of pretty cages, containing birds of every kind. While the jailers were moving about around him, Fabrizio entertained himself by listening to the birds' singing, and watching their farewells to the last rays of the setting sun. This aviary window was not more than five-and-twenty feet from one of his own, and some five or six feet below it, so that he looked down upon the birds.

There was a moon that night, and just as Fabrizio entered his prison, she rose in majesty over the horizon on the right, from behind the Alps toward Treviso. It was only half past eight, and at the other end of the horizon, where the sun had just set, a brilliant red light, tinged with orange, lay on the clear-cut outlines of Monte Viso, and the other Alpine peaks, piled one above the other from Nice toward the Mont Cenis and Turin. Without another thought for his misfortunes, Fabrizio gave himself over to the emotion and delight roused by this splendid sight. "This, then, is the wonderful world in which Clelia Conti lives. To her serious and pensive soul this view must be specially delightful. One feels here just as one does in the lonely mountains a hundred leagues from Parma." It was not till he had spent more than two hours at his window, admiring the view which appealed so strongly to his heart, and casting many a glance, meanwhile, at the governor's pretty palace, that Fabrizio suddenly exclaimed: " But is this a prison? Is this what I have dreaded so intensely?" Instead of discovering discomforts and causes for bitterness at every step, our hero was falling in love with the delights of his dungeon.

Suddenly a frightful noise roughly recalled his attention to the realities of life. His wooden room, which rather resembled a cage, and was especially remarkable for its resonant qualities, was violently shaken; the barking of a dog and a number of little shrill squeaks made up a most extraordinary pandemonium. " What is this? Shall I be able to escape so soon? " thought Fabrizio. A moment afterward he was laughing, as perhaps no prisoner ever laughed before. By the general's orders, the jailers had brought up with them an English dog, very savage, which had been told off to keep guard over the more important officers, and which was to spend the night in the space so ingeniously contrived all round Fabrizio's cage. The dog and the jailer were both to sleep in the aperture, three feet deep, between the flag-stones of the original flooring of the room and the wooden boards, upon which the prisoner could not take a step without being heard.

Now, when Fabrizio entered the room called " Passive Obedience," it had been in possession of about a hundred huge rats, who had taken to flight in all directions. The dog, a sort of cross between a spaniel and an English fox-terrier, was not good-looking, but was exceedingly sharp. It had been fastened to the flagged pavement below the floor of the wooden room, but when it smelled the rats close beside it, it struggled so desperately that it contrived to slip its collar. Then began the mighty battle, the noise of which had disturbed Fabrizio, and roused him out of his anything but unpleasant dream. The rats, which had been able to escape the first onset, took refuge in the wooden room, and the dog followed them up the six steps which led from the stone pavement to Fabrizio's shed. Then a far more terrible racket began. The wooden shell was shaken to its very foundations. Fabrizio laughed like a lunatic, till the tears ran down his cheeks; Grillo, the jailer, who was laughing just as heartily, had shut the door. The dog was not the least incommoded in his hunt by the furniture, for the room was absolutely bare; the only thing to interfere with his bounds upon his prey was an iron stove standing in one corner. When the dog had destroyed all his enemies, Fabrizio called to him, patted him, and succeeded in making friends with him. " If ever this fellow should see me jumping over some wall," said he to himself, " he will not bark at me." But this cunning policy was a mere pretence on his part. In his state of mind at that moment, it was a delight to him to play with the dog. By a strange whimsicality, on which he did not reflect, there was a sense of secret joy at the bottom of his heart.

When he had run about with the dog till he was out of breath—

" What is your name? " said Fabrizio to the jailer.

" Grillo, at your Excellency's service, in everything that the regulations will permit."

" Well, my good Grillo, a fellow of the name of Giletti tried to murder me in the middle of the road. I defended my life, and killed him. I should kill him again, if it had to be done. But none the less I will live a cheery life as long as I am your guest. Ask leave from your chiefs, and then go fetch me some linen from the Palazzo Sanseverina, and bring me plenty of *nébieu d'Asti*."

This is a fairly good effervescent wine, made in Piedmont, in the country of Alfieri, and which is highly esteemed, especially by that class to which jailers generally belong. Eight or ten of these gentry were engaged in moving various ancient and highly gilt pieces of furniture, taken from the prince's apartments on the first floor, into Fabrizio's wooden room, and they all carefully treasured up their prisoner's remark in favour of Asti wine. In spite of all their efforts, the arrangements for Fabrizio's first night were rather pitiful; but the only thing that seemed to distress him was the absence of a bottle of good *nébieu*. " He seems a good' fellow," said the jailers as they departed, " and we must only hope one thing—that our chiefs will let his friends pass money in to him."

When he was left alone, and had settled down a little after all the noise, " Is it possible that this can be a prison?' said Fabrizio to himself, as he looked out over the mighty horizon stretching from Treviso to the Monte Viso, the huge chain of the Alps, the snow-covered peaks, and the stars above them. " And this my first night in a prison, too! I can imagine that Clelia Conti must delight in this aerial solitude. Here we are a thousand leagues above the meannesses and wickednesses which make up our life down there. If those birds there, under my window, belong to her, I shall see her. . . . Will she blush when she sees me?" When slumber overtook him, in the small hours of the morning, the prisoner was still debating this great question.

On the very morning after that first night in prison, during which Fabrizio had not once felt impatient, he was reduced to holding conversations with Fox, the English dog. Grillo, the jailer, still looked at him with the most kindly eyes, but a newly issued order had sealed his lips, and he brought his prisoner neither linen nor *nébieu*.

" Shall I see Clelia?" thought Fabrizio as he woke. " But do those birds really belong to her?" The birds in question were beginning to chirp and sing, and at that height, theirs was the only noise that fell upon the air. The deep silence which reigned at that altitude was a most novel and pleasurable sensation to Fabrizio. He listened with delight to the little fitful, lively warbling with which his neighbours the birds greeted the sun. " If they are hers, she will come for an instant into that room under my window." And while he watched the huge ranges of the Alps, against the nearer tier of which the citadel of Parma seemed to project like an outwork, his eyes came back perpetually to the splendid satin-wood and mahogany cages, with their gilded wires, which stood in the middle of the bright room which had been transformed into an aviary. It was not till later that Fabrizio found out that this room was the only one on the second floor of the palace which had any shade between eleven o'clock and four; it was screened by the Farnese Tower.

"What will my grief be," said Fabrizio to himself, "if, instead of that modest and thoughtful face which I expect, and which, perhaps, will blush a little at the sight of me, I behold the coarse countenance of some vulgar waiting-maid, who has been sent to supply the birds' necessities? But if I do see Clelia, will she condescend to notice me? Faith, I must risk some indiscretion, so as to attract her attention. Some privileges must surely be allowed to a man in my position. And besides, we two are alone here, and far away from all the world. I am a prisoner, and what General Conti and wretches of his kind probably regard as their inferior, . . . but she has so much cleverness, or rather so much heart, as the count believes, that perhaps, even as he says, she despises her father's trade. That would account for her melancholy. A noble reason, truly, for her sadness. But, after all, I am not a complete stranger to her. . . . What modest grace there was in her greeting to me yesterday evening! I remember very well that when I met her near Como I said to her, 'Some day I shall go to see your beautiful pictures at Parma. Will you then remember this name—Fabrizio del Dongo?' Has she forgotten it? She was so young!

"But now I think of it," said Fabrizio in astonishment, and breaking off the thread of his thoughts, "I am forgetting to be angry! Can it be that I possess a mighty courage, like that of which the ancients gave a few instances to the world? Am I a hero, with no suspicion of the fact? What! I, who dreaded prison so bitterly, here am I in a dungeon, and I can not remember to be sad! How true it is that the dread of the evil is a hundred times worse than the evil itself! How is this? Must I argue myself into grief at finding myself in this prison, which, so Blanès said, may as likely last ten years as ten months? Can it be the strangeness of

my new surroundings which diminishes the distress I ought
to feel? Perhaps this unreasoning cheerfulness, which is
quite independent of my own will, will come to a sudden
end? Perhaps in another instant I shall fall into the black
gloom which ought to overwhelm me?

"In any case, it is a very astonishing thing that I should
be in prison, and that I should have to argue with myself
before I can feel sad. Upon my word, I come back to my
old inference; perhaps I am a great man, after all!"

Fabrizio's musings were broken by the arrival of the carpenter of the fortress, who came to take measurements for
a screen for his windows. This was the first occasion on
which this room had been occupied as a prison, and its completion in this essential particular had been overlooked.

"Then," said Fabrizio, "I shall be deprived of that
splendid view?" and he tried to feel sad over the loss. "But
what," he cried suddenly, speaking to the carpenter, "I shall
not be able to see those pretty birds!"

"Ah, the signorina's birds, that she's so fond of," said
the man, a kind-looking fellow. "They will be hidden,
blocked out, swallowed up, like all the rest."

Talking was as strictly forbidden to the carpenter as to
the jailer, but this man pitied the prisoner's youth. He
told him that the huge screens, which were to rest on the
sills of the two windows, and run outward from the walls
in proportion to their height, were to prevent the prisoners
from seeing anything but the sky. "It is done," he added,
"with the view of impressing their minds, so as to increase
a salutary feeling of sadness, and fill the prisoners' souls
with a desire to amend their ways. Another invention of the
general's," added the carpenter, "is to take out the window-
glass and replace it with sheets of oiled paper."

Fabrizio was much taken with the epigrammatic tone of
this conversation, seldom met with in Italy.

"I should very much like to have a bird to cheer me,
I am so fond of them. Buy me one from the Signorina Clelia
Conti's maid."

"What!" exclaimed the carpenter; "you must know
her, if you tell her name so plainly."

"Who is there that has not heard of that famous beauty? But I have had the honour of meeting her several times at court."

"The poor young lady has a very dull life here," continued the carpenter. "She spends her whole time over there with her birds. This morning she has had some fine orange trees bought, and has ordered them to be placed at the door of the tower, just under your window. If it were not for the cornice you would be able to see them." Certain words in this reply had been very precious to Fabrizio; he devised some friendly pretext for bestowing a gift of money upon the carpenter.

"I am doing wrong twice over," said the man. "I am talking to your Excellency, and taking your money. When I come back the day after to-morrow, about these screens, I will have a bird in my pocket, and if I am not alone, I will pretend to let it escape. And, if I can manage it, I will bring you a prayer-book. It must be very painful to you not to be able to say your prayers."

"So," said Fabrizio, as soon as he was alone, "those are her birds! But after another two days I shall not be able to see them."

The thought brought a tinge of sadness to his face. But near midday, at last, to his inexpressible delight, after long waiting and much watching, Clelia came to attend to her birds. Fabrizio, motionless and almost breathless, stood upright, close against the huge bars of his window. He remarked that she did not raise her eyes to him, but there was a something shy about her movements, as though she felt she was being looked at. Even if she had desired it, the poor girl could not have forgotten the subtle smile which had flickered on the prisoner's lips, just as he was being led out of the guard-room on the preceding night.

Though according to all appearances she was keeping the most careful watch upon her actions, she reddened visibly as she drew near the window of the aviary. Fabrizio's first impulse, as he stood close against his iron window bars, was to indulge in the childish freak of rapping a little on the iron, so as to make a slight noise. But the very idea of such a lack of delicacy disgusted him. " It would serve me right if she sent her maid to look after her birds for a week afterward." This tender scruple would not have occurred to him at Naples or at Novara.

He watched her hungrily, saying to himself: " She will surely not go away without condescending to glance at this poor window, and yet she is just opposite it." But as she moved from the back of the room, into which, thanks to the superior height of his position, Fabrizio could clearly see, Clelia could not prevent herself from glancing up at him as she walked, and this was sufficient to make Fabrizio venture to salute her. " Are we not alone in the world here? " said he, to give himself courage. When he saluted her the young girl stopped short and dropped her eyes. Then Fabrizio saw her raise them again, very slowly and with an evident effort, and she greeted the prisoner with the gravest and most distant gesture. But she could not prevent her eyes from speaking. Without her knowledge, probably, they held, for one instant, an expression of the liveliest pity. Fabrizio noticed she was colouring so deeply that the rosy tinge was spreading rapidly even on to her shoulders, from which the heat had caused her to drop a black lace shawl, as she entered the aviary. The involuntary glance by which Fabrizio answered her salute doubled the young girl's agitation. " How happy that poor woman would be," said she to herself, thinking of the duchess, " if she could only see him as I see him, just for one moment! "

Fabrizio had nursed a tiny hope that he might have been able to send her another greeting ere she departed, but to avoid this fresh attention, Clelia executed a skilful retreat *in échelon* from one cage to another, as though she had necessarily to end her task by attending to the birds nearest to the door. She left the room at last, and Fabrizio stood motionless, gazing at the door through which she had just disappeared. He was a changed man.

From that instant the one object of his thoughts was to discover how he might continue to see her, even after that odious screen should have been placed over the window looking on to the governor's palace.

The Chartreuse of Parma

Before going to bed on the previous night, he had performed the tedious and tiresome duty of concealing most of his gold coins in several of the rat holes which adorned his wooden room. " To-night," he thought, " I must hide my watch. Have I not heard that with patience and the jagged spring of a watch, a man may cut through wood and even through iron? So I may be able to saw through the screen." The work of hiding the watch, which lasted for several hours, did not seem lengthy to him. He pondered over the various methods whereby he might attain his end, and his own knowledge of carpentering matters. " If I set about it properly," he mused, " I can simply cut out a compartment of the oaken board of which the screen will consist, at the place where it will rest on the window-sill. I will take this bit of wood in and out, according to circumstances. I will give everything I have to Grillo, so as to induce him to overlook this little manœuvre." All Fabrizio's future happiness seemed to depend on the possibility of carrying out this undertaking, and he thought of nothing else. " If I can only contrive to see her, I am happy. . . . But, no," he went on, " she must see that I see her." All night long his head was full of carpentering schemes, and in all probability he never gave a thought to the court of Parma, the prince's anger, and all the rest. We must acknowledge, too, that he did not trouble himself a whit concerning the distress in which the duchess must be plunged. He waited eagerly for the morning, but the carpenter did not reappear. He was apparently considered too much of a Liberal by the prison authorities, and they carefully sent another, a gruff-looking fellow, who deigned no answer except a threatening grunt to all the pleasant things which Fabrizio was inspired to say to him. Some of the duchess's endless attempts to enter into correspondence with Fabrizio had been discovered by the marchesa's numerous agents, and General Fabio Conti received daily warnings from her, which both startled him, and nettled his vanity. Every eight hours six soldiers relieved each other in the great ground-floor hall, with its hundred pillars. Besides this, the governor placed a jailer on each of the three iron gates in the passage, and poor, unlucky Grillo, the only person who saw the prisoner, was forbidden to go outside the Farnese Tower oftener than once a week, which vexed him sorely. He made Fabrizio conscious of his ill-temper. Fabrizio had wit enough to reply with these words only, " Plenty of *nébieu d'Asti*, my good fellow," and he gave him some money.

" Well, even this, which consoles us for every misfortune," exclaimed the angry Grillo in a voice so low that the prisoner could hardly catch it, " we are forbidden to accept, and I ought to refuse it. But I shall take it. Yet, indeed, it is money wasted, for I can not tell you anything about nothing. Why, you must be guilty indeed! The whole citadel is upside down because of you, and the duchess's fine tricks have got three of us sent away already."

" Will the screen be ready before noon? " That was the great question which made Fabrizio's heart thump all through that long morning. He counted up every quarter of an hour as it rang on the citadel clock. However, when the third quarter after eleven struck, the screen had not yet arrived, and Clelia reappeared to attend to her birds. Cruel necessity had so emboldened Fabrizio, and the danger of never seeing her again seemed to him so greatly to exceed anything else in the whole world, that he dared, as he gazed at Clelia, to make a gesture with his finger as of sawing the wooden screen. It must be added that as soon as she perceived this very seditious gesture on the part of the prisoner, she made him a sort of half bow, and retired.

" Bless me! " exclaimed Fabrizio in astonishment. " Can she have been so unreasonable as to take a sign dictated by the most imperious necessity for a piece of ridiculous familiarity? I wanted to entreat her to condescend to look up sometimes at my prison window when she came to see her birds, even if she should find it masked by a huge wooden shutter! I wanted to make her understand that I would do everything that was humanly possible to contrive to see her. Good God! Will she abstain from coming to-morrow on account of that indiscreet gesture of mine? " This dread, which disturbed Fabrizio's slumbers, was thoroughly well founded. By three o'clock the

next day, when the two huge screens were set up on each
of Fabrizio's windows, Clelia had not appeared. The various sections of these screens had been drawn up from the
platform of the great tower, by means of cords and pulleys,
fastened outside the iron bars of the windows. It is true,
indeed, that Clelia, hidden behind one of the sun blinds in
her room, had anxiously watched all the workman's actions.
She had clearly perceived Fabrizio's mortal anxiety, but,
nevertheless, she had found courage to keep the promise she
had made herself.

Clelia was an eager little Liberal. In her first youth
she had taken all the Liberal talk she had heard in her father's
society in the most serious earnest, while her father's only
view of it was to make a position for himself. This had
given her a scorn and almost a horror of the pliability of
courtiers; hence arose her dislike to marriage. Since Fabrizio's arrival she had been harried by remorse. "Now,"
said she to herself, "my unworthy heart is taking up the
cause of those who would betray my father. He dares to
make me signs, as if he would saw through a door. . . .
But," she went on, and her heart was wrung at the thought,
"the whole city talks of his approaching death. . . . To-
morrow may be the fatal day. . . . Under such monsters as
those who govern us, what is there in the world that is not
possible? How soft, how nobly calm, are those eyes,
doomed, perhaps, soon to close forever! Heavens, what
anguish the duchess must be enduring! . . . And, indeed,
every one says she is in despair. . . . If it were I, I would
go, like the heroic Charlotte Corday, and stab the prince."

During the whole of his third day in prison, Fabrizio
was beside himself with rage, simply and solely because
Clelia had not returned. "If she was to be angry with me,"
he exclaimed, "I should have done much better to tell her
that I loved her," for he had arrived at this discovery.
"No, it is not my nobility of soul that prevents me from
fretting in my prison, and makes me bring Father Blanès's
prophecy to naught. I do not deserve so much honour. In
spite of myself, I dream of the gentle pitying look Clelia
cast on me as the gendarmes were leading me out of the

guard-room—that look has wiped out all my past life! Who would have told me I should have met such gentle eyes in such a place! and at the very moment when my own sight was polluted by the appearance of Barbone, and of the general who rules this fortress! Heaven opened, in the midst of those vile creatures. And how can I help loving beauty, and seeking to see it again? No, it is not my nobility of soul which makes me indifferent to all the petty annoyances with which imprisonment overwhelms me." Fabrizio's imagination, running rapidly over every possibility, reached that of being set at liberty. "No doubt the duchess's affection will work miracles for me. Ah, well, I should thank her but very coldly for my liberty; there is not much coming back to such places as these. Once I was out of prison, living as we do in different societies, I should hardly ever see Clelia again. And, after all, what harm does the prison do me? If Clelia would only not crush me with her displeasure, what more need I ask of Heaven?"

On the evening of that day on which he had not seen his lovely neighbour, a great idea occurred to him. With the iron cross of the rosary given to each prisoner when he entered the fortress, he began, and successfully, to work a hole in the screen. "This is not very prudent, perhaps," thought he, before he began. "The carpenters have said in my presence that they will be followed to-morrow by the painters. What will the painters say when they find a hole in the window screen? But if I do not commit this imprudence I shall not be able to see her to-morrow. What! shall I deliberately spend another day without seeing her, and after she has left me in anger?" Fabrizio's imprudence had its reward; after fifteen hours' labour he did see Clelia, and, by an excess of good fortune, as she thought he did not see her, she stood motionless for a long time, gazing at the great screen. He had ample time to read symptoms of the tenderest pity in her eyes. Toward the end of her visit it became evident that she was neglecting the care of her birds to spend whole minutes in contemplation of his window. Her soul was sorely troubled; she was thinking of the duchess, whose extreme misery had inspired her with so much pity, and yet she was beginning to hate her. She could not comprehend the profound melancholy which was taking possession of her whole nature, and she was angry with herself. Two or three times during the course of her visit Fabrizio's eagerness led him to try to shake the screen; he felt as if he could not be happy unless he could make Clelia understand that he saw her. "Yet," said he to himself, "shy and reserved as she is, no doubt if she knew I could see her so easily, she would hide herself from my sight."

He was much more fortunate the next day (on what trifles does love build happiness!). While she was looking up sadly at the great screen, he managed to slip a small piece of wire through the hole he had made with his iron cross, and make signs to her which she evidently understood—at all events in so far as that they were intended to convey "I am here, and I see you."

Bad luck followed Fabrizio on the following days. He was anxious to take a bit of wood the size of his hand out of the monster screen, which he would have replaced whenever he chose, and which would have allowed of his seeing and being seen, and thus of speaking, by signs at all events, of that which filled his heart. But the noise of the little and very imperfect saw which he had fashioned out of his watch-spring and notched with his cross gave the alarm to Grillo, who spent long hours in his room. He thought he observed, indeed, that Clelia's severity seemed to diminish in proportion as the material difficulties, which prevented any correspondence between them, increased. Fabrizio noticed clearly that she no longer affected to drop her eyes or look at the birds whenever he attempted to make her aware of his presence with the help of his paltry bit of iron wire. He had the pleasure of seeing that she never failed to appear in her aviary exactly as the clock struck a quarter to noon, and he was almost presumptuous enough to believe that he himself was the cause of this exact punctuality. Why so? The idea does not appear reasonable, but love catches shades which are invisible to the careless eye, and deduces endless consequences from them. For instance, since Clelia could not see the prisoner she would raise her eyes toward his window almost as soon as she entered the aviary. These were the gloomy days when no one in Parma doubted that Fabrizio would soon be put to death. He was the only person unaware of the fact. But the horrible thought was never out of Clelia's mind, and how could she reproach herself for the excessive interest she took in Fabrizio? He was about to perish, and for the cause of liberty, for it was too ridiculous to put a Del Dongo to death for giving a sword thrust to an actor. It was true, indeed, that the charming young man was attached to another woman. Clelia was profoundly miserable, though she did not clearly realize the nature of the interest she took in his fate. "If he is led out to death," said she to herself, " I shall certainly take refuge in a convent, and never again will I reappear in this court society. It fills me with horror; they are polished murderers, every one of them!"

On the eighth day of Fabrizio's imprisonment she endured a great humiliation. Absorbed in her sad thoughts, she was gazing fixedly at the prisoner's window. He had given no sign of his presence that day. All at once he removed a small bit of his screen, a little larger than his hand. He looked at her cheerily, and she read greeting in his eyes. This unexpected experience was too much for her; she turned quickly to her birds, and began to attend to them; but she trembled so much that she spilled the water she was pouring out for them, and Fabrizio could see her emotion quite plainly. She could not face the situation, and at last, to escape it, she ran away.

That moment was, without any comparison, the happiest in the whole of Fabrizio's life. If his liberty had been offered to him at that moment, how joyously would he have refused it!

The following day was that of the duchess's deepest despair. Every one in the city was convinced that all was over with Fabrizio. Clelia had not the dreary courage to treat him with a harshness which found no echo in her heart. She spent an hour and a half in the aviary, looked at all his signs, and often replied to them by the liveliest and sincerest expression of interest, at all events. Every now and then she would slip away to conceal her tears. Her womanly instincts made her vividly conscious of the imperfection of the language they were employing. If they could have spoken, in how many different ways might she not have endeavoured to discover the real nature of Fabrizio's feeling for the duchess? Clelia could hardly deceive herself now; she felt a hatred for the Duchess Sanseverina.

One night Fabrizio happened to think somewhat seriously about his aunt. He was astonished to find he hardly recognised his recollection of her. His memory of her had completely altered; at that moment she seemed fifty years old to him. " Good God!" he cried enthusiastically, " how right I was not to tell her that I loved her!" He went so far as hardly to be able to understand how he had ever thought her so pretty. In that respect the alteration in his impression of little Marietta was less remarkable. This was because he had never dreamed that his heart had anything to do with his love for Marietta, whereas he had frequently imagined that the whole of his heart was possessed by the duchess. The duchess of A—— and Marietta now appeared in his memory as two young turtle-doves, whose whole charm resided in their weakness and their innocence, whereas the noble image of Clelia Conti, which absorbed his whole soul, actually filled him with a kind of terror. He felt, only too clearly, that the happiness of his whole life would depend on the governor's daughter, and that she had it in her power to make him the most miserable of men. Every day he was tortured by the mortal fear of seeing some inexorable caprice end the strange and delightful life he led in her vicinity. At all events, she had filled the first two months of his imprisonment with happiness. This was the period during which, twice every week, General Fabio Conti assured the prince: " I can give your Highness my word of honour that the prisoner Del Dongo never speaks to a human being, and spends his whole life either in a state of the deepest despair or else asleep."

Clelia came every day, two or three times over, to see her birds. Sometimes she only stayed a few moments. If

The Chartreuse of Parma

Fabrizio had not cared for her so much he would soon have found out that he was loved. But he was in deadly doubt upon that subject. Clelia had ordered a piano to be placed in the aviary. While her fingers wandered over the keys, so as to account for her presence in the room, and occupy the attention of the sentries who marched to and fro under her windows, her eyes answered Fabrizio's questions. On one subject only she would make no response, and on certain great occasions she even took to flight, and thus would sometimes disappear for a whole day. This was when Fabrizio's signs indicated feelings the nature of which it was impossible for her to misunderstand. On that point she was quite inexorable.

Thus, closely imprisoned as he was, within a narrow cage, Fabrizio's life was a very busy one. It was entirely devoted to the solution of the all-important problem, " Will she love me? " The result of endless observation, perpetually renewed, but as perpetually shadowed by doubt, was as follows : " All her deliberate gestures answer ' No,' but every involuntary movement of her eyes seems to betray her growing regard for me."

Clelia hoped to escape any open avowal of his love, and it was to avoid this risk that she had refused, and very angrily, to grant a request which Fabrizio had proffered several times over. One would have fancied the miserable expedients to which the poor prisoner was reduced would have touched Clelia's heart with greater pity. He wanted to correspond with her, by means of letters which he wrote upon the palm of his hand with a piece of charcoal he had been so lucky as to find in his stove. He would have made up the words letter by letter, showing them one after the other. This plan would have facilitated their intercourse twofold, for it would have allowed of his putting things in a clear form. His window was some five-and-twenty feet away from Clelia's, and it would have been too risky to talk over the heads of the sentries, who marched up and down in front of the governor's palace. Fabrizio was uncertain whether he was loved or not. If he had possessed any experience in such matters he would have had no doubt at all. But till now no woman had ever filled his heart. And further, he had no suspicion of a fact which would have driven him to despair, if he had been aware of it. There was serious likelihood of a marriage between Clelia Conti and the Marchese Crescenzi, the wealthiest gentleman at the court of Parma.

CHAPTER XIX

GENERAL FABIO CONTI'S ambition, goaded to madness by the difficulties that had arisen in the way of the Prime Minister, Count Mosca, and which seemed to threaten his fall, had driven him into violent scenes with his daughter. Perpetually and angrily he told her that she would ruin his prospects unless she made up her mind to choose a husband at last. She was past twenty; it was high time she should come to some decision. An end must be put, once for all, to the cruel state of isolation in which her unreasonable obstinacy placed him, and so forth.

Clelia's first object, when she took refuge in her aviary, had been to escape from her father's constant ill-humour. The only means of access to the room was by climbing a small and very inconvenient staircase, a serious obstacle to the governor's gouty feet.

For the past few weeks, Clelia's soul had been so storm-tossed, she was so puzzled, herself, to know what she ought to desire, that without actually giving her father her word, she had almost drifted into an engagement. In one of his fits of rage the general had exclaimed that he would thrust her into the gloomiest convent in Parma, and leave her there to fret her heart out until she condescended to make a choice.

"You know that our family, old though it is, can not command more than six thousand francs a year, whereas the Marchese Crescenzi's income amounts to over a hundred thousand crowns. Every soul at court gives him the character of being the kindest of men; he is a very good-looking fellow, young, high in the prince's favour, and I say that nobody but a mad woman would refuse his suit. If this refusal had been your first, I could have endured it, but this is

343

the fifth or sixth offer, the very best at court, at which you turn up your nose, like the little fool you are! What would become of you, may I inquire, if I were put on half-pay? A fine triumph it would be for my enemies, who have so often heard me spoken of as a possible minister, to see me living in some second-floor apartment! No, 'pon my soul! my good nature has misled me often enough into playing the part of Cassandra. You will either give me some valid reason for your objections to this poor fellow Crescenzi, who does you the honour to be in love with you, to be ready to marry you without a fortune, and to insure you a dowry of thirty thousand francs a year, which will, at all events, insure me a home—you will talk sense to me, or—devil take it! I'll make you marry him within the next two months."

The only word in all this speech that had impressed Clelia was the threat about the convent, which would remove her from the citadel at a moment when Fabrizio's life still seemed to hang upon a thread. For not a month passed but that the report of his approaching death was noised afresh about the town and court. However severely she argued with herself, she could not make up her mind to run this risk. To be parted from Fabrizio, and at the very moment when she was trembling for his life, was, in her eyes, the greatest—at all events, it was the most pressing—of all possible misfortunes.

It was not that proximity to Fabrizio fed her heart with any hope of happiness. She believed the duchess loved him, and her soul was torn by deadly jealousy. Her mind dwelt incessantly on the advantages possessed by a lady who commanded such general admiration. The extreme reserve with which she carefully treated Fabrizio, the language of signs to which, in her dread of some possible indiscretion, she had restricted him, all seemed to combine to deprive her of the means of reaching some clearer knowledge of his feelings about the duchess. Thus, every day made her more cruelly conscious of the terrible misfortune of having a rival in Fabrizio's heart, and every day her courage to expose herself to the danger of giving him an opportunity of telling her all the truth as to what that heart felt, grew less and less.

The Chartreuse of Parma

Yet what exquisite joy would it have been to hear him express his real feelings! How happy it would have made Clelia to be able to lighten the hideous suspicions that poisoned her existence.

Fabrizio was a trifler. At Naples he had borne the reputation of being a man who was always changing his mistresses. In spite of all the reserve natural to an unmarried girl, Clelia, since she had been a canoness, and had frequented the court, had made herself acquainted—not by questioning, but merely by a process of careful listening—with the reputation of each of the young men who had successively sought her hand in marriage. Well, compared with all these young men, Fabrizio's reputation, as regarded his love-affairs, was the most fickle. He was in prison, he was bored, he was making love to the only woman to whom he had a chance of speaking. What could be more simple? What, indeed, more usual? And that was the thought which distressed Clelia. If some full revelation convinced her that Fabrizio did not love the duchess, what confidence, even then, could she place in his vows? And even if she had believed in the sincerity, what trust could she place in the durability of his feelings? And finally, to make her heart overflow with despair, was not Fabrizio already high up in the ecclesiastical career? Was he not on the very eve of taking permanent vows? Were not the highest dignities in that special line of life in store for him? "If I had the faintest spark of good sense," thought the unhappy Clelia to herself, "should I not take to flight? Ought I not to beseech my father to shut me up in some far distant convent? And to crown my misery, it is my very terror of being sent away from the citadel, and being shut up in a convent, which inspires all my actions. It is this terror which drives me into deceit, and forces me into the hideous and shameful falsehood of publicly accepting the Marchese Crescenzi's attentions."

Clelia was exceedingly reasonable by nature; never once in her life, hitherto, had she had reason to reproach herself with an ill-considered action. Yet in this matter her behaviour was the very acme of unreasonableness. Her misery

345

may be imagined. It was all the more cruel because the girl was under no illusion; she was giving her heart to a man with whom the most beautiful woman at court, a woman who was her own superior in numerous particulars, was desperately in love. And this man, even if he had been free, was incapable of any serious attachment, whereas she, as she felt only too clearly, would never care but for one person in her life.

During her daily visits to her aviary, then, Clelia's heart was torn by the most cruel remorse. Yet when she reached the spot, the object of her anxiety was changed; almost in spite of herself, it became less cruel, and, for an instant, her remorse died away. With beating heart she awaited the moments when Fabrizio was able to open the little shutter he had made in the huge wooden screen that masked his window. Often the presence of the jailer Grillo in his room prevented him from communicating by signs with his friend.

One evening, about eleven o'clock, Fabrizio heard the strangest sounds within the citadel. By lying on the window-sill and slipping his head through his shutter-hole, he could contrive, at night, to make out the louder noises on the great stairway, called the "Three Hundred Steps," which ran from the first courtyard within the Round Tower to the stone terrace on which the governor's palace and the Farnese Prison, in which he was confined, were built.

Toward the middle of its course, somewhere near the hundred and eightieth step, this staircase was carried from the southern to the northern side of a great courtyard. At this point there was a very light and narrow iron bridge, the centre of which was kept by a porter. The man was relieved every six hours, and he was obliged to stand up and flatten his body against the side of the bridge before any one could cross it. This bridge was the only method of access to the governor's palace and the Farnese Tower. Two turns of a screw, the key of which the governor always kept upon his person, sufficed to drop this iron bridge more than a hundred feet down into the court below. Once this simple precaution had been taken—as no other staircase existed in

The Chartreuse of Parma

the citadel, and as every night, as twelve o'clock struck, an adjutant brought the ropes belonging to every well in the fortress into the governor's house, and placed them in a closet beyond his own bedroom—access to the governor's palace was utterly impossible, and it would have been equally impossible to get into the Farnese Tower. Fabrizio had clearly realized this fact on the day of his entrance into the citadel, and Grillo, who, like every jailer, was fond of boasting about his prison, had re-explained the matter to him several times over. His hopes of escape were therefore very faint. Yet one of Father Blanès's sayings lived in his memory: " The lover thinks oftener of reaching his mistress than the husband thinks of guarding his wife; the prisoner thinks more often of escape than the jailer thinks of locking the doors. Therefore, in spite of every obstacle, the lover and the prisoner are certain to succeed."

That evening Fabrizio distinctly heard a numerous party of men cross the iron bridge—called the " Bridge of the Slave," because a Dalmatian slave had once contrived to escape by throwing the keeper of it over into the courtyard below.

" They are coming to carry somebody off; perhaps they are going to take me out and hang me. But there may be some confusion; I must take advantage of it." He had taken his arms, and was just withdrawing his money from some of his hiding-places, when he suddenly stopped short.

" Man is a strange animal; there's no denying that," he exclaimed. " What would any invisible spectator think if he saw my preparations? Do I really want to escape at all? What would become of me the day after that on which I returned to Parma? Should I not make every possible effort to get back to Clelia? If there is any confusion, let me take advantage of it to slip into the governor's palace. Perhaps I might get speech of Clelia; perhaps the confusion would provide me with an excuse for kissing her hand. General Conti, who is as naturally suspicious as he is constitutionally vain, keeps five sentries on his palace, one at each corner and one at the entrance door. But luckily for me the night is as dark as pitch." Fabrizio crept on tiptoe to find out what Grillo, the jailer, and his dog were about. The jailer was sound asleep, wrapped in an ox-skin slung by four cords, and supported by a coarse net. Fox, the dog, opened his eyes, rose, and crawled over to Fabrizio to be patted.

Our prisoner went softly back up the six steps which led to his wooden shed. The noise at the base of the tower, and just in front of the door, had grown so loud that he quite expected Grillo would wake up. Fabrizio, fully armed and prepared for action, believed this night was to bring about some great adventure. But suddenly he heard the first notes of a most beautiful symphony. Somebody had come to serenade the general or his daughter. He burst into a violent fit of laughter. "And I was already prepared to deal dagger thrusts in all directions. As if a serenade were not an infinitely more probable thing than an abduction that necessitated the presence of eighty persons in a prison, or than a revolt!" The music was excellent, and to Fabrizio, whose soul had been a stranger to such delights for many weeks, it seemed exquisite. He shed happy tears as he listened, and poured out the most irresistible speeches to the fair Clelia in his delight. But at noon next day she looked so deeply sad, she was so pale, and the glances she cast at him were occasionally so wrathful, that he did not venture to ask her any question about the serenade; he was afraid of appearing rude.

Clelia had good reason to be sad; the serenade had been offered her by the Marchese Crescenzi. Such a public step was tantamount to a kind of official announcement of her marriage. Until that very day, and even until nine o'clock that evening, she had stood out nobly. But she had given in at last, on her father's threat that he would instantly send her to the convent.

"Then I should never see him again," she said to herself, weeping. In vain did her reason add: "I should never see him again—that man who will bring me every sort of sorrow, the lover of the duchess, the fickle being who is known to have had ten mistresses at Naples, and to have forsaken them all. I should never see him again—that am-

bitious youth, who, if he escapes the sentence now hanging
over him, will immediately re-enter the service of the
Church. It would be a crime if I were ever to look at
him again, once he has left the citadel, and his natural inconstancy will spare me that temptation. For what am I
to him? A mere pretext for lightening his boredom for a
few hours of each of his days in prison." Even while she
thus reviled him the memory of his smile, as he looked at
the gendarmes round him when he was leaving the jailer's
office on his way to the Farnese Tower, came back to
Clelia's memory. Her eyes overflowed with tears. " Dear
friend, what would I not do for you! You will be my ruin,
I know; that is my fate. I work my own destruction, and
in the vilest way, when I listen to this terrible serenade to-
night. But at noon to-morrow I shall look into your eyes
again!"

It was on the very morrow of that day on which Clelia
had sacrificed so much for the young prisoner whom she
loved so passionately—it was on the morrow of the day
on which, conscious though she was of all his faults, she
had sacrificed her life to him, that her coldness almost drove
Fabrizio to despair. If, even through the imperfect language of signs, he had done the least violence to Clelia's
feelings, she would probably not have been able to
restrain her tears, and Fabrizio would have obtained her
confession of all she felt for him. But he was not bold
enough; he was too mortally afraid of displeasing Clelia.
The punishment she had it in her power to inflict on him
was too severe for him to face. In other words, Fabrizio
had no experience of the nature of the emotion stirred in a
man by the woman he really loves. It was a sensation he had
never felt before, even to the very faintest extent. It took
him a week from the night of the serenade to recover his
accustomed terms of friendship with Clelia. The poor girl,
terrified lest she should betray herself, took refuge in severity, and every day Fabrizio fancied his favour with her grew
less.

One day—Fabrizio had then been in prison almost three
months, without holding any communication with the outer

world, yet without feeling unhappy—Grillo had remained in his room far into the morning. Fabrizio was in despair, not knowing how to get rid of him. Half-past twelve o'clock had struck before he was able to open the two little traps, a foot high, which he had cut in his hateful screen. Clelia was standing at the aviary window, her eyes fixed on Fabrizio's room. The deepest despair hovered over her drawn features. Hardly had she caught sight of Fabrizio than she made him a sign that all was lost; then, hurrying to her piano and pretending to sing a recitative out of an opera then in vogue, she said, in sentences broken by her despair and the fear of being understood by the sentinels marching up and down under the window:

"Good God! you are still alive! How deeply I thank Heaven! Barbone, the jailer whose insolence you punished on the day of your arrival here, had disappeared, and left the citadel altogether. He returned the night before last, and since yesterday I have had reason to think he is trying to poison you. He comes and hangs about the private kitchen in the palace, where your meals are cooked. I know nothing for certain, but my waiting-woman believes that vile countenance only comes into the palace kitchens with the object of destroying your life. I was beside myself with anxiety when you did not appear; I thought you were dead! Do not eat any food that is brought you, until I give you leave. I will contrive some means of sending you a little chocolate. In any case, at nine o'clock to-night, if, by Heaven's mercy, you happen to have a thread, or can make a line out of some of your linen, let it drop from your window on to the orange trees below. I will fasten a cord to it, which you will draw up, and by means of that cord I will send you bread and chocolate."

Fabrizio had treasured up the scrap of charcoal he had found in the stove in his room. He made haste to take advantage of Clelia's emotion, and to write on his hand a succession of letters which made up the following words:

"I love you, and the only reason my life is precious to me is because I see you. Above all things, send me paper and a pencil."

The Chartreuse of Parma

As Fabrizio had hoped, the excessive terror he had read in Clelia's face prevented the young girl from breaking off their conversation after his bold declaration that he loved her. All she did was to look very much displeased. Fabrizio was clever enough to add: "There is so much wind to-day that I can hardly make out the counsels you are good enough to give me as you sing; the noise of the piano drowns your voice. What is the poison of which you speak?"

At his words all the young girl's alarm broke out afresh; she began hastily writing large letters in ink on pages which she tore out of a book, and Fabrizio was beside himself with delight at seeing the method of correspondence he had so vainly begged, established at last, after three months of effort. He carefully clung to the little deception which had served his purpose so well. What he wanted to do was to write letters, and he kept pretending he could not catch the sense of the words, the letters of which Clelia held up to his gaze one after the other.

She was obliged to leave the aviary and hurry to her father. Her greatest terror was that he might come to look for her there. His suspicious instinct would have been very much offended by the close vicinity of the aviary window to the screen concealing that of the prisoner's room. It had occurred to Clelia herself, a few minutes previously, when Fabrizio's non-appearance was causing her such mortal anxiety, that a piece of paper wrapped round a small stone might be thrown over the top of the screen. If, by good luck, the jailer in charge of Fabrizio should not happen to be in his room, this would be a quite reliable method of correspondence.

Our prisoner lost no time in fashioning a kind of line out of some of his under-linen, and a little after nine o'clock in the evening he distinctly heard a slight tapping on the boxes of the orange trees under his window. He let down his line, and brought up, fastened to the end of it, a very long, thin cord, by means of which he drew up, to begin with, a supply of chocolate, and then, to his inexpressible satisfaction, a roll of paper and a pencil. In vain did he drop his cord down again; nothing more was sent up. Probably the sentries had approached the neighbourhood of the orange trees. But he was beside himself with delight. He instantly wrote an endless letter to Clelia, and the moment it was finished he fastened it to his line and let it down. For more than three hours he waited vainly for her to come and take it, and several times he drew it up again to alter expressions in it. "If Clelia does not see my letter to-night," he thought, "while she is still softened by her idea about the poison, she may, when morning comes, utterly refuse to receive any letter from me at all."

The real truth was that Clelia had not been able to get out of going down into the town with her father. This idea occurred to Fabrizio when he heard the general's carriage drive up, about half an hour after midnight. He knew the sound of his horses' feet. What was his joy when, a few minutes after he had heard the sentries salute the general as he crossed the terrace, he felt a tremor shake the cord, which he had kept wound about his arm. Something very heavy was being fastened to the end of it. Two slight pulls gave him the signal to draw it up. He had some difficulty in getting the heavy object past a very projecting cornice that ran below his window.

The object he had found it so difficult to draw up was a bottle filled with water, wrapped in a shawl. In a passion of delight the poor young fellow, who had lived so long in such complete solitude, covered the shawl with kisses. But no words of mine can depict his emotion when, after all those many days of disappointed hope, his eyes fell on a little scrap of paper, fastened to the shawl with a pin.

"Drink no water but this; live on the chocolate. To-morrow I will make every effort to send you up some bread. I will mark it all over with little crosses in ink.

"It is a horrible thing to say, but you must be told, that Barbone may possibly be sent here to poison you. How comes it that you have not felt the subject of your pencil letter must be most displeasing to me? And, indeed, I would not write to you at all but for the excessive danger that threatens us. I have just seen the duchess; she is very well, and so is the count. But she has grown much thinner. Do not write to me again upon that subject. Do you want me to be angry with you?"

It required a great effort of virtue on Clelia's part to write the last line but one of her note. Everybody about court was declaring that the Duchess Sanseverina was beginning to feel a great regard for Count Baldi, that very good-looking young man who had been the Marchesa Raversi's friend. One point was quite certain—he had broken in the most scandalous fashion with the aforementioned marchesa, who had been a mother to him for six years, and had established his social position. Clelia had been obliged to write her hasty note twice over, because in the first copy she had allowed something of the new love affair ascribed to the duchess by public spite to appear.

"What a mean creature I am," she exclaimed, "to speak evil of the woman he loves to Fabrizio!"

The next morning, long before daylight, Grillo entered Fabrizio's room, put down a rather heavy parcel, and disappeared without a word. The bundle contained a good-sized loaf of bread, covered all over with little pen-and-ink crosses. Fabrizio covered them with kisses; he was very much in love. With the loaf he found a "rouleau," containing six thousand francs in sequins, wrapped in numerous paper coverings, and finally a beautiful new breviary. On the margin of the book the following words had been traced, in a handwriting he was beginning to know:

"*Poison!* Beware of water, of wine, of everything! Live on chocolate; try to make the dog eat the dinner you will not touch. Do not betray your suspicions. The enemy would seek out some other means. Let there be no imprudence, in God's name, and no carelessness!"

Fabrizio immediately removed the precious words, which might have compromised Clelia, and, tearing a great number of leaves out of the breviary, he made up several alphabets, each letter clearly written with charcoal crushed up and moistened with wine. These alphabets were dry by the time a quarter to twelve struck, and Clelia made her appearance two paces from the aviary window. "Now," said Fabrizio to himself, " the great thing is to get her to make use of them." But by good luck, she had many things to tell the young prisoner about the attempt to poison him. A dog belonging to the servant girls had died after eating of a dish which had been cooked for Fabrizio. So that Clelia, far from objecting to the use of alphabets, had prepared a splendid one of her own, written in ink. The conversation thus carried on—not a very easy matter during the first few minutes—lasted no less than an hour and a half; that is to say, for as long as Clelia could stay in the aviary. Two or three times, when Fabrizio ventured on forbidden subjects, she deigned him no answer, and turned away for a moment to bestow some necessary care upon her birds.

Fabrizio had induced her to promise that at night, when she sent him water, she would also send him one of her own alphabets, written in ink, which was much more easily deciphered. He did not fail to write her a very long letter, from which he was careful to exclude all expression of tenderness, or any, at all events, likely to give offence. This method proved successful, and his letter was accepted. When their alphabet conversation began next day Clelia did not reproach him. She told him the danger of poison was growing less; the serving-men who made love to the governor's kitchen-maids had fallen upon Barbone and half murdered him. He would probably not venture to reappear in the kitchens. Clelia confessed that for Fabrizio's sake she had dared to steal an antidote in her father's possession; this she would send him. The great point was that he should instantly reject any food the taste of which was unusual.

Clelia had questioned Don Cesare very closely, without being able to discover the source of the six thousand sequins Fabrizio had received. But in any case it was an excellent sign; his captors' severity was softening.

This poison episode advanced our prisoner's business mightily. He could not, indeed, extract the slightest confession of anything like love. But he had the delight of living on the most intimate terms with Clelia. Every morning, and sometimes in the evenings, too, they held a long conversation with their alphabets. Every night at nine o'clock,

The Chartreuse of Parma

Clelia accepted a long letter, and sometimes returned a few words in reply. She sent him up the newspaper and a few books, and Grillo had been coaxed into bringing Fabrizio wine and bread, with which he was supplied every day by Clelia's waiting-maid. The jailer had concluded that the governor was not in agreement with the persons who had sent Barbone to poison the young monsignore, and he, as well as his comrades, was heartily glad of it, for it had become a proverb in the prison that if a man only looked Monsignore del Dongo in the face he was sure to give him money.

Fabrizio had grown very pallid. The total absence of exercise tried his health, but except for that, he had never been so happy in his life. The tone of his conversations with Clelia was intimate, and sometimes very merry. The only moments in Clelia's life that were not embittered by terrible forebodings and remorse were those she spent talking to him.

One day she was so imprudent as to say:

" I admire your delicacy. As I am the governor's daughter, you never speak to me of your desire to recover your liberty."

" That is because I have no such ridiculous desire," replied Fabrizio. " If I once got back to Parma how should I ever see you? And life would be unendurable to me, henceforth, if I could not tell you all my thoughts. . . . No, not exactly all my thoughts. You take good care of that. But, after all, in spite of your unkindness, to live without seeing you every day would be far worse suffering to me than this imprisonment. I never was so happy in my life. Is it not comical that my happiness should have been waiting for me in a prison? "

" There are a great many things to be said upon that subject," replied Clelia, suddenly growing very grave, and almost gloomy.

" What! " cried Fabrizio in great alarm, " am I in danger of losing that little corner I have won in your heart, the only happiness I have in all the world? "

" Yes," she replied. " I have every reason to think you

355

are not acting honestly by me, although in the world you are considered a very honourable man. But I will not go into this matter to-day."

This curious confidence made that day's conversation very awkward, and tears often stood in the eyes of both speakers.

Chief-Justice Rassi still pined to change his name. He was very weary of the one he had made himself, and longed to be called the Baron Riva. Count Mosca, on his side, was working, with all the skill he possessed, to feed the venal judge's passion for his barony, and to double the prince's mad hope of making himself constitutional King of Lombardy. These were the only two methods of delaying Fabrizio's execution he had been able to discover.

The prince kept saying to Rassi : " A fortnight's despair, and a fortnight's hope. By patiently carrying out this treatment we shall contrive to break down that haughty woman's temper. It is this alternation of gentleness and severity which is used to break in the most unmanageable horses. Apply the caustic with a steady hand."

So every fortnight a fresh report of Fabrizio's approaching death spread over Parma. Each of these stories plunged the unhappy duchess into the deepest despair. Faithful to her resolve not to drag the count down into her own ruin, she would only see him twice in the month. But her cruelty to the poor man was punished by the continual alternations of hope and dark despair in which her own life was spent. In vain did Count Mosca, in spite of the bitter jealousy caused him by the attentions of the good-looking Baldi, write to the duchess when he could not see her, and acquaint her with all the information he owed to the future Baron Riva. To make a stand against the horrible reports concerning Fabrizio, which were in such constant circulation, the duchess should have spent all her time with a clever and kind-hearted man such as Mosca. Baldi's stupidity, which left her alone with her own thoughts, rendered existence hideous to her, and the count could not succeed in inspiring her with his own reasons for hope.

By means of certain ingenious pretexts the minister induced the prince to consent to send the documents concerning all the very complicated intrigues which, according to Ranuzio Ernest IV's wild hope, were to make him constitutional King of Lombardy, to the house of an accomplice near Sarono, in the very middle of that fair country.

More than a score of these very compromising papers were either in the prince's own hand or bore his signature, and the count intended, if Fabrizio's life should be seriously threatened, to inform his Highness that he was about to place these proofs in the hands of a great Power which could crush him with a word.

Count Mosca thought himself sure of the future Baron Riva. Poison was the only thing he feared. Barbone's attempt had greatly alarmed him—to such a point, indeed, that he had made up his mind to risk what looked like an act of madness. One morning he drove to the citadel gate, and sent for General Fabio Conti, who came down to him on the bastion above the gate. As they walked up and down in friendly fashion, the count did not hesitate to say, after a little preface, which, though civil enough, was decidedly bitter-sweet:

" If Fabrizio should die in any suspicious manner, his death may be ascribed to me, and I should bear the reputation of a jealous fool. That would make me look utterly ridiculous, a thing to which I am resolved never to submit. Therefore, if he should die of any sickness, I shall kill you with my own hands to clear myself; of that you may be perfectly certain."

General Fabio Conti made a very fine answer, and talked big about his courage. But he never forgot the look the count had given him as he spoke.

A few days later, and as if he had arranged it with the count, Chief-Justice Rassi ventured on an imprudence very remarkable in such a man. The public scorn which clung to his name and made it a proverb with the lowest of the populace, was sickening him, now that he had a reasonable hope of escaping it. He forwarded General Fabio Conti an official copy of the sentence condemning Fabrizio to twelve years in the citadel. Legally speaking, this ought to have been done the very morning after Fabrizio entered the prison. But what was unheard of in Parma, that country of secret measures, was that the justiciary should have ventured on such a step without an express order from the sovereign. For what hope could there be of doubling the duchess's terrors every fortnight, and so breaking down her haughty temper, as the prince expressed it, once an official copy of the sentence had passed out of the office of the Ministry of Justice? On the evening before the day on which ·General Fabio Conti received Chief-Justice Rassi's official letter he was informed that Barbone, the clerk, had been thoroughly thrashed on his way back to the citadel, rather late at night. From this he concluded that there was no longer any desire in high quarters to get rid of Fabrizio, and by an instinct of prudence which saved Rassi from the immediate consequences of his folly, he did not mention the transmission of the official copy of the prisoner's sentence at his next audience with the prince. The count, mercifully for the poor duchess's peace of mind, had discovered that Barbone's clumsy attempt had been inspired solely by his own private vengeance, and it was he who had provided the clerk with the warning to which we have just referred. It was a pleasant surprise for Fabrizio, when, after a hundred and thirty-five days in his somewhat cramped cage, Don Cesare, the worthy chaplain, came one Thursday to take him for a walk on the leads of the Farnese Tower. Before Fabrizio had been there for ten minutes, the fresh air overcame him, and he fainted away. Don Cesare made this incident a pretext for allowing him half an hour's walk every day. This was a folly. The frequent outings soon restored our hero to a strength which he abused.

Several more serenades were given. The only reason that induced the punctilious governor to permit them was that they helped to bind his daughter Clelia, whose character alarmed him, to the Marchese Crescenzi. He had an uneasy feeling that there was nothing in common between himself and his daughter, and lived in perpetual dread of some freak on her part. She might take refuge in a convent, and then he would be helpless. Otherwise the general had his fears that all this music, the sound of which must reach the deepest dungeons reserved to the blackest Liberals, might screen the making of signals. He was jealous, too, of the musicians on their own account. Therefore, the moment the serenade was over, they were locked up in those great, low-ceilinged rooms of the governor's palace which were used as offices by his staff in the daytime, and the doors were not opened till broad daylight the next morning. The governor himself stood on the " Bridge of the Slave " while the men were searched in his presence, and never restored them to liberty without telling them, several times over, that he would instantly hang any man who dared to undertake to carry the most trifling message to any prisoner. It was well known that in his terror of displeasing the prince he was certain to keep his word; so, to overcome their horror of the night's imprisonment, Crescenzi was obliged to pay his musicians triple fees. All the duchess could wring out of the cowardice of one of these men, and this with great difficulty, was that he should carry a letter in, and give it to the governor. The letter was addressed to Fabrizio, and deplored the sad fact that during the five months he had been in prison his friends outside had never been able to establish the smallest correspondence with him.

When the musician entered the citadel he cast himself at General Fabio Conti's feet, and confessed that a priest, a stranger to him, had so insisted on his taking charge of a letter addressed to Signor del Dongo, that he had not ventured to refuse, but that, faithful to his duty, he now hastened to place it in his Excellency's hands.

His Excellency was highly flattered. He know how great the duchess's resources were, and was terribly afraid of being fooled by her. In his joy the general carried the letter to the prince, who was equally delighted.

" Then the firmness of my government has avenged me at last! For five months that haughty woman has been in anguish. But one of these days we will build a scaffold, and her wild imagination will not fail to convince her it is for young Del Dongo."

CHAPTER XX

ONE morning, toward one o'clock, Fabrizio, stretched upon his window-sill, had slipped his head through the opening he had made in the screen, and was gazing at the stars, and at the wide horizon visible from the top of the Farnese Tower. As his eyes wandered over the country lying toward the lower Po and Ferrara, they chanced to notice a very small, but exceedingly bright, light, seemingly placed on the top of a tower. "That light can not be visible from the plain," said Fabrizio to himself. "The thickness of the tower would prevent any one from seeing it from below. It must be a signal to some distant point." All at once he remarked that this light appeared and disappeared at very close intervals. "It must be some young girl signalling to her lover in the next village." He counted nine successive flashes. "That's an 'I,'" said he, "and certainly 'I' is the ninth letter in the alphabet." Then, after a pause, there came fourteen flashes. "That's an 'N.'" Then, after another pause, there came a single flash. "That's an 'A'; the word is 'Ina.'"

What were his joy and astonishment when he realized that these successive flashes, punctuated by short pauses, made up the following words:

"Ina pensa a te,"

which evidently meant, "Gina is thinking of thee." Instantly he replied by successive displays of his own lamp through the aperture in his shutter:

"Fabrizio loves thee."

This correspondence was kept up till daylight. It was the hundred and seventy-third night of his captivity, and these signals, he was informed, had been made every night

The Chartreuse of Parma

for four months. But any one might notice and understand the signs; that very night a system of abbreviations was agreed upon. A series of three rapid flashes was to stand for the duchess, four for the prince, two for Count Mosca. Two quick flashes, followed by two slow ones, was to mean "escape." It was settled that for the future they would use the ancient alphabet "*alla monaca*," which, to baffle indiscreet curiosity, alters the usual position of the letters in the alphabet, and gives them others of its own devising. Thus, "A" becomes the tenth letter, and "B" the third; so that three successive eclipses of the lamp stand for "B," ten for "A," and so forth. The words were separated by a short interval of darkness. A meeting was arranged for an hour after the following midnight, and that next night the duchess came to the tower, which stood about a quarter of a league from the town. Her eyes filled with tears when she beheld signals made by Fabrizio, whom she had so often given up for dead. She signalled to him herself, with the lamp: "I love you! Courage! health! hope! Use your muscles in your room; you will want all the strength of your arms."

"I have not seen him," thought the duchess to herself, "since that concert when the Fausta sang, and he appeared at my drawing-room door dressed as a footman. Who could have dreamed, then, of the fate that was awaiting us!" The duchess apprised Fabrizio by signal that he would soon be rescued, "thanks to the goodness of the prince" (there was always a chance that the signals might be read). Then she began to say all sorts of tender things; she could not tear herself away from him. Nothing but the entreaties of Ludovico, whom she had made her confidential servant, because he had been useful to Fabrizio, could induce her to discontinue the signals, even close upon daybreak, when they might possibly attract the attention of some evil-disposed person. This reiterated assurance of his approaching deliverance threw Fabrizio into the deepest melancholy. Clelia remarked this next morning, and was imprudent enough to inquire its cause.

"I see I am on the point of giving the duchess serious cause for displeasure."

The Chartreuse of Parma

" And what can she possibly ask of you that you could
refuse ? " exclaimed Clelia, pricked by the most eager curiosity.

" She wants me to leave this place," he replied, " and
that is what I will never consent to do."

Clelia could not answer; she looked up at him, and
burst into tears. If he could have spoken to her then at
close quarters he might perhaps have induced her to confess
feelings, his uncertainty concerning which often cast him
into the deepest sadness. He was keenly conscious that for
him life without Clelia's love could only be a succession of
bitter sorrows, or one long unbearable weariness. Life did
not appear worth living if he was only to go back to those
pleasures which had seemed to interest him before he had
known what love really was, and although suicide has not
yet become the fashion in Italy, he had thought of it as
a final refuge, should fate part him from Clelia.

The next day he received a long letter from her.

" It is necessary, my friend, that you should know the
truth. Very often, since you have been shut up here, the
whole town of Parma has believed your last hour had come.

" It is true that you are only sentenced to twelve years
in the fortress, but it is an undoubted fact, unhappily, that
an all-powerful hate pursues you, and twenty times I have
trembled at the thought that your days might be ended by
poison. You must, therefore, snatch at every *possible* means
of escape. You see that for your sake I fail in my most
sacred duties. You may judge how imminent your danger is,
by the things I dare to tell you, and which are so unfit for
me to say. If it be absolutely necessary, if you can find no
other means of safety, you must fly. Every instant you
spend within this fortress may place your life in greater
peril. Remember that there is a party at court which has
never allowed its plans to be checked by any likelihood of
crime. And do you not perceive that all the plans of that
party are constantly foiled by Count Mosca's superior cunning? Certain means have now been devised to insure his
banishment from Parma. This throws the duchess into despair. And does not her despair become a certainty, if the

young prisoner is put to death? This one fact, which is
unanswerable, will enable you to gauge your own position.
You say you feel affection for me. Think, in the first place,
that insurmountable obstacles must prevent this feeling from
ever becoming a solid one between us. We shall have met
each other in our youth; we shall have held out friendly
hands to one another, in a moment of misfortune. Fate
will have sent me to this stern place to soften your suffering, but I should reproach myself eternally if fancies which
have not, and never will have, any true foundation, led you
to neglect any possible opportunity of saving your life from
such a frightful peril. The cruel imprudence I committed
when I exchanged some friendly signs with you, has cost
me my peace of mind. If our childish games with alphabets
have filled you with illusions so unjustifiable, and which may
be so fatal to you, I shall never be able to justify myself in
my own eyes, by recalling Barbone's attempt upon you to
my memory. I myself, even when I thought I was saving
you from a momentary danger, shall have placed you in
far more terrible and far more inevitable peril, and never,
to all eternity, can my wrongdoing gain pardon, if it has
inspired you with feelings which might lead you to neglect
the counsels of the duchess. This, then, is what you force
me to reiterate: Save yourself! I command you!"

The letter was a very long one. Some passages, such as
that "I command you," which we have just quoted, were
full of an exquisite encouragement to Fabrizio's love. The
actual feeling of the letter struck him as being fairly tender,
although its expression was remarkably prudent. At other
moments he paid the penalty of his complete ignorance of
this kind of warfare, and saw nothing but ordinary friendship, or even the most commonplace humanity, in Clelia's
letter. None of its contents, however, shook his resolve for
a single instant. Supposing all the dangers she described
to be very real, was it anything too much to purchase the
daily joy of seeing her by facing some momentary risk?
What would his life be if he were to find refuge, once more,
at Bologna or Florence? For if he should escape from the
citadel, he could never hope for leave to reside anywhere

within the state of Parma. And if the prince altered his views so far as to set him at liberty—a very unlikely contingency, seeing he, Fabrizio, had become, to a powerful faction, a useful element for the overthrow of Count Mosca —what would life be, even at Parma, parted from Clelia by the bitter hatred of the two parties? Once or twice in a month, perhaps, chance might bring them both into the same drawing-room. But even then, what could the nature of their conversation be? How were they ever to recover the tone of absolute intimacy he now enjoyed for several hours every day? What would their drawing-room talk be like, compared with the intercourse they kept up through their alphabets? "What matter if I have to pay for this life of delights, this unique chance of happiness, by taking some trifling risks? And is it not happiness, again, to find this poor opportunity of proving my love to her?"

Fabrizio's only view of Clelia's letter, then, was that it gave him an excuse for craving an interview with her. This was the one and constant object of all his longing. He had never spoken to her but once, and only for an instant, just as he was being led to his prison. And that was more than two hundred days ago. There was a method by which a meeting with Clelia might be easily arranged. The worthy Don Cesare allowed Fabrizio to walk for half an hour every Thursday, in the daytime, on the terrace of the Farnese Tower. But on the other days his exercise, which might have been observed by all the dwellers in and around Parma, and thus seriously compromised the governor, was taken after nightfall. The only staircase by which the terrace of the Farnese Tower could be reached was that in the little bell tower of the chapel, with its gloomy black and white marble decorations, of which my reader may retain some recollection. Grillo was in the habit of taking Fabrizio into the chapel and opening the door leading to the little staircase in the tower for him to pass up it. He ought to have followed him, but the evenings were growing chilly, and the jailer allowed him to go up alone, turned the key upon the tower, which communicated with the terrace, and went back to sit in his warm room. Well, why should not Clelia and her waiting-woman meet him, some night, in the black marble chapel?

All Fabrizio's long letter in answer to Clelia's was written with the object of obtaining this interview. And further, with the most absolute sincerity, and as though he had been speaking of another person, he confided to her all the reasons which made him resolve not to leave the citadel.

"I would risk a thousand deaths, every day, for the happiness of talking to you with our alphabets, which do not now give us a moment's difficulty. And you would have me commit the blunder of banishing myself to Parma, or perhaps to Bologna, or even to Florence! You expect me deliberately to remove myself farther away from you. Such an effort, let me tell you, is impossible to me. It would be vain for me to give you my word. I could not keep it."

The result of this plea for a meeting was a disappearance on Clelia's part, which lasted no less than five days. For five whole days she never came near the aviary, except when she knew Fabrizio would not be able to open the little shutter in his screen. Fabrizio was in despair. This absence convinced him that, in spite of some glances which had filled him with foolish hopes, he had never really inspired Clelia with any warmer feeling than one of friendship. "In that case," thought he, "of what value is my life to me? Let the prince rid me of it. I shall be grateful to him. That is another reason for my staying in the fortress." And it was with a sense of deep disgust that he replied to the signals flashed by the little lamp. The duchess was convinced he had gone quite crazy when, in the report of the signalled conversations which Ludovico presented to her every morning, she read the extraordinary assertion: "I do not desire to escape. I choose to die here."

During those five days of Fabrizio's misery, Clelia was even more wretched than he. The following idea, a very bitter one to a generous soul, had occurred to her: "It is my duty to flee to some convent far from the citadel. When Fabrizio knows I am not here—and I will take care he does know it, from Grillo and all the other jailers—he will make up his mind to attempt to escape." But to go into a convent meant to give up all hope of ever seeing Fabrizio again. And how could she bear not to see him, now that he had given her so clear a proof that the feeling which might once have bound him to the duchess no longer existed? What more touching proof of devotion could any man have offered? After seven long months of an imprisonment which had seriously undermined his health, he refused to regain his liberty. A frivolous being, such as the courtiers had given Clelia cause to believe Fabrizio to be, would have sacrificed twenty mistresses to shorten his stay in the fortress by one day, and what would he not have done to escape from a prison where he might be poisoned at any moment!

Clelia's courage failed her; she committed the signal mistake of not taking refuge in a convent, a step which would likewise have given her a quite natural excuse for breaking with the Marchese Crescenzi. Once this mistake was made, how could she stand out against this young man, so lovable, so natural, so devoted, who was exposing his life to the most frightful peril, simply for the sake of the happiness of looking at her out of his window? After five days of the most terrible struggle, interspersed with fits of bitter self-scorn, Clelia made up her mind to answer the letter in which Fabrizio besought her to grant him an interview in the black marble chapel. She refused the meeting, indeed, and in somewhat harsh terms; but from that instant all her peace of mind departed. Every moment her imagination showed her Fabrizio dying from the effects of poison; six or eight times a day she would go up into the aviary to satisfy her passionate need of seeing with her own eyes that he was alive.

"If he remains in the fortress," said she to herself, "if he is still exposed to all the vile things that the Raversi party is plotting against him, in order to overthrow Count Mosca, the only reason is because my cowardice has prevented me from going into a convent. What pretext would he have had for remaining here, if he had known for certain that I had gone forever?"

This girl, with all her shyness and innate pride, even

faced the risk of encountering a refusal from Grillo, the jailer. She humbled herself to the extent of sending for him, and telling him, in a voice the trembling tones of which betrayed her secret, that in a few days Fabrizio would gain his freedom; that the Duchess Sanseverina was taking the most active steps with this object; that it was frequently necessary to obtain the prisoner's instant reply to certain proposals made to him, and that she begged him, Grillo, to allow Fabrizio to make an opening in the screen which masked the window, so that she might communicate to him, by signs, the intelligence she was receiving several times each day from the duchess.

Grillo smiled, and assured her of his respect and obedience. Clelia was intensely grateful to him for saying nothing more. It was quite clear that he was perfectly cognizant of everything that had been going on for some months.

Hardly had the jailer left her presence, when Clelia gave the signal agreed on for summoning Fabrizio on great occasions, and she confessed all she had done to him. " Your heart is set on dying by poison," she added. " I hope to gather courage, one of these days, to leave my father, and take refuge in some distant convent. That will be my duty to you; and then, I hope, you will not oppose the plans which may be suggested to enable you to escape. As long as you are here, I must endure moments of horrible distress and perplexity. Never in my life have I done anything to harm anybody, and now it seems to me that I shall be the cause of your death. Such an idea, even concerning a person utterly unknown to me, would drive me to despair. Imagine, then, what I feel at the thought that a friend, whose folly gives me grave cause for complaint, but with whom, after all, I have had daily intercourse for so long a time, may at that very moment be in the throes of death. Now and then I feel that I must make sure for myself that you are alive.

" To save myself from this horrible anguish I have just humbled myself so low as to ask a favour from an inferior, who might have refused it, and who may yet betray me. After all, it would be happier for me, perhaps, if he did denounce me to my father. I should instantly go to my convent, and I should no longer be the very unwilling accomplice of your cruel folly. But, believe me, this state of things can not last long, and you will obey your orders from the duchess. Are you content, my cruel friend? It is I who beseech you to betray my father! Call Grillo, and give him money!"

Fabrizio was so desperately in love, the slightest expression of Clelia's will filled him with such dread, that even this extraordinary communication did not make him feel certain he was beloved. He called Grillo, rewarded him generously for his past complaisance, and told him, as regarded the future, that for every day on which he allowed him to make use of the opening in his screen, he would give him a sequin. Grillo was delighted with this arrangement.

"Monsignore," he said, "I am going to speak to you quite frankly. Will you make up your mind to eating a cold dinner every day? That is a very simple method of escaping the risk of poison. But I will beg you to practise the most absolute discretion; a jailer must see everything, and guess nothing. Instead of one dog, I will keep several, and you yourself shall make them taste every dish you intend to eat. As for wine, I will give you mine, and you must never touch any bottle except those out of which I have drunk. But if your Excellency wants to ruin me forever, you have only to confide these matters even to the Signorina Clelia. All women are alike, and if she should quarrel with you to-morrow, the day after, in her vengeance, she will tell the whole story to her father, whose greatest joy would be to find some excuse for hanging a jailer. Next to Barbone himself, the general is the most spiteful man in the citadel, and there lies the real danger of your position. He knows how to use poison, be sure of that, and he would not forgive me if he thought I was keeping two or three little dogs."

There was another serenade.

Grillo now answered all Fabrizio's questions; he had resolved, indeed, that he would be prudent, and not betray the Signorina Clelia, who, as it appeared to him, though just about to marry the Marchese Crescenzi, the richest man in the state of Parma, was nevertheless carrying on a love affair, as far as prison walls allowed, with the handsome Monsignore del Dongo. He had just been replying to Fabrizio's questions about the serenade, and blunderingly added, " He is expected to marry her soon." The effect of this simple sentence on Fabrizio may be imagined. That night, his only response to the lamp signals was to the effect that he was ill. The next morning, at ten o'clock, when Clelia appeared in the aviary, he asked her, with a ceremonious politeness quite unusual between them, why she had not frankly told him that she loved the Marchese Crescenzi, and was just about to marry him.

" Because none of all that is true," she answered petulantly. The rest of her reply, indeed, was not so explicit. Fabrizio pointed this out to her, and took advantage of the occasion to make a fresh request for an interview. Clelia, who saw her good faith called in question, agreed almost at once, begging him, at the same time, to note that she would be dishonoured forever in the eyes of Grillo.

That evening, when it had grown quite dark, she appeared, with her waiting-woman, in the black marble chapel. She stopped in the middle, close by the night lamp. Grillo and the waiting-maid turned back, and stood about thirty paces off, near the door. Clelia, shaking with emotion, had made ready a fine speech; her object was not to let any compromising confession escape her. But the logic of passion is very merciless; its deep interest in discovering the truth forbids the employment of useless precautions, and its intense devotion to its object deprives it of all fear of giving offence. At first Fabrizio was dazzled by Clelia's beauty. For over eight months he had not looked so closely at any human being save his jailers, but the name of the Marchese Crescenzi brought back all his fury, and this was increased when he clearly perceived Clelia's answers to be full of a prudent discretion. Clelia herself recognised that she was increasing his suspicions, instead of dispelling them. The painfulness of the thought was more than she could endure.

" Would it make you very happy," she said, with a sort
of rage, and with tears standing in her eyes, " to think you
have made me forget everything I owe to myself? Until the
third of August last year, I never felt anything but distaste
for the men who sought to please me. I had a boundless
and probably exaggerated scorn for the character of all
courtiers ; everybody who was happy at court disgusted me.
But I noticed remarkable qualities in a prisoner who was
brought to the citadel on the third of August. First of all,
and almost unconsciously, I endured all the torments of jealousy. The charms of an exquisite woman, whom I knew
well, were so many dagger thrusts in my heart, because I
believed, and I still believe it a little, that this prisoner was
attached to her. Soon the persecutions of the Marchese
Crescenzi, who had asked my father for my hand, increased
twofold. He is a very rich man, and we have no fortune at
all. I refused his advances with the most absolute independence. But my father pronounced the fatal word, 'a
convent,' and I realized that if I left the citadel, I should
not be able to watch over the life of the prisoner in whose
fate I was interested. Until that moment, the chief object of
my care had been to prevent his having the smallest suspicion of the terrible dangers which threatened his life.

" I had been quite resolved never to betray either my
father or my secret, but the woman who protects this prisoner, a woman of the most splendid activity, a woman of
superior intelligence and indomitable will, offered him, as
I believe, the means of escape. He refused them, and endeavoured to persuade me he would not leave the citadel
because he would not leave me. Then I committed a great
fault. I struggled for five days ; I ought instantly to have
betaken myself to a convent, and left the fortress. That step
would have provided me with a very easy method of breaking with the Marchese Crescenzi. I had not courage to
leave the fortress, and I am a ruined girl. I have set my
affections on a fickle man. I know what his conduct was
at Naples, and what reason have I to suppose his nature
has changed? During a very severe imprisonment he has
paid court to the only woman he could see ; she has been

an amusement to him in his boredom. As he could not speak to her without a certain amount of difficulty, this amusement has taken on a false appearance of passion. The prisoner, who has made himself a reputation for courage, has taken it into his head to prove that his love is more than a mere passing fancy by risking considerable danger, so as to continue seeing the person whom he believes he loves. But once he is back in a great city, and surrounded by all the temptations of society, he will again be that which he has always been—a man of the world, addicted to dissipation and gallantry; and the poor companion of his prison will end her days in a convent, forgotten by this fickle being, and weighed down with the deadly regret of having confessed her love to him."

This historic speech, of which we have only indicated the principal features, was, as may well be imagined, broken twenty times by Fabrizio's interruptions. He was desperately in love, and he was perfectly convinced that before meeting Clelia he had never known what love was, and that the destiny of his whole life was bound up with her alone.

My reader will doubtless imagine all the fine things he was pouring out when the waiting-woman warned her mistress that the clock had just struck half-past eleven, and that the general might be coming in at any moment. The parting was a cruel one.

" Perhaps this is the last time I shall ever see you," said Clelia to the prisoner. " A measure which is so evidently to the interest of the Raversi cabal may give you a terrible opportunity for proving that you are not inconstant." Choking with sobs, and overcome with shame because she could not altogether stifle them in the presence of her maid, and more especially of the jailer, Clelia parted with Fabrizio. No second conversation would be possible until the general gave out that he was going to spend an evening in society. And as, since Fabrizio's imprisonment, and the interest it inspired among the curious courtiers, he had thought it prudent to suffer from an almost unintermitting fit of the gout, his expeditions into the town, which were directed by the necessities of a cunning policy, were frequently not decided upon till just before he stepped into his carriage.

After that evening in the marble chapel, Fabrizio's life was one succession of transports of joy. Great obstacles, indeed, still stood between him and his happiness, but at all events he had the supreme and unlooked-for bliss of being loved by the divine creature on whom his thoughts unceasingly dwelt. On the third day after the interview the lamp signals ended very early, close upon midnight, and just at that moment Fabrizio's head was very nearly broken by a large leaden ball which was thrown over the upper part of his window screen, came crashing through the paper panes, and fell into his room.

This very bulky ball was by no means as heavy as its size gave reason to suppose. Fabrizio opened it with ease, and within it he found a letter from the duchess.

Through the archbishop, whom she sedulously flattered, she had won over a soldier belonging to the citadel garrison. This man, who was most skilful in the use of the catapult, had either fooled the sentries placed at the corners and on the door of the governor's palace, or had come to an understanding with them.

" You must save yourself with ropes. I shudder as I give you this strange counsel. For a whole month I have shrunk from speaking the words. But the official horizon grows darker every day, and we may expect the worst. You must instantly begin to signal with your lamp, so that we may know you have received this dangerous letter. Show ' P,' ' B,' and ' G,' *alla monaca*—that is to say, four, twelve, and two. I shall not breathe freely until I have seen this signal. I am on the tower, and will answer by ' N ' and ' O,' ' seven ' and ' five.' Once you have received this answer, do not signal any more, and apply your whole mind to understanding my letter."

Fabrizio instantly obeyed, made the signals indicated, and received the promised response. Then he resumed his perusal of the letter.

" We may expect the very worst. This has been affirmed to me by the three men in whom I have most confidence, after I had made them swear on the Gospels to tell me the truth, whatever agony it might cost me. The first of these men threatened the surgeon at Ferrara, who would have denounced you, that he would fall upon him with an open knife in his hand; the second told you, when you returned from Belgirate, that you would have been more strictly prudent if you had put a pistol shot into the man-servant who rode singing through the wood, leading a fine horse, rather too lean. The third man is unknown to you; he is a highway robber of my acquaintance, a man of action, if ever there was one, and as brave as you are yourself. That reason, above all others, induced me to ask him what you had better do. All three, without knowing that I had consulted the other two, have assured me you had far better run the risk of breaking your neck than spend another eleven years and four months in perpetual fear of a very likely dose of poison.

"For a month you must practise climbing up and down a knotted rope in your own room. Then, on a feast day, when the garrison of the citadel will have received an extra ration of wine, you will make your great effort. You will have three ropes of silk and hemp, as thick as a swan's quill. The first, eighty feet long, to carry you down the thirty-five feet from your window to the orange grove; the second, of three hundred feet—there the difficulty comes in, on account of the weight—to carry you down the hundred and eighty feet of the great tower; and a third, of thirty feet, to take you over the rampart. I spend my whole life studying the great wall on the east—that is, on the Ferrara side; a crack caused by an earthquake has been filled up by means of a buttress which forms an inclined plane. My highway robber assures me he would undertake to get down on that side, without too much difficulty, and with no damage beyond a few grazes, simply by letting himself slip down the slope of this buttress. There are only twenty-eight feet of vertical drop quite at the bottom; this side of the citadel is the least well guarded.

"Nevertheless, taking it altogether, my robber—who has escaped from prison three times over, and whom you would like if you knew him, although he hates all men of your caste—my highway robber, I say, who is as active and nimble as you are yourself, thinks he would rather make the descent on the western side, exactly opposite that little palace which you know so well as having once been occupied by the Fausta. What makes him inclined to choose that side is that, though the slope of the wall is very slight, it is almost entirely covered with briers. There are plenty of twigs as thick as one's little finger, which may indeed scratch and tear you if you are not careful, but which also supply an excellent hold. Only this morning I was looking at this western side, through an excellent glass. The place to choose is just below a point where a new stone was inserted in the balustrade, about two or three years ago. From this stone downward you will first of all find a bare space of about twenty feet. Down that you must move very slowly (you may imagine how my heart trembles as I write these horrible instructions, but courage consists in knowing how to choose the lesser evil, however terrible that may be); after this bare space you will find eighty or ninety feet covered with very large brambles and bushes, in which the birds fly about; then a space of about thirty feet, with nothing on it but grass, wall-flowers, and pellitories; and at last, as you get closer to the ground, twenty feet more of brambles, and some twenty-five or thirty feet which have been lately plastered.

" What would make me choose this side is that exactly below that new stone on the upper balustrade there stands a wooden hut, built by one of the soldiers, in his garden, and which the captain of engineers attached to the fortress is anxious to make him pull down. It is seventeen feet high, with a thatched roof, and the roof touches the main wall of the fortress. It is this roof which tempts me. If such a dreadful thing as an accident should happen it would break your fall. Once you get there you will be within the ramparts, but these are rather carelessly guarded. If any one should stop you there, fire off your pistols, and defend yourself for a few minutes. Your friend from Ferrara and another brave man, he whom I call the highway robber, will be provided with ladders, and will not hesitate to scale the rampart, which is not very high, and to fly to your help.

"The rampart is only twenty-three feet high, with a very gradual slope. I shall be at the foot of this last wall, with a good number of armed servants.

"I hope to be able to send you five or six letters by the same hand which brings you this one. I shall constantly reiterate the same things in different terms, so that we may be thoroughly agreed. You will guess what I feel when I tell you that the man who would have had you fire your pistol at the man-servant—who is, after all, the kindest of beings and is half killing himself with remorse—thinks you will escape with a broken arm. The highway robber, who has more experience in such expeditions, thinks that if you will come down very slowly, and above all, without hurrying yourself, your liberty should not cost you more than a few raw places. The great difficulty is to get the ropes, and that has been the one object of my thoughts during the fortnight for which this great plan has occupied every instant of my time.

"I do not reply to that piece of madness, the only foolish thing you ever said in your life, 'I do not desire to escape.' The man who would have had you shoot the man-servant exclaimed at once that the dulness of your life had driven you crazy. I will not conceal from you that we dread a very imminent danger, which may perhaps hasten the day of your flight. To warn you of that danger, the lamp will signal several times over:

"'*The castle is on fire.*'

"You will answer:

"'*Are my books burned?*'"

There were five or six more pages in this letter, all crammed with details. They were written in microscopic characters, on very thin paper.

"All that is very fine, and very well arranged," said Fabrizio to himself, "and I owe eternal gratitude both to the duchess and to the count. Perhaps they will think I am afraid, but I will not escape. Did any man ever escape from a place where he is perfectly happy in order to cast himself into the most hideous banishment, where he will find nothing, not even air that he can breathe? What should I do at the end of the first month, if I were at Florence? I should put on a disguise and come and hover round the gate of this fortress to try to catch a glimpse of her."

The next morning Fabrizio had a fright. He was standing at his window, toward eleven o'clock, looking out at the magnificent view and waiting for the happy moment when Clelia would appear, when Grillo, quite out of breath, bustled into his room.

"Quick, quick, monsignore! Throw yourself on your bed—pretend to be ill. Three judges are coming up; they are going to question you. Think well before you speak; they have come here to entangle you." As Grillo spoke the words he was hastily shutting up the little trap-door in the screen. He thrust Fabrizio on to his bed, and threw two or three cloaks over him.

"Say you are in great pain, and speak as little as you can. Above all things, make them repeat their questions, so as to give yourself time to think."

The three judges entered the room. "Three escaped convicts," said Fabrizio to himself, as he noted their vile countenances, "not three judges at all." They wore long black gowns; they bowed to him solemnly, and sat themselves down without a word, in the only three chairs the apartment contained.

"Signor Fabrizio del Dongo," quoth the senior of the three. "We are distressed by the sadness of the duty we are here to fulfil. We have come to inform you of the death of His Excellency, the Marchese del Dongo, your father, late Grand Steward, Major-Domo of the Lombardo-Venetian Kingdom, Knight Grand Cross of the Orders of ——, and so forth." Fabrizio burst into tears. The judge proceeded:

"The Marchesa del Dongo. your mother, has sent you a letter communicating this news, but as she has added improper remarks of her own to her announcement, the court of justice yesterday decided that you were only to be given extracts from her letter, and these extracts will now be read to you by Registrar Bona."

When the passages had been read out by this functionary, the judge came over to Fabrizio, who was still lying on his bed, and pointed out the paragraphs in his mother's letter, copies of which had just been read to him. In the letter Fabrizio caught sight of such phrases as " unjust imprisonment," " cruel punishment for a crime that is no crime," and understood the motive of the judge's visit. Nevertheless, in his scorn for these unworthy magistrates, he said nothing at all to them, except these words: " I am ill, gentlemen; I am half dead with weakness, and you must excuse my not getting up."

The judges departed, and Fabrizio shed many more tears. At last he questioned with himself: " Am I a hypocrite? I used to think I did not care for him."

On that day, and those following it, Clelia was very sad. She called him several times over, but she had hardly courage to say anything to him. On the morning of the fifth day from that of their first interview, she told him she was coming to the marble chapel that night.

" I can only say a few words to you," she said as she entered. She was trembling to such an extent that she had to lean on her waiting-woman. Having sent her back to the chapel door, she spoke again, in a voice that was barely intelligible. " You will give me your word," she said, " your sacred word of honour, that you will obey the duchess, and try to escape on the day and in the manner in which she will command you. Otherwise I shall immediately take refuge in a convent, and I swear to you, here, that I will never open my lips to you again."

Fabrizio stood dumb.

" Promise," said Clelia, with tears in her eyes, and almost beside herself, " or else this talk will be our very last. You have turned my life into something horrible. You are here because of me, and any day of your life here may be your last." Clelia was so weak at this moment that she had to support herself against a huge arm-chair which had been placed in the centre of the chapel in former days for the use of the imprisoned prince. She very nearly fainted away.

"What must I promise?" said Fabrizio in a despairing voice.

"You know what."

"Then I swear to cast myself knowingly into hideous misery, and to condemn myself to live far from everything I love in this world."

"Promise clearly!"

"I swear I will obey the duchess, and take to flight when and how she wills. And what is to become of me when I am far away from you?"

"Swear you will save yourself, whatever happens!"

"What! Have you made up your mind to marry Crescenzi as soon as I am gone?"

"My God, what a creature you must think me!—But swear, or my soul will never know peace again!"

"Well, then, I swear I will escape from here the day the duchess commands me to do so, and whatever may come to pass beforehand."

Once Clelia had extracted the oath, she grew so faint that she had to retire as soon as she had expressed her thankfulness to Fabrizio.

"Everything," she said, "was ready for my flight to-morrow, if you had insisted on staying on here. At this moment I should have looked my last on you. That was my vow to the Madonna. Now, as soon as I am able to leave my room I will go and look at the wall below the new stone in the balustrade."

The next day she looked so deadly white that it cut him to the heart. She said to him, from her aviary window:

"We must not deceive ourselves, dear friend; our affection is a sinful one, and I am sure some misfortune will overtake us. If nothing worse happens, your attempted flight will be discovered, and you will be utterly lost. Nevertheless we must obey the dictates of human prudence, and that commands us to make every effort. To get down the outside of the great tower you must have over two hundred feet of the strongest rope. With all my endeavours I have not been able, since I knew of the plan, to get together more than fifty feet. The governor has issued an order that every cord and rope found in the citadel is to be burned, and every night the ropes belonging to the wells—which are so weak that they often break even under the light weight they have to carry—are carefully removed. But you must pray God to pardon me, for I am betraying my father, and labouring, unnatural daughter that I am, to cause him mortal grief. Pray to God for me, and if your life is saved, make a vow to consecrate every instant of it to his glory.

" Here is an idea which has occurred to me. In a week from now I am to go down from the citadel to be present at the wedding of one of the Marchese Crescenzi's sisters. I shall return at night, of course, as propriety demands. But I will use all my endeavours to come in as late as possible, and perhaps Barbone will not venture to look at me too closely. All the great ladies of the court, and among them, no doubt, the duchess, will be present at the wedding. In Heaven's name, let one of those ladies pass me a bundle of fine rope, not too thick, and packed as small as possible. If I have to risk a thousand deaths, I will dare every means, even the most dangerous, of getting the bundle into the fortress, and so fail, woe is me, in every duty. If my father finds me out, I shall never see you again. But whatever fate awaits me, I shall be happy, as a sister may be happy, if I can help to save you."

That very evening, by means of his nightly signals with the lamp, Fabrizio informed the duchess of the unique chance that presented itself for sending him a sufficient quantity of rope. But he besought her to keep the matter secret, even from the count, which seemed to her a most extraordinary thing.

" He is mad," thought the duchess. " His imprisonment has altered his nature; he looks at everything from the tragic point of view." The next morning a leaden ball, cast by the catapult, brought the prisoner news that he stood in the greatest possible danger. The individual, he was told, who had undertaken to bring in the ropes was thereby positively and absolutely saving his life. Fabrizio lost no time in apprising Clelia of this fact. The leaden ball also brought Fabrizio a very exact sketch of that portion of the western wall lying between the bastions, by which he was to descend from the top of the great tower. Once he had got so far, his escape would become fairly easy, the ramparts, as my readers are aware, being only twenty-three feet in height. The back of the plan bore a splendid sonnet, written in a small delicate hand. In these lines, some high-hearted person adjured Fabrizio to take to flight, and not to permit his soul to be debased, and his body worn out, by the eleven years of captivity which still lay before him.

And at this point a necessary detail, which partly explains how the duchess had found courage to counsel Fabrizio to attempt so dangerous an escape, obliges us to break the thread of the story of this bold enterprise for a short space.

The Raversi faction, like all parties when they are out of power, was anything but united. Cavaliere Riscara hated Chief-Justice Rassi, who, so he declared, had caused him to lose an important lawsuit, in which, as a matter of fact, Riscara had been in the wrong. Through Riscara, the prince received an anonymous warning that Fabrizio's sentence had been officially reported to the governor of the citadel. The Marchesa Raversi, like the clever party leader she was, was exceedingly annoyed by this false step, and at once sent warning of it to her friend the Chief Justice. She thought it perfectly natural that he should have desired to get something out of Mosca, so long as Mosca remained in power. Rassi betook himself boldly to the palace, making sure a few kicks would settle the matter as far as he was concerned. The prince could not do without some clever lawyer about him, and Rassi had carefully procured the banishment, as Liberals, of a judge and a barrister, the only two men in the country who might possibly have taken his place.

The prince, in a fury, poured out a volley of abuse upon him, and was in the act of moving forward to thrash him.

"Well, well," replied Rassi, with the most perfect calmness, "it is only some clerk's mistake, after all. The matter is prescribed by law. It ought to have been done the very morning after Del Dongo was sent to the citadel. The zealous clerk thought he had forgotten something, and got my signature to the letter as a mere matter of form."

"And you think you will get me to believe such clumsy lies as these!" shouted the prince, in a rage. "Why can't you say honestly that you've sold yourself to that scamp Mosca, and that he has given you your decoration for doing it? But, by my soul, a thrashing shall not finish the job for you. I'll have you tried, and you shall be dismissed in disgrace."

"I defy you to have me tried," answered Rassi boldly. He knew this to be a sure means of quieting the prince. "The law is on my side, and you've no second Rassi who will know how to elude it. You will not dismiss me, because at certain moments your nature grows severe, and then you thirst for blood, while at the same time you desire to retain the esteem of all reasonable Italians, because that esteem is essential to your ambition. At all events, you'll recall me the first time your temper makes you hanker after some severe sentence, and, as usual, I shall provide you with a correct verdict, found by fairly honest judges, to satisfy your spite. Try and find another man in your dominions as useful to you as I."

This said, Rassi took to flight. He had escaped with one hearty blow from a ruler and five or six kicks. He left the palace and departed straight to his country house at Riva. He was rather afraid of a dagger thrust while the prince was in his first fury. Still he was quite sure that before a fortnight was out a courier would be sent to recall him to the capital. He devoted the time he spent in the country to organizing a safe means of correspondence with Count Mosca; he was desperately in love with the title of baron, and thought the prince had too high an opinion of that whilom sublime dignity known as "noble rank" to allow of his ever conferring it upon him; whereas the count, who was very proud of his own birth, thought nothing of any nobility that could not show proofs of its existence before the year 1400.

The Chartreuse of Parma

The Chief Justice had not been mistaken in his forecast;
he had hardly been a week in his country house before one
of the prince's friends paid him a chance visit, and advised
him to return to Parma without delay. The prince gave
him a smiling reception, but presently he turned very grave,
and made him swear on the Gospels that he would keep
what he was about to confide to him secret. Rassi swore in
the most solemn manner, and the prince, his eyes blazing
with hatred, exclaimed that so long as Fabrizio del Dongo
was alive he should never be master in his own house,
adding:

"I can neither drive the duchess out, nor endure her
presence. Her looks defy me, and half kill me."

After Rassi had allowed the prince to explain himself
at great length, he pretended to be greatly puzzled himself,
and then—

"Your Highness shall be obeyed, no doubt," cried he.
" But it is a horribly difficult business. There are no
grounds for condemning a Del Dongo to death for having
killed a Giletti. It is an astonishing feat, already, to have
given him twelve years in a fortress for it, and besides, I
have reason to suspect the duchess has laid her hand on
three of the peasants who were working at the Sanguigna
excavations, and were outside the ditch when that villain
Giletti attacked Del Dongo."

"And where are these witnesses?" cried the prince
angrily.

"Hidden in Piedmont, I suppose. Now, we should want
a conspiracy against your Highness's life."

"That plan has its dangerous side," said the prince. " It
stirs up the idea."

"Well, but," said Rassi, with an air of innocence, " there
you have the whole of my official arsenal."

"We still have poison."

"But who would give it? That idiot of a Conti?"

"Well, according to all we have heard, it would not be
his first attempt."

"He would have to be in a rage himself," replied Rassi,
" and besides, when he got rid of the captain, he was not

thirty years old, and he was desperately in love and far less of a coward than he is now. Reasons of state must, no doubt, override every other, but, taken at a disadvantage, as I am now, and at the first glance, the only person I can think of to carry out the sovereign's orders is a man of the name of Barbone, the jail clerk in the fortress, whom Del Dongo knocked down the first day he was there."

Once the prince was set at his ease, the conversation was endless; he closed it by giving his chief justice a month's law. Rassi had begged for two. The next morning he received a secret gratuity of a thousand sequins. He thought the matter over for three days. On the fourth he came back to his original argument, which seemed to him quite evident. "Count Mosca is the only person who will be inclined to keep his word to me, because in making me a baron he gives me something he does not value himself. *Secondo*, if I warn him, I probably save myself from committing a crime the full price of which I have pretty nearly received in advance. *Tertio*, I avenge myself for the first humiliating blows bestowed on the Cavaliere Rassi." The following night, he acquainted Count Mosca with the whole of his conversation with the prince.

The count was still paying his court to the duchess in secret. It is true that he did not see her more than once or twice a month in her own house, but almost every week, and whenever he could contrive any opportunity for speaking to her about Fabrizio, the duchess, attended by Cecchina, came, late in the evening, and spent a few minutes in the count's garden. She contrived to deceive even her coachman, who was devoted to her, and who believed her to be paying a visit in a neighbouring house.

My readers will easily imagine that the moment the count had received the Chief Justice's hideous communication he made the signal agreed on with the duchess. Though it was midnight, she sent Cecchina to beg him to come to her at once. The count, as delighted as any young lover by this appearance of intimacy, hesitated to tell the duchess the whole story. He feared he might see her go wild with grief. Yet, after having cast about for equivocations which might mitigate the fatal announcement, he ended by revealing the whole truth. He was not capable of keeping back any secret she begged him to tell her. But nine months of excessive misfortune had greatly altered her passionate soul; her nature was strengthened, and the duchess did not break out into sobs or lamentations. The next evening she caused the signal of imminent danger to be made to Fabrizio:

> *" The castle is on fire."*

He answered quite clearly:

> *" Are my books burned? "*

That same night, she had the happiness of sending him a letter inside a leaden ball. A week after that day came the wedding of the Marchese Crescenzi's sister, at which the duchess was guilty of a desperate piece of imprudence, which shall be duly related in its place.

CHAPTER XXI

ABOUT a year before the period of her misfortunes, the duchess had made acquaintance with a strange being. One day, when, as they say in that country, " *aveva la luna,*" she had betaken herself, quite unexpectedly, toward evening, to her country house on the hill overlooking the Po, at Sacca, beyond Colorno. She delighted in making improvements in the place; she loved the huge forest that crowns the hill and grows close up to the house. She was having paths cut through it to various picturesque spots.

" You'll be carried off by brigands, fair lady," said the prince to her one day. " A forest where you are known to walk can not possibly remain deserted." The prince cast an eye on the count, whose jealousy he was always trying to kindle.

" I have no fears, Most Serene Highness," replied the duchess, with an air of innocence. " When I walk about in my woods, I reassure myself with the thought that I have never done any one any harm; therefore, who should there be to hate me ? " The remark struck the hearers as a bold one; it recalled the insulting language employed by the Liberals of the country, a most impudent set of people.

On the day of which we speak, the duchess was reminded of the prince's remark by the sight of a very poorly dressed man, who was following her, at a distance, through the trees. In the course of her walk she made an unexpected turn, which brought her so close to the stranger that she was frightened. Her first impulse was to call to her game-keeper, whom she had left about a thousand paces off, in the flower-garden, close to the house. But the stranger had time to approach her, and cast himself at her feet. He was young, very handsome, miserably clad—there were rents a foot long in his garments—but his eyes blazed with the fire of an ardent soul.

"I am condemned to death; I am Dr. Ferrante Palla; I am starving, and so are my five children."

The duchess had noticed that he was frightfully thin, but his eyes were so beautiful, and their expression at once so fervent and so tender, that any idea of crime never occurred to her. "Pallagi," thought she to herself, "should have given such eyes to the St. John in the Desert he has just placed in the cathedral." The thought of St. John had been suggested by Ferrante's incredible thinness. The duchess gave him the only three sequins she had in her purse, apologizing for the smallness of the gift, on the score that she had just paid her gardener's account. Ferrante thanked her fervently. "Alas!" he said, "in old days I lived in cities; I saw beautiful women. Since I have been condemned to death for performing my duties as a citizen I have dwelt in the woods, and I was following you, just now, not to rob you, nor to ask for alms, but, like some savage, fascinated by a dainty beauty. It is long since I have seen two fair white hands."

"But pray rise," said the duchess, for he was still kneeling.

"Let me stay where I am," answered Ferrante. "The position makes me realize I am not stealing at this moment, and that thought calms me. For you must know that since I have been prevented from following my profession, I have lived by theft. But at this moment I am only a humble mortal adoring a sublime beauty." The duchess realized that the man was a little mad, but she was not frightened, she read the poor fellow's fervent and kindly soul in his eyes, and besides, she was not at all averse to people of extraordinary appearance.

"I am a doctor, then, and I made love to the wife of Sarasine, the apothecary at Parma. He discovered us, and drove her out, with three children whom he suspected, and justly, to be mine, and not his own. She has borne me two more since then. The mother and her five children live in the deepest poverty about a league from here, in a sort of hut in the wood, which I built with my own hands. For I must keep out of the gendarmes' way, and the poor woman will not be parted from me. I was condemned to death, and very justly, too, for I was a conspirator; I loathe the prince, who is a tyrant. I could not take to flight, for I had no money. But my misfortunes have grown far greater now, and if I had killed myself it would have been better for me, a thousand times. I have no love, now, for the unhappy woman who has borne me these five children, and sacrificed everything for me. I love another. But if I kill myself, the five children and the mother must literally die of hunger." There was truth in the man's voice.

"But how do you live?" exclaimed the duchess, greatly affected.

"The children's mother spins; the eldest girl is fed by a farmer of Liberal opinions, whose sheep she tends. As for me, I rob on the highway between Piacenza and Genoa."

"How can you reconcile robbery with your Liberal principles?"

"I keep note of the people whom I rob, and if ever I have anything of my own, I will return the sums I have stolen from them. I reckon that a tribune of the people, such as I, performs a work, considering its danger, well worth a hundred francs a month, and I take care not to steal more than twelve hundred francs a year. But I am mistaken; I steal a little more than that, and the overplus enables me to pay for the printing of my works."

"What works?"

"Will the —— ever have a chamber and a budget?"

"What!" cried the duchess in astonishment. "Then you, sir, are one of the most famous poets of our century, the renowned Ferrante Palla!"

"Renowned, that may be; but most unhappy, that is sure."

"And a man of such powers, sir, is forced to live by theft!"

"Perhaps that is the very reason why I have some talent. Up till now all our best-known authors have been paid either by the government or by the faith they were endeavouring to undermine. Now, in my case, first of all, I carry my life in my hand, and secondly, consider, madam, the thoughts that stir within me when I set out to rob! 'Am I doing right?' I say to myself. 'Are my services as a tribune really worth a hundred francs a month?' I've two shirts, the coat you see upon me, some poor weapons, and I shall certainly end by being hanged. I venture to think I am disinterested. I should be happy, but for the fatal love which prevents my finding anything but misery in the company of the mother of my children. The ugliness of my poverty is what makes me suffer. I love rich dresses, white hands"—and he began to look at the duchess's hands in a way that frightened her.

"Farewell, sir," she said. "Can I serve you in any matter at Parma?"

"Give a thought, sometimes, to this question: His profession is to stir men's hearts, and prevent them from falling asleep in that false and utterly material happiness which monarchies bestow. Is the service he renders his fellow-citizens worth a hundred francs a month?—My misfortune," he added very gently, "is that I love. For nearly two years you have filled all my soul, but until this day I had looked at you without causing you any fear," and he took to flight with a rapidity so prodigious that it both astonished and reassured the duchess. "The gendarmes would find it difficult to catch him," she thought. "He certainly is mad."

"He is mad," her servants told her. "We have all known for ever so long that the poor man is desperately in love with the signora. When she is here, we see him wandering about in the upper parts of the wood, and as soon as she is gone he never fails to come down and sit wherever she has stopped. He carefully picks up any flowers which may have fallen from her nosegay, and carries them about for a long time, fastened to his shabby hat."

"And you never told me of these follies?" said the duchess, almost reproachfully.

"We were afraid the Signora Duchessa might tell Count Mosca. Poor Ferrante is such a good fellow, he never does any one any harm, and because he loves our Napoleon, he has been condemned to death."

Not a word did she say to the minister about this meeting, and as it was the first secret she had kept from him for over four years, she found herself stopped short in the middle of a sentence at least ten times over. When she went back to Sacca she brought gold with her, but Ferrante did not appear. A fortnight later she went again. Ferrante, after having followed her for some time, bounding along in the wood about a hundred paces from her, bore down upon her as swiftly as a sparrow-hawk and cast himself at her knees, as on the first occasion.

" Where were you a fortnight ago? "

" In the mountains beyond Novi, robbing some muleteers on their way back from Milan, where they had been selling oil."

" Accept this purse."

Ferrante opened the purse, took out a single sequin, which he kissed and thrust into his bosom, and then gave the purse back to her.

" You give me back this purse—you, who are a robber! "

" No doubt about that. My rule is that I must never have more than a hundred francs. Now, at this moment, the mother of my children has eighty francs and I have twenty-five; I am out of my reckoning by five francs, and if I were to be hanged at this moment I should be stung by remorse. I have taken one sequin, because it comes from you, and I love you! "

The tone in which these simple words were spoken was perfect. " He really does love! " thought the duchess to herself.

That day he seemed quite off his balance. He said there were some people at Parma who owed him six hundred francs, and with that sum he would repair his hut, in which his poor children were now constantly catching cold.

" But I will advance the six hundred francs to you," exclaimed the duchess, greatly moved.

" But, then, would not my political opponents slander me, and say that I, a public man, am selling myself? "

The Chartreuse of Parma

The duchess, deeply touched, offered to conceal him at Parma if he would swear to her that for the moment he would not exercise his functions in the town, and above all that he would not carry out any of the death sentences which he declared he had *in petto*.

"And if I am hanged as the result of my imprudence," said Ferrante seriously, "all those wretches who do the people so much harm will live for years and years, and whose fault will that be? What would my father say to me when I meet him up yonder?"

The duchess talked to him a great deal about his little children, who would very likely die of the damp. At last he accepted her offer of a hiding-place in Parma.

During the one and only half-day which the Duke Sanseverina had spent at Parma after his marriage, he had shown the duchess a very curious secret chamber in the southern corner of the palace which bore his name. The outer wall, which dates from the middle ages, is eight feet thick. It has been hollowed out within, and a chamber has been thus formed, some twenty feet high, and only two wide. Just beside it is that much-admired "reservoir," quoted by all travellers—a famous piece of twelfth-century work, erected during the siege of Parma by the Emperor Sigismund, and included, at a later period, within the inclosure of the Palazzo Sanseverina.

To enter the hiding-place, a huge block of stone, set toward its centre on an iron pivot, must be swung aside. So deeply touched was the duchess by Ferrante's condition of madness and the melancholy fate of his children, for whom he obstinately refused to accept any gift of value, that for some considerable time she allowed him to make use of this chamber. About a month later she saw him again, still in the woods at Sacca, and, being a trifle calmer on that occasion, he recited one of his sonnets, which struck her as being equal, if not superior, to all the finest things produced in Italy during the two previous centuries. Ferrante was granted several interviews. But his passion grew more ardent and importunate, and the duchess perceived that it was following the laws of every love which is allowed the smallest oppor-

tunity for conceiving a gleam of hope. She sent him back
to his woods, and forbade him to speak to her. He obeyed
her instantly, with the most perfect gentleness.

Thus matters stood when Fabrizio was arrested. Three
days afterward, just at nightfall, a Capuchin friar knocked at
the door of the Palazzo Sanseverina. He had, he said, an
important secret, which he desired to communicate to the
mistress of the mansion. She was so wretched that she admitted him to her presence. It was Ferrante. "A fresh
iniquity is taking place here—one with which the tribune of
the people must concern himself. Moreover, as a private
individual, all I have to give the Duchess Sanseverina is my
life, and that I offer her."

This heartfelt devotion on the part of a thief and a madman touched the duchess deeply. For a long time she conversed with this man, held to be the greatest poet of northern
Italy, and she shed many tears. "This man understands my
heart," said she to herself. The next day, at the Ave Maria,
he reappeared, disguised as a liveried servant.

"I have not left Parma. I have heard a horrible thing
which my lips shall never repeat—but here I am. Consider,
madam, what it is that you refuse! The being you see before you is no court puppet, but a man." He knelt as he
spoke the words, as though to increase their weight, and
added: "Yesterday I said to myself, 'She wept in my presence, therefore she is a thought less wretched!'"

"But, sir, think of the risks you are running. You will
be arrested in this city."

"The tribune, madam, will reply, 'What is life when
duty calls?' The unhappy man whose penance it is that he
feels no passion for virtue since he has been consumed by
love, will add: 'Madam, Fabrizio, a brave-hearted man, is
perhaps about to perish. Do not drive away another brave
man who offers you his service. Here you have a frame of
steel and a heart that fears nothing in the world save your
displeasure!'"

"If you mention your feelings to me again, I will close
my doors to you forever."

It did occur to the duchess, that evening, to tell Ferrante she would provide a small income for his children. But she was afraid he might go out from her presence and destroy himself.

Hardly had he left her, when, haunted as she was by gloomy forebodings, she began to muse. " I, too, may die—would to God it might be so, and soon! If I could only find a man worthy of the name, to whom I might confide my poor Fabrizio ! "

An idea flashed across the duchess. She took a sheet of paper, and in a document into which she introduced all the few law terms with which she was acquainted, she acknowledged that she had received the sum of twenty thousand francs from Signor Ferrante Palla, on the express condition that she should pay a yearly pension of fifteen hundred francs to Signora Sarasine and her five children. The duchess added : " I further leave a yearly income of three hundred francs to each of her five children, on condition that Ferrante Palla shall professionally attend my nephew Fabrizio del Dongo, and be as a brother to him—I implore him to do this ! " She signed the paper, antedated it by a year, and put it away.

Two days later Ferrante reappeared. It was just at the moment when the whole town was stirred by reports of Fabrizio's approaching execution. Was this gloomy ceremony to take place within the citadel, or under the tree in the public square? Many men of the humbler classes walked up and down in front of the citadel gates that evening, to try and see whether the scaffold was being built. This sight had moved Ferrante. He found the duchess dissolved in tears, and quite unable to speak. She greeted him with her hand, and pointed him to a seat. Ferrante, who was disguised, that day, as a Capuchin friar, behaved magnificently. Instead of seating himself, he knelt down, and began to pray devoutly in an undertone. Seizing a moment when the duchess was a little calmer, and without changing his position, he broke off his prayer for an instant, with the words : " Once again he offers his life."

" Consider what you say," exclaimed the duchess, and in her eye there was that wild look which follows upon tears, and warns us that rage is getting the better of emotion.

"He offers his life to place an obstacle in the way of Fabrizio's fate, or to avenge it."

"There is a circumstance," replied the duchess, "in which I might accept the sacrifice of your life."

She was looking at him, closely and sternly. A flash of joy shone in his eyes; he rose swiftly to his feet and stretched out his arms toward heaven. The duchess fetched a document hidden in a secret drawer in her walnut-wood cabinet. "Read it," said she to Ferrante. It was the gift in his children's favour, of which we have just spoken.

Tears and sobs prevented Ferrante from reading to the end; he fell on his knees.

"Give me back that paper," said the duchess, and she burned it at the taper before his eyes.

"My name must not appear if you are taken and executed," she added, "for this matter affects your very life."

"It is a joy to me to die by injuring the tyrant; it is a much greater joy to die for you. Now that is said, and clearly understood, do me the kindness not to speak of money again. It gives me a painful feeling that you may doubt me."

"If you are compromised I may be so too," replied the duchess, "and Fabrizio after me. For that reason, and not at all because I doubt your courage, I insist that the man who will pierce my heart shall be poisoned, and not stabbed. For the same reason, a most important one to me, I command you to do everything in the world to save yourself."

"I will perform all—faithfully, punctually, and prudently. I foresee, madam, that my vengeance will be bound up with yours. Even if it were otherwise, I would still obey—faithfully, punctually, and prudently. I may not succeed, but I will strive with all the strength a man can use."

"Fabrizio's murderer must be poisoned."

"I had guessed it; and during the seven-and-twenty months of this wandering and hateful life of mine, I have often thought of committing such an action on my own account."

"If I am detected and condemned as your accomplice," continued the duchess, and there was pride in her voice, "I do not choose to have it imputed to me that I have tempted you. I command you to make no attempt to see me before the moment of our vengeance. There is to be no question of his being put to death until I give you the signal. At this moment, for instance, his death, far from being a service, would be a misfortune to me. His death will probably not have to take place for several months, but it will take place! I insist that he shall die by poison, and I would rather let him live on than see him killed by a bullet. For reasons which I do not choose to explain, I insist that your life shall be saved."

The tone of authority the duchess used to him filled Ferrante with delight. A mighty joy shone in his eyes. As we have said, he was frightfully thin, but it was easy to see that he had been exceedingly handsome in his early youth, and he fancied he still was what he had been in former days. "Am I mad?" he thought, "or does the duchess intend, some day, when I shall have given her this proof of my devotion, to make me the happiest of all living men? And why not, after all? Am I not quite as good as that puppet Mosca, who has not been able to do anything for her in her need—not even to help Monsignore Fabrizio to escape?"

"I may desire his death even to-morrow," continued the duchess, still in the same authoritative tone. "You know that huge reservoir of water, at the corner of the palace, close by the hiding-place you have occasionally occupied? There are secret means whereby all that water can be turned into the street. Well, that shall be the signal for my vengeance. If you are at Parma you will see, if you are living in your woods you will hear, that the great reservoir at the Sanseverina Palace has burst. Act then, at once! But use poison, and, above all things, risk your own life as little as may be. Let no one ever know that I have had a finger in the matter."

"Words are useless," replied Ferrante, with ill-restrained enthusiasm. "I have already decided on the means I shall employ. That man's life becomes more odious to me than before, since as long as he lives I shall not dare to look on you again. I shall await the signal of the reservoir bursting on to the street." He bowed swiftly, and went out. The duchess watched him go.

When he had reached the next apartment she called him back. " Ferrante," she cried, " noble fellow ! "

He returned, as though impatient at being delayed; at that moment there was something magnificent about his face.

" And your children? "

" Madam, they will be richer than I. You will perhaps grant them some trifling income."

" Here," said the duchess, holding out a sort of large olive-wood case, " here are all the diamonds I have left. They are worth fifty thousand francs."

" Ah, madam, you humiliate me," exclaimed Ferrante, with a horrified gesture, and his whole countenance changed.

" I shall never see you again before the thing is done. Take this, I desire it," added the duchess, with a haughty expression which crushed Ferrante. He slipped the case into his pocket and retired.

He had closed the door behind him when the duchess called him back, and he returned, wearing an anxious expression. The duchess was standing in the middle of the drawing-room. She threw herself into his arms. After a moment Ferrante almost fainted from sheer happiness. The duchess freed herself from his embrace, and glanced meaningly at the door.

" This is the only man who has ever understood me," said the duchess to herself. " Fabrizio would have behaved like that if he could have understood me."

The duchess possessed two special characteristics. What she had desired once she desired always, and she never deliberated a second time concerning anything she had once decided. In this last connection she would quote a remark made by her first husband, the kind-hearted General Pietranera. " What an insolence to my own self! Why should I think I am cleverer to-day than I was when I made the decision? "

From that moment a sort of cheerfulness reappeared in

the duchess's temper. Before that fatal resolution was taken, at every step her mind took, at every new point she noticed, she had felt her own inferiority to the prince, her weakness, and the vile fashion in which she had been tricked. The prince, as she held, had shamefully deceived her, and Count Mosca, as the result of his courtier-like instinct, had, though innocently, seconded the prince's efforts. Once vengeance was decided on, she felt her own strength, and every fresh working of her mind brought her happiness. I am rather disposed to think that the immoral delight the Italian nature finds in vengeance is connected with the strength of the national imagination. The natives of other countries do not, strictly speaking, forgive—they forget.

The duchess did not see Palla again till toward the end of Fabrizio's prison days. He it was, as my readers may perhaps have guessed, who suggested the idea of the escape. In the woods, about two leagues from Sacca, stood a half-ruined tower, dating from the middle ages, and over a hundred feet high. Before mentioning the idea of flight a second time to the duchess, Ferrante besought her to send Ludovico with some trusty men, to set a succession of ladders against this tower. In the presence of the duchess he climbed to the top by the ladders, and came down simply on a knotted rope. Three times over he made the experiment, and then set forth his notion again. A week afterward Ludovico also came down from the top of the tower on a knotted rope. Then it was that the duchess suggested the idea to Fabrizio.

During the last days before the attempt, which might possibly, and that in more than one fashion, result in the prisoner's death, the duchess never knew an instant's repose, except when Ferrante was with her. The man's courage stirred her own, but it will be easily understood that she felt obliged to hide this strange connection from the count. She was not afraid of his being horrified by it, but she would have been worried by his objections, which would have doubled her own anxiety. "What! choose an acknowledged madman, sentenced to death, to be her closest counsellor!" "And," the duchess would add, talking to herself, "a man capable, in the future, of doing such strange things!" Ferrante was in the duchess's drawing-room when the count entered it to inform her of the prince's conversation with Rassi. She had much ado, after the count's departure, in preventing Ferrante from proceeding instantly to the execution of his terrible project.

"I am strong now," cried the crazy fellow. "I have no doubt at all as to the legitimacy of my action."

"But in the moment of rage which must inevitably follow, Fabrizio would be put to death."

"Well, then he would be spared the danger of his descent. It is possible, it is even easy," he added, "but the young man has had no practice."

The marriage of the Marchese Crescenzi's sister was duly celebrated, and at the *fête* given on that occasion, the duchess was able to meet Clelia, and talk to her, without rousing the suspicions of well-bred lookers-on. In the garden, whither the two ladies had betaken themselves to get a moment's breath of air, the duchess herself gave Clelia the packet of ropes.

These ropes, most carefully made of hemp and wool mixed, and knotted, were very slight, and fairly flexible. Ludovico had tested their strength, and every yard of them would safely carry eight hundredweight. They had been compressed into several packets, exactly resembling quarto volumes. Clelia took possession of them, and promised the duchess she would do everything that was humanly possible to get them into the Farnese Tower.

"But your natural timidity alarms me; and besides," added the duchess politely, "what interest can you feel in a man you do not know?"

"Monsignore del Dongo is unfortunate, and I promise you *that he shall be saved by me.*"

But the duchess, who had no particular confidence in the presence of mind of a young lady of twenty, had taken other precautions, which she took care not to reveal to the governor's daughter. As may naturally be supposed, the said governor was present at the festivities in honour of the marriage of the Marchese Crescenzi's sister. The duchess said to herself that if she could give him a strong narcotic, it might be concluded, on the first blush, that he had been seized with a fit of apoplexy, and then, instead of putting him into his carriage to take him back to the citadel, she might, by dint of some little cunning, contrive to have him carried in a litter, which should chance to be in the house in which the guests were assembled. There, too, should be found intelligent men, dressed as workmen employed about the festivities, who, in the general confusion, should obligingly offer themselves to carry the sick man up to his palace on the height. These men, headed by Ludovico, carried a considerable quantity of rope, skilfully concealed about their persons. It will be observed that since she had been seriously considering the subject of Fabrizio's flight, the duchess had quite lost her head. The peril in which that beloved being stood was more than she could bear, and above all, it had lasted too long. By the very excess of her precautions, as we shall see, she almost brought about the failure of his escape. Everything was carried out as she had planned, with this single exception—that the effect of the narcotic was far too powerful. Every one, even professional men, believed the general had an attack of apoplexy.

Fortunately Clelia, in her despair, never for a moment suspected the duchess's criminal attempt. So great was the confusion, when the litter in which the general lay half dead was borne into the citadel, that no objection was made to the entrance of Ludovico and his men, and they were only subjected to a purely formal search on the " Bridge of the Slave." When they had carried the general to his bed, they were taken to the servants' quarters, and hospitably entertained. But after the meal, which did not end till toward morning, they were informed that according to the rules of the prison, they must be locked up for the remainder of the night in one of the lower rooms of the palace. After daylight the next morning they would be set at liberty by the governor's lieutenant.

The men had contrived to convey the ropes they had been carrying to Ludovico. But Ludovico found great difficulty in attracting Clelia's attention for a moment. At last, as she was passing out of one room into another, he made her see that he was laying the packets of rope in a dark corner in one of the drawing-rooms on the first floor. Clelia was profoundly impressed by this strange incident, and horrible suspicions at once started up in her mind.

" Who are you? " said she to Ludovico, and when he gave her a very ambiguous answer she added:

" I ought to have you arrested. Either you or those employing you have poisoned my father. . . . Tell me, this instant, what poison you have used, so that the doctor of the citadel may give him the proper remedies! Confess instantly, or else neither you nor your accomplices shall ever leave this citadel again."

" The signora does wrong to be alarmed," replied Ludovico, with the most perfect grace and civility. " There is no question of poison at all. Some one has imprudently given the general a dose of laudanum, and the servant commissioned to commit this crime has apparently put a few drops too many into the glass. This will cause us eternal remorse. But the signora may rest assured that—thank Heaven for it!—there is no danger of any sort. The governor must be treated for having taken an overdose of laudanum by mistake. But I have the honour of assuring the signorina, once more, that the footman employed about the crime used no real poisons, such as those used by Barbone when he tried to make away with Monsignore Fabrizio. There has been no attempt to avenge the danger run by Monsignore Fabrizio; all the clumsy footman was given was a flask of laudanum. I swear that to the signorina on my oath. But of course she understands that if I were cross-questioned officially I should deny everything. Besides, if the signorina were to speak to any one, even to the good Don Cesare, either of laudanum or of poison, Fabrizio would be slain by the signorina's own hand. She would make any attempt at flight impossible, and the signorina knows, better than I, that the people who desire to poison Monsignore will not use laudanum only, and she knows, too, that a certain person has only granted one month's grace, and that more than one week has already passed by since the fatal order was received. Therefore, if she has me arrested, or if she even says a single word to Don Cesare, or any other person, she will throw back all our undertakings for much more than a month, and I speak the truth when I say that she will be killing Monsignore Fabrizio with her own hand."

Clelia was terrified by the strange calm with which Ludovico spoke.

"So here I am," she thought, "in close conversation with a man who has poisoned my father, and who addresses me with the utmost politeness; and it is love which has led me into all these crimes!"

So great was her remorse that she had hardly strength to speak. She said to Ludovico:

"I am going to lock you up in this room. I must run and tell the doctor that the illness is caused by laudanum. But, great heavens! how am I to tell him that I have found it out myself! Then I will come back and release you. But," said Clelia, hurrying back from the door, "did Fabrizio know anything about this laudanum?"

"No, indeed, signorina. He never would have consented. And besides, what was the good of confiding in an unnecessary person? We act with the strictest caution; our object is to save Monsignore Fabrizio, who will be poisoned within three weeks. The order has been given by a person whose will meets, as a rule, with no obstacles. But if the signorina must know all, it is believed that the duty has been confided to the terrible Chief-Justice Rassi!"

Clelia fled in horror. She had such confidence in Don Cesare's perfect uprightness that she ventured to tell him, with a certain amount of reticence, that the general had been given laudanum, and nothing more. Without replying, without asking a question, Don Cesare hastened to the doctor.

Clelia returned to the drawing-room into which she had locked Ludovico, intending to ply him with questions concerning the laudanum. She did not find him there; he had contrived to escape. Lying on a table, she perceived a purse of sequins and a little box containing several sorts of poisons. The sight of the poison made her shudder. "How can I be sure," she thought, "that nothing but laudanum has been administered to my father, and that the duchess has not tried to avenge herself for the attempt made by Barbone?

"Great God!" she exclaimed, "I am holding intercourse with my father's poisoners, and I have allowed them to escape. And perhaps, if that man had been closely questioned, he would have confessed to something more than laudanum."

Bursting into tears, Clelia instantly fell upon her knees, and prayed fervently to the Madonna.

Meanwhile the doctor of the citadel, greatly astonished by the information conveyed to him by Don Cesare, according to which laudanum was the cause of all the trouble, administered suitable remedies, which soon removed the most alarming symptoms. At daybreak the general came to his senses a little. His first act on returning to consciousness was to pour volleys of abuse on the colonel, his second in command of the citadel, who had ventured, while the general lay unconscious, to give a few orders of the most simple description.

The governor then flew into a violent rage with a kitchen maid who had brought him a bowl of broth, and who ventured to pronounce the word "apoplexy."

"Is a man of my age," he exclaimed, "likely to have an apoplexy? Only my bitterest enemies could possibly take pleasure in putting such a story about. Besides, have I been bled, so as to give even slanderers a right to talk about apoplexy?"

Fabrizio, deep in preparations for his own departure, could not conceive the meaning of the strange noises that filled the citadel when the governor was carried back to it half dead. At first he fancied his sentence had been altered, and that he was about to be put to death. Then, when nobody appeared in his room, he concluded that Clelia had been betrayed, that the ropes which she had probably been conveying back into the fortress had been taken from her, and that, in fact, all the plans for his escape had been rendered impossible. At dawn the following morning he saw

an unknown man enter his room, and, without uttering **a** word, set down a basket of fruit. Under the fruit was hidden **a** letter, couched in the following terms:

" Filled with the bitterest remorse for what has been done—not, thank Heaven, by my consent, but in consequence of an idea of mine—I have made a vow to the Most Holy Virgin that if, by her blessed intercession, my father's life is saved, I will never again refuse to obey an order of his. I shall marry the marchese as soon as he requires me to do it, and I shall never see you again.

" Nevertheless, I believe it to be my duty to carry through that which has been begun. On Sunday next, when you come back from mass, to which you will be taken at my request—forget not to prepare your soul for death; you may lose your life in your difficult undertaking—when you come back from mass, I say, do all you can to delay the moment when you re-enter your room. There you will find that which is indispensable for your intended enterprise. If you perish it will break my heart! Will you be able **to** accuse me of having had a hand in your death? Has not the duchess herself told me, over and over again, that the Raversi faction is winning the day? It is bent on binding the prince to it by an act of cruelty which will separate him forever from Count Mosca. The duchess has sworn to me, with tears, that no resource save this remains. If you make no attempt you will certainly perish. I can not look at you again; I have made my vow. But if, toward the evening on Sunday, you see me at the usual window, dressed entirely in black, it will be a sign that on the following night everything will be ready, as far as my feeble powers will permit. After eleven o'clock—perhaps at midnight, or one in the morning—a little lamp will stand in my window. That will be the decisive moment; commend your soul to your patron saint, put on the priestly habit with which you are provided, and depart.

" Farewell, Fabrizio! I shall be at my prayers, and shedding the bitterest tears, you may be sure of that, while you are running these terrible risks. If you perish I shall not survive you—great God, what have I said? But if you succeed, I shall never see your face again. On Sunday, after mass, you will find in your prison the money, the poisons, the ropes sent you by that terrible woman who loves you so passionately, and who has told me, three times over, that this thing must be done. May God and the blessed Madonna preserve you!"

Fabio Conti was a jailer whose soul was always anxious, miserable, wretched, constantly dreaming that some prisoner was escaping from his clutches. He was loathed by every soul in the citadel. But misfortune inspires all men with the same sentiments, and the unhappy prisoners, even those chained up in dungeons three feet high and wide, and eight feet long, in which they could neither stand nor sit upright—all the prisoners, even these, I say, joined in having a Te Deum sung at their expense, when they heard that the governor was out of danger. Two or three of the poor wretches even wrote sonnets in honour of Fabio Conti. Such is the effect of misery upon mankind. Let that man blame them whose fate has condemned him to spend a year in a dungeon three feet high, with eight ounces of bread a day, and fasting on Fridays!

Clelia, who never left her father's room except to say her prayers in the chapel, announced that the governor had decided that the rejoicings were not to take place until the Sunday. On that Sunday morning, Fabrizio was present at the mass and the Te Deum. In the evening there were fireworks, and the soldiers in the lower halls of the castle received wine, four times as much as the quantity authorized by the governor. Some unknown person had even sent in several barrels of brandy, which the soldiers broached. The soldiers who were drinking themselves drunk were too good-natured to allow their five comrades, who were doing sentry duty on the palace, to suffer from that fact. As fast as they reached their sentry-boxes a trusty servant gave them wine. Further, some unknown hand provided those on duty from midnight onward with a glass of brandy, and (as was ultimately proved at the trial) at each glass the brandy bottle was forgotten in the sentry-box.

The merry-making lasted longer than Clelia had expected, and it was not till toward one o'clock that Fabrizio, who, more than a week previously, had sawn through the bars of the window which did not look toward the aviary, began to take down the wooden screen. He was working almost over the heads of the sentries on the governor's palace, but they heard nothing. All he had done to the immensely long rope necessary for carrying him down the terrible descent of a hundred and eighty feet was to make a few fresh knots. He had slung this line over his shoulder; it was very much in his way, on account of its bulk; the knots prevented it from falling together, and it stood out more than eighteen inches from his body. "This will be my great difficulty," said Fabrizio to himself.

Having arranged this rope as best he could, Fabrizio took the length which he intended should carry him down the thirty-five feet between his window and the terrace on which the governor's palace stood. But seeing he could hardly, drunk though the sentinels were, come down on the very tops of their heads, he got out, as we have already said, by the second window of his room, which looked on to the roof of a sort of huge guard-room. Some sick whim of General Fabio Conti's had filled this old guard-room, which had not been used for a century, with a couple of hundred soldiers, whom he ordered up as soon as he could speak. He declared that the people who had tried to poison him would murder him in his bed, and that these two hundred soldiers must protect him. The effect of this unexpected measure on Clelia's feelings may be imagined. The pious-hearted girl was very deeply conscious of the extent to which she was deceiving her father, and a father who had just been very nearly poisoned in the interests of the prisoner whom she loved. The unexpected advent of these two hundred men almost struck her as a decree of Providence, forbidding her to go forward, and restore Fabrizio to liberty.

But the prisoner's approaching death was the universal topic of conversation in Parma. Even at the festivities in honour of the marriage of Signorina Julia Crescenzi, the melancholy subject had been discussed. Since a man of Fabrizio's birth, imprisoned for such a trifle as an unlucky sword thrust given to an actor, was not set at liberty after nine months' detention, although he was favoured by the Prime Minister, there must be something political about his story. That being so, it was said, there was no use in thinking more about it. If it did not suit the authorities to put him to death in the public square, he would soon die of sickness.

A locksmith who had been sent for to do some work in General Fabio Conti's palace referred to Fabrizio as a prisoner who had been put to death long since, and whose death was concealed for reasons of policy. When Clelia heard that man speak, she made up her mind.

CHAPTER XXII

In the course of that day Fabrizio was assailed, several times over, by certain serious and disagreeable reflections. But as he heard the hours strike, each one of which brought him nearer to the moment of action, he felt himself grow brisk and cheerful. The duchess had written to him that the fresh air was sure to overcome him, and that he would hardly have got outside his prison before he would find it impossible to walk. In that case it would certainly be better to run the risk of being retaken than to throw himself from the top of a wall a hundred and eighty feet high. " If that misfortune overtakes me," said Fabrizio to himself, " I will lie down close to the parapet; I will sleep for an hour, and I will start again. As I have sworn my oath to Clelia, I would rather fall from the top of a rampart, however high, than spend my life considering the taste of every bit of bread I eat. What horrible suffering there must be at the end when a man dies of poison! And Fabio Conti would make no bones about it; he would just give me the arsenic with which he kills the rats in his fortress."

Toward midnight one of those thick white fogs which the Po sometimes casts over its banks rose over the town, and thence to the esplanade and the bastions, in the midst of which stands the great tower of the citadel. Fabrizio thought he perceived that the little acacias round the soldiers' gardens, at the foot of the great wall below, were no longer visible. " This is capital! " thought he to himself.

A little after the stroke of half-past twelve the tiny lamp appeared in the aviary window. Fabrizio was ready; he crossed himself, then he fastened the thin rope which was to carry him down the twenty-five feet between his room and the platform on which the palace stood to his bed. He reached the roof of the guard-room occupied, since the previous night, by the two hundred extra men of whom we have spoken, without any mishap. Unluckily, at that hour —a quarter to one—the soldiers were not yet asleep, and while Fabrizio stepped stealthily over the great curved roof tiles he heard them saying that the devil was on their roof, and that they must try and shoot him with a musket. Some voices declared this wish to be exceedingly impious; others said that if they fired a shot without killing anything the governor would put them all in prison for having alarmed the garrison unnecessarily. All this fine discussion caused Fabrizio to hurry over the roof as quickly as he could, and thus make much more noise than he might have done. As a matter of fact, when he passed, clinging to his rope, in front of the windows, and fortunately for him, owing to the projection of the roof, some four or five feet away from them, they were all bristling with bayonets. Some people have declared that Fabrizio, who was always a wild fellow, took it into his head to play the devil's part, and threw a handful of sequins to the soldiers. He certainly did scatter sequins all over the floor of his room and across the platform, as he passed from the Farnese Tower to the parapet, on the chance of their distracting the attention of the soldiers who might try to pursue him.

Once he had reached the platform, surrounded by sentries, who, as a rule, shouted a complete sentence, " All's well round my post," every quarter of an hour, he moved toward the western parapet, and looked about for the new stone.

What appears incredible, and might induce one to doubt the facts, if their consequences had not been witnessed by a whole city, is that the sentries along the parapet did not catch sight of Fabrizio and lay hands on him. It is true that the fog to which we have referred was beginning to rise, and Fabrizio has related that when he was on the platform the fog seemed to him to have reached half-way up the Farnese Tower. But it was not a thick fog, and he could clearly distinguish the sentries, some of whom were moving about. He used to add that, driven by some supernatural force, he placed himself boldly between two sentries, not very far from each other, and quietly unwound the long rope he was carrying slung round his body, and which got entangled twice over. It took him a long time to disentangle it, and lay it out upon the parapet. He could hear the soldiers talking all round him, and was quite resolved to stab the first who came near him. "I was not in the least agitated," he used to add; "I seemed to myself to be performing some ceremony."

At last he cleared his rope, and fastened it into an opening in the parapet, made for the rain-water to run through. Then he climbed on to the parapet, and prayed earnestly to God. Next, like a hero of the days of chivalry, he thought for an instant of Clelia. "What a different man I am," said he to himself, "from the careless and libertine Fabrizio who came into this place nine months ago!" At last he began to let himself down the tremendous height. He moved mechanically, he said, as he would have done if he had been coming down before friends, in broad daylight, to win a wager. About midway he suddenly felt the strength in his arms fail; he even thinks he lost his grip of the rope for a moment. But he soon grasped it again. Perhaps, he said afterward, he held on to the brambles against which he was slipping and which tore him. Every now and then he felt a most agonizing pain between his shoulders, which almost took away his breath. The undulating motion was most trying; he was constantly being swung away from the rope against the brambles; he was touched by several birds of considerable size, which he disturbed, and which blundered against him as they flew away. He took the first of these for people in pursuit of him, who were descending from the citadel in the same manner, and made ready to defend himself. At last he reached the base of the great tower, unhurt, except that his hands were bleeding. He related that over the lower half of the tower the outward slope of the wall was of great assistance to him. He rubbed against it as he went down, and the plants growing between the stones held him up. When he reached the bottom he fell on an acacia in the sol-

diers' gardens, which, looking at it from above, he had taken
to be four or five feet high, but which really was fifteen or
twenty. A drunken man who was sleeping under it took
him for a robber. When Fabrizio fell out of this tree he
almost put out his left arm. He began to hurry toward the
rampart, but according to his own story his legs seemed
made of wadding; he had no strength left. In spite of the
danger he sat down, and drank a little brandy which still
remained to him. For some minutes he slept, so soundly as
not to remember where he was. When he woke up he
thought he was in his room, and could not understand how
it was he saw trees. At last the awful truth dawned on him.
Instantly he moved toward the rampart, and reached it by a
wide flight of steps. A sentry was snoring in his box close
by. He found a cannon lying in the grass, and fastened his
third rope to it. It was a little too short, and he fell into a
muddy ditch, with about a foot of water in it. Just as he was
getting up, and trying to make out where he was, he felt himself seized by two men; for a moment he was alarmed, but
soon, close to his ear, and in a very low voice, he heard the
words, "Ah, monsignore, monsignore!" He realized dimly
that the men came from the duchess, and instantly he fainted
dead away. A little while after he felt himself being carried
by men who walked swiftly and silently. Then they stopped,
which terrified him very much. But he had no strength
either to speak or to open his eyes. He felt somebody embrace him, and suddenly he recognised the perfume of the
duchess's clothes. That perfume revived him; he was able
to open his eyes and say "Ah, dearest friend!" and then he
fainted again.

The faithful Bruno, with a squad of police officers, all devoted to the count, was waiting two hundred paces off. The
count himself was hiding in a little house close to the spot
where the duchess was waiting. He would not have hesitated, had it been necessary, to draw his sword, assisted by
several half-pay officers, his own intimate friends. He considered himself bound to save Fabrizio's life. He believed
him to be in the most imminent danger, and felt the prince
would have signed his pardon if he (Mosca) had not com-

mitted the folly of endeavouring to save his sovereign from writing another.

Ever since midnight the duchess, surrounded by men armed to the teeth, had been wandering up and down, in dead silence, close to the citadel ramparts. She could not stay quiet for an instant; she expected to have to fight to save Fabrizio from his pursuers. Her fervent imagination had inspired her with a hundred precautions, too long to mention here, and all of them incredibly imprudent. More than eighty persons are calculated to have been on foot that night, expecting to fight on some extraordinary occasion. Fortunately Ferrante and Ludovico were at the head of the business, and the Minister of Police was not hostile. But the count himself remarked that nobody betrayed the duchess, and, in his ministerial capacity, he knew nothing at all.

The duchess utterly lost her head when she saw Fabrizio. First of all she clasped him in her arms, and then, when she saw he was covered with blood, she grew beside herself with alarm. The blood had flowed from Fabrizio's hands, but she thought he was dangerously hurt. Helped by one of her servants, she was taking off his coat, to dress his wounds, when Ludovico, who fortunately was present, insisted on placing the duchess and Fabrizio in one of the little carriages, which had been kept hidden in a garden near the gate of the city, and they started full gallop to get across the Po at Sacca. Ferrante, with twenty well-armed men, formed the rear-guard, and had staked his own life that he would stop all pursuit. The count did not leave the vicinity of the citadel—and then alone and on foot—till two hours later, when he saw that nothing was stirring. "Now," said he, "I am steeped in high treason," and he was half wild with joy.

Ludovico hit upon the excellent idea of putting a young surgeon attached to the duchess's household, and who was very much of Fabrizio's build, into a carriage.

"Fly," said he to him, "toward Bologna! Blunder as much as ever you can, try to get yourself arrested, then refuse to give clear answers, and end by owning that you are Fabrizio del Dongo. Above all things, gain time. Use all your skill to be as stupid as you can. You will get off with a month's imprisonment, and the duchess will give you fifty sequins."

"Does anybody think of money when it's a question of serving the duchess?"

Off he started, and was arrested some hours later, to the deep delight of General Fabio Conti and Rassi, who saw his barony take to itself wings and fly away together with Fabrizio's peril.

It was not till six o'clock in the morning that the escape became known in the citadel, and it was ten before anybody dared tell the prince. So well had the duchess been served, that in spite of Fabrizio's profound slumber, which she took for a dangerous fainting fit, and consequently stopped the carriage three times over, she was crossing the river in a boat as the clock struck four. Relays of horses awaited them on the farther bank; they drove two more leagues very swiftly, then they were stopped for more than an hour to verify their passports. The duchess had passports of every kind, both for herself and Fabrizio, but she was half mad that day; she took it into her head to give ten napoleons to the Austrian police official; she took his hand and burst into tears. The official, very much startled, did all his verification over again. They now took post-horses. The duchess paid so lavishly, that in a country, where every stranger is looked at doubtfully, she aroused universal suspicion. Once more Ludovico came to the rescue; he declared the duchess was mad with grief on account of the long-continued fever of young Count Mosca, the son of the Prime Minister of Parma, whom she was taking to Pavia, to consult the doctors there.

It was not till they were ten leagues beyond the Po that the prisoner thoroughly woke up. One of his shoulders was dislocated, and he was covered with abrasions. The duchess was still behaving in such an extraordinary fashion that the host of the village inn in which they dined thought he had to do with one of the imperial princesses, and would have rendered her the honours he believed to be her due, when Ludovico warned him that the princess would certainly have him thrown into prison if he ventured to have the bells rung.

At last, toward six o'clock in the evening, they reached Piedmontese soil. Not till then was Fabrizio in perfect safety. He was conveyed to a little village, standing off the high-road, his hands were dressed; he slept for a few hours longer.

It was at this village that the duchess indulged in an action which was not only a hateful one from the moral point of view, but the effect of which on the tranquillity of the remainder of her life was grievous in the extreme. Some weeks before Fabrizio's escape, on a day when the whole of Parma had betaken itself to the citadel gates to try and catch sight of the scaffold being erected in the courtyard for his benefit, the duchess had shown Ludovico, who had become her household factotum, the secret whereby one of the stones forming the bottom of the famous reservoir attached to the Palazzo Sanseverina, that work of the thirteenth century to which we have already referred, might be driven out of its skilfully concealed iron bed. While Fabrizio was sleeping soundly in the little village tavern, the duchess sent for Ludovico. So strange were the glances she cast at him that he thought she had lost her reason.

"No doubt you expect me to give you several thousand francs," said she. "Well, I am not going to do that. You are a poet; you would soon have squandered all the money. I shall give you the little property called the Ricciarda, a league from Casal Maggiore." Beside himself with delight, Ludovico cast himself at her feet, protesting, in heartfelt accents, that it was not for the sake of earning money that he had helped to save Monsignore Fabrizio, and that he had always loved him with a special affection since the time when he had been third coachman to the duchess, and had had the honour of driving his carriage. When the man, who really was a faithful-hearted fellow, thought he had sufficiently encroached on this great lady's time, he would have taken his leave, but she, with flashing eyes, said to him, "Stay here!"

She was walking silently up and down the tavern room,

from time to time casting the most extraordinary glances on Ludovico. At last the man, perceiving no apparent end to her strange march, ventured to address his mistress:

"The signora has granted me such an excessive gift, so far beyond anything a poor man like myself could have imagined, and above all so immensely superior to the poor services I have had the honour of doing her, that I think I can not, in all conscience, keep the lands of the Ricciarda. I have the honour to return the property to the signora, and to entreat her to grant me a pension of four hundred francs a year."

"How many times in your life," said she to him, with the gloomiest air of pride, "how many times have you heard it said that I relinquished a plan I had once mentioned?"

Having said these words, the duchess walked up and down again for some minutes, then, stopping suddenly short, she cried:

"It is by accident, and because he won that little girl's favour, that Fabrizio's life has been saved. If he had not made himself charming he would have died; can you deny me that?" she cried, sailing down upon Ludovico, her eyes flashing with the darkest rage. Ludovico stepped several paces backward, and concluded she was certainly mad, a fact which inspired him with serious alarm regarding his ownership of the Ricciarda.

"Well, well," said the duchess, changing suddenly to the gentlest and most cheerful tone, "I desire my good people at Sacca shall have a delightful day—one they shall remember for ages. You shall go back to Sacca. Have you any objection? Do you think you will be in any danger?"

"Very little, signora. Nobody in Sacca will ever let out that I have been in attendance on Monsignore Fabrizio, and besides, if I may venture to say so to the signora, I am longing to see *my* property of the Ricciarda. It seems so comical to me to be a landowner."

"Your pleasure delights me. I think the tenant of the Ricciarda owes me some two or three years of his rent. I make him a present of one half of what he owes me; the other half of all his arrears I give to you, but on this condition: You will go to Sacca, you will say that the day after to-morrow is the *fête* day of one of my patron saints, and the night after your arrival you will have my house illuminated in the most splendid manner. Spare neither money nor pains. Recollect that this has to do with the greatest happiness of my life.

"I have been making ready for this illumination for a long time. For more than three months I have been collecting everything needful for this splendid festivity in the cellars of my house. I have deposited all the fireworks for a magnificent display in the gardener's care. You will have them let off on the terrace facing the Po. There are eighty-nine great hogsheads of wine in my cellars. You will set up eighty-nine fountains running wine in my park. If a single bottle remains undrunk on the following day, I shall say you do not love Fabrizio. When the fountains of wine are running, and the illumination and the fireworks are in full swing, you will slip away cautiously, for it is possible, and that is my hope, that in Parma all these fine doings will be taken as an insult."

"That is not possible only; it is certain. And it is certain, too, that Chief-Justice Rassi, who signed monsignore's sentence, will be bursting with rage. And," added Ludovico somewhat timidly, "if the signora desired to give her poor servant even a greater pleasure than that of receiving half the arrears of the Ricciarda, she would give me leave to play a little joke upon that same Rassi."

"You're a good fellow," exclaimed the duchess, delighted. "But I absolutely forbid you to do anything at all to Rassi. I intend to have him publicly hanged at some future time. As for yourself, try not to get yourself arrested at Sacca; everything would be spoiled if I lost you."

"Me, signora! Once I have said I am keeping the feast of one of the Signora Duchessa's patron saints, you may be sure that if the police sent thirty gendarmes to interfere, not one of them would be on his horse by the time they reached the red cross in the middle of the village. They are not to be trifled with, those Sacca men—first-rate smugglers every one of them, and they worship the signora."

"Well," the duchess began again with a curiously off-hand air, "while I give wine to my good people at Sacca, I want to drench the people of Parma. On the very night when my castle is lighted up, take the best horse in my stables, hurry off to my palace in Parma, and open the reservoir."

"Ah, that's a fine idea of the signora's," cried Ludovico in fits of laughter, "wine for the good folks at Sacca, water for the Parmese townsmen, who had made so certain, the wretches, that monsignore was going to be poisoned like poor L——."

Ludovico could not get over his delight. The duchess watched his ecstasies with evident satisfaction. "Wine for the Sacca men," he kept saying, "water for the Parmese! The signora doubtless knows, better than I do, that twenty years ago, when the reservoir was imprudently emptied, the water ran a foot deep in many of the streets of Parma."

"And water for the Parmese," answered the duchess, laughing. "The square before the citadel would have been crammed with people if Fabrizio's head had been cut off. . . . Everybody calls him the *great culprit.* . . . But above all things, do it cunningly! Let no living being ever know that the inundation was your work, nor done by my order. Fabrizio, even the count himself, must remain in ignorance of this wild joke. . . . But I was forgetting my poor people at Sacca. Go you, and write a letter to my man of business, which I will sign. You will tell him he is to distribute a hundred sequins among the poor of Sacca, in honour of my patron saint, and that he is to take all your orders about the illumination, the fireworks, and the wine. Above all things, be sure there is not one full bottle in my cellars the next morning."

"The signora's steward will only find one difficulty. The signora has owned the castle now for five years, and she has not left ten poor persons in Sacca."

"And water for the Parmese!" quoth the duchess, humming it like a tune. "How shall you carry out my joke?"

The Chartreuse of Parma

"I see my plan quite clearly. I shall start from Sacca at nine o'clock. At half past ten my horse will be at the inn of the Three Blockheads on the road to Casal Maggiore, and *my* property of the Ricciarda. At eleven I shall be in my room at the palace, and at a quarter past the townsfolk of Parma will have water, and more than they want of it, to drink the *great culprit's* health. Ten minutes later I shall go out of the city by the Bologna road; as I pass it by I shall make a deep bow to the citadel on which monsignore's bravery and the signora's wit have just heaped dishonour. I shall take a country path with which I am well acquainted, and so I shall make my way back to the Ricciarda."

Ludovico raised his eyes to the duchess's face, and felt a thrill of terror. She was staring fixedly at the bare wall, six paces from.her, and it must be acknowledged that there was something awful in her glance. "Ah, my poor land!" thought Ludovico to himself. "She certainly is mad." The duchess looked at him and guessed his thought.

"Aha, Signor Ludovico, the great poet! You would like the gift in writing. Fetch me a sheet of paper." Ludovico did not wait for a repetition of the injunction, and the duchess wrote out, in her own hand, a lengthy acknowledgment, antedated by twelve months, whereby she declared she had received the sum of eighty thousand francs from Ludovico San-Michele, and had given him the Ricciarda as security for that sum. If, at the expiration of twelve months, the duchess had not returned the said eighty thousand francs to Ludovico, the lands of the Ricciarda were to remain his property. "There is something fine," said the duchess to herself, "in giving a faithful servant very nearly a third of all that remains to myself."

"Hark!" said the duchess to Ludovico. "After you have played my joke with the reservoir I can only give you two days in which to enjoy yourself at Casal Maggiore. To insure the validity of the sale, you must say the business dates more than a year back. You must rejoin me at Belgirate, and that without any delay. Fabrizio may possibly go to England, and you must follow him thither."

The Chartreuse of Parma

Early the next morning the duchess and Fabrizio were at Belgirate.

They settled themselves down in that enchanting village. But a mortal sorrow awaited the duchess on the shores of the beautiful Lago Maggiore. Fabrizio was an altered man. From the very first moments of his awakening out of the lethargic slumber which had followed on his flight, the duchess had perceived that something extraordinary was passing within his soul. The deep feeling which he hid with so much care was a somewhat strange one—it was nothing less than his despair at finding himself out of prison. He carefully abstained from confessing the cause of his sadness; that would have elicited questions which he did not choose to answer. "But," said the duchess in her astonishment, "the hideous sensation, when hunger forced you to stave off inanition by eating some of the horrible food sent from the prison kitchen, the sensation—Is there any odd taste about this? Am I poisoning myself at this moment? Did not that feeling fill you with horror?"

"I thought of death," replied Fabrizio, "just as I suppose soldiers think of it. It was a possibility, which I fully believed I should escape by my own skill."

What an anxiety, what a grief was this to the duchess! She watched this being whom she adored, who had once been so unlike other men, so lively, so full of originality, a prey now to the deepest reverie. He preferred solitude even to the pleasure of talking over everything, in utter frankness, with the best friend he had in the world. His behaviour to the duchess was still kindly, attentive, full of gratitude. As in the old days, he would have given his life for her a hundred times over. But his heart was elsewhere. Often they sailed four or five leagues over the lovely lake without exchanging a word. Conversation, the chilly exchange of thought still possible to them, might, perhaps, have seemed agreeable to others. But they, and more especially the duchess, still recollected what their conversations had been before that fatal fray with Giletti had parted them. Fabrizio owed the duchess the story of the nine months he had spent in a hideous prison, and now it appeared that all

417

he had to tell of that time amounted to a few short and unfinished phrases.

"This was sure to happen, sooner or later," said the duchess to herself, drearily. "Sorrow has aged me, or else real love has come to him, and I only hold the second place in his heart." Humbled, crushed, by this greatest of all possible sorrows, the duchess would sometimes murmur to herself, "If it had been Heaven's will that Ferrante should have gone quite mad, or that his courage should have failed, it seems to me I should have been less wretched." From that moment, this partial regret poisoned the duchess's esteem for her own character. "So," she mused bitterly, "I repent me now of a resolution I have once taken. I am no longer a Del Dongo."

"Heaven willed it so," she began again. "Fabrizio is in love, and what right have I to desire he should not be in love? Has one single word of love ever been exchanged between us?"

This thought, sensible as it was, prevented her from sleeping, and at last—this proves that age and a weakening soul had overtaken her, simultaneously with her hope of a condign vengeance—she was a hundred times more wretched at Belgirate than she had been at Parma. As to the identity of the person who had cast Fabrizio into so strange a reverie, there was no possibility of any reasonable doubt. Clelia Conti, that pious maiden, had deceived her father, since she had consented to make the garrison drunk, and Fabrizio never mentioned Clelia's name. "But," the duchess added, beating her breast in her despair, "if the garrison had not been intoxicated, all my inventiveness and all my care would have come to naught. Therefore it is she who has saved him."

It was only with the most extreme difficulty that the duchess could induce Fabrizio to give her any details of the events of that night, which, so the duchess said to herself, "would otherwise have been the subject of never-ending conversation between us. In those happy days he would have talked all day long, and with incessant spirit and gaiety, about the veriest trifle it came into my head to suggest."

The Chartreuse of Parma

As it was necessary to provide for every contingency, the duchess had established Fabrizio at the port of Locarno, a Swiss town at the end of the Lago Maggiore. Every day she fetched him, in a boat, for long expeditions on the lake. One day she took it into her head to go up to his room, and found the walls covered with a quantity of views of the city of Parma, for which he had sent to Milan, or even to Parma itself—that country which he should have held in detestation. His little sitting-room had been transformed into a studio, fitted with all the *impedimenta* of a water-colour artist, and she found him just finishing a third sketch of the Farnese Tower and the governor's palace.

"All you need do now," said she, with a look of vexation, "is to draw the portrait of that delightful governor who wanted to poison you, from memory. But now I come to think of it," continued the duchess, "you really should write him a letter of apology for having taken the liberty of escaping and bringing ridicule upon his citadel."

The poor lady little thought how truly she was speaking.

Fabrizio's first care, the moment he had reached a place of safety, had been to indite General Fabio Conti a perfectly polite and, in a sense, a very ridiculous letter, in which he begged him to forgive him for having escaped, alleging, as his excuse, that he had been given reason to believe that a person occupying a subaltern position in the prison had been ordered to poison him. Fabrizio cared little what he wrote. His one hope was that the letter might fall under Clelia's eyes, and his own face was wet with tears as he traced the words. He closed his epistle with a very whimsical phrase: he ventured to say that now he was at liberty, he very often regretted his little chamber in the Farnese Tower. This was the ruling thought of his letter, and he hoped Clelia would understand it. Still in a writing humour, and still hoping that a certain person might read what he wrote, Fabrizio penned his thanks to Don Cesare, the good-natured chaplain who had lent him theological books. A few days later Fabrizio persuaded the small bookseller at Locarno to travel to Milan, where this worthy, who was a friend of the celebrated book-fancier, Reina, bought

him the most splendid editions to be discovered of the
works lent him by Don Cesare. The kind chaplain received
these books, with a fine letter telling him that the poor prisoner, in moments of impatience which might perhaps be
forgiven him, had covered the margins of his books with
absurd notes. He therefore besought him to replace those
volumes in his library by these now despatched to him, with
a most lively sense of gratitude.

Fabrizio was not exactly correct when he described his
endless scribblings on the margins of a folio copy of the
works of St. Jerome as " notes." Hoping he might be able
to send the book back to the good chaplain and exchange
it for another, he had written on its margins, from day to day,
a most careful journal of everything that happened to him
in prison. These great events amounted to nothing but the
expression of his ecstasies of *divine love* (the word divine was
used instead of another, which he dared not write). Sometimes this " divine love " cast the prisoner into the deepest
despair ; then, again, a voice heard in the air would give him
some hope, and lift him into transports of happiness. All
this was written, fortunately, in prison ink, composed of
wine, chocolate, and soot, and Don Cesare, when he put the
volume of St. Jerome back on his library shelves, had
scarcely glanced at it. If he had looked closely over the
margins he would have become aware that one day the prisoner, believing himself to have been poisoned, was rejoicing
in the thought that he was to die within forty paces of that
which he had loved best in this world. But other eyes besides those of the kind-hearted chaplain had perused the
page since Fabrizio's escape. The beautiful idea of *dying
near the object of one's love*, expressed in a hundred different
forms, was followed by a sonnet, which set forth that the
soul, parted after hideous torments from the weak body
which it had inhabited for the past three-and-twenty years,
and impelled by that instinctive desire for happiness natural to everything which has had life, would not, even if the
great Judge granted pardon for all its sins, betake itself to
heaven, to join the angelic choir, the moment it obtained its
freedom ; but that, more happy after death than it had been

In life, it would join itself to its earthly love, within a few paces of the prison in which it groaned so long. " Thus," ran the last line of the sonnet, " I shall have found my paradise on earth."

Although within the citadel of Parma Fabrizio was never mentioned, except as a vile traitor who had violated the most sacred laws, the worthy priest was delighted at the sight of these beautiful books, sent him by an unknown hand—for Fabrizio had been careful not to write for a few days after their arrival, lest the sight of his name should induce the indignant return of the whole consignment. Don Cesare did not mention this attention to his brother, who flew into a fury whenever Fabrizio's name was spoken. But since the prisoner's escape he had fallen back into all his former intimacy with his charming niece, and as he had at one time taught her a little Latin, he showed her the beautiful books he had received. This had been the traveller's hope. Clelia suddenly reddened deeply; she had recognised Fabrizio's handwriting. Long narrow pieces of yellow paper had been placed, like markers, in different parts of the volume, and how true is it that amidst the sordid money interests, and the cold and colourless vulgarity of the considerations which fill our lives, the acts inspired by a genuine passion seldom fail to produce their due effect! On this occasion, as though some favouring goddess led her by the hand, Clelia, guided by instinct, and by one overmastering thought, begged her uncle to allow her to compare his old copy of St. Jerome with that he had just received. How shall I describe the joy that brightened the gloomy sadness into which Fabrizio's absence had plunged her, when she found, on the margins of the old St. Jerome, the sonnet of which we have spoken, and the recital, day by day, of the love she had inspired!

That very first day she knew the lines by heart, and sang them to herself, leaning on her own window, opposite that lonely one at which she had so often seen the tiny opening appear in the wooden screen. The screen in question had been taken down, to be produced in court, and used as a proof in an absurd trial which Rassi was now instituting against Fabrizio, who was accused of having escaped, or, as the Chief Justice put it, laughing himself, of *having snatched himself from the clemency of a magnanimous prince.*

Every step Clelia had taken caused her bitter remorse, and now that she was so unhappy, her self-reproach was all the deeper. She struggled to soften the blame she cast upon herself by recalling the vow she had made to the Madonna, when the general had been half poisoned, and renewed every day since—*that she would never see Fabrizio again.*

Fabrizio's escape had made the general very ill, and besides, he had very nearly lost his post, when the prince, in his rage, discharged all the jailers in the Farnese Tower, and sent them as prisoners to the city jail. The general had been partly saved by the intercession of Count Mosca, who preferred having him shut up in the top of his citadel to having to deal with him as an active and intriguing rival in court circles.

It was during this fortnight of uncertainty as to the disgrace of the general, who was really ill, that Clelia found courage to perform the sacrifice of which she had spoken to Fabrizio. She had been clever enough to fall ill on that day of general rejoicing, which had also, as my readers recollect, been that of Fabrizio's flight. The next day, again, she was ill, and, in a word, she managed so cleverly that, except for the jailer Grillo, whose special charge Fabrizio had been, not a soul suspected her complicity, and Grillo held his peace. But as soon as Clelia's fears from this quarter were quieted, her legitimate remorse tortured her yet more cruelly. "What earthly reason," said she to herself, "can possibly lessen the crime of a daughter who betrays her father?"

One evening, after having spent almost the whole day in the chapel, and in tears, she begged her uncle, Don Cesare, to come with her to the general, whose fits of rage now terrified her all the more because they were constantly mingled with curses of that abominable traitor Fabrizio.

When she reached her father's presence she found courage to tell him that if she had always refused to give her hand to the Marchese Crescenzi it was because she felt no inclination toward him, and that she was convinced the union would not bring her happiness. At these words the general flew into a fury, and Clelia had considerable difficulty in speaking again. She added that if her father, tempted by the marchese's fortune, thought himself obliged to give her a formal order to marry him, she was ready to obey. The general was quite taken aback by this conclusion, which he did not in the least expect. He ended, however, by being very much delighted. " So," said he to his brother, " I shall not have to live in rooms on the second floor, after all, even if this scamp Fabrizio's vile behaviour does cost me my place."

Count Mosca took care to be very much shocked by the escape of " that good-for-nothing fellow Fabrizio," and seized every opportunity of repeating Rassi's vulgar phrase as to the dull behaviour of the young man who had turned his back on the sovereign's clemency.

This witty remark, beloved by the smart set, did not take at all among the populace. The people, left to their own good sense, and though they held Fabrizio a very guilty man, admired the courage he had shown in climbing down from so great a height. There was not a soul about court who felt any admiration for his courage. As for the police, which was sorely humiliated by its mishap, it had officially discovered that twenty soldiers, bought over with money distributed by the duchess—that vilely ungrateful woman whose name could not be pronounced without a sigh—had brought Fabrizio four ladders, each forty-five feet long, and all bound together. Fabrizio had thrown down a rope, which had been fastened to these ladders, and his only exploit had been the very ordinary one of hauling them up. Certain notoriously imprudent Liberals, and among them a Doctor C——, an agent in the prince's direct pay, added, and compromised themselves by saying so, that this merciless police had been so cruel as to cause eight of the soldiers who had abetted the ungrateful Fabrizio's flight to be barbarously shot. Hence Fabrizio was blamed, even by genuine Liberals, because his foolhardiness had brought about the death of eight poor soldiers. Thus do small despots whittle down the value of public opinion.

CHAPTER XXIII

AMIDST the general storm of invective, Archbishop Landriani alone stood faithful to his young friend's cause, and ventured, even at the princess's court, to quote that maxim of jurisprudence, according to which the justification of an absent person must always be received with unprejudiced ears.

On the very morning after Fabrizio's escape, several persons received a tolerable sonnet, which acclaimed his flight as one of the finest actions of the century, and likened Fabrizio to an angel descending upon earth on outspread wings. On the evening of the third day, every tongue in Parma was repeating a really magnificent piece of verse. This purported to be Fabrizio's soliloquy as he swung himself down the rope, and reviewed the various incidents of his life. Two magnificent lines insured this second sonnet its proper place in public estimation. Every connoisseur recognised the hand of Ferrante Palla.

But at this point, I myself ought to fall into the epic style. What colours are bright enough to paint the torrents of indignation that submerged the hearts of all well-conditioned folk at the incredible news of the insolent illumination at Sacca! One shriek of horror went up against the duchess; even genuine Liberals thought she had risked the safety of the poor suspects in the various prisons in a most barbarous fashion, and unnecessarily exasperated the sovereign's feelings. Count Mosca declared that only one course was left to the duchess's old friends—they must forget her. The concert of execration was quite unanimous. Any stranger passing through the town must have been struck by the strength of public opinion. Still, in this country, where the delights of vengeance are thoroughly appreciated, the illuminations and the splendid *fête* given to over six thousand peasants in the park at Sacca had a huge success. Everybody in Parma was saying that the duchess had given a thousand sequins to her peasants, and this, it was added, explained the somewhat rough reception given the thirty gendarmes the police had been foolish enough to send into the village, thirty-six hours after the splendid festivities, and the general drunkenness which had followed on them, had come to an end. The gendarmes had been received with volleys of stones, had taken to flight, and two of them had been thrown into the river.

As to the bursting of the great reservoir at the Palazzo Sanseverina, that had hardly been noticed. A few streets had been flooded during the night, and in the morning people might have thought it had been raining. Ludovico had carefully broken the glass in one of the palace windows, which accounted for the entrance of the thieves, and a short ladder had actually been found hard by. Count Mosca was the only person who recognised the finger of his friend.

Fabrizio was quite resolved to get back to Parma as soon as he could. He sent Ludovico with a long letter to the archbishop, and that faithful servant came back to the first village in Piedmont—Sannazaro, to the west of Pavia—and there posted the Latin epistle addressed by the worthy prelate to his young friend. We must here add a detail, which, like many others, doubtless, may strike people as wearisome, in a country where caution is no longer necessary. The name "Fabrizio del Dongo" was never written; all letters intended for him were addressed to Ludovico San-Michele, either at Locarno in Switzerland, or at Belgirate in Piedmont. The envelope was made of coarse paper, it was clumsily sealed, the address was hardly legible, and occasionally adorned with additions worthy of a cook, and all these letters were antedated, by six days, from Naples.

From the Piedmontese village of Sannazaro, near Pavia, Ludovico hurried back to Parma. He was charged with a mission which Fabrizio regarded as of the utmost importance. He was ordered to do no less a thing than to send

The Chartreuse of Parma

Clelia Conti a silken handkerchief, on which one of Petrarch's sonnets had been printed. One word in the sonnet had, indeed, been altered. Clelia found it on her table, two days after she had received the thanks of the Marchese Crescenzi, who declared himself the happiest of men; and I need not describe the impression this mark of unfailing recollection produced upon her feelings.

Ludovico had received orders to collect every possible detail as to what was happening in the citadel. He it was who brought Fabrizio the sad news that the marriage with the Marchese Crescenzi appeared to be a settled thing. Hardly a day passed that he did not offer Clelia some form of festivity within the citadel walls. One decisive proof that the marriage was settled was that the marchese, who was excessively rich, and consequently, like most wealthy people in northern Italy, exceedingly stingy, was making huge preparations—and that, although he was marrying a dowerless girl. It is true that General Fabio Conti, whose vanity had been sorely stung by this remark—the first which occurred to all his fellow-countrymen—had just bought a landed property costing over three hundred thousand francs, and that, though he had nothing of his own, he had paid for it with ready money, presumably money belonging to the marquis. He had also given out that he bestowed the property on his daughter as a wedding gift. But the expenses of drawing up the deeds, and others, which came to more than twelve thousand francs, struck the Marchese Crescenzi, a man of very logical mind, as a very ridiculous outlay. He, on his part, was having magnificent hangings—admirably devised for delighting the eyes, by the famous Pallazzi, a Bolognese painter—woven at Lyons. These hangings, each of which bore some part of the Crescenzi family arms (the family, as all the world knows, is descended from the famous Roman Consul Crescentius, who lived in 985), were to furnish the seventeen saloons composing the ground floor of the marchese's palace. The hangings, clocks, and chandeliers, delivered in Parma, cost over three hundred and fifty thousand francs. The value of the new mirrors, added to those the house already contained, reached two hundred thousand francs. With the exception of two rooms, famous as the work of Parmegiano, the greatest painter of that country next to the divine Correggio, all the apartments on the first and second floor were now occupied by the most famous Florentine and Milanese painters, who were adorning them with frescoes. Fokelberg, the great Swedish sculptor, Tenerani, from Rome, and Marchesi, from Milan, had been working for a year on ten bas-reliefs representing as many noble acts in the life of that truly great man Crescentius. Most of the ceilings, which were also painted in fresco, contained some allusion to his career. One particular ceiling— on which Hayez, of Milan, had depicted Crescentius received in the Elysian Fields by Francesco Sforza, Lorenzo the Magnificent, King Robert, the Tribune Cola di Rienzi, Macchiavelli, Dante, and the other great figures of the Middle Ages —was most generally admired. Expressed admiration for these elect beings was considered to hint scorn of the people in power at the moment.

All these splendid details absorbed the attention of the nobles and burghers of Parma, and wrung our hero's heart, when he read them, related with artless admiration, in a long letter of over twenty pages which Ludovico had dictated to a customs-officer at Casal Maggiore.

" And I am so poor! " said Fabrizio to himself. " I have four thousand francs a year in all, and for everything. It is downright insolence for me to dare to be in love with Clelia Conti, for whom all these marvels are being prepared."

One item in Ludovico's letter, written in his own clumsy hand, informed his master that he had happened, one night, on poor Grillo, his former jailer, who had been thrown into prison and subsequently released, and who now bore all the appearance of a man who was hiding. Grillo had begged him, of his charity, to give him a sequin, and Ludovico had given him four in the duchess's name. The former jailers, twelve of them, who had just been set at liberty, were making themselves ready to give the new men who had succeeded them a " knifing entertainment " (*trattamento di coltellate*) if they could contrive to come upon them outside the citadel. Grillo had reported that there was a serenade at the fortress every night, that the Signorina Clelia Conti looked very pale, was often ill, and *other things of that sort*. As a consequence of this absurd expression, Ludovico received orders, by return of post, to come back to Locarno. He came, and the details he supplied by word of mouth were still more distressing to Fabrizio's feelings.

My readers may imagine how pleasant he made himself to the poor duchess; he would have died a thousand deaths rather than have pronounced the name of Clelia Conti in her presence.

The duchess loathed Parma, and to Fabrizio everything that reminded him of that city was at once sublime and tender.

Less than ever had the duchess forgotten her vengeance. She had been so happy before Giletti's death, and now, what a fate was hers! She was living in constant expectation of a frightful event, not a word of which she dared mention to Fabrizio—she who, when she had made her arrangement with Ferrante, had dreamed that one day she would rejoice Fabrizio's heart by assuring him that his day of vengeance would surely come.

My readers may conceive some idea of the agreeability of the conversations between Fabrizio and the duchess. The dreariest silence generally reigned between the two. To increase the enjoyment of their intercourse the duchess had allowed herself to be tempted into playing a trick upon her too beloved nephew. The count wrote to her almost every day. Apparently he still sent couriers, as in the first days of their love, for his letters always bore the postmark of some small Swiss town. The poor man taxed his wits so as not to speak too openly of his affection, and to devise amusing letters. All she did was to glance over them carelessly. What, alas, is the fidelity of a lover she esteems, to a woman whose heart is wrung by the coldness of the man she prefers!

In two months the duchess only sent him back one answer, and that was to request him to sound the princess, and find out whether, in spite of the insolent display of fireworks, a letter from the duchess would be well received. The letter he was to present, if he thought it wise, prayed the princess

to appoint the Marchese Crescenzi to the post of lord in
waiting to her Serene Highness, which had lately fallen
vacant, and begged the position might be given him in consideration of his marriage. The duchess's letter was a masterpiece, full of the tenderest respect, most perfectly expressed.
Its courtier-like language did not contain a single word of
which the consequences, even the most distant, could have
been otherwise than agreeable to the princess, and the answer it elicited breathed a tender friendship, which separation was putting to the torture.

"My son and I," wrote the princess, "have not had one
fairly pleasant evening since your sudden departure. Has
my dear duchess forgotten that it is to her I owe the fact
that I have regained a consulting voice in the nomination of
the officers of my household? Does she feel herself obliged
to give reasons for appointing the marchese, as though her
expressed desire were not the best of reasons to me? The
marchese will have the post if I can do anything toward it,
and in my heart there will always be a place—and the very
first—for my delightful duchess. My son uses absolutely
the same expressions—though indeed they are rather strong
in the mouth of a great fellow of one-and-twenty—and begs
you will send him specimens of the minerals of the valley of
Orta, near Belgirate. You can address your letters to the
count, who still detests you, and whom I love all the better
on account of this sentiment. The archbishop, too, has remained faithful to you. We all hope to see you back some
day; remember, that must be! The Marchesa Ghisleri, my
mistress of the robes, is about to leave this world for a
better one. The poor woman has given me a great deal of
trouble, and she displeases me now by departing at such
an unseasonable moment. Her illness makes me think of
the name which I should once have found such pleasure in
substituting for hers—if, indeed, I could have succeeded in
obtaining this sacrifice of her independence from the unique
being who, when she left us, carried away with her all the
delights of my little court," and so forth.

Thus, day after day, when the duchess met Fabrizio,
she felt conscious of having done all that in her lay

to hurry on the marriage which was driving him to despair, and they often spent four or five hours sailing together upon the lake, without uttering a single word to each other. Fabrizio's kind-heartedness was complete and perfect, but he was thinking of other things, and his simple and artless mind supplied him with no subjects of conversation. The duchess saw this, and therein was her torture.

I have forgotten to relate, in its proper place, that the duchess had taken a house at Belgirate, a lovely village which fulfils all the promise of its name (the view of a beautiful curve of the lake). Out of the French window of the drawing-room, the duchess could step into her boat. She had chosen a very ordinary one, for which four rowers would have sufficed, but she hired twelve, and was careful to have one man from each of the villages in the neighbourhood of Belgirate. The third or fourth time she found herself in the middle of the lake, with all these well-chosen men about her, she signed to them to cease rowing.

" I look upon you all as my friends," she said, " and I am going to trust you with a secret. My nephew Fabrizio has escaped from prison, and perhaps some treacherous attempt may be made to lay hands upon him, although he is on your lake, and in a free country. Keep your ears open, and warn me of everything you may hear. I give you leave to come into my room either by day or night."

The men responded in the most enthusiastic manner; she had the talent of making herself loved. But she did not think there would be any question of trying to seize Fabrizio; it was for herself she was taking these precautions, and before she had given the fatal order to open the reservoir at the Palazzo Sanseverina, she would never have dreamed of them.

Prudence had also led her to hire Fabrizio's lodging in the Port of Locarno. Every day he either came to see her, or she herself went to see him in Switzerland. The delights of their perpetual *tête-à-tête* may be gauged by the following detail. The marchesa and her daughters came to see them twice, and they were glad of the presence of these strangers —for ties of blood notwithstanding, a person who knows nothing of one's dearest interests, and whom one does not see more than once a year, may fairly be called a stranger.

One night, the duchess, with the marchesa and her two daughters, was at Fabrizio's rooms in Locarno. The archpriest of the neighbourhood and the village priest had both come to pay their respects to the ladies. The archpriest, who was interested in some commercial house, and kept himself informed of the current news, happened to say:

" The Prince of Parma is dead."

The duchess turned very pale. She could hardly find courage to inquire, " Have you heard any details?"

" No," replied the archpriest, " the report only mentions his death; but that is quite certain."

The duchess looked at Fabrizio. " It was for him I did it," she said to herself, " and I would have done a thousand times worse. And there he sits in front of me, utterly indifferent, and thinking of another woman!" It was beyond the duchess's power to endure the dreadful thought; she swooned away. Every one hastened to her assistance, but when she came back to her senses she noticed that Fabrizio was far less perturbed than the two priests; he was dreaming, as usual. " He is thinking he will go back to Parma," said the duchess to herself, " and perhaps that he will break off Clelia's marriage with the marchese. But I shall know how to prevent that." Then, recollecting the presence of the two ecclesiastics, she hastily added:

" He was a great prince, and has been sorely slandered. He is a sore loss to us all."

The two priests took their leave, and the duchess, who longed to be alone, announced her intention of going to bed.

" No doubt," said she to herself, " prudence forbids my returning to Parma for a month or two. But I feel I shall never have that patience; I suffer too much here. Fabrizio's perpetual silence and absorption are more than my heart can bear. Who would have told me I ever could have felt weary of sailing alone with him over this beautiful lake! And just at the moment when, to avenge him, I have done more than I can ever tell him! After such a sight as that, death seems nothing at all. Now, indeed, I am paying for the ecstasies of happiness and childish delight I felt in my palace at Parma, when Fabrizio joined me there on his return from Naples. If I had said one word then, it would all have been settled; and perhaps, if he had been bound to me, he never would have thought of that little Clelia. But that word filled me with a horrible repugnance. Now she has the better of me, and what can be more natural? She is only twenty, and I, besides being altered by trouble and illness, am twice her age. . . . I must die, I must make an end of it! A woman of forty is nothing to any man, except those who have loved her in her youth. The only joys left to me now are those of vanity. And do they make life worth living? That's another reason for going to Parma and amusing myself. If certain things happened, I should be put to death; well, what matter? I will die nobly, and just before the end, but not till then, I will tell Fabrizio, ' Ungrateful boy, it was for you I did it!' . . . Yes, Parma is the only place where I can find occupation for what little life remains to me. I'll play the great lady there. What a blessing it would be if I could find enjoyment, now, in the glories which used to make the Raversi sick with envy! In those days I only became aware of my happiness by seeing it mirrored in jealous eyes. . . . My vanity has one piece of good fortune. Except for the count, perhaps, not a soul can have guessed at what has cut my affections at their root. . . . I will love Fabrizio, I will devote myself to his fortunes, but he shall not break off Clelia's marriage and marry her himself. . . . No, that shall never be! "

So far had the duchess proceeded in her melancholy soliloquy when she heard a great noise in the house.

" Hark! " she cried; " they are coming to arrest me! Ferrante has been taken and has confessed. Well, all the better. I shall have something to do; I must fight for my life. But to begin with, I mustn't let them take me! "

Half dressed, the duchess fled to the bottom of her garden. She was just meditating climbing over a low wall, and escaping into the open country, when she caught sight of some one going into her room, and recognised Bruno, the count's confidential man. He was alone with her maid. She approached the open window; the man was telling the maid about the wounds he had received. The duchess came back into her room, and Bruno, casting himself at her feet, besought her not to tell the count the absurd hour at which he had arrived.

"The moment the prince was dead," he added, "the count sent orders to all the posting-houses that no horses were to be given to any Parmese subject; consequently I travelled as far as the Po with our own horses. But when we were getting off the ferry-boat my carriage was over-turned, smashed up, and destroyed, and I was so seriously hurt that I could not ride, as it was my duty to have done."

"Very good," said the duchess, "it is three o'clock in the morning. I'll say it is midday. But don't you dare to con-tradict me!"

"That is like the signora's usual kindness."

In a literary work, politics play the part of a pistol shot in the middle of a concert—something rough and disagreeable, to which, nevertheless, we can not refuse our attention.

I am now going to speak of very ugly matters, concern-ing which, for more than one reason, I would gladly be silent. But I am compelled to refer to certain events which come within our purview, seeing they are connected with the lives of the persons I describe.

"But good God," said the duchess to Bruno, "how did that great prince come by his death?"

"He went out to shoot birds of passage in the marshes by the river, a few leagues from Sacca. He fell into a hole, hidden by a tuft of grass; he was in a violent perspiration, and the cold struck him. He was conveyed to a lonely house, and there he died, within a few hours. Some declare that Signore Catena and Barone are dead too, and that the whole accident was caused by the saucepans in the peasant's house, into which they were taken, being full of verdigris—they all breakfasted in that house. Then the hot-headed folk, the Jacobins, who say whatever suits them, talk about poison. I know that my friend Toto, one of the court serv-ants, would have died but for the care lavished on him by a sort of lunatic who seemed to know a great deal about medicine, and made him use very strange remedies. But nobody talks about the prince's death any more, and, indeed, he was a cruel man. When I was starting, the populace was collecting to murder Chief-Justice Rassi, and the people wanted to set the gates of the citadel on fire, so as to try and save the prisoners. But some people declared Fabio Conti would fire his cannon on them, while others vowed the gunners in the fortress had poured water on their gunpowder, and would not destroy their fellow-citizens. But here is something far more interesting: While the surgeon at Sandolaro was binding up my poor arm, a man came in from Parma, and told us that when the people saw Barbone, that clerk from the citadel, in the streets, they first of all thrashed him mercilessly, and then hanged him on the tree in the square, nearest to the citadel. Then they set out to destroy that fine statue of the prince that stands in the royal gardens, but the count sent for a battalion of the guard, drew it up in front of the statue, and sent the people word that no man who came into the garden should leave it alive, and then every one was frightened.

"But a very strange thing, which the man from Parma, a former gendarme, told me, over and over again, is that the count kicked General P——, the commandant of the prince's guard, tore off his epaulettes, and had him marched out of the garden by two fusileers."

"That's just like the count!" exclaimed the duchess, in a transport of delight, which she would have thought impossible a moment previously. "He would never allow any one to insult our princess, and as for General P——, he was so devoted to his legitimate masters that he would never serve the usurper, whereas the count, whose feelings were less delicate, fought through all the Spanish campaigns, a thing which was often cast in his teeth at court."

The duchess had opened the count's letter, but over and over again she stopped reading it to question Bruno.

It was a very comical letter. The count used the most lugubrious language, and yet the most lively joy was evident in every word. He gave no details as to the manner of the prince's death, and ended his letter with the following words:

" You will come back, of course, my dearest angel. But I would advise your waiting a day or two for the messenger whom the princess will send you, as I hope, either to-day or to-morrow. Your return must be as magnificent as your departure was bold.

" As to the *great culprit*, who is with you, I fully expect to have him tried by twelve judges, selected from every party in the state. But to punish the wretch as he deserves, I must first of all be in a position to make curl-papers out of the first sentence, if it exists."

The count had reopened his letter:

" Here's quite another business. I have just had cartridges served out to the two battalions of the guards, I am going to fight, and do my best to deserve that surname of ' Cruel ' with which the Liberals have so long honoured me. That old mummy, General P——, has dared to talk in barracks of parleying with the populace, which is in a state of semi-revolt. I write this in the middle of the street. I go hence to the palace, which no one shall enter except across my dead body. Farewell! If I die, I die as I have lived, worshipping you *in any case*. Don't forget to send for the three hundred thousand francs lodged in your name with D—— at Lyons.

" Here comes that poor devil Rassi, wigless and as pale as death; you've no idea what a figure he is. The populace is bent on hanging him. That would be too hard on him; he deserves to be drawn and quartered as well! He would have taken refuge in my palace, and has run after me into the street. I hardly know what to do with him. . . . I do not want to take him to the prince's palace; that would bring about a revolt in that quarter. F—— will see whether I care for him. My first words to Rassi were, ' I must have the sentence on Monsignore del Dongo, and all the copies you have of it, and you will tell all those shameless judges, who have brought about this revolt, that I will have them all hanged, and you, my friend, into the bargain, if they breathe a single word of this sentence, which has never existed.' I am sending a company of grenadiers to the arch-bishop, in Fabrizio's name. Farewell, dear angel. My house will be burned, and I shall lose those delightful pictures I have of you. I am hurrying off to the palace to get that vile General P—— cashiered. He is working for his own hand, flattering the populace as basely as he used to flatter the late prince. All these generals are frightened out of their wits; I think I'll have myself appointed commander-in-chief."

The duchess was spiteful enough not to send and rouse Fabrizio. She felt a glow of admiration for the count, which strongly resembled love. "All things considered," said she to herself, "I really must marry him." She wrote him instantly to that effect, and sent off one of her servants. That night the duchess had no time to feel unhappy.

The next day, toward noon, she saw a boat with six rowers swiftly cleaving the waters of the lake. Fabrizio and she soon recognised a man wearing the Prince of Parma's livery. He was, in fact, one of his couriers, who, before he jumped on shore, called out to the duchess: "The revolt is put down." This courier brought her several letters from the count, a charming missive from the princess, and a parchment decree from Prince Ranuzio-Ernest V which created her Duchess of San Giovanni, and appointed her Mistress of the Robes to the Princess-Mother. The young prince, who was learned in mineralogy, and whom she believed to be a simpleton, had been clever enough to write her a little note, but there was love at the end of it. The note began thus:

"The count says, my Lady Duchess, that he is pleased with me. As a matter of fact, I have faced a few musket shots beside him, and my horse was wounded. The fuss made over so small a thing has made me earnestly desire to be present at a real battle, so long as it be not against my own subjects. I owe everything to the count; all my generals, who know nothing of war, have behaved like hounds. I believe two or three of them have run away as far as Bologna. Since the day when a great and deplorable event called me to power, I have signed no decree which gives me so much pleasure as this, which appoints you my mother's mistress of the robes. My mother and I have remembered that one day you admired the beautiful view from the Palazzetto San Giovanni, which once belonged to Petrarch—at least, so we are told. My mother desired to give you this little property, and I, not knowing what to give you, and not daring to offer you all that belongs to you already, have made you a duchess in my own country. I do not know whether you are so learned as to be aware that Sanseverina is a Roman title. I have just given the ribbon of my Order to our excellent archbishop, who has displayed a firmness very uncommon in a man of sixty-two. You will not be angry with me for having recalled all the banished ladies. I am told that in future I must never sign my name without having written the words ' *your affectionate.*' It vexes me that I should be thus made to squander an assurance which is not fully true, except when I write myself ' *your* affectionate, Ranuzio-Ernest.' "

Who would not have thought, judging from this language, that the duchess was about to enjoy the highest favour? Nevertheless, she found something very odd in other letters from the count, which reached her two hours later. These advised her, without further explanation, to put off her return to Parma for a few days, and to write the princess word that she was exceedingly unwell. Notwithstanding, the duchess and Fabrizio started for Parma immediately after dinner; the duchess's object, which, however, she did not admit to herself, was to hurry on the Marchese Crescenzi's marriage. Fabrizio, for his part, performed the journey in a state of wild happiness, which seemed perfectly ridiculous to his aunt. He had hopes of seeing Clelia soon, and fully reckoned on carrying her off, in spite of herself, if that should be the only means of breaking off her marriage.

The journey of the duchess and her nephew was a very cheerful one. At the last posting station before Parma, Fabrizio stopped a moment to put on his churchman's garb. As a rule he wore ordinary mourning dress. When he came back to the duchess's room—

" There seems to me something very odd and inexplicable," she said, "in the count's letters. If you will be ruled by me you will stay here for a few hours. I'll send you a messenger as soon as I have had a talk with the mighty minister."

It was only very unwillingly that Fabrizio bowed to this sensible piece of advice. The count received the duchess with transports of joy worthy of a boy of fifteen, calling her "his wife." It was long before he would talk of politics. When they came back, at last, to the dull realms of common sense—

"You did very wisely," he said, "to prevent Fabrizio from arriving openly. There is a great reaction going on here. Just guess the name of the colleague the prince has imposed on me as Minister of Justice. Rassi, my dear soul, Rassi, whom I treated like the blackguard he is, on the day of our great excitements. By the way, I must warn you that everything that happened here has been suppressed. If you read our Gazette, you will perceive that a clerk at the citadel, of the name of Barbone, has been killed by a fall from a carriage. As for the sixty-odd rogues I had shot when they tried to wreck the prince's statue in the gardens, they are all quite well, but they have gone on long journeys. Count Zurla, the Minister of the Interior, has personally visited each of these unlucky heroes' homes, and has made over fifteen sequins to their family or friends, with strict orders to say that the dead man is travelling, and a very direct threat that any one who ventures to hint anybody has been killed will be forthwith shut up in prison. A man from my own office at the Ministry for Foreign Affairs has been sent to the journalists of Milan and Turin, to prevent any mention of the 'unfortunate event'—that's the correct term—and this man is to go as far as Paris and London, so as to give an almost official denial to any newspaper reference to our disturbances. Another agent has gone toward Bologna and Florence. I shrug my shoulders.

"But the comical thing, at my age, is that I felt a flash of real enthusiasm when I was addressing the soldiers of the guard, and when I tore the epaulettes off that contemptible fellow, P——. At that moment I would have given my life for the prince without the smallest hesitation. I confess, now, it would have been a very silly way of ending it. At this moment the prince, kind-hearted young fellow as he is, would give a thousand crowns if I would die of some sickness. He dares not ask me to resign, as yet, but we see each other as seldom as possible, and I send him a quantity of small written reports, just as I did with the late prince after Fabrizio was imprisoned. By the way, I have not turned his sentence into curl-papers, for the excellent reason that that villain Rassi never gave it to me. That is why you have done so wisely to prevent Fabrizio from arriving publicly. The sentence is still valid. However, I do not believe Rassi would dare to arrest our nephew to-day. Still, he may possibly dare to do it within a fortnight. If Fabrizio absolutely insists on coming into the city, let him come and live in my house."

" But what is the reason of all this? " exclaimed the astonished duchess.

" The prince has been persuaded that I give myself the airs of a dictator, and of the saviour of the country ; that I want to lead him like a child, and even that, in speaking of him, I used those fatal words ' that child.' This may be true ; I was very much excited that day. But, indeed, I really looked on him as a thorough man, because he was not frightened in face of the first musketry firing he had ever heard in his life. He is by no means a fool. His tone, indeed, is much better than his father's, and—I can not say it too often—at the bottom of his heart he is both good and upright. But his honest young soul is stung when the story of some piece of rascality is told him, and he thinks his own nature must be vile to perceive such things. Think what his education has been."

" Your Excellency should have remembered that he was to be our master some day, and should have placed a clever man about his person."

" In the first place, we have the instance of the Abbé de Condillac, who was appointed by my predecessor, the Marchese di Felino, and turned his pupil into a very king of simpletons. He walked in religious processions, and in 1796 he failed to make terms with General Buonaparte, who would have tripled the size of his dominions. And in the second place, I never dreamed I should have been Prime Minister for ten successive years. Now that my mind is disabused of that idea—that is to say, for the last month—I am resolved to put together a million of francs before I leave this Bedlam I have saved, to its fate. But for me, Parma would have spent two months as a republic, with the poet Ferrante Palla as dictator!"

The duchess reddened at the words. The count knew nothing of that story.

"We are coming back, now, to the regular eighteenth-century monarchy, ruled by the confessor and the mistress. At heart, all the prince cares for is mineralogy—and perhaps, madam, for you! Since he has succeeded, his body-servant, whose brother, a fellow with nine months' service, I have just made a captain—this body-servant, I say, has put an idea into his head that he ought to be the happiest of men, because his profile will appear on the coinage. That fine notion has brought boredom in its train.

"Now he must have an aide-de-camp to help him out of his boredom. Well, even if he were to offer me that precious million of money, which is so necessary to insure our comfort at Naples or Paris, I would not undertake to cure him of his boredom, and spend four or five hours every day in his Highness's company. Besides, as I am cleverer than he is, he would think me a monster before the first month was out.

"The late prince was spiteful and envious, but he had fought as a soldier, and commanded troops, and that had given him a certain sense of deportment. There were the makings of a prince in him, and with him I could behave as a minister, whether good or bad. But with this honest son of his, in spite of all his candour and real kind-heartedness, I am obliged to resort to intrigue. I find myself the rival of the veriest old woman among his courtiers, and a rival in an inferior position, too, for I shall certainly despise scores of precautions which I ought to take. For instance, three days ago, one of those women who lay out clean towels in all his rooms contrived to mislay the key of one of the prince's English writing-tables. Whereupon his Highness refused to attend to any of the business, the papers for which were in that particular receptacle. For twenty francs we might have had the board at the back of the writing-table removed, or have had the lock opened with a false key. But Ranuzio-Ernest V informed me that such a proceeding would give the court locksmith bad habits.

"So far he has never contrived to be of the same mind three days running. If the young prince had been born a marquis, with a large fortune, he would have been one of the most worthy men about his own court—a sort of Louis XVI. But how is that pious simplicity of his to escape all the skilful ambushes that surround him? Thus your friend the Raversi's *salon* is more powerful than ever. Its frequenters have discovered that I, who had the populace fired on, and who was resolved, if necessary, to kill three thousand of them, sooner than permit any insult to the statue of the prince, who had been my master, am a violent Liberal; that I tried to get a constitution signed, and more stuff of the same kind. With such republican stories, these madmen would prevent us from enjoying even the best of monarchies. . . . You, madam, in fine, are the only existing member of that Liberal party at the head of which my enemies have placed me, of whom the prince has not spoken in harsh terms. The archbishop, who is still a perfectly upright man, is in thorough disgrace, because he used reasonable language about what I did on the *unlucky day*.

"On the day after that which was not then, as yet, known as 'unlucky,' while it was still true that a revolt had taken place, the prince told the archbishop that he was going to make me a duke, so that you might not have to take an inferior title when you married me. To-day, I fancy, it is Rassi, whom I ennobled for selling me the late prince's secrets, who will be made a count. In face of such promotion as that, I should look like a fool."

"And the poor prince will degrade himself."

"No doubt of that. But, after all, *he is master* here, and in less than a fortnight, that fact will still the voice of *ridicule.* Therefore, dear duchess, let us do as we should do if we were playing *tric-trac.* *Let us withdraw* "

" But we shall be anything but rich ! "

" After all, neither you nor I need luxury. If you will give me a seat in your box at the San Carlo, and a horse to ride, I shall be more than content. It will never be the luxury, greater or less, in which we live, that will insure our position; it will be the pleasure the clever folk of the place may find in drinking a cup of tea in your drawing-room."

" But," replied the duchess, " what would have happened on the *unlucky day* if you had held yourself apart, as I trust you will do in future? "

" The troops would have fraternized with the populace, there would have been three days of killing and burning ;— for it will be a century, yet, before a republic can cease to be an anomaly in this country. After that, a fortnight's pillage, until two or three foreign regiments had been sent in to quell the disorder. Ferrante Palla was in the midst of the populace, as brave, and as raging mad, as usual. He had some dozen friends backing him up, no doubt, and out of that Rassi will make a fine conspiracy. One thing is certain; that, though he wore an incredibly tattered coat, he was distributing money by handsful in every direction."

Astounded by all this news, the duchess hurried off to present her acknowledgments to the princess. The moment she entered the royal apartment, the lady-in-waiting presented her with the little gold key, to be worn at the waist, which is the symbol of supreme authority in that portion of the palace ruled by the princess. Clara Paolina lost no time in dismissing all her attendants. For the first moments after she was left alone with her friend, her manner and speech were neither of them absolutely frank. The duchess, who could not understand what this meant, was very cautious in her answers. At last the princess burst into tears, and throwing herself into the duchess's arms, exclaimed :

" My misfortunes are beginning afresh. My son will treat me worse than his father did."

" I'll take good care he does not," replied the duchess vehemently. " But in the first place," she went on, " I must

The Chartreuse of Parma

beg your Most Serene Highness to condescend to accept all my gratitude and my humblest duty."

"What do you mean?" exclaimed the princess, alarmed at the thought of a possible resignation.

"What I mean is, that whenever your Most Serene Highness gives me leave to turn the shaking chin of yonder Chinese monster on the chimneypiece to the right, you will give me permission, too, to call things by their real names."

"Is that all, my dear duchess?" exclaimed Clara Paolina, rising, and herself placing the monster's chin in the required position. "Speak now, with perfect freedom," she added, in the most gracious fashion.

"Madam," replied the duchess, "your Highness has grasped the position perfectly. Both you and I are in a most dangerous position. Fabrizio's sentence is not annulled. Consequently, whenever there is any desire to get rid of me, and insult you, he will be cast into prison again. Our position is as bad as ever it was. As regards myself personally, I am going to marry the count, and we shall settle at Naples or in Paris. The final stroke of ingratitude from which the count is suffering at the present moment, has thoroughly sickened him; and save for your Serene Highness's sake, I should not advise him to have anything more to do with this mess, unless the prince were to give him an enormous sum of money. I will ask your Highness's leave to explain that the count, who had a hundred and thirty thousand francs when he first entered politics, owns barely twenty thousand francs a year at the present time. In vain have I besought him, this ever so long, to consider his own pocket. During my absence he has picked a quarrel with the prince's farmers-general, who were scoundrels. The count has replaced them by other scoundrels, who have given him eight hundred thousand francs."

"What!" exclaimed the astonished princess. "Good heavens, how sorry I am to hear that!"

"Madam," replied the duchess, with the most absolute coolness, "shall I turn the monster's head to the left?"

"No, no, indeed!" exclaimed the princess; "but I am

sorry that a man of the count's character should have thought of gain of that description."

" But for this theft he would have been despised by all honest folk."

" Good God! can that be possible? "

" Madam," replied the duchess, " except my friend the Marchese Crescenzi, who has four or five hundred thousand francs a year of his own, every soul in this place steals. And how should they not steal, in a country where gratitude for the greatest services does not last quite a month? Therefore the only real thing which outlives disgrace is money. Madam, I am about to venture on some terrible truths."

" I give you leave," said the princess with a deep sigh; " and yet they hurt me cruelly! "

" Well, then, madam, the prince, your son, a perfectly upright man, may make you far more wretched than his father did. The late prince's nature was very much like that of other men. Our present sovereign is never sure of desiring the same thing for three days on end. Consequently, to be sure of him, one must live perpetually with him, and never let him speak to any one else. As this truth is not very difficult to divine, the new ultra party, led by those two wise heads, Rassi and the Marchesa Raversi, will endeavour to provide the prince with a mistress. This mistress will be given ' carte blanche ' to make her own fortune, and to dispose of some inferior posts. But she will have to answer to the party for her master's constant goodwill.

" To be thoroughly well-established at your Highness's court, I must have Rassi spurned and banished. Further, I must have Fabrizio tried by the most upright judges who can be found. If, as I hope, these judges recognise his innocence, it will be only natural to grant the archbishop's wish that Fabrizio shall be his coadjutor, and his ultimate successor. If I fail, the count and I will forthwith retire. In that case I leave your Serene Highness this farewell advice: You must never forgive Rassi, and you must never leave your son's dominions. So long as you keep near him, your good son will never do you any serious harm."

" I have followed your arguments with all the attention

they deserve," replied the princess with a smile. " But am I, then, to undertake the care of finding a mistress for my son?"

" Not that, indeed, madam! But see to it that your drawing-room shall be the only one in which he finds amusement."

On this subject the conversation ran on endlessly. The scales were falling from the eyes of the innocent and intelligent princess. The duchess sent a courier to Fabrizio, to tell him he might enter the city, but that he must conceal himself. Hardly any one saw him. Dressed as a peasant, he spent his whole time in the wooden booth which a chestnut seller had set up under the trees of the square, just opposite the citadel gates.

CHAPTER XXIV

THE duchess arranged the most delightful evenings at the palace, where so much gaiety had never been seen before. Never did she make herself more attractive than during this winter, in spite of the fact that she was living in circumstances of the greatest danger. Nevertheless, through all this critical time she never gave a thought of sadness, save on one or two occasions, to the strange alteration which had taken place in Fabrizio. The young prince used to come very early to his mother's pleasant evening parties, and she never failed to say to him:

" Do go and attend to your government duties! I am certain there are more than a score of reports lying on your table, waiting for a ' yes ' or ' no ' from you, and I do not choose to have it said all over Europe that I am trying to turn you into a ' Roi fainéant,' so that I may reign in your stead."

These remarks always suffered from the drawback of being dropped at the most inopportune moment—that is to say, just when his Highness had overcome his natural shyness and was enjoying himself very much, acting some charade. Twice a week there were parties in the country, to which the princess, on the plea of reconquering the affections of his people for the young sovereign, invited the prettiest women of the middle class. The duchess, who was the soul of the merry court, was in hopes that these fair ladies, who all looked with an eye of mortal jealousy on the success of their fellow *bourgeois*, Rassi, would make the prince acquainted with some of that minister's endless rascalities. For, among other childish notions, the prince claimed to possess a moral ministry.

446

The Chartreuse of Parma

Rassi had too much good sense not to realize how much harm these brilliant parties, managed by his enemy at the princess's court, were likely to do him. He had not chosen to make over the perfectly legal sentence passed on Fabrizio, to Count Mosca. It had therefore become necessary that either he or the duchess should disappear from court.

On the day of that popular tumult, the existence of which it was now the correct thing to deny, money had certainly been circulated among the people. Rassi made this his starting-point. Dressed even more shabbily than was his wont, he found his way into the most wretched houses in the city, and spent whole hours in close confabulation with their poverty-stricken denizens. His efforts were richly rewarded. After a fortnight spent in this fashion, he had made certain that Ferrante Palla had been the secret leader of the insurrection, and further, that this man, who had been as poor as a great poet should be, all his life, had sent eight or ten diamonds to be sold at Genoa.

Among others, five valuable stones were mentioned, really worth more than forty thousand francs, but for which thirty-five thousand francs had been accepted *ten days before the prince's death*, because, so the vendors said, *the money was wanted*.

The minister's transports of delight over this discovery were indescribable. He had perceived that fun was being constantly poked at him in the princess dowager's court, and several times over, when the prince was talking business with him, he had laughed in his face, with all the artlessness of youth. Rassi, it must be confessed, had some singularly vulgar habits. For instance, as soon as he grew interested in a discussion, he would cross his legs, and take hold of his shoe. If his interest deepened he would spread out his red cotton handkerchief over his knee. The prince had laughed heartily at a joke played by one of the prettiest women of Rassi's own class, who, well aware that she herself possessed a very pretty leg, had given him an imitation of the graceful gesture habitual to the Minister of Justice.

Rassi craved a special audience, and said to the prince:

" Would your Highness be disposed to give a hundred

447

thousand francs to know the exact nature of your august father's death? With that sum we should be able to bring the culprits to justice, if they exist."

The prince's answer was a foregone conclusion.

Within a short time, Cecchina informed the duchess that she had been offered a large sum of money if she would allow a jeweller to see her mistress's diamonds—a proposal which she had scornfully refused. The duchess scolded her for having refused, and a week later Cecchina was able to show the diamonds. On the day fixed for their inspection, Count Mosca placed two reliable men to watch every jeweller in Parma, and toward midnight he came to tell the duchess that the inquisitive jeweller was no other than Rassi's own brother. The duchess, who was in very gay spirits that evening (there was acting going on at the palace —a *commedia dell'arte,* in which each personage invents the dialogue as he proceeds, only the general plan of the play being posted up in the side scenes), the duchess, who was playing one of the parts, was to be supported, as the lover of the piece, by Count Baldi, the former friend of the Marchesa Raversi, who was present. The prince, who was the shyest man in his dominions, but very good-looking, and exceedingly soft-hearted, was under-studying Count Baldi's part, which he desired to play at the second performance.

" I have very little time," said the duchess to the count. " I come on in the first scene of the second act. Let us go into the guard-room."

There, in the presence of a score of the body-guard, sharp fellows every one of them, and eagerly watching the colloquy between the Prime Minister and the mistress of the robes, the duchess said to her friend, with a laugh:

" You always scold me if I tell secrets which need not be told. It is I who brought Ernest V to the throne. I wanted to avenge Fabrizio, whom I loved much more than I do now, though very innocently, even then. I know very well you have not much belief in my innocence, but that matters little, since you love me in spite of my crimes. Well, this crime is a very real one. I gave all my diamonds to a very interesting kind of madman, by name Ferrante Palla, and I even kissed him, so as to induce him to destroy the man who wanted to have Fabrizio poisoned. Where was the harm?"

"Ah, then that's how Ferrante got the money for his revolt!" said the count. "And you tell me all this in the guard-room!"

"I'm in a hurry, you see, and this fellow Rassi is on the track of the crime. It's very true that I never hinted at insurrection, for I abhor Jacobins. Think it all over, and tell me your advice, after the play is over."

"I will tell you at once that you must make the prince fall in love with you . . . but in all honour, of course!"

The duchess was being called for on the stage, and fled.

A few days later, the duchess received, by post, a long ridiculous letter, signed with the name of a person who had once been her waiting-maid. The woman asked for employment about the court, but at the first glance the duchess realized that neither the writing nor the style were hers. When she unfolded the sheet, to read the second page, the duchess saw a little miraculous picture of the Madonna folded within another leaf, that seemed to belong to an old printed book, flutter to her feet. After having glanced at the picture, the duchess read a few lines of the old printed leaf. Her eyes began to shine; these were the words she had read:

"The tribune took a hundred francs a month, no more. With the rest he strove to stir the sacred flame in souls which had been frozen by selfishness. The fox is on my track; that is why I made no attempt to see the adored being for the last time. I said to myself: 'She has no love for the republic—she, who is so superior to me in mind, as in grace and beauty.' And besides, how can I set up a republic where there are no republicans? Can I have been mistaken? In six months I shall be wandering, microscope in hand, through the small American towns. So shall I discover whether I should continue to love your sole rival in my heart. If you receive this letter, baroness, and if no profane eye has seen it before yours, cause one of the young ash trees which grow twenty paces from the spot where I first

dared to address you, to be broken down. Then I will cause
to be buried, under the great box tree in the garden, which
you once noticed, in my happy days, a coffer containing those
things which bring slander on men of my opinions. Be
sure I should never have ventured to write this, but that
the fox is on my track, and may possibly reach that angelic
being. Look under the box tree a fortnight hence."

" If he has a printing press at his command," said the
duchess, " we shall soon have a collection of sonnets! God
knows what name he will give me in them ! "

The duchess's vanity inspired her with an experiment.
She was laid up for a week, and there were no parties at
court. The princess, who was very much scandalized by all
that the fear of her son had forced her to do during the earlier period of her widowhood, spent that week in a convent
attached to the church where the late prince had been buried.
This break in the series of entertainments threw an enormous amount of time on the prince's hands, and brought
about an evident diminution in the credit of the Minister of
Justice. Ernest V realized all the dulness that threatened
him if the duchess should leave his court, or even cease to
shed gaiety upon it. The evening parties began again, and
the prince took more interest than ever in the *commedie
dell'arte*. He was dying to play a part himself, but did not
dare to acknowledge this desire. At last, one day, he said
to the duchess, reddening very much, " Why should I not
act, too ? "

" We are all at your Highness's command. If you will
honour me with the order I will have the plan of a play made
out. All your Highness's chief scenes shall be with me, and
as every beginner must hesitate a little, if your Highness
will be good enough to watch me a little closely, I will suggest the answers you should make." Thus everything was
settled, and in the most skilful manner. The prince, shy
as he was, was ashamed of his shyness, and the care the
duchess took to prevent his suffering from this inherent
nervousness impressed the young sovereign deeply.

On the day of his first appearance, the performance began
earlier than usual, and when the company moved into the

The Chartreuse of Parma

theatre there were not more than eight or ten elderly women in the drawing-room. Their faces caused the prince no particular alarm, and besides, they had all been brought up at Munich, in the most thoroughly monarchical principles, and applauded dutifully. The duchess, by virtue of her authority as mistress of the robes, locked the door by which the mass of the courtiers usually passed into the theatre. The prince, who had considerable *literary* intelligence, and was very good-looking, got through his first scenes very well, cleverly repeating the sentences he read in the duchess's eyes, or which she suggested in an undertone. Just when the few spectators were applauding with all their might, the duchess made a sign; the great doors were thrown open, and in a moment the room was filled with all the pretty women of the court, who, thinking the prince's face charming, and his whole demeanour thoroughly happy, burst into applause. The prince flushed with delight. He was playing the part of lover to the duchess. Far from suggesting words to him, she was soon obliged to beg him to shorten his scenes. He dilated on "love" with a fervour which frequently put the actress quite out of countenance; some of his speeches were five minutes long. The duchess was no longer the dazzling beauty she had been a year previously. Fabrizio's imprisonment, and still more, her stay on the Lago Maggiore with the Fabrizio who had grown gloomy and silent, had added ten years to the fair Gina's appearance. Her features had grown sharper; there was more intelligence, and less juvenility, about them. Very seldom, nowadays, did they display the sprightly humour of her youth. Yet on the stage, rouged, and with the advantage of all that art does for an actress's appearance, she was still the prettiest woman at the court. The prince's passionate speeches roused the courtiers' suspicions. That evening, every man said to his neighbour, "This is the Balbi of the new reign." The count raged within himself. When the play was over, the duchess said to the prince, before the whole court:

"Your Highness acts too well. People will begin to say you are in love with a woman of eight-and-thirty, and that will spoil my marriage with the count. So I will not act any more with your Highness unless your Highness will promise you will only address me as you would a woman of a certain age—the Marchesa Raversi, for instance."

The performance was repeated three times over. The prince was wild with delight, but one evening he looked very much worried.

"Unless I am very much mistaken," said the mistress of the robes to the princess, "Rassi is trying to play us some trick. I would suggest that your Highness should have some acting to-morrow night. The prince will act badly, and in his despair, he will tell you something."

As a matter of fact the prince did act very ill; he was hardly audible, and could not contrive to wind up his sentences. By the end of the first act the tears were almost standing in his eyes. The duchess kept close beside him, but she was cold and unmoved. The prince, finding himself alone with her for a moment in the green room, went over to the door and shut it. Then he said:

"I shall never be able to get through the second and third acts. I will not submit to being applauded out of good nature. The applause I was given to-night almost broke my heart. Advise me. What am I to do?"

"I will go upon the stage; I will make a deep courtesy to her Highness, and another to the audience, and I will announce that the actor who was playing the part of Lelio has been taken suddenly ill, and that therefore the play will be wound up with a little music. Count Rusca and the little Ghisolfi will be too delighted to have a chance of showing off their thin voices before such a brilliant assembly."

The prince seized the duchess's hand and kissed it passionately. "Why are you not a man?" he cried. "You would give me good advice! Rassi has just laid a hundred and eighty-two depositions against the persons accused of murdering my father on my writing-table, and besides the depositions there is an indictment which covers more than two hundred pages. I shall have to read them all, and further, I have given my word not to say anything about them to the count. All this is sure to end in executions. Already he is pressing me to have Ferrante Palla, that great poet whom I admire so much, carried off from a place near Antibes, in France, where he is living under the name of Poncet."

"From the day when your Highness hangs a Liberal, Rassi will be bound to the ministry by iron chains, and that is what he most earnestly desires. But it will not be safe for your Highness to let it be known you are going to take a drive, two hours before you start. Neither the princess nor the count shall hear, through me, of the cry of anguish which has just escaped you, but as my oath forbids me to keep any secret from the princess, I shall be glad if your Highness will tell your mother what you have just permitted me to hear."

This idea diverted the sovereign's mind from the distress with which his failure as an actor had overwhelmed him.

"Very good. Go and call my mother. I will go straight to her cabinet."

The prince left the theatre, crossed the drawing-room leading to it, and haughtily dismissed the great chamberlain and the aide-de-camp in waiting, who had followed him. The princess, on her part, hastily left the auditorium. As soon as she had reached her own apartments the duchess courtesied profoundly to mother and son, and left them alone together. The excitement of the courtiers may be conceived; that is one of the things which makes a court so entertaining. In an hour's time, the prince himself appeared at the door of the cabinet, and summoned the duchess. The princess was in tears, the prince looked very much disturbed.

"Here are two weak beings in a bad temper," said the mistress of the robes to herself, "and looking about for some good pretext for being angry with somebody else." To begin with, mother and son took the words out of each other's mouth in their anxiety to relate all the details of the matter to the duchess, who, when she answered, was most careful not to put forward any idea. For two mortal hours the three actors in this wearisome scene never ceased playing the parts we have just indicated. The prince himself went to fetch the two huge portfolios Rassi had laid upon his writing-table. Coming out of his mother's cabinet, he found the whole court waiting for him. "Take yourselves off and leave me alone!" he exclaimed with a rudeness which had never been known in him before. The prince did not choose to be seen carrying the portfolios himself—a prince must never carry anything. In the twinkling of an eye the courtiers disappeared. When the prince came back, he found nobody in the apartment except the footmen, who were putting out the candles. He packed them off in a rage, and treated poor Fontana, the aide-de-camp in waiting, who, in his zeal, had stupidly stayed behind, in the same fashion.

"Every soul is set on trying my patience this evening," he said to the duchess crossly, as he re-entered the cabinet. He believed in her cleverness, and was furious at her evident determination not to put forward any opinion. She, on her part, was quite resolved she would say nothing unless her advice was expressly asked. Thus another full half-hour went by before the prince, who was keenly alive to his own dignity, could make up his mind to say, "But you say nothing, madam!"

"I am here to wait on the princess, and to forget everything that is said before me, instantly."

"Very good, madam," said the prince, reddening deeply. "I command you to give me your opinion."

"The object of punishing crimes is to prevent a repetition of them. Was the late prince poisoned? That is very doubtful. Was he poisoned by the Jacobins? That is what Rassi pines to prove; for thenceforward he becomes indispensable to your Highness for all time. In that case your Highness, whose reign is just opening, may expect many an evening like this one. The general opinion of your subjects, and it is a perfectly true one, is that your Highness's nature is full of kindness. So long as your Highness does not have any Liberal hanged, this reputation will remain to you, and you may be very certain that no one will think of giving you poison."

"Your conclusion is quite clear," exclaimed the princess peevishly. "You don't desire to have my husband's murderers punished."

The Chartreuse of Parma

" Madam, that, I suppose, is because I am bound to them by ties of the tenderest friendship."

The duchess read clearly in the prince's eyes that he believed her to be thoroughly agreed with his mother on some line of conduct to be dictated to him. A somewhat rapid succession of bitter repartees was exchanged between the ladies, at the end of which the duchess vowed she would not say another word, and to this resolution she steadily adhered. But the prince, after a long discussion with his mother, ordered her once more to tell him her opinion.

" I can assure both your Highnesses I will do nothing of the kind."

" But this is mere childishness! " exclaimed the prince.

" Duchess, I beg you will speak," said the princess with much dignity.

" I beg your Highness will excuse my doing so. But," continued the duchess, addressing herself to the prince, " your Highness reads French beautifully. To soothe our agitated feelings, would your Highness read *us* one of La Fontaine's fables? "

The princess thought the expression " *us* " exceedingly impertinent, but she looked at once astonished and amused when the mistress of the robes, who had calmly gone over to the bookcase and opened it, came back carrying a volume of La Fontaine's Fables. She turned over the leaves for a few minutes, and then, handing the prince the book, she said: " I beseech your Highness to read the *whole* fable."

LE JARDINIER ET SON SEIGNEUR

Un amateur de jardinage
Demi-bourgeois, demi-manant,
Possédait en certain village
Un jardin assez propre, et le clos attenant.
Il avait de plant vif fermé cette étendue :
Là croissaient à plaisir l'oseille et la laitue,
De quoi faire à Margot pour sa fête un bouquet,
Peu de jasmin d'Espagne et force serpolet.
Cette félicité par un lièvre troublée
Fit qu'au seigneur du bourg notre homme se plaignit.
Ce maudit animal vient prendre sa goulée
Soir et matin, dit-il, et des piéges se rit ;

The Chartreuse of Parma

Les pierres, les bâtons y perdent leur crédit :
Il est sorcier, je crois. — Sorcier ! je l'en défie,
Repartit le seigneur : fût-il diable, Miraut,
En dépit de ses tours, l'attrapera bientôt.
Je vous en déferai, bonhomme, sur ma vie.
— Et quand ? — Et dès demain, sans tarder plus longtemps
La partie ainsi faite, il vient avec ses gens.
— Çà, déjeunons, dit-il : vos poulets sont-ils tendres ?
.   .   .   .

L'embarras des chasseurs succède au déjeuné.
    Chacun s'anime et se prépare ;
Les trompes et les cors font un tel tintamarre,
    Que le bonhomme est étonné.
Le pis fut que l'on mit en piteux équipage
Le pauvre potager. Adieu planches, carreaux ;
    Adieu chicorée et poireaux ;
    Adieu de quoi mettre au potage.
.   .   .   .

Le bonhomme disait : Ce sont là jeux de prince.
Mais on le laissait dire ; et les chiens et les gens
Firent plus de dégât en une heure de temps
    Que n'en auraient fait en cent ans
    Tous les lièvres de la province.

Petits princes, videz vos débats entre vous ;
De recourir aux rois vous seriez de grands fous.
Il ne les faut jamais engager dans vos guerres,
    Ni les faire entrer sur vos terres.

After the reading a long silence ensued. The prince put the book back in its place himself, and began to walk up and down the room.

"Well, madam," said the princess, "will you deign to speak ?"

"No, indeed, madam ; not until his Highness has appointed me his minister. If I were to speak here I should run the risk of losing my post as mistress of the robes."

Silence fell again, for a full quarter of an hour. At last the princess bethought her of the part once played by Marie de Medicis, mother of Louis XIII. Every day, for some time previously, the mistress of the robes had caused Mons. Bazin's excellent History of Louis XIII to be read to her Highness. The princess, vexed though she was, considered

456

that the duchess might very likely leave the country, and that then Rassi, of whom she was horribly afraid, would quite possibly follow Richelieu's example, and induce her son to banish her. At that moment the princess would have given anything she had on earth to be able to humiliate her mistress of the robes. But she was powerless. She rose from her seat, and with a smile which had a touch of exaggeration about it she took the duchess's hand, and said:

"Come, madam, prove your affection for me by speaking!"

"Two words then, and no more. All the papers collected by that viper Rassi should be burned in this fireplace, and he must never know they have been burned." Whispering in the princess's ear, she added, with a familiar air:

"Rassi may be a Richelieu."

"But, devil take it," cried the prince, much vexed, "these papers have cost me more than eighty thousand francs!"

"Prince," replied the duchess passionately, "now you see what it costs you to employ low-born rogues! Would to God you might lose a million rather than that you should ever place your faith in the vile scoundrels who robbed your father of his peaceful sleep for the last six years of his reign!"

The word *low-born* had given great pleasure to the princess, who held that the count and his friend were somewhat too exclusive in their esteem for intelligence—always nearly related to Jacobinism.

During the short moment of deep silence filled up by the princess's reflections, the castle clock struck three. The princess rose, courtesied profoundly to her son, and said: "My health will not permit me to prolong this discussion any further. Never employ a *low-born* minister! You will never convince me that Rassi has not stolen half the money he made you spend on espionage." The princess took two tapers out of the candlesticks, and set them in the fireplace, so that they still remained alight. Then, drawing nearer to her son, she added: "In my case, La Fontaine's fable over-

'rides my just longing to avenge my husband. Will your Highness give me leave to burn these writings?"

The prince stood motionless.

"He really has a stupid face," said the duchess to herself. "The count is quite right, the late prince would never have kept us till three o'clock in the morning before he could make up his mind."

The princess, who was still standing, continued:

"That lawyer-fellow would be very proud if he knew his papers, all of them crammed with lies, and cooked up to secure his own advancement, had kept the two greatest personages in the state awake all night!"

The prince flew at the portfolios like a fury, and emptied their contents on to the hearth. The weight of the papers very nearly stifled the two candles; the room was filled with smoke. The princess saw in her son's eyes that he was sorely tempted to seize a water-bottle, and save the documents that had cost him a hundred thousand francs.

She called to the duchess sharply, "Why don't you open the window?" The duchess hastened to obey. Instantly all the papers flamed up together; there was a great roar in the chimney, and soon it became evident that it, too, had caught fire.

In all money matters, the prince was a mean man. He fancied he saw his palace blazing, and all the treasures it contained destroyed. Rushing to the window, he shouted for the Guard, and his tone was quite wild. At the sound of the prince's voice, the soldiers ran tumultuously into the court. He came back to the fireplace, up which the air from the open window was rushing, with a noise that was really alarming. He lost his temper, swore, took two or three turns up and down the room, like a man beside himself, and finally ran out of it.

The princess and her mistress of the robes were left standing, facing each other, in the deepest silence.

"Is she going to be in a rage again?" said the duchess to herself. "Well, my cause is won, at any rate!" and she was just making up her mind to return very impertinent answers, when a thought flashed across her—she had noticed the second portfolio standing untouched. "No, my cause is only half won," she thought, and she addressed the princess, somewhat coldly, "Have I your Highness's commands to burn the rest of these papers?"

"And where will you burn them, pray?" inquired the princess crossly.

"In the drawing-room fireplace. If I throw them in one after the other there will be no danger."

The duchess thrust the portfolio, bursting with papers, under her arm, took a candle in her hand, and went into the adjoining drawing-room. She gave herself time to make sure that this particular portfolio held the depositions, hid five or six packets of papers under her shawl, burned the rest very carefully, and slipped out without taking leave of the princess.

"Here's a fine piece of impertinence," she said with a laugh. "But with her affectations of inconsolable widowhood, she very nearly brought my head to the scaffold."

When the princess heard the noise of the duchess's carriage, she was filled with anger against her mistress of the robes.

In spite of the lateness of the hour, the duchess sent for the count. He had gone to the fire at the palace, but he soon appeared, bringing news that it was all over. "The young prince really showed a great deal of courage, and I paid him my heartiest compliments."

"Look quickly over these depositions, and let us burn them as fast as we can."

The count read and turned pale.

"Upon my word, they had got very near the truth. The investigation has been most skilfully conducted. They are quite on Ferrante Palla's track, and if he speaks, we shall have a difficult card to play."

"But he won't speak," cried the duchess. "That man is a man of honour! Now into the fire with them!"

"Not yet. Let me take down the names of ten or fifteen dangerous witnesses, whom I shall take the liberty of spiriting away, if Rassi ever attempts to begin again."

"Let me remind your Excellency that the prince has

given his word not to tell the Minister of Justice anything about our nocturnal performance."

" And he will keep it, out of cowardice, and because he hates a scene."

" Now, my dear friend, this night's work has done a great deal to hasten on our marriage. I never would have brought you a trial in the criminal courts as my dowry, more especially for a wrong I did on account of my interest in another person."

The count was in love. He caught her hand protestingly; tears stood in his eyes.

" Before you leave me, pray give me some advice about my behaviour to the princess. I am worn out with fatigue. I have been acting for an hour on the stage, and for five hours in her Highness's cabinet."

" The impertinent manner of your departure has avenged you amply for the princess's disagreeable remarks, which were only a proof of weakness. When you see her to-morrow, take the same tone as that you used this morning. Rassi is neither an exile nor a prisoner yet, nor have we torn up Fabrizio's sentence.

" You pressed the princess to make a decision; that always puts princes, and even prime ministers, out of temper. And besides, after all, you are her mistress of the robes; in other words, her humble servant. A revulsion of feeling which is invariable with weak natures will make Rassi's favour higher than ever within three days. He will strive to ruin somebody, but until he has compromised the prince, he can be sure of nothing.

" There was a man hurt at the fire to-night—a tailor. Upon my soul, he showed the most extraordinary courage. To-morrow I will suggest that the prince should walk out, leaning on my arm, and pay a visit to that tailor. I shall be armed to the teeth, and I will keep a sharp lookout. And, indeed, so far, no one hates this young prince. I want to give him the habit of walking about in the streets—a trick I shall play on Rassi, who will certainly succeed me, and who will not be able to allow him to do anything so imprudent. On our way back from the tailor's house, I'll bring the prince past his father's statue; he'll see how the stones have broken the skirt of the Roman tunic with which the fool of a sculptor has adorned the figure, and he must be a prince of very limited intelligence indeed if he is not inspired with the remark, ' This is what one gets by hanging Jacobins,' to which I shall reply, ' You must either hang ten thousand, or not a single one; the massacre of St. Bartholomew destroyed Protestantism in France.'

" To-morrow, dearest friend, before I start on my expedition, you must wait upon the prince, and say to him: ' Last night I acted as your minister; I gave you advice, and in obeying your orders I incurred the displeasure of the princess. You must reward me.' He will think you are going to ask him for money, and will begin to knit his brows. You must leave him to struggle with this unpleasant thought as long as possible. Then you will say: ' I entreat your Highness to give orders that Fabrizio shall be tried after hearing *both* parties—that is to say, that Fabrizio himself shall be present—by the twelve most respected judges in your dominions,' and without losing a moment you will beg his signature to a short order written by your own fair hand, which I will now dictate to you. Of course I shall insert a clause to the effect that the first sentence is annulled. To this there is only one objection, but if you carry the business through quickly, it will not occur to the prince.

" He may say, ' Fabrizio must give himself up again at the fortress.' You will reply, ' He will give himself up at the city jail ' (you know I am master there, and your nephew will be able to come and see you every evening). If the prince answers, ' No; his flight has smirched the honour of my citadel, and as a matter of form, I insist on his going back to the room he occupied there,' you in your turn will say, ' No; for there he would be at the mercy of my enemy Rassi,' and by one of those womanly hints you know so well how to insinuate, you will make him understand that to work on Rassi, you might possibly inform him as to this night's *auto da fé*. If the prince persists, you will say you are going away to your house at Sacca for ten days.

" You must send for Fabrizio, and consult with him

about this step, which may bring him back into his prison. We must foresee everything, and if, while he is under lock and key, Rassi loses patience, and has me poisoned, Fabrizio might be in danger. But this is not very probable.

" You know I have brought over a French cook, who is the cheeriest of men, always making puns; now, punning is incompatible with murder. I have already told our Fabrizio that I have discovered all the witnesses of his brave and noble behaviour. It is quite clear it was Giletti who tried to murder him. I had not mentioned these witnesses to you, because I wanted to give you a surprise. But the plan has failed; I could not get the prince's signature. I told our Fabrizio I would certainly procure him some high ecclesiastical position, but I shall find that very difficult if his enemies at the court of Rome can put forward an accusation of murder against him. Do you realize, madam, that if he is not tried in the most formal manner, the name of Giletti will be a bugbear to him all the days of his life? It would be a very cowardly thing to avoid a trial when one is quite sure of one's innocence. Besides, if he were guilty I would have him acquitted. When I mentioned the subject, the eager young fellow would not let me finish my story; he laid hands on the official list, and together we chose out the twelve most upright and learned of the judges. When the list was complete we struck out six of the names, and replaced them by those of six lawyers who are my personal enemies, and as we could only discover two of these, we made up the number with four rascals who are devoted to Rassi."

The count's remarks filled the duchess with deadly and not unreasonable alarm. At last she submitted to reason, and wrote the order appointing the judges, at the minister's dictation.

It was six o'clock in the morning before the count left her. She tried to sleep, but all in vain. At nine she was breakfasting with Fabrizio, whom she found consumed with longing to be tried; at ten she waited on the princess, who was not visible; at eleven she saw the prince, who was holding his *lever*, and who signed the order without making the slightest objection. The duchess sent off the order to the count, and went to bed.

I might give an entertaining account of Rassi's fury when the count obliged him, in the prince's presence, to counter-sign the order the prince himself had signed earlier in the morning. But events press too thickly upon us.

The count discussed the merits of each judge, and offered to change the names. But my readers may possibly be growing as weary of my details of legal procedure as of all these court intrigues. From all of them we may draw this moral—that the man who comes to close quarters with a court imperils his happiness, if he is happy, and in any case, risks his whole future on the intrigues of a waiting-woman.

On the other hand, in a republic, such as America, he must bore himself from morning to night by paying solemn court to the shopkeepers in the street, and grow as dull as they are, and then, over there, there is no opera for him to go to.

When the duchess left her bed that evening, she endured a moment of extreme anxiety. Fabrizio was not to be found. At last, toward midnight, during the performance of a play at the palace, she received a letter from him. Instead of giving himself up at the city jail, which was under the count's jurisdiction, he had gone back to his old room in the fortress, too delighted to find himself once more in Clelia's neighbourhood.

This was an immensely important incident, for in that place he was more than ever exposed to the danger of poison. This piece of folly drove the duchess to despair, but she forgave its cause—her nephew's wild love for Clelia—because that young lady was certainly to be married, within a few days, to the wealthy Marchese Crescenzi. By this mad act Fabrizio recovered all his former influence over the duchess.

"That cursed paper I made the prince sign will bring about Fabrizio's death! What idiots men are, with their notions of honour! As if there were any necessity for thinking about honour under an absolute government in a country where a man like Rassi is Minister of Justice! We ought simply and solely to have accepted the pardon which the prince would have given, just as willingly as he gave the order convoking this extraordinary court. What matter is it, after all, whether a man of Fabrizio's birth is accused, more or less, of having killed a strolling player like Giletti with his own hand and his own sword?"

No sooner had the duchess received Fabrizio's note, than she hurried to the count. She found him looking quite pale.

"Good God, my dear friend!" he cried. "I certainly bring bad luck to this poor boy, and you will be frantic with me again. I can give you proofs that I sent for the keeper of the city jail yesterday evening. Your nephew would have come to drink tea with you every day. The awful thing is that it is impossible for either you or me to tell the prince we are afraid of poison, and poison administered by Rassi. He would regard such a suspicion as immoral to the last degree. Nevertheless, if you insist upon it, I am ready to go to the palace. But I know what answer I shall receive. I will say more; I will offer you a means which I would not use for myself. Since I have held power in this country I have never caused a single man to perish, and you know I am so weak-minded in that particular, that when evening falls I sometimes think of those two spies I had shot, a trifle hastily, in Spain. Well, do you wish me to rid you of Rassi? There is no limit to Fabrizio's danger at his hands. Therein he holds a certain means of driving me to take my departure."

The suggestion was exceedingly pleasing to the duchess, but she did not adopt it.

"I do not choose," said she to the count, "that in our retirement under the beautiful Neapolitan sky your evenings should be darkened by sad thoughts."

"But, dearest friend, it seems to me we have nothing but sad thoughts to choose from. What will become of you, what is to become of me, if Fabrizio is carried off by illness?"

There was a fresh discussion over this idea. The duchess closed it with these words: "Rassi owes his life to the fact that I love you better than I do Fabrizio. No; I will not poison every evening of the old age we are going to spend together."

The duchess hurried to the fortress. General Fabio Conti was delighted to have to refuse her admittance, in obedience to the formal provisions of military law, whereby no one can enter a state prison without an order signed by the prince.

" But the Marchese Crescenzi and his musicians come into the citadel every day."

" That is because I have obtained a special order for them from the prince."

The poor duchess was unaware of the extent of her misfortune. General Fabio Conti had taken Fabrizio's escape as a personal slight upon himself. He had no business to admit him when he saw him enter the citadel, for he had no orders to that effect.

" But," thought he, " Heaven has sent him to me, to repair my honour, and save me from the ridicule which would have blighted my military career. I must not lose my chance. He will be acquitted—there is no doubt of that— and I have only a few days in which to wreak my vengeance."

CHAPTER XXV

OUR hero's arrival threw Clelia into a condition of despair. The poor girl, earnestly pious and thoroughly honest with herself, could not blink the fact that she could never know happiness apart from Fabrizio. But when her father had been half poisoned, she had made a vow to the Madonna that she would sacrifice herself to him by marrying the marchese. She had also vowed she would never see Fabrizio again, and she was already torn by the most cruel remorse, on account of the admission into which she had slipped in her letter to Fabrizio the night before his flight. How shall I describe the feelings that swelled that shadowed heart when, as she sadly watched her birds fluttering hither and thither, she raised her eyes, instinctively and lovingly, to the window whence Fabrizio had once gazed at her, and saw him stand there once again, and greet her with the tenderest respect.

At first she thought it was a vision, which Heaven had sent her as a punishment. At last the hideous truth forced itself on her mind. "They have taken him," she thought, "and now he is lost!" She remembered the language used within the fortress after his escape—t e very humblest jailer had felt himself mortally humiliated by it. Cleli looked at Fabrizio, and in spite of herself, her eyes spoke all the passion that was driving her to despair. "Can you believe," she seemed to say to Fabrizio, "that I shall find happiness in the sumptuous palace that is being prepared for me? My father tells me, till I am sick of hearing it, that you are as poor as we are. Heavens! how gladly would I share that poverty! But, alas, we must never see each other again!"

Clelia had not the strength to make any use of the alphabets. Even as she gazed at Fabrizio, she turned faint, and dropped upon a chair beside the window. Her head rested upon the window ledge, and as she had striven to look at him till the last moment her face, turned toward Fabrizio, was fully exposed to his gaze. When, after a few moments, she opened her eyes, her first glance sought Fabrizio. Tears stood in his eyes, but they were tears of utter happiness. He saw that absence had not made her forget him. For some time the two poor young creatures remained as though bewitched by the sight of each other. Fabrizio ventured to say a few words, as though singing to a guitar, something to this effect: " It is to see you again that I have come back to prison; I am to be tried."

These words seemed to stir all Clelia's sense of virtue. She rose swiftly to her feet, covered her eyes, and endeavoured to make him understand, by the most earnest gestures, that she must never see him again. This had been her promise to the Madonna, which she had forgotten when she had looked at him. When Fabrizio still ventured to give expression to his love, Clelia fled indignantly, swearing to herself that she would never see him again. For these were the exact terms of her vow to the Madonna : " *My eyes shall never look on him again.*" She had written them on a slip of paper which her uncle Cesare had allowed her to burn on the altar, at the moment of the elevation, while he was saying mass.

But in spite of every vow, Fabrizio's presence in the Farnese Tower drove Clelia back into all her former habits. She now generally spent her whole day alone in her room, but hardly had she recovered from the state of agitation into which Fabrizio's appearance had thrown her, than she began to move about the palace, and renew acquaintance, so to speak, with all her humbler friends. A very talkative old woman, who worked in the kitchens, said to her, with a look of mystery, " Signor Fabrizio will not get out of the citadel this time."

" He will not commit the crime of getting over the walls," said Clelia, " but he will go out by the gate if he is acquitted."

The Chartreuse of Parma

"I tell your Excellency, and I know what I am saying, that he will never go out till he is carried out feet foremost."

Clelia turned deadly pale; the old woman remarked it, and her eloquence was checked. She felt she had committed an imprudence in speaking thus before the daughter of the governor, whose duty it would be to tell every one Fabrizio had died of illness. As Clelia was going back to her rooms she met the prison doctor, an honest, timid kind of man, who told her, with a look of alarm, that Fabrizio was very ill. Clelia could hardly drag herself along; she hunted high and low for her uncle, the good priest Cesare, and found him at last in the chapel, praying fervently; his face betrayed the greatest distress. The dinner bell rang. Not a word was exchanged between the two brothers at table, but toward the end of the meal the general addressed some very tart remark to his brother. This latter looked at the servants, who left the room.

"General," said Don Cesare to the governor, "I have the honour to inform you that I am about to leave the citadel. I give you my resignation."

"Bravo! Bravissimo! . . . to cast suspicion on me! And your reason, may I inquire?"

"My conscience."

"Pooh! you're nothing but a shaveling priest. You know nothing about honour."

"Fabrizio is killed!" said Clelia to herself. "They've poisoned him at his dinner, or else they'll do it to-morrow." She flew to her aviary, determined to sing and accompany herself on the piano. "I will confess it all," said she to herself. "I shall be given absolution for breaking my vow to save a man's life." What was her consternation, on reaching the aviary, to perceive that the screens had been replaced by boards, fastened to the iron bars. Half distracted, she endeavoured to warn the prisoner by a few words, which she screamed rather than sang. There was no answer of any sort. A deathlike silence already reigned within the Farnese Tower. "It's all over," she thought. Distraught, she ran down the stairs, then ran back again, to fetch what money she had, and her little diamond earrings. As she went by she snatched up the bread remaining from dinner, which had been put on a sideboard. " If he is still alive, it is my duty to save him." With a haughty air she moved toward the little door in the tower. The door was open, and eight soldiers had only just been stationed in the pillared hall on the ground floor. She looked boldly at the soldiers. Clelia had intended to speak to the sergeant who should have been in charge, but the man was not there. Clelia hurried up the little iron staircase which wound round one of the pillars; the soldiers stared at her, very much astonished, but presumably on account of her lace shawl, and her bonnet, they dared not say anything to her. There was nobody at all on the first floor, but on the second, at the entrance to the passage, which, as my readers may recollect, was closed by three iron-barred doors, and led to Fabrizio's room, she found a turnkey, a stranger to her, who said, with a startled look:

" He hasn't dined yet."

" I know that quite well," said Clelia loftily. The man did not venture to stop her. Twenty paces farther on, Clelia found, sitting on the first of the six wooden steps leading up to Fabrizio's room, another turnkey, very elderly, and exceedingly red in the face, who said to her firmly, " Signorina, have you an order from the governor? "

" Do you not know who I am? "

At that moment Clelia was possessed by a sort of supernatural strength. She was quite beside herself. " I am going to save my husband," she said to herself.

While the old turnkey was calling out, " But my duty will not permit me," Clelia ran swiftly up the six steps. She threw herself against the door. A huge key was in the lock; it took all her strength to turn it. At that moment the old turnkey, who was half drunk, snatched at the bottom of her skirt. She dashed into the room, slammed the door, tearing her gown, and, as the turnkey pushed at it, to get in after her, she shot a bolt which she found just under her hand. She looked into the room and saw Fabrizio sitting at a very small table, on which his dinner was laid. She rushed at the

table, overturned it, and, clutching Fabrizio's arm, she cried,
" Hast thou eaten? "

This use of the second person singular filled Fabrizio
with joy. For the first time in her agitation, Clelia had forgotten her womanly reserve and betrayed her love.

Fabrizio had been on the point of beginning his fatal
meal. He clasped her in his arms, and covered her with
kisses. " This food has been poisoned," thought he to himself. " If I tell her I have not touched it, religion will re-
assert its rights, and Clelia will take to flight. But if she
looks upon me as a dying man I shall persuade her not to
leave me. She is longing to find a means of escape from her
hateful marriage; chance has brought us this one. The
jailers will soon collect; they will break in the door, and
then there will be such a scandal that the Marchese Crescenzi
will take fright, and break off his marriage."

During the momentary silence consequent on these reflections, Fabrizio felt that Clelia was already endeavouring
to free herself from his embrace.

" I feel no pain as yet," he said to her, " but soon I shall
lie at thy feet in agony. Help me to die! "

" Oh, my only friend," she answered, " I will die with
thee! " and she clasped her arms about him with a convulsive
pressure.

Half dressed as she was, and half wild with passion, she
was so beautiful that Fabrizio could not restrain an almost
involuntary gesture. He met with no resistance.

In the gush of passion and generous feeling which follows on excessive happiness, he said to her boldly: " The
first instants of our happiness shall not be soiled by a vile lie.
But for thy courage I should now be nothing but a corpse,
or struggling in the most hideous tortures. But at thy entrance I was only about to dine; I had not touched any of
the dishes."

Fabrizio dilated on the frightful picture, so as to soften
the indignation he already perceived in Clelia's eyes. Torn
by violent and conflicting feelings, she looked at him for
an instant, and then threw herself into his arms. A great
noise arose in the passage, the iron doors were roughly

opened and violently banged, and there was talking and shouting.

"Oh, if only I was armed!" exclaimed Fabrizio. "They took my arms away before they would let me come in. No doubt they are coming to make an end of me. Farewell, my Clelia! I bless my death, since it has brought me my happiness!" Clelia kissed him, and gave him a little ivory-handled dagger, with a blade not much longer than that of a penknife.

"Do not let them kill thee," she said. "Defend thyself to the last moment. If my uncle hears the noise—he is brave and virtuous—he will save thee. I am going to speak to them!" and as she said the words, she rushed toward the door.

"If thou art not killed," she said feverishly, with her hand on the bolt and her head turned toward him, "starve rather than touch any food that is brought thee. Keep this bread about thy person always." The noise was drawing nearer. Fabrizio caught hold of her, took her place by the door, and throwing it open violently, rushed down the six wooden steps. The ivory-handled dagger was in his hand, and he was just about to drive it into the waistcoat of General Fontana, the prince's aide-de-camp, who started back in alarm, and exclaimed, "But I have come to save you, Signor del Dongo!"

Fabrizio turned back, up the six steps, said, within the room, "Fontana has come to save me," then, returning to the general, on the wooden steps, he conversed calmly with him, begging him, in many words, to forgive him his angry impulse. "There has been an attempt to poison me; that dinner you see laid out there is poisoned. I had the sense not to touch it, but I will confess to you that the incident annoyed me. When I heard you coming up the stairs, I thought they were coming to finish me with daggers. . . . General, I request you will give orders that nobody shall enter my room. Somebody would take away the poison, and our good prince must be informed of everything."

The general, very pale, and very much horrified, transmitted the order suggested by Fabrizio to the specially selected jailers, who had followed him. These gentry, very much crestfallen at seeing the poison discovered, lost no time in getting downstairs. They made as though they were going in front, to get out of the way of the prince's aide-de-camp on the narrow staircase; as a matter of fact, they were panting to escape and disappear. To General Fontana's great astonishment, Fabrizio halted for more than a quarter of an hour at the little iron staircase that ran round the pillar on the ground floor. He wanted to give Clelia time to conceal herself on the first floor.

It was the duchess who, after doing several wild things, had succeeded in getting General Fontana sent to the citadel. This success had been the result of chance. Leaving Count Mosca, who was as much alarmed as herself, she hurried to the palace. The princess, who had a strong dislike to energy, which always struck her as being vulgar, thought she was mad, and did not show the least disposition to attempt any unusual step to help her. The duchess, distracted, was weeping bitterly. All she could do was to repeat, over and over again, " But, madam, within a quarter of an hour Fabrizio will be dead of poison! "

When the duchess perceived the princess's perfect indifference, her grief drove her mad. That moral reflection, which would certainly have occurred to any woman educated in one of those northern religions which permit of self-examination—" I was the first to use poison, and now it is by poison that I am destroyed "—never occurred to her. In Italy such considerations, in moments of deep passion, would seem as commonplace as a pun would appear to a Parisian, under parallel circumstances.

In her despair, the duchess chanced to go into the drawing-room, where she found the Marchese Crescenzi, who was in waiting that day. When the duchess had returned to Parma he had thanked her fervently for his post as lord in waiting, to which, but for her, he could never have aspired. There had been no lack of asseverations of devotion on his part. The duchess addressed him in the following words:

" Rassi is going to have Fabrizio, who is in the citadel, poisoned. Put some chocolate and a bottle of water, which

The Chartreuse of Parma

I will give you, into your pocket. Go up to the citadel, and save my life by telling General Fabio Conti that if he does not allow you to give Fabrizio the chocolate and the water yourself, you will break off your marriage with his daughter."

The marchese turned pale, and his features, instead of kindling into animation, expressed the most miserable perplexity. He " could not believe that so hideous a crime could be committed in so well-ordered a city as Parma, ruled over by so great a prince," and so forth. And to make it worse, he enunciated all these platitudes exceedingly slowly. In a word, the duchess found she had to deal with a man who was upright enough, but weak beyond words, and quite unable to make up his mind to act. After a score of remarks of this kind, all of them interrupted by her impatient exclamations, he hit on an excellent excuse. His oath as lord in waiting forbade him to take part in any machinations against the government.

My readers will imagine the anxiety and despair of the duchess, who felt the time was slipping by.

" But see the governor, at all events, and tell him I will hunt Fabrizio's murderers into hell!"

Despair had quickened the duchess's eloquence. But all her fervour only added to the marchese's alarm, and doubled his natural irresolution. At the end of an hour he was even less inclined to do anything than he had been at first.

The unhappy woman, who had reached the utmost limit of distraction, and was thoroughly convinced the governor would never refuse anything to so rich a son-in-law, went so far as to throw herself at his feet. This seemed only to increase the Marchese Crescenzi's cowardice—the strange sight filled him with an unconscious fear that he himself might be compromised. But then a strange thing happened. The marchese, a kind-hearted man at bottom, was touched when he saw so beautiful and, above all, so powerful a woman, kneeling at his feet.

" I myself, rich and noble as I am," thought he, " may one day be forced to kneel at the feet of some republican."

The marchese began to cry, and at last it was agreed that

the duchess, as mistress of the robes, should introduce him to the princess, who would give him leave to convey a small basket, of the contents of which he would declare himself ignorant, to Fabrizio.

The previous night, before the duchess had become aware of Fabrizio's folly in giving himself up to the citadel, a *commedia dell'arte* had been acted at court, and the prince, who always kept the lovers' parts for himself, and played them with the duchess, had spoken to her so passionately or his love that had such a thing been possible, in Italy, to any passionate man, or any prince, he would have looked ridiculous.

The prince, who, shy as he was, took his love-affairs very seriously, was walking along one of the corridors of the palace, when he met the duchess, hurrying the Marchese Crescenzi, who looked very much flustered, into the princess's presence. He was so surprised and dazzled by the beauty and the emotion with which despair had endued the mistress of the robes, that for the first time in his life he showed some decision of character. With a gesture that was more than imperious, he dismissed the marchese, and forthwith made a formal declaration of his love to the duchess. No doubt the prince had thought it all over beforehand, for it contained some very sensible remarks.

"Since my rank forbids me the supreme happiness of marrying you, I will swear to you on the Holy Wafer that I will never marry without your written consent. I know very well," he added, "that I shall cause you to lose the hand of the Prime Minister—a clever and very charming man— but, after all, he is fifty-six years old, and I am not yet twenty-two. I should feel I was insulting you, and should deserve your refusal, if I spoke to you of advantages apart from my love. But every soul about my court who cares about money speaks with admiration of the proof of love the count gives you, by leaving everything he possesses in your hands. I shall be only too happy to imitate him in this respect. You will use my fortune much better than I, and you will have the entire disposal of the annual sum which my ministers pay over to the lord steward of the crown. Thus it will be you, duchess, who will decide what sums I may expend each month."

The duchess thought all these details very long-winded. The sense of Fabrizio's peril was tearing at her heart.

" But don't you know, sir," she exclaimed, " that Fabrizio is at this moment being poisoned in your citadel. Save him! I believe everything!" The arrangement of her sentence was thoroughly awkward. At the word *poison* all the confidence, all the good faith which had been evident in the poor, well-meaning prince's conversation, disappeared like a flash. The duchess only noticed her blunder when it was too late to remedy it, and this increased her despair—a thing she had thought impossible. " If I had not mentioned poison," said she to herself, " he would have granted me Fabrizio's liberty. Oh, dear Fabrizio," she added, " I am fated to ruin you by my folly!"

It took the duchess a long time, and she was forced to employ many wiles, before she could win the prince back to his passionate declarations of affection. But he was still thoroughly scared. It was only his mind that spoke; his heart had been frozen—first of all by the idea of poison, and then by another, as displeasing to him as the first had been terrible, " Poison is being administered in my dominions without my being told anything about it. Rassi, then, is bent on dishonouring me in the eyes of Europe. God alone knows what I shall read in the French newspapers next month."

Suddenly, timid as the young man was, his heart was silent, and an idea started up in his mind.

" Dear duchess," he cried, " you know how deeply I am attached to you. I would fain believe your terrible notion about poison is quite unfounded. But, indeed, it set me thinking, too, and for a moment it almost made me forget my passionate love for you, the only one I have ever felt in my life. I feel I am not very lovable; I am nothing but a boy, very desperately in love. But put me to the test, at all events!"

As the prince spoke he grew very eager.

" Save Fabrizio, and I will believe everything! No doubt

The Chartreuse of Parma

I am carried away by a foolish mother's fears. But send instantly to fetch Fabrizio from the citadel, and let me see him. If he is still alive, send him from the palace to the city jail, and keep him there for months and months, until he has been tried, if that be your Highness's will!"

The duchess noticed with despair that the prince, instead of granting so simple a petition with a word, had grown gloomy. He was very much flushed; he looked at the duchess, then dropped his eyes, and his cheeks grew pale. The idea of poison she had so unluckily put forward had inspired him with a thought worthy of his own father, or of Philip II. But he did not dare to express it.

"Listen, madam," he said at last, as though with an effort, and in a tone that was not particularly gracious. "You look down upon me as a boy, and further, as a creature possessing no attraction. Well, I am going to say something horrible to you, which has been suggested to me, this instant, by the real and deep passion I feel for you. If I had the smallest belief in the world in this poison story, I should have taken steps at once; my duty would have made that a law. But I take your request to be nothing but a wild fancy, the meaning of which, you will allow me to say, I may not fully grasp. You expect me, who have hardly reigned three months, to act without consulting my ministers. You ask me to make an exception to a general rule, which, I confess, seems to me a very reasonable one. At this moment it is you, madam, who are absolute sovereign here; you inspire me with hope in a matter which is all in all to me. But within an hour, when this nightmare of yours, this fancy about poison, has faded away, my presence will become a weariness to you, and you will drive me away, madam. Therefore I want an oath. Swear to me, madam, that if Fabrizio is restored to you, safe and sound, you will grant me, within three months, all the happiness that my love can crave; that you will ensure the bliss of my whole life by placing one hour of yours at my disposal, and that you will be mine!"

At that moment the castle clock struck two. "Ah, perhaps it is too late now!" thought the duchess.

The Chartreuse of Parma

" I swear it," she cried, and her eyes were wild.

Instantly the prince became a different man. Running to the aide-de-camp's room at the end of the gallery—

" General Fontana," he cried, " gallop at full speed to the citadel; hurry as fast as you can to the room where Signor del Dongo is confined, and bring him to me. I must speak to him within twenty minutes—within fifteen, if that be possible."

" Ah, general! " exclaimed the duchess, who had followed on the prince's heels. " My whole life may depend on one moment. A report—a false one, no doubt—has made me fear Fabrizio may be poisoned. The moment you are within earshot, call out to him not to eat. If he has touched food, you must make him sick; say I insist upon it—use violence if necessary. Tell him I am following close after you, and believe I shall be indebted to you all my life! "

" My lady duchess, my horse is saddled; I am thought a good rider; I will gallop as hard as I can go, and I shall be at the citadel eight minutes before you."

The aide-de-camp vanished. He was a man whose one merit was that he knew how to ride.

Before he had well closed the door the young prince, who apparently knew his own mind now, seized the duchess's hand. " Madam," he said, and there was passion in his tone, " deign to come with me to the chapel." Taken aback for the first time in her life, the duchess followed him without a word. She and the prince ran down the whole length of the great gallery of the palace, at the far end of which the chapel was situated. When they were inside the chapel the prince cast himself on his knees, as much before the duchess as before the altar.

" Repeat your oath! " he exclaimed passionately. " If you had been just, if the misfortune of my being a prince had not injured my cause, you would have granted me, out of pity for my love, that which you owe me now, because you have sworn it."

" If I see Fabrizio again, and he has not been poisoned— if he is alive within a week from now—if your Highness appoints him coadjutor to Archbishop Landriani, and his ultimate successor—I will trample everything, my honour, my womanly dignity, beneath my feet, and I will give myself to your Highness."

"But, *dearest friend*," said the prince, with a comical mixture of nervous anxiety and tenderness, "I am afraid of some pitfall I do not understand, and which may destroy all my happiness; that would kill me. If the archbishop makes some ecclesiastical difficulty which will drag the business out for years, what is to become of me? I am acting, you see, in perfect good faith; are you going to treat me like a Jesuit?"

"No, in all good faith. If Fabrizio is saved, and if you do all in your power to make him coadjutor and future archbishop, I will dishonour myself, and give myself to you. Your Highness will undertake to write '*approved*' on the margin of a request which the archbishop will present within the week?"

"I will sign you a blank sheet of paper! You shall rule me and my dominions!" Reddening with happiness, and thoroughly beside himself, he insisted on a second oath. So great was his emotion that it made him forget his natural timidity, and in that palace chapel where they were alone together, he whispered things which, if he had said them three days previously, would have altered the duchess's opinion of him. But in her heart, despair concerning Fabrizio's danger had now been replaced by horror at the promise which had been torn from her.

The duchess was overwhelmed by the thought of what she had done. If she was not yet conscious of the frightful bitterness of what she had said, it was because her attention was still strained by anxiety as to whether General Fontana would reach the citadel in time.

To stem the boy's wild love talk, and turn the conversation, she praised a famous picture by Parmegiano, which adorned the high altar in the chapel.

"Do me the kindness of allowing me to send it to you," said the prince.

"I accept it," replied the duchess. "But give me leave to hurry to meet Fabrizio."

The Chartreuse of Parma

With a bewildered look she told her coachman to make his horses into a gallop. On the bridge that spanned the fortress moat she met General Fontana and Fabrizio coming out on foot.

" Have you eaten? "

" No, by some miracle."

The duchess threw herself on Fabrizio's breast, and fell into a swoon, which lasted for an hour, and engendered fears, first for her life, and afterward for her reason.

At the sight of General Fontana, General Fabio Conti had grown white with rage. He dallied so much about obeying the prince's order, that the aide-de-camp, who concluded the duchess was about to occupy the position of reigning mistress, had ended by losing his temper. The governor had intended to make Fabrizio's illness last two or three days, and " now," said he to himself, " this general, a man about the court, will find the impudent fellow struggling in the agonies which are to avenge me for his flight."

Greatly worried, Fabio Conti stopped in the guard-room of the Farnese Tower, and hastily dismissed the soldiers in it. He did not care to have any witnesses of the approaching scene.

Five minutes afterwards, he was petrified with astonishment by hearing Fabrizio's voice, and seeing him well and hearty, describing the prison to General Fontana. He swiftly disappeared.

At his interview with the prince, Fabrizio behaved like a perfect gentleman. In the first place, he had no intention of looking like a child who is frightened by a mere nothing. The prince inquired kindly how he felt.

" Like a man, your Serene Highness, who is starving with hunger, because, by good luck, he has neither breakfasted nor dined."

After having had the honour of thanking the prince, he requested permission to see the archbishop, before proceeding to the city jail.

The prince had turned exceedingly pale when the conviction that the poison had not been altogether a phantom of the duchess's imagination had forced itself upon his childish brain. Absorbed by the cruel thought, he did not at first reply to Fabrizio's request that he might see the archbishop. Then he felt obliged to atone for his inattention by excessive graciousness.

"You can go out alone, sir, and move through the streets of my capital without any guard. Toward ten or eleven o'clock you will repair to the prison, and I trust you will not have to stay there long."

On the morrow of that great day, the most remarkable in his whole life, the prince thought himself a young Napoleon. That great man, he had read, had received favours from several of the most beautiful women of his court. Now that he too was a Napoleon by his success in love, he recollected that he had also been a Napoleon under fire. His soul was still glowing with delight over the firmness of his treatment of the duchess. The sense that he had achieved something difficult made quite another man of him. For a whole fortnight he became accessible to generous-minded argument; he showed some resolution of character.

He began, that very day, by burning the patent creating Rassi a count, which had been lying on his writing-table for the last month. He dismissed General Fabio Conti, and commanded Colonel Lange, his successor, to tell him the truth about the poison. Lange, a brave Polish soldier, terrified the jailers, and found out that Signor del Dongo was to have been poisoned at his breakfast, but that too many persons would have had to have been let into the secret. At his dinner, measures had been more carefully taken, and but for General Fontana's arrival, Monsignore del Dongo would have died. The prince was thrown into consternation. But, desperately in love as he was, it was a consolation to him to be able to think, "It turns out that I really have saved Monsignore del Dongo's life, and the duchess will not dare to break the word she has given me." From this thought another proceeded: "My way of life is much more difficult than I supposed. Every one agrees that the duchess is an exceedingly clever woman. In this case my interest and my heart agree. What divine happiness it would be for me, if she would become my Prime Minister!"

The Chartreuse of Parma

So worried was the prince by the horrors he had discovered, that he would have nothing to do with the acting that evening.

"It would be too great a happiness for me," said he to the duchess, "if you would rule my dominions, even as you rule my heart. To begin with, I am going to tell you how I have spent my day." And he began to relate everything very exactly. How he had burned Rassi's patent, his appointment of Lange, Lange's report on the attempted poisoning, and so forth.

"I feel I am a very inexperienced ruler. The count's jokes humiliate me. Even at the council-table he jokes, and in general society he says things which you will say are not true. He declares I am a child, and that he leads me wherever he chooses. Though I am a prince, madam, I am a man as well, and such remarks are very vexatious. To cast doubt on the stories Mosca put about, I was induced to appoint that dangerous scoundrel Rassi to the ministry. And now here I have General Fabio Conti, who still believes him to be so powerful that he dares not confess whether it was he or the Raversi who suggested his making away with your nephew. I have a good mind to have General Fabio Conti tried. The judges would soon find out whether he is guilty of the attempted poisoning."

"But have you any judges, sir?"

"What!" said the prince, astounded.

"You have learned lawyers, sir, who look very solemn as they walk through the streets. But their verdicts will always follow the will of the dominant party at your court."

While the young prince, thoroughly scandalized, was saying a number of things which proved his candour to be far greater than his wisdom, the duchess was thinking to herself.

"Will it answer my purpose to have Conti dishonoured? Certainly not, for then his daughter's marriage with that worthy commonplace individual Crescenzi becomes impossible."

An endless conversation followed on this subject between the duchess and the prince. The prince's admiration quite blinded him. Out of consideration for Clelia's marriage with the Marchese Crescenzi, but on this account solely, as he angrily informed the ex-governor, the prince overlooked his attempt to poison a prisoner. But, advised by the duchess, he sent him into banishment until the date of his daughter's marriage. The duchess believed she no longer loved Fabrizio, but she was passionately anxious to see Clelia married to the marchese. This came of her vague hope that she might thus see Fabrizio grow less absent-minded.

In his delight, the prince would have disgraced Rassi openly that very night. The duchess said to him laughingly:

" Do not you know a saying of Napoleon's, that a man in a high position, on whom all men's eyes are fixed, must never allow himself to act in anger? But it is too late to do anything to-night. Let us put off all business until to-morrow."

She wanted to get time to consult the count, to whom she faithfully repeated the whole of the evening's conversation, only suppressing the prince's frequent references to a promise the thought of which poisoned her existence. The duchess hoped to make herself so indispensable that she would be able to get the matter indefinitely adjourned by saying to the prince, "If you are so barbarous as to make me endure such a humiliation, which I should never forgive, I will leave your state the next morning."

The count, when the duchess consulted with him as to Rassi's fate, behaved like a true philosopher. Rassi and General Fabio Conti travelled to Piedmont together.

A very peculiar difficulty arose in connection with Fabrizio's trial. The judges wanted to acquit him by acclamation at their very first sitting.

The count was obliged to use threats to make the trial last a week, and insure the hearing of all the witnesses. " These people are all alike," said he to himself.

The day after his acquittal, Fabrizio del Dongo took possession, at last, of his post as grand vicar to the good Archbishop Landriani. On that same day the prince signed the despatches necessary to insure Fabrizio's appointment as the archbishop's coadjutor and ultimate successor, and within less than two months, he was installed in this position.

Everybody complimented the duchess on her nephew's serious bearing. As a matter of fact, he was in utter despair.

Immediately after his deliverance, which had been followed by General Fabio Conti's disgrace and banishment, and the duchess's accession to the highest favour, Clelia had taken refuge in the house of her aunt, the Countess Cantarini, a very rich and very aged woman, who never thought of anything but her health. Clelia might have seen Fabrizio, but any one acquainted with her former engagements, and seeing her present mode of behaviour, would have concluded that her regard for her lover had departed when the danger in which he stood had disappeared. Fabrizio not only walked past the Palazzo Cantarini as often as he decently could ; he had also succeeded, after endless trouble, in hiring a small lodging opposite the first floor of the mansion. Once, when Clelia had thoughtlessly stationed herself at the window, to watch a procession pass by, she had started back, as though terror-struck. She had caught sight of Fabrizio, dressed in black, but as a very poor workman, looking at her out of one of his garret windows, filled with oiled paper, like those of his room in the Farnese Tower. Fabrizio would have been very thankful to persuade himself that Clelia was avoiding him on account of her father's disgrace, which public rumour ascribed to the duchess. But he was only too well acquainted with another cause for her retirement, and nothing could cheer his sadness.

Neither his acquittal, nor his important functions, the first he had been called on to perform, nor his fine social position, nor even the assiduous court paid him by all the clergy and devout persons in the diocese, touched him in the least. His charming rooms in the Palazzo Sanseverina were no longer large enough. The duchess, to her great delight, was obliged to give him the whole of the second floor of her palace, and two fine rooms on the first floor, which were always full of people waiting to pay their duty to the youthful coadjutor. The clause insuring his succession to the archbishopric had created an extraordinary effect in the country. Those resolute qualities in Fabrizio's character, which had once so scandalized the needy and foolish courtiers, were now ascribed to him as virtues.

It was a great lesson in philosophy to Fabrizio to find himself so utterly indifferent to all these honours, and far more unhappy in his splendid rooms, with half a score of lackeys dressed in his liveries, than he had been in his wooden chamber in the Farnese Tower, with hideous jailers all about him, and in perpetual terror for his life. His mother and his sister, the Duchess V——, who had travelled to Parma to see him in his glory, were struck by his deep melancholy. So greatly did it alarm the Marchesa del Dongo, who had become the most unromantic of women, that she thought he must have been given some slow poison in the Farnese Tower. Discreet as she was, she felt it her duty to speak to him about his extraordinary depression, and Fabrizio's tears were his only answer.

The innumerable advantages arising out of his brilliant position produced no impression on him, save one of vexation. His brother, that vainest of mortals, eaten up with the vilest selfishness, wrote him an almost formal letter of congratulation, and with this letter he received a bank bill for fifty thousand francs, to enable him, so the new marchese wrote, to purchase horses and carriages worthy of his name. Fabrizio sent the money to his younger sister, who had made a poor marriage.

Count Mosca had caused a fine Italian translation to be made of the Latin genealogy of the Valserra del Dongo family, originally published by Fabrizio, Archbishop of Parma. This he had splendidly printed, with the Latin text on the opposite page; the engravings had been reproduced by magnificent lithographs, done in Paris. By the duchess's desire a fine portrait of Fabrizio was inserted, opposite that of the late archbishop. This translation was published as Fabrizio's work, executed during his first imprisonment. But in our hero's heart every feeling was dead, even the vanity inherent in every human creature. He did not condescend to read one page of the volume attributed to him. His social position made it incumbent on him to present a magnificently bound copy of it to the prince, who, thinking he owed him some amends for having brought him so near an agonizing death, granted him his " *grandes entrées* " to the sovereign's apartment—an honour which confers the title of " *Eccellenza.*"

CHAPTER XXVI

THE only moments when Fabrizio's deep sadness knew a little respite were those he spent lurking behind a glass pane which he had substituted for one of the oiled-paper squares in the window of his lodging, opposite the Palazzo Cantarini, to which mansion, as my readers know, Clelia had retired. On the few occasions, since he had left the fortress, on which he had caught sight of her, he had been profoundly distressed by a striking change in her appearance, from which he augured very ill. Since Clelia's one moment of weakness her face had assumed a most striking appearance of nobility and gravity. It might have been that of a woman of thirty. In this extraordinary change of expression Fabrizio recognised the reflection of some deep-seated resolution. " Every moment of the day," said he to himself, " she is swearing to herself that she will keep her vow to the Madonna, and never look at me again."

Fabrizio only guessed at part of Clelia's misery. She knew that her father, who had fallen into the direst disgrace, would never be able to return to Parma and reappear at the court (without which life was impossible to him) until she married the Marchese Crescenzi. She wrote her father word that she desired to be married. The general was then lying ill from worry at Turin. This fateful decision had aged her by ten years.

She was quite aware that Fabrizio had a window facing the Palazzo Cantarini, but only once had she been so unfortunate as to look at him. The moment she caught sight of the turn of a head or the outline of a figure the least resembling his, she instantly closed her eyes. Her deep piety, and her trust in the Madonna's help, were to be her only

486

support for the future. She had to endure the sorrow of feeling no esteem for her father; her future husband's character she took to be perfectly commonplace, and suited to the dominant feelings of the upper ranks of society. To crown it all, she adored a man whom she must never see again, and who, nevertheless, had certain claims upon her. Taking it altogether, her fate seemed to her the most miserable that could be conceived, and it must be acknowledged that she was right. The moment she was married she ought to have gone to live two hundred leagues from Parma.

Fabrizio was acquainted with the extreme modesty of Clelia's character; he knew how much any unusual step, the discovery of which might cause comment, was certain to displease her. Nevertheless, driven to distraction by his own sadness, and by seeing Clelia's eyes so constantly turned away from him, he ventured to try to buy over two of the servants of her aunt, the Countess Cantarini. One day, as dusk was falling, Fabrizio, dressed like a respectable countryman, presented himself at the door of the palace, at which one of the servants he had bribed was awaiting him. He announced that he had just arrived from Turin with letters for Clelia from her father. The servant took up his message, and then conducted him into a huge antechamber on the first floor. In this apartment Fabrizio spent what was perhaps the most anxious quarter of an hour in his whole life. If Clelia repulsed him he could never hope to know peace again. "To cut short the wearisome duties with which my new position overwhelms me," he mused, "I will rid the Church of an indifferent priest, and will take refuge, under a feigned name, in some Carthusian monastery." At last the servant appeared, and told him the Signorina Clelia was willing to receive him.

Our hero's courage quite failed him as he climbed the staircase to the second floor, and he very nearly fell down from sheer fright.

Clelia was sitting at a little table, on which a solitary taper was burning. No sooner did she recognise Fabrizio, under his disguise, than she rushed away, and hid herself at the far end of the drawing-room. "This is how you care for my salvation," she cried, hiding her face in her hands. "Yet you know that when my father was at the point of death from poison, I made a vow to the Madonna that I would never see you. That vow I have never broken except on that one day—the most wretched of my life—when my conscience commanded me to save you from death. I do a great deal when, by putting a forced and, no doubt, a wicked interpretation on my vow, I consent even to listen to you."

Fabrizio was so astounded by this last sentence that, for a few seconds, he was incapable even of rejoicing over it. He had expected to see Clelia rush away in the most lively anger. But at last he recovered his presence of mind, and blew out the candle. Although he believed he had understood Clelia's wishes, he was trembling with alarm as he moved toward the far end of the drawing-room, where she had taken refuge behind a sofa. He did not know whether she might not take it ill if he kissed her hand. Throbbing with passion, she cast herself into his arms.

"Dearest Fabrizio," she said, "how slow you have been in coming! I can only speak to you for a few moments, for even that is certainly a great sin, and when I promised that I would never see you again, there is no doubt I understood myself to promise that I would never speak to you either. But how can you punish my poor father's vengeful thought so barbarously? For, after all, he was nearly poisoned, first, to facilitate your flight. Should you not have done something for me, who risked my fair fame to save you? Besides, now you are altogether bound to the priestly life, you could not marry me, even if I found means of getting rid of this detestable marchese. And then, how could you dare to attempt to see me in full daylight, on the day of that procession, and thus violate my holy vow to the Madonna, in the most shocking manner?"

Beside himself with surprise and happiness, Fabrizio clasped her closely in his arms.

A conversation which had to begin by explaining so many things was necessarily a long one. Fabrizio told Clelia the exact truth as to her father's banishment. The duchess had had nothing whatever to do with it, for the very good reason that she had never thought, for a single instant, that the idea of poison had emanated from General Conti. She had always believed that to be a witticism on the part of the Raversi faction, which was bent on driving out Count Mosca. His long dissertation on this historical fact made Clelia very happy; she had been wretched at the thought that it was her duty to hate any one belonging to Fabrizio, and she no longer looked on the duchess with a jealous eye.

The happiness consequent on that evening's meeting only lasted a few days.

The worthy Don Cesare arrived from Turin, and found courage, in his perfect single-heartedness, to seek the presence of the duchess. After having obtained her word that she would not betray the confidence he was about to repose in her, he confessed that his brother, misled by a false idea of honour, and believing himself defied and ruined in public opinion by Fabrizio's escape, had believed himself bound to seek for vengeance.

Before Don Cesare had talked for two minutes his cause was won; his absolute honesty had touched the duchess, who was not accustomed to such exhibitions; its novelty delighted her.

"Hurry on the marriage of the general's daughter with the Marchese Crescenzi, and I give you my word of honour that I will do everything I can to have the general received as if he were coming back from an ordinary journey. I will ask him to dinner myself. Will that satisfy you? No doubt there will be a stiffness at first, and the general must not be too hasty about asking to be reappointed governor of the citadel. But you know my regard for the marchese; I shall bear no grudge against his father-in-law."

Armed with these assurances, Don Cesare sought his niece, and told her that her father's life lay in her hands; he had fallen ill from sheer despair, not having appeared at any court for several months.

Clelia insisted on going to see her father, who was hiding under a false name in a village near Turin; for he had taken it into his head that the court of Parma would request his extradition, with the object of bringing him to trial. She found him in bed, ill, and almost out of his mind. That very night she wrote a letter to Fabrizio, breaking with him forever. On receiving the letter, Fabrizio, whose character was growing very like that of his mistress, went into retreat at the Convent of Velleia, in the mountains, some thirty leagues from Parma. Clelia had written him a letter that covered ten pages. She had solemnly sworn she would never marry the marchese without his consent. That consent she now besought, and Fabrizio granted it in a letter written from his retreat at Velleia, and breathing the purest friendship.

When Clelia received this letter—the friendly tone of which nettled her, we must acknowledge—she herself fixed her wedding-day, and the festivities connected with it added to the splendour which rendered the court of Parma specially noticeable that winter.

Ranuzio-Ernest V was a miser at heart, but he was desperately in love, and he hoped to keep the duchess permanently at his court. He begged his mother's acceptance of a considerable sum of money, to be spent in entertaining. The mistress of the robes made admirable use of this addition to the royal income; the festivities at Parma that winter recalled the best days of the Milanese court, and of Prince Eugene, that lovable viceroy of Italy, the memory of whose goodness has endured so long.

The archbishop's coadjutor had been recalled to Parma by his duties. But he gave out that, from religious motives, he should continue to live in retirement in the small apartment in the archiepiscopal palace which his protector, Monsignore Landriani, had insisted on his accepting, and thither he retired, with one servant only. He was not present, therefore, at any of the brilliant court entertainments, and this fact earned him a most saintly reputation in Parma, and all over his future diocese. An unexpected result of this retirement, which had been inspired solely by Fabrizio's profound and hopeless sadness, was that the worthy archbishop, who had always loved him, and who, in fact, had been the person who had first thought of having him appointed coadjutor, began to feel a little jealous. The archbishop, and very rightly, conceived it his duty to attend all the court functions, according to the usual Italian custom. On these occasions he wore his gala costume, very nearly the same as that in which he appeared in his cathedral choir. The hundreds of servants gathered in the pillared anteroom of the palace never failed to rise and crave the archbishop's blessing as he passed, and he, as invariably, condescended to stop and bestow it. It was during one of these moments of solemn silence that Monsignore Landriani heard a voice saying: " Our archbishop goes to balls, and Monsignore del Dongo never goes out of his room."

From that moment the immense favour in which Fabrizio had stood at the archiepiscopal palace came to an end. But he was able, now, to stand on his own feet. The behaviour which had only been actuated by the despair into which Clelia's marriage had cast him, was taken to be the result of his simple and lofty piety, and devout folk read the translation of his family genealogy, which exemplified the most ridiculous vanity, as though it were an edifying work. The booksellers published a lithographed edition of his picture, which was bought up in a few days, and more especially by the lower classes. The engraver, out of ignorance, surrounded Fabrizio's portrait with several adornments, which should only have appeared on the portrait of a bishop, and to which a coadjutor could lay no claim. The archbishop saw one of these pictures, and his fury exceeded all bounds. He sent for Fabrizio, and spoke to him in the harshest manner, and in terms which his rage occasionally rendered very coarse. Fabrizio had no difficulty, as my readers will readily believe, in behaving as Fénelon would have done in such a case. He listened to the archbishop with all possible humility and respect, and when the prelate ceased speaking, he told him the whole story of the translation of the genealogy by Count Mosca's orders, at the time of his first imprisonment. It had been published for worldly ends—such, indeed, as had seemed to him (Fabrizio), by no means suited for a man in his position. As to the portrait, he had had as little to do with the second edition as with the first. During his retreat the bookseller had sent him twenty-four copies of this second edition addressed to the archiepiscopal palace. He had sent his servant to buy a twenty-fifth copy, and having thus discovered that the price of each to be thirty sous, he had sent a hundred francs in payment for the first twenty-four portraits.

All these arguments, though put forward in the most reasonable manner, by a man whose heart was full of sorrow of a very different kind, increased the archbishop's fury to madness. He even went so far as to accuse Fabrizio of hypocrisy.

" This is what comes of being a common man," said Fabrizio to himself, " even when he is clever."

He had a more serious trouble at that moment, in the shape of his aunt's letters, which absolutely insisted on his returning to his rooms at the Palazzo Sanseverina, or, at all events, on his coming occasionally to see her. In that house Fabrizio felt he was certain to hear talk of the Marchese Crescenzi's splendid entertainments in honour of his marriage, and he was not sure he would be able to endure this without making an exhibition of himself.

When the marriage ceremony took place, Fabrizio had already kept utter silence for a week, after having commanded his servant, and those persons in the archbishop's palace with whom he had to do, never to open their lips to him.

When Archbishop Landriani became aware of this fresh piece of affectation he sent for Fabrizio much oftener than was his wont, and insisted on holding lengthy conversations with him. He even made him confer with certain of his country canons, who complained that the archbishop had contravened their privileges. Fabrizio took all this with the perfect indifference of a man whose head is full of other things. " I should do much better," thought he, " to turn Carthusian. I should be less wretched among the rocks at Velleia."

He paid a visit to his aunt, and could not restrain his tears when he kissed her. He was so altered, his eyes, which his excessive thinness made look larger than ever, seeming ready to start out of his head, and his whole appearance, in his threadbare black cassock, was so miserable and wretched, that at her first sight of him the duchess could hardly help crying too. But a moment later, when she had told herself it was Clelia's marriage that had so sorely changed this handsome young fellow, her feelings were as fierce as those of the archbishop, though more skilfully concealed. She was cruel enough to dilate at length on various picturesque details which had marked the Marchese Crescenzi's delightful entertainments. Fabrizio made no reply, but his eyes closed with a little convulsive flutter, and he turned even paler than before, which at first sight would have been taken to be impossible. At such moments of excessive misery his pallor took a greenish tint.

Count Mosca came into the room, and the sight he beheld (and which appeared to him incredible) cured him, once for all, of that jealousy of Fabrizio which he had never ceased to feel. This gifted man made the most delicate and ingenious endeavours to rouse Fabrizio to some interest in mundane affairs. The count had always felt an esteem, and a certain regard for him. This regard, being no longer counterbalanced by jealousy, deepened into something approaching devotion. "He really has paid honestly for his fine position," said Mosca to himself, as he summed up Fabrizio's misfortunes. On pretext of showing him the Parmegiano, which the prince had sent the duchess, the count drew Fabrizio apart.

"Hark ye, my friend, let us speak as man to man. Can I serve you in any way? You need not fear I shall question you. But tell me, would money be of any use to you? Can interest serve you in any fashion? Speak out; you may command me—or, if you prefer it, write to me."

Fabrizio embraced him affectionately, and talked about the picture.

"Your behaviour is a masterpiece of the most skilful policy," said the count, returning to an ordinary light conversational tone. "You are laying up a most admirable future for yourself. The prince respects you. The populace venerates you. Your threadbare black suit keeps Archbishop Landriani awake o' nights. I have some acquaintance with political business, and I vow I don't know what advice I could give you to improve it. Your first step in society, made at five-and-twenty, has placed you in a position that is absolutely perfect. You are very much talked about at court, And do you know to what it is you owe a distinction which, at your age, is unique? To your threadbare black garments. The duchess and I, as you know, are in possession of the house Petrarch once owned, which stands on a beautiful hill in the forest, close to the river. It has struck me that if ever the small spites of envious folk should weary you, you might become Petrarch's successor, and his renown would set off yours." The count was racking his brains to bring a smile to the wasted melancholy face. But he could not do it. What made the alteration in Fabrizio's countenance all the more striking was that until quite lately its fault, if it possessed one, had been its occasionally unseasonable expression of sensuous enjoyment and gay delight.

The count did not allow him to depart without telling him that in spite of the retirement in which he was living, it might look somewhat affected if he did not put in an appearance at court on the following Saturday—the princess-mother's birthday. The words went through Fabrizio like a dagger thrust. "Good God!" thought he, "what possessed me to enter this house?" He could not think of the meeting he might have to face at court, without a shudder. The thought of it overrode all others. He made up his mind that his only remaining chance was to reach the palace at the very moment when the doors of the reception rooms were thrown open.

As a matter of fact, Monsignore del Dongo's name was one of the first to be announced at the great state entertainment, and the princess received him with all imaginable courtesy. Fabrizio kept his eyes on the clock, and as soon as the hand pointed to the twentieth minute of his visit, he rose to take his leave. But just at that moment the prince entered his mother's apartment. After paying him his duty, Fabrizio was skilfully edging toward the door, when to his great discomfiture, one of those trifles of court etiquette with the use of which the mistress of the robes was so well acquainted, was suddenly sprung upon him. The chamberlain in waiting ran after him to say he had been named to join the prince's whist party. This, at Parma, is an excessive honour, far transcending the rank the archbishop's coadjutor occupies in society. To play whist with the sovereign would be a special honour for the archbishop himself. Fabrizio felt the chamberlain's words go through him like a dart, and mortally as he hated any public scene, he very nearly told him he had been seized with a sudden attack of giddiness. But it occurred to him that this would expose him to questions, and complimentary condolences, even more intolerable than the game of cards would be. He hated to open his mouth that day.

Luckily, the superior general of the Franciscan Friars happened to be among the important personages who had come to offer their congratulations to the princess. This monk, a very learned man, and worthy follower of Fontana and Duvoisin, had taken his stand in a distant corner of the reception room. Fabrizio placed himself in front of him, turning round so as not to see the doorway into the room, and began talking theology with him. But he could not prevent himself from hearing the Marchese and Marchesa Crescenzi announced. Contrary to his own expectation, Fabrizio experienced a sensation of violent anger.

" If I were Borso Valserra " (one of the first Sforza's generals), said he to himself, " I should go over and stab that dull marchese, with the very ivory-handled dagger Clelia gave me on that blessed day, and I would teach him to have the insolence of showing himself with his marchesa anywhere in my presence." His face had altered so completely that the superior general of the Franciscans said to him :

" Is your Excellency ill ? "

" I have a frightful headache . . . the light hurts me . . . and I am only staying on because I have been desired to join the prince's whist party."

At these words the superior general of the Franciscans, who was a man of the middle class, was so taken aback, that, not knowing what else to do, he began bowing to Fabrizio, who, on his side, being far more agitated than the superior general, fell to talking with the most extraordinary volubility. He noticed that a great silence had fallen on the room behind him, but he would not look round. Suddenly the bow of a violin was rapped against a desk, some one played a flourish, and the famous singer, Signora P——, sang Cimarosa's once celebrated air, *Quelle pupille tenere*. Fabrizio stood his ground for the first few bars. But soon his anger melted within him, and he felt an intense longing for tears. "Good God," he thought, "what an absurd scene! and with my priestly habit, too!" He thought it wiser to talk about himself.

"These violent headaches of mine, when I fight against them as I am doing to-night," said he to the superior general of the Franciscans, "always end in crying fits, which might give rise to ill-natured comment, in the case of a man of our calling. So I beseech your most illustrious reverence will give me leave to look at you while I weep, and will make no remark on my condition."

"Our provincial at Catanara suffers from just the very same discomfort," said the general of the Franciscans, and he began a long story in an undertone.

The absurdity of the tale, which involved a recital of everything the provincial ate at his evening meal, made Fabrizio smile, a thing he had not done for many a day. But he soon ceased listening to the superior general. Signora P—— was singing, in the most divine fashion, an air by Pergolese (the princess had a fondness for old-fashioned music). There was a slight noise three paces from Fabrizio. For the first time that evening he turned his head. The chair which had scraped on the parquet floor was occupied by the Marchesa Crescenzi, whose eyes, swimming with tears, met Fabrizio's, which were in no better case. The marchesa bowed her head. For some seconds Fabrizio went on gazing at her. He was studying that diamond-laden head. But his eyes were full of anger and disdain. Then, repeating to himself, "*And my eyes shall never look on thee again*," he turned back to the superior general and said:

"My complaint is coming on again, worse than ever."

The Chartreuse of Parma

And, indeed, for over half an hour Fabrizio wept abundantly. Fortunately, one of Mozart's symphonies—vilely played, as they generally are in Italy—came to his rescue, and helped to dry his tears.

He held his ground, and never looked toward the Marchesa Crescenzi. But Signora P—— began to sing again, and Fabrizio's soul, relieved by the tears he had shed, passed into a state of perfect calm. Then life looked different to him. "How can I expect," he mused, "to be able to forget her at the very outset? Would that be possible?" Then the idea occurred to him: "Can I possibly be more wretched than I have been for the last two months? And if nothing can increase my misery, why should I deny myself the pleasure of seeing her? She has forgotten her vows, she is fickle—is not every woman fickle? But who can deny her heavenly beauty? A glance of hers throws me into an ecstasy, and I have to do myself violence even to look at other women, who are supposed to be the loveliest of their sex. Well, why should I not enjoy that ecstasy? At all events, it will give me a moment's respite."

Fabrizio knew something of mankind, but as regards passion he was without experience. Otherwise he would have told himself that the momentary delight in which he was about to indulge would stultify all the efforts he had been making for the past two months to forget Clelia.

The poor lady had only attended the reception under her husband's compulsion. She would have departed, after the first half-hour, on the score of illness. But the marchese assured her that to send for her carriage and drive away, while many other carriages were still driving up, would be a most unusual proceeding, and might even be taken as an indirect criticism of the entertainment offered by the princess.

"As lord in waiting," the marchese went on, "I am bound to remain in the room, at the princess's orders, until all the guests have retired. There may, and there no doubt will, be orders to be given to the servants—they are so careless. Would you have me allow a mere equerry to usurp this honour?"

The Chartreuse of Parma

Clelia submitted. She had not seen Fabrizio. She still hoped he might not be present at the reception. But just as the concert was beginning, when the princess gave the ladies permission to be seated, Clelia, who was anything but pushing in such matters, allowed herself to be shouldered out of the best seats, near the princess, and was forced to seek a chair at the back of the room, in the very distant corner to which Fabrizio had retired. When she reached her seat the dress of the Franciscan superior general, an unusual one in such company, caught her attention, and at first she did not notice the slight man in a plain black coat who was talking to him. Yet a certain secret impulse made her rivet her eyes on that person.

"Every man here is in uniform, or wears a richly embroidered coat. Who can that young man in the plain black suit be?" She was gazing at him attentively, when a lady, passing to a seat near her, jerked her chair. Fabrizio turned his head. So altered was he that she did not recognise him. She said to herself at first: "Here is somebody who is like him. It must be his elder brother. But I thought he was only a few years older, and this man must be five-and-forty." Suddenly she recognised him by the way his lips moved.

"Poor fellow, how he has suffered!" she thought. And she bowed her head, not on account of her vow, but crushed by her misery. Her heart was swelling with pity. He had not looked anything like that, even after he had been shut up nine months in prison. She did not look at him again. But though her eyes were not exactly turned toward him, she was conscious of his every movement.

When the concert came to an end, she saw him go over to the prince's card-table, which was set out a few paces from the throne. When she saw Fabrizio thus removed some distance from her she breathed more freely.

But the Marchese Crescenzi had been very much disturbed at seeing his wife banished so far from the throne. He spent the whole evening trying to persuade a lady who was sitting three chairs from the princess, and whose husband was under pecuniary obligations to himself, that she had better change places with the marchesa. The poor lady objected, as was natural. Then he went and fetched the husband, who owed him money. This gentleman made his better-half listen to the dreary voice of reason, and at last the marchese had the pleasure of arranging the exchange, and went to fetch his wife. "You are always far too retiring," he said. "Why do you walk about with your eyes cast down? You will be taken for one of these middle-class women who are astonished at finding themselves here, and whom everybody else is astounded to see. That crazy woman the mistress of the robes is always doing that sort of thing. And then they talk about checking the progress of Jacobinism! Recollect that your husband holds the highest position of any man at the princess's court. And supposing the republicans should succeed in pulling down the court, and even the nobility, your husband would still be the richest man in this country. That is a notion you do not consider half enough."

The chair in which the marchese had the pleasure of seating his wife stood not more than six paces from the prince's card-table. Clelia could only see Fabrizio's profile, but she was so struck by his thinness, and especially by his air of utter indifference to anything that might happen to him in this world—he, who in old days had his word to say about every incident that occurred—that she ended by coming to the frightful conclusion that Fabrizio was completely altered, that he had forgotten her, and that his extreme emaciation must result from the severe fasting his piety had enjoined. Clelia was confirmed in this sad conviction by the conversation of all who sat near her. The coadjutor's name was on every tongue: every one was seeking the reason of the special favour which had been shown him. How was it that he, young as he was, had been admitted to the prince's card-table? A great effect was produced by the indifferent politeness and haughty air with which he dealt his cards, even when he cut them for his Highness.

"It really is incredible," exclaimed the old courtiers. "The favour his aunt enjoys has quite turned his head. . . . But Heaven be thanked, that will not last long! Our sov-

ereign does not like people who assume such airs of superiority." The duchess went up to the prince, and the courtiers, who remained at a respectful distance from the card-
table, so that they could only catch a few chance words of the
prince's conversation, noticed that Fabrizio flushed deeply.
" No doubt," thought they, " his aunt has chidden him for
his fine show of indifference." Fabrizio had just overheard
Clelia's voice; she was answering the princess, who, in her
progress round the room, had addressed a few words to the
wife of her lord in waiting. At last the moment came when
Fabrizio had to change his place at the whist-table. This
brought him exactly opposite Clelia, and several times he
gave himself up to the delight of looking at her. The poor
marchesa, feeling his eyes upon her, quite lost countenance.
Several times she forgot what she owed her vow, and in
her longing to read Fabrizio's heart, she fixed her eyes upon
his face.

When the prince had finished playing, the ladies rose to
go into the supper room. There was some little confusion,
and Fabrizio found himself close to Clelia. His resolution
was still strong, but he happened to recognise a very slight
perfume which she was in the habit of putting in her dress,
and this sensation overmastered all his determination. He
drew near her, and murmured, in an undertone, and as if to
himself, two lines out of the sonnet from Petrarch which he
had sent her printed on a silken handkerchief from the Lago
Maggiore. " How great was my happiness when the outer
world thought me wretched! and now, how altered is my
fate ! "

" No, he has not forgotten me," thought Clelia in a passion of joy. " That noble heart is not unfaithful."

> " Non ! vous ne me verrez jamais changer
> Beaux yeux, qui m'avez appris à aimer ! "

She ventured to say these two lines from Petrarch to herself.

Immediately after supper the princess retired. The prince
had followed her to her own apartments, and did not reappear
in the reception-room. As soon as this news spread, every

one tried to go away at once, and confusion reigned supreme
in all the anterooms. Clelia found herself quite near Fabrizio. The deep misery of his expression filled her with
pity. " Let us forget the past," she said, " and keep this in
memory of our *friendship*." As she said the word she put
out her fan, so that he might take it.

In one moment everything changed to Fabrizio's eyes.
He was another man. The very next morning he announced
that his retreat was at an end, and went back to his splendid
rooms in the Palazzo Sanseverina.

The archbishop said, and believed, that the favour the
prince had shown Fabrizio by summoning him to his card-
table had turned the new-fledged saint's head. The duchess
perceived that he had come to an understanding with Clelia.
That thought, which increased twofold the pain of the memory of her own fatal promise, made her finally resolve to
absent herself for a while. People were astonished at her
folly. " What! Leave court at the very moment when her
favour appeared to know no limits! "

The count, who was perfectly happy now that he was
satisfied there was no love between Fabrizio and the duchess,
said to his friend : " This new prince of ours is the very in-
carnation of virtue, but I once called him ' *that child.*' Will
he never forgive me? I only see one means of thoroughly
regaining my credit with him, and that is by absence. I will
make myself perfectly charming and respectful, and then I
will fall ill, and ask leave to retire. You will grant me permission to do so, now that Fabrizio's fortunes are assured.
But," he added, with a laugh, " will you make the immense
sacrifice of changing the high and mighty title of duchess
for a much humbler one, for my sake? I am entertaining
myself by leaving all the business here in a state of the most
inextricable confusion. I had four or five hard-working
men in my various ministries; I had them all pensioned
off, two months ago, because they read the French newspapers, and I have replaced them with first-class simpletons."

" Once we are gone, the prince will find himself in such
difficulties that, in spite of his horror of Rassi's character, I

have no doubt he will be obliged to recall him, and I only await my orders from the tyrant who rules my fate to write the most affectionate and friendly letter to my friend Rassi, and tell him I have every reason to hope his merits will soon be properly recognised."

CHAPTER XXVII

This serious conversation took place the day after Fabrizio's return to the Palazzo Sanseverina. The duchess still felt sore at the sight of Fabrizio's evident happiness. "So," said she to herself, "that pious little minx has deceived me! She has not been able to hold out against her lover for even three months."

The certain expectation of happiness had given that cowardly being, the young prince, courage to love. He heard a rumour of the preparations for departure at the Palazzo Sanseverina, and his French *valet de chambre*, who had but scant faith in any fine lady's virtue, inspired him with courage as to the duchess. Ernest V ventured on a step that was severely blamed by the princess, and by all sensible people about the court. In the eyes of the populace, it set the seal on the astounding favour the duchess enjoyed. The prince went to see her in her palace.

"You are going!" said he, and there was a gravity about his tone which made it hateful to the duchess. "You are going! You mean to deceive me, and break your oath. And yet, if I had delayed ten minutes about granting you Fabrizio's pardon, he would have died! And you would leave me behind you in misery! But for your oaths I never should have dared to love you as I do. Have you no honour?"

"Consider well, my prince. Have you ever been so happy, all your life long, as during the four months which have just gone by? Your glory as a sovereign, and, I venture to think, your happiness as a kind-hearted man, have never reached such a point before. This is the arrangement I propose to you. If you condescend to accept it, I will not be your mistress for a passing moment, and in virtue of an oath extorted from me by fear, but I will devote every instant of my life to making you happy. I will be to you, always, what I have been for the last four months, and perhaps, some day, love may crown friendship. I would not say that might never be."

" Well," said the prince, overjoyed, " be something else, and something more! Rule me and my dominions, both at once. Be my Prime Minister. I offer you such a marriage as the necessities of my rank permit me. We have an instance of the kind quite near us—the King of Naples has just married the Duchess of Partana. I offer you all I can—a marriage of the same kind. I will add a piece of shabby policy, to convince you that I am no longer a child, and that I have thought of everything. I will not lay stress on the position I thus impose on myself, of being the last sovereign of my race, nor on the grief of seeing the great powers dispose of my succession during my lifetime. I hail these drawbacks—very real ones—as a blessing, since they provide me with a further means of showing you my regard and passionate devotion."

The duchess did not feel a moment's hesitation. The prince bored her, and she thought the count perfectly charming. There was only one man in the world whom she could have preferred to him. And besides that, she ruled the count, and the prince, as the natural outcome of his rank, would more or less have ruled her. Finally, he might grow inconstant and take mistresses. Before many years were out, their difference of age would almost appear to give him a right to do so.

From the very first, the prospect of being bored had settled the whole question. Nevertheless the duchess, in her desire to be charming, asked to be allowed to think it over.

Space will not permit me to repeat the almost tender expressions, and the infinitely gracious terms, in which she wrapped her refusal. The prince got into a rage; he saw all his happiness slipping through his fingers. What was he to do with himself after the duchess had left his court? And then there was the humiliation of being rebuffed; and besides, "What will my French servant say when I tell him I have failed."

The duchess was artful enough to calm the prince, and little by little, to bring the negotiation back to its proper limits.

"If your Highness will only consent not to insist on the result of a fatal promise, which fills me with horror, because it makes me despise myself, I will spend my whole life at your court, and that court shall always be what it has been this winter. Every instant of my life shall be devoted to increasing your happiness as a man, and your glory as a sovereign. But if your Highness insists on my keeping my oath, you will have blighted the rest of my life, and you will see me depart from your dominions that instant, never to return. The day on which I lose my honour will be the last day on which I shall ever look upon you."

But, like all pusillanimous men, the prince was obstinate; and besides, her refusal of his hand had stung his pride as a man and as a sovereign. He thought of all the difficulties he would have had to surmount to insure the acceptance of this marriage, and which, nevertheless, he had been resolved to overcome. For three hours the same arguments were repeated on each side, and frequently interlarded with very bitter expressions. The prince exclaimed: "Do you then want to make me believe, madam, that you have no honour? If I had hesitated as long that day, when General Fabio Conti was poisoning Fabrizio, you would be building his tomb now in some church in Parma."

"No, not in Parma indeed—a country of poisoners!"

"Very well, madam," retorted the prince angrily. "You can depart and take my scorn with you."

As he was going out the duchess said in a low tone: "Well, sire, come here at ten o'clock to-night, in the most absolute *incognito*, and you will make a fool's bargain. You will see me for the last time in your life—and I would have devoted the whole of mine to making you as happy as an absolute sovereign can be, in this Jacobin century. And pray consider what your court will be like when I am no longer there to drag it out of its natural dulness and spitefulness!"

"On your part, you refuse the crown of Parma, and something better than a crown. For you would not have been an every-day princess, married out of policy, and without love. My heart is wholly yours, and you would have been absolute mistress of my actions, and of my government, forever."

"Yes, but the princess, your mother, would have had the right to despise me as a vile schemer."

"Pooh! I would have given the princess an income, and banished her."

Three quarters of an hour were spent in sharp rejoinders. The prince, who was a fastidious-minded man, could neither make up his mind to insist on his rights, nor to allow the duchess to depart. He had been told that once the first victory was won, no matter how, women always came round.

Dismissed in anger by the offended duchess, he ventured to reappear, trembling and very miserable, at three minutes before ten o'clock. At half past ten the duchess got into her carriage and started for Bologna. As soon as she was beyond the boundary of the prince's dominions she wrote to the count:

"The sacrifice is accomplished. Do not expect me to be cheerful for a month. I shall never see Fabrizio again. I am waiting for you at Bologna, and I will be the Countess Mosca whenever you choose. One thing, only, I ask of you: never force me to reappear in the country I am now leaving; and remember always that instead of a hundred and fifty thousand francs a year, you are going to have thirty or forty thousand at the outside. All the fools about you have stared at you open-mouthed, and now your whole reputation will depend upon how far you choose to condescend to understand their small ideas—'*Tu l'as voulu, Georges Dandin!*'"

A week later, the marriage took place at Perugia, in a church which contains the tombs of the count's ancestors. The prince was in despair. He had sent the duchess three or four couriers, and she had carefully sent him back envelopes which covered his letters, with the seals unbroken.

The Chartreuse of Parma

Ernest V had conferred a splendid income on the count, and had given Fabrizio the ribbon of his Order.

"That was what pleased me most about our farewells," said the count to the new Countess Mosca della Rovere. "We parted the best friends in the world. He gave me a Spanish Order, and diamonds which are worth quite as much as the Order. He told me he would make me a duke, only that he wanted to keep that method of drawing you back to his dominions in his own hands; consequently I am commissioned to inform you (and it is a fine mission for a husband!) that if you will condescend to return to Parma, even for a month, I shall be made a duke, with any title you choose, and you will be given a fine property."

All this the duchess refused with a sort of horror.

After that scene at the court ball, tolerably decisive as it had appeared, Clelia betrayed no recollection of the love she had momentarily seemed to share. The most vehement remorse had surged over that virtuous and pious nature. Fabrizio understood this very well, and in spite of all the hope he tried to feel, a gloomy sadness overcame his soul. This time, however, his misery did not force him into retirement, as at the period of Clelia's marriage.

The count had begged his nephew to keep him exactly informed of everything that happened at court, and Fabrizio, who was beginning to realize all he owed him, had resolved to fulfil this mission faithfully. Like every one in the city and at court, Fabrizio had no doubt that his friend nursed the project of returning to the ministry, and wielding greater power than he had ever held before. The count's forecasts were soon verified. Within six weeks of his departure, Rassi was Prime Minister. Fabio Conti was appointed Minister of War, and the prisons, which the count had well-nigh emptied, began to fill again. When the prince summoned these men to power he fancied he would thereby avenge himself on the duchess. He was crazed by passion, and he hated Mosca as his rival.

Fabrizio had a great deal on his hands. Archbishop Landriani, now seventy-two years old, had fallen into a very weak condition, and hardly ever went beyond his palace doors. His coadjutor was obliged to represent him on almost every occasion.

The Marchesa Crescenzi, overwhelmed by remorse, and terrified by what her religious director said to her, had hit upon an excellent plan for keeping out of Fabrizio's sight. On the plea that her first confinement was approaching, she had shut herself up within her own palace; but to this palace a huge garden was attached.

To this garden Fabrizio contrived to find access, and along Clelia's favourite walk he placed nosegays of flowers, arranged in an order which constituted a language, like those she had sent him every evening during the last days of his imprisonment in the Farnese Tower.

This attempt caused the marchesa great annoyance. Her heart throbbed, sometimes with remorse, and then again with passion. For several months she would not go into the palace garden at all; she even scrupled to cast a glance in that direction.

Fabrizio began to believe he was parted from her forever, and despair was taking possession of his soul. The society in which he spent his life was hateful to him, and if he had not been convinced in his heart that the count would never find peace of mind out of office, he would have retired to his little rooms in the archiepiscopal palace. It would have been a comfort to him to live alone with his thoughts, and never to hear a human voice except when he was performing his ecclesiastical functions. " But," said he to himself, " no one but I can serve the interests of Count and Countess Mosca."

The prince still treated him with a respect which insured him the foremost rank at court, and this favour was largely owing to his own behaviour. Fabrizio's extreme reserve, the result of an indifference to all the affections and petty passions that fill the lives of ordinary men, which amounted to positive disgust, had piqued the young prince's vanity. He would often remark that Fabrizio was as clever as his aunt. The prince's candid nature had realized half the truth, that no one else about him possessed the same methods of feeling as Fabrizio. A fact which could escape no one, not even the most ordinary courtier, was that Fabrizio's credit was by no means that of an ordinary coadjutor, but even exceeded the consideration displayed by the sovereign for the archbishop. Fabrizio wrote word to the count that if ever the prince should be clever enough to perceive the muddle into which such ministers as Rassi, Fabio Conti, Zurla, and others of the same calibre had brought his affairs, he, Fabrizio, would be the natural channel whereby the sovereign might make some friendly demonstration, without too great a risk to his own vanity.

"But for the recollection of the fatal words, ' *that child,*' " he wrote to Countess Mosca, "applied by a man of genius to an august personage, that august personage would already have exclaimed ' Come back at once, and rid me of all these vagabonds.' Even now, if the wife of the man of genius would condescend to any step, even the slightest, the count would be recalled with the greatest joy. But if he will wait till the fruit is thoroughly ripe he will return in far more brilliant fashion. And indeed, the princess's receptions have grown deadly dull; the only amusement they afford consists in the ridiculous behaviour of Rassi, who, now he is a count, has developed a mania for noble birth. Strict orders have just been issued that no person who can not prove eight quarterings of noble descent is to dare to appear at the princess's evening receptions. These are the exact terms of the edict. The men who have hitherto had the right to go into the great gallery in the morning, and be present when the sovereign passes through to mass, are to continue in the enjoyment of this privilege. But all new arrivals will have to prove their eight quarterings. *À propos* of which somebody said, ' It's very clear that Rassi knows no quarter.' "

My readers will readily imagine that such letters as these were not confided to the ordinary post. Countess Mosca wrote back from Naples: "We have a concert every Thursday, and a party every Sunday. Our rooms are absolutely crowded. The count is delighted with his excavations; he sets apart a thousand francs a month for them, and has just brought down labourers from the mountains of the Abruzzi, who only cost him twenty-three sous a day. You really ought to come and see us. This is more than the twentieth time that I have summoned you, ungrateful boy!"

Fabrizio had no intention of obeying the summons. Even his daily letter to the count or countess was an almost unendurable weariness to him. My readers will forgive him when they learn that a whole year had thus passed away without his being able to address a single word to the marchesa. All his attempts to enter into some kind of correspondence with her were repulsed with horror. The habitual silence which, out of sheer weariness of life, Fabrizio kept everywhere, except at court, and when performing his religious functions, added to the perfect purity of his morals, had won him such extraordinary veneration that he made up his mind, at last, to follow his aunt's advice.

"The prince," she wrote, "venerates you so deeply that you must expect to fall into disgrace shortly. Then he will shower marks of neglect upon you, and the vile scorn of the courtiers will follow on his. All these small despots, however honest-hearted they may be, change like the fashions, and on the same account—out of boredom. The only way in which you can insure yourself support against the sovereign's whims is by preaching. You improvise poetry so well! Try to talk, for half an hour, about religion! You will talk heresy at first, but pay a learned and discreet theologian to listen to your sermons, and point out their faults to you, and the next time you preach you can correct them."

The misery of mind engendered by a crossed love makes any effort requiring attention and activity an odious burden. But Fabrizio reminded himself that his influence over the populace, if he acquired any, might some day be useful to his aunt and to the count, for whom his admiration daily increased, in proportion to his own knowledge of life and the wickedness of men. So he made up his mind to preach, and his success, the way to which had been prepared by his emaciation and his threadbare coat, was unexampled. His sermons breathed a deep sadness, which, combined with his handsome face, and the stories of the high favour in which he stood at court, conquered every woman's heart. The ladies discovered that he had been one of the bravest captains in Napoleon's army, and before long, this ridiculous story was absolutely believed. The seats in the churches in which he was to preach were kept beforehand; the poorer folk would take possession of them at five o'clock in the morning, and turn money by the speculation.

So great was Fabrizio's success, that at last an idea which changed his every feeling flashed across his brain. Might not the Marchesa Crescenzi come some day, were it out of mere curiosity, to hear him preach? And of a sudden the delighted public perceived that his eloquence increased twofold. In moments of excitement he ventured on word-pictures, the boldness of which would have made the most practised orators tremble. Occasionally, quite forgetting himself, he would be swept away by a wave of passionate inspiration, and the whole of his audience would be melted into tears, but in vain did his *aggrottato* * eye scan every face turned toward the pulpit, in search of that one being whose presence would have meant so much to him.

" But if ever that happiness does come to me," he thought, " I shall either faint away, or I shall stop dead short in my discourse." To protect himself from this last difficulty, he composed a sort of tender and passionate prayer, which he always laid on a stool in his pulpit. His intention was to begin to read this composition if the marchesa's presence should ever make it impossible for him to improvise a word.

One day he heard, through those of the marchesa's servants who were in his pay, that orders had been given to make the box belonging to the Casa Crescenzi, at the principal theatre, ready for the next evening. It was more than a year since the marchesa had appeared in any theatre, and she was breaking her habit now, in order to hear a tenor who had created a *furore*, and crammed the building every evening. Fabrizio's first feeling was one of the greatest joy. " At last I shall be able to look at her for a whole evening. They say she has grown very pale." And he

---

* Raised in a frown from intensity of search.

tried to fancy how that lovely head must look, with all its tints dulled by the struggle that had passed within its owner's soul. His faithful Ludovico, quite alarmed by what he called his master's madness, secured, though with much difficulty, a box on the fourth tier, almost opposite the marchesa's. An idea occurred to Fabrizio. " I hope I may put it into her head to come and listen to my sermon, and I will choose a very small church, so that I may be able to see her well." Fabrizio usually preached at three o'clock. Early in the morning of the day on which the marchesa was to go to the theatre he announced that as some duty connected with his office would keep him at the archiepiscopal palace the whole day long, he would preach, as an exception, at half past eight, that night, in the little Church of Santa Maria della Visitazione, which stood just opposite one of the wings of the Palazzo Crescenzi. He sent Ludovico to the Nuns of the Visitation with an enormous quantity of tapers, and begged them to light their church up brilliantly. He obtained a whole company of grenadiers of the guard, and a sentry, with fixed bayonet, was set on each chapel, to prevent any thieving. His sermon was not to begin until half past eight, but at two o'clock in the day the church was completely filled. My readers will conceive what a stir there was in the usually quiet street overlooked by the noble outlines of the Palazzo Crescenzi. Fabrizio had given out that, in honour of Our Lady of Pity, his subject would be the pity which a generous heart should feel for a person in misfortune, even if that person be a guilty one.

Disguised with every possible care, Fabrizio entered his box at the theatre as soon as the doors were opened, and before it was lighted up. Toward eight o'clock the performance began, and a few minutes afterward he experienced a joy which no one who has not felt it can conceive. He saw the door of the Crescenzi box open, and very soon the marchesa entered it. He had not obtained such a good view of her since the day when she had given him her fan. Fabrizio thought he would have choked with joy. His sensations were so extraordinary that he said to himself: " Perhaps I am going to die. What a blessed ending to my sad life! Perhaps I shall fall down in this box. The good people waiting for me in the Church of the Visitation will wait in vain, and to-morrow they will hear their future archbishop has been found in an opera box, disguised as a servant, and dressed in livery. Farewell, then, to all my reputation! And what care I for my reputation?"

However, toward a quarter to nine Fabrizio made a great effort, and leaving his box on the fourth tier, he proceeded on foot, and with the greatest difficulty, to the place where he was to change his undress livery for more appropriate habiliments. He did not reach the Church of the Visitation till near nine o'clock, and then, so white and weak did he appear, that a report spread through the church that the co-adjutor would not be able to preach that night. My readers will imagine all the attentions that were lavished on him by the nuns, through the grating of their inner parlour, in which he had taken refuge. The good ladies talked a great deal. Fabrizio asked them to leave him alone for a few minutes, and then he hurried off to his pulpit. One of his faithful adherents had told him, about three o'clock, that the church was quite full, but full of people of the lowest class, apparently attracted by the sight of the lighted tapers. When Fabrizio entered the pulpit he was agreeably surprised to find all the chairs occupied by young people of fashion, and older ones holding the most important positions in the city. He began his sermon with a few apologetic sentences, which were received with suppressed exclamations of admiration. Then came a passionate description of the unhappy being whom all men must pity if they would worthily honour the Madonna of Pity, who herself suffered so sorely upon earth. The orator was very much agitated; at times he could hardly speak so as to make himself heard in the far corners of the little church. In the eyes of all the women, and many of the men, his own excessive pallor made him look like the unhappy being they were called upon to pity. A very few minutes after the words of excuse with which his sermon opened, his audience perceived that he was not in his ordinary condition. His sadness, that evening, was deeper and more tender than it generally was; at one moment tears were visible in his eyes, and the whole audience broke into a sob, so loud that it quite interrupted his discourse.

This first interruption was followed by half a score. There were cries of admiration, bursts of tears, and incessant exclamations, such as "O Holy Madonna!" "O great God!" So general and so inexpressible was the emotion of this select audience, that nobody was ashamed to cry out, and the people who did so were not considered ridiculous by their neighbours.

During the rest which is usually taken in the middle of a sermon, Fabrizio was told that not a soul remained in the theatre. Only one lady, the Marchesa Crescenzi, was still in her box. During this interval of rest, a great noise suddenly rose in the building; the faithful were voting a statue to the coadjutor. The reception of the later half of his discourse was so extraordinary, and unrestrained outbursts of Christian repentance were so frequently replaced by exclamations of admiration which were utterly profane, that before he left the pulpit he felt himself obliged to address a sort of reprimand to his auditors. Whereupon every one walked out of the church in a sedate and formal manner, and, once the street was reached, indulged in an outburst of fervent applause, and shouts of "Evviva del Dongo!"

Fabrizio hastily looked at his watch, and rushed to a little grated window which lighted the narrow passage from the organ to the convent. As a civility to the incredible and unusual crowd which filled the street, the porter of the Palazzo Crescenzi had garnished the iron hands which we often see projecting from the walls of palaces built in the middle ages, with a dozen torches. After a few moments, and long before the shouting had ceased, the event which Fabrizio was awaiting with so much anxiety occurred—the marchesa's carriage, bringing her back from the theatre, appeared in the street. The coachman was obliged to pull up, and it was only at a foot's pace and by dint of much shouting that he was able to bring the vehicle to the door.

The marchesa's heart, like that of any person in sorrow, had been touched by the noble music. But the utter solitude of the theatre, once she had learned its cause, had affected her far more. In the middle of the second act, and while the splendid tenor was on the stage, even the people in the pit had suddenly left their seats to go and try their chance of getting inside the Church of the Visitation. When the crowd stopped the marchesa before she could get to her own door, she broke into tears. " I had not chosen ill! " said she to herself.

But just on account of this moment of emotion, she steadily repulsed the suggestions of the marchese, and all the *habitués* of the house, who could not conceive why she did not go to hear such an astonishing preacher. " Why," they cried, " he triumphs over the finest tenor in Italy! "

" If I once see him I am lost! " said the marchesa to herself.

In vain did Fabrizio, whose powers seemed to grow more brilliant every day, preach again, several times over, in the little church near the Palazzo Crescenzi. He never beheld Clelia, who, indeed, ended by being seriously vexed, at last, by his affectation in coming to disturb her quiet street, after having driven her out of her garden.

Fabrizio, as his eyes ran over the faces of the women listening to him, had for some time noticed a very pretty dark-complexioned countenance, and a pair of eyes that blazed. These splendid eyes were generally swimming in tears by the time he had reached the eighth or tenth sentence in his sermon. When Fabrizio was obliged to say things that were lengthy and wearisome to himself, he was rather fond of looking at this pretty head, the youth of which attracted him. He found out that the young lady was called Annetta Marini, the only child and heiress of the richest clothier in Parma, who had died some months previously.

Soon the name of Annetta Marini was on every one's lips. She had fallen desperately in love with Fabrizio. When these wonderful sermons had begun, it had been already settled that she was to marry Giacomo Rassi, the eldest son of the Minister of Justice, a young man who had appeared by no means displeasing to her. But when she had heard Monsignore Fabrizio preach twice, she vowed she would not marry at all, and when she was asked the reason of this strange alteration, she replied that it was not worthy of any honest girl to marry one man when she felt she was desperately in love with another. At first her family vainly sought to discover who that other might be.

But the scalding tears Annetta shed during Fabrizio's sermons put them on the track. When her mother and uncles asked her whether she loved Monsignore Fabrizio, she answered boldly, that, as the truth had been found out, she would not soil herself by telling a lie. She added that as she had no hope of marrying the man she adored, she was at all events resolved her eyes should no longer be offended by the sight of young Count Rassi's ridiculous figure. Within two days the scorn thus cast on the son of a man who was the envy of the entire middle class was the talk of the whole town. Annetta Marini's answer was reckoned delightful, and every soul repeated it.. It was talked of at the Palazzo Crescenzi, as everywhere else.

Clelia took good care never to open her lips on such a subject in her drawing-room. But she questioned her waiting-woman, and on the following Sunday, after she had heard mass in the chapel within her palace, she took her waiting-woman with her in her carriage, and went to a second mass in the Signorina Marini's parish church. Here she found all the fine gentlemen in the town, attracted by the same object. They were standing round the door. Soon a great stir among them convinced the marchesa that Signorina Marini was entering the church. From the place she occupied she could see her very well, and, pious though she was, she did not pay very much attention to the mass. Clelia thought this middle-class beauty wore a resolute look, which to her mind would only have been appropriate in a married woman of several years' standing. Otherwise her figure and waist were admirably neat; and her eyes, as they say in Lombardy, seemed to hold conversations with everything they looked at.

Before mass was over the marchesa slipped out.

The very next day the *habitués* of the Palazzo Crescenzi, who came there every evening, were retailing another story of Annetta Marini's absurdities. As her mother, fearing she might do something foolish, kept her very short of money, Annetta had gone to see the famous painter Hayez, who was then at Parma, decorating the drawing-room of the Palazzo Crescenzi, and had offered him a magnificent diamond ring given her by her father if he would paint her Monsignore del Dongo's picture. But she desired the monsignore might be represented in ordinary black, and not in priestly garb. Consequently, on the previous evening, the fair Annetta's mother had been greatly surprised and sorely scandalized at discovering a splendid picture of Fabrizio del Dongo, in the finest gold frame that had been gilded at Parma for the last twenty years, in her daughter's chamber.

CHAPTER XXVIII

So rapidly have events followed one on the other, that we have had no time to give any sketch of the comical race of courtiers that swarmed at the Parmesan court, and indulged in the strangest comments on the incidents we have been relating. In that country, the qualifications necessary to enable some small sprig of nobility, with his yearly income of two or three thousand francs, to figure in black stockings at the prince's *levers* was, first and foremost, that he never should have read Rousseau or Voltaire; this condition is not difficult of fulfilment. In the second place, it was essential to be able to refer with emotion to the sovereign's cold, or to the last case of mineralogical specimens sent him from Saxony. If, besides all this, our gentleman religiously attended mass every day of his life, and if he could reckon two or three fat monks among his intimate friends, the prince would condescend to speak to him once in every year, either a fortnight before, or a fortnight after, the first of January. This endowed the person so honoured with great importance in his own parish, and the tax-collector dared not worry him overmuch, if he should happen to fall into arrears with the annual tax of one hundred francs imposed on his modest property.

Signor Gonzo was a sorry wight of this description, an individual of very noble birth, and who, besides his own small fortune, held, thanks to the credit of the Marchese Crescenzi, a magnificent post which brought him in the princely sum of one hundred and fifty francs a year. This gentleman might have dined at home if he had chosen. But he had a mania. He was never happy and easy in his mind unless he was sitting in the room of some great personage who said to him every now and then: "*Hold your tongue, Gonzo; you are nothing but a fool.*" This verdict was always the outcome of bad temper, for Gonzo almost always showed more wit than the great person in question. He talked, and talked fairly well, about everything, and further, he was ready to change his opinion if the master of the house only pulled a wry face. As a matter of fact, though full of cunning as regarded his own interests, he had not a single idea in his head, and if the prince did not happen to have a cold, he was sometimes very much puzzled what to say on entering a drawing-room.

Gonzo had earned himself a reputation at Parma by means of a splendid three-cornered hat, adorned with a somewhat dishevelled plume, which he wore even when he was in morning dress. But my readers should have seen the fashion in which he carried that plume, whether upon his head or in his hand—therein lay his talent and his importance. He would inquire with real anxiety after the health of the marchesa's little dog, and if the Palazzo Crescenzi had caught fire he would have risked his life to save any one of those splendid arm-chairs covered with gold brocade, on which his black silk knee-breeches had caught for so many years whenever he ventured to sit himself down for a moment.

Every evening toward seven o'clock, several individuals of this type made their appearance in the marchesa's drawing-room. Before they had well seated themselves, a lackey —splendidly attired in a pale-yellow livery, covered, as was the red waistcoat which completed its magnificence, with silver embroidery—relieved the poor gentlemen of their hats and canes. Close on his steps came a servant, carrying very small cups of coffee, set in cases of silver filigree, and every half-hour a steward, wearing a sword and a gorgeous coat in the French style, handed round ices.

Half an hour after the arrival of the threadbare little courtiers, came five or six officers of the most military appearance, who talked very loud, and generally discussed the number of buttons a soldier must wear on his coat if the general commanding him was to win battles. It would not have been prudent to quote a French newspaper in that drawing-room, for even if the news imparted had been pleasant—as, for instance, that fifty Liberals had been shot in Spain—the person telling the story would still have stood convicted of having perused the French publication. The acme of skill, as recognised by these people, consisted in getting their pensions increased, once in ten years, by the sum of a hundred and fifty francs. In this fashion does the prince share the delight of reigning over all peasants, and over the middle classes, with his nobles.

The chief figure in the Crescenzi drawing-room was, without any contradiction, a Cavaliere Foscarini, a perfectly straightforward gentleman, who had consequently been in prison more or less under every *régime*. He had been a member of that famous Chamber of Deputies at Milan which threw out Napoleon's law of registration—a very uncommon occurrence in history. The Cavaliere Foscarini, who had been the devoted friend of the marchese's mother for twenty years, had retained his influence in the family. He always had some entertaining story to tell; but nothing escaped him, and the young marchesa, who felt herself guilty at the bottom of her heart, trembled in his presence.

As Gonzo was possessed by a real passion for great folks who abused him and made him weep once or twice a year, he had a mania for rendering them small services. And but for the paralysis caused by habits engendered by excessive poverty, he might occasionally have succeeded, for he was not devoid of a certain amount of cunning, and a far greater amount of effrontery.

This Gonzo, even as we know him, rather despised the Marchesa Crescenzi, for she had never said an uncivil word to him in his life. But, after all, she was the wife of that powerful Marchese Crescenzi, lord in waiting to the princess, who would say to Gonzo once or twice a month, " Hold your tongue, Gonzo, you are nothing but a fool."

Gonzo noticed that all the talk about little Annetta Marini roused the marchesa, for an instant, out of the state of reverie and indifference in which she usually sat, until the clock struck eleven. When that happened, she would make tea, and offer it to every man present, addressing him by name. After which, just before she retired to her own rooms, she would seem to brighten up for a moment, and this was the time always chosen by her guests to recite satirical sonnets to her.

Excellent sonnets of this kind are produced in Italy. It is the only form of literature in which some life still stirs. It must be acknowledged that they are not submitted to the censure, and the courtiers of the Casa Crescenzi always prefaced their sonnet with the words, " Will the Signora Marchesa give us leave to recite a very poor sonnet? " Then, when every one had laughed at the lines, and they had been repeated two or three times over, one of the officers was sure to exclaim, " The Minister of Police ought really to see about hanging a few of the authors of these vile performances." In middle-class society, on the contrary, the sonnets were received with the frankest admiration, and many copies were sold by the lawyers' clerks.

The curiosity betrayed by the marchesa led Gonzo to augur that too much had been said about the beauty of Signorina Marini, who owned a fortune of a million francs to boot, and that his hostess was jealous. As Gonzo, with his never-failing smile and his utter insolence with regard to everything that was not nobly born, went whithersoever he would, he made his appearance, the very next day, in the marchesa's drawing-room, wearing his plumed hat with a certain triumphant cock, in which he only indulged once or twice a year, when the prince had said to him " Addio, Gonzo."

Having respectfully greeted the marchesa, Gonzo did not retire, as was his custom, to the chair which had been put forward for his accommodation. He stood himself in the middle of the circle, and brusquely exclaimed : " I have seen the picture of Monsignore del Dongo." Clelia was so taken aback that she was obliged to support herself on the arms of the chair ; she strove to make head against the storm, but finally she was obliged to leave the drawing-room.

" My poor dear Gonzo," haughtily exclaimed one of the officers who was just finishing his fourth ice, " you certainly do blunder in the most extraordinary manner. How comes it that you do not know that the coadjutor, who was one of the bravest colonels in Napoleon's army, once played a vile trick on the marchesa's father, by getting out of the citadel where General Conti was commanding, just as he might have got out of the Steccata (the principal church in Parma)."

"Indeed, my dear captain, I am ignorant of many things, and I am a poor idiot who makes mistakes all day long."

This reply, which was quite in the Italian style, raised a laugh at the gay officer's expense. Soon the marchesa came back; she had armed herself with courage, and was not without some vague hope that she might have a chance of herself admiring Fabrizio's portrait, which was said to be excellent. She praised the talents of Hayez, who had painted it. All unconsciously, she smiled delightfully at Gonzo, who looked slyly at the officer. As all the other household courtiers indulged in the same pleasure, the officer departed, but not without vowing a mortal hatred against Gonzo. Gonzo was triumphant, and that evening when he took his leave he was invited to dinner on the following day.

"Here's a fresh story," exclaimed Gonzo the next day, after dinner, when the servants had retired. "It really would seem as if our coadjutor had fallen in love with the little Marini girl." The tumult in Clelia's heart, on hearing so extraordinary an assertion, may be conceived; the marchese himself was disturbed.

"But, Gonzo, my dear fellow, you are talking nonsense, as you generally do. And you really should speak with a little more respect of a man who has had the honour of playing whist with his Highness eleven times over."

"Very good, Signor Marchese," said Gonzo, with the coarseness of men of his kidney. "I'll dare swear he would be very glad to play with the little Marini too. But for me it is enough that these details should offend you. As far as I am concerned, they have no further existence. For, above all things, I desire not to shock my dearest marchese."

The marchese always retired to take a *siesta* after his dinner. This day he was willing to go without it. But Gonzo would rather have cut out his tongue than have said another word about Annetta Marini; and every moment he would begin some speech calculated to rouse the marchese's hopes of hearing him revert to the young lady's love-affairs. Gonzo possessed, in the highest degree, that Italian instinct which delights in holding back the longed-for word. The poor marchese, who was dying of curiosity, was reduced to making advances. He told Gonzo that when he had the pleasure of dining in his company he always ate twice as much as usual. Gonzo would not understand. He began to give an account of a splendid gallery of pictures collected by the Marchesa Balbi, the late prince's mistress. He mentioned Hayez two or three times, lingering over his name with an accent of the deepest admiration. " Good," said the marchese to himself; " now he's coming to little Annetta's picture." But Gonzo took care to do nothing of the kind. Five o'clock struck at last, to the great vexation of the marchese, who was in the habit of getting into his carriage at half past five, after his *siesta*, and driving to the Corso.

" Just like you and your stupidity," he exclaimed to Gonzo. " You will make me, the princess's lord in waiting, get to the Corso after her, and she may have orders to give me. Come, be quick about it; tell me shortly, if you are capable of that, all about these pretended love-affairs of the coadjutor's."

But Gonzo intended to keep that story for the marchesa, who had asked him to dinner. Very curtly, therefore, he despatched the tale, and the marchese, half asleep, went off to take his *siesta*. With the poor marchesa Gonzo followed quite a different system. So youthful and so simple had she remained, in spite of all her riches, that she thought herself obliged to atone for the roughness with which the marchese had just spoken to Gonzo. Delighted with his success, the little man recovered all his eloquence, and made it his pleasure, no less than his duty, to supply her with endless details.

Little Annetta Marini paid as much as a sequin for every place kept for her at the sermons. She always attended them with two of her aunts, and her father's old bookkeeper. The seats, which she had kept for her overnight, were generally opposite the pulpit, rather toward the high altar, for she had remarked that the coadjutor frequently turned toward the high altar. Now, what the public had also remarked, was that, *not unfrequently*, the young preacher's speaking eyes rested complacently on the youthful heiress, in her piquant beauty, and apparently, too, with some attention. For once his eyes were fixed on her, his discourse became learned; it bristled with quotations, the emotional note in his eloquence disappeared, and the ladies, whose interest in the sermon instantly disappeared likewise, began to look at Annetta, and speak evil of her.

Three times over Clelia made him repeat these extraordinary details. At the end of the third time she grew very thoughtful. She was reckoning up that it was just fourteen months since she had seen Fabrizio.

"Would it be very wrong," said she to herself, "if I spent an hour in a church, not to see Fabrizio, but to listen to a famous preacher? Besides, I would sit far away from the pulpit, and I would only look at Fabrizio once when I came in, and another time at the end of his sermon. . . . No," she added, "it is not to see Fabrizio that I am going, it is to hear this extraordinary preacher." In the midst of all these arguments the marchesa was pricked with remorse. She had behaved so well for fourteen months! "Well," she thought at last, to pacify herself a little, "if the first woman who comes this evening has been to hear Monsignore del Dongo preach I will go too; if she has not been, I will refrain."

Once she had made up her mind, the marchesa filled Gonzo with delight by saying to him:

"Will you try to find out what day the coadjutor is going to preach, and in what church? This evening, before you leave, I may perhaps have a commission for you."

Hardly had Gonzo departed for the Corso than Clelia went out into the palace garden. The objection that she had never set her foot in it for ten months did not occur to her. She was eager and animated, the colour had come back to her face. That evening, as each tiresome guest entered her drawing-room, her heart throbbed with emotion. Gonzo was announced at last, and he instantly perceived that for the next week he was destined to be the one indispensable person. " The marchesa is jealous of the little Marini girl, and on my soul," he thought, " a comedy in which she will play the leading part, with little Annetta for the soubrette, and Monsignore del Dongo for the lover, will be something worth seeing. Faith, I'd go so far as to pay two francs for my place." He was beside himself with delight, and the whole evening he kept taking the words out of everybody's mouth and telling the most preposterous tales (as, for instance, that of the Marquis de Pecquiny and the famous actress, which he had heard the night before from a French traveller). The marchesa, on her part, could not sit quiet ; she walked about the drawing-room, she moved into the adjacent gallery, into which the marchese would admit no picture which had not cost more than twenty thousand francs. That evening those pictures spoke so clearly to her that they made her heart ache with emotion. At last she heard the great doors thrown open, and hurried back to the drawing-room. It was the Marchesa Raversi. But when Clelia endeavoured to receive her with the usual compliments, she felt her voice fail her. Twice over the marchesa had to make her repeat the question, " What do you think of this fashionable preacher ? " which she had not caught at first.

" I did look upon him as a little schemer, the very worthy nephew of the illustrious Countess Mosca. But the last time he preached, look you, at the Church of the Visitation, opposite your house, he was so sublime that all my hatred died down, and I consider him the most eloquent man I have ever heard in my life."

" Then you have attended at his sermons ? " said Clelia, shaking with happiness.

" Why, weren't you listening to me ? " said the marchesa, laughing. " I would not miss them for anything on earth. They say his lungs are affected, and that soon he won't preach any more."

The Chartreuse of Parma

The moment the marchesa had departed Clelia beckoned Gonzo into the gallery.

" I have almost made up my mind," she said, " to hear this much-admired preacher. When will he preach? "

" On Monday next—that is, three days hence; and one might almost fancy he had guessed your Excellency's plan, for he is coming to preach in the Church of the Visitation."

Further explanation was indispensable. But Clelia's voice had quite failed her. She walked up and down the gallery five or six times without uttering a word. Meanwhile Gonzo was saying to himself: " Now revenge is working in her soul. How can any man have the insolence to escape out of prison, especially when he has the honour of being kept under watch and ward by such a hero as General Fabio Conti! "

" And, indeed," he added, with skilful irony, " there is no time to be lost. His lungs are affected; I heard Dr. Rambo say he would not live a year. God is punishing him for having broken his arrest . . . by his treacherous escape from the citadel."

The marchesa seated herself on the couch in the gallery, and signed to Gonzo to follow her example. After a few moments she gave him a little purse, into which she had put a few sequins. " Have four places kept for me."

" Might your poor Gonzo be permitted to follow in your Excellency's train? "

" Of course; tell them to keep five places. . . . I do not at all care," she said, " to be near the pulpit, but I should like to see the Signorina Marini, whom every one tells me is so pretty."

During the three days that were still to elapse before the Monday on which the sermon was to be preached, the marchesa was in an agony. Gonzo, who felt it the most excessive honour to be seen in public in the following of so great a lady, had put on his French coat and his sword. Nor was this all. Taking advantage of the close neighbourhood of the palace, he had a magnificent gilt arm-chair carried into the church for the marchesa's use—a proceeding which was

The Chartreuse of Parma

looked on as a piece of the greatest insolence by the middle-class portion of the audience. The feelings of the poor marchesa, when she beheld this arm-chair, which had been set immediately opposite the pulpit, may easily be imagined. Shrinking, with downcast eyes, into the corner of the huge chair, Clelia, in her confusion, had not even courage to look at Annetta Marini, whom Gonzo pointed out to her with a coolness which perfectly astounded her. In the eyes of the true courtier, people who are not of noble birth have no existence at all.

Fabrizio appeared in the pulpit. So pale and thin was he, so devoured with grief, that the tears instantly welled up in Clelia's eyes. Fabrizio spoke a few words, and then stopped short, as if his voice had suddenly failed him. Vainly he strove to bring out one or two sentences. At last he turned and took up a written sheet.

" My brethren," said he, " a most unhappy being, and very deserving of all your pity, beseeches you, through me, to pray for the conclusion of his torture, which can only end with his own life."

Fabrizio read the rest of the document very slowly, but so expressive was his voice that, before he reached the middle of the prayer, everybody, even Gonzo himself, was in tears. " At least nobody will notice me," said the marchesa to herself, as she wept.

While Fabrizio was reading this written paper, two or three ideas concerning the condition of the unhappy man on whose behalf he had just asked for the prayers of the faithful, occurred to him. Thoughts soon came crowding on him thickly. Though he seemed to be addressing the public at large, it was to the marchesa that he really spoke. He brought his sermon to a close a little earlier than usual, because, in spite of all his efforts, his own tears came so fast that he could no longer speak intelligibly. The best judges considered the sermon a strange one, but equal, at all events, in its pathetic qualities, to the famous discourse preached among the lighted tapers. As for Clelia, before she had heard the first ten lines of Fabrizio's prayer, she felt it was an atrocious crime to have been able to spend fourteen months without seeing him. When she went home she retired to bed, so that she might be able to think about Fabrizio in peace; and the next morning, tolerably early, Fabrizio received a note in the following terms:

"The writer depends on your honour. Find four 'bravos' on whose discretion you can rely, and to-morrow, when midnight strikes at the Steccata, be close to a little door marked No. 19, in the Street of St. Paul. Remember that you may be attacked, and do not come alone."

When Fabrizio recognised that adored handwriting he fell on his knees and burst into tears.

"At last," he cried, "at last, after fourteen months and eight days! Farewell to preaching!"

The description of all the wild feelings which raged that day in Fabrizio's heart and Clelia's would be a long one. The little door mentioned in the note was no other than that of the orangery of the Palazzo Crescenzi, and a dozen times that day Fabrizio found means to look at it. A little before midnight he armed himself, and was walking quickly, and alone, past the door, when to his inexpressible joy he heard a well-known voice say very low:

"Come in hither, beloved of my heart." Very cautiously Fabrizio entered, and found himself within the orangery, indeed, but opposite a window strongly grated, and raised some three or four feet above the ground. It was exceedingly dark. Fabrizio had heard some noise in the window, and was feeling over the grating with his hand, when he felt another hand slipped through the bars, that took hold of his, and carried it to lips which pressed a kiss upon it.

"It is I," said a beloved voice, "who have come here to tell you that I love you, and to ask you if you will obey me."

My readers will imagine Fabrizio's answer, his joy, his astonishment. When the first transports had subsided, Clelia said: "I have vowed to the Madonna, as you know, that I will never see you. That is why I receive you now in the dark. I am very anxious you should know that if you ever oblige me to look at you in daylight everything will be over between us. But to begin with, I will not have you preach before Annetta Marini; and do not think it was I who committed the folly of having an arm-chair carried into the house of God."

" My dearest angel! I shall never preach again before anybody. The only reason I preached was my hope that by so doing I might some day see you."

" You must not speak to me like that! Remember that I am forbidden to see you."

At this point I will ask my readers' permission to pass in silence over a period of three years. When our story begins afresh, Count Mosca has long been back at Parma as Prime Minister, with greater power than ever.

After these three years of exquisite happiness, a whim of Fabrizio's heart altered everything. The marchesa had a beautiful little boy two years old, Sandrino. He was always with her, or on the marchese's knee. But Fabrizio hardly ever saw him. He did not choose that the boy should grow into the habit of loving another father, and conceived the idea of carrying off the child before his memories were very distinct.

During the long daylight hours, when the marchesa might not see her lover, Sandrino's presence was her consolation. For we must here confess a fact which will seem strange to dwellers on the northern side of the Alps. In spite of her failings, she had remained faithful to her vow. She had promised the Madonna that she would never see Fabrizio; those had been her exact words. Consequently she had never received him except at night, and there was never any light in her chamber.

But every evening Fabrizio visited his mistress, and it was a very admirable thing that, in the midst of a court which was eaten up by curiosity and boredom, his precautions had been so skilfully taken that this *amicizia*, as people call it in Lombardy, had never even been suspected. Their love was too intense not to be disturbed by occasional quarrels. Clelia was very subject to jealousy. But their disagreements almost always arose from a different cause—Fabrizio having

The Chartreuse of Parma

taken unfair advantage of some public ceremony to introduce himself near the marchesa and look at her; she would then seize some pretext for instant departure, and would banish her friend for many days.

Residents at the court of Parma were astonished at never being able to discover any intrigue on the part of a woman so remarkable for beauty and intelligence. She inspired several passions which led to many mad actions, and very often Fabrizio, too, was jealous.

The good Archbishop Landriani had long been dead. Fabrizio's piety, his eloquence, and his exemplary life, had wiped out his predecessor's memory. His elder brother was dead, and all the family wealth had devolved on him. From that time forward he divided the hundred and odd thousand francs which formed the income of the archbishopric of Parma between the priests and curates of his diocese.

It would have been difficult to conceive a more honoured, a more honourable and useful existence, than that Fabrizio had built up for himself when this unlucky fancy of his came to disturb it all.

"According to your vow, which I respect, and which, nevertheless, makes my life miserable, since you will not see me in daylight," said he one day to Clelia, "I am forced to live perpetually alone, with no relaxation of any kind except my work, and even my work fails me sometimes. In the midst of this stern and dreary manner of spending the long hours of each day, an idea had come into my head, which torments me incessantly, and against which I have struggled in vain for the last six months. My son will never love me; he never hears my name. Brought up, as he is, in all the pleasing luxury of the Palazzo Crescenzi, he hardly even knows me by sight. On the rare occasions when I do see him, I think of his mother, for he reminds me of her heavenly beauty, at which I am not allowed to look, and he must think my face solemn, which, to a child's eyes, means gloomy."

"Well," said the marchesa, "whither does all this alarming talk of yours tend?"

The Chartreuse of Parma

"To this: I want my son back. I want him to live with me. I want to see him every day. I want him to learn to love me. I want to love him myself, at my ease. Since a fate such as never overtook any other man has deprived me of the happiness which so many loving souls enjoy—since I must not spend my whole life with all I worship—I desire, at all events, to have one being with me who shall remind my heart of you, and, in a certain sense, replace you. In my enforced solitude, business and men alike weary me. You know that ever since the moment when I had the happiness of being locked up by Barbone, ambition has been to me an empty word, and in the melancholy that overwhelms me when I am far from you, everything which is unconnected with the deep feelings of my heart seems preposterous to me."

My readers will realize the lively sorrow with which the thought of her lover's suffering filled poor Clelia's soul. And her grief was all the deeper because she felt there was a certain reason in what Fabrizio said. She even went so far as to debate with herself whether she ought not to seek release from her vow: then she could have seen Fabrizio in the light, like any other member of society, and her reputation was too well established for any one to have found fault with her for doing so. She told herself that by dint of spending a great deal of money she might obtain release from her vow, but she felt that this thoroughly worldly arrangement would not ease her own conscience, and feared that Heaven, in its anger, might punish her for this fresh crime.

On the other hand, if she consented to grant Fabrizio's very natural desire, if she endeavoured to avoid fresh misery for the tender-hearted being whom she knew so well, and whose peace was already so strangely imperilled by her own peculiar vow, what chance was there of carrying off the only son of one of the greatest gentlemen in Italy without the fraud being discovered? The Marchese Crescenzi would lavish huge sums of money, would put himself at the head of the searchers, and sooner or later, the abduction would be known. There was only one means of avoiding this danger—to send the child far away, to Edinburgh, for instance, or to Paris. But this alternative her mother's heart could not face. The other method, which Fabrizio suggested, and which was indeed the most reasonable, had something threatening about it, which made it almost still more dreadful in the agonized mother's eyes. There must be a feigned sickness, Fabrizio declared; the child must grow worse and worse, and must die, at last, while the Marchese Crescenzi was away from home.

Clelia's repugnance to this plan, which amounted to absolute terror, caused a rupture which could not last long.

Clelia declared that they must not tempt God; that this dearly loved child was the fruit of a sin, and that if anything more was done to stir the divine wrath, God would surely take the child back to himself. Fabrizio recurred to the subject of his own peculiar fate. "The state of life to which chance has brought me, and my love for you, force me to live in perpetual solitude. I can not enjoy the sweetness of an intimate companionship, like most of my fellow men, because you will never receive me except in the dark, and thus the portion of my life I can spend with you is reduced, so to speak, to minutes."

Many tears were shed, and Clelia fell ill. But she loved Fabrizio too dearly to refuse to make the frightful sacrifice he asked of her. To all appearances Sandrino fell sick. The marchese hastened to send for the most famous doctors, and Clelia found herself confronted by a terrible difficulty which she had not foreseen. She had to prevent this idolized child from taking any of the remedies prescribed by the physicians, and that was no easy matter.

The child, kept in bed more than was good for his health, fell really ill. How was she to tell the doctor the real cause of the trouble? Torn asunder by these conflicting interests, both so near her heart, Clelia very nearly lost her reason. Fabrizio, on his side, could neither forgive himself the violence he was doing to the feelings of his mistress, nor relinquish his plan. He had found means of nightly access to the sick child's room, and this brought about another complication. The marchesa was nursing her son, and sometimes Fabrizio could not help seeing her by the light of the tapers. This, to Clelia's poor sick heart, seemed a horrible wickedness, and an augury of Sandrino's death. In vain had the most famous casuists, when consulted as to the necessity of keeping a vow in cases where such obedience would evidently do harm, replied that no breaking of a vow could be considered criminal, so long as the person bound by a promise toward God failed, not for the sake of mere fleshly pleasure, but so as not to cause some evident harm. The marchesa's despair did not diminish, and Fabrizio saw that his strange fancy would soon bring about both Clelia's death and her child's.

He appealed to his intimate friend, Count Mosca, who, hardened old minister as he was, was touched by this love story, of the greater part of which he had been quite unaware.

" I will have the marchese sent away for five or six days at least. When shall it be? "

Within a short time Fabrizio came to the count with the news that everything was prepared to take advantage of the marchese's absence.

Two days later, while the marchese was riding home from one of his properties in the neighbourhood of Mantua, a band of ruffians, who appeared to be in the pay of a private individual, carried him off, without ill-treating him in any way, and put him into a boat which took three days to drop down the river Po—exactly the same journey Fabrizio had performed after his terrible business with Giletti. On the fourth day the ruffians landed the marchese on a lonely island in the river, having previously and carefully emptied his pockets, without leaving him any money or valuable of any kind. It was two whole days before the marchese could get back to his palace at Parma. When he arrived he found it all hung with black, and the whole household in the deepest grief.

The result of this abduction, skilfully as it had been carried out, was melancholy in the extreme. Sandrino, who had been secretly removed to a large and handsome house in

The Chartreuse of Parma

which the marchesa came to see him almost every day, was dead before many months were out. Clelia fancied that a just punishment had come upon her, because she had been faithless to her vow to the Madonna—she had so often seen Fabrizio by candlelight, and twice even in broad daylight, and with the most passionate tenderness, during Sandrino's illness! She only survived her much-loved child a few months. But she had the comfort of dying in her lover's arms.

Fabrizio was too desperately in love, and too faithful a believer, to have recourse to suicide. He hoped to meet Clelia again in a better world, but he was too intelligent not to feel that there was much for which he must first atone.

A few days after Clelia's death he signed several deeds, whereby he insured a pension of a thousand francs a year to each of his servants, and reserved a like income for himself. He made over lands, bringing in almost a hundred thousand francs a year, to the Countess Mosca, a like sum to the Marchesa del Dongo, his mother, and the residue of his patrimony to one of his sisters, who had made a poor marriage. The next day, having sent his resignation of his archbishopric, and of all the posts which had been showered upon him by the favour of Ernest V and the affection of his Prime Minister, to the proper quarter, he retired to the Chartreuse de Parme, which stands in the woods, close to the river Po, two leagues from Sacca.

The Countess Mosca had fully approved her husband's reassumption of the ministry, when that had taken place, but nothing would ever induce her to set her foot within Ernest V's dominions; and she held her court at Vignano, a quarter of a league from Casal Maggiore, on the left bank of the Po, and consequently within Austrian territory. In the magnificent palace which the count had built her at Vignano, she received the *élite* of Parmese society every Thursday, and saw her numerous friends on every other day. Fabrizio would never let a day pass without going to Vignano. In a word, the countess apparently possessed every ingredient of happiness. But she only lived a very short time longer than

The Chartreuse of Parma

Fabrizio, whom she adored, and who spent only one year in his *chartreuse*.

The prisons of Parma stood empty. The count was immensely rich, and Ernest V was worshipped by his subjects, who compared his government with that of the Grand Dukes of Tuscany.

°   °   .   .   .   .   °   °

TO THE HAPPY FEW!

THE PORTRAITS
OF STENDHAL

THE PORTRAITS OF STENDHAL

" I WILL confess to you," wrote Stendhal, one day, toward 1838, " that I pin my pride to the hope of possessing a certain amount of reputation in the year 1880." This

HENRI BEYLE-STENDHAL.
Aged 25 years, after a
chalk drawing.

yearning on the part of Henri Beyle may be said to have developed into a prophecy. It was not until about 1880, that his posthumous glory assumed any great proportions in France. Before that date, there was no recognised and authentic portrait of the author of *La Chartreuse de Parme,* and none of the very few reprints of his works had included any representation of his features, under the guise of frontispiece.

The general conception of the author of the theory of " crystallization " in his work *De l'Amour* was that of a dandy —so much indifference and so many confessions of self-conceit did the style of that book reveal. The literary circle which admired him so vastly, toward the close of the nineteenth century, and built him up a sort of sacrosanct popularity in the literary world, was sorely taken aback when the pictured countenance of the object of its worship was unearthed. The first portrait discovered was David d'An-

The Portraits of Stendhal

ger's medallion, executed in 1829. This was by no means calculated to excite admiration, either by its beauty of feature, or the delicacy of its lines. Charles Mongelet, though a fervent admirer of Beyle, thought his idol " looked like an apothecary." There was nothing for it but to bow to the evidence, and relinquish imaginary dreams concern-

STENDHAL.
Aged 46 years, after a medallion by David d'Angers.

ing Stendhal, of whom Berlioz, who saw him at Rome, writes in his *Memoirs,* " A little pot-bellied man with a spiteful smile, who tries to look grave."

The friend of Mérimée, whose Letters and Journal affect so much gay wit and love of adventure—in the style of Casanova and Seingalt (?)—was far, very far indeed, from being our ideal *cavaliere servente.* " Physically," writes Ste. Beuve, referring to Stendhal, " his figure, though not short, soon grew thickset and heavy, and his neck short and full blooded. His fleshy face was framed in dark curly hair and whiskers, which, before his death, *were assisted by art.* His forehead was fine : the nose turned up, and somewhat Kalmuck in type. His lower lip, which projected a little, betrayed his tendency to scoff. The eyes were rather

The Portraits of Stendhal

small, but very bright, deeply set in their cavities, and very pleasing when he smiled. His hands, of which he was proud, were small and daintily shaped. In the last years of his life he grew heavy and apoplectic. But he always took great pains to conceal the symptoms of physical decay, even from his own friends."

The portraits of Stendhal as a young man (such as the miniature discovered at Grenoble, and reproduced after Mme. Strienka, which forms the charming frontispiece to the present edition—and the portrait at the head of this note)—present him to us in more attractive guise, although already inclined to stoutness. It was at this period that he was remarked, at the Court Balls, on account of the beauty of his leg—an advantage much noticed in those days. In the picture in the Grenoble Museum, signed "Dreux d'Orcy," Henri Beyle, then probably about forty years of age, with thinning locks, shows us a countenance to which the blood has already flown, and eyes that are fairly fine and tender, with a kindly and sensual mouth. It was this portrait, with its revelation of subtlety, which gave birth to the following amusing definition of the author of *Rouge et Noir*, then Consul at Civita Vecchia—"He had the wit of a diplomatist in the body of a grocer."

PORTRAIT OF STENDHAL.
After a painting by Dreux d'Orcy in the museum at Grenoble.

The remaining portraits of Stendhal are less authentic. One, after an etched engraving, strikes one as a concoction. Another, after a drawing dated 1832, is more sincere, cer-

The Portraits of Stendhal

tainly, but it is not graceful. Here we have an unexpected Stendhal, hideously common and ugly—a sort of foretaste of the Joseph Prudhomme type immortalized by Henri Monnier. This portrait makes one inclined to believe in the authenticity of a caricature by Monnier, said to have been an extraordinarily exaggerated presentment of Henri Beyle, under the name of M. de Fougeray, which appears on the first page of a book called *Les Soirées de Neuilly*.

This comic portrait, which figures as a tail-piece in the present edition, represents a full-bellied individual, with a bulldog muzzle, and baldheaded, but for a few hairs

HENRI BEYLE.
After a picture by Boilly, 1807.

on his poll. This burlesque-looking and obese personage, in black satin breeches, with his umbrella tucked under his arm, hat in hand, of obsequious air, and unclean aspect, is, we are told, none other than the biographer of Roffini. Henri Monnier is said to have assured Charles Asselineau, the romantic writer, that in this composition, he had "*barely caricatured the outline of Henri Beyle who had posed as his model.*"

Here we have the sum total of the portraits of this remarkable writer. They do not flatter their subject, and they somewhat frustrate

HENRI BEYLE.
After a drawing, 1832.

The Portraits of Stendhal

our conception of this "master of the elegancies." Regard for truth makes us feel it incumbent on us to publish them as they stand. In every one of these heads there is a touch of the hydrochephalous: their effect is massive, thickset, rustic. Yet Beyle was a man to whom love was given. According to his own account, he was a "bourreau de cœurs."

In love, as in the case of genius, such miraculous transformations do occur. In the ancient days, the gods were veiled in clouds. The symbol may be carried down to ours. Beyle, too, was veiled.

OCTAVE UZANNE.

HENRI BEYLE.
Caricature by Henri Monnier, under the name
of M. de Fougeray.